SAVANNAH
FROM SAVANNAH

SAVANNAH
COMES UNDONE

DENISE HILDRETH

THOMAS NELSON
Since 1798

NASHVILLE   DALLAS   MEXICO CITY   RIO DE JANEIRO

D0106575

Published in Nashville, Tennessee, by Thomas Nelson. Thomas Nelson is a registered trademark of Thomas Nelson, Inc.

Thomas Nelson, Inc., titles may be purchased in bulk for educational, business, fund-raising, or sales promotional use. For information, please e-mail SpecialMarkets@ThomasNelson.com.

Publisher's Note: This novel is a work of fiction. Names, characters, places, and incidents are either products of the author's imagination or used fictitiously. All characters are fictional, and any similarity to people living or dead is purely coincidental.

ISBN 978-1-59554-559-6

Printed in the United States of America
10 11 RRD 5 4 3 2

SAVANNAH
FROM SAVANNAH

This book is dedicated to those who have ever known loss,
and those who have had a dream only to watch it crumble.
May you realize this side of heaven that God redeems
all things, even those that seem unredeemable.

CHAPTER ONE

Savannah is my name. It's also my world, my home. I didn't cherish it until I left. And when I returned, it was because I had something to prove.

My mother, Victoria, was born and reared in Savannah. My name is explained by her love for this city—that and my belief that she had a craving to spend the rest of her life announcing her daughter to every living creature as "Savannah from Savannah." For a time I thought she was just being cute. Then I realized that this was really how she intended to introduce me for the rest of my natural existence.

"Savannah," she said when I confronted her, "one day you will thank me. When you are famous and the whole world knows you as 'Savannah from Savannah,' children will envy you and long to be named after you. And me, well, I will be your mother."

By the age of thirteen, having no desire to be any child's envy, I went around my eighth-grade class and had all my friends sign a petition requesting my name be legally changed. Afterward, I walked straight up to the courthouse and into the office of Judge Hoddicks, one of my father's best friends. I withdrew my two sheets of moderately legible names from the pages of *The Hobbit,* where I'd stashed them for safety, spread them on Judge Hoddicks's desk, and informed him I would like to change my name to Betty.

"Why Betty?"

"Because my mom doesn't like any name that ends in a *y.* Just try calling her Vicky and see what happens to that southern charm of hers. It will fade like a vapor."

He directed me to a chair in his stunning office, with its rich mahogany bookcases and coffered ceiling. I passed the time reading my well-worn copy of Tolkien's classic until the glass-paned door opened and my mother made her entrance. I thought maybe he wanted to witness the meltdown of a southern woman in high heels and Mary Kay. But her arrival proved it was all about her ability to command any room as well as this city's inhabitants.

She looked fabulous—perturbed, but fabulous. Vicky always looks fabulous. She has never appeared in public in anything lower than a two-inch heel. She doesn't own a pair of jeans, and she wouldn't be caught dead with curlers in her hair, without makeup on her face, or without being fully accessorized by seven a.m.

Ten minutes later, as we left the office, I vowed that even if I called her Victoria to the world, she would always be Vicky in my mind. I took one last look back and asked Judge Hoddicks to give me a call if there was anything he could do. He assured me he would.

Today, eleven years later, my legal name is still Savannah Grace Phillips. To Judge Hoddicks, however, I will forever be Betty.

I have spent a considerable amount of my life trying to convince people that Vicky isn't my real mother. I mean how could I come from a woman I don't understand, a woman no one understands? Anyone with half a pea-pickin' ounce of perception can tell that Vicky and I are nothing alike. We don't talk alike, act alike, or do anything else alike.

And you wouldn't know I was hers by my looks, either. I have two inches on her five-foot-four frame. And I don't think our hair is the same color, although no one really knows what her original hair color was. My hair has always been golden brown and straight as a stick. Vicky has been blond, frosted, and redheaded. The best color of all was when she wanted to be platinum blonde, and woke up the morning of the annual Savannah Chamber of Commerce Ball with the majority of her hair lying broken off on her pillow. But we don't talk about that much.

The only remote proof that Vicky could actually be my mother is that I do, on rare, necessary occasions, feel the need to freely express myself in, shall we say, clear tones. My father, Jake Phillips, has the amazing ability to sit back and breathe before responding. I, however, like Vicky, tend to speak before thought has had a chance to register. This is a most exhilarating, dangerous trait that we share. Vicky has managed to envelop hers in charm. I have only managed to envelop mine in something begging to be refined.

I have tried to channel this intense need to freely express myself into the written word. Every Big Star notebook I've saved from school contains either words to songs, short stories, or entire movie scripts. In high school, I ran for student-body president just so I could write a speech. The speech was so good I didn't even have to campaign to win. I appealed to the students' deepest cravings: food, exemption from finals, and football. Tie those three things together and then close with a poem called "The Man Who Thinks He Can," and, well . . . my fellow students were mush. The poor girl who lost had her own campaign manager and spent so much money on pencils and posters that I almost felt bad for beating her.

That moment allowed me to catch a glimpse of how words can impact the human spirit. A few months later, a short story about an eighty-year-old named Lula who wore purple hats and sang show tunes at area nursing homes, à la a Victoria biography, secured me a scholarship to the School of Journalism at the

University of Georgia. College taught me how to craft my gift, a gift that would propel me into the highbrow world of publishing. I envisioned my books in the window of Barnes & Noble and day-dreamed of people rushing in to catch the latest novel by Savannah Phillips—or "Savannah from Savannah," as people back home would forever require me to be identified. And that probably would have been my life, had it not been for some intervening circumstances and a newspaper.

For four years of college and two years of graduate school, Vicky sent me a subscription to our local paper, the *Savannah Chronicle*. She never acknowledged it, but when there is a half-page ad on page 3 that reads "To our Savannah from Savannah, wishing you all the best in your new passage, Love, Mom and Dad," you just kind of know. My first week of college, feeling somewhat liberated yet homesick, I picked up my mail and headed to a McDonald's right off-campus to grab a Coke. Then I would take my Coke over to a small café across from my apartment and get a chef's salad with Thousand Island and blue-cheese dressing on the side. There, along with caffeine and fat grams, I consumed every article and ad in the paper.

For years, I considered Savannah a town of the near-dead and dying, a place frequented by people who'd come to pick out retirement facilities. I had never realized that it was so vibrant, alive. The main reason for this newfound impression appeared every Wednesday and Friday at the bottom of the front page of section B. Beside her column in the local section was a picture of a distinguished-looking lady with frosted hair, probably in her mid-fifties. Gloria Richardson. Her smile looked genuine, and her human-interest stories made me believe that unexpected kindness and prevailing strength just might exist in Savannah after all. So twice a week for six years, I spent lunchtime rediscovering the place I thought I knew and had longed to leave.

One Wednesday in the last weeks of the final semester of my master's work, I picked up my mail and my *Chronicle* and headed to McDonald's, and then the café. With Coke and salad at the ready, I flipped through the envelopes first and paused at a return address labeled "Fiction Achievement Award." I couldn't believe the results were already in.

Over the past six years, I had dedicated myself to consuming other writers' work and sharpening my own. For my thesis, I turned in a 450-page novel about four female college dropouts who left home to discover the world. It was a delightful tale of searching and survival, crafted over an agonizing two years. My dean entered the novel in a fiction contest for unpublished writers. A portion of the winning story would be published in a leading literary magazine, and leading fiction houses would consider the manuscript for publication.

Surely I held in my hands a rejection letter, sent out first to the really bad entries. Not only was I not picked to win, but my book was so bad they wanted me to know two weeks early how truly pathetic I am!

I sat up straighter in my booth and tore the letter open. "Let the guillotine fall quickly," I said.

Dear Ms. Phillips,

After careful consideration, we are pleased to inform you that your novel, *Road to Anywhere,* has been selected for the Fiction Achievement Award. An excerpt from your novel will appear in a future edition of the *National Literary Review.* We look forward to meeting you in person on May 15 with Taylor House Publishing in New York. All pertinent information has been sent to Dean Hillwood at the University of Georgia. The awards ceremony will be held on May 16 at the Waldorf Astoria. We have reserved a table for you and nine of your guests.

Congratulations. We are pleased to help you pursue
your dreams of becoming a successful author.

Sincerely,
Jeff Peterson
Chairman, Awards Committee

"Oh my stars! Oh my stars!" I said, throwing the letter into the air and jumping out of my booth. I caught my Coke before it traveled south and smiled at a surprised couple at the closest table. This was a moment to savor. I had finally achieved what I'd spent years working for.

I have no idea who I passed or who passed me on the dance back to my apartment. I'm not even sure what route I took, but I made it back, walked upstairs to my room, and sat down on the edge of my bed. I opened the letter and read the words again and again. I walked over to the phone and laid the envelope and letter down on the desk. For the first time, the addressee information on the envelope registered with me. Though the letter itself was addressed to me, the envelope read, "Victoria Phillips."

At first I laughed, thinking how funny that they had mistakenly used my mother's name instead of mine. Then reality surfaced. There was no way in the world they would know my mother's name unless they knew my mother. A weight drove me into my chair. I couldn't move. I couldn't breathe.

What had she done? Why in the world would she get involved? I had worked so hard, trying to make this novel good enough to win on its own merits. Two hours passed, as did two classes. Around three that afternoon my eyes turned from the window to the phone. I picked it up and dialed.

A thick New York accent greeted me. "Taylor House Publishing."

"Jeff Peterson, please."

"May I tell him who's calling?"

"Yes, yes you can. Would you tell him it is Victoria Phillips from Savannah, Georgia," I spread the southern belle accent so thick the receptionist would be talking about it for the rest of the day.

"One moment, Ms. Phillips," and with the press of a button, I was dumped into the land of Muzak.

"Well, Mrs. Phillips. So, good to hear from you," said a lackey's voice. Disgusting. "So your daughter has received the results of the contest. I trust she's happy."

After all the years of mimicking Vicky, I could have auditioned for *Saturday Night Live*. "Oh, she is, Jeff, she is. She got the letter today, as a matter of fact, and she was thrilled."

"It turned out to be a really fabulous piece of work." Was that a smirk in his voice?

"Well, I just wanted to thank you again for your help and discretion in this matter."

"Don't mention it. I look forward to meeting you and your daughter next month."

"Oh, you don't know how much I look forward to meeting you. Good-bye."

"Good-bye, Mrs. Phillips."

And with that, my dream ended and my mission began.

CHAPTER TWO

I need you, now," was the only other call I made.

"I'll be there as fast as I-16 will take me," said the voice from the other end.

To kill the next three and a half hours, I did what any normal college student would do in her moment of uttermost stress—I cleaned. But I didn't clean just anything. I cleaned the bathroom. From top to bottom, spic-and-span, take-a-nap-in-the-shower kind of clean.

Screams from my best friend, Paige, snapped me out of the world of the ceramic celestial. "Oh my word, this is worse than I ever dreamed. You could have a picnic in here. I came as fast as I could." She walked over to help me pull off the kneepads, rubber gloves, and galoshes.

"I'm not well," I said as I derubberized. I stood to give her a hug, realizing only then that my body had participated in contortionist activity. Paige threw her arms around me, then, forcing me back, stared at me eyeball-to-eyeball. "You look horrible. Let's go get a Coke." And she headed for the door.

I never moved. With no inflection or emotion I said, "I don't want a Coke." For a moment Paige was paralyzed.

"What?" Her flip-flops brought her back over to me. "Come in here." She led me into my bedroom and pushed me across the room to a small sofa at the foot of my bed. "Sit down. You *aren't* well, are you? You talk; Paige will listen." She took the floor and wrapped her petite frame into a ball, positioning herself as she had countless times through the years, ready for me to let loose.

I wanted to pace, but I didn't have the energy. So, I just began at the beginning. I told her of the letter, Vicky's name, and the call to New York. She listened intently. "Paige, I've tried for years to figure out what I wanted to do with my life. Years, I tell ya! Finally, finally I figured out I love books. I love to read them, and I love to write them. So, I changed my major to English and literature, you know, and I felt like the world opened up to me.

"Through all of this, the one thing Little Miss Vicky couldn't do was stay out of it. First she tried to get me a job hosting the Athens news before I had even finished my first semester. Then, she tried to get me a radio broadcasting gig covering the capitol."

"But she hates Atlanta," Paige said, getting up to search the room for food.

"There are chips in the top drawer of the dresser and some bottled water in the closet."

"No Diet Coke?"

"No! Just water. No ice, no cup, just room-temperature water kept in a closet. Now, please, this is my crisis."

"Who keeps chips in a dresser and water in a closet?" she asked.

"You are here to console, not critique."

"I can't console well without food." Paige finally discovered the Doritos and some water, and she walked back to the sofa with a look of hungry dismay.

After a full minute of Paige's futile attempts to open the bag, I jerked it from her hand, ripped it open, and gave it back.

"Focus," I said.

"I am, I am, continue." She munched a Dorito.

"Then she tried to get me the role of the narrator in *Joseph and the Amazing Technicolor Dreamcoat.*"

"Oh, I remember that," Paige said, starting to laugh hysterically. "The whole role is singing, and you're the worst this side of Arkansas."

"Yes, well, thankfully, I know I can't sing and declined the audition. But that's just what she's poked her nose into since college. Who has time to talk about the previous eighteen years!" I was finally coming alive.

Paige pulled her fingers through her hair, trying to push her bangs out of her eyes. "You just put cheese powder in your hair," I told her.

"Oh, it's just us. Who cares?" She put her hand back into the bag to retrieve another chip. "But you know what? I think it's time you quit whining about your mama and get on with your life." She stuffed another chip in her mouth. "You know what really amazes me?"

"What?"

"I can't believe you figured this out. Me? I would have spent the rest of my life thinking what a coincidence it was that my mother's name was on *my* letter." She was totally serious. "But you've always been that way. You could figure out just about anything, about anyone. You remember when someone stole your student-council speech from your locker?" She snickered.

"Yeah," I said, laughing myself at the memory.

"You turned that school and half its students and staff upside down until you finally sneaked into Kimberly Malloy's house and found it in a shoebox in her closet. You are shameless!" Now her snicker had turned into a belly laugh.

"Hey, I was doing good until her mother sneaked up on me with a can of Mace, ready to attack the behind that was poking out of her daughter's closet." That image made us both hysterical.

"At least you weren't cleaning her bathroom," Paige said, laughing so hard she fell off of the sofa.

"Maybe that's it," I said after we wiped our tears and regained our composure. "Maybe I don't need to write books. Maybe I need to uncover stories. Maybe I need to write for a newspaper or something."

"Yeah! You could move back home and write for our paper."

For the first time in the last six hours, I was actually having a rational thought. "You're right, Paige. I could. Maybe this book-writing thing isn't what I was really supposed to do. Maybe I'm supposed to be a journalist after all." That said, I began to pace. "Maybe I could go home, write for the paper, and uncover stories. The first will be 'Tales of Victoria.' That's what I need to do. I need to go home and write stories that terrorize my mother." I was beginning to like this whole idea.

"You need to just go home and do what you're good at."

"I was able to prove that Victoria rigged this contest. There's no telling what I could uncover around our fair city. We've had a very productive evening, my fine friend."

"Yes, we have. Can we eat now?" she asked as she stood to brush the Dorito crumbs off her shirt.

"Are you not totally sick? You just ate an entire bag of chips."

"We'll call that an appetizer," she said, then she threw her arm around me and led me toward the door.

"OK. I need a Coke anyway."

Leo's has the hottest chicken wings north of Hades, accompanied by what Leo calls "raw fries," thinly sliced potatoes cooked either almost raw or crispy, like I like them. Paige and I munched on celery and blue cheese and ate ourselves sick, then we headed back to my apartment to crash. Around three a.m. we had exhausted both conversation and ourselves. Paige got up with me at seven thirty, and by eight I was in class and she was headed home.

After my second class, I went to the mailroom and reached into my mailbox, excited to examine the paper and discover where the *Savannah Chronicle* could most effectively utilize an investigative reporter. But that morning's edition held more distracting information. "Local Humanitarian and Writer, Gloria Richardson, Dead at 62" announced the headline. I read in disbelief, feeling as if a friend I loved deeply was gone. This woman, who had made such an impact on my life, was dead of cancer.

Who knew how many articles she had written about people who overcame insurmountable odds and helped others, in spite of their own circumstances? All the while, she could have been writing her own story. She chose, instead, to keep her battle a secret. Maybe it was the cancer itself that drove her to write some of her more moving pieces. Who could be sure?

As I closed the paper, I thought about the last six years. Lines from past columns began to fit themselves together in my recollection, as if taking over my senses. Then came thoughts of short stories and novels I had written, chased by images of my misguided mother and the decisions I was now forced to make because of them.

It was time for me to become a writer. A good writer. A life-altering writer. A Gloria writer. I knew what I would do. I would decline the award. Better yet, Vicky would decline the award on my behalf and with sincere regret for all of Mr. Peterson's troubles. I would return to Savannah. I would make my own mark right on Vicky's doorstep.

The front page of the *Savannah Chronicle* declared a Mr. Samuel Hicks the editor at large. Within the hour I dialed the number, went through a truly southern receptionist, a rude secretary, and finally landed a rather winded-sounding Mr. Hicks.

"Uh . . . uh, Mr. Hicks, my name is Savannah. And this is probably not the way you normally handle business, but I, well I, uh, I really felt like I needed to speak to you immediately. I'm here at the University of Georgia, and for the last six years, I've consumed every article Gloria Richardson has written. Each one seemed more, well, more powerful than the one before."

The phone was so quiet on the other end, I finally asked, "Are you still there?"

"I'm here," said a perturbed voice.

"I know her death has left a tremendous void at the *Chronicle*. I also know that no one will ever totally fill the place that she has left, but I believe I am capable of carrying on her vision, and—"

"Young lady, I'm not sure who you are or what you think you are capable of, but I won't be hiring anyone to fill Gloria's shoes. No one can. We have only entry-level positions available at this time. If you are interested in a job, you can send in a résumé and some writing samples to our human resources department. Now, I have to get to work." And he hung up.

I decided at that exact moment that I would have Gloria's column in less than a month. Vicky wouldn't be allowed to know. At least not until I decided to tell her.

CHAPTER THREE

After graduation, I hit the road for home in Old Betsy, my eight-year-old black Saab. She's a little tired. The fabric on the ceiling is beginning to detach in a couple of places, but that will be an easy fix. When I actually have time to fix it.

Vicky wanted my dad to buy me a Lincoln Town Car for graduation. She felt it would be safer. "Safe" being the operative word. Safe from anything and everybody. No one would want to be seen with an eighteen-year-old girl in a Lincoln Town Car. My dad graciously salvaged my reputation and refused.

Something happens to me just north of downtown. Savannah begins to fill my senses. No matter what the time of year, I'm forced to roll down my windows and tug open my sunroof, allowing myself to both feel and smell home. I've memorized the story that the streets tell in progression, culminating in the enchantment of the place I call home, the Historic District.

I know this city. I know it the way a couple who have been married fifty years know where the lines came from around each other's eyes. I know its stately oak trees covered in moss, its Bradford pear trees blooming in clouds of white. Savannah holds all my secrets shared with best friends, my first kiss, my once-upon-a-time dreams of foreign lands and great adventures, and my discovery of faith. It is 2.2 square miles of history and life's simple pleasures. It was built of twenty-four squares, many of which held a church, cathedral, or synagogue, and a neighbor who knew not only your name, but your dreams.

During my high-school years, these were the streets we drove in unforgettable joy, riding with heads stuck out the window. These streets were also home to our own Barney Fife, Sergeant Millings. He always hid on the corner of Oglethorpe and East Jones Streets, waiting for any opportunity to pull one of us kids over and fortify his claim that no one under the age of forty-five should be driving.

We Phillipses lived in Atlanta until my eleventh birthday, when my father, Jake, sold his multimillion-dollar accounting firm at the ripe old age of forty. My mother had longed to return to the place she called home since I could remember. So Dad said good-bye to insane hours, the pressure of a hundred employees, and an hour-and-a-half commute. He bought a small coffee shop on East State Street in Savannah, packed up the Phillips clan, and settled in to spend the rest of his life enjoying his family and his job.

Jake's Coffee Shop is located on Wright Square, between the Chatham County Legislative Building and the courthouse. His shop is the place where people start their days with some good old-fashioned brew, as he likes to call it. "If you can't spell it or pronounce it, you surely shouldn't drink it," he is fond of saying.

I proved to be his most difficult customer. I hate coffee. I've tried. I've tried it every way but in milkshake form, and I may have had it that way as well. But I hate it. I am a confessed Coca-Cola addict. It is one of life's greatest joys, especially McDonald's Cokes. They are magical. Their magic lies in that powerful, burning sensation that brings alive every sensory organ known to man. My first taste of a McDonald's Coke sent me soaring. I had more energy than a carpool of five-year-olds and never forgot the taste. Sure, I had had Coke before—but this, this wasn't Coke; this was an experience.

When we moved to Savannah, I commenced my search for the Golden Arches immediately. A quick survey of the area revealed not one within the Historical District. Appalled and persistent, I did what any committed McDonald's Coke connoisseur would do: I picketed. For one week, I picketed in front of our house before and after school, even sacrificing my after-school recreational reading hour. "Do you people not think I deserve a break today?" I asked the passersby. "Don't you know I need to start my day with a Coke and a smile? Well, do you see me? I'm not smiling."

Mother was mortified. "My stars, Savannah Phillips, I'll build you one in the backyard with its own play land if you will just get yourself inside." I refused to be swayed, because we don't *have* a backyard. We have a courtyard, overtaken by a lap pool and flowers with names that no one on the face of the earth beside Victoria and Martha Stewart can pronounce.

By the end of the week, I was worn down. I had been honked at, laughed at, and exploited on the evening news. To top it off, I was dying of thirst. That Friday, Dad picked me up from school and took me straight to his shop. He blindfolded me and led me to the back room. The removal of my blindfold revealed my very own McDonald's Coke fountain, courtesy of a good friend who owned a franchise. Dad knew an eleven-year-old prepubescent girl didn't need any extra drama, especially when she had no trouble creating her own already.

On this beautiful May afternoon, when the front of my house on Abercorn Street came into view, the world was in perfect order. And I was certain I was home. Why so certain? Easy. There were two six-foot signs spanning both of our front balconies. The sign on the balcony to the left of the front door read "Welcome Home," and the sign to the right read "Savannah." I truly wished Vicky could have found a more discreet way to express her excitement.

The house was built with brick made by slave laborers. The people of Savannah in that time believed that if the brick was so

inexpensive, it couldn't be good enough. So they covered the brick with stucco and scored it to make it look like stone. By the 1970s, the same brick that years before had been deemed worthless and in need of covering began to be valued for its actual worth at ten dollars a brick. Its value had homeowners all over Savannah removing their stucco. The brick on our home is undeniably stunning.

There is more ironwork in the city of Savannah than in any other city in America, the majority of it unquestionably on my house. Two balconies in front of the second-floor windows flank ornate black-painted wooden doors. They are rather simple, but beautiful nonetheless—well, before they were mercilessly draped with vinyl communiqué. Ivy climbs the brick wall and reaches around the front of the house from East Jones to Abercorn. There is also a beautiful iron fence that follows the curves of the house in front of the lower windows.

When I pulled into the driveway, my little brother, Thomas, who is all of six-foot-one, came flying out of the side door. He had my door opened before I could even reach for the handle.

"I'm sure you hate the sign," he burst, "but you would have hated Mom's first one even more. She had it evenly distributed with 'Home' cut in half." Thomas turned to face our front stoop, pointing first to the left side. "Welcome Ho"—he stopped long enough to point to the right—"me Savannah. We'd've had tourists making you the next Savannah attraction."

"The eighth wonder of the world, I'm sure."

He planted a kiss on my head. "Don't think so highly of yourself. Fortunately for you, she declared you would rather she cook for you anyway. By now she thinks the whole thing was her idea, and she's totally satisfied."

"Thank you for preserving my reputation." Duke, Dad's golden retriever, came pounding out the side door and stood stately at Thomas's side.

"Duke, you haven't changed a bit. Except maybe gained about

fifty extra pounds!" I grunted as he put both paws on my shoulders and licked me, obviously expecting me to reciprocate. "Someone has got to get this dog on a meal plan."

"He's on Mom's-leftovers meal plan. She refuses to spend money on actual dog food for him."

"Who does that surprise?"

"Well, she might not have a choice. The vet told Dad Duke needs to lose fifty pounds. So Dad started walking him." He stopped and patted Duke on the head. "I think Dad's lost more than Duke has, though."

"Yeah, there's not much pleasure in a fifty-pound bag of Alpo when compared to pork tenderloin." Duke's ears perked up at the mere mention of pork.

"What are you doing here anyway?" I asked, finally stopping long enough to give him a hug. "I thought you had another week of school." As he walked around to open the trunk, I smiled at his neatly cropped hair.

Thomas was in his third year at The Citadel Military Academy in Charleston, South Carolina. Vicky was sure he had enrolled to embarrass her, but he had dreamed of going to The Citadel ever since Judge Hoddicks's son Roger filled his head with stories of life as a cadet. When Thomas came home after his first month with his head shaved, Vicky called the general who was the head of The Citadel and threatened abuse charges.

"Have you seen my child?"

"Yes, ma'am. In fact, I have another five hundred that look just like him."

"Well, it is criminal, I tell you. Criminal." She then headed to her room. Dad followed her and, legend has it, made it clear she would call and apologize. Now, Dad lets Vicky think what she will, but trust me, he is the one who has this ship under control. She made that call to the general, albeit brief and very private, then gathered herself, returned downstairs, declared Thomas too thin, and began to cook a feast.

"I finished up exams early," Thomas said, bringing me back to the present.

"Lucky you."

"I'd say lucky *you* by the way Mom has tried to make your graduation the talk of the town. You might need me here to keep you out of the limelight. Especially if you plan to tell Mom about your new career move. All I have to do is bring up women in the Corps, and she will resurrect her letter-writing campaign to the South Carolina Legislature."

I had called Thomas to warn him of what I was doing, knowing he could help me with the excruciating task of adjustment. We walked around the sidewalk to the front of the house and up the stairs to the double front doors. In old Georgian homes, the entrances were built on the second floor in an effort to limit the dust and dirt that entered the houses from the horse-drawn carriages traveling the dirt streets. The servants lived on the lower level. Today, most homeowners rent out the lower levels as apartments, but Vicky never has. She, instead, made it a haven where Thomas foolishly relocated his room. Vicky walks around in sheer delight, believing her baby will never want to leave.

As we reached the top of the front steps, I stopped and turned around to take a moment to breathe in the essence of my life.

"Been a while, huh, Vanni?"

Wrapping my arm around the young man who alone could call me by such a name, I closed my eyes and allowed a smile to cross my face. "Mmm hmm . . . it's been too long." We walked inside.

I hadn't been home at all my last semester, trying to finish my story and finals. It seemed like forever. Yet, the looming foyer bombarded me with familiarity, right down to the smell in the air, which proclaimed that fried chicken was on the menu.

The oriental rug still encompassed the majority of the black-marble floor. Two black Armthwaite chairs flanked the opening to the left of the foyer, which held the dining room. One massive arrangement of flowers that Mother replenished on a weekly basis brought it all together, creating an abode that could compete with the pages of *Veranda*.

The magnificent staircase with a wrought-iron banister and an oriental stair runner in complimentary tones of rich black, peach, and pink curved around the back of the foyer. I peeked into the "parlor," as Vicky called it. A living room to any normal person, but not to any person living in Savannah. In front of the window sat the early 1900s burlwood petite grand piano, one of my mother's most treasured keepsakes. My father had it shipped from London as a wedding gift.

Above the fireplace in the parlor hangs a picture of Vicky in a white organza gown with hand-beaded flowers all over it, adorned by a bow on each sleeve. All I can say about her hair is that it is big. I have no idea what it is with pageant people and big hair. Maybe they are just trying to make themselves look taller, but most of the time it spreads as wide as it does high. Draped across her is a sash declaring her "Miss Georgia United States of America." She stands stately in this twenty-seven-year-old photograph, her hand draped ever so deliberately, yet casually, across the back of a French colonial chair. Below the portrait in an acrylic box rests her Miss Georgia United States of America crown. Thomas and I call it the "Ode to Vicky." This parlor is her own private sanctuary, where she comes often just to stare at her picture, remembering who knows what.

Thomas came back through the front door, setting down the rest of my bags. "Happy thoughts, I hope."

I couldn't help but laugh as I picked up my bags. "Humorous thoughts. I'm going to get cleaned up for dinner. What about you? Because I have something I want you to do."

"What? I'm not telling Mom anything for you."

"I need you to go take down those banners. Please, they are humiliating. And as long as we keep her inside, she won't even know they're gone."

"Would you like me to hang them up in your room?"

"I will refrain from telling you what to do with them, because I am a southern lady." I turned my back to him and headed up the stairs to a landing that connected four bedrooms. Mine was in the far left corner.

Mother has revamped this house completely three different times and rearranges furniture and accessories on a bimonthly basis. But she is not allowed to touch my room. It is where I can come and know that things will be like I left them. The color of my room is yellow. It reminds me of sunshine. My bedroom suite consists of a wrought-iron bed and a pine dresser that sits to the left of my bed in front of the windows. A pine armoire stands directly across from the bed, housing those things that make young adulthood tolerable: a TV, a stereo, a VCR, and a recently added DVD player. My mother, an only child, had wanted to put my grandmother's antique bedroom suite in my room after my grandparents died, he from a heart attack, she from heartbreak. But I don't do dead people's furniture. I'm more than glad to love 'em while they're living, but once they're gone, well, I don't want to be sleeping on their furniture.

My bed is flanked by floor-to-ceiling bookcases. On these shelves lie my greatest treasures. Pictures of some of my best memories with my closest friends are stuck between the books that have shaped me. Chaucer's *Canterbury Tales,* Lewis's *Chronicles of Narnia,* and Fitzgerald's *The Great Gatsby.* Brontë's *Wuthering Heights* is still wuthering as far as I'm concerned, but some things were just required reading. I also have numerous biographies, some that were authorized and others that weren't. There is the one about the Onassis women that is rather enlightening; a book of Ronnie's love letters to Nancy Reagan, which leaves little room for most men to stand a chance; one of Hillary Clinton that my mother told me I couldn't leave in her house; and the one of George W. Bush she bought to replace it.

When he won the election over Al Gore, she acted like a giddy school girl. She even calls him by the pet name his wife gave him, "Bushie." I told her she needed to get a grip. She told me I needed to appreciate her respect for world leaders. I asked her to name one other world leader she actually knew.

"Oh, you know, the lady with all the shoes. I hear she's pretty good."

"Imelda Marcos?"

"Yes, that's her," she said, acting as if she had said it herself.

"Did anyone ever tell you she went to prison?"

She told me I was getting a little snippy and needed to watch my tone, that she was still my mother. But I saw through the protest. My mother has a crush on the president. I know it, she knows it, and anyone who catches her watching Fox News knows it.

Some books inside this bookcase have changed me. *Roots* by Alex Haley first came to television when I was in elementary school. Mom wouldn't let me watch it, thinking it would be too troubling for my tender years. But she was so glued to the TV set downstairs that I sneaked in the first four nights of viewing without her knowing. My father eventually caught me and held me in his arms while we watched together. He did his best to explain, at least as much as he was able to understand himself. For the next week's show and tell, I brought no show, just tell, and all I told was the story of *Roots*. My teacher finally assured me I had covered all that could possibly be covered. I assured her there was more, but one week was all I got. For my thirteenth birthday, Dad gave me the book.

Gone with the Wind rests there too. That one was Vicky's gift for my thirteenth birthday. "Everyone needs to know her heritage."

"It's fiction, Mother," I told her.

"Fiction to some; reality to truly southern women." I will never tell her that I have actually read the book, or that Scarlett is my secret heroine. In fact, no living soul will ever know, because my mother would see it as cause for public celebration.

Scanning to the bottom of my bookcase, my eyes caught the biography of John Wesley. It is one of my two most precious books, and the sight of it caused me to laugh. I was forced to read it by the pastor of Wesley Monumental United Methodist Church. My longtime friend and eventual boyfriend, Grant Lewis, conned me into sneaking inside the church one Saturday night during our eleventh-grade year, all because he wanted to see who could stay inside the longest without getting freaked out by the shadow figures coming through the fifteen stained-glass windows. We both lost it at the same time when we heard footsteps on the hardwood floor.

"What was that?" Grant whispered.

"God coming to tell us we shouldn't be messing in His stuff."

"No, He only comes on Sunday. It has to be John Wesley's ghost."

"Well, rest assured, he'll know for certain whose inane idea this was by the time he heads home."

About that time, Pastor Mason walked up the stairs and laid his Sunday sermon on the pulpit, eliciting from me a scream loud enough to make Grant scream too. All this lively noise culminated in a scream from Pastor Mason louder than the aforementioned. Not to mention he also went airborne, jumping so high that his knee hit the edge of the pulpit. By the time he hobbled over to turn on the lights, Grant and I were frozen. I couldn't have run had I tried. I knew then that, just like in dreams, fear prevents retreat.

Pastor Mason hobbled calmly toward us, removed us from the red-carpeted runner, and sat us firmly on the front row of the stiff wooden pew. I was too scared to speak, and Grant never opened his eyes.

Then Pastor Mason decided that if we felt it necessary to come to church so early for the Sunday service, we must be in need of a powerful sermon. So he climbed to his pulpit—well, limped actually—and proceeded to preach.

You would think, due to my state of mind, that I'd have trouble remembering his sermon, but I think it is precisely because of my state of mind that I do remember. Surely part of my punishment in heaven for pulling such a stunt would be to recite the sermon verbatim. And I still pretty much can. His message was titled "The Door."

He began by describing the front doors to people's homes and likened them to Jesus being the door to life. Then he compared Jesus to shepherds and spoke of how shepherds are the door to the sheep pen. No one gets to the sheep unless they go through the shepherd. Then he finished with this word: "Each of us should be a bridge builder to that door, the door of Jesus Himself." I wasn't sure I got it, what with all those mixed metaphors, but I'd certainly remember it.

For the benediction, Pastor Mason made us sing four stanzas of "Christ Is Risen" and assigned a twenty-five-page report on the life of John Wesley. Somewhere between the message and the singing, Grant passed out from holding his breath. When Pastor Mason finally left us alone, I was at the altar praying that God would somehow forgive me, and Grant came to long enough to roll around underneath the pew in hysterics. I didn't speak to Grant again until I had written my report, and I have kept the book on John Wesley's life safely tucked away ever since.

John Wesley is known for starting Sunday school in Savannah. It is told that as a little boy he escaped his room in the attic one night when his house caught on fire. He said that night he realized there was a destiny for his life. Wesley loved people, all people. He preached to the Spanish, the Italian, the French, and the English. "The world is my parish," he said. So I guess you could say he was a door to the world. His only desire was to leave something life-changing in his wake. I didn't know if I'd ever leave a wake, but I hoped I could leave something, be a door to someone, somehow.

The other book that has changed my life is my grandmother's Bible. Though I wasn't willing to take her bed, I was pleased to take her Bible. So, it rests here as well, with all her hopes and markings, and new hopes and markings of my own. My greatest treasures are in this room. The past six years, however, have led me to believe they are in this home, in this city.

I only hope I'm still Vicky's treasure by the time dinner is over.

CHAPTER FOUR

In the land of lard you don't have to be told what's for dinner; each offering has a distinct smell of its own. There is the fried-steak smell, the fried-pork-chop smell, the fried-green tomatoes, squash, or okra smell; and the greatest of them all, the fried-chicken smell. As for the smell of Victoria's fried chicken, well, let's just say it is so sinfully delicious that I am forced to call her Victoria when referring to it. My mother is in her element in the kitchen, where she dances around like a virtuoso in apron and high heels.

My first evening back revealed all things as they were: Dad at the table going through the mail, Duke at his feet, Thomas nowhere in sight; he rarely was. This world of mine was still mine.

I set the table and pulled out serving dishes. When all was ready, a yell went out for Thomas to come to dinner. Upon his arrival, we all took our usual seats—me across from Dad and Thomas across from Vicky. And there in front of us was a piece of heaven, a platter of fried chicken à la Victoria.

We also had fresh corn on the cob, butter beans, macaroni and cheese—and not that boxed kind either. Vicky would have needed rehabilitation if anyone in her home cooked something out of a box. The only thing she bought in boxes was cereal, and that only after my father took a liking to Frosted Flakes. If it wasn't homemade, Vicky declared it wasn't worth eating. This caused a bit of a controversy every now and then, but I'll just leave that to the imagination.

No, OK, I'll tell. One evening some new neighbors invited us for dinner. Vicky usually liked to have new families over to our house so she could supervise all culinary activities, but this couple was insistent that they cook for her after all she had done to help them get acclimated to the city.

Upon arrival, Vicky gave me a dirty look for having gum in my mouth. "Would you mind telling me where your trash can is?" I asked our lovely hostess.

She stopped putting ice in the glasses and pointed me in the direction of the pantry. "Sure, honey, it's right over there."

Vicky was standing next to me when I swung the pantry door open to get to the trash can. There, in full view, were boxes for just about anything you could imagine. There was macaroni in boxes, rice in boxes, soups in boxes, cakes in boxes—and the crowning transgression—entire meals in boxes.

Poor Vicky grew white as a sheet. She politely excused herself, grabbed my father, and pulled him into the half bath beneath the stairs.

I heard snippets of "I wouldn't feed Duke . . ." and ". . . snowball's chance in Dixie." Then I heard a male voice say, "You will and you'll like it."

Dad must have been immensely clear, because she returned and we all convened at the dinner table, where Vicky sat staring at her plate. As our hostess passed her a perfectly acceptable meal, she asked, "Victoria, is anything wrong tonight? You look kind of peaked."

Vicky came out of her trance long enough to say, "No, nothing's wrong." She then picked up her fork and let it slowly work its way through the food without ever bringing it to her mouth.

My dad glared at her from across the table, but even that didn't work. Finally she asked the lady, "So, how do you make this, this, this lovely casserole?"

"Oh, it's really easy. In fact, I think I have another box of it in the pantry that I'll give you to take home."

Well, I honestly thought Vicky was going to expire right there. But with one more glance at my father, she ever so slowly put a minuscule amount of food on her fork. It crept to her lips, where she placed only the tiniest bit into her mouth. I was mesmerized.

When the first bite entered, she feigned chewing. The next thing I knew, her eyes were watering, and she started coughing and gagging and holding her throat. She jumped up and asked the lady, fist clinched around her throat. "What's in here?" The poor hostess, horrified, ran to the trash can, pulled out the empty box with my chewing gum stuck on top, and began to read out loud every ingredient on the back.

When the lady got to an ingredient she couldn't pronounce, Vicky said, "That's it! I'm deathly allergic to that." Waddling over to my father, still holding her throat, she grabbed his arm and feigned gasping, "Jake, you'd better get me to the emergency room immediately."

My dad hadn't budged and didn't budge. He simply looked at her and said, "You can walk yourself home, get the car, and drive yourself to the emergency room. The kids and I are going to finish dinner with this kind family, and we will check on you when we get home."

I don't know if our poor hostess was more horrified by what she had done to my mother or by how my father was treating her. Her husband did his best not to break out in sheer hysterics, and I just sat back and enjoyed the drama. Thomas never looked up. He was still enjoying every bite of his boxed dinner. Vicky glared at my father, touched the lady's arm gently, apologized, grabbed her purse, and waddled home.

When the door closed behind her, Dad looked at the sweet

hostess about to collapse in tears and touched her arm. "Victoria has episodes like this quite often, but trust me, she'll be back to normal, oh, I'd say by early morning. Now, let's enjoy this excellent meal." He looked at both of us, smiled a smile we knew all too well, and we stayed another two hours.

"Lord, we thank You that Savannah is home. We thank You that we can be together. We thank You for this meal we are about to receive and the amazing hands that so sacrificially and lovingly prepared it for us from scratch." I thought it rather shameless to try to schmooze your mother through prayer, but I would take whatever worked. "Amen," Thomas closed.

Vicky started right in. "Savannah, has Dean Hillwood let you know when you could expect to hear the results of the contest?"

Thomas was on that like a duck on a June bug. "Mom, did I tell you that I'm going to bring some of the guys home this summer? They haven't quit talking about your biscuits since the last away game and—"

"Thomas, that will be great, but I was speaking to Savannah. She and I haven't had time to talk in weeks. She's been so busy." She turned back to me. "So if you win, will you move to New York or try to stay here?"

I wiped my mouth and refolded my napkin. "There is something you need to know about the contest."

"Tell your mother anything, darling."

"I spoke with my dean before I left school, and he totally agreed and is supporting me. I hope you can do the same."

"Now, honey, your mother loves you more than Dean Hillwood. I'm sure anything you do I will support." My eyes caught Dad's. I knew he would support whatever decision I made. As long as I was making an honest living and enjoying what I did, he would be happy for me.

"Well, I've been doing a lot of thinking over the last couple of months, and I've made some decisions for my life. I did receive the results of the contest." Poor Vicky leaned in so far her chin was about to touch the gravy. "And I won, actually."

"Oh my stars! I knew you would win," she said with a little too much enthusiasm. "I just knew you would. You were created for this, Savannah. You are just going to be amazing! Oh, but you can't move. Will you have to move? Surely you won't have to move immediately, if you have to move at all. I mean, can't you write books from anywhere?"

"Yes, I can write from anywhere."

"Yes! Right! You could. You could write them from right up there in your bedroom."

"Yes, I could, actually."

"Oh my stars! Oh, well, let's eat. Let's just eat and eat and eat and then go get dessert and eat some more," she said, laughing at her own delight.

"I'm not finished, Mother," but she didn't hear a word. I was forced to reach over and touch her hand. "Mother, Mother . . ."

"Oh, yes, darling, what is it? If you have something else to tell your Mother, just go right ahead."

"I did win the contest," I said, pausing to take a deep breath, "but I am not accepting the award."

"You what?"

"I turned it down. But before you go off in the other direction, let me finish."

"Savannah Grace Phillips, I cannot—" she began. Dad reached over and touched Vicky's arm and nodded in my direction. She looked slightly perturbed but conceded. "Continue, Savannah," she said through pursed lips.

"Go ahead, Savannah. We're listening," Dad said, softening his brow.

"I've been doing a lot of thinking. I love to write. I really do. In fact, until this contest, I thought that really was what I wanted to do with my life. But when the opportunity came, something didn't feel right." I studied Vicky's expression, but she offered nothing but staged melodrama.

"I can't believe this! Something didn't *feel* right," she started.

"Victoria, let her finish."

"Do please finish, Savannah," she said, stabbing at a butter bean.

I looked over at Thomas for support. He gave me a wink and a smile. "It just isn't right for me. I believe there is something else."

"Something else? What? A street hustler? A Falcons cheerleader? Heaven help us all." A brief clutch of her chest caused the entire table to flinch.

"I believe I have a different mission in life than to simply write novels. And that's basically all I have to say." I picked up my fork to eat my now-cold dinner. Then I let fly the arrow that would certainly strike with practiced precision. "Oh, there is one more thing. I want to live here, here in Savannah. And if I can, Mother, I'd really like to stay at home, at least until I can find an apartment."

My, my, my, a verse and a chorus of "Sweet Beulah Land" could have been sung about that time. You would have thought the last five minutes were a distant memory by the light that came on in Vicky's black eyes and the smile that crept its way back into position. I knew it was evil, but it was necessary. For a moment, my thoughts went to visions of the inevitable Vicky meltdown when I indeed found my new place. All could be certain she would die a thousand deaths, each of which we would suffer with her.

On the whole, the entire adventure went well. She offered a few brief groans, a few sighs, and a few, well, I'm not sure what they were, but they didn't quite fit the gasp category. Dad sat meditatively across from me as well, never picking up a bite of food. Thomas looked up only between bites.

As the production came to a close, Dad got up calmly from his seat, kissed me on the head, and whispered in my ear, "I'm not sure what you are up to, but I know you have a plan." I looked up and he smiled at me—that smile that is definitively Dad. Then he sat back down, content to finally eat his chicken.

I felt a hand on mine. I looked over at Vicky and saw tears coming down both cheeks. She just smiled at me, either out of pity or pleasure, I'm not quite sure, and patted my hand like she does. Then she said, "Eat your chicken, darling." Even cold, Victoria's chicken was still the best I had ever eaten.

"Jake, why don't you and Thomas clear the table so Savannah and I can go for a walk?"

Dad hesitated, thinking I'm sure that the whole pat-on-the-hand, tears-in-the-eyes presentation at the table was a momentary diversion, and that I might be in for the reeling of my entire human existence. "Victoria, she's a grown woman. You can't make her decisions for her."

She kissed him on the forehead and headed to the foyer. "Yes, but she'll always be my daughter. We'll be back shortly, I promise."

She never asked me if I wanted to go for a walk, but I followed her to the foyer, and Duke followed close behind, both of us with our tails tucked between our legs.

"Grab your sweater. It might be cool," she said. Vicky took her elegantly embroidered sweater from the coatrack by the door, and I grabbed my gray sweatshirt off the armchair. Duke seemed content to stay behind, but I made him come for protection. He and Vicky have issues. She's had little regard for him since Dad refused to name him Magnolia.

As we walked down the stairs and turned the corner to East Jones Street, the air still held a slight chill, but I could feel the hint of summer in the distance. We headed straight to walk the squares.

It took an entire square for Vicky to get to the point of this excursion. We had taken only two other walks like this one since we moved to Savannah. One was the prerequisite birds-and-the-bees talk. I'm not sure how it ended. I just know that by the time she was through and I realized that she had participated in birds-and-bees behavior on at least two separate occasions—well, it absolutely rocked my world. Then there was the going-off-to-college talk: always be a lady, wear clean underwear in case you get in a wreck, don't give your heart away, don't talk back, and call home once a day. I obliged by calling three times a week. And I never understood the clean underwear part anyway, because after a wreck, who could be sure what was bad hygiene and what was simply a by-product of the wreck itself?

I had a feeling, however, that this conversation was going to be different. Why? Because for the first two blocks Vicky never said a word. She didn't talk about the weather. She didn't talk about the McCollums, who live next door, and their grandchildren, Penelope and Priscilla. She didn't tell the latest gossip about crazy Mrs. Weitzer, who lives across the street, or dirty old Mr. Dickerson, who lives two doors down and has a habit of gazing through windows. She didn't even talk about the new flowers planted around Lafayette Square. She didn't talk about what was happening down at the Chamber of Commerce, where she served the city as director, or the coffeehouse. She didn't talk about her latest recipe or award. She didn't even talk about how glad she was to have both of her children home. No, for two solid blocks, my mother remained absolutely and miraculously silent. Then, it began like this.

"Savannah, I remember those countless times as I would rock you in the wee hours of the morning and stare into your precious face, dreaming of what you would become. For years I tried to make you me, but I realized some women weren't meant to be like me," she said, placing her hand daintily on her chest while I nodded in adamant agreement.

"I used to think you would be a great pianist, until I heard you play."

That gave us both a moment of confirming laughter. "Ain't that the truth."

"Savannah, don't say 'ain't.'"

"OK," I said in mock appeasement.

"We tried you in ballet, and then we saw you dance."

"Thank you for saving me," I said, laughing again. We were coerced into stopping so Duke could take care of his business. We both stopped talking because it was hard to have any meaningful conversation with that going on.

"I don't know why that dog has to do that," she said, crinkling her nose and turning away.

"Because he's a dog."

"I don't care. He should be more discreet. Out here where anyone can see. Did you bring something to pick it up with?"

"There is no way I'm picking that up!"

"That is the law around here, Savannah."

"Well, you should have told me that before we started this thing."

Victoria sighed in disgust. "I knew we should have gotten a lap dog."

When Duke was finished, we picked up our walk and she picked up her thoughts.

"But when you brought home your first creative-writing piece in middle school, I knew then what you had been created for. I don't believe I have ever read words more simple, yet profound, more compelling or endearing in my entire life."

"That's a bit overstated."

"No, it's not. You engulfed me with your story, and you made me cry at your ability to express yourself so tenderly yet with such strength."

Duke yawned and shook his head.

"All that at thirteen?"

"Yes! You were a very gifted child." Her use of the past tense gave me pause. "You got that from your mother. So I nurtured your imagination. You went into theater and writing. And I always believed that one day you would be one of the greatest writers of your generation—melodramatic, maybe, but phenomenal nonetheless."

"Can you imagine, someone from our family melodramatic?"

"Well, they say every family has one."

"Yes, they do." I could not believe the poster child for melo-drama had just labeled me the same.

"I've pictured your face in the bookstore windows and thought about how we could advertise your first book signing here in Savannah. Well, anyway, tonight, listening to you, I realized that your life isn't about what I want. Your life is about doing what you believe is the absolute best thing for you."

When we reached the edge of the Dueling Zone in front of the cemetery, Victoria stopped and turned to face me. The dueling zone was used years before for unresolvable conflicts. It had been avoided by us since our last flip-flop confrontation. Duke didn't realize we had stopped until his leash extended fully and he was forced to come back or gag to death. Victoria looked down and patted his head. I thought about checking her temperature, her pulse, her latest psychiatric evaluation, but I figured this was one of those once-in-a-lifetime moments that just needed to be left as is.

"Savannah, everything in my life that I ever wanted I have achieved. I was crowned Miss Georgia United States of America."

"Yes, you were."

"I married the man I have always loved, and he has loved me better than I probably deserve," she said hesitantly but not totally convincingly. I held my tongue.

"I have two children who are exactly what I wanted. I live in the city I adore. I have a job I love and the anticipation of some-thing eternal beyond this world. I don't need anything else except to see my children achieve the same happiness I have been fortu-nate enough to enjoy. If you find that in staying here and seeking out a new dream, then I will support you wholeheartedly." And with that she kissed me and hugged me as only a mother can do.

Somehow Vicky made me believe her. How she could try so hard to secure my victory in that contest and not fight harder at this moment wasn't clear, but she didn't. And it felt genuine. She really seemed, at that moment at least, to want for my life what-ever I wanted for my life. We would see.

"Thanks."

"Well, we believe you will make the right choices because we believe in you. Now, let's go home before your father thinks I've killed you and thrown you into the river," she said, and she hooked her arm in mine.

As we headed home, I took in all the changes that had taken place while I'd been gone. "I see the Adamses repainted their house. When did they do that?"

"Oh, that was an issue. Jane Ann wanted a rich cream and her husband wanted a gray. They were both wrong; I thought yellow would be perfect." We continued up the street, leaving the yellow painted-brick house behind us.

CHAPTER FIVE

I have always been a jogger, well, since the eighth grade. It is the one form of enjoyable exercise that middle-school P.E. offered, and since then, running has been a way of life. I conned Paige into joining me for all of two days. Then she lost interest and retreated to her indoor life.

My freshman year in high school, though, my motivation for jogging changed. It happened one Sunday morning at the church we attend on Tybee Island, in my usual place on the tenth pew, left-hand side. I had not expected to encounter any life-altering milestone that morning, and so I was caught unaware. Pastor Brice took his place behind the acrylic podium and began his simple message titled "The State of Your Soil." It was all about a gardener's inability to plant a crop of any substance or value unless he first prepares his soil. He used the parable of the sower and the seed from the Gospel of Matthew. And he let us know in the most tender of ways, that unless we spent time preparing the soil of our hearts through prayer and actually dusting off the coffee-table Bible, no seed would ever take root.

Since that day, morning has been my "tilling time," beginning with a jog. I put on my earphones and play some inspirational music. Then I head home and read from my grandmother's Bible, digging for the same treasures she did before me.

I've come to realize that those moments in the morning have done exactly what Pastor Brice said they would. Focusing on my heart, focusing on my life, taking time to actually ask the Lord to show me His will—I've seen things take root.

This particular morning I grabbed Duke and we headed toward Forsythe Park. I greeted the lightness in the air with thankfulness that the heavy heat had not yet arrived. Spring in the South is simply a wish.

As Duke and I trotted along, a curly-headed beast on a bicycle attacked from out of nowhere. Duke turned around so fast that his leash wrapped up my legs like a bad mess of Christmas-tree lights, leaving me in a dreadfully knotted heap. The maniac came to an abrupt stop, and I tried to unwind my legs from my neck as graciously as possible.

"I'm so sorry," he said, half apologetic, half laughing. "Here, let me help you." He tried to untangle Duke's leash from around my legs. Duke thought this whole thing was a game and couldn't decide who needed licking more, me or Evel Knievel, so he just lavished us both.

"I'm OK. Really, it's no big deal," I said, trying to act cool as my feet finally touched the sidewalk again. He helped me up and handed me Duke's leash. Duke clearly wanted him to stay, but I was ready for him to go. "Really, I'm OK. But *you* need to slow down a tad on that thing," I said, raising my right eyebrow.

"Yeah, slow down a tad. I haven't heard that word in a very long time."

"What word?"

"Tad."

"I didn't say tad!"

"Well, I don't have time to argue over a young, attractive woman like yourself using the word *tad,* because I'm kind of late for work. I'm really sorry. Are you sure you're OK?" he asked again as he headed over to pick up his blue bike off the concrete.

"Yes, I'm OK, really," I said, making it clear I was oblivious to the fact that he had called me both young and attractive. "It's all of five thirty in the morning. Where on earth do you work?" I asked, trying not to notice how toned and tanned his arms were as they grabbed the handlebars and his muscles flexed magnificently.

"Oh, just up the street. Maybe we'll bump into each other again," he said, an irritatingly straight, beautiful white smile lighting up his annoyingly dramatic dark eyes. "But if you're OK, I really have to go."

"I'm OK. So just go," I said, shoving my hand at him.

He departed with a smirk, and Duke watched as he and his bouncing black curls rode up the street in the direction of Bay Street, forcing me to have to watch as well. Grant was the only man who had ever turned my head, and that head had been stuck inside books for so long, even Grant hadn't been able to turn it in years. Duke and I had a long talk about his leash, and I tried to "till" as best I could, but I confess I was a tad distracted.

How do newspaper people dress? Do they wear their *hair back, or down, or what?* I pulled up my wet, stringy hair, then let it fall, then pulled it up just to let it fall again. Duke was sitting at my bathroom door with a cocked eyebrow. "Do they walk around with pencils behind their ears and their shirttails out, always racing around on a deadline? I should have gone in yesterday before I came home and scoped out the joint."

After great deliberation, I settled on a simple black pantsuit with a pale blue tank underneath, slid myself into my black mid-heeled mules, certain flip-flops were inappropriate, and pulled my hair back in what I hoped was a Lois Lane do. She's about the only newspaper reporter I knew. Then I was on my way, sneaking out to join the world of the employed.

When I turned left onto Bay Street off of Abercorn, I could see the sign SAVANNAH CHRONICLE hanging vertically from the side of the building up ahead. Those two words seemed to mock me, "SAVANNAH CHRONICLE, and you don't know anything about us."

True, but that was all about to change. I walked into the office and wasn't greeted by anyone. I came early, wanting to catch Mr. Hicks fresh before the onslaught of appointments and crises. The receptionist's desk was empty, and the people who were there were running around in such a tizzy that they noticed nothing but the path ahead of them, if that. I decided to make myself at home and find Mr. Hicks's office without assistance.

I searched the first and second floors without encountering so much as a hello, and decided to make my way to the third floor. As the elevator ascended, the fear in my mind did as well. *Maybe this is the week he decided to take his wife and kids to the south of France. Or maybe he doesn't even have a wife. And he probably doesn't like kids. In fact, he probably would hate the south of France. Or maybe he's a nice man who likes everyone and was just upset the day I called because of the loss of Gloria. Who knows?*

The elevator doors opened, and I heard his booming personality before sighting the body that went with it. "So much for fresh, free from crisis, and no appointments." I eased up the maze of aisles, following the noise toward a half-open door. The words coming from the office were loud and direct. "I told you yesterday I didn't want to see you here this morning. So go to your office, pack it up, and get out of here. And if I see your face around here at lunch, I'll pack you up and throw you out myself."

I began to perspire. Southern ladies don't "sweat," Vicky says. She could have been proven wrong ten times over that morning, however. As I neared the door, the name placard that read "Mr. Samuel Hicks, Editor at Large" confirmed my fear. From my vantage point, his office looked rather sparse but possessed a fabulous view of Bay Street. Then, the object of his torment came into view—an elderly woman, whose black hair had strands of gray, and whose etched chocolate hands made it evident she was in her glory years. I couldn't make out her soft words, but Mr. Happy Hicks's roaring verbosity didn't allow for much of a reply anyway.

I sat down in a chair on the other side of the door, which kept me out of view. "So that's Mr. Hicks," I said to myself. "Just like I thought, a man who takes vacations in his recliner with the remote control, who hates children, his wife left him years ago because he didn't know how to be nice, and when he dies, only a handful of people will come to his funeral, and they will only be there because he owes them money."

And the longer I sat there contemplating this afflicted life, the madder I became. I should have let it go. But who could? Someone stronger maybe, but self-control was a quality I had yet to successfully till. I saw no reason to start today. When I heard her faint whisper and then the power of his voice begin to consume the air again, I stood and took a moment to set my course. Fortunately, one of my professors had been a hard one to melt, until I stole his heart with my Georgian graciousness. Well, maybe not completely stole his heart, but he did at least quit glaring at me. I wasn't confident that a similar tactic would work here. But wars had been won with less. Then the spirit of Vicky welled up inside me, and I decided this wasn't a moment for graciousness. The only appropriate approach for this brute was "The Vicky." No lady should ever be spoken to in such a rude, ungentlemanly, and unacceptable manner. So, I spun my little heels around, steeled my jaw, and let Vicky take over.

As Mr. Hicks jerked his head to see me standing there, I realized he was a rather calm-looking man in his late fifties. The precious lady turned and smiled a beautiful white smile. She sensed rescue had come. I pushed the door open the rest of the way, and it flew so fast, I'm certain the doorknob stuck in the wall. For a moment, I wished he had been standing behind it. I walked over to his desk, where he had already assumed a seated position, his slight belly from too many fast-food lunches poking out in front. I put both hands on his desk and leaned over where he could see me clearly.

"What can I do for you, young lady?"

"Actually, I don't need anything from you now. At first I thought I wanted to work at your newspaper. But I can tell you're not a man who appreciates talent or even people, for that matter."

That statement caught his attention, and the lady crossed her arms and leaned back in amusement.

"No, anyone that would speak to a precious lady like this"— I patted her on the arm— "the way I've heard you speak to her isn't a man that deserves fine, raw talent. This lady has probably worked for you for years. Met your deadlines, listened to your rantings, spent sleepless nights wondering what would possibly make someone like you happy. She comes into the office every day and isn't allowed to drink McDonald's Coke or even have pictures of her golden retriever on her desk."

"She doesn't have a golden retriever, and she drinks coffee."

"Like you know what kind of dog she has."

"Yes, I do. She has a cocker spaniel."

I looked at the lady, hoping he was bluffing, but she nodded with a smile.

"Well, the point isn't what kind of dog she has; it has to do with who she is. She's a human being who deserves your respect. She deserves to be treated like a lady and respected for her, well, for her age if for nothing else. There's wisdom behind these gray hairs, gray hair you probably contributed to. Lord knows she's probably spent a lifetime having to make sure you're happy. And frankly, I don't want to spend the rest of my life doing the same."

Mr. Hicks was having trouble stifling a grin, which incensed me all the more. "Are you through?" he asked as he folded his arms and rested them on the top of his stomach.

"No, not quite. I came here today to get a job. Gloria Richardson's job. But I am leaving here disillusioned and dismayed. You wouldn't appreciate me. You probably didn't appreciate Gloria any more than you appreciate this fine lady."

"It's Ruby," she said with a smile and a nod of apparent satisfaction in Mr. Hicks's direction.

"Thank you, Ruby, nice to meet you. I'm Savannah. Anyway, I have decided I wouldn't want to work for someone who would treat anyone the way Miss Ruby has been treated here today. So for all of the beleaguered souls, I quit."

"Is that so?"

"Yes, and remember you could have had your Gloria back by next week, only her name would have been Savannah. You could have published stories the next generation could appreciate and the older generation would have respected."

"Yeah, that the older generation would have respected." Miss Ruby snickered.

I looked at her, shook Miss Ruby's hand, and turned on my heels, not so gracefully. Fortunately, I gathered myself prior to disaster, and proceeded to walk toward the door. Vicky was good, but Savannah had just raised the bar.

"Hold it just one moment, young lady." I turned around cautiously to face the now-standing and rather looming figure in front of me. "Do you mean you are just going to come in here and rant and rave and then leave without ever allowing anyone else to speak?"

"Well, I . . ."

"Now it is time for you to listen. Miss Ruby, would you like to tell her what was happening here today?"

Miss Ruby walked over to me and took me by the hand. "I just want you to know, Miss Savannah, that is the kindest thing I've seen anyone do for someone else in a long time. I thought kids your age didn't think about much else than the opposite sex and mooching off their parents." I decided then never to introduce her to Paige. "But on Mr. Hicks's behalf, I must tell you, he was making me go on vacation."

Her face lit up and every ounce of blood drained from my own. "Oh."

"Yes, that's what I was telling her. This woman, as you can tell, is here before anyone else and works after everyone else leaves. She doesn't go on vacation unless absolutely forced and hasn't taken a sick day in thirty years."

"Don't need a sick day, Samuel. I'm healthy as a horse. My husband's no longer living, all the kids are grown, and I just enjoy being here," she said, looking at me with a wink. I tried to smile back, but I was totally incapable. I no longer had a book deal and had just successfully rejoined the world of the unemployed without ever having left.

"So see, Savannah. Things aren't always as they appear. Now, if you'll excuse us, I'd like to talk to this lady for a minute," he said.

"Sure, I'm sorry. I hope you have a great vacation," I said, nodding to Miss Ruby. "And I hope you have a pleasant day as well, sir."

"Savannah, I was actually talking to Miss Ruby. I'd like you to stay for a moment," he said, smiling. "Ruby, I meant every word I said. Get going."

"I'm going, I'm going. Savannah, if you don't make it in the newspaper world, you'd make an excellent defense attorney," she said, patting me on the arm. She left the room, and her chuckle trailed her up the hall.

Then there were two. I looked at him with a pathetic grin, and he motioned for me to have a seat. "So you're the one I told to send me some of her writing. Do you always follow instructions this well?"

"Well, I wanted to make sure you read my articles. I didn't know where they would end up if I simply mailed them."

"You're a brave soul, Savannah."

"I believe I just knocked on the door of stupidity myself."

"Well, that too," he said chuckling, his belly bouncing as he laughed. "I've only seen that kind of passion one other place before."

"Where's that, sir?"

"In Gloria Richardson. She had it from the moment she arrived and it left with her. Don't get me wrong. We've got excellent journalists. But passion and an ability to write are two different things. You'll have to learn to harness your passion, Savannah. And I'm not sure if you can even write, seeing as I never got what I asked for."

"I have some samples with me, though I can't imagine you'd actually want to read them now."

"Well, I do. Leave them with me, and I'll call you later."

I retrieved what I had brought and placed them on his desk. "Does she really have a cocker spaniel?"

"Yes, his name is Sam, after me, and he just turned eight. And she takes her coffee with cream, no sugar. I know the people who work with me, Savannah. And I know them well."

"Hmm." And with that I pulled the embedded door closed, certain I had left a couple of lingering impressions.

CHAPTER SIX

I needed a Coke. A Coke and a good book. I headed to Jake's.

Only eight fifteen and Jake's was already lively. The atmosphere and the company, even more than the coffee, is why people return. In the past thirteen years, I don't think Dad has lost a customer. Judge Hoddicks, Jake's most loyal patron, is in every morning at eight, and Mr. and Mrs. Leonard Culpepper, who live above the coffee shop, follow moments behind. The Culpeppers have two decafs with no sugar and extra cream. They firmly believe that caffeine after seven a.m. will keep them awake.

Jennifer, Hope, and Karen from the Legislative Plaza next door pick up their usuals around eight thirty, before they head into the office. They get cappuccinos later in the day at that other coffee shop, the mere mention of which is not allowed at Jake's. But they wouldn't miss seeing my dad at the beginning of their day for anything.

Most everything in the Savannah Historic District, besides restaurants and that other coffee shop, closes around five. My father's main business comes from his square alone, and he figures when they are gone, he can go home too. Dad is home no later than five fifteen. Oh, and he is closed on Sunday. He, like Chick-fil-A, operates by the motto "After six days of work, everyone needs a day of rest."

As my face registered with old friends, there were hugs all around. Louise and Mervine, twins who came out of retirement to work with Dad, stopped midpour, abandoning countless customers.

"Mervine, this child is too thin. Savannah Phillips," Louise continued, "sit yourself down while we try to find you some food." They flitted around the counter that separates the tables from the back offices, storage rooms, and Coke machine, leaving their customers to fill their own cups.

Richard, one of the sweetest men I know and Dad's right-hand man, was standing behind the counter refilling a couple of obvious tourists' cups when he heard Louise's commotion. Richard's sixty-five years showed only faintly on his dark skin, as gray had begun to infiltrate his coarse black hair. He grabbed me and hugged me the way only Richard can, hugging me so hard it would take hours before I would breathe correctly again.

"Savannah Phillips, I can't believe you finally got out of school. I thought you were going to stay until they made you leave," he told me, his beautiful smile lighting up his face.

"You didn't hear, Richard? They did kick me out. Vicky came by and told them unless they changed the color of the brick on campus, she wasn't going to pay the rest of my tuition." Richard laughed with me as I pulled up a chair at the counter.

Since the death of notorious Savannian Jimmy Williams, my mother has done more for Savannah's architectural integrity than anyone in recent history. Jimmy Williams is the man from the acclaimed book *Midnight in the Garden of Good and Evil,* a book that put Savannah on the map for things many like my mother would rather have kept off. He came into this city bringing his own demanding perspective and rather extravagant taste and colorful lifestyle. Prior to his death he purchased and restored seventy-two homes. The publication of his story caused this city's tourism to increase by 46 percent.

Since Williams's death, Vicky, a member of the Historic Review Board, started a program in conjunction with the Savannah College of Art and Design, a co-op in which the students work with the city on the restoration of historic homes and landmarks. They have beautifully restored more than fifty of the downtown-area homes, turning them into museums of Savannah's history and stores reflecting Savannah's taste and style.

Vicky also helped to pass a law that banned changes on the outer structure of any home in the Historic District without those changes first being approved by the city. It passed easily in the state legislature. The only thing that still rankles her is that some modern buildings were grandfathered in, including one up the street that she refuses to drive by, walk by, or discuss. She wanted to have them torn down, but no one was brave enough to tackle that one. She is this city's greatest lobbyist and advocate. She is the government's greatest thorn. But Savannah loves her. I think one day she'll run for mayor. I also think she does most of this in hopes that someone will write a book about her. Then she can say, "Jimmy Williams may have increased tourism 46 percent, but I, Victoria Inez Phillips, increased tourism 54 percent and didn't have to murder a soul to do it." Not that a few of us haven't died a thousand deaths in the process.

"Your mother will eventually learn that not everything requires her opinion," Dad said as he appeared from the back room, Coke in hand, and pulled up a chair next to me at the counter. His six-foot-one frame is still sturdy at the age of fifty-three, a brief eight years older than my mother. He was probably considered "fine" when he was young, though I can't say I'm comfortable ascribing that kind of adjective to my father.

"Well you can dream in Technicolor if you wish," I pronounced, "but as long as there is breath in ol' Vicky, there will be a helpless victim on the other side of her opinion."

"Dreaming in Technicolor is something I do often," he said, laughing that genuine laugh I have grown to love. None of that fake southern stuff just to make you feel good. Jake only laughs if it's funny. He also cries when his kids make him proud and lights up like a fifteen-year-old schoolboy when Vicky enters the room. "But you don't need to talk that way about your mother. And it is 'Mother,'" he added. Dad got up to wipe off a table that had just been vacated by two businessmen. "What've you been doing this morning?"

I stopped for a moment to watch him in this environment that he loved. He looked happy. "Oh, nothing much really. Just rode around for a bit to see what has changed."

"You look mighty nice to have been just riding around," he said, giving Richard a wink.

"Oh, well, I've been trying to look a little more professional. You know, with graduating and everything," I said, apparently unsuccessful in my attempt to convince anyone, including the two women who had just come out of the back room with a banana and a muffin.

"Do you have a busy morning?" Dad asked.

"Nope." I pulled a book out of my bag and waved it around. "I have a little time to kill before lunch."

"Well, we could use an extra pair of hands round here," Richard said. "Why don't you go grab an apron so you don't mess up your new look?"

I gave Richard my best woeful sigh and put the book away. Then I headed to the back of the store, grabbed an apron, and proceeded to fill cups.

Above the counter at Jake's hangs a blackboard that features daily pieces of wisdom or, as my father calls them, "Thoughts for the Journey." Some folks take these little thoughts to heart, like the one that read, "A man who works hard is guaranteed success." Dad said he saw more activity on the square that day than he had seen in years. Or the other that had people falling all over themselves trying to live right: "Live righteously and rewards will seek you out. Live like the devil and misfortune will pursue you."

Some people, like Vicky, take the ones they like and leave the ones they feel don't apply. She was especially offended the day Dad had written, "A quarrelsome wife is like a constant dripping." She thought he had it up all day, but he only put it up when he saw her come out of the courthouse and head over toward the shop.

"Are you calling me 'a constant dripping,' Jake Phillips?"

Dad simply smiled, removed her hands from her hips, wrapped his arms around her defensive body, and whispered in her ear, "No. You, my love, are a consistent nurturer." To this day, whenever Vicky begins her constant dripping, Dad, or any of us nearby, lets her know that she is consistently nurturing that which has been nurtured enough.

Today Dad's thought for the journey read, "Anxiety in the heart of man can make him depressed, but it takes only one nice word to make him happy." Surely I had caused enough anxiety for the entire population of Savannah already that morning, making this a justifiable penance. So for the next three hours, Dad and I determined to get rid of everyone's anxieties with a nice word. We complimented suits, hairdos, grandchildren's pictures—we even complimented things that really shouldn't have been complimented at all, like Mrs. Taylor's new wiry-haired, rat-looking dog. When it came through the door, Duke ran to the other side of the counter where he would be safe from such a rodent. Dad made over that dog until Mrs. Taylor was beaming from ear to ear.

By the time the morning and midmorning rushes had cleared, depression had vacated the streets around Jake's Coffeehouse. I was even feeling better myself.

As I walked to my car, I could feel the heat challenge the coolness of my skin. Crawling into the black car and its warming conditions made me dread what the actual summer would hold. I pulled out of my parking place and was forced to stop as a group of ubiquitous tourists made their way across the street in front of me.

They give themselves away too easily what with their visors, hanging cameras, walking shorts (which no one should be walking in), sneakers with crumpled-up socks, and even colored socks with loafers. Fanny packs and guidebooks usually finish off the colorful ensembles. Some visitors take the opportunity to wear hats they aren't brave enough to wear in their hometowns. And everyone over fifty has a jacket on, just in case our 100-degree, humidity-filled afternoons might turn into a chilled breeze. Tourists keep Savannah alive, however, and they love to try locally owned places like Jake's, or Clary's Café, the restaurant I was aiming for before this flock of poorly attired geese stopped me.

Clary's is perched directly across the street from my house. Paige and I have patronized Clary's for their BLTs since I can't remember when. We have been friends since my second week at the Massie School. We were paired up for a history project in Mr. Gilbert's class, and the rest, as they say, is . . . When I left for the University of Georgia, she stayed here in Savannah to go to the Savannah College of Art and Design.

I parked my car beside my house, crossed the street to Clary's, and arrived inside to, no surprise, Paige's absence. Paige was always late, whether it was fashionable or not.

Her parents—Sheila, my mother's best friend since childhood, and Patterson Long—own a beautiful antique shop on Abercorn Street right across from Saint John the Baptist's Catholic Church. Paige doesn't care much for antiques, but she is one of the most skilled painters I have ever met. I would've commissioned her to create the cover for my first book, had my original dream still been intact. Paige has been selling paintings since she was in high school. Her parents, out of sheer pride, put her first paintings up in their store. By the time she graduated college, she was so popular and had sold so many paintings, she opened up her own little area in the back of the antique shop. But Paige had recently declared at least partial independence by moving into her own apartment in the Lafayette Building—right next to her shop on the square.

Paige entered Clary's in total Paige style: out of breath. "You are not going to believe what happened."

"Try me," I said, leaning back in my chair and knowing I was in for an interesting narrative.

"I got pulled!"

"You got pulled?"

"Yeah! There he was. Mr. I-don't-have-anything-better-to-do-than-pull-over-people-for-no-reason Millings."

"He does need a life."

"He needs a mint. Have you smelled that man's breath?" she asked as her entire face contorted in horror.

"Can't say I've gotten that close."

"Well, hold on to your hat, Hannah; it won't be long," she said, flipping her hair, which was really too short to flip.

"Did you flash him a smile? Offer him money? Bribe him with a portrait?" I laughed as I took a sip of the chocolate shake my favorite waitress, Helen, set down in front of me the very moment of my arrival.

Paige slumped back in her chair. Then, as if getting a second wind, she sat up, patted me on the arm. "So, how did your meeting go?"

Before I could reply, Helen returned. The waitresses here rarely change, and Helen is an icon. She cusses like a sailor, smokes like a forest fire, and talks like a man. She has been reprimanded for the first two offenses a trillion times; the third is out of her control. Oh, and she has a photographic memory. She has never written down an order, and she gets each one right every time. Even down to a table of ten. "Girls, I'm so glad to see you both. But, Savannah, you are too skinny and, Paige, your hair is too blond. I'll have your BLTs out in a minute." And away she went.

"Why is it that you are always skinny, and all she notices about me is my hair color? I've had this same color for five years."

"And I've weighed the same since my senior year in high school."

"Anyway, didn't I ask you about you and your job?"

"Well, I have successfully told Vicky about forgoing the book deal and kept it a secret that I am trying to get this job at the paper."

"Aren't you the woman?"

"Well, I'm not so sure I'm all that, not after this morning."

"Savannah, what did you do?"

"Why would your first thought be, what did I do? Why couldn't it possibly be something someone else did?"

"Please. What did you do?"

"I pulled a Vicky," I told her, crinkling my nose.

"No!" Both hands slammed down on the table, her eyes wider than a hoot owl. "You pulled a Vicky on the very man who could give you a job? That's a tad audacious."

"Did you just say tad?"

"Probably. My mother uses it all the time."

"Well, thank the Lord! I must have picked it up from you. I was afraid I had picked it up from my mother. Well, it was really a huge mistake." Paige sat in complete and total silence and listened to the rest of my story. Helen brought our lunch and Paige finished most of her BLT before I'd taken my first bite.

By the time I was through, all she could say was, "Get out."

"I did!" I told her, laughing.

"Do you think you'll hear from him?"

"Honestly?"

"Honestly."

"Well, since he didn't call security, odds are I'll hear something." I took a sip of my shake.

Paige looked up and nodded, then swallowed and said, "There is something I need to tell you."

"OK. You are way too serious. What is it?"

She paused long enough to make me look her in the eye. Then as she always does in her rare serious moments, she placed her hand underneath her porcelain chin. She gave up on tanning years ago after a severe burning episode. Now she wears SPF-105. "I heard that Grant is getting married."

"Well, we all want to get married one day, don't we?" I said, hoping she was just joking.

"Savannah, I'm not joking. He met this girl from Converse College while he was at Clemson. They started dating after he got out of school and started working for his dad's firm. She is graduating this month, and they are supposed to get married this summer."

Grant and I had only seen each other a couple of times since I started graduate school. He had been my best friend through middle school. Then in high school we realized that we felt more for each other than just friendship, and we dated through my senior year in college. Until this halting moment, I had somehow thought that he and I would one day get married. He was the only guy I had ever cared about. Now, I knew that things had changed since graduate school, but we still talked.

Our last serious conversation had taken place one morning at my dad's shop, right before I went back to school for my master's and he started full-time at his dad's architectural firm on Oglethorpe Square. I'll never forget how beautifully golden his skin was from spending most of his summer on the ocean. I stared at him through the front window at Jake's, where I sat at a table facing the sidewalk.

He walked in wearing wrinkled khaki shorts and a T-shirt, which, like the majority of his wardrobe, bore the name of a local store or a race he had recently participated in. "Out for a day of fun?"

He gave me a gentle kiss and sat down. "Actually, I'm working today."

"Dressed like that?"

"I'm helping Dad do some things in the yard," he said, laughing.

"When do you start your real job with your father?"

Instead of answering, Grant sat and reached across the table to take my hand. "Savannah, I think we have some decisions to make. We've done this relationship thing for four years now. Except I'm not sure I would even call it a relationship. I need more. I think it's time. I want us to take our relationship to the next level. Really focus on our future."

I blinked, wishing I had an answer he would want to hear. But school required everything of me. And at that time, I was so consumed with writing, I didn't know how I could offer a real, committed relationship much of anything. "We've got all the time in the world for that," I responded. "You know I love you. I've always loved you. And next to Paige, you're the best friend I've ever had. I just need to get this master's behind me. And I just can't commit to any more right now."

I'll never forget the look in his eyes when he left that afternoon. He hugged me a little longer than usual. But school would be over eventually. Then there would be time to solidify our relationship. Obviously, Grant hadn't been clear on the plan.

"Earth to Savannah," Paige said, waving her hand in front of my face.

"Do you even know her name?"

"I think it's Eliza or something like that. One of those real southern kind of names."

"Oh, more southern than *Savannah?*"

Paige rolled her eyes.

"Do you think he really loves her or does he just want to get married?"

"Savannah, you know Grant isn't going to marry someone he's not in love with."

"Maybe she's dog ugly."

"No such luck, my friend. I saw her over the Christmas holidays. He brought her to an exhibit. She was very tall and very gorgeous." Paige turned up her nose in mock disgust. "I mean legs up to—"

"That really is enough. I bet she's fake. I bet there isn't a thing on her that's real."

We wrapped up our lunch and declared that we would do this every Monday.

"Call me as soon as you hear something about the job. And no cleaning excursions. It's going to be OK." She sealed her solace with a hug.

I watched as she faded up the street, the consummate artist, from the way she dresses to the way she walks. If she weren't my best friend, I would hate her, so irritatingly perky and cute.

Looking out over the same street I had viewed only hours before, I was amazed by how a morning could change things.

CHAPTER SEVEN

The beauty of Savannah is that it is a place where people come to fulfill dreams. Sure, we have a lot of old money, the kind that joins the Oglethorpe Club and are members of the Garden Club. But there are a number of people who simply come to make their own way, start a business, raise a family, and leave their mark on their own little corner of the world through life and love and loss.

As I walked down River Street, I took a left on Perry, crossing in front of Chippewa Square, which holds the familiar statue of General Oglethorpe, Savannah's founding father, and the concrete wall behind the bench where Forrest Gump had his box of chocolates. The city was planned on paper before Oglethorpe even arrived and before Forrest was a thought. Oglethorpe's friend Robert Casteel was an architect in England and later jailed in debtor's prison. It is said that England's prisons were dismal beyond comprehension. Casteel died there of smallpox, and Oglethorpe dreamed of creating a new life for the poor, the debtors, and the religiously persecuted. Savannah was his canvas.

In 1733, Oglethorpe's Savannah had four laws. Law Number

One: No hard liquor, only beer and wine allowed. He didn't want any lushes in his society. That lasted only in dreams. Law Number Two: No slaves. Oglethorpe wanted Savannah built as a place of equals. That was repealed in 1751, thanks in large part to Eli Whitney and the cotton gin. Law Number Three: No Catholics. Oglethorpe feared they would be sympathetic to the Spanish and try to take over this new colony. So much for the religiously persecuted. Law Number Four: No lawyers. That was repealed in 1755, you guessed it, by a lawyer. But until there were lawyers, Savannians needed a way to settle their disputes. So the citizens built the Dueling Field, on the backside of Colonial Park Cemetery.

As I turned my gaze from the familiar square, I couldn't help but notice the gray-sided home on the corner whose basement had been transformed into a quaint little bookstore. I have never passed a bookstore without going inside; it's sacrilegious.

During my school years, I spent most of my time and money at E. Shavers Booksellers on the corner of Bull and East Harris Streets. My life's original plan was to open up a little bookstore in the basement of my own home. Since reading William Golding's *Lord of the Flies,* I believed kids needed a place to experience the world of adventure and make-believe, a safe place to get lost in the turmoil of undisciplined youth. Remembering *my* dreams made me realize I had left little room for someone else's. Grant had probably figured that out long before.

Trying not to contemplate Miss Converse's false beauty any further, I opened the tucked-away door and stepped into an enchanted land, Katherine's Corner Bookstore.

Everything was neatly categorized and organized. There was history, fiction, nonfiction, new releases, and, of course, local-interest titles in a prominent display in the front. I laughed when I saw the book that featured pictures of my home—well, not exactly my home. A local publisher doing a new book about Savannah asked Vicky if she would allow them to shoot a couple of our rooms for the book, because our home is on the Historical Register. Well, you would have thought she had been crowned Miss Saint Patrick's Day Queen. We thought she was going to make us move to a hotel for a week so nothing would be touched once her interior designer came in and did a "fluff."

My mother worked frantically to make sure everything was perfect. But in the end, the only pictures that didn't develop correctly were the ones they had taken of the inside of our house. By the time this was discovered, it was too late to do another photo shoot. Dad would have refused to go through the torture again anyway. So instead of this lovely book having pictures of Vicky's décor, the publishers used photos someone had taken of the previous owners' interior.

You won't find this lovely picture book lying around in Vicky's parlor, that's for sure, but a very nice book it is, even if Vicky's fluffing has been omitted.

A striking lady, probably in her late forties, appeared from behind a bookcase. She caught my eye and smiled, her beautiful dark eyes reflecting the soft track lighting. "Can I help you find anything, honey?" she asked.

She was carrying a stack of magazines to the rack by the front door, and the sun caught her salt-and-pepper hair, a rarity in these parts. Southern women, for the most part, don't want you to think their hair has ever seen gray, even if they're eighty and walking with a cane. She wore little makeup, but a stunning color of red lipstick and simple jewelry complemented her natural olive complexion perfectly.

"No, I was just walking and saw your great little store here. How long have you been open?"

"Only about a month. But the remodeling took over a year, so it's really nice to just feel settled."

"Where are you from?"

"Here originally, but I moved to Birmingham with my husband when we were first married so he could work in his father's business. When my husband passed away, I decided to come back home," she said, taking outdated magazines to the counter.

"Oh, I'm really sorry."

"Well, thank you. Jim suffered for almost two years with cancer. So I was ready to let him go. Don't take that the wrong way, but when you love someone like that, the last thing you want is to see them suffer."

I nodded.

"Eventually, letting go is easier than holding on. Our children are grown and have all moved away, so I decided there was no better time than now to try out my dreams," she said, indicating the store with a sweeping gesture.

"Well, I think you've done a wonderful job with your dream. It's perfectly quaint."

"I hope you'll feel free to stop by anytime. Do you live around here?"

"Yes, ma'am. On Abercorn Street across from Clary's."

A flicker of recognition came to her eyes as she posed my most dreaded question. "Oh, are you Victoria Phillips's daughter?"

"Yes, ma'am. And Jake's too," I added for my own peace of mind. "Savannah, Savannah Phillips," I said, holding my hand out, hoping she would not hold my heritage against me. "Do you know them?"

"Well, I've met your father," she said, grasping my hand in a solid, confident shake. "Hello, Savannah, I'm Katherine Owens."

I smiled back, still wondering.

"I stop in at your father's place now and then. He is a doll. And so is that sweet Richard. Now, your mother I haven't met yet, but I've heard a lot about her."

"I can only imagine."

"I heard your mother is responsible for much of the recent restoration around here."

"Yes, she is. There's something about her and this city."

"Then perhaps that explains your beautiful name?"

For some reason Katherine's question didn't irritate me. I smiled. "Maybe so."

She smiled back. "So are you just here for the summer?"

"No, I just finished my master's and moved back here to find a job," I said, then added, "Actually, I've found the place I want to work, but I'm not so sure if they're going to want me."

"Oh, really! What do you mean?"

"That's a long story. But let's just say that I should hear something by this evening."

"You sound like a rather interesting character," she said with a faint laugh. "Well, Savannah, it was a pleasure to meet you. I'm going to go back to my cataloging. New fiction is on the back wall, and new nonfiction is right beside it."

"What do you suggest?"

"Well, this one isn't new, but I've been rereading some classics lately," she said, reaching into a shelf and pulling out Harper Lee's *To Kill a Mockingbird*. "It takes me back."

"I love that one too," I said, taking the book from her extended hand. "Atticus Finch, a man to be admired."

Leaving the bookstore to head back home, I noticed the decorative fish spout she had put on her gutters. Another indication of the lady she was, so understatedly overstated. She captured my attention without ever changing the volume of her voice. Not like my mother, who had a Chamber-of-Commerce Victoria voice, and a hold-on-to-your-britches "Mama's home" kind of voice. Katherine was just a lady. A lady to be admired.

The note on the kitchen counter read, "Vanni, Mom has a late Chamber meeting. I'm meeting Dad after work to do some things at the shop. Dinner is on your own, unless you want to come grab a bite with us later. Love, Thomas."

The phone rang, commencing a desperate search for it. Thomas never left it on its cradle, so I didn't stand a chance of getting to it before the person on the other end hung up or was sent off to voice mail heaven. Fortunately, it was close by, underneath the newspaper on the kitchen table.

"Hello."

"Savannah Phillips, please." I knew immediately who it was.

"This is she," I replied, trying to hide the terror in my voice.

"Ms. Phillips, this is Mr. Hicks. I've been reading your work this afternoon, and, well, it's not bad."

"Thank you, sir." *I think.*

"I've decided I'm willing to give you a month to prove yourself. I'd like you to start a week from Monday. You can run one human-interest story each week, in two parts. And I'm not going to tell anyone you are Gloria's replacement until I know that you can handle the pace around here."

"I understand."

"Most of our entry-level positions start at four hundred dollars a week, with one week's vacation after the first year. We offer one week's sick leave your first year and pay health insurance."

"I don't believe this position is entry-level, sir. My articles will probably be the most-read next to your headline news. Doesn't that alone make me more valuable?"

"So what do you think you should be paid, young lady?"

Put on the spot, I backtracked. "You know, Mr. Hicks, four hundred will be fine, actually. I really need six hundred to be able to move out into an apartment. But I'll just work up to that."

He probably believed I was playing him. But I really did need six hundred dollars a week. "How about we meet in the middle, Savannah? I'll give you five hundred and a week's vacation this year. But you need to remember, the newspaper business isn't a place for getting rich; it's a place for creating change."

He got the no-rich part right. I just hoped I could eat. But decided it would be a good excuse for having to eat at my mother's. Then I almost got mad, realizing if she hadn't ruined my publishing deal, there's no telling what I could be making right now. "That will be wonderful. Thank you."

"Oh, and one more thing, you'll make sure you don't interrupt conversations you are not privy to."

I simply replied, "I'll be there."

"Very well. I'll see you Monday. Your first story is due Tuesday."

Tuesday? One could spend a year or two writing a book. How in the world was I going to have two articles ready in a little over a week? "That's no problem," I said. "Would you mind if I came in tomorrow and went through Gloria's research materials?"

"Not at all. I'll make sure Rich Greer, our weekend editor, knows you're coming. I'll see you in a week." And with that he hung up the phone.

I set down the phone and did a jig around the kitchen. I was going to be Gloria. I was going to be a newspaper writer. Grabbing my cell phone, I got in the car to go to Jake's and called Paige immediately.

"You goob! I can't believe you are not answering the phone!" I said when her voice mail answered. "I got a call from Mr. Happy Hicks! He's giving me the job! For at least a month, he says, but in one month he'll be mine. Call me!" I pulled up right in front of Dad's store, almost knocking over two elderly people in plaid shorts. I apologized as best I could.

Richard was behind the counter pouring some decaf for a young woman. "Put the cup down, Richard." As soon as he did, I gave him a bear hug and a big kiss on the cheek. Then I grabbed him by both arms, looked straight into his eyes, and said, "I got a job, Richard. A real job."

Richard let out a big whoop and spun me around behind the counter. My foot caught an empty coffeepot, and it crashed to the floor. Out came Dad, Thomas, Louise, and Mervine.

"Savannah, you got a job?" my dad asked.

"Yes, I got a job. Can you believe it? I pulled a Vicky and it worked. I got a job! I mean it could have blown up in my face. But really, it was the perfect thing to happen. He saw my tenacity, my drive, my passion he called it. He—"

"Breathe, Savannah," Dad said.

Louise and Mervine scurried away and were back in no time with a cherry floating in a big old Coke. "Special occasions require special things," Louise said. Mervine, well, she just shook her head. In thirteen years I had never heard Mervine do much more than agree. Maybe she was mute, but now didn't seem like the right time to ask.

"Vanni, you're the man!" Thomas hooted. "I never dreamed you could get a job so quick. Who's paying who?" He leaned against the door that led to the back.

"And what kind of job did you actually get?" Dad asked.

"Well"—I spread my arms wide and grinned—"You are looking at the next human-interest writer for the *Savannah Chronicle*."

Richard, who was trying to clean up the mess we had made and actually give coffee to the lady at the counter, set down the cup and said, "That was what Gloria Richardson did. My, my, my Savannah, those are some mighty big shoes for your dainty little feet."

"Savannah, that's fantastic. When did you decide you wanted to do this?" Dad straightened his apron over his crisp short-sleeve green polo shirt.

"Well, it all started with that paper Mother kept sending me." I filled him in while everyone else returned to thirsty sojourners. When I finished, he said, "I'm very proud of you."

"I learned something along the way, too. Ya wanna hear?"

"Shoot," he said, leaning on his elbow and giving me his undivided attention. Something he had always done. From skinned knees to broken hearts, Dad knew when the world needed to stop.

"I saw a lot of people pass through the halls of academia, Dad. But they were so caught up in themselves. Everyone wanted to be the best, you know, have the perfect talent or the loudest applause. But no one seemed to see the real joy in the fact that they had a gift at all. Do you know what I mean?"

"How about I see where you're going to land."

"Well, it's like they missed it. Like the guys who sacrificed everything to be the first in the college draft, even if it meant giving up their character. They had the gift but missed the purpose."

"A lot of people do that."

"Well, I don't want to, Dad."

"Then always be gracious, Savannah." Dad paused in a way that said I'd better listen up. "Your gift will make room for you. Sometimes it will bring you before great people. But it isn't *your* gift, Savannah; it's simply been entrusted to you. So hold it modestly. And remember, wisdom will be needed for every decision you make, just like you needed it for this one."

"That's why you're here, isn't it? To keep me humble and give me wisdom?" I kissed him on the cheek and raised my half-empty glass. "Here's to gifts."

Dad raised his coffee cup and added, "Here's to a paycheck."

We closed up the shop, but everyone stayed, and we spent the next three hours talking over Chinese takeout. Everyone had suggestions for what my first story should be. Then they all added their two cents about how I should tell my mother. The real beauty of the moment, however, was that I had a job she didn't even know about.

Everything was perfectly situated—the pillow, the light, the book, my water—when the slight tap on the door interrupted the quiet. Vicky peeked in.

"I hear you had a rather eventful day!" she said, sitting down on the edge of the bed.

"Yes, I did. But who told you?" I asked, laying my book across my chest and trying to conceal my annoyance.

"Your father, but that was about all he gave me. He said you would want to tell me yourself."

"Oh, he did, did he?"

"So what happened that is so exciting?"

"Well, first tell me about your day. You're in mighty late." I knew this would buy me a little time to get my story in place. And like Paige, it never took much to sidetrack my mother. Past adventures proved that.

Like after she tired of decorating our home she went on a Fact Finding mission for our fair city. When Vicky found out there was a store named Jezebel on River Street, you would have thought the sun had stopped shining on the South. Vicky worked herself into a lather, sure the heathens had come to town and pretty soon we were going to have massage parlors on every corner doing "Lord knows what!"

"I'm sure the Lord knows what," I told her.

She got mad that I would even suggest that the Lord would know what went on inside a massage parlor.

Then one day we heard that she had actually gone inside Jezebels. Well, we figured whoever owned that store had been subjected to a big-time come-to-Jesus meeting. But the store owner, now one of Mother's best friends, told us later that Vicky was so overtaken by the green linen ensemble in the window that she stayed until three that afternoon, trying on clothes and telling her life story. She denied it was true. But then we saw her leave the house in an outfit in the lovely shade of green.

"Oh, a few members of the Chamber are trying to change my mind about some of the tour guides having to dress in original southern dresses. They want everyone to wear those khaki shorts and logoed button-up shirts. I still can't believe you were able to talk me into allowing that in the first place," she said, poking me under the covers. "It's so unprofessional."

Vicky is colossally concerned with the impression Savannah visitors take home with them. She feels if they don't want, even long, to return, then she has failed as the head of the Chamber. So she decided a couple of years ago to make sure that every aspect of our social graces was operating, well, with grace. It began with her incognito rides on the local Savannah touring trolleys, horse-drawn carriages, or walks in one of the walking tours. If the tour guides didn't entertain the visitors, if they didn't know Savannah history as well as they did the ins and outs of their own families, if they didn't create a total feeling of consummate hospitality, Vicky would inform the guides' bosses of their inability to "capture their audience."

"Just remember," established tour guides tell the new recruits, "real tourists don't wear high heels. If you spot one, it's her. And if she doesn't leave your tour crying, you are over."

She still has no idea they are onto her. And I'm not about to tell her. There's nothing more amusing than driving past a trolley car and watching the guide with more motions than a synchronized swimmer, while Vicky sits in the back in her pink hat and large sunglasses. She looks like a bad Susan Lucci impersonator, thinking no one knows who she is.

Where I really feel Mother has gone over the edge, however, is in this crinoline controversy. Back when I was in high school, I passed one of the tour guides in a full-length peach dress, with about forty-five layers of crinoline and a huge bonnet with roughly the same number of flowers on top. She was giving a tour dressed up in this garb with the heat index at 110 degrees. Her makeup had melted, and she had mascara tracks all the way to her chin. Most of it had pooled at the top of her lace collar, which looked as if it was choking her. Poor thing was trying to blot herself with a tissue and spin a parasol at the same time.

I came home and told Mother, "This is totally inhumane. You should at least give those poor pitiful souls a choice." I didn't figure anyone would choose to wear those ridiculous getups, and Vicky didn't either, so she compromised by breaking it up half and half. God bless the miserable creatures who were at the cutoff line of the crinolines.

I closed my book and laid it on the nightstand and put my arms behind my head, thinking we might be here for a while.

"People get enough of the authentic here without making others endure human torture."

"Well, you start snipping away, and pretty soon we're no better than Charleston."

"Mother, Charleston is beautiful, and I doubt they make their people dress up like bad southern belle impersonators just to make tourists feel they've had a real cultural experience."

"You don't think they wear those kind of dresses in Charleston?"

"No, Mother. Charleston is progressive, and you need to be careful not to hold Savannah back from what most would see as progress."

"But I love those dresses. The girls look so sweet in them," she said, having no recollection as to why she had come into my room.

I rolled over on my side and yawned, hoping this would not be a terminal discussion.

"Well, I still haven't decided," she said, not moving.

"You mean you kept those people in a meeting for almost five hours without reaching a decision?" I asked in mock disbelief.

"Yes, but I'm too tired to worry about it anymore tonight. I'll think about it tomorrow." She leaned over and kissed me good night. When she reached the door, she turned back around and cut out the light. Standing in the doorway, the hall light created her silhouette. "I know you think I forgot why I came in here, but you obviously aren't ready to tell me your news. So I'll just let you tell me when you're ready." The door closed behind her.

"The lady is good," I said to the door.

CHAPTER EIGHT

"Good morning, Mother," I said, greeting her with a kiss. I sat down at the counter to enjoy my breakfast. *Maybe she would still let me come by for breakfast and dinner even after I move out,* I thought. *My word, I'm not going to be so well off that I can do it all. Everyone needs a gradual transition, don't they?*

She was prancing around in a beautiful cream linen sundress with matching cream mules when I entered. "How did you rest, darling?" Her hair was somewhere in the brown family today. This is as close to her real color as we'll be seeing this side of heaven.

"I rested great. It's nice just to be home in my own bed."

"Well, I'm so glad you're here, precious. This is exactly where you belong, with your mother and your father and everything that makes you comfortable," she said, fixing me a plate. I knew why she was there. She knew why she was there. And even cleaning my bathroom from stem to stern wouldn't prevent this conversation from having to take place eventually.

"OK, you've been patient long enough. I'll tell you," I said, trying to scarf down some bacon before I began. "I got a job."

"You got a job? Already? Where?"

I knew she didn't think I could get one without her, but I refrained from needless gloating. I responded, "At the paper. I am going to write human-interest stories."

"Savannah, oh my word, well, that, that is wonderful. Is that what you really want to do?"

"Yes, it is. It's exactly what I want to do. Well, I've got a busy day, so I'd better get going." I poured myself just enough juice to wash down the entire scrambled egg I had just crammed in my mouth.

"But, Savannah, I had our day planned," she said, puffing out her lip like a spoiled two-year-old child. "There are some new neighbors I told we would meet for lunch, and then I was going to take you and show you some of the houses that the college finished since you were home last. And I'd like to know more, more about this, this job thing."

"Mother, we'll do all those things, I promise. I have to go to the paper today. And I have to start early."

"Today? So soon? And in those shoes?"

"Yeah, I've only got a little over a week before my first story is due." Then I went in for the kill. "And while we're talking change here, I think you need to know that I'm going to move out as soon as I get enough money."

"But, Savannah …"

With my hand in the air to try and stop her graciously, I headed to the door. "You know, the funny thing is, I never would've even thought about the paper had it not been delivered every day while I was at college. It was so strange too, because I never ordered it, nor did I ever have to pay for it. Oh, well, I guess it was just meant to be. I'll be home for dinner."

Most things in the South run slowly even Mondays through Fridays, but tack on a weekend and, well, let's just say, snails could outrace a southerner. But not at Jake's. The environment was rather frenzied for a Saturday in Savannah.

"Big day?" He handed me a Coke glass filled to the brim.

"Yes, and an eventful morning too. I told Mother that once I get a couple of paychecks I'm going to get my own place."

"I think you should, Savannah. You're a grown woman, and you need to pave your own course and create a life for yourself. So where are you going to live?"

"I have no idea." I leaned back against the counter and took a long swig of my Coke. Dad picked up his coffee and took a drink himself.

"How did your mother handle such eventful news?"

"Didn't give her time to do anything!"

"How did you accomplish that?" he said with a laugh.

"Walked out the door after revealing that her newspaper was what led me down this whole path in the first place."

"You are shameless."

"I know."

"No dramatic unfoldings? No emergency-room scares?"

"No, but I expect to be confronted eventually with everything from heart palpitations to the fact that 'criminals loom in the streets seeking single females who live in apartments all by themselves,'" I said in perfected Victoria.

"Ooh, that one might even scare me."

From my parking place across the street, I could see through the windows that lights were on everywhere, and people were obviously working feverishly preparing the Sunday morning copy. I tried to forget that the only thing I knew about newspapers I learned reviewing books for the Massie School *Ledger*, a job I was given because I was the only one who actually read them.

The second semester of my junior year at UGA, I decided to take a literature class with a required-reading list of fifteen books. It included Emily Brontë's *Wuthering Heights*, F. Scott Fitzgerald's *The Great Gatsby*, Hemingway's *The Sun Also Rises*, other titles you might recognize, and some that might make you cock your head the way Duke does when he has no clue what you're trying to tell him. That course was a turning point for me. After that class, I knew there was a place for me. I needed to hone my craft, polish my abilities, and learn how to place my words on a page the way they were uniquely formed in my mind before my fingers ever typed them. This was my masterpiece to create. No one alive could create it the way I could. No one could copy it or duplicate it exactly. So I poured myself into what I already loved. I thought it had proven faithful.

Yet here I was, staring at a newspaper building with a questionable sting still in my gut. *I should be staring at the front door of the largest publishing house in the nation,* she thought. *But, no, I had to have some intervening circumstances.* Circumstances that had diluted my world into a city. With all the changes of the past month, I still wanted to leave a mark that would last. A mark that would change something or, dare I believe, someone the way Gloria's mark had changed me. Whether I liked it or not, destiny hovered in front of me, daring me to enter. Before leaving the comfort of my car, I decided to leave all preconceived ideas behind with it, taking in my confidence instead. If I left that behind as well, I might never find it again.

Between her continual *"Savannah Chronicle,* please hold," the receptionist mouthed she would be with me in a moment. After putting the 111th caller successfully on hold with or without permission, I told her I was here to meet Mr. Greer. She declared it loud and clear over the intercom and went back to find that caller number one had hung up hours ago.

Mr. Greer was a small, elderly gentleman with a nice smile, strong hands, and a round little bowling-ball tummy. "Savannah, nice to meet you. Follow me, and I'll show you Gloria's office." We walked through a maze of cubicles to the back of the building. He walked with such a spry step it was hard to keep up. As I wove my way through the great gray abyss, I pitied the poor people who had to spend their lives staring into such a dismal sea. I had spent six years of college writing in parks, sitting in coffee shops, or staring out my window into a stunning courtyard. We proceeded to the same elevator I had ridden only once before. The numbers on the buttons were nearly invisible from years of being poked, and the elevator creaked so loudly, I held on in hope that the doors would open to actually reveal the next floor and not some helpless state of in-between.

The doors opened to the infamous third floor, and we walked straight ahead in the direction of Mr. Hicks's office. Situated next door, looking out over Bay Street, her name still declared on the door, was Gloria Richardson's office. I was almost afraid to go in. I stopped by the door and looked up at Mr. Greer to make sure it was OK to enter. It almost felt wrong, almost disrespectful. "It's OK, Savannah. I'll check on you in a little while. If you need anything, my office is right around the corner there. I hope you find what you're looking for."

"Thanks. Me too," I said. I peered through the glass wall for a moment, wanting to be absolutely certain I should enter at all. It was clear that all of Gloria's personal things were gone, but everything else was in pristine and perfect order. I finally gathered the courage to enter, slowly turning the knob, and letting the door slide gently open. The sun was already illuminating the office, but my aversion to dead-people's belongings prompted me to turn on the lights anyway. For a moment I took in the fact that this office was amazing. "Can you believe this view?" I asked out loud to no one.

A faint scent of lavender was in the air. Maybe her fragrance or a scented candle. I sat down slowly in her chair and ran my hands across the smooth leather arms. The stapler and tape dispenser were in exemplary condition and fastidiously positioned. The Post-it notes and paper clips looked as if they had rarely been used. I opened her top drawer to find nothing more than some notepads.

I swiveled the chair around to stare out the wall-length window and repressed my intense need to grin. My eyes made their way to the two black metal filing cabinets against the wall. I walked over and opened the top drawer to find everything perfectly labeled and color-coded. Though an amazing writer, the woman obviously suffered from an obsessive-compulsive neatness disorder. My only neatness disorder manifested itself in the bathroom area.

I sifted through each folder, feeling as if I was somehow violating her privacy. I was sorting through this woman's life. These files held the questions, mysteries, and discoveries never revealed in her columns. They held her decisions of what to print and what not to print. They held her legacy. They held secrets I was sure I shouldn't see but couldn't keep myself from opening.

Four hours passed before the startling sound of knocking broke the spell. I looked up and felt the burning sensation in my neck muscles. "Come in."

"Savannah, you've been in here a long time. You OK?" Mr. Greer asked, tugging at his pants to pull them up frighteningly higher.

"Yes, sir. I'm doing fine."

"Would you like some lunch? I'm going out to grab a quick bite."

"Oh, that would be great. I'll have whatever you're having."

"Oh, you will, will you?" he said with a chuckle. "Need you some cottage cheese and prunes? You look a little young for those things."

I laughed myself. "Well, how 'bout you grab me something more accustomed to my dietary tract."

"That would be a cheeseburger and French fries, I presume."

"You would be a phenomenal presumer." I returned to my work, and he returned quickly for someone who should probably move a little slower. The prunes probably kept him in a hurry everywhere he went. I ate simply to keep my stomach from distracting me and went straight back to reading.

Each story was like a life lesson. And each article was neatly cut out and paper-clipped to the inside of each folder that housed the related interviews and research. In the last drawer of the second file cabinet, I came upon closed files. Some were closed due to lack of

information, some for lack of validity, and others because the subject
had changed his mind. By all notions of modern journalism, not
many reporters kept stories from going to press because the subject
changed his mind.

After peering at the clock and seeing it was already five thirty, my
stiffening body made it clear it was time to go home. Mr. Greer had
said good-bye an hour ago. I stood up to close the file drawer and
heard something bang inside. I reopened it and looked to make sure
the files hadn't fallen. I closed the door again and heard the same sliding, banging noise. Opening it once more, I reached my hand between
two files to feel down inside the bottom of the drawer. At the back,
my hand found something square, about the size of my palm.

It was a tape recorder. I pulled it out and found a tape inside. I
pushed "play" and immediately heard a woman's voice asking a
question. It had to be Gloria. It freaked me out, sitting there in her
office, holding her voice in my hand, so I shut the tape off. I put the
tape player in my purse, knowing it wasn't stealing, because it would
be returned to its rightful place. But I wasn't about to sit there and
listen to it in her office.

I could smell dinner from the street. Duke was at the
door and politely rolled over so his stomach could be rubbed with
my foot. I took my flip-flop off and gave him a courtesy rub.

Vicky wanted a lap dog. Duke would oblige, but he's not
exactly what she had in mind. She told Dad that if Duke knocked
over one more antique with his tail, the dog would be living in the
coffee shop. I believe Vicky might be gone before Duke, but we'll
let time play that hand.

In the kitchen, Dad was already setting the table and Thomas
was filling the tea glasses, both talking to Vicky as she set dinner on the
counter. She had prepared fried pork chops, fried potatoes, steamed
cabbage, and fried cornbread patties. No wonder Dad and Duke were
having to go for walks. It was that or become terminally clogged.

"Savannah, were you at the newspaper all day?" Vicky asked.

"Yes, I was. And it was so interesting. And you should see my office. It's awesome. It overlooks Bay Street and has a wall of windows. I know it will be a lot of work, but I'm totally prepared."

We fixed our plates and sat down at the table. With grace said, Vicky revealed her latest idea. "I've been thinking about our talk this morning."

"Our talk?" I asked.

"The apartment, darling. I understand that a young woman would want her own place." Poor Thomas about spewed pork chops at that. Dad even perked up to listen.

"Well, thank you, Mother. I'm glad to hear that."

"And you know, I know a place that just came on the market that I think would be perfect for you."

"Well, that really isn't necessary. I want to do this on my—"

"I insist, Savannah. I've already called, and we have an appointment to see it tomorrow after lunch." And without any further conversation or debate, she proceeded to recount the events of a day worthy of a movie script. How so much can happen to one lady on a Saturday is beyond my power of imagination. I zoned out somewhere between the hair salon and manicure and picked back up with Duke taking a dip in the swimming pool.

"Well, it is warm for May," I said. It wouldn't have mattered, however, if Duke had been teetering on the edge of heatstroke and utter demise; the fact that the pool would have to be excavated of dog hair was reason enough to keep him out.

"I don't know why you didn't take him with you this morning," she said to Dad.

"Because he was sound asleep on Thomas's bed, and I didn't figure they would get up before noon. I couldn't imagine Duke doing much damage in an afternoon," he said, smiling at me across the table.

"Well, Thomas didn't actually get up until one and left around two, so the damage that Duke caused happened in less than an afternoon. Your dog is amazingly talented."

Duke had been called "your dog" since the naming episode. Now, if she had gotten her way, Magnolia probably could have taken a dump in her pool and she wouldn't have thought a thing about it.

"Well, we'll get the pool cleaned out," Dad calmly assured her.

I sneaked away somewhere between Duke's need for obedience training and the city's need for a flowering fish garden in front of the Chamber of Commerce. I had a more important conversation to listen to.

CHAPTER NINE

M y purse rested on one of the glass tables that flanked each side of my bed. I knew what was in there; I just wasn't sure it was for me to hear.

It has to be OK, I assured myself. *She would want her work continued.* I took my purse and retrieved the tape recorder, popping the tape out. Side A was clearly marked, but there was no other labeling of any kind. Odd for a woman who could have won the Savannah Labeler of the Year Award.

A scratching and sniffing noise at the door distracted me. I cracked it open to see Duke wearing a look that cried, "Rescue me. Bring me into your sanctuary. Save me from the wicked throes of men. Purge me from this madness."

I opened the door wider and he ran straight to my bed, perched his hairy body on my cream coverlet, and sprawled himself out where his back paws reached my duvet. I made him scoot over and proceeded to rewind the tape.

I pushed play, and that voice, that unfamiliar voice, the one I had heard in my head for years, was more commanding than I had ever imagined. The tape began with questions of the interviewee's past. I listened intently. The woman who responded to Gloria's questions seemed familiar, but I couldn't place her voice. "So, tell me," Gloria asked, "When did you begin competing in the Miss Georgia United States of America Pageant?" For a moment I thought the other voice would betray itself as my mother's. But when the answer came, it was certainly not the voice of Victoria. This was driving me crazy.

Apparently, the lady Gloria was interviewing was there to tell the tale of why she believed the pageant was rigged the year she competed.

"Can you tell me the events that led you to your conclusions?"

The lady paused before saying in a soft and kind voice, "You know, Gloria, I really don't think I want to talk about this. It's been a long time, and I've moved past this. I really don't think it's necessary to go over such silly events. I hope I haven't wasted your time."

Gloria responded just as kindly, "Of course not; here, I'll just cut this off . . ." And with that, the tape went dead. I tried both sides. There was nothing else.

I leaned back against Duke almost afraid of what I held in my hand. Downstairs resided not only the queen of pageants, but the queen of the Miss Georgia United States of America Pageant. If this pageant was rigged—if it had ever been rigged—I needed to know. She needed to know. Everyone needed to know. "But who cares about pageants anyway?" I said to Duke. He put his head on his paws. "They're silly. They have no value. You prance around the stage in your skivvies. You wear heels of inhumane height. We're just going to put this back inside my purse here and forget we ever even heard such nonsense. Gloria was right not to pursue such a silly story. That's not a human-interest story. That's silliness. Don't you agree?" His expression said he did.

I walked into the bathroom to brush my teeth. In the mirror, a little bit of mildew in the bottom of my shower caught my eye.

Two hours later, Thomas found me. "What's wrong with you now?"

Some of my hair had come loose from its knot on the back of my head, and I blew it out of my eyes. "What do you mean, what's wrong with me? There's nothing wrong with me. Does something have to be wrong with a person simply because they want to have a clean bathroom?"

"Chill, Homer."

"Just because you're totally comfortable living in filth doesn't mean I am. Bathrooms carry more germs than Duke's mouth. Ever thought about that when you step into that shower of yours?" I finished off the grout in the far corner of the bathroom, underneath the farthest cabinet. Then I sat down, took off my rubber gloves, and looked up at Thomas, giving my hair one more quick blow. "There, I'm through."

"You are your mother's child."

"Why in the world did you say that?"

"Because Dad has more money than—"

"Do not say God; that's totally sacrilegious."

"I was going to say Bill Gates."

"No, he doesn't."

"Well, more money than most, and Mom refuses to have anyone clean her house."

"She doesn't think anyone can do it as well as she can."

"That's sick. Why would you clean your own house when you could afford to have someone else clean it?"

"Thomas, I'm way too tired to talk about our mother's issues. She does it because she is a control freak. And besides, someone might try to steal her tiara."

Thomas began staring at Duke's mouth. "Did you know dogs' mouths are supposed to be one of the cleanest places known to man?"

"You are here why?"

He came over to kneel down beside me. "To say good night. You can deny it if you want, but between dinner and now something happened. No one cleans the bathroom for pleasure, my dear

Vanni. Especially you. Are you sure you don't want to tell me what's wrong?"

"There's nothing wrong, Thomas," I said, standing up in front of him. "I simply wanted to take a shower in a clean one, that's all. Now if you'll excuse me . . ." With that, I closed the door on his perfectly positioned nose.

"OK. Whatever you say. But I'm just two floors down," he hollered. I heard Duke pad after him.

After a nice long, hot shower, bed captured me. Reading would be nice, but sleep was persistent. Dreams of tiaras, big hair, spiked heels, and that voice held me captive. Everyone in my dream had that voice. I woke up one time in the middle of the night with fists flailing, trying to prevent someone from wrapping a sash around me. By the time morning came, I was simply glad to have survived the night.

Sunday in the South means church. Sunday in this house, even if we lived in California, would still mean church. I hadn't been to our church in months: Babies had been born, people had been buried, and marriage vows had been spoken, and no doubt Vicky knew about each one. But bless her heart, I hadn't given her enough time to tell me what she had been doing, much less what anyone else had been doing.

Mother descended the staircase as though it were a runway. She had brought back hats on Sundays in Savannah. And everything always matched. Today she had chosen a pale blue ensemble trimmed in cream, her feet adorned by lovely Via Spigas in cream as well. She was accessorized with pearls this morning, and the whole grouping was topped off by a beautiful cream hat encompassed by a stunning pale blue bow, accentuated in the center by pristine blue silk hydrangeas.

Dad looked sharp in one of his navy suits, white crisp shirt, and light blue tie with white polka dots. He only wore suits on

Sundays anymore. He wouldn't even wear them on Sunday if he didn't feel one should wear one's very best to church. Mom thought one should look divine. I chose pleasant; Thomas settled for doable. In fact, I don't know how he got past her, in his wrinkled no-pleat khakis, flip-flops, and stretch-cotton shirt sleeves rolled up, but he did. He pulled off flip-flops on a Sunday! In fact, he pulled off a million things I never could.

I wore a simple black skirt and white blouse. Feeling rebellious, I let the blouse hang outside of my skirt. I pulled my shoulder-length hair back in a sleek ponytail, about the only way I wore it anymore, valuing the thirty minutes it saved me by not having to blow it dry. I debated wearing flip-flops but didn't desire war. A pair of black mules completed the look, and I was off to accomplish the day.

Dad and Vicky left about thirty minutes early so she wouldn't miss greeting anyone. Through the years, many in the city have thought of my father as a pushover when it comes to Vicky. This perception is usually reversed when they meet him. Dad was the one who let her know that we would travel thirty minutes to Tybee Island to go to church, because he thought it was best for the family. Pastor Brice's church has a little bit of everything; it is an integrated place of culture and worship. My dad believes that you should worship in places where all people are accepted.

"If you only see people there who look like you, you're missing what you've come for," he told us.

Mother loved the church but felt that as the head of the Chamber of Commerce she should attend church in one of the historical churches downtown. "You are more than welcome to attend any church you want," he said, "but you will attend it alone. The kids and I are going to Pastor Brice's church, with or without you." Today, Sister Victoria is one of our church's official greeters.

Thomas and I got to spend some time together on the ride over. He opened the door to his 1995 Jeep, a gift for graduation—not new of course, but nice nonetheless. "Glad to see you're learning how to be a gentleman."

"Glad to see you're still too chicken to wear flip-flops."

I slid into the car, and he closed the door. Dad didn't even buy new cars for himself, so he sure wasn't going to buy one for us. He knew you lost ten thousand dollars by driving a car off the lot, so he made sure the ten thousand was lost by someone else before he drove it away. It wasn't by frivolousness that he had retired at forty. Now Vicky, she would pay extra just so she could have it.

The Jeep was unusually clean. "Did Mother make you take her someplace?"

"No, things were growing in the back, so I figured yesterday was a good day to get it cleaned up. You just lucked out," he laughed.

"No, I would have just driven myself. What else did you do yesterday?"

"Well, me and Jeff Bryson—you remember him from Louisiana?"

"Yeah, sure . . . no, I honestly have no idea."

"You know, the guy from New Orleans who goes to The Citadel with me? He came home with me last summer for a couple of weeks. He won Mom over because he told her Savannah was far more beautiful than Charleston."

"Oh yeah, I remember."

"Well, he was here visiting his girlfriend, Mary Thomas, who went to Saint Vincent's and now goes to the College of Charleston. I went with them to the beach to surf and hang out. After your meltdown, we went to City Market to listen to a jazz band. I got so sunburned, though, I could hardly sleep," he added. "What did you do?"

"It wasn't a meltdown. My bathroom needed cleaning."

"Was it the apartment thing? Because I'm not ever leaving."

"Why should you? Free room, free laundry."

"Don't forget the food."

"No, how dare I forget the food."

"Why would you leave?"

"If you have to ask, you wouldn't understand." I knew he would continue to think it was the apartment that had me troubled. No one else needed to carry the burden of that tape until it was clear what it was really about. Not even Thomas.

We pulled up to the church just a couple of minutes before service started at ten. You could see Vicky's brim a mile away. She greeted us as she had every Sunday for the last thirteen years, straightening our shirts, spitting on her fingers to flatten one of Thomas's cowlicks. We often went in one of the other entrances just to avoid her spit and shine, but because we had parked in the front of the church today, we had to go through the front entrance.

"You two go get a seat and sit quietly." As if that thought would be lost on us in some way. We just smiled and did as we were told. Wonder what would've happened if, instead, we had chosen to stand in the back and carry on loud conversations, just to prove we were too inept at coming up with such a conclusion ourselves.

Inside, Thomas and I hugged necks, said hellos, and sat down about midway back on the left-hand side. Vicky and Dad sat on the second row on the right-hand side. The music started, and no one saw their seat again for almost forty-five minutes. The music rocked the house, then came down to a soothing pace. Each song gave me a reason to rejoice, reflect, or respond. Some clapped, some stood silent, others raised their hands in a form of surrender, but each responded in the way that expressed his own heart.

When the special song was over, Pastor Brice took the platform in his usual unpretentious way. He acquired his congregation's respect without demanding it. Today's message was titled "The Life You're Looking For." For the next forty minutes, Pastor Brice made it clear that the direction for our lives could be something we've yet to discover. Then he told us what was necessary in a person's character to achieve the ultimate destiny for his or her life. I listened as if every word was spoken directly to me. I felt as if he had followed me around for the last two months, cataloging my life and culling a message from my mayhem. But somewhere between his reading of the Scripture and his final point I felt a calming, even an assuring, that the decision I had made was necessary for wherever I was going.

After a magnificent meal of roast and potatoes, Vicky was sitting in wait. "OK, let's go. I want to show you your new apartment."

I eased myself out of the chair and followed her reluctantly to the front door. "Don't get too excited. There are no guarantees that I'm going to move into this apartment."

"You're going to love it. I promise." And she took off out the front door and across the street. I had barely closed the door behind me when she turned around in front of a townhouse almost directly in line with her own front door, flung her arms wide open, and declared, "Ta-da! Isn't it perfect?!" I sat down right on our top step. "Savannah, get up. You're going to love this."

I got up and walked over to the Mini-Me. It was made with brick, just like her house; had an iron railing in front of the door, just like her house; and had ivy growing halfway up the wall, just like her house. The only difference was the red front door. "Why didn't you pick the one next to it?" I asked as I stood beside her. "Its door is black."

"It didn't have as much charm. Come on, Bett loaned me her MLS key." Bett Thomas is the only *real* real estate agent in town. Others try, but she's the master.

"Of course she did. But there is really no reason for me to see this, Mother. I'm not going to live across the street from you. I may as well not move out at all."

"Oh, OK. Well, good, let's just go home then," she said, turning her little three-inch heels around quicker than she could rename a street Victoria Valley Drive.

"Is that what this is about? Did you do all of this so I would stay home? Well, get your hiney in that house and show it to me then."

"Savannah! I'm going to have whiplash if you keep spinning me in circles like this." She opened the door.

The place was breathtaking. It had plantation shutters, hardwood floors, built-in bookcases, and a newly remodeled kitchen and master bath. It had three bedrooms and two baths. And it was simply perfect.

As she closed the door behind us, I stood my ground. "Well, if I was even willing to live across the street, it wouldn't matter, because I couldn't afford this place anyway. It's probably $1,500 a month."

"Actually, it's $2,500 a month," she said, "but I'll help you pay what you can't afford."

"How would that have me independent and making my own way?"

"Savannah, give me a break. You'll be living by yourself. I won't even bring you dinner, unless we have tons of leftovers." She smiled. We walked back through our front door. "Well, I think it's perfect, and if you let it go, you'll be sorely disappointed," she said to my back as I dragged myself up the stairs.

"It won't be the first time," I called back. I spent the rest of the evening in travail over the fact that I needed a story. She and Dad went up the street for a Bible study, allowing me to use that time to get a snack and head back upstairs.

Duke and I conversed about the Abercorn address and relocation. He was all for it. And the thoughts of how nice it would look decorated did have a certain appeal. "I would technically be out on my own." Duke panted in agreement. "No one would have to know Vicky was supplementing the rent. It would look nice with some furniture and my bedroom suite." Somewhere between choosing toile or damask, we both surrendered to sleep. And somewhere in the middle of the night, Vicky slipped me a lovely sample of a new-address acknowledgment for one Savannah Phillips at the address across the street.

CHAPTER TEN

There is something about dogs that just makes life better: they have a way of listening without giving opinions, following you wherever you go, and being totally comfortable with no agenda at all. What an ideal relationship. After slipping on my Nikes, I headed out with Duke. I talked to him for a couple of blocks, then I put my earphones on to listen to my new weekly tilling CD, Jonathan Pierce's *Run to You,* I put the button on repeat. "I could walk to you, but I'd rather run," came the lyrics, giving me the motivation to keep up the pace.

After the second mile, I stopped to give Duke a break at the doggy fountain. The break was really more for me, because Duke was in much better shape since he and Dad started working out. I sat down on a bench at the south side of the park and saw a familiar face approaching out of the corner of my eye.

"Savannah?" Grant called.

I took off my earphones and swung them over my shoulder. "Hey, Grant," I said, wondering if hugging him was appropriate anymore. Hard to believe I was actually having to ask myself that question.

He bent down and hugged me instead. "I saw Duke and knew you weren't your father. I heard you were home. How're you doing?" he asked.

"Oh, I'm doing great!" I said, sounding ridiculously fake. "How're you doing?"

"I'm doing pretty well. Work is good. Dad and I manage pretty well together." He was wiping his beautiful tan face with a white towel. "I have had some things change, though. Do you mind if I sit down?" he asked, waving to the empty side of the bench.

"No, not at all," I answered. Duke came up from his water break and shook his head right in front of us, soaking us both. "Oh, that's attractive, Duke," I said, laughing. Grant smiled, causing both his green eyes and perfectly white teeth to flash, as they did any-time something amusing or thought-provoking happened.

"Savannah," he began rather cautiously, "I've wanted to call you for a while, but I didn't know where to begin. I met someone my last semester at school. Her name's Elisabeth." So much for Paige's accuracy. "She's a sweet girl. After you and I had our talk, I decided that I had to get on with life. So she and I started dating after I graduated. We've been dating almost two years now, and we're getting married next month. I wanted to tell you myself, but figured your mom would tell you first," he said, laughing. I had long since grown accustomed to people laughing after they said my mother's name.

"Well, she didn't tell me anything, which means somehow this has escaped her realm of knowledge. How that is at all possible, I am totally unaware. But Paige told me yesterday."

"Well, we haven't had a need to tell that many people around here. Elisabeth's from North Carolina, so we're getting married there, but then we'll move back here after the honeymoon." He spoke in such a matter-of-fact tone. Did he not know this news was only a day old to me?

"So do you love her?" I blurted, then slapped my hand over my mouth. "I'm sorry. I can't believe I said that. Of course you love her. You wouldn't marry someone you didn't love. Why would any-one marry someone they didn't love? No one marries someone they don't love. Well, maybe if it were for money, but I'm sure this isn't about money . . ."

"Yes." He paused, then softly touched my arm. "I do love her, and you're right. I wouldn't marry someone I didn't love. She's a wonderful girl, and she really loves me. And she's Methodist too!" Another laugh.

"Well, what more could you ask for?" I asked, all the while wishing he would say, "I could have asked for you." But he had asked for me. And two years ago, I had let him get away.

He looked me directly in the eyes. "Not much. I'm a lucky man. I've loved well, Savannah. And I loved you well."

"I loved you too, Grant. No, I *love* you too. But you know me, I believe that the decisions we make are for a reason. You've been one of my best friends for as long as I can remember. I know what your expressions mean. I can tell what you're thinking by the way you squint your nose when you're perplexed, or by the different rubs you have for your head. There's the stressed rub"—I demon-strated—"and the thinking rub." My laugh was much more awk-ward than his. "I know all of these things about you, and I still let you walk out of my life. And that day led us to this day, a day I didn't plan, but apparently a day that was meant to be. You deserve to be loved well," I said. Grant looked down at the top of Duke's head. I touched the bottom of his face and lifted his chin so I could see those green eyes as we closed this chapter of our lives. "You're a wonderful man. One I always appreciated, but never quite the way that you deserved. I wish you the greatest happiness." I turned to go and heard him call out my name, differently than I had ever heard before. He was letting go.

"Savannah, you would like her. She would have been your kind of friend."

"If she likes you, I know I would like her," I said.

He stood up and brushed himself off. "And she would like

you," he said. "Everyone likes you." He smiled at me as only he can, then he turned and jogged away.

Duke and I stood there. Walking away felt somehow treasonous. Downright sacrilegious. But Grant—Grant hadn't just walked away; he had jogged. There was no slow step, no hung head, no discreet wipe of the eyes. But I couldn't move. Moving meant letting go. Moving meant good-bye.

Duke's whimper forced me back to Forsythe Park. "Me too, boy. Me too."

Dad's Land Rover was sitting in the street when I rounded Abercorn Street. My mother was perched at the door, his hand eclipsing hers as they rested on the edge of his open window. This was how love looked: undivided attention and last-minute conversations. It looked through the same eyes after twenty some years and yet still held a reluctance to part, an anticipation of the next time they would see one another. I looked at Duke sadly. He looked at me as if he knew what I was thinking. Well, he had never known love either. There was the chocolate lab up the street, but Dad wouldn't let him anywhere near her. I walked up the steps a tad slower than usual.

I distracted myself by taking inventory of my closet. It was certain—I possessed no appropriate newspaper reporter attire. It was time to shop. I decided to walk because summer would be here soon, and months would pass before I could again walk without perspiration settling behind my knees and in the creases of my arms. Today was beautiful and warm, but not cruel. As I passed Katherine's bookstore, a customer emerged with a sack full of books. Thinking maybe something inside could spark my interest and give me an idea for a human-interest story that might actually interest a human, I decided to go inside.

People were browsing most every nook and cranny. Many looked like tourists. An elderly gentleman dressed in plaid pants picked up Vicky's book with pictures of someone else's home. He skimmed through and set it down and progressed to another about ghosts. Savannah has a ghost story around almost every corner, which appalls Vicky to no end. When she found out Disney World copied the exterior of the Hamilton Turner Inn for the facade of their haunted mansion, well, she wrote Mr. Disney himself, totally oblivious to the fact that he had been dead for years. And this past year, Savannah was voted the most haunted city in North America; and well, let's just say, had my mother learned of it, Washington would have been notified.

Katherine was behind the counter when I came in, and she saw me immediately. A customer was waiting to check out, and she thanked him and invited him to stop by again before leaving Savannah. With her greeting, my pulse went haywire. The voice on the tape. Katherine was the one who had a story to tell. A story she never finished. Afraid my expression would give me away, I pretended to interest myself in a display. My new friend had a secret.

When she spoke again, I jumped. "Well, Savannah. I hoped I'd see you again soon. I didn't know it would be this soon, though. I see you've got your book with you. Wanting to return it already?"

"No, no, I usually carry one around. You know, in case there's any lag time. And I . . . well I . . . I hadn't planned on stopping in so soon, but I just needed to do a little research, you know, take a few minutes to browse." I picked up the closest thing to me, to show that I hadn't really come to expose her deep, dark, buried secret.

"Well, you research all you need to," she said, turning her attention to Mr. Plaid Pants's wife, Mrs. Polka Dot.

More people came and went, so I spent some time browsing through the new autobiography section, trying hard not to stare at Katherine. My mind raced with a thousand questions, all begging for immediate answers. Katherine walked around the bookstore like she owned the place. Well, you know what I mean. She has a quiet confidence that invites you in and encourages you to stay, but you know you're in her domain. I tried to act interested in the autobiographies.

There were more stars' faces on the covers of books than you could find on the walls at the Chamber of Commerce office. Vicky had all the stars take a picture with her and the Chamber staff before they left town after filming their movies. Then she would shoo everyone out of the way and get one of her own. She has pictures with Julia Roberts, Tom Hanks, Denzel Washington, Kevin Spacey, and Clint Eastwood. They all hang in her office at home. Not that anyone knows what that office is for. Come to think of it, no one knows what her office is for at the Chamber either, because she's usually standing in someone's front yard talking or sitting on the back of a trolley car acting like she's not who everyone knows she is.

Eventually, Katherine got a moment of reprieve from her busy spurt and came back to where I was. "We just got a lot of new books in. You should look through the titles and see what you find."

"Do you read a lot?" I asked, not wanting to blurt out the real question lying beneath the surface: "What on earth were you doing in a pageant and what on earth do you know?"

"As often as I can."

"Do you mind if I ask what you're reading now?"

"You'll laugh," she said, putting her hand up to her mouth to hide her blushing face.

"Trust me, after the books I tell people I've read and loved, you won't find me laughing at you. Try me." I hoped she would reveal that she had just picked up the latest edition of *Pageant Scandals and Recovering Drama Queens,* which would be a perfect segue into my questions.

"Well, I was going through our young-reader section the other day and found one I hadn't read in years. I couldn't remember much about it except how much I enjoyed reading it the first time. So, I picked it up again."

"OK . . . and it is . . . ?"

"It's been a crazy journey for me."

She turned her attention back to me. "Really? How so?"

"Can we sit down?" I asked, motioning to the steps beside us. "Sure."

For the next hour, we had the luxury of uninterrupted time. Absolutely no other customer entered the store. It was a divine appointment. I told her about the fiction award and publishing opportunity, leaving out the part about my mother but adding the revelation of my destiny and the countless papers that had made their way to UGA.

"Those articles consumed me. And now I'm here, back where I started. So, we'll see if it works. But none of it will work without a story," I said, getting to my feet, hoping she would burst from the exhaustion of having held such a tale of disrepute for so long that she could no longer control herself. But control herself she did.

She stood up. "Well, I'm sure you'll find exactly what you need."

"I'm sure I will. Thanks for listening. I've got to run and buy some appropriate clothes for this new job," I said, motioning to the T-shirt and denim Capris I had on.

"You'll do wonderfully, Savannah. Now go get beautiful."

"I'm not looking for miracles, just closed-toed shoes."

She laughed and walked me to the door. "I hope I'll see you soon."

"Oh, I'll see you soon. Very soon, I'm sure." And with that, I walked out the door, realizing I had a story. The story just needed to admit it should be told.

CHAPTER ELEVEN

I entered through the back gate that leads directly to Paige's portion of the antique shop. I did this to avoid any questions her mother might ask, because they would be the same as my mother's. She, like Vicky, never wears jeans and prefers heels over anything else. The fact that Paige and I came out so alarmingly normal still amazes us both.

As I came through the door, Paige was wrapping up a painting for a customer, a lady who owned one of the hospitality centers up the street. She was planning to send the piece to her daughter in Augusta for her birthday. We said our hellos, and I went behind the counter to unwrap the lunch I'd brought. Before Paige sat down, she turned the Open sign around to Closed.

"You're going to have people so confused on when you're open and closed that they're going to start coming by at night just to try to catch you."

"The joy of having your own business," she mused.

"Speaking of having your own business, have you met Katherine Owens? She owns Katherine's Corner Bookstore."

"How long have you known me?"

"Too long."

"Have you ever seen me with a book in my hand?"

"She carries magazines too."

"Oh, well then, no, I haven't met her yet. But I have all intents and purposes of meeting her soon." She took a bite of her chicken wrap.

I told her all about Katherine and how lovely she was and about going into Gloria's office and finding the tape and then realizing it was Katherine's voice. "Why do you think she didn't want to tell her story?"

"Maybe she's really the Beauty Queen Serial Killer and decided at the last minute that she liked her life of freedom. She didn't want to chance the world knowing her deeds of devastation," she said, slurping like Hannibal Lecter.

"You have too much imagination," I said, rolling my eyes and taking another bite of my sandwich. "Would you help me think? OK, she mentioned the pageant was rigged. But then she closed down. I mean, if Miss Georgia United States of America is rigged, that could mean that Vicky's win was rigged."

"Savannah, if you think you've had trouble with your mama in the past, you are asking for trouble of colossal proportion if you go tampering with her tiara."

"Who does beauty pageants? Who would know something about this? You know everyone, Miss Social Queen."

"Hey now, I've never been the queen of anything. You beat me, remember?"

"Homecoming queen doesn't count. Besides, Vicky bribed half the campus with promises of pizza and Coke for lunch."

"There was Emma Riley," she said, hardly stopping to breathe as she engulfed what was left of her wrap.

"Emma Riley. Oh, that's right. Emma did pageants forever. She was one of the most beautiful girls I've ever seen. Didn't she win Miss Queen of Everything and move out to California with a beach bum or something?"

"You haven't heard about Emma?"

"*No,* I haven't heard about Emma. What? What!"

"Well, after she lost Miss Georgia Whatever, her life went to pot. She didn't come out of her house for about six months, married the biggest loser in Savannah. Now she comes out every now and then, but no one hardly recognizes her because she looks so terrible. Has a busload of children with dirty faces and nasty tempers."

"You've got to be kidding me."

"Nope. That is the truth as I see it from here."

"And you see pretty much everything from here."

"Absolutely. That's why I chose this corner."

"Maybe I need to visit Miss Emma."

"Maybe you need to get your inoculations first. She's a scary lady now."

"You are such the overreactor."

"Fine. Go see for yourself."

"Watch me chase this crazy story. I'll waste my first week and end up coming here to interview you and make you sound like you're some great gift to the community. I'll be writing obituaries by next week."

"You laugh. You probably are supposed to be writing about me. I'm a human-interest story," she said seriously.

"You're a human-interest story all right. A young girl with rich parents who let her sell her paintings in the back of their store on the days she chooses to show up. People will only be interested in seeing if your parents ever thought of adoption," I told her, picking up my fork to dig into my key-lime square.

"I've accomplished extraordinary things for my age."

"Yes, you have. And I probably will share your story one day, but most everyone around here knows your story, and mine too probably, thanks to our respective mothers. But my first article has to be a bang. I have to leave them knowing that someone worthy of Gloria's position has arrived."

Paige swallowed the first bite of her key-lime square. "Oh, Savannah, this thing is delicious. Who made this? And if it's a man, is he married?"

"Yes, it's a man, and I have no idea if he's married."

"Where did you get this food?"

"It's a new place. Wright's Café, over off of West York."

"Well, it's divine." Then, with her mouth full, she managed to say, "No, I know you're right. And it sounds like this could be, hopefully, a wonderful discovery."

"Yes, I really think it will." We talked for a while longer, and I told her about my run-in with Grant. We both agreed that I should leave it at that and spend the rest of my life avoiding him and Miss Converse, but I wasn't sure how long I'd be able to keep that up. Paige loved my new clothes, hated the shoes, and sent me off with instructions to check for a wedding band the next time I was at Wright's Café.

Things were running as usual when I entered Dad's coffee shop. Customers were coming in and out, giving Duke the usual devoted attention. Duke had decided to spend some time lying out on the sidewalk in hopes that some unwitting lady from the courthouse would forget Dad's ban on feeding Duke the remainders of bagels and muffins.

Inside, Judge Hoddicks was at the counter, picking up his late-afternoon fix. He had an assistant, but not a day went by that he didn't step out of his robe and into the Savannah sunshine for a little banter with Jake. "Hi, Judge."

"Hi, Betty!" he said, grabbing me in a bear hug. I love that he still calls me Betty. "I hear you're here to stay."

"Can you believe it?"

"No, I thought for sure we'd lose you to one of those states up there in the North, writing your books, getting famous, and referring to us as those crazy people from the South."

I laughed. "I did too! But then I came to the conclusion that I'm as crazy as the rest of you."

"Well, you may not be happy about it, but I sure am," he said with a kiss on the cheek and a smile as he headed for the door. "Jake, give Betty whatever she wants, and put it on my tab!" He walked out, never turning around.

"You got it, Judge," Dad said, wiping off the counter and laughing at his old friend. Before I got situated good, Mervine came from the back, set a Coke down in front of me with a little nod and a sheepish smile, and disappeared again.

"Dad, have you ever in all these years asked why Mervine never talks?"

"Well, I just figured that Louise talks enough for the both of them, and Mervine's never felt that anything else needed to be said. But I overheard Louise telling Richard one day not to let her shy, quiet personality fool you, because she talks a blue streak at home. So how was the apartment?"

"The Mini-Victoria across the street? I looked at it, realized I would have to have ten roommates to afford it, and said thanks but no thanks."

"Has that stopped her?"

"You are such a funny man. What do you think?"

"I figure she's got a contract on it as we speak."

"And new-address postcards for me to mail out."

"So what are you going to do?"

"Keep looking. But I must admit, it was fabulous."

"With your mother, I have no doubts," he said, getting up from his chair and heading toward the back. "So why are you declining?"

"Because it would defeat the purpose," I said, following behind. "You aren't making your way in the world if your mother is paying your rent and bringing you dinner."

"I'm glad to hear you say that," he said. He turned around and started two new pots of coffee.

"I'm sure you are. But I'll find one. My friend Claire's got her real-estate license and she's going to look for some things."

"Well, that will be nice," he said, giving me a kiss.

My mother's voice was coming from the top of the stairs, sounding loud and irritated. I rounded the corner, peeked inside her room, and was greeted by her derrière protruding from underneath the bed skirt. I leaned up against her door, not wanting to miss whatever might be unfolding.

Her head finally popped out from under the bed, most of her hair all crowned nicely on the top, giving her a nouveau-retro kind of undone look. In her hand she held the shoe that matched the one already adorning her right foot—except for the nicely mangled heel and chewed up sling-back strap, evidence of a bored golden retriever with bitterness issues.

The look on her face was priceless. She grabbed her heart, feigning a heart attack from my unsuspected presence, and proceeded to tell me that Duke was going to be living at Jake's.

I went into my bedroom to hide out until she left. I heard the clicking of what I assumed to be a different pair of heels go down the stairs and out the door. I gave her a few seconds to come back in case she forgot something, having learned this trick after getting caught on two occasions by her return for forgotten things.

The first time she caught me with a BB gun shooting at squirrels. The next time she caught me talking on the phone to Grant after we had both been put on phone restriction for the episode at John Wesley's church. I wasn't sure why she was leaving so late in the day, but then I remembered that it was Monday, and every other Monday evening she hosted a meeting of the local historical society at the Owens-Thomas house right after work, to discuss issues that needed to be dealt with in the Historical District regarding renovations and gaudy décor.

Having waited a sufficient amount of time, I headed to the attic and found a box marked "Pageant Keepsakes." I opened it, trying to disturb as little as possible. Inside her box of keepsakes rests what most would consider trinkets of self-absorption. We all had a sneaking suspicion that Vicky crawled up here to peruse her little box of mementos, because every now and then you would see her walking around with pieces of insulation in her hair.

I've often wondered what it was that took her all the way to first runner-up at the Miss United States of America Pageant. After all, it's hard for any young woman to look at her mother objectively. Young women see their mothers with guarded fear, ever cognizant that they are looking at what they could become.

Vicky competed in the Miss United States of America Pageant in 1976, the 200th anniversary of our Declaration of Independence. She chose a Statue of Liberty costume for the introduction of contestants. To her dismay and horror, over half of the girls wore their own Statue of Liberty costumes. I don't know how she thought her costume would be original, but obviously, common sense wasn't a prerequisite for competition in 1976. I told her she should have dressed up like Uncle Sam, because no other woman at a beauty pageant would dare dress up like a man. She could have won most original for sure. She didn't laugh.

After moving aside her rather torched torch and gingerly placing her lovely silver-sequined statue costume on the floor, there on top of dried and crushed roses, banners, and other memorabilia was the 1976 program book. I pulled it out and laid it aside, then replaced everything with hopes that she would never notice. I was kind of surprised that her box wasn't wired.

I began to flip through the pages carefully. If a beauty contest was rigged, the tampering would most logically begin with the judges or the auditors. I studied the page bearing their photos. Judge number one, Marcus Smythe, hailed from South Carolina. He looked kind of cartoonish, with thick gray hair, bow tie, and a sports coat. He was a local television personality there in the Low Country.

The second judge was a lady named Dr. Beverly Corzine from Tennessee, a Vanderbilt graduate and a physician in Nashville. She looked rather elegant, despite the super-fixed hairdo from the seventies.

The third judge was a dowdy-looking lady named Madeline Taylor. She looked downright manly and mad. My, what a combination for a pageant judge! She was a retired schoolteacher, and she wore her hair in a pageboy with chopped-off bangs that looked as if her granddaughter had made Grandma a beauty-school guinea pig. She wore glasses on a cord around her neck. Well, all you saw in the picture was the cord, but with those squinty, shifty eyes, you were sure glasses were hanging somewhere nearby. She hailed from Florida. So much for her joy of retirement in the Land of Sunshine.

Then there was judge number four, a distinguished-looking gentleman from Jackson, Mississippi. Wearing a coat and tie, he looked to be in his late forties. His name was Randolph Cummings III. He was a Mississippi attorney who also ran the local community theater in Jackson.

The final judge was a former Miss Georgia United States of America herself, Francis Margaret McEntire. She was from Atlanta and was a graduate of the University of Georgia, recently married and with a new baby on the way, her bio declared. So these were the five people who would decide which young lady would be dedicated to hosting local barbecues and talent competitions, visiting snotty-nosed kids in schools and kissing all over them, and cutting ribbons at the openings of local funeral homes and furniture stores. What excited a woman about all of that was beyond the power of my imagination. In 1976 at least, twenty-one women apparently found such a lifestyle worth coveting.

I turned the page. A section with no pictures read, "Auditors for the evening are Lynn and Larry Templeton of Templeton and Associates Accounting Firm of Macon."

After looking at my mother's program I didn't know much more about pageants than I did when I began, but I was intrigued by the thought that anyone would bother rigging a pageant in the first place. It seemed ridiculous and petty. Even so, it had happened at least one time, at least as far as Katherine was concerned. I had a week to kill, and I might as well kill it well. Then I caught myself. "I don't have a week to kill," I said out loud. "I have a week to produce a human-interest story. Lord, help us all." Fortunately, the Lord knew I really meant it.

CHAPTER TWELVE

Before anyone came home for the evening, I left a note on the kitchen counter that I was having dinner out. Across the street at Clary's, maybe, but it was "out" nonetheless. I ate dinner and consumed two shakes and three Cokes, all the while staring at my house. I watched as every light turned off, including the ones inside Clary's, and they told me to go home or clock in.

Standing on the steps to my house, I knew my growing dread wasn't over the apartment taunting me from across the street. My real concern was how to confront Vicky with the possibility that the Miss Georgia United States of America pageant had once or ever or always been rigged. Over dinner and liquid chocolate, I had asked myself a million questions, most of them regarding my mother's reaction.

If for one moment she thought she had not won her title because she was the best in the show . . . well, it would be a ruin like no other. I would be released from the family. My scooping abilities would become the bane of my mortal existence. My name would never be spoken again.

The more I thought about it, however, the more I concurred

the drama might actually be worth watching. But then again, this claim of Katherine's, accompanied by proof I would have to uncover, could destroy my mother's greatest achievement. That in and of itself was, at its core, unfair.

And so I decided I would not share an ounce of this with my family until I could prove that it was true. At least for tonight, I wanted my mother to lay her head on her pillow believing that she was still a former Miss Georgia United States of America simply because the judges thought she should be. I wasn't willing to take that from her . . . unless I absolutely had to.

I tried to be as quiet as possible, slipping up the stairs and closing the door behind me. No sooner had I turned the light on and flung my shoes across the room than there was a knock at my door. I opened it to find Thomas and Duke peering back at me.

"Can we come in for a minute?" he asked.

They plopped themselves on the bed, and I headed to the bathroom to apply Noxzema and brush my teeth. "It looks like you already have."

He watched me lather my face.

"Is that what all girls do before they go to bed?"

"Well, I'm not sure what all girls do, but it works for this one."

"I kind of always imagined that Mom just took off her entire face and sat it on a foam head next to her bed, then put it back into position in the morning," he said, rolling on his back and sticking his feet up in the air as if he himself were Duke.

I couldn't help but laugh, and I accidentally stuck a Noxzema-covered finger in my eye. "Ow! You are just wrong. But, in my twenty-four years of existence I have only seen her without makeup on one occasion, and I was in preschool. I asked her to hurry up and put it on, and I've never seen her without it since." I wiped my face clean and started to brush my teeth.

"Well, she looks good even without it. Anyway, I just wanted you to know that she told me tonight about the apartment she found you. Dad told her to let you make your own decisions."

I stopped in the middle of my brushing. "Wellimnodgonatakit. Whaddoyouthankshe'ldoweniteler?"

"Besides attach a tracking device to your car, who knows?"

I spit, rinsed, and wiped my mouth, then walked back into the bedroom and sat on the edge of the bed. Looking straight ahead into my bathroom, I spotted a glimpse of dirt. "Do you think my bathroom is clean enough?"

"Have you ever thought of therapy?" He jumped up and patted me on my head as if I was Duke and they departed. I just watched as he closed the door.

"Have you ever thought of therapy?" I mimicked. "Blah, blah, blah." I decided to go downstairs to grab a glass of water before I put my pajamas on and went to bed. I rounded the corner to walk through the den that is attached to the kitchen, flipped on the light, and let out a scream. Sitting there on the sofa in the now brightly lit family room was Vicky. The last thing I had been expecting to see was a person in that room, and the last one I actually wanted to see at that moment was my mother.

Once I retrieved my nerves from the far corners of the earth, I continued to walk past her to the kitchen. "What are you doing sitting here in the dark?"

"I was waiting on you, actually," she said. She turned around to face me but remained in her chair. "I wanted to talk to you about your new place."

I kept my back to her as I filled up a cup with ice and water from the door of the refrigerator. "Mother, I'm not taking that apartment."

"Why not? It's beautiful. And it's right here."

"Mother, it's like I wouldn't have even moved away. I would be right across the street. I may as well stay here. And that's not going to happen," I added quickly.

"Savannah, I don't know why on earth you would think you

need your own apartment anyway. It's just silly. You have a beautiful room upstairs. You have someone to cook and clean for you. You don't have to worry about paying rent or any of those other things that could happen to a young lady . . . alone . . . all by herself . . . in a strange place . . . with strange people," she said in a rather entertaining form of mock fear.

I turned to look at her. She had still not moved from her chair, but she now had her arms wrapped around her knees and the most exaggerated of wide-eyed expressions. I walked over to her and sat on the moss-green velvet ottoman directly across from her floral chair. "Mother, let me tell you something. There comes a time when a young woman has to take the opportunity to become just that, a woman. Lest you forget, I have lived the last several years in my own apartment at school. Now, instead of living in my own apartment hours away, I'll be living in my own apartment possibly blocks away. But not across the street." I took a moment to be a touch melodramatic and reached out to pat her leg, then I stood to be able to part the room after my final statement.

"You should actually treasure this experience, Mother. This move is a testament to how competently you have raised me to be self-sufficient and a major contributor to this city, your city. That fact alone should make you as excited for this new adventure of mine as I am. I will now become part of your city, something you can share with your countless visitors, an asset to your community. I will now officially be a part of Savannah, all because of the excellent way in which I was raised," I finished, feeling manipulative but successful, because with each sentence her lamentable stature straightened in confidence and pride. And with the knowledge that I had probably just created an even greater monster, I departed.

The moment I saw him, I ducked behind the edge of the building. Grant made this walk every morning, from his house on 345 Habersham to his dad's architectural building. In years past

I had craved discovery, even choreographed it a time or two. But now, sight of Grant brought rejection and undue trauma. So as he rounded the corner of Lincoln Street, I rounded the corner of Jake's and entered the back door slightly winded.

Coming through the door, Dad spotted me. "Grant's out front grabbing a coffee. Would you like to say hey?"

"Grant hates coffee."

"Doesn't seem to anymore. Maybe he's picking it up for his dad."

"Or maybe for his floozy."

"Savannah Phillips! What did you say?"

"I said I'm feeling a little woozy. I might need a double this morning."

"That's what I thought you said." He placed the cups in the sink and wiped his hands on his apron while I got what I needed from the Coke machine. "It sounds like you had a rather eventful evening last night with your mother," he said, heading to the coffee maker.

"It was a rather brilliant performance, if I do say so myself. However, it was all true. And I have been raised exceptionally well." I kissed him on his cheek and headed for the door.

"Yes, and educated in the art of manipulation by the master."

"I'm not sure what time I'll be home," I added on my way out. "Would you let Mother know I'm going to grab dinner out?"

"No, you can call your mother. I am not your messenger, young lady."

"OK, OK, I'll call her. But I'm not sure if I'll get her. I might have to simply leave the message on her voice mail. Oh, that wretched piece of machinery. It has totally devoured a culture's ability to address each other personally. Modern technology will be our society's eventual downfall."

"Technology and wimpy children will be our death."

As I grabbed the door handle and pulled it open, the smell of Savannah mingled with the brewing of freshly roasted coffee. I turned around. "Dad, if you knew something that could possibly hurt someone you love, but the knowledge of that truth could prevent its ability to hurt even more people, would telling it be worth the risk?"

Dad set down his pot and turned to me. "I have no idea what you are talking about, Savannah, and Lord knows if I really want to. I can tell you, though, that life has taught me that revealing truth isn't always easy. But allowing someone to be hurt knowingly is unforgivable. Just make sure that what you reveal is actually true."

"That's what I thought too," I said. I headed out the door and into the alley, then back to the front of the building. Richard was outside standing by the door, watching Duke watch his beloved chocolate lab cross to the other side of the square.

He never turned to look at me. "Poor thing. Never gets quite close enough."

"He is a woeful creature." I turned to look at the lines that had now grown distinctively deeper through the years in the corners of Richard's eyes. They were from his endless smiles and bouts of laughter. Next to my mother, Richard knew most everything happening in this town. The reason was that he did more listening than talking. Richard listened as people shared their stories, and he knew when they wanted his advice and when they simply wanted his ear. He was like your best hairdresser or priest.

"Richard, I have a question for you."

"Shoot, Savannah," he said, still observing Duke's frustration.

"Do you remember Emma Riley? She graduated from Massie School a couple of years before me? Really pretty girl who won all the local pageants?"

"Oh, that's a sad story, Savannah," he drawled. "A very sad story. Seems she married herself a drunk, had four children like stairsteps, and barely gets by. I hear he beat her and the children. It's a very sad story."

"Do you know where she lives?"

"Actually, I hear she finally listened to reason and moved away from that jerk."

"Richard! That doesn't sound like you."

"Sorry, Savannah. Things like that just make my southern gentlemanly ways fade out with the northern breeze. Seems she moved into the apartment underneath her mother and father's home once her divorce was final, changed her name back to Riley, and her folks help her take care of her children. But I don't know that she's any better than before." He stopped and looked at me as if to remove himself from the land he had drifted to. "What in the world you readin' now, Savannah Phillips?"

"Oh, it's *To Kill a Mockingbird.*"

"Child, you haven't changed a lick. We're going to bury you with a book."

"Eww. No talk of such things." I kissed Richard and patted Duke. "She probably drinks out of toilets, Duke. I'm sure she's not worth it." He sighed a heavy sigh, refusing to be consoled, and dropped himself back to the heated pavement.

CHAPTER THIRTEEN

The Savannah morning sun had shifted into assault position. No one in this square would be able to escape it until late in the afternoon. It had already attacked the sides of my Coca-Cola cup and left me with a wet hand. I just about ended up bathed in Coke as I tried to find a napkin in my glove compartment, put my cup in a cup holder, and answer my ringing cell phone all at the same time. I grabbed the Coke before it cascaded down the front of my white linen pants.

"Hello," I answered, sounding rather discomposed for such an early hour.

"Well, Miss Sunshine apparently has already forgotten that she has a real job and the possibility of moving out of her home in a very short while."

"Miss Sunshine just about rained on herself. Did you decide to work today, or do you want to come out and play with me?"

"If I don't sell some artwork, I can't pay rent."

"Yeah, right, and if I hadn't gotten a job, I'd've been kicked out of Vicky's house. Anyway, I'm headed to Emma's house now. Sure you don't want to come?"

"You mean you're just going to go over to her house, show up on her doorstep, and say, 'Do you want to tell me your story?'"

"Well, I was planning on it until you said it like that. Do you have a better idea?"

"No, I don't have any idea. I just hope you're still packing that BB gun in your trunk. You might need it. And don't tell her I said anything about her. I don't want her sending her children over to me for art lessons, if you know what I mean."

"I have no idea what you mean. Well, I've got to go. I'm here."

"Good luck, brave soul."

The front of the Riley's house was as beautiful as it had always been. Mr. and Mrs. Riley were well-respected in the city. They ran a local restaurant down on River Street that was a favorite of tourists and locals alike. They weren't very assuming people, but they were stunningly beautiful, thus Emma's flawlessness. I couldn't imagine that this beauty from high school could be as haggard as Paige and Richard made her out to be.

There wasn't a doorbell by the apartment door, but there was a beautiful gold-plated lion's-head door knocker. I clutched the ring that it held in its jaws and tapped it with three determined strokes. There was no sign of the door opening for an extremely long moment, but I could hear movement. Every shade in the downstairs apartment was drawn. After what seemed like enough time for Vicky to both groom and accessorize, a hand lifted the corner of the blind and a blue eye peeked out.

"Who is it?" the eyeball asked.

"It's Savannah Phillips from up the street. I would like to speak with Emma, if it's possible."

The door opened to reveal something I wouldn't have believed possible. The natural beauty from high school was now just natural. Truth be told, she didn't even seem natural. She was only two years older than I, but she looked as if she were my mother's age. In fact, my mother looked better than Emma. Emma's once sun-kissed blond hair looked as if it hadn't had contact with a brush in years.

Her skin, which used to be so golden and fresh, now looked sallow and worn. Her eyes were once a stunning blue. Now they lacked any life at all.

Almost too shocked to speak, I mustered up something to the effect of, "I just finished my master's work and heard you had moved back home, and I wanted to see how you were." I felt like an idiot and knew I probably sounded more like an idiot than I actually felt.

She stared at me, revealing she didn't believe much of what I'd said. "Savannah, we hardly ever talked in school. Why would you want to talk to me now?"

I decided since honesty had worked in my life up to that point, there was no reason to ruin my track record. The worst that could happen would be a door slammed in my face, or a challenge to make her beautiful again. "Emma, actually you're right. I'm not here to just talk. I wanted to ask you a few questions for a story I'm working on. Do you mind if I come in for a minute?" She just stood there, staring, glaring. "I promise I won't take long, and if you don't want to talk to me, I will take my things and leave," I said, motioning to my satchel that was hanging on my side.

To my surprise, she opened the door to let me in. I didn't know, however, that I was going to need a backhoe to make it past the foyer. The place was dirty, excessively cluttered, and filled with the stale smell of cigarette smoke. Emma walked ahead of me in a white tank top covered in I didn't want to know what. She had on what looked like men's boxers, and she kicked the toys out of her way to get down the hall to the small living room in the back. She never apologized or even spoke in the process; she just sort of shuffled. She shuffled stuff out of her way and removed clothes from the sofa, motioning for me to sit.

If Vicky had come with me, she would have snatched up Emma, told her to get ahold of herself, then taken her to the bathroom and scrubbed her from head to toe. I, on the other hand, planned to sit there on that sofa and hope I didn't have Cheerios stuck to my behind when I got up. Emma lit a cigarette, revealing the early lines that had formed around her mouth and the yellowness of her teeth. She really was a pitiful sight.

"What do you want, Savannah?" she said flatly.

"Emma," I paused for an extremely long time, having no idea how in the world to even begin this conversation. "Emma, I'm sure you know people around town have speculated for years about what has happened to you. Some say your life turned upside down when you lost the Miss Georgia United States of America Pageant."

She took a long drag from her cigarette, but her face registered a moment of shock. "Is that so?"

For a moment I believed she might put her cigarette out on my arm. So I responded quickly. "Well, yes, and if I told you I was working on a story that might reveal that the pageant was in some way rigged, would you be willing to tell me your story?"

At that question, I was sure I saw a scant ounce of emotion in Emma's eyes. I'm not sure what kind of emotion, but something. Something there reflected a brief recollection of a life past, a faded memory. It was almost as if in one transient expression I saw her experience a reality long since forgotten. As if with one volatile query she was confronted with the reason for who she had become. But it left before I could catch it with my own expression. Her original apathy returned. "I wouldn't care to tell you anything about beauty pageants. Now if you'll leave, I need to go get my children from upstairs." She stood up and headed back to the door.

I would make one last-ditch effort, see if I could retrieve her past and make her confront it. I stood as if to follow her but remained at the edge of the sofa. "Emma, you were once one of the most beautiful women in this city. What happened to you?" I was probably crossing a line, but I believed someone needed to shake this girl up and make her confront her demons. And if my mother wasn't here to do it, who better than me?

She turned around and glared at me in the most menacing of ways. I decided this was probably how all beauty queens looked without sequins and tiaras, false eyelashes, and imitation body parts. For a moment, I thought about escaping out the back, not sure what women like her were capable of; but I decided, whether I ever published a story or not, this girl needed serious help. It was time for intervention. And if I was to be the interventioner (if that's even a word), then so be it.

"I mean, well, um . . . look at you!" I said, pushing back my fear, getting even bolder, and taking a determined step forward. "When is the last time you have taken care of yourself: brushed your hair, washed your clothes, picked up after your children?" I asked, gesturing at the mayhem. "When is the last time you looked in the mirror and saw someone you liked? I may not have known you well growing up, but I'm not dumb enough to think this is the real you." The more I talked, the stiffer her upper lip became and the redder her face. Right before I thought she was going to explode on my head, I decided I would show myself out, but not without one last statement. Unfortunately she beat me to it.

"Who do you think you are coming into my home, with your little preppy-looking self? You have no idea what my life is. You live in your little fantasy world, with no responsibility and no one tugging at your sleeve twenty-four hours a day. You spend time sipping lattes and hanging out with your prissy mama."

Well, heaven help the child who talks that way about my mama. I can tell you any story about her I dare please. But Emma's words brought me to life in a way that, honestly, to that point I had never seen myself. "First, let me tell you one thing. I don't drink lattes. I drink Coca-Cola. Second, I have responsibilities. But I actually take care of them."

"So do I," she said, glaring.

"Oh, do you? Well, I make sure at the end of the day when I lay my head on my pillow that I did the right thing, the right way, and at the right time, with hopefully the right motives. I don't let others suffer at my hands."

"Does anyone look like they're suffering around here?"

"Well, I don't call ten years of T-shirts living the high life. And third, my mother is one of the finest women you will ever meet. It would do you good to learn how to be half the woman that she is. No, it would do us both good." With that, I passed her in the carved-out path and turned around to add one final thought.

"Emma, I don't care if you tell me anything about your experience. I might've been sent here for one reason alone today, and that was to let you know you need to remember how to live. You have four reasons upstairs. They should be enough to clean yourself up, make something out of your life, and do those things you were created for. Because I assure you this isn't it. And if you need to figure out where to start, you would benefit from talking to my mother. She has a way of helping people see the good in themselves. I think you've forgotten that you have any."

She walked over to the door and opened it, making it clear she had tired of my dissertation.

"I'm sorry to bother you. I hope you have a good afternoon." With that, I walked out of the already opened door, and she slammed it behind me.

"Well, that went well."

I needed a mandatory rest period. There was only one place that ever gave me real quiet—the Savannah College of Art and Design Library. I took my station next to the window, so I could keep my eye on who was coming and going up the street.

As I opened up my satchel, I saw him. His bike was still blue and his curls still curly. He passed by the window, and just as I turned my head to watch his departure, he turned back and caught my eye and smiled a "I know you're watching me but don't want me to know" kind of smile. I returned a raised eyebrow and upturned lip. *Cocky little something, aren't you? I wasn't even looking at you. I was just looking out the window trying to create an adequate opening for my first article. You need to get a job anyway and quit riding around the street like some troubled youth with nowhere to go.*

I began an Internet search to find out how I could get copies of the Miss Georgia United States of America program books. The Miss Georgia United States of America Pageant Web site opened to the playing of their theme song. "What a lady, dressed as royalty. With such grace, she has arrived. Can't you see her magic and splendor? Isn't this world greater for having her?"

Ooh, bad rhyme, I thought to myself as the song continued. "Here she comes. Walking on air, she comes. Don't you wish you were her? The lady divine, Miss Georgia United States of America."

"Ooh, so sad. So very, very sad," I actually said out loud. I had heard the song a thousand times. Vicky walked through the house singing it to herself. But hearing it from a computer speaker solidified the fact that it truly was wretched.

Searching the Web site, I found the past issues. Some poor soul had been forced to scan every page of every program book over the last fifty years. Grateful, I began the tedious search for Katherine's picture. She would have to be somewhere before Victoria, who was crowned in 1976.

I found her in 1972. I couldn't believe it. Despite more than thirty years, she looked exactly the same, without the gray, of course. And the few laugh lines from a good life that had since formed around her eyes were undetectable in the photo. Underneath her picture it read "Katherine Powers, Miss Savannah United States of America, sponsored by the Savannah Chamber of Commerce."

Finding Katherine, I began to research the judges for her the year she competed. There I saw Mr. Randolph Cummings III himself. I began to scan through the years and learned that Mr. III was a judge from 1970 through 1992. Then in 1993, Mr. Randolph Cummings IV came into the picture as a judge. I went back to Katherine's program and looked at the auditors. Her auditors were Mr. Lyle Wilcox and Mr. Stanley Harvard. But looking through the programs from '71 and '73, Mr. Wilcox and Mr. Harvard hadn't audited before or since. The Templetons audited from 1973 until 1996, and then a different set of auditors was used every year after that.

My mind raced with a thousand questions. *If the pageant was rigged, by whom? Was it by the directors, a rotund older fella named Mr. Carl Todd, or his daughter, Miss Carline Todd? Was it this Mr. III judge, who never seemed to go away? Or was it these one-time auditors? And were they fired for what they did that year?* It was up to me to make this puzzle work. It was up to me to make it all work before Tuesday. Because by Tuesday, Savannah needed a story and Mr. Hicks needed a reason to fire me. I determined I would have mine; I only hoped that it wouldn't afford him his in the process.

The Atlanta phone book popped up on the Internet and pulled up Wilcox, Harvard, Pratt, and Dean. What could it hurt to call and ask for a meeting? The worst they could do would be to say no. I dialed right there on my mobile phone and heard a friendly voice. "Wilcox, Harvard, Pratt, and Dean, may I help you?"

"Yes, hello. I was trying to reach Mr. Lyle Wilcox or Mr. Stanley Harvard."

"Oh," she said, pausing. "Well, they have both retired, but Mr. Wilcox's son, Raymond, and Mr. Harvard's daughter, Suzanna, both work here. Would you like to speak to one of them?"

"Do you mean they've retired from the company or have they retired, period?"

"Well"—she dropped her voice to a whisper—"Mr. Wilcox retired about two years ago from the company and died immediately after his retirement. Mr. Harvard retired over ten years ago and just passed away last month. So, I guess you could say they have both retired, retired."

"Well, in that case, how about I just speak with Mr. Wilcox, Mr. Raymond Wilcox?" I said.

"Oh, he's in a meeting right now, so you can't speak with him."

I decided not to remind her that she had just asked me if I

would like to speak with him, so I went on to request to speak to Suzanna Harvard.

"Oh, well, she's in that same meeting. In fact they are all in that meeting. By the way, who is this?"

"My name is Savannah Phillips. I'm from Savannah, Georgia, and—"

"Oh, isn't that cute. I bet you go around telling people you are Savannah from Savannah." Her laugh was increasingly irritating.

"Actually, no I don't say that to anyone. You know what, I don't think I'll leave a message. I think I'll just try back another time." I hung up and decided to see if maybe Mr. Wilcox's or Mr. Harvard's wives were still living. Searching under their personal names, I could find no listing for Mr. Wilcox, but Mr. and Mrs. Stanley Harvard were in Buckhead. I picked up my phone to try again.

"Hello," said a voice from the other end.

"Hello, Mrs. Harvard?"

"Yes, this is she. May I ask who is calling?" she responded warmly.

"My name is Savannah Phillips, and I am calling you from Savannah, actually," I said, pausing to see if she would want to add anything of her own to my recent statement. She didn't, so I continued. "I'm working on a story about the Miss Georgia United States of America Pageant. I know it has been a long time, but I saw your husband's firm was the auditor in 1972, and I wanted to know if I could discuss that event with you."

"Young lady, that was a lifetime ago and an experience we don't fondly recall. I'm not sure what you are working on, but I can assure you, you won't find any information here."

"Well, I understand that it's been a long time, and to you it probably isn't even worth discussing. But what if I told you that what happened could still be affecting the pageant today? Would it matter at all to you then? I mean, I'm not sure that pageants matter at all to you. They don't matter much to me myself. But—"

"Pageants are of no consequence to me one way or the other. But whatever some women want to do is their own business.

Stanley had nothing to do with those pageants. He only audited them for one year, and then he quit. So I don't really have any information to give you. Are you some kind of reporter or something?"

The way she said "reporter" had an air of sleaze to it. I had never thought that people might see what I do as somehow less than ethical or necessary. But if they hadn't met Gloria or read her work, then their only point of reference was the media they were forced to endure on 24/7 news. The kind that can make news from nothing during a slow news cycle. "Actually, I write human-interest stories for the *Savannah Chronicle*." No point in her knowing that I had yet to write my first story. "I believe I have found something of interest to Savannah. It revolves around the year your husband was an auditor. I just wanted to come and talk with you about it."

"You and I have nothing to talk about."

"I'm not asking you to promise anything. I'm just asking for the opportunity to talk with you."

"This would be a waste of both of our time, young lady."

"Ma'am, I know I'm young, but I believe that everyone should have the opportunity to do their best in anything and be granted their due successes accordingly. I'm not a big beauty pageant person, but if that is a young woman's dream, she ought to at least have the opportunity to pursue that dream fairly."

The other side of the line was quiet for a while. "I'll meet you tomorrow at noon at the Buckhead Diner. Do you know where that is?"

"Yes, ma'am. It's my favorite restaurant in Atlanta, and I'll be there by eleven thirty. I'm sure we'll leave liking each other."

"Well, we will leave, but I don't know how much we will like each other." All that followed was a dial tone.

CHAPTER FOURTEEN

I parked Old Betsy a couple of houses down from 13 Oglethorpe Avenue, where Claire was waiting. We hadn't seen each other since my fall break, when we had spent a morning catching up over breakfast at The Lady & Sons in the City Market. She was already looking tan, and it was just May. She looked like a real real-estate agent in her seersucker pantsuit and strappy pumps. I walked toward her and we greeted each other in the only acceptable way below the Mason-Dixon line—with a hug. A real hug. Not a half-pat or a half-tap. But a grab-you-and-let-you-know-somebody's-got-you kind of hug.

"Claire, I can't believe how tan you are. It's only May. When have you had time to lay out?" I asked her.

"Savannah, where have you been? We don't lay out anymore around here; that stuff will kill you. We use Tan Beautiful that they sell on TV. You just wipe it on, let it sit, and vavoom, you've got a tan. Looks natural, doesn't it?"

"It looks amazing. But I'll stick to the real thing. What's the joy of living this close to the ocean if you don't ever lay out on the beach?"

She laughed. "Wait until we hit thirty. Then you'll be asking me what the number is to QVC."

I turned to look at the cute white house in front of us. "This is a charming place."

"You're going to love it. It just came on the market yesterday. I heard some young couple bought it and want to rent out the bottom. Number 13A, that could be you," she said as she opened the iron gate.

"That would be amazing. You should see where my mother wanted me to move."

"Already heard and already have."

"This city is pathetic."

"This city is Savannah," she said as she flipped on the light inside. We entered the quaint little apartment in the den area. Directly behind it was an open kitchen and a small area for a breakfast table. Down a small hall toward the back of the house was a bedroom and bath. All in great condition, with what appeared to be the original hardwood floors and moldings. "Isn't this quaint?"

"Yeah, it really is. What's the rent?"

"It's eight hundred a month. It's a little more than you said you could afford, but this is Savannah."

"Well, I think I could swing that. At least until I have to get a new car."

"Oh, that car will outlive you!"

I laughed. "You're probably right." We walked through one more time and I checked out the closets, which were small but doable; and then tested the appliances, which were older but in good condition. "This really is great. I think it will be perfect. Do you think I have a couple of weeks, until I get paid?"

"I can find out who the owners are and ask. I don't even think they are moving in for another month. Heard they wanted to do a few renovations."

"Well, maybe it would work out perfectly," I said as we made our way outside and headed to our cars.

As we went to the other side of the street, Grant came walking toward us. "Well, hello, girls. What are you doing over here on this side of town?"

"We could ask you the same question," Claire chimed in.

"Oh, I'm coming to check on my house. I just bought #13, the white one right up there," he said, pointing. I simply watched another dream slip its way into the sewer that was quickly becoming my life.

"You've got to be kidding—" Claire started.

"Well, you must be doing well at the architectural firm." I glared at Claire, who retreated. "It looks like a beautiful place."

"Yeah, times are good, I guess. I thought it was a great place, and Elisabeth loved it. We're trying to rent out the bottom, though, so if you hear of anyone, let me know."

"We'll do that," I assured him. "Well, we've got to run."

"Yeah, me too. See ya'll soon, I'm sure."

"I guess you'll want me to look for something else," Claire said in shared hurt as we watched Grant walk into his new house.

"Yeah, that would be a good idea," I said, opening my door.

"We'll find something. Keep your chin up."

"We've nowhere left to go but up. Call me." And I drove away from my second lost opportunity at freedom.

I could hear Vicky before I even entered the kitchen.

"People are just tacky. Who would spend millions on a home and just put tacky right out in plain view? They'll have to get rid of it. They didn't get it approved, and they'll have to get rid of it." Vicky added the clanging of pots and pans along with her own jaws for effect.

"Victoria, you don't need to be involved in everyone's business. When a person spends that much money for a home, they should be able to paint it purple and attach a helicopter pad on the top if they want to."

"Jake, that's not how it works."

"Yes it is, Victoria. Whether you and your little fashion committee think it is fashionable."

"I don't have a fashion committee. I have a historical review committee."

"Call it what you will, but you spend too much time in people's business."

My mother was still grumbling like a food processor, preparing what looked to be spaghetti when I came in and sat on the stool by the island. "What's all the commotion about?" I suspected this little ruckus just might prevent me from having to have any conversation about my day at all.

The pots were clanging louder than had been heard in a good year. "Oh, you wouldn't believe it, I tell you. People are just crazy. Just lack the sense God gave a pea turkey."

"What in the world is a pea turkey?"

"Savannah, don't bother me about the way I talk. You know good and well a pea turkey isn't anything more than a pea turkey."

"OK. So who lacks the sense God gave a pea turkey?"

She turned to stare at me, waving around a small frying pan in her left hand. "This couple down the street invited me over today to see how everything had been decorated since they moved in. They're from South Carolina. What does that tell you?"

I was sure at that moment my mother had ADD. Decorating and South Carolina had nothing to do with each other. In fact, most of what she said didn't seem connected. She could change the direction of conversation as quickly as she changed the color of her hair. Why did it take me so long to notice things? Apparently, I had spent my life too preoccupied, and at that moment I needed to pay more attention to what was going on around me.

"Savannah, are you listening to me?" I was surprised that she noticed I had wandered off the subject as well. Maybe I had ADD too. I didn't think so. But who could be sure?

"They're from South Carolina."

"Oh, right. So you can just imagine where I'm going with this. I go inside, and their house is horrendous. I mean everything is Pepto pink. The walls, the trim, half the furniture."

"The furniture?"

"Yes, and their poodle even looked like she was pink. It could have been the tones bouncing off of the walls, but by the time I left I thought my aubergine suit had turned pink."

I dodged the waving pan and added, "Well, aubergine is a variation of the pink-purple family."

"Savannah, stop. I know what color aubergine is."

"OK, continue."

"Now, anyway, beyond the house being horrendous, she told me they had just gotten a satellite. It had come in today. I told her that was great. That she would love it. That we had one as well. Then we proceeded to her patio and gardens." Her eyes went so wide you would have thought she had seen a two-headed pink pelican. "Well, this, honey, was a satellite big enough to call in Star Trek, Alien Nation, and any other outer space extraterrestrial you would desire. It was big enough for E.T. to phone home, I tell you."

"Ooh, E.T., huh?"

"Yes, and it had its own concrete slab. It takes up half of their backyard and can be seen from two different streets. All I said was, "Well, honey, I do believe that's the largest television apparatus I have ever seen."

"Half the backyard?"

"Savannah, small children could get overtaken by that thing. They could be snatched up by Galaxy Network and lost for eternity. But it won't stay. I won't allow it. They are in the Historical District, and that home is on the Register, and I'm not allowing some big canker sore—"

"I think you mean eyesore."

"Thank you, I mean eyesore like that to exist in this city. Pretty soon people would be calling it artwork and hanging it off the sides of their houses. It wouldn't end, I tell you. And then we would be known as the satellite capital of the world. I can hear the advertisements: 'Come to Savannah, where you'll get beaches, good food, and any channel in the galaxy.' Now that's just not what I intend to let happen." And with that, she turned back around to actually use the frying pan she had been torturing me with.

By the time we actually ate, watched a little TV, and went to bed, Vicky was still mumbling under her breath. I washed my face and spent some time in prayer. I crawled into bed not knowing what tomorrow would bring, but certain my future was much brighter than Satellite Lady's.

CHAPTER FIFTEEN

I got up before anyone else so I could make a quiet exit. I wrote a quick note saying I had some work to do until late that evening (which I did), I wouldn't be home until late (which I wouldn't), and I would see them in the morning (which I would). Adding the only thing necessary to prevent a return to a thousand questions, I jotted a note to my mother offering lunch tomorrow. That invitation alone would save me from being accosted by a woman perched atop a chair in the dark when I got home.

A new bronze button-down with a patterned skirt in cream and bronze seemed appropriate for my lunch appointment. I pulled my hair back in a low ponytail and slipped on a pair of cream-colored slides, which I'm certain Vicky paid entirely too much for. The entire ensemble was topped off with a Louis Vuitton backpack, a graduation gift I never asked for.

Heading west on Interstate 16 allowed me about two and a half hours to drive, catch my breath, and sort my thoughts. How was I possibly going to be able to write a story about a rigged beauty pageant and not make a debauchery of Gloria's good name? She wrote stories of conviction. She wrote articles that made readers believe in something, even someone. She unearthed a moral compass that came from something more profound than herself.

I wasn't sure which way my own compass pointed half the time, and I probably wouldn't be able to help anyone else find theirs. The only thing I knew on this day was that I had her job, a possible first story, and a knowing in my heart that this was what I was supposed to do. At that point, those were the only things I could trust.

This is for a purpose. This is for justice. If Emma really lost because of unethical behavior and her pathetic existence is the end result, then this does have a purpose. Emma needs me. She might not know it, but she'll thank me for this when it is over, I thought.

The parking lot at Buckhead Diner off of Piedmont was pretty full at eleven thirty. As I pulled up, I realized that neither Mrs. Harvard nor I knew what the other looked like. Voice recollection would be our only connection, other than the "are you her?" look in each other's eyes.

The hostess put my name on the waiting list. I told the supermodel hostess my guest would be a Mrs. Harvard and then sat down at the curved booth under the window. Scanning the waiting area, no one seemed to look like a Mrs. Harvard, not that I had any idea what a Mrs. Harvard would look like. There was a couple all cozied up in the corner, acting as if there was no other person around their love nest. They were totally unsympathetic to the fact that someone in the room had just been forced to hear her one-time boyfriend and future husband tell her he was marrying another woman. I found them annoying.

A group of thirty-something women chattered away by the door, as if this was their first day of adult conversation in the last millennium and they were making up for lost time. With each woman hardly taking time to breathe between sentences, it was a miracle that they even knew what the others were saying. I'm sure as long as the words returning weren't "Mama" or "gimme," it didn't matter much.

The young couple took their seats without ever removing their hands from each other. *I'd love to see what you two look like in fifty years.* Looking back now, Grant and I had never been that way. He hadn't competed with another man, just my own selfishness. It made me wonder if I had ever loved him the way real lovers do, those who finish each other's sentences and can't walk without holding hands.

The group of jabbering women forced me back into the moment as they walked to their table. Around eleven forty-five, the supermodel led me to mine. A young waitress made her way to my booth by the far window to take my drink order. Coke seemed adolescent, so I asked for water with lemon.

At noon sharp, Mrs. Harvard walked through the door, looking just like the seventy-some-year-old wife of a "retired" accountant from Atlanta should. As her low-heeled, closed-toed, cream pumps brought her stately frame to our table, I stood to greet her. She placed her small and wrinkled hand into mine. We made our introductions, and I invited her to sit down.

"It's a pleasure to meet you, Mrs. Harvard. Thank you so much for coming." I waited for her to get comfortable in the booth.

She nodded her freshly styled, frosted gray hair. She straightened her dainty pink-and-white striped piqué skirt, then ran her hands across the matching short-sleeved jacket accented with pearl buttons. I glanced at her matching pink purse. "Well, if I hadn't given you my word, I would've canceled this silly meeting. I don't know why on earth you are fooling around with something that is thirty years old and of little importance to most people."

"Well, I'm bringing it up because of the people it was important to at one time."

"'At one time' may be the key words, young lady."

That "young lady" thing was so irritating. "Well, apparently not. After thirty years, a woman I know actually felt she should tell someone." Mrs. Harvard seemed to debate whether she would stay. Her pause allowed me to add another thought. "And it was obviously something that either your husband or his partner was troubled enough by, or caught red-handed doing, that they never performed the task again."

The waitress arrived in time to prevent her from grabbing her knife and flinging it in my direction. "I think I'm going to need a Coke, young lady," she said, looking at the waitress and then returning her glare to me. I figured if I was the source of causing a seventy-something woman to actually "need" a Coke, then we might get somewhere.

"Savannah, is it?" she asked. I nodded back at her with as genuine a smile as I could muster. "Savannah, let me tell you something about my husband, God rest his soul," she said with a quick bowing of her frosted head and crossing of the chest. "If there is one thing that Stanley was, it was honest. He never wanted anything to do with anything or anyone that wasn't totally honest. So, if you are here questioning his character, then I'll let you know right now our conversation is finished."

"Mrs. Harvard, I'm not here to destroy anyone's character. I am simply here to find out why in 1972 a young lady who competed in the Miss Georgia United States of America Pageant left feeling rather confident that the wrong girl was chosen."

"I'm sure girls feel that way every year. It's a beauty pageant; only one girl can win."

"I know that. But this is a different situation, and I'm here to find out what Mr. Harvard might have known, or Mr. Wilcox for that matter. Did a judge have a complete change of mind? Or, for some ridiculous reason, did your husband change the scores?" I asked, keeping my eyes on her knife.

The waitress came back again, and Mrs. Harvard, who had never opened a menu, looked at her and ordered blue cheese chips. "I would like a Coke too," I added.

"Well, you're just an adventurous little soul, aren't you?" Mrs. Harvard said, moving her straw around in her glass and never taking her eyes off me. "So, Nancy Drew, why would my husband quit if he had something to gain? I would think he would continue forever if he was making a profit, wouldn't you?"

The giggling sounds from the booth across from us pulled my attention in their direction. There they sat. The two young lovers, oblivious to common decency. I wanted to slap them. By George, for a moment I wanted to slap her. But I was too busy watching them to remember her. And when I did, she was still in full discourse.

"Let me tell you why: Because he didn't. Because my husband was the auditor for that pageant for one year. One year too many. And, to kill your curiosity, it was my husband who realized that something underhanded was going on. So if you thought this is where you would find your story, you are sadly mistaken, young lady." I noticed her run her frail fingers around a simple gold wedding band that still graced her ring finger.

"Then who is the story, Mrs. Harvard?"

"You're the reporter, Savannah."

"So you're not going to give me anything?"

"Oh, yes, young lady. I'm going to give you something. I'm going to give you a piece of advice. You need to decide first if this is even a story worth telling. If it is, you need to make sure my husband's name is never mentioned. And then you need to figure out where the real story is, because you've looked in the wrong place."

"Can't you throw me a bone?" I asked, exhausted.

"Yes, I'll give you a bone. Longevity is the key here, and what would be gained is the question. If you're going to be a reporter, you need to ask all the questions." With that, she stood up, laid her unused napkin on the table, picked up her pink purse, and pranced herself out of the diner.

The waitress arrived with a plate of blue cheese chips. "I'll need another Coke," I said, staring at the plate in front of me. "And you can keep them coming."

Mrs. Harvard left me feeling like an idiot, totally speechless and with the check. I didn't even have my first paycheck, and she had left me with the stupid bill, which I paid only after I had successfully made myself sick on blue cheese chips. Walking out to my car in a stupor, I was half-fuming, half utterly confused, and completely full.

Why in the world would she even agree to meet me if she wasn't going to tell me anything? I thought as I drove. *My word, I drove three hours to talk to her. This is a joke. I'm going to go work for Paige. That's what I'll do. I'll stay at home, make the basement an apartment, and work for Paige on the weekends, live on Daddy's money and Mother's cooking. And I'll make prank phone calls in the wee hours of the morning to a little old frosted-haired, pink-and-white-striped prima donna in Atlanta.*

CHAPTER SIXTEEN

Thursday brought rain inside and out. *Lord, let it be a monsoon and every restaurant in town flooded. And let Vicky be forced to go into work for crisis management.* Then I heard her voice downstairs and knew there was no such luck. The alarm clock read ten. I hadn't slept in until ten in years. Of course, with my usually uneventful life, I usually slept like a baby. But all my new adventures proved tiring.

The knock on the door had to be one of a perfectly manicured hand.

"Ugh."

She opened the door anyway. When she saw me still under the covers, she walked over and placed her hand on my forehead. "Savannah, are you feeling OK?"

Removing my head from underneath her hand, I scooted past her to the restroom to brush my teeth. "Yes, ma'am. I'm fine. I just had a longer day than I thought."

She followed right behind. "Well, I thought you would meet us at Bible study last night. But when you didn't come, I got worried. Then, you were resting so soundly when we got home, we didn't want to wake you. What in the world were you doing all day yesterday?"

Fortunately I had already crammed the toothbrush in my mouth, and most of what I said was purposely unintelligible. "Welunfortenlswthsu."

"Oh?"

"Thniwentwfentishrwolkintomir."

"Hmm, really."

"Yehannremtadlokrutsfioiinhn."

She just nodded and continued anyway. "OK, well, sounds like fun. I want you to meet our new director of tourism. She's an absolute doll, and I just know that you'll love her. I invited her to lunch with us."

I was about to look at her with an "I can't believe you invited someone else to lunch with us" kind of look, but then I realized that with someone else there it would give me the opportunity to avoid discussion about what I had been up to. I rinsed out my mouth and straightened. "That's a wonderful idea."

"I knew you would think so. It's too late for you to eat breakfast, or you won't want lunch. We're going to meet her at eleven thirty at the Gryphon Tea Room for tea and sandwiches," she added as she left. "I'd say you need to get a move on, and please try to dress a smidgen more, well, more delicate, OK?"

I peeked my head around the corner and watched as her Karen Kane blue linen sundress and matching blue linen overshirt swayed behind her, and her camel-colored BCBG mules clicked on the hardwood until she was gone.

Staring at my closet, I tried to deduce what Vicky defined as a "smidgen more delicate." But since I didn't even know what that meant, there was no way to accomplish it, was there? The best solution when I couldn't read minds—comfort. I chose a comfortable, long, and loosely fitting black skirt with tiny white polka dots and a black linen vest. There was a mysterious shoebox in the front of my closet that said Kate Spade. I pulled it out and opened it to find a pair of black open-toed sandals with one wide strap across the top.

Inside was a "delicately" written note. "I thought these might be a pleasant alternative to flip-flops." They were rather cute, and they would make her happy, so I caved. They were undeniably comfortable too, but she didn't need to know everything.

"I wondered if you were ever going to get here," Dad said as I came through the back door around eleven.

I poured myself a Coke and sat down at a stool by the prep table in the back. "I had a rough day and even longer night. I had to go to Atlanta to interview someone for the story I'm working on. Then I forgot I had promised Mother lunch, and that thought kept me up another six hours."

"Your mother is looking forward to your lunch, so you need to be nice," he said in all seriousness. "So, when are you going to tell us about this story?"

"Well, I haven't really told anyone anything about it. I'm not sure when I'm going to talk about it. I'm trying to get all of my sources and facts together first."

"Like a reporter?"

"Yeah, that real-reporter kind of thing. Can't give all my stuff away."

"So how was the apartment Claire showed you?" he asked, sitting down beside me.

"Great, just great."

"Oh, that good?"

"Yeah! Grant and Miss Converse would be my landlords!"

He laughed, then stood up and went toward his office. "Ooh, nice. Your mother's offer is looking better and better, isn't it?"

I followed him. "No way! I'll just keep looking. Stay focused. I'll find it. Something safe, affordable, and conveniently located to my life."

He rummaged through his mail, smiling. "You think all that's out there?"

"Yes, I do. Anyway, I don't have any more time. I've got to go meet Mother and this new director of tourism she invited to have lunch with us," I said, walking to the back door.

"Oh, you're meeting Amber today."

"Why are you smirking? I hate it when you smirk."

"Well, you should have a wonderful time. Yep, you're going to have a fabulous day," he said. I heard him laughing all the way out to the front of the store.

The Gryphon Tea Room is off Madison Square on Bull Street. Mother was sitting in the front window waving at me as if we hadn't seen each other in a week. It was then this figure leaned up from behind her, as if they had gone to the same how-to-wave-like-a-beauty-queen school. Then it all came together: the wave, Dad's laugh, hair that looks like a Pantene commercial: I was having lunch with Miss Savannah United States of America. "You will pay, old man."

I walked in and went up the few steps that led to the elevated area of tables that flanked the big picture window in the front of the store. They both sized me up and down. But when Vicky spotted the shoes, it was evident she approved. I smiled back at her knowingly.

"Hey, I'm Amber," she said. The six-foot-tall frame stood up to shake my hand like an overexcited Jack Russell terrier. "Your mother has told me so much about you," she added, still shaking. I pulled my hand from her grip.

Casting a raised right eyebrow in my mother's direction, I said, "Well, I haven't heard much about you."

"Oh, well, I've heard Savannah this and Savannah that. Everyone in this whole entire town knows you and loves you. And your mother. Oh, Miss Victoria is just the sweetest thing," she said, patting my mother on the leg as my mother smiled at her and looked at me, wanting to see me nod in agreement. I thought I was going to gag at the "Miss Victoria" thing and was too bewildered at this creature in front of me to realize that my mother wanted my element of approval.

"Your mother and I have been friends since I was Miss Queen of Tulips United States of America three years ago. And now that I'm Miss Savannah United States of America, well, let's just say, we've been practically inseparable," she said with a giddy laugh. I raised my right eyebrow, gave a nod in the direction of my mother, made mental note of my father's torture to come, followed by a deep breath for the woman in front of me who had yet to breathe herself. With the same thought, I realized that Amber's experience was exactly what I did need to talk about. Maybe this was providence. Maybe this was exactly what was supposed to happen to me today.

"Then, she helped me get this job and, well, I just know you and I are going to be the best of friends. I mean, I feel like we are sisters already because your mother has treated me like a daughter." I settled in, certain we would never be good friends, nor sisters. She may act like my mother, look like my mother—in a pageant, fixed sort of way—she might even be a better fit for my mother, but Vicky was still my mother.

"Well, it sounds like you and my mother have a lot in common," I said, looking up gratefully at the waitress who had come to save me from another Amber monologue on her joyous entrance into our world.

While "Miss Victoria" and "Miss Amber" placed their orders, I mentally orchestrated the conversation for the afternoon. There were two choices: Let them dictate the next hour to hour and a half and leave exhausted and in need of therapy or dictate it with my developing journalistic skills, which, unbeknownst to them, had failed miserably the day before.

"So, Amber, is it?" I asked. I paused, trying to use up minutes.

"Yes, Amber. It was my mother's favorite stone, and she has

always said I was exactly what she ordered, and so she named me Amber. How did you get the name Savannah?" she asked. Then she flipped her hair back with her perfectly French-manicured nails, revealing her absolutely flawless skin, but not following my lead in the slightest.

"Oh, it's a long story."

Vicky missed the clue. "I named her Savannah because I grew up here and have always loved this city. It was my favorite place and she was exactly what I ordered as well."

"Oh, that is one of the sweetest things I've ever heard. Isn't she the sweetest lady you would ever want to meet? I could just put her in my purse and take her home," she said, lifting up her pretty little designer bag and opening it up like she wanted Vicky to hop in. I knew at that exact moment that attempting to follow any journalistic agenda was hopeless.

I was sitting at a table with two women who didn't quite measure all the way up to the normal scale. They were normal on their own scale, the beauty queen, live and breathe, never-had-a-greater-dream kind of scale. That scale required little interactive conversation. So, I just sat back, drank my Earl Grey tea, ate my crab cakes, and watched them dine on skimpy salads, water with lemon, and the fancy house tea while they told their own stories back and forth as if hearing them for the first time. That is exactly what I did for two solid hours.

Amber sipped her water with her left pinkie sticking out as if she was competing even now. "Savannah, your mother said you were never interested in beauty pageants." I nodded emphatically, assuring her she was exactly right. "Well, I've competed in pageants ever since I was little. I'll never forget the very first one. It was called 'Little Miss Savannah.' I've lived here all my life, so that's why I competed in 'Little Miss Savannah.'" I about rolled my eyes, figuring she was certain I couldn't have come up with that on my own. This made me feel fortunate that I hadn't moved here until I was old enough to ensure my escape from such things.

"I was pathetic. I'd never been in a pageant before, and my mother had never seen a pageant for little girls, but I entered it anyway. We had to compete in swimsuit and "party dress," they called it. So, my mom bought me a metallic fuchsia swimsuit and white sandals, that are back in style now, you know, the kind where the strap goes between the toes, not those flip-flop kind of things. I can't believe people even wear those today. Can you, Miss Victoria?" she asked, looking over at my mother.

"Well, they do make some cute ones nowadays," my mother said rather diplomatically. I propped my foot up on her side of the booth.

"Well, I don't think ladies should be caught dead in those things. They ought to outlaw them this side of the Mason-Dixon line. They are just ghastly. Anyway, my mother bought me those cute ones where the strap comes up between your toes then con-nects to a strap that buckles around your ankle. Now, the white and fuchsia kind of clashed. I probably looked like all feet," she said, laughing at her own story. She put her hand over her chest as if it was almost more than she could handle.

During her treatise I gave a few nods, a few smiles, and a few raised right eyebrows, assuring them I was mentally present. My mother kept looking at me to gauge my politeness level. She even cast a couple of "this girl is a little too much" expressions my way. I was glad she had us to compare to each other.

"Oh, I bet it was as cute as it could be," Vicky said to re-assure her.

"Well, I doubt it, and it only gets worse from there. Then, Mama bought me a pretty little pastel pink church dress—notice I didn't say party dress—and she put black patent-leather shoes on my feet, with white knee-socks," she said, doubling over in laughter. Even I knew that would have been a pretty pathetic combination.

"You're not serious," Vicky exclaimed in true horror. "She put a pink dress on you and black patent-leather shoes?"

"Yes, and sent me out there on that stage to compete against eight-year-old pros with absolutely no modeling experience of my own. I clomped around on that stage from one end to the other. I had no idea what in the world I was doing, but I was too young to know any better," she said, beside herself in hysterics now.

"That is just awful. You poor thing. Were you scarred?" Vicky asked in all seriousness.

She paused long enough to pick up a piece of lettuce and place it in her mouth as if she might blow up like a house. "No. In fact, when we were walking to the car, my mother said, 'I bet you won't ever want to do that again, will you?' I told her that if I could get a new swimsuit, a new dress, and two new pairs of shoes, I would do it anytime. At that moment, she created a beast. That was how the journey of my career began," she said, meaning every word she had just spoken. She had made a career out of beauty pageants.

Mother picked up a slightly larger bite of her own salad. Vicky at least appreciated food. She had a great figure for her age, but she wasn't obsessed about her weight. And her excellent cooking was something she wasn't going to let only other people appreciate. But in public, she ate a little more refined. "So what did you do next?"

"Well, my next pageant was the Miss Snow White Pageant. My mother had gotten it down by now. I had me a great party dress. This pageant actually had talent too, and I am a rather fabulous little singer. I mean *American Idol* didn't appreciate me when I competed for them last year, but, well, that Simon Cowell, he's just a mean ol' meany."

I determined she was of the ADD family too. "A mean ol' meany, huh?" I tried to stop myself, but it came out anyway.

"Yes, just downright rude. I told him he needed to come to the South and learn some manners. I didn't know what they taught him over there in England, but here we didn't say such cruel things to people."

"What did he say to you?"

"It's just too horrible to repeat, Savannah."

"Oh, we won't tell anyone. I promise." I figured I could blame rumors on any one of the other thirty million viewers who'd already heard. "Your secret is perfectly safe with us. Right, Mother?"

Even Vicky was dying to know about this, so she chimed in, "Yes, absolutely. Not a word to another living, breathing soul."

"Well, OK. But I promised I would never even give him the privilege of repeating it. He had the audacity to tell me I sounded like the girl in the movie *Shrek* that made the bird explode. And if I sang much longer, he was certain he would have exploded."

My hysterics were lost on her. "So anyway," she continued. "In that pageant I competed in talent and swimsuit. And I won. I didn't win talent but I did win the overall title, which let me compete in the state pageant. The girl who had won first runner-up and talent here in Savannah was able to go to the state pageant too. She beat me at state, which I still don't understand how that happened, and I won't tell you her name, because you probably know her, and I don't want to sound petty." She came up for air. "But after that, I had the bug and knew that one day I wanted to be Miss United States of America."

"Oh, Amber, you've got to tell Savannah some of those stories you told me, about what the girls did while you competed in pageants. They are just hysterical," Vicky prodded.

"Oh yes, do tell," I added.

"Oh, I did see some funny things through the years. The funniest though was this one poor soul who I competed with my first year in Miss Savannah," she said. She must have noticed my perplexed look, when she said "first year." "Yeah, I competed in Miss Savannah United States of America three times before I won. And this will be my fourth time in Miss Georgia United States of America.

"Anyway, one of the girls was going to wear a dress her mother had made for her evening-gown competition. It was a one-shoulder-strapped evening gown in royal blue." I had no idea how this girl remembered all of this stuff and wasn't about to stop her to ask. "So, when she competed she didn't think her gown fit well, but she went out there anyway. After the pageant was over and she went to take her gown off, she realized that she had worn it backward. Worn it backward!" she said, heehawing and slapping the table. Vicky laughed as if she were hearing it for the first time too.

"Can you imagine walking out in a dress where your, your"— Amber leaned in closer and said in the most delicate of whispers— "where your boobies are in the back?"

I was ashamed I had even leaned in for that one. "She didn't know she had her dress on backward because it didn't have a tag in it since her mother had made it. Her mother came backstage and asked her if she couldn't tell"—here we went again, as she leaned in—"that her boobies were in the back."

I could only picture that poor girl being traumatized for the rest of her life. She would forever be known as the girl with her "boobies in the back."

"I bet her mother dressed her for the rest of her competitions," Vicky said, finding her own self rather charming.

Amber showed a hint of compassion for the young lady who would forever be checking the tags in her clothes before donning her attire for the day. "Actually she never competed again." Her sadness left as quickly as it had come, and the giddy storyteller was back.

"Yeah, I've seen a thousand incredible sights in my years. I've seen girls add 'extra personality' by winking at the judges during their swimsuit competitions when their mothers meant for them to add it in their talent competition. I've seen girls play drums who shouldn't have, dance who couldn't, and sing who, well, let's just say dogs in the near vicinity are still not the same." There was a final pause as she placed her napkin over her half-remaining salad.

"Oh, this has been fun, hasn't it, girls?" she said, getting a nod and a smile from Vicky and as much as I could muster from myself. "I do hope we can do this again soon. I have a thousand more stories. And, Savannah, I just loved getting to know you. You are one of the neatest people I have ever talked to."

"Thank you, I'm glad we had this time together too."

"Well, I need to get home. I'm meeting with a dress designer today to see if she can copy a dress I saw Julia Roberts wear to the Academy Awards last year. I think it would be simply elegant to compete in. You know Julia Roberts filmed a movie here? I was an extra in it. She and I would have been great friends too, but they wouldn't let me get near her," she said, rolling her eyes. I was amazed at the discernment of the Hollywood elite.

"Well, kisses, kisses!" she said, leaning over to my mother and pretending to kiss her on the cheek. She came at me, but I shot out a hand and practically punched her in the stomach. And after another ferocious shake, she turned to descend the stairwell in true beauty-pageant style. Her tight white Capris were paired with a black sweater that had one shoulder out and a small sleeve on the other arm, seemingly similar to that backward-dressing victim. Her three-inch heels met each step with grace and ease. But she turned back suddenly, her pretty, preppy purse dangling from a dainty arm. "Oh, my word, I almost forgot. I've got to run to the drugstore and refill my subscription. I have allergies, you know. And no one wants to see a beauty queen with her nose dripping."

"I think you mean prescription," I said, trying to stifle my embarrassment for her. My mother cut me a glance because she knew it wasn't polite to correct people in such a manner. But as far as I was concerned, my politeness quota had been tapped an hour and a half earlier.

"Yes, that's what I said, prescription. So see you precious little ladies later." And she went back into cascading mode.

I could not control myself any longer. "Oh, Amber." With the mention of her name, she stopped and turned in model pose to see whatever it could be that I wanted now.

"Yes?" she asked still in full stance.

"I think . . . oh my goodness . . . I think I see your tag sticking out in the front of your sweater." The look on her face was worth the two hours I had been forced to surrender. As she pulled the front of her shirt out to make sure there wasn't a tag resting on her neckline, I decided to deliver her.

"I'm just joking," I said, laughing. She didn't laugh back. "Actually, I was hoping you'd let me see your Miss Georgia United States of America program book sometime." Vicky looked at me with wide-eyed disbelief. Why in the world would I be asking for such a thing from Amber? I tried to dispel her thousand questions by adding, "The one thing I always enjoyed about Mother's was checking out the hairstyles." I know it sounded totally lame, but Amber would think I thought it was chic and Mother would think I just wanted to make fun of them. Both would believe that either was reason enough.

"Sure. I'll drop it by this evening," she said with a quick wave and a wink, and with that, pageant's greatest ode to itself walked out the door, and the eyes of every man in the room followed close behind.

Mother wiped her mouth and placed her own napkin in her plate. "Savannah, thank you for being so kind. At least until those final moments."

"It wasn't too hard when you don't have to say anything for two hours," I said emphasizing the last five words. "Mother, truly, you must think that girl is over the top," I said, getting up from my seat and holding out my hand to help her up as well.

She smiled and took my extended hand, "Slightly!"

"Slightly?"

Then she laughed, wrapped her arm around my shoulder, and walked with me down the stairs and out the door to the street, whispering in my ear, "Drastically! But you have to admit she is very entertaining."

"If that's your choice of entertainment," I said. It was a comfort for me to remember that somewhere underneath it all Mother was more human than I often gave her credit for. She gave me a kiss and said she was going to shop awhile. I sat in my car watching her walk down the street. She entered a quaint shop up from the Tea Room. In spite of it all, I was thankful that she was mine. And even more grateful that she wasn't the girl who would be for-ever known as Miss Boobies in the Back. Some things were just too horrific even for willing participants.

CHAPTER SEVENTEEN

Amid thoughts of high heels, bad talent, and evening-gown malfunctions, Mrs. Harvard's words raced through my mind again and again: "Longevity is the key, and the question is what could be gained." As far as I could tell, only two people had been involved in this pageant promenade longer than dirt: Mr. Cummings III and the director himself. As most things dysfunctional start at the top, that seemed the place to begin.

I headed back to the library to see what Mr. Cummings III was up to now. I wasn't even sure if he was alive to be up to something at all, since his son had taken over judging for him, but I'd start at the top and work my way through those Cummingses until I reached Adam if need be. The Jackson, Mississippi, phone book held a Mr. Randolph Cummings III and IV.

I was probably stupid to just pick up the phone and call cold. What was I going to say, "Hey, Mr. Cummings, are you a creep? Do you take pleasure in rigging a beauty pageant? Do you not have a life?" As soon as I asked myself that, it was clear the real question was missing: Why? Why would Mr. Cummings be willing to fix a beauty pageant? What would he gain? Why was he the one chosen to change his scores, if indeed he had? Either he was a man with no backbone or he was a man who had something to lose.

I didn't stand much to gain by a phone call. What was he going to do, give me a confessional right over the telephone line? This would take a trip to Jackson, Mississippi. Work started Monday, so unless I was planning to do a story on why people had fish heads on the downspouts of their gutters, I needed to head to Jackson.

I wrote down both the business and home addresses and phone numbers of all of the Cummingses, then made my way to Jake's for a talk. Nearly there, I heard the clicking of high heels and the whooshing of cascading following close behind. My greatest horror and newest fear called out, waving her arms in front of her face and all but skipping down the sidewalk. "Savannah, hey it's me, Amber. Remember, we just had lunch together?"

"Yeah, I remember!"

"I have that program book you wanted. In fact I brought you all of mine. I was going to run them by your house, but figured you probably hadn't even had time to get home yet. Do you want to sit down and look at them together?" she asked, hopeful. Looking at the stack of rather large program books, I politely declined.

"So you've done this three times already?"

"Yes, I know they say third time's a charm, but to be honest with you, the third time su— Oh, my word, I almost said something very unladylike. Slap me and call my mama. But I believe four is fabulous, fantastic, and philanthropic. I'm not exactly sure what *philanthropic* means, but it is just a great word to say."

"No, it's OK, I understand," I said, looking at her with pity at the possibility that she actually thought *philanthropic* started with an *f*. I was still trying to gauge whether she was imbalanced or simply overprocessed. "And sorry, I would love to sit down and go through these with you, but I have to take a really quick trip. But

I promise, I will get these back to you very soon. Maybe we can even have lunch again." I could have slapped myself.

"Oh, that would be wonderful. Let's do it soon. I have a thousand more pageant stories to tell you. I know, let's meet Monday."

"Actually, I start work on Monday and my friend Paige and I, well, we set aside that day every week to catch up. How about Tuesday?"

"Oh, that'll be just fabulous. I'll try to go back and see if I can find some more pictures to show you. I could even bring my crown. Oh, Savannah, we are going to have so much fun! You take care now. I'll see you soon," she said, beaming. "I just know we are going to be the best of friends."

I smiled the best I could, thanked her for the books, and headed for my car.

"Oh, yoo-hoo! Savannah!" the voice came again from behind.

"Yes," I said, slowly turning to take in her radiant glory once more.

"There is a pageant tomorrow night in Hinesville."

"Where in the world is Hinesville?"

"Just a hop and a skip up the interstate. Seeing as you wanted to see my program books and all, I thought you might want to go with me. I love to scope out the competition."

At that moment I was presented with one of the greatest dilemmas I had been forced to encounter in my young life: whether to actually go see a pageant of my own free choice or refuse to allow my reputation to fall under such ill repute. *Well, it would only be for research,* I thought. *I haven't been to a pageant since I was old enough to say no. I probably need to be abreast of what happens in pageants. Did I just say* abreast? *If I go to that pageant, let alone spend an entire evening with Amber, I might come out of there robed in velvet and clogging. I can't do it. I just can't put myself through such needless affliction.*

"You know, that might not be such a bad idea," I said. "I haven't been to a pageant in years. But I'll need to meet you there.

I'll have to leave as soon as it's over because I have to get out of town early the next morning."

"Oh, Savannah Phillips, you will have the most wonderful time of your life. There's singing and dancing," she said, twirling herself around the sidewalk. "It's sheer magic. I'll get you directions and save you a seat, and I'll give you all the inside information on the contestants. You'll wish you had entered." And with that, she skipped, sauntered, and cascaded away.

I got in behind the wheel and hated myself. I was almost certain I hated my job at this point too, but the one thing Amber had accomplished was make me feel amazingly better about my mother. In light of this new acquaintance, I realized Vicky wasn't quite so unnatural after all. Then I was consumed with intense desire to see what Amber looked like in these program books resting on my lap.

The first one I opened was 1998. There she was, Amber Topaz Childers, Miss Rose Petal Queen United States of America. Both she and her mother must have had a thing for jewelry. This was the first time Amber had gone to Miss Georgia United States of America. She looked exactly the same. She was obviously dedicated to her look.

I perused the remainder of the contestants because they captivated me. My eyes couldn't help themselves. They were drawn to the hair, the makeup, the smiles, the queens. A picture snapped me out of my hypnosis. The portrait of Emma Elizabeth Riley, Miss Savannah United States of America, rested beneath Amber's.

This was the Emma Riley I had known. She was undeniably the most beautiful girl in the entire school, possibly all of Savannah. She was perfect without being plastic. She was every beauty pageant's dream contestant, and she won every pageant around town. She even won Miss Massie School her freshman year. She was the first freshman to ever hold the title. My mother said she waited two years after high school to compete in Miss Savannah United States of America. She wanted to be prepared, older, and more mature. Town talk has it that the entire city was shocked when Emma didn't return Miss Georgia United States of America. She never competed again and, according to Paige, thus began her spiral to spandex.

The beautiful face stared back, forcing the question of how she had lost. And having witnessed her ability with the flute, even I knew she was talented. The girl could kick behind on that little sideways piece of machinery. Flipping over to the judges' page, there I saw the face of Mr. Randolph Cummings IV. The director, Mr. Todd, had turned the reins over to his heir apparent as well, Carline Todd. The Templetons were still around, tallying up all of these fine scores.

The 1999 program book showed Miss Amber decked out in sequins, mane pulled up and sitting aloft her head. This was the year following Emma's defeat, and Amber was now Miss Macon United States of America. But this year, Mr. Cummings IV was gone and the Templetons had been replaced by another Atlanta firm. I scanned her next book, and neither Mr. Cummings IV nor the Templetons had returned. It was definitely time to head to Mississippi. Questions needed answers. And as soon as I was through being terrorized by tiaras, I would see what stories Mississippi had to tell.

For a woman with no job, a flight to Mississippi would be impossible. For a father with a credit card, all things were possible. So I headed in his direction. I would broach the subject on two levels, honesty and flattery. Oh, and the fact that he owed me for sending me off to lunch knowingly with those two. When these three merged to form a plan, the humidity of May turned into nothing more than a gentle breeze. I spent an undue amount of time outside Jake's with Duke, talking through my rhetoric. He got bored, so I reluctantly entered, heading in the direction of the Coke.

I caught Dad's eye and motioned him in the back room. "I need to speak with you for a moment."

He finished wiping remnants of the afternoon tourist traffic off the counter and followed me into his office. "What's wrong, Savannah? Surely lunch couldn't have done enough damage to require a private conversation."

"What you did was wrong."

"Welcome home, Savannah."

"Oh, so now you're saying I really owe you."

"Let's just be thankful your reputation is still intact."

"Well, the thing I need to talk about is . . . well . . . I don't feel like I can tell you everything right now, mostly due to the fact that I don't know everything right now. But I do know that I need to go to Jackson, Mississippi, this weekend to do some research, and unfortunately the Bank of Savannah is empty."

"I wasn't aware there was a Bank of Savannah."

"Well, there is, in its dwindling state. So I need to make a withdrawal from the Bank of Jake."

"Oh, yes! I know that one very well. Your account there is busted, however."

"I promise you, I wouldn't ask if it wasn't essential. I also promise I will pay you back everything even if I have to stay at home a week longer than I want. But I really need to do this, and I really need you to trust me without asking a lot of questions."

Dad reached into his pocket and pulled out his wallet, from which he took his platinum American Express. "Savannah, if there is one thing I know about you, it's that you wouldn't be asking me for money and offering to stay at home another week longer if you didn't feel it was absolutely necessary."

"You're a smart man."

"Very smart, don't forget it. I also know you have bigger reasons for everything you're doing that I will learn about soon enough. Whatever it is, all I ask is that you do it well and that you be careful," he said, handing me his card, kissing me on my cheek, and walking toward the door.

"Dad, thanks. I love you totally separate of the fact that I'm holding your credit card in my hand," I said, laughing.

He turned back around, laughing himself. "I love you too. And trust me, it is *totally* separate of the fact that you are holding my credit card in your hand."

With that he disappeared to continue his commission for the day. "Listen to the wise people around you, and live a life that is always learning."

Richard said people had been asking Dad and him questions all day long. "There's been more learning going on in here than I've seen happenin' in a schoolhouse in fifty years!"

CHAPTER EIGHTEEN

My entrance caused most eyes to turn my way, except those belonging to the elderly man in the back, who squinted at the books in front of him. I watched as Katherine headed to a little boy who was sitting in her reading corner. "Well, Savannah, good morning. I think I'm going to offer you a part-time job. You're here almost as much as I am."

I closed the door behind me. "Too much time on my hands. But that will change come Monday."

"Is that when you officially begin your new job?"

"Yes, and my first story is due Tuesday."

"Well, tell me all about it," she said, patting the stool next to her behind the counter. "And did you find you some reporter clothes?"

"I'm not sure I even know what reporter clothes are, but I found some clothes to wear to the newspaper and at least act like a reporter."

"So what's your first story going to be?"

I had prepared myself for this question on my walk over. This was why I had come. "Well, all the details haven't been worked out yet. So, I'm really not certain at the moment. I've got to do some more research and make sure all the facts are accurate."

"Well, that's wise of you, Savannah." The squinty, elderly man made his way to the cash register with a large-print book in hand. I could tell by the way he squinted at the bills in his wallet that this checkout would take a while.

The magazine rack was nearby. I picked up a couple of magazines to add to Paige's library while Katherine waited for the gentleman to exit. He packed up book and billfold, and I paid for Paige's literary advancement. "Well, I hope you have a great night, Katherine. I've been snookered into some rather interesting activities myself."

"Did you just say snookered?"

"I'm absolutely certain I did not just say snookered."

"So what is your big activity?"

"Oh, there's a pageant up the road, and the reigning Miss Savannah United States of America, who is certain I'm her new best friend, wants me to attend. I haven't been to one in years. So, it will be interesting to see what happens. Have you ever been to a pageant?" I asked. I am shameless.

"I've gone to a few in my time. But not for many years. I'm sure you'll have an interesting time. Come back and see me soon." She closed the register, patted my hand, and headed to the back of the store.

"OK," I said, trying not to sound deflated. I whispered to her disappearing back, "But if you get bored and want to come along, let me know." A few tourists, who had dressed, well, just wrong, watched my departure. Who knew how they could justify such attire, but they did.

Sergeant Millings was on West Harris Street at Madison Square, writing up a ticket for a shiny blue bicycle leaning against a light pole. "Hello, Sergeant Millings. Heard you saw Paige the other day."

"Gave her a ticket, all right. That little thing flittin' round here doin' thirty-five in a twenty. She shouldn't even have a car. You kids ought to ride the trolley or somethin'."

I stopped in front of the bike. "Yeah, I know. So why are you giving a bicycle a ticket? I'm certain it wasn't exceeding the speed limit."

"Are you trying to be smart, Miss Savannah?" he asked, looking up from his notepad.

"Now, have you ever known me to act smart?" I asked, smiling from ear to ear as I continued past him. "Now, you have a wonderful afternoon, you hear?" About the time I approached Drayton Street, the cries of one bicycle boy pierced the everyday noise. There was no need to turn around to watch his curls bounce in the wind.

Miss Amazon Amber had left directions no fewer than four times on the voice mail. I erased them all right before my departure in hopes no others would be left for my family to retrieve.

At the Hinesville High School Auditorium, the princess of pink came cascading down the steps to meet me. Her pink pantsuit was complemented by the tiara sitting atop her blanched tresses. There were as many rhinestones on her suit as her tiara. I was sure my subtle attire of blue jeans and leather jacket would be appreciated by overstimulated observers. She scampered and sparkled toward me, calling out my name for every entering entourage to hear. "Ooh, Savannah, we've got to hurry. You do *not* want to miss the opening number," she said, grabbing my arm and pulling me inside. "I've got your ticket, and Trina and Tina, my good friends—of course I just call them the twins—well, they're saving us a seat."

"Yea!" I said, clapping my hands together in feigned excitement.

The auditorium was abuzz. Faces were flying everywhere. Pictures of women's heads had been stapled or taped atop paint stirrers and people were waving them all around like bad Home Depot advertisements. We made our way to our seats, which were close enough to the judges to read their scorecards. I prayed no one would know me. Our seating companions, Trina and Tina, were adorned in splendor as well. Trina's tiara hailed from Sandersville,

Georgia, and Tina earned hers in Swainsboro. "Hey!" they sang in unison.

Sure of the fact I would never say "hey" again as long as I lived, I said, "Hello."

"Oh, Amber, she's just as cute as you said she was," Trina—or was it Tina?—exclaimed. There was no way I was capable of spending the evening figuring out which was which. "Yes, you are, Savannah. You're just cute as pie. And you look just like your mother."

"Yeah, we all just love Miss Victoria," they said, finishing each other's sentences. I was like a spectator at a tennis tournament.

The curtain rose, whisking us away into the wonderful world of waving and whipping. *Whipping* was the term I created for young ladies as they came to the edge of the runway and whipped themselves back around. "Ooh, she shouldn't have worn those tacky shoes with that dress," Amber said as she leaned over to my ear. "I don't know who told that child strappy was in, but she looks like Elvira."

Then Tina or Trina chimed in and said, "Oh, my goodness. Would you looka there? Tinisha Tettweiller has entered herself in another pageant. That child has competed in twenty-four preliminaries in the past two years. She should just stop."

I hoped they didn't truly know how many pageants Tinisha had been in. The fact that they were counting would be far more disturbing than Tinisha's obsessive-compulsive pageant disorder. When swimsuit started, I couldn't help but ask, "*Where* did she get *those*?"

Amber leaned over. "Honey, that's what we call taping."

"Taping?"

"Some girls have cleavage by natural graces. And others have to create their own. They just lift those babies up, tape 'em underneath, and voilà—you've got cleavage."

Why am I here? I slumped even further into my chair.

"Honey, you think that's bad," Amber continued, not noticing my discomfort. "I've seen girls tape their entire stomachs!"

I turned to stare at her in disbelief, but the commentary continued for the next two and a half hours.

As fifteen ladies competed in swimsuit, I endured talk of thighs, taped parts, and cellulite. For talent, I tolerated commentary on pitch, poor choices of songs, and bad Barbra Streisand impersonations. And for evening gown, those three girls were downright shameless. They ripped those poor girls apart for wearing velvet in May or insufferable shades of purple. One girl could be seen only from the nose up because of the boa that flanked the top of her purple velvet dress. Throughout the evening, a petite brunette, who sang the tar out of "Quiet Please, There's a Lady on Stage" and donned, shall we say, a stunning dress that looked to be hand crocheted, captured the audience's attention and applause. Even Amber and Friends seemed to like her.

While the trio was captivated by what was going on onstage, I turned my attention to the judges and their interaction with the auditors. And as the late-forties, overmanufactured hostess bantered and babbled to kill time, the auditors feverishly tallied the scores in full view of the audience.

When the hostess declared it was time to announce the winner, a young, tall drink of water named Lancy took home second runner-up honors. Tinisha was going to have to live with the title of first runner-up and another notch on her tally. And the petite brunette named Valerie was declared the winner. Being the novice I was, it seemed the proper lady had won. As far as I could tell, Hinesville could rest tonight knowing its pageant wasn't rigged.

Amber took me by the arm and escorted me from the building. "Well, did you enjoy yourself or what? Have you ever had so much fun in your entire life? I'm telling you, I could go to one of these a night!"

"Oh, well, wouldn't that be exciting? I'm afraid that might just send me over the edge though. I mean, how could a girl stand such a ruckus every night? Those people got wild in there," I said, politely extricating myself from her embrace.

"You should see it when they get nasty. That's when it gets really good. When mamas are yelling at each other across the auditorium, and daddys want to meet in the parking lot. Oh, girl, Hollywood couldn't write things as good as I've seen over the years. So what did you think about the winner?"

"I thought she was cute. She seemed like she was the best on the stage to me."

"She's a little short, though. It's hard to distribute all that weight when you've got less of an area of distribution."

"She didn't look like she had much weight on her at all."

"Well, she wore a black bathing suit. And you know what they say about black bathing suits."

"I'm certain I have no idea."

"You only wear black when you're trying to cover up something. So, we'll see how she looks when we get to Miss Georgia United States of America."

"Do you ever get tired of saying that entire phrase?"

"No, not really."

"What do you say we shorten it?"

"What did you have in mind?" She looked at me as if I might be close to committing some form of sacrilege.

"Nothing major. I just thought maybe we could call it Miss Georgia US of A."

"No, I don't think that would be appropriate," she said, heading toward her car.

"Are you serious?" I asked, stopping in the middle of the parking lot.

"Yes, I am. Women spend years trying to achieve such an honor. I think it cheapens their efforts not to give them the courtesy of announcing their complete title."

"Well, I will hereby take note of such an argument."

"Thank you, and I will take note of your desire to be proficient." I knew she meant efficient, but there was no point in correcting her. "Now, I've got to head to the victory party up the street at the mayor's house. All the queens are invited. Sure you don't want to come?"

"Oh, well, I would love to, but I've got such an early morning."

"OK, well, I'll see you for lunch on Tuesday," she unlocked the doors to her Mercedes coupe with the click of a button.

"Oh, yeah, Tuesday!" I said under my breath, inserting my key into Old Betsy and giving the door a tug.

"Don't forget!" she said, climbing into her plush car.

"I wouldn't dare," I said, straightening my cushion so I wouldn't fall to the floorboard.

CHAPTER NINETEEN

needed to talk to my mother. Crazy, but true. Because in the middle of this madness lay a dream of Victoria Phillips. And swirling around it like a vulture was me. Even though she had ruined my dream, the thought of destroying hers ate away at me. I needed peace. I needed my mother.

"Hello, darling. I just love caller ID. What are you doing up and out this early?"

"I could ask you the same thing."

"Oh, a ladies' store is having a sale and the owner is letting me come by early to look through things before the rush."

I knew good and well she was talking about Jezebel's, but I would let her maintain her anonymity.

"Mother, do you know what a wonderful lady I think you are?"

For a moment she did not respond. Then, totally serious: "Savannah, are you drunk?"

"You know I'm not drunk. I do not get drunk, and besides, it's too early to be drunk. I know we clash every now and then over dumb things, but I really do love and appreciate you." I almost felt like a knot was forming in my throat.

"Savannah, are you crying? Is someone holding a gun to your head? Are you about to be murdered? Where are you, darling?" I could see her making a mad dash up the street past the Francis McNary Antique Store.

"Mother! I'm fine. Really. I just needed you to know how I feel."

Sounding as if she were slightly winded, she managed, "Well, I love you too, darling. So if you're not dying, are you needing something?"

"No! You act like I've never told you I loved you before in your life."

"Well, you've never said it quite like this before."

"OK, so let me say it like this, and don't ruin the moment."

"Well, thank you. Those are some of the kindest words I've ever heard," she said, now tearing up herself.

"Don't cry. Please, Mother."

"OK. Thank you." Then the sound of a horn blow pierced the receiver. There she was, standing on the sidewalk in front of an antique store in heels, cell phone attached to her ear and snot running down her nose, stopping to pant and blow. It was most Victoria.

"So, where are you? Do you want to come join me?"

"Actually, that's why I'm calling. I just need you to listen for one moment and not ask me any questions. I need you to just trust me."

"Savannah, I do trust you. You know that."

"Mother, you just asked me if I was drunk!"

"Well, I knew you weren't," she said, trying to sound convincing.

"I have to go to Jackson, Mississippi—"

"Jackson, Mississippi? For what? Why in the world are you going to go to Jackson, Mississippi?"

"Mother, I told you, no questions. Trust, remember?"

"OK, right, no questions, just trust. No questions. All right, I think I'm ready."

"I'm working on a story. But I need more facts on it before I can put it to print. I'll be back as soon as I can tomorrow."

"But what about—"

"Mother, no questions. Dad has given me all the money I need, and he knows no more than you, so please don't hound him. OK?"

"OK. But I don't like it. And that wasn't a question. That was a statement," she said all rushed so I wouldn't interrupt her.

I decided to turn to my method of distraction. "Oh, and I really like my shoes, Mother. Thank you for getting them for me."

"I knew you would like them. Kate Spade, she's the in thing right now. I think you would love a lot of her things. She makes the best handbags you have ever seen. And her stuff is timeless, you know, not trendy. I hear she even makes luggage now. Oh, Savannah, that would have been great for your trip. Not that I think you should be taking this trip. Again, that was not a question."

I figured Mother realized there was no one on the other end of her phone by the time I reached the airport. I checked in at the American Airlines counter and traveled with only one carry-on. The restaurant and small shopping area at the airport betrayed my mother's touch. Her influence seemed to surpass reasonable jurisdiction. Here, twenty miles away from Savannah, I sat in a town square that she had created in the middle of the airport. She felt people should have the "Savannah experience," as she called it, as soon as they stepped off the plane. So all of the small shops and stores were built on a square with real trees and small park benches.

Thomas said that when the square was initially finished, Vicky came by to make sure everything met with her approval. When she touched the ficus tree next to the women's restroom, she let out a yell. The tree was artificial. Today, Savannah's rumor mill has it that every tree, plant, bush, and phony flower ended up on the sidewalk in front of the designer's house, accompanied by a note that read, "Whatever you sow, that will you reap. Enjoy! Victoria

Phillips." Then she hired Thomas and about six of his high-school buddies, paid them with food, and created the parklike setting travelers now sit in.

The passengers on my flight were rather sparse, and I had a row to myself. The relative peace gave me time to reflect on the week's activities. But Emma kept coming to the front of my mind. If loss had the power to destroy someone's life, then a multitude of issues were at stake in Emma's. I mean, I had lost a thousand things through the years, but none of them—not even Grant—caused me to surrender myself to defeat.

Maybe my defeat was different. Maybe I wanted to lose. But everyone should know how to lose with grace. How can you ever appreciate winning, truly appreciate winning, if you've never known what it's like to lose? Even as whacked as my mother is, I have seen her face defeat gracefully. She has shaken hands with the winner of the annual Rose Day event, when her roses, though stunning before the tornado, looked a little haggard after. Then she shook the hand of Dolores Armstrong, Judge Hoddicks's secretary, after Dolores won the annual Fried Chicken Cookoff. Now I will tell you, on that one Victoria got bamboozled. There is no way anyone can touch my mother's chicken. But ever the pro that she is, she walked up to Dolores, hugged her, and even held up a piece of Dolores's chicken for the picture in the paper.

But Emma . . . Emma had given up on life. She had let defeat swallow her whole. She had even allowed it to steal her own family from her. This beautiful woman had come to the unthinkable place where she saw beauty in nothing. All because of a loss.

There was a deeper lesson here, I knew. I would search for it later. For now, I would search for the story that would bring her and Katherine vindication.

The clock on the dashboard of the rented Jeep Liberty read 12:09. My notebook held the street address of both Mr.

Cummingses. I scoured the map, searching for the location. I turned the key and the car started, eliminating my half-hope that I would be forced to spend the night in the airport, leave with nothing, and start work on something far less complicated.

Confrontation was nothing new to me. Twenty-four years of living with Vicky had freed me of trauma or trepidation at the prospect, and the Mr. Hicks and Emma episodes had recently sharpened my skills in this area. But I was about to confront people who lived by a different code. People who for some reason chose to select pageant winners based on something other than merit. The thing that gnawed at me was the fact that I had no idea what that something was.

Maybe it was just because of friendship. Maybe Mr. Cummings and the pageant director were so close that they would do anything for each other to make sure that the other was delivered the greatest results for his efforts. No, real friends have character. You can't be one without it. Maybe it was blackmail. No, that wouldn't last for thirty years. If it did, one of them was really smart and the other remarkably stupid. No, it had to be greed. People do amazing things for money. Yes, it had to be money.

As I processed my thoughts, it became clear that my destination was wrong. When I turned onto the interstate, the Golden Arches greeted me. Once I had acquired the necessary Coke, I knew what I had to do. This couldn't begin on Mr. Cummings's doorstep. It had to begin behind the scenes of his life. If the fraud was about money, then we were headed for one more ride. I just hoped I would still be in the driver's seat when we reached the destination. I pulled out my cell phone.

The voice on the other end sounded like it was chewing something. "Hello."

"Hello. Judge Hoddicks, it's Betty. I hope I didn't catch you at a bad time."

"No, honey. We're just finishing up some pork chops. A big ol' Saturday afternoon spread. Do you want to join us? All the kids are here too. I'm sure they would love to see you." I heard him tell everyone it was me. A resounding group "hello" came through on my end of the phone.

"Actually, Judge, I'm in Jackson, Mississippi, and I need a huge favor."

"You aren't in jail down there, are you? I'll have someone's head if they've done anything to you. Where—"

"No! No! I'm fine. Actually I'm working on a story and wondered if you knew anyone who could let me into the courthouse today. I know most courthouses are closed on Saturday, but I need to do some research. I only have today and tomorrow to get everything accomplished. I might end up in the unemployment line before I even see a paycheck if I don't."

"Betty, you hold on. I have an old college buddy who's a judge right there in Jackson. Hang on the line and I'll call him real quick on my cell." The hand-off went to Mrs. Hoddicks first, who said hello and then passed me around the table. By the time the judge returned, I had been fully updated on every cold, engagement, death, and baptism within the last six months of the entire Hoddicks family.

"Betty! His law clerk will meet you there. Where are you, anyway?"

"I'm only about five minutes from downtown."

"Well, the courthouse is right in the heart of their city. The clerk will meet you at the side door on the south side. He has been told to get you whatever information you need. If you have one ounce of frustration, honey, you just call me back. I'll come down there myself and get you what you need. You hear me?"

"Yes, sir. I'm sure I'll be fine. I can't thank you enough. And if this goes well, I'll get you free coffee at Jake's for the rest of your tenure."

That made him cackle. "Well, that would be great! Jake will appreciate it."

"He'll appreciate you helping me even more. Thanks again."

The Jackson County Courthouse looked imposing in the glow of the afternoon sun. I parked in front and walked around to the south side. Standing by the side door was a handsome young law clerk, probably about my age. He held out his dark hand and introduced himself.

"Gregory Taylor."

"Hello. Savannah Phillips. Nice to meet you. Thank you for doing this."

He did not seem at all perturbed at having been called in on the weekend. "Well, follow me, and we'll try to find what you need." He opened the side door and led me down a dark hallway lined by frosted-glass doors. The hall deposited us into the lobby. The vastness of the courthouse was impressive and possessed a sense of awe and quiet reverence. The hallowed halls brought to mind the lives salvaged and lost inside. "I sure am sorry to take away your Saturday. I know how people in the law field enjoy a moment of reprieve."

He surrendered a beautiful smile. "Oh, it's no big deal. I needed to come in and get some work done. You just gave me a reason to have to do it. So, what exactly do you need?"

"I need whatever information you have on Randolph Cummings III and Randolph Cummings IV." At the mention of their names, Gregory stopped dead in his tracks.

"Do you know that Mr. Cummings, both of them, are two of the most respected and influential men in this city? If you are trying to dig up anything unseemly about them, you won't find it here." His drawl took the edge off his charming but matter-of-fact tone.

"I hope I don't. But there is only one way to know. I need to see every certificate, every license, every death notice you have on record for this family." Then I added my own southern charm for good measure. "And Judge Hoddicks said if I had any problems he would be more than glad to come up here and help me get whatever information I need."

"Well, let's not waste any time then," Gregory replied politely.

He led me to a door that took us to the basement. "Are there any lights down here?"

He flicked on the light. "Don't worry. There's nothing down here but thousands of boxes and a few rats. And the lights usually scare off the rats."

I looked at him, grateful for lights. "How long have you been here?"

"I've clerked for Judge Tucker for two years now. I finished law school last year, but I worked for him every summer during those long years, so coming here full-time just seemed like a natural progression."

"Sounds like it."

"Well, this is it. Almost everything you want to know about anyone in the city: tax records, licenses, certificates, all right here." He pointed to about a hundred separate rows of shelving that ran the full length of the courthouse and were stacked with boxes from floor to ceiling. "It looks like you'll have everything you'll need. Everything is filed alphabetically, so that will help."

"Immensely."

"There are some cubicles over there in the corner," he said, motioning to four small work stations that lined the front wall. "I'll be in my office, and you can buzz me at #22 if you need anything."

"You can't bring your work down here?"

He laughed, "No, but I'm just a phone call away. I promise."

"I hope you were planning on working late, because I don't know if I'll be through before morning," I said, heading to one of the cubicles to unload my stuff.

"Honestly, I'm in no hurry. If it's morning, I'll just be that much further ahead. If you get hungry later, call me and I'll order us some pizza. And if you can't find something and need my help, just let me know."

"I'll forget to call, I'm sure. How about we just decide now on six o'clock? I'll buy if you'll order."

"That would be fine by me."

"Thanks, Gregory. I really appreciate your help. I know this is no one's idea of a good time on a Saturday."

"Obviously, you and I have different measures of that. Working until sunrise has always been my idea of a good time."

As he disappeared up the stairway, the masses of cardboard boxes brought me back to reality. Having no idea what I was looking for or what I was doing here, the only thing I was sure of was that if one rat trespassed on my territory, Gregory was going to find his hiney firmly planted in the cubicle in front of me.

As I worked my way down the aisle marked CU, I found a box that read "CUMMINGS, Randolph II, III & IV." These people had so much stuff, the three of them were worthy of their own box. The box was bulging. I slid it off the shelf with a thud and scooted it across the floor with both hands until it rested beside my work area. Then I grabbed my cell, called the hotel, and asked them to cancel my reservation. I wouldn't be needing a bed tonight, just caffeine. I would definitely need caffeine.

CHAPTER TWENTY

The Cummingses' box was sectioned off in three different places, by II, III, and IV. Each Cummings had his own section of business ventures and licenses and records, with IV being smaller than the first two. Mr. Cummings II's file began with the title deed to what was apparently his first home. It was followed by a marriage certificate, only one that I found, and then numerous business licenses.

"Well, at least he's the husband of only one wife. That's a nice place to start." Someone was going to have to talk to me or I would go crazy down here. Mr. II had his own law firm, which was now Cummings & Cummings Attorneys at Law. The formal corporation name change was enclosed. His son had been added in 1962, and he held a partnership in a local grocery store and owned a Burger King franchise and numerous other business ventures that seemed to be locally operated companies right here in Jackson. The file ended with the death certificate of one Cora Lee Cummings on September 14, 1985, at the age of seventy-five, followed by Randolph Cummings Jr. on October 19, 1991, at the age of eighty-nine.

The file of Randolph Cummings III, like his father's, began with a marriage certificate. On June 20, 1956, at the age of twenty-three, he married Patricia "Patty" Gwendolyn Stryker, who was only seventeen. "That's just sick. She was only a baby, snatched up by some worldly-wise attorney."

The IIIs purchased their first home only two weeks after their marriage, the address of which matched the one I'd written down. Mr. III joined his father's law firm in 1962. He then purchased a local theater, an arcade, a pizzeria, and a coffee shop. Dare Jake know he and this man had anything in common! As I rummaged through the rest of his papers, most documenting his numerous real-estate investments, absolutely nothing seemed to suggest he would care at all who in the world won a beauty pageant.

Heading to Mr. IV's folder, a tiny file in the back caught my attention. It was marked "Patricia Cummings." Her folder held evidence of two businesses: a local jewelry store and P&R Printing Co. The jewelry store seemed a logical business for any woman. But the printing company, for some reason, I found rather odd.

About that time, I heard someone coming down the stairs. Not even imagining that almost five hours had passed, the hair on the back of my neck stood up. But then I saw the pizza box and Gregory's face.

"Surely it isn't six already?" I tried to stand up, realizing quickly how long I'd been sitting. *"Ow!"*

"Yes, it's six. Have you been sitting there this entire time?" he asked, laughing at my pitiful attempt to rise. He reached out his hand to steady me.

"I didn't realize I'd been looking at this stuff for so long. Do you have any way for us to find old newspaper articles around here, or could we only do that at the paper?"

"Whoa, Snoop Dogg, why don't you sit down, eat a bite, and tell me your story?" He set the pizza on top of my desk and pulled up a chair. He had brought two extra Cokes down with him. I had finished off mine hours earlier, so I was grateful for the thoughtfulness.

"Good idea. I *am* starving."

He grabbed a piece of pizza, propped his Nikes up on the table, and leaned back in his chair, letting me know he was ready for the scoop. As he took a bite of pizza, I noticed his muscular calves. They made me confident his favorite pastime was running. "So, Miss Savannah. What in the world are you doing here on a Saturday night, hundreds of miles from home, in a basement at a courthouse in Jackson, Mississippi, snooping into the lives of some of Jackson's most prominent and influential citizens? Surely, this is a good story."

I leaned back as well. "You'll think I'm an idiot. Shoot, half the time *I* think I'm crazy, chasing some wild concoction of a story that no one gives a horsefly's rear end about."

"Did you just say 'a horsefly's rear end'?" He slapped his hands on his khaki shorts in amusement.

"Yes, have you never heard that before?" I realized then that I myself had only ever heard my mother say it.

"No, can't say that I have. And I don't know that you need to say it around anyone else," he said, going back to his pizza.

I started eating my pizza with fervor, trying not to chew and talk at the same time. "Thanks for the advice. So, if I tell you what I'm working on, do I have attorney-client privilege?"

"Only if you pay me."

"How much do you charge?"

"Well, tonight I have a special going. Tonight I am only charging one dollar per client per visit."

"Are you telling me I only have to pay you one dollar for the entire visit and I will have the undivided attention of your services?"

"It is your lucky day."

"That's a mighty cocky smile, Mr. Attorney Wannabe. But here." I grabbed the satchel beside me, pulled out a dollar bill, laid it on the table, and pushed it toward him. "I hereby pronounce you my attorney. And whatever I tell you is strictly confidential and can never be repeated."

"Absolutely. I'm all yours. Compensation has been exchanged and privilege is granted. Shoot with your concoction." He took a long swig of his Coke. He was a tall, good-looking fellow, with a quick wit and true southern charm. His blue-and-white T-shirt complemented his flawless dark skin, and his calm demeanor made him easy to talk to. For the next hour my new attorney listened to everything that had transpired in my life in the last two weeks. He sat rather mesmerized and quiet the entire time until I mentioned P&R Printing. Gregory's wheels began turning themselves.

I wiped my mouth and took another drink of my Coke. "What are you thinking?"

"I'm thinking, what would a pageant need with either jewelry or a printing company?"

"All beauty pageant women wear jewelry; that's a given. But money, not jewelry, causes people to rig pageants. So unless she's selling diamond tiaras and has the market on the whole Miss United States of America Pageant, that's not where she's making the money. Now for printing, they have to print these." I reached down and pulled out Amber's and my Mother's ridiculously large programs. You'd better not touch this one without gloves," I said, pointing to Vicky's book. "You might be a lawyer, but she, my friend, is CIA material."

He feigned difficulty lifting them as he brought each one to his side of the desk. "These things are huge! Why in the world would they need something this large?"

"This is how pageants make money for their prizes."

"I thought they had sponsors for prizes."

"They do for some, but the girls also sell program pages to businesses in their local cities. The money from those pages, at five hundred dollars a pop, offsets the expenses of the pageant and pays for scholarships."

"Savannah, there are over five hundred pages in here. That's $250,000. Combine that with sponsors' goodies and ticket sales, and somebody's making some money. I think your story is on the money. Follow the money, Savannah," he said, and he closed up the empty pizza box and walked it to the trash can.

Turning around so I could see him, I said, "What am I going to do, break into bank records and find out if someone received large sums of cash after the pageant money was collected? I don't have the time or the capability to do something like that."

He walked back and sat down. "Savannah, you don't always have to *prove* things, sometimes you just need to *know* things."

"I have no idea what you're saying," I told him, putting my head in my hands and sighing from sheer exhaustion.

"I'm saying, what do you know?"

"What do I know?"

"Yes, what do you know?"

"Nothing."

"OK, what do you *think* you know?"

"I *think* I know a judge changed his scores."

"Go on."

"I think I know which judge, who at face value has no motive and a wife who owns a printing company."

Gregory opened two program books in front of him. Each had its own list of acknowledgments to vendors who had donated their work. In both books, some twenty-five years apart, on line three, thank-yous went out to P&R Printing Company for the printing of program books, letterhead, and the new Miss Georgia United States of America personalized stationery. "Look, it's right here in black and white. Now, even if P&R printed these monster books out of the goodness of their hearts, it's unseemly at best. No judge should have any dealings with a pageant in a manner like this. It muddies the water."

"Well, sure it does, but it all but says right here that they did the work free for sponsorship purposes."

"Sure, they did it free. Can you imagine the stink if they had charged for it? That would be blatant misconduct. But what if their free services are a cover-up for a kickback? And what if their kickback comes with a perk for the pageant director? 'You help me and I'll help you.' The Cummings get a whopping tax deduction, and the pageant weasels their way out of a whopping printing bill. This really isn't that hard to see."

"What am I going to do, walk up to their door with a bunch of what ifs? 'Um, ma'am, I think, though there is no way on God's green earth I can prove it, that you are taking a kickback on the inflated price of advertising pages in a pageant program book in order to manipulate scores for a pageant director in Georgia. Now, don't let your foot kick me in the behind too hard as you *throw me out your door!*' Are you whacked? *I'm* going to be the human-interest story by the time you're through with me."

"Savannah, you should have gone to law school. You don't go in there declaring what you don't know. You put them on the stand, letting them assume you know everything. Then, eventually, they give themselves away. They're either frustrated you've got it wrong, or their expression reveals how right you really are." He stood and paced as if he were trying the case of a lifetime.

"You're saying I need to act like I know all this as fact in order to prompt a response?" I asked. "Would you please quit pacing?"

"That's exactly what I'm saying."

"What do you think we are doing here, acting out parts in a John Grisham novel?"

"Well, at least he knows how to write a good legal thriller, plus, he's good-looking like me and from Mississippi too."

"You are incorrigible."

"Yes ma'am, I know I'm adorable, but back to the business at hand."

"So, after I get sued for slander, you'll be my attorney, right?"

He waved my dollar in front of my face.

I couldn't help but smile back. "And that's about all you're worth, too. We'll probably end up in jail together."

"Well, at least you like me!"

"Yeah, at least I like you!"

After spending two more hours examining possibilities, I felt I needed more. I needed facts, not assumptions. "Let's go on a tour of Jackson. Let's go check out some printing companies and some of Cummings's office buildings."

"We can go look, but I will not allow you to step out of the car."

"You can lock the doors."

"I can and I will," he said, getting up himself. We walked out to his car and he opened the door for me to climb in.

"Nice car for a law clerk," I said, admiring his shiny silver Volvo.

"Thank you. A man's got to have a nice ride."

The tour of Jackson began. We traveled through the Historical District, and Gregory gave me a tour of some of the oldest African-American churches in the nation. He also showed me where Medgar Evers lived. Then we progressed to an area of town where the Cummingses owned the entire block. All in a row on West Capital Street stood Cummings Enterprises, Patricia's Precious Stones jewelry store, and P&R Printing at the top of the street.

"Here's the Cummings Compound, as we like to call it here in Jackson."

"So they're not quite the sweethearts of Jackson as you first led me to believe?"

"Well, they're high-profile, influential people. They own most everything in this city, including a few people. So, it is my job to protect this city. It is your job to protect your own behind."

"So, since behind protection is my job, what do you say we get out and take a walk up the street?"

"You're a persistent little creature."

"Yes, I am. Let's walk." Things were pretty quiet for a Saturday evening. A few people were walking about, and I could hear music and laughter coming from up the street.

"So how did you get here?"

"I was born and raised here."

"And law school? Was that always the plan?" I asked as we admired the grand entrances of the Cummings Compound.

"That was a father's dream for his son. Then it became the son's dream for himself."

"My dad would be happy at this point if I were simply self-sufficient, seeing as I had to use his credit card to get here."

"I would agree with him, seeing as you've yet to pay for the pizza."

"I haven't left yet. I'll pay you for that pizza."

"Savannah, you've had me so distracted I didn't even realize where we were. If someone sees us back here, we'll have more tongues wagging than a carpool of St. Bernards," he said as he noticed that I had drifted to the back of the Cummings's buildings.

"I just wanted to see what they had back here," I said, walking over to the back door of Cummings Enterprises and wiggling the handle, knowing it would be locked. It was.

"You can't go inside. You're going to get yourself arrested and who's going to come get you out?"

"That would be your job, Counsel."

"Not on your life."

"Gregory, look," I whispered, pointing to an open window. "Give me a lift."

"I will not. I will leave you behind, right here all by yourself."

"OK, then, I'll lift myself," I said, reaching as high as I could, barely able to grasp the tip of the window sill. I jumped up and was able to get a weak hold on the inside trim, all the while trying to glide my right foot up the side of the brick building. But with nothing to hold on to, I collapsed into a heap on the asphalt parking lot.

"You're pathetic."

"You're pathetic for not helping me."

"This is breaking and entering. This is a federal offense, a reason people go to jail and others are disbarred."

"This is not breaking and entering. The window is open. So, technically it is only entering. And I've seen enough *Law & Order* to know that many a defense is won on a technicality. Now please, you don't have to enter. Just give me a boost."

"That is being an accomplice to a crime."

"I will tell anyone who asks that I forced you."

"With what, a high heel?"

"I don't wear high heels," I said, pointing to my flat black sandals.

"Well, whatever you are going to do, you need to hurry. In Jackson, Mississippi, a black man in an alley with a white woman makes for nothing good in the eyes of busybodies."

"Just a quick hoist. You go back to the car, drive around the block, and I'll meet you at the courthouse."

"You don't even know how to get back to the courthouse," he said, exasperated. He bent down.

"Trust me, I'll find it. And you can go back to work. Now please, hoist!" Gregory relented. As I put my foot in his hands, he hefted me with enough effort to give me a firm grip on the window.

"How in the world . . . is *this* . . . a human-interest story?" He panted as he struggled to push me the rest of the way through.

"I'm a human and I'm interested. That's all you need to know." In reply, he pushed me so hard I flew through the window, landing on both head and shoulders and causing a loud crash as I toppled a picture frame.

"What happened? Are you all right?" he called in a half-whisper, half-petrified yell.

I poked my head out of the window and peered out. "Let's just say it is now officially *breaking* and entering. Go; I'll catch up with you later." I closed the window that separated us. I used my shirt tails to collect the broken glass as best I could, all my years of watching courtroom dramas having made me cautious. I laid them all back neatly on an unsuspecting employee's desk and headed through the dark corridors in search of . . . anything. I found a rag in a kitchen area and used it to open and close doors, searching by the dim parking-lot lights streaming in the windows.

When I began to think my first crime spree would prove utterly pointless, I noticed a cracked door. Behind the door was a dark staircase that led to purgatory for all I knew. But I had to go. While descending the dark stairwell, it became undeniably clear that I had taken leave of every good sense I had ever possessed. "Mercy," I said out loud, "I am in Jackson, Mississippi, breaking into an office building, searching for something, I don't even know what. I've sunk low. Desperately low." Sinking even further into blackness, it was evident by the lack of any light that this room had no windows. I felt safe enough to search for the light and finally found a switch. The light was blinding.

Once my eyes adjusted, I began to take in the environment around me. The room resembled the courthouse basement, with row upon row of shelving bearing boxes upon boxes of documents. I meandered down each aisle, searching for anything marked P&R Printing. Near the back were about six rows full of boxes for P&R Printing, which had been in business for over thirty-five years according to the dates on the labels. About halfway through row three, I found thirty-some boxes marked "banking records." I began in 1972, the year of Katherine, and searched for anything linking P&R Printing to the Miss Georgia United States of America pageant. I found absolutely nothing.

After what felt like hours of absolutely nothing, I turned the corner and saw a box marked "Personal." Pulling out my handy-dandy rag, I carefully opened the lid. It, like the last thirty-something boxes I had drifted through, was filled with nothing but papers and cards. Then the name Todd caught my eye. But this name wasn't Carl Todd, the director of the Miss Georgia United States of America pageant or of Carline Todd, his daughter. This name was Catherine Todd.

I painstakingly pulled the file out and laid it in front of me. Inside were twenty-two neatly rubber-banded notes. I opened each one. They were personal notes from Catherine Todd, thanking "Patty" for the jewelry and printing. In each she made reference to the "special gift enclosed," and each note was dated. Going immediately back to the bank statements and following the date of each note, a major deposit, identified simply as "Gift," was made exactly one week after the date of each letter into Patricia's personal account. Each deposit ranged from fifty to seventy-five thousand dollars, far more than any reasonable printing bill would have been.

I sneaked back upstairs and pilfered around until I found a copy machine. I made copies of each letter and each deposit, then returned the originals to their proper places. Exiting the same way I had entered, I took extra care to wipe the window and sill free of any fingerprints. As I turned the corner to return to West Capital Street, I tucked the photocopies underneath my shirt. I sensed a car come alongside me and heard a voice say, "Get in the car."

I hopped in, and every ounce of adrenaline left me, causing me to go limp. "I thought I told you I'd meet you back at the courthouse."

"You would have never made your way back there, even by morning," Gregory said as he pulled into his parking place in front of the courthouse.

"Well, thank you. Let's get inside, so I can show you what I got."

We descended to the basement, and for the next couple of hours I told him what I had found. He determined that no matter what the money was for, whether for jewelry or for the printing, it was unethical at best and, at worst, motivation enough for a judge to alter his vote.

I decided I wanted to meet the Cummingses before I left. Gregory decided I was certifiable. But he prepped me nonetheless on how I would need to present myself. I wasn't sure I would take all of his advice, but I would use what I thought was worth using.

Somewhere in the wee hours of the morning we both fell asleep in our chairs, our heads lying on opposite sides of the desk.

"Hello," I said, not sure where I was or how I got there.

"Savannah? Did I wake you up, darling? It's nine o'clock," said the familiar voice from the other end.

"Yes. But that's OK. I needed to get up anyway." I slowly tried to extract myself from the chair I had become one with during the night.

"Savannah, I heard through the grapevine that you made a visit to Emma Riley the other day." She stopped for a moment, but I knew what was coming.

Who knew how she knew, but no one here was surprised. "Oh, you did?"

"Yes, now I don't know what you are doing or what you are working on or why in the world you went to talk to Emma. But you and I are going to talk tonight and I want to hear everything. I have a feeling that what you are working on involves pageants because there is no way this side of Texas that you would voluntarily ask someone to show you her pageant program book."

"Now, that's not necessarily true."

"Oh, yes it is. You would rather be hog-tied and drug through cow manure across the whole state of Georgia than to have to sit down and look at one of those books." I wasn't sure where she came up with that, but she was pretty accurate on this point. "Nor is there any reason that after all these years you would seek out Emma Riley. So, just plan on me being up whenever it is you get home. I love you, and be safe. We'll talk tonight. Good-bye now."

CHAPTER TWENTY-ONE

The Edison Walthall Hotel is where everyone goes for Sunday brunch, mostly because the food is fabulous, but also, though no one would admit to it, to be seen. Gregory knew that Mr. and Mrs. Cummings III and IV went to the ten o'clock service at Saint Peter the Apostle at 123 NW Street, followed by an eleven fifteen brunch at the hotel. This was Judge Tucker's normal routine as well, when he was in town, which he wasn't this weekend, which was why Gregory knew it. At least that is what he testified to. He also knew that the Cummingses were usually home by twelve thirty and enjoyed working in their yard on Sunday afternoons. "I see them there working when I get out of church," he told me.

"I thought we'd take our own trip to the Edison for some Mississippi brunch," he said in his most southern of accents. "That way you can see what all the highfalutin Jacksonians look like."

I returned with my best Scarlett impersonation: "Well, that is a wonderful idea. How about I let you drive since you know the way?"

After cleaning ourselves up, we walked outside into a beautiful Sunday morning. He opened the door for me, and we traveled a short distance to the hotel. It was only about eleven, but the place was already busy.

"Do you people not go to church around here?"

"We go to the early service, Miss Savannah. We might miss something happening if we go any later than ten or ten thirty. But if you want to go to a happening place, come with me. We don't get out until about one. Then everyone goes to my mother's house for fried chicken."

"Gregory, are you sure we aren't related? We stay in church till pretty late too, and fried chicken is our favorite Sunday meal."

"It is the South, Savannah. I could be your cousin."

"Wouldn't that be a hoot!"

"Yes, I would find it rather amusing."

"Sorry I kept you out of church today. I'm sorry I kept myself out too."

"That's OK. Even though you need extra repentance for your escapades last night."

The Edison was a beautiful hotel, with a brunch I hadn't seen the likes of in years. They had eggs, bacon, sausage, beautiful fresh fruit with real cream, and a place to make omelets or pancakes. They even had a beautiful display of desserts, if you had another sweet tooth after you got through licking Aunt Jemima off of your plate. The waitress smiled at us politely but gave us the once-over, trying to figure out if we were a couple. She sat us at a small booth near the back of the room. As the waiter poured the water for us, I asked Gregory a question I had never asked a person before.

"Gregory, do you still find it difficult living as a black man here? I mean, not just in the South, but in America in general?"

"You'd be surprised, Savannah. Sometimes you see it in their eyes or hear it in the inflections in their voices. Sometimes it's subtle; other times they don't even try to hide their feelings. You even see it in churches."

"In churches?"

"What rock have you been under?"

"I'm not sure. We have every imaginable race in our church."

"You are the exception. Racism exists on both sides on what should be the most unsegregated day of the week. But it's everywhere. I see it in the way people refuse my gaze or move to the other side of the street. You want to scream at them, 'I'm a lawyer, not a criminal.'" Then he added with a laugh, "Of course, most people think lawyers *are* criminals."

I had to laugh at that one too. "They need to meet my lawyer, because he's dirt cheap."

"Well, I hear his prices might be going up."

"Not mine. I'm locked in at a lifetime rate."

"Well, anyway," he said, looking down and putting a lemon in his water, "it does get old at times, but some things have become a way of life."

"Some things should never become a way of life." I took a drink of water. "Thank you. You have been a great help and have come up with many wonderful ideas, I might add. I don't know that I'll use them all, but they were good nonetheless."

"Savannah, look casually at the door. That's Mr. and Mrs. Cummings III. Oh, and that's their son and his wife coming in right behind them," he whispered.

The presence of the stately looking older couple commanded the room. They moved spryly for their age, and I could tell they were regulars. People rushed immediately to service them. Mr. Cummings was tall and had an air of authority about him. His hair was totally gray, and he wore tailored glasses. Mrs. Cummings was statuesque. Her hair was white and she wore a vibrant red suit with matching red pumps. Even her lipstick was a bold red.

The son followed, looking like a younger version of his father. His wife followed him, looking like a cartoon character.

"Where did he get her?"

"From the hills of Tennessee, they say. Dumped wife number one, brought this beauty in, cleaned her up, and now he takes her out. Kind of like I did for you," he said, flashing his big smile. I raised my right eyebrow and he kept on. "They say she's had more sucked out of her than the Mississippi River. I think she's been pulled and plucked so much she'd probably bounce back if you threw her up against a wall."

"You are cruel."

"But knowledgeable."

We watched as the foursome took their seats. Every time someone came through the door and walked by their table, they would stop to speak to the Cummingses.

"This town loves these people."

"As I said. They are all but gods here, and you're going up against them with recent-college-graduate bravado and, dare I say, a few stolen facts."

"I'll be hung by morning."

"You'll be fabulous, Savannah." His tone had become serious. I looked at him. "You know something happened. Something that was wrong. You had gut instinct. You did your research, albeit somewhat criminal. You hold a smoking gun, and if by chance there are more rounds in the chamber, you at this moment are the only one who can do something about it."

We finished our breakfast and kept our eyes on the Cummingses as they finished their own and eventually left. We paid our check, and Gregory took me back to my car. For the thousandth time, we rehearsed how I should play my hand. I retrieved my stuff from his trunk and climbed into my car. Before we left, he walked over to my window. "It was nice to meet you, Savannah. You are proof that good things come out of Georgia."

"You are proof that good people become lawyers. Atticus Finch would have liked you," I said, patting his hand as it rested on my rolled-down window.

"I would have liked him too. Good luck. You'll be a great journalist. I expect to read that article you're going to write," he said, smiling and standing back up to return to his own car.

"I'll make sure you get a copy of that article," I said, smiling back. With that, Gregory climbed in his car and led the way to a grand house on the outskirts of downtown. The sign at the entrance of their driveway read "Cummings Estate." As he pulled away, I saw him wave through his rearview window. I returned the wave and hoped I could recollect our plan of attack. But I knew the one detail I would never forget—Gregory.

The straight driveway ran for almost a quarter-mile. The house was directly in front, so as I drove, it was always in my sight, becoming larger and larger the closer I got. Stopping in front of their home, I took a deep breath. Who knew how this was going to work? But the only way to know would be to actually evacuate the car and find out. Even removing my seat belt seemed like a daunting task.

As I closed the car door behind me and began to approach the house, the front door swung open. The older lady who only moments earlier had been in her Sunday best was now changed into denim trousers, a white T-shirt, tennis shoes, and a wide-brimmed straw hat, her red lips still vibrant. In her left hand were a pair of gardening gloves, and in her right, what appeared to be fruit tea. Following close behind was the rather intimidating figure of her husband. Well, intimidating until I got a look at his bad case of chicken legs in old Bermuda shorts and the same black socks he had surely worn to church under his suit. He also wore a white T-shirt and a large straw hat to protect him from the glare of the intense sun.

They didn't see me until they reached the bottom of their steps.

"Well, hello, young lady. You startled me," Mrs. Cummings said, almost tossing her glass and forcing me to catch it.

"Oh, I'm sorry, ma'am. I thought you might have heard me pull up."

She laughed, "My hearing's not as good as it used to be. I probably wouldn't hear a burglar if he was standing in my bedroom."

"Well, don't spread that around town."

That caused her to eye me suspiciously. Eventually she relaxed, realizing I didn't seem the burglar type. And a burglar probably wouldn't drive straight up the driveway and head to the front door on a Sunday afternoon. No, burglars climb into open windows and rummage through people's private, personal files.

"So how can we help you, young lady?" Mr. Cummings asked, turning his back to me and beginning his Sunday gardening ritual. "I hope you're not selling something."

I walked up and extended my hand to Mrs. Cummings, who hadn't moved from the bottom of the stairs since her initial discovery of me. "No, sir, I'm not. My name is Savannah Phillips. I live in Savannah, Georgia."

She put down her gloves and iced tea and shook my hand. Then laughed, adding, "Well hello, Savannah from Savannah. People probably call you that all the time!"

I tried not to glare or smirk, but I knew immediately this lady and I were not going to like each other. "Did you say 'Phillips'?" Mr. Cummings asked, looking over his shoulder briefly.

"Yes, sir, I did," I answered.

"So why are you here, Savannah?" Mrs. Cummings continued, turning to find her own spot in the garden.

There I sat with two backs staring at me. I decided to go for the jugular. After all, I had been suspected as a burglar and I had been called "Savannah from Savannah."

"Actually, I'm here on business."

"Oh?"

"Yes, I'm working on an article investigating voting irregularities and possible bribery at work in the Miss Georgia United States of America pageant," I stated calmly. Both pairs of hands stopped gardening. Neither head turned around. "Yes, it seems that thirty years ago some questions were raised about the possibility of a rigged pageant. I met with Mrs. Stanley Harvard of Atlanta's Wilcox and Harvard accounting firm. I've also met with a couple of former contestants."

With that, Mr. Cummings turned around and rose. He seemed much nicer seated. He approached me in what was still a frightening swagger for a man of some seventy years. "I have judged many a pageant in my day, young lady. Girls make accusations all the time. They get upset and start screaming foul. But if you came here looking for some story to quench a thirty-year-old question, you might want to take your assumptions and head on back home to Savannah." Then he just stared at me.

"So, does this mean you don't want to give me any type of statement?"

"I don't give statements to accusations or conjecture. So, no, I'm not giving you a statement on anything," he said, remaining perfectly still. By this time, Mrs. Cummings had turned in front of her hydrangeas to view the action.

Seeing that everything was going pretty much as rehearsed, I turned around to head back to my car. The walk back allowed me to take some deep breaths and collect my parting words. Opening my car door to make it clear that I was leaving, I turned around, letting one foot rest on the frame and keeping the other planted firmly on the ground. They needed one final thought to ponder on their Sunday afternoon among azaleas, boxwoods, and hostas.

"Well, it was nice to meet you both. I hope we see each other again. You know, before I leave, I'll share one more thought with you. As I was down at the courthouse last night, going through all of your records with the blessings of Judge Tucker, I discovered that Mrs. Cummings owns a printing business and a jewelry store. I also noticed that a printing company by the same name does all the printing for the Miss Georgia United States of America program books and has for roughly the last thirty years. The one thing that didn't seem to make sense however, was"—I paused for *Law & Order* effect—"why the Miss Georgia United States of America Pageant would use a printing company in Mississippi." Slapping myself in the head I added, "Then, I realized that P&R

Printing Company wouldn't register with anyone as being yours. So I put two and two together and came up with this scenario: Maybe your printing company has a deal worked out with Mr. Todd, the Georgia state pageant director, that for every page that is sold, your printing company gets a kickback and, for those kickbacks, Mr. Todd gets a vote of his choice."

Mr. Cummings put his hand under his chin and took one step forward. I pulled my door to me for protection. "Then I came across some banking sheets," I said, reaching inside and pulling a copy of the sheets from the front seat. "They showed a large deposit, every year, exactly one week after the pageant." Then risking the possibility that they might investigate my breaking and entering, I proceeded cautiously.

"Then I found someone to help me." They never had to know who. With any luck they would spend the next two months interrogating their staff. "And with their help I found these letters," I said, holding up copies of Catherine's letters as well. "This wasn't hard to get. There are even dates and transaction amounts here. So, I'm sure that if I need any further information, Judge Tucker will get me anything I need to help progress this little Mississippi steamboat right on up the river."

I bent down to act as if I was getting in the car, but popped back up for the *coup de grâce*. "It would be nice if I found nothing, but a good journalist must be thorough. If you change your mind about giving a statement, you can reach me at the *Savannah Chronicle*. You can just ask for Savannah from Savannah, OK?" With that I gave a big smile and a wink and climbed into my car. Mr. Cummings didn't move a muscle as my car turned in front of him. I rolled down the passenger window and leaned toward it. "Oh, and tell your son I'd like to talk to him as well. I won't bother him today though, seeing as Sunday should be a day of rest. But, I would love to discuss his years of service, specifically the year that Emma Riley lost. He might want to know what she's up to now. Take care." I gave a final nod to each and drove off.

I couldn't tell by either one's expressions if I'd receive a call. But I didn't figure any of us would sleep much tonight. If I was right, they'd call. If I was wrong, well, my story on Victoria's violets would have to be one of the most creative pieces I had ever written.

CHAPTER TWENTY-TWO

I used the twenty-five-minute drive from the Savannah airport to listen to my Jonathan Pierce CD. He was a cutie, that one. I couldn't help but wonder if he was married. But a guy like that wouldn't want a newspaper writer from Savannah who was doing her first story on a rigged beauty pageant.

On the outskirts of town, I picked up my cell phone and checked my messages. There were three. The first was from Vicky, telling me what was for dinner, saying she hoped I got home safely, and that we would talk later. I had no doubt. The second message was from Paige, wanting to get together for dinner. And the third message was from Gregory, wanting to know how my encounter had gone. He left his number.

I wasn't about to address Vicky any sooner than necessary, so I decided to call Gregory. He picked up on the second ring.

"Hello."

"Is this Mr. Grisham?"

He laughed. "You couldn't afford him so you had to settle for me, remember?"

"Oh, yeah, that's right. You're the cheap attorney."

"So go ahead. What happened? I've been waiting all afternoon for you to call me."

"Well, I don't know that anything was accomplished, but I laid it out there like you told me to."

"What was their reaction?"

"Mr. Cummings had none. He just stared a hole through me. Mrs. Cummings stopped her yard work long enough to turn around, but I didn't get more than a stare from her either. They are a stoic couple."

"All you could do was lay your evidence out there. Now you're going to have to play the waiting game. Even lawyers have to endure this type of thing."

"I'm not a lawyer, remember. I'm a journalist. No, I'm not even a journalist. I don't know what I am. But I know what I'm about to be: a tour guide wearing fifty layers of crinoline, melting makeup, and a bonnet that no self-respecting woman should be forced to don. How is it possible that I have already descended from published author to Scarlett O'Hara reject? I ask you, how is such a thing humanly possible?"

"At least you're positive."

"Oh, I am? You call that scenario positive?"

"Yes, you have a career to fall back on. Most put all of their hopes into one thing. But not you. You are a multifaceted individual with many gifts. If you can't write about Savannah, you can just tell people about Savannah." He laughed himself into a tizzy.

"I'm glad you find my life so amusing."

Gregory collected himself. "I believe you will probably have a phone call by Monday."

"You really think so?"

"I absolutely think so. I know you did extremely well. Were you nervous?"

"I was until she called me 'Savannah from Savannah.' Then all nerves vanished and I was ready for the kill."

"They'll call. I don't know what they'll tell you, but they will call."

"I hope you're right."

"Let's get us some dinner and those key-lime, I-need-to-marry-that-man squares."

"You are sad."

"Yes, I know. Then we'll watch *Law & Order*," Paige said from the other end.

"Ooh, yeah. I need to sharpen my skills, plus it will keep me from going home. I'll be there around six."

I retrieved dinner, made a fool of myself trying to catch a glimpse of the chef's left hand, and was headed back to the car when I heard the familiar siren. "Savannah! Yoo-hoo, Savannah!"

There she was, Miss Amber Topaz, waving as if from a runway on the opposite side of the street. She had to be stalking me. If I hadn't looked up so quickly, I would have tried to pretend I hadn't heard her holler my name. But dumb me had looked.

I waved as nonchalantly as possible, hoping my open car door would give her the signal I was headed somewhere. It didn't faze her a bit. Direct insults probably wouldn't faze her either, unless they were related to her clothing, hair, or makeup. She came to an abrupt halt right in front of my trunk. "Hey, Savannah. I just keep running into you all over the place. I think this has to be another sign that you and I are just destined to be lifelong friends. Don't you?"

I sat down in the driver's seat and placed dinner on the passenger's side, then put my keys in the ignition, trying to look hurried. "Well, we have seen each other a lot lately."

"Are we still on for Tuesday? I love The Lady & Sons and thought that would be a great place for us to go and tell each other more stories about our lives. And drink sweet tea until we burst," she said, patting me on the leg.

Turning the car on, I said, "I might have to reschedule our

lunch. I've run into a few deadlines and I'm trying to make sure I have my first article ready to go to press by Tuesday. So we might have to play lunch by ear, if that's OK."

"Oh, sure. We have the rest of our lives to have lunches. But I'll keep in touch with you just to make sure you're not working too hard," she said in that mock voice of concern, giving me another irritating pat. "So, did you enjoy looking at my program books? Weren't some of those girls just ghastly?"

"I thought all the girls were rather attractive. But I can't stay and chat, I've got a dinner appointment that I have to get to."

"Well, I just think some of those girls look like they've been rode hard and put up wet. You know that's an old saying in the South."

"Yes, I think I've heard of that one."

"I mean, in that book I gave you there were girls who couldn't even win the Miss Fried Okra Pageant, but somehow they made it to Miss Georgia United States of America. I figure they were the only ones who even competed in their local pageants. Some people's parents should just tell them, 'Honey, you're not really right for pageants; why don't we put you in mud-wrestling. With those thighs you could beat anybody.' You know what I'm saying?"

"Actually, I don't. And, not to be rude, but I have an appointment, and if I don't leave, I'm going to be extremely late," I said.

"Oh, OK. Well, I've got to go too. I have a mock interview rehearsal," she said, standing to her feet.

Before I could catch myself, I said, "What's a mock interview rehearsal?" I was now officially the biggest idiot in Georgia. It is one thing to be an unwilling participant in lunacy, but it is another thing altogether to become a willing one

She began like a whirlwind, arms flailing, hands patting, eyes sparkling, voice dancing. "Oh, Savannah, mock interview rehearsal is the most awesome thing. I get all three of my aunts and my mother and my stepmother, and for about two hours they bombard me with every type of question, from who the president is to how many pairs of shoes Imelda Marcos has."

"Imelda, huh?"

"Yeah, she's my favorite world leader. Then, they ask me what my thoughts are on everything from world peace and universal health care to what my favorite song is and why I named my dog Aqua Marine Lewis."

I did prevent myself from asking why she named her dog Aqua Marine Lewis. Instead, I put the car in park and leaned back in my seat. My watch read five forty-five. Paige's was only two minutes away. Surely she would be through in ten minutes. Wouldn't she?

I stared at her moving lips, realizing I might be forced to run her over. But I would at least be willing to write her obituary. "Miss Cubic Zirconia Childers was killed graciously by Miss Savannah Phillips after Ms. Phillips was tortured mercilessly for thirty minutes by the beauty-pageant junkie. In lieu of flowers, please send cash donations to the Miss Georgia United States of America Pageant for new opening-number outfits. Every dress will be emblazoned with precious stones symbolizing the precious jewel that Miss Childers was to all of us."

As I rested my eyes, she continued her lesson in interviewing techniques. "See, at the pageant—you know those five judges you saw at the pageant the other night?"

I nodded.

"Well, during interview, they sit in front of you at a big long table and for ten minutes they shoot you with questions and you answer them as rehearsed, yet as natural as possible, of course. They have a bio on each of the girls that they get before the pageant begins. Sometimes they ask you questions off your bio, and other times they ask you whatever comes off the tops of their heads. I've seen girls leave interviews crying. The judges asked such tough questions they couldn't hardly answer any of them. Then the next girl will go in and come out all smiles, saying it was the easiest thing she has ever done."

"Hmm," I said, keeping my eyes closed.

"One girl got asked a question one time about what she

would do to reform the EPA. Poor girl didn't even know what it was. She thought EPA stood for the Equal Protection for Animals, and she went on for two minutes talking about how she felt that every cow, duck, frog, and cat should be treated with the same respect as people. Then she gave four solutions, declaring that her plan would make the system better. She said the only thing the judge said was, 'I'm sure it would honey, I'm sure it would.'" When her roommate informed her that EPA stood for the Environmental Protection Agency, the poor girl walked straight into the bathroom and tossed her cookies. Her mother took her home that night. I'm telling you, you have to be prepared for anything."

"For anything," I agreed, nodding my head. And that was when I made my move. I reached out my hand, grabbed the doorknob, looked her squarely in the eye, and said, "I have to leave now. I'm sorry. But we'll talk this week."

"OK. Always great to talk to you. I love hearing all about you. You're just the neatest person," she said with a Vaseline-slathered-on-your-teeth kind of grin. "I'll talk to you soon. Toodeloo," and she skipped into the dusk. It was a wretched sight, but she nevertheless caught the attention of an elderly gentleman in the car across the street. He almost took out a fire hydrant. His wife slapped him with her purse.

CHAPTER TWENTY-THREE

O h, that was so good," Paige said, all but licking her plate for any leftover key-lime residue.

"Yes, it was."

"I want to marry him."

"Get a new line."

"It's true. I want a guy who can cook."

"I want a guy who can figure out the minds of sociopathic killers."

"I'm going to start making you watch comedies."

"Speaking of sociopaths, let's rehearse again what I'm going to say to my mother. There is the possibility I will never be seen alive again." I really had no idea how my mother would react to my discoveries, assumptions, and speculations. This was the woman who had been caught walking around with a tiara on her head, singing show tunes in the middle of the afternoon, when a group of tourists passed by her house and spotted her through the window. This is the same woman who invites former queens over to her house every year to watch the Miss United States of America Pageant in their old pageant dresses. This is a woman slightly off balance when it comes to beauty pageants. She was liable to horse-whip me with her sash. Her next ad in the *Savannah Chronicle* would probably read "New daughter wanted for extremely gracious, fun-loving, pageant-watching mother-daughter experience."

"Well, if you think I'm going to tell you how to handle your mama . . . Girl, you are the master with her. You just treat her gentle, compliment her shoes, and offer to go out to lunch with her this week. She'll forget everything else you have to say. You know that."

"That won't work this time. This will cut to her core. She lives and breathes pageants. If she thinks I think her beloved pageant is rigged or remotely less than authentic, well, she might think death would be sweeter."

"Well, at least you have a job, a place to live, a father who will provide you with Coke to cure your ills, and a best friend who can support you for a while if need be. And who will never, and I do mean never, force you to watch another pageant as long as you live."

"Say it's true!"

"It's so true! Now go. You can do it. Remember, gentle. Be very gentle. And compliment, don't forget to compliment. And call me. No matter what time. Don't forget to call me," she said, opening the door to let me out.

"I won't. But be fasting and praying."

"I'm starting now. But hurry, I'd like to get a bowl of cereal around eleven."

"You're sick."

"But I love you."

"I'll call you later."

"I'll be waiting, rest assured."

I entered through the front door. This simply needed to be faced head-on. A ball came bouncing in from the kitchen, and Duke came barreling out behind it. The ball hit the wall, bounced against the iron console, ricocheted to the other wall, hit my leg, and then landed at my feet. Duke took roughly the same path. His front paws slid across the hardwood as his back paws tried to slow his speed. Eventually his full body weight hit the foyer rug, causing his front paws to curve under his body, creating an odd somersault effect. The carpet ended up in a heap. He tried to recover himself, but his feet scrambled when he hit the hardwood, resulting in a bad Scooby-Doo impersonation. Finally, he landed at my feet, panting. I patted his head.

"No way, champ, will I touch that ball."

Dad called him a second later, and Duke gave up on me, retrieved his ball, and took it back to his faithful companion. I turned the corner to the kitchen and saw Dad sitting on the floor for the dog and ball show.

"Hey, sweetheart," he said, standing up to hug me.

"Do not touch me with those hands. You've been playing ball with a spit wad."

"Oh, but it's lovely spit," he said, still reaching out to me.

I ran to the other side of the kitchen island. "Where's Mother?"

Dad walked over to the sink to wash his hands. "You're a brave soul. She is wondering what in the world you are up to. I'm wondering the same, but her curiosity is exceptionally piqued since she got word you went to see Emma. Are you ready to talk to her?"

"Do I have a choice?"

"There's always a choice."

"Yes, to deal with or to delay. I'm too busy to delay."

"Do you want to practice on me?"

I gave him a hug. "You would not be practice for what I'm about to face. You wouldn't even be a warmup. Just wish me luck."

"Good luck," he said, hugging me back and pointing upstairs.

I slowly climbed the stairs, wishing I was in one of those magical children's novels, like *The Lion, the Witch and the Wardrobe,* and that my stairs would lead me to an enchanted forest where I would be crowned the queen of something. The queen of anything. I would settle for queen of the Dukes at this point, spitball and all.

Her door was shut. I turned to glance into my room before knocking and noticed that there was stuff all over my bed. It was like a Kate Spade store. There were four Kate Spade handbags, ten pairs of shoes, even some that looked like flip-flops. There was an entire travel ensemble, with a wheeled carry-on and makeup cases. There was an executive ensemble, with what looked like a new satchel and a Day-Timer, with a coordinating wallet and key ring. I couldn't help but smile. I also couldn't help but wonder how long it must have been since I had told my mother I appreciated something about her. This overkill was evidence that it had been a very long time. I was glad I'd seen all this before I entered her room.

Her door opened just as I was about to knock. She looked beautiful, as always. She was wearing a pale blue silk Christian Dior robe, with a nightgown of the same color peeking out at the top. She had on her one-and-a-half-inch heeled bedroom shoes and stood exquisitely finished in full makeup and surprisingly subtle accessories.

"Hello, darling! When did you get home?" She opened the door wider.

"Just a few minutes ago," I told her, coming into this room that held so many memories. During our at-home years, Thomas and I would always come up to Mother and Dad's room at night, sit in their sitting room in front of the fireplace, and talk about our days. Mother would read to us while Dad read his own book. Then we would watch a television show, pray, and they would tuck us in.

"Mother, I love all the stuff in there on my bed. That was very thoughtful. I even saw a couple pairs of flip-flops," I said, smiling at her and truly meaning it, not that I'd fight anything that worked.

She just beamed. "I'm glad you do. I thought it might help you with your new job. And if you have a lot of traveling to do, well, then you'll have some things for that as well."

I put my arm around her and led her to the chairs that we hadn't sat in together for so long. "I was going to take you for a walk outside. But since you already have your gown on, why don't we just sit here," I said, motioning for her to sit down in her chair. I sat across from her in Dad's well-worn chair.

She gestured to the closet. "Well, I could get dressed and we could walk down past the cemetery again."

"No, I really think this will be more comfortable, and I'm not really in the mood for being that close to dead people. And we haven't sat in here together for a long time. This will be a nice change of pace for us."

"Savannah, I declare, you sound like you've grown into a woman," she said as she perched her feet daintily atop her ottoman and wrapped her robe around her legs. "I remember how you and I used to cuddle in this chair every night. You would tell me the greatest made-up stories. One of my favorites was how you had written the president of McDonald's asking him to boycott the entire city of Savannah until he put a McDonald's downtown next to your father's store," she said, laughing.

"Mother, that wasn't a story. I did write him."

"Savannah, you did not!" she said, laughing even louder. "How many times have you written them?"

"Well, in total, about twenty-five. Some were to report poorly maintained Coke machines, others were to report poor carbonation, and my last was a letter of special thanks," I told her, not revealing it was for the machine they let my dad put in his store.

"What did you write to thank them for?"

"Just to tell them I appreciated their willingness to meet the needs of young children." She would think I was talking about the Ronald McDonald house.

"Savannah, you are like no child I've ever met. You're beautiful, yet not snooty. A trait you got from me, I might add," she said in absolute seriousness.

"Mother, I really need to talk to you about something important."

"Yes, I know you do. You have for a while. I figure it has something to do with beauty pageants. At first I thought you might be telling the stories of past queens. However, I figured out that wasn't it or you would have wanted to interview me and not Emma. Then, I figured you must have found something intriguing, or someone intriguing, who spiked your interest."

"Yes, I have."

"And since I thought I had revealed about everything possible to be known regarding the world of pageants, I knew I would just have to wait for you to tell me yourself. So, Savannah, what has prompted your sudden interest in pageants?" At that moment she looked so vulnerable, so delicate, so . . . my mother, so the last person in the world that I would ever want to hurt. And she was Jake's wife, and Jake's rare wrath caused me far greater concern than this woman facing me. So I proceeded gently.

"Mother, the last thing I would ever want to do is hurt you. And please know that I don't even know all the facts yet. There might not be a story here at all," I said.

"Well, tell me, and we'll see."

"Well, you need to know first that the story came to me. I didn't seek it out. And for that reason alone, it seemed necessary to pursue it. I hope you'll understand when I tell you what I know. But I hope you'll understand even more what I think."

"I trust you, Savannah."

I began with the day I had first walked into Katherine's store and finished with the events of the weekend, leaving out a few of my questionable activities. For almost two hours, Vicky did nothing but listen intently and nod her head when it was appropriate. She never asked a question, and for the majority of the time her head just rested on her hands as she watched every word come out of my mouth. When I was finished, she leaned back in her chair, rested her head, and closed her eyes.

"Are you going to say anything?"

"Well, first I'm going to say that that was a very long story, and you need to learn to go easy on the details."

"I'll work on that."

"Second, I'm going to tell you that truth is more important than anything. Your father and I have taught you that from the beginning. If there is truth here and you find it, then you should rightly reveal it. My only request is that you make sure you know the truth, that you don't reveal speculations. People have been ruined by speculation."

"I wouldn't want to ruin anyone."

"Savannah, if all the speculation that was said about me was believed, I would probably be locked up in a cell with former beauty pageant queens forced to watch reruns of *Miss Congeniality* all day. But I know what is true about me, and so do the people I love. So, make sure you never contribute to faleshoods about others. Those are the values we raised you by, Savannah. I don't expect you to act any other way."

"Nor would I want to."

She leaned in to make her point clear. "I know on Wednesday, whatever is in the paper will be the truth that you found. And I know that if it leads to speculation about me and how I won, or if I should have won, I will still know what is true and so will my family. All I ask for is excellence, and that's all you've ever given. I trust you, young woman. I trust you because I know you."

"Thank you, Mother."

"You're welcome. And I know that inside of you is a continual struggle to do what is right, especially if there is the possibility you might hurt someone. What is right is always right. The cost doesn't change that. And I will be just as proud of you no matter what you decide, because I know you'll do the right thing. You always have. Now, it's late, my mind's taxed, and I need some rest. If you need any help, let me know." With that she got up, walked over to me and kissed me on my head, and made her way to the bathroom to remove her face.

I rose in a stupor. I had expected flash and fireworks. I had expected screaming fits and tears. I had expected drama. But I got a lady. A gentle, understanding lady. A woman who at that moment cared more about my doing what was right than the conflict, speculation, or questions about her that it would cause. That was the depth of this woman's love for me.

Since tomorrow was my first day working a "real job," as they call it, I needed to make sure I had myself fully prepared to enter the world of the employed. I'd held down plenty of jobs before, but this was different. This wasn't one of those college standbys where I could call in at the last minute if I had a stomachache, boyfriend matter, or just felt more like taking in a movie. This one had designated sick time, vacation leave, working hours, and an actual desk I would have to sit behind. The thought of all of it began to make me extremely nervous.

I had really thought that I would spend my years strolling through parks, sitting in diners, carrying my laptop around with me, and documenting the life that passed by. My life would be devoted to developing characters and enlightening imaginations, with little structure and unlimited lunches with friends, being my own boss and creating my own schedule. In short, my life would be like Paige's.

Until now, these newly defined rules for living had been lost on me. Everything had been such a whirlwind since I had pulled the car up in front of my "Welcome Home" banner, that I hadn't thoroughly explored the concept of having a real job. Had I, I might not have shown up at all. Needing to redirect my energies, I focused on what I was going to wear. Vicky had provided me with substantial options.

I located a light-gray pair of silk pants with a nice line. I decided to pair them with a pale-pink cotton sweater and gray open-toed shoes.

The outfit wasn't truly me, but I wasn't going to be truly me until I could relocate my office to a front table in Jake's Coffeehouse. Looking out over Bay Street would be nice, but I would much prefer the view at the shop. As good as I was at the art of persuasion, I imagined I could negotiate that by the end of the first month. The possibility gave me added energy.

There I stood, staring at all those shoes and handbags, when this overwhelming feeling urged me to try it all on. For me this was strangely odd. I'm not the kind of person who cares about fashion. As long as an item remotely fits, remotely matches, remotely works, I'm remotely happy. I'm not obsessive about outerwear. I like to look nice, neat, clean, all of those things. But let's just say I've never left a store wearing my new shoes. I'm the kind of person that could bring home a pair of new shoes, throw them in the back of the closet, and forget they were there until I stumbled upon them searching for an old pair of flip-flops. So, this feeling, this need, this momentary weirdness, almost frightened me.

Still, I reached into the first box and pulled out a pair of shoes that certainly were from another time. They were espadrilles. There were a couple pairs of different-colored tennis shoes, and two beautiful pair of slip-on open-toed sandals with a slight heel. One was in camel and the other in black. These would go with anything. Though I wasn't a big heel wearer, these were so attractive I decided to slip my foot in one, then the other. Staring at my feet in the mirror, they looked slimmer, older, more refined. They didn't look like mine.

At that moment I was posing. I, Savannah Phillips, was striking a pose. My right foot went in front of my left, in kind of perpendicular form. It was a beauty pageant stance. I was metamorphosing! Then, I grabbed a handbag and slung it over my shoulder. Before I knew it, I was prancing toward the mirror, striking a pose and turning back, flinging myself around so my hair would whip around my face. It was the whipping action that did it. I whipped a tad too fast and about broke my neck. The fall was slow and methodical, but the results extremely fascinating.

Then I caught a really good look at myself in the mirror. There I was—rear in the air, one shoe off, the strap of a purse hanging around my neck, and my hair so whipped my face was invisible. The sight of myself and pathetic genes caused me to laugh so hard I fell over in the floor. "So much for my attempts at striking a pose," I said out loud.

Collecting myself, I turned my attention to Vicky's executive ensemble purchases, I picked up the Day-Timer. It was a little black number, fastened with a silver clasp. I transferred all my numbers into it and decided to record my upcoming activities. Monday, May 5, 2002, first day of work 8:00 a.m., lunch with Paige at Clary's 12:00 p.m., Tuesday, May 6, first article due! Now, I was ready: an outfit, matching shoes, a Day-Timer . . . absolutely no story.

I laid my outfit across the chair by the window to iron in the morning, picked up a gray purse and matching wallet and laid it by my outfit, then placed my newly organized organizer inside my purse. Then I crawled into bed; but feeling the need to say my prayers kneeling tonight, crawled back out. "Lord, I'm not sure what I'm about to embark on tomorrow. I'm not even sure if I've been chasing the right story, but help me know. Somehow, please help me know." I thanked Him for the day and even the new shoes with the heels. I got back into bed, and somewhere between thoughts of Amber's cockamamie stories, Emma's nappy hair, and Vicky's continual surprises, I fell asleep.

CHAPTER TWENTY-FOUR

At five a.m., only Duke had perked. The sun wasn't ready, and I was too nervous.

I jogged and tilled and rummaged through my thoughts. My CD of the week was by CeCe Winans. My first lap was consumed with Mrs. Harvard, my first meeting with Katherine, Emma's first appearance at her door, and the mean old lady who wanted to make jokes with my name. I considered Gregory's question of whether this was a human-interest story at all.

As my thoughts grew more frustrating, I decided I needed one more lap around the park. This lap was for tilling and not thinking. Duke looked at me as if he would just as soon go back home, but I encouraged him to give it one more shot. After the pain in my right side began and the half-dead dog next to me stopped cold, we headed toward home.

Knowing I had to face work eventually, I showered, ironed, dressed, and made my way to the kitchen for something to nourish me until lunch. Mother was already downstairs. She had made a tremendous breakfast: bacon, eggs, homemade biscuits, cheese grits, and homemade hash-brown potatoes. At that moment, Victoria needed to be kissed. I was most willing to oblige.

"Thank you. Thank you! Thank you!" I said, planting a big one on her cheek.

"You're welcome," she said, laughing. "I knew you would be excited and would need some extra energy."

"You were so right!" I said, stuffing a piece of bacon in my mouth as I fixed my plate and sat down.

Mother leaned across the counter and watched me devour my food. "Savannah, you need to quit chomping like that. You have to make a good impression with these people, so if you are going to eat in front of them, you need to get ahold of yourself."

"I'm sorthwy," I said with my mouth full, then swallowed a mouthful of juice. "I'm just so nervous."

"You're going to do great. You just give them your best story and put your personality in it, and you'll do great," she said, standing back up and turning around to put the dirty dishes in the dishwasher.

"Do you have any more thoughts on your story?"

"No, ma'am. I'm just going to see what I find out today. I hope Mr. Cummings will call me, give me some more information, but who knows. I hope I haven't spent the last four days chasing a ridiculous story for no reason. If I have, then, we'll just have to pull out my handy-dandy 'Painting with Paige' article from sophomore year creative-writing class. I figure I'm creative enough to give even that a different twist."

She still had her back to me, but I could see she was laughing. "I'm sure you can."

I got up and headed for the door. "I love you, Mother. Have a great day."

"I love you too, darling. And I know you'll do a great job. I like your shoes."

"I do too."

"I wish you would have worn your hair down. You look so

much more ladylike with it down. Don't you want some jewelry? I have a great silver bauble necklace that would accentuate your gray pants perfectly. I even have a gray straw hat, if you would like that." I headed for a Coke.

When I entered the coffeehouse, everyone paused and then stared at me with their mouths hanging open.

"I know, I know, I look like a real person," I said in mock disgust, walking straight for the Coke machine. I picked up a glass that was far too small. "Please tell me you have something bigger than this. I am requiring extreme caffeine." Mervine smiled and headed into the stockroom behind Dad's office. She came out holding one of the biggest cups I'd ever seen.

She set it down beside me, patted me on the back, and simply said, "Enjoy, honey."

I was almost startled. In thirteen years, I had probably heard her speak no more than once per year.

"Savannah, what time do you have to be at your new job?" Louise asked.

"Well, I'm getting there a little early. I want to figure out where everything is and make a good impression," I said, filling up my thirty-two-ouncer.

"Well, you look wonderful, darling," Dad said, coming over to give me a kiss on the cheek.

Taking a long drink of my Coke, I took a breather to say, "Well, I'm not sure what newspaper people are supposed to look like, but this is my best shot at acting like I do."

Then as if a dam had burst, Mervine spoke. "Well, I think you look like a princess, Savannah. You're going to blow the roof off that paper, and I am so looking forward to reading your first article. You're going to set this city on its ear." By this time she had more motions than a tent-revival preacher on a Saturday night.

"And it's about time we had some fresh faces and new life around here. I think that editor up there needs some new perspectives, and I believe you're just the kind of person to give it to him. I also believe these young people with their pierced parts need to see a young and refined lady. Sure you have a little edge, but a little edge never hurt anybody. It's about time someone your age left a mark on their own culture. Who knows, us old people might even learn something ourselves." Then she stopped talking, returned to the counter, and simply smiled at us.

"I told you she talked," Louise said. "Doesn't even take a breath either. That's what she does from the time she wakes up. Talk, talk, talk. Talks to her kids' pictures, talks to the TV, my word, even talks to the Braves on TV." And she walked to the front of the store just shaking her head.

Mervine grinned from ear to ear. Didn't say another word, just grinned as she followed Louise. Dad and I just stared at each other, dumbfounded. "I have never . . ." was all I could say.

"I have never myself," Dad agreed, still looking through the door that led to the front of the store. "In all these years, that woman hasn't so much as asked what time it was. You might better watch out today, Savannah. I believe a new day has come."

"Well, it's calling my name. I've got to run. Wish me luck!" I did look back one more time, just to make sure that whole occurrence hadn't been a brief apparition. But when my eyes revealed Dad still leaning against the counter staring in the direction of Mervine and Louise, I knew it was true. Mervine had spoken.

There was little activity at seven at the *Savannah Chronicle*. People were beginning to mill about, but only a few. I drove to the back of the building and parked my car in what appeared to be the newspaper's parking lot.

Gathering myself and my new backpack, which I had settled on this morning instead of the purse, I decided to leave my Coke in the car and feel everyone out first. Who knew if they even allowed drinks inside? I wanted to fit in the best I could for the girl whose name had appeared in the paper more times than the mayor's.

I walked through the front door and at first glance saw no one at the front desk. Then a bright lady with a determined step headed in my direction.

"You look new," she said as she came around the corner with her hands full of papers. She smiled at my expression.

"So much for hiding my real feelings," I told her, smiling back at her.

"Well, my name is Doris, Doris Berry. I've worked here at this paper for over fifty-five years. Yes, ma'am, fifty-five years. I started when I was eighteen, right after high-school graduation." She looked good for seventy-three. Her hair was unashamedly silver and she wore little makeup. Only her hands told her age. I imagined this woman had lived well and enjoyed life. And the way she talked about this place caused me to believe she ran the ship tighter than Mr. Hicks.

I tried awkwardly to shake one of her hands, but they were encumbered with the files she was carrying. "Nice to meet you, Ms. Berry. I'm Savannah, Savannah Phillips."

"Well, it's Doris, and I know exactly who you are. Yes, ma'am, I know exactly who you are. You look like both your father and your mother. You have her nose and mouth and his everything else. Time will tell whose personality you have," she said with a wink. "Follow me and I'll show you to your desk." I followed her after first offering to help her carry her load. She refused. I didn't want to make her feel bad, so I never told her I had already seen my office.

We passed a small waiting area and the payment desk. "This is your corner," she said, leading me to a corner cubicle in the very back of the first floor—no windows, no fraction of a view of the outside world, nothing to see but gray, fabric-covered, Styrofoam-like walls all around me. Perched atop the desk was a computer and a desk calendar. Underneath the drab gray desk was a drab gray wastebasket. I guess the shock of my surroundings must have registered on my face. "Is something wrong?"

"Well, kind of," I said, hoping not to embarrass her. "I'm replacing Gloria. And I was here Saturday to do some work, and I've already seen my office upstairs, next to Mr. Hicks."

I could tell that she was trying to stifle a grin. "Oh, well, I see, and I hate to tell you this, but you have to work your way to that office, Savannah. Geraldine O'Malley, who has been here for twenty years and runs our classified section, is getting that office. This," she said, pointing to our dreary surroundings, "well, this, my dear, is your office."

"Oh," I said, mortified. "That was pretty presumptuous of me, wasn't it?" I was thankful no one else was around.

"It's totally understandable. And it will be our little secret," Doris whispered. I could tell by her kind smile she meant it, and my gratefulness increased. "So, Savannah, this is the world of newspapers. It's fast and furious with little glamour and long hours. Pretty soon you'll forget you can't see the world outside that you're writing about in here."

"Is it always this messy?" I asked, referring to the papers strewn about in every cubicle and corner.

"It's a newspaper, Savannah. Paper is a part of our name."

"After fifty-five years, haven't you gotten tired of staring at gray partitions?" I asked her as I stared aimlessly at the sea of blandness in front of me and the chaos that surrounded me.

"Oh, Savannah," she said, laughing. "After fifty-five years, you get an office on the third floor, surrounded with windows and looking out over Bay Street. Trust me, you'll adjust. You'll eventually adjust." Then she added, "Just an FYI: Most people have laptops today, if you know what I mean. Work is where you make it. Just get acclimated here, then you can work wherever you need to. The only requirement is that your work gets done."

I knew immediately I was going to like her. "Come on," she continued. "Let me drop these papers off and I'll give you the tour.

It doesn't get hopping around here until around eight thirty." She dropped the papers off on a desk settled even deeper in the mono-chrome dimness. It was a glassed-in office, however, with a win-dow and a view of the alley. Doris informed me that this office belonged to the editor of the news division, Don Jefferson. Then she informed me that she was the head of advertising.

"No wonder you know me so well."

"Your mother has about kept this paper in business," she said laughing.

"My mother has about kept this city in business."

"That she has, my dear, that she has."

"Does everyone know that Victoria's daughter is coming to work here?"

"I'm afraid so. But they expect you to arrive in rhinestones, tiara, and four-inch heels, shouting orders and redecorating, so they're liable to be disappointed," she said, scanning my outfit.

"This will probably be the first time that I'm glad I've disap-pointed someone."

"I'm with you there, honey, I'm with you there. So let me show you where we eat around here," she said, going to the third floor. "This is our quaint break room." *Quaint* wasn't quite the word. It was old and tired, but it had a Coke machine, snack machine, and refrigerator. "Most people eat out," she said matter-of-factly. "These are the restrooms for this floor. I'll show you the others as we go," she said, pointing out the two doors next to the break room. "These are the major points. Printing has all of the fourth floor. Advertising and the main offices take up the third floor. Business, life and living, and classifieds take up the second floor. And the first floor is the news department, which handles every-thing from national to local. You are governed by Mr. Hicks, however. He edits all local articles himself. He was really fond of Gloria, Savannah. I'm honestly shocked that he hired anyone for that position at all. How did you do it anyway?" she asked, stop-ping to face me.

"The story hasn't gotten around?"

"No. No one is quite sure how you did it. Now, there has been a lot of speculation: new advertising from your mother, threats, bribery, and the like. But no one really believes any of that. And they sure won't when they meet you. So how did you do it?"

"That will be Mr. Hicks's story to tell," I said with a raised right eyebrow.

"You're good, Savannah. You're really good."

I stared at a computer I had never used, with the word IBM written across it. I had been a Mac girl since I learned how to use the computer in middle school. With each new one that came out, I would forgo anything—clothes, trips, food, anything but Coke—to get the next one available. My current models were the new iBook laptop and an iMac Cube, graduation gifts. That day I wished I had used an IBM at least once. If all else failed, though, the iBook was in my backpack.

After ten minutes of searching, I found the turn-on switch at the back of the computer. The screen popped up. Where was my AppleWorks, my Quark, my intimate friends? I decided to wait until someone came to show me how to use it, lest I begin my first day by melting down the mainframe. Hey, Mervine had spoken today; anything was possible.

Around eight o'clock, more people began to enter. I decided to unload my backpack and try to make this square, lusterless closet homey. I took out my pens, notebooks, pencils, Post-its, and my Day-Timer. Not that I had anything in the Day-Timer except my lunch plans, but no one else had to know that. By eight thirty the place was coming alive with chatter and people. I tried to look like I was working hard. Trying to write notes on my Emma conversation was virtually impossible, because it was so one-sided there wasn't much to tell.

People were busy even as they walked through the door, so

busy in fact that no one even noticed me. About eight forty-five, however, footsteps headed toward my desk. I heard them before I saw them—flip-flops. The flip-flops came around the corner; my eyes moved upward to the face of their owner. Curly Locks with the blue bike was standing in front of me. And to top it off, he held a cup of coffee in his hand. It was a white cup with that brown wrapper around the center. Coffee from that other place.

His eyes spotted me, registering shock at first before being over-taken by a wide, chafing little grin. "My, my, my. If it isn't the girl without a name. But now I know your name. Because we've all been wondering when Victoria's daughter was going to get here." As if my new cell wasn't enough, Curly Locks was going to be my cell mate.

Forget not having a story; being Victoria's daughter would be my greatest challenge in this new job. I would face it head-on. I would face it like Savannah. And I would begin today with the man in flip-flops.

"Actually, the name is Savannah," I said, rising to face him eye to eye. Well, eye to chest, but that's neither here nor there. I reached out my hand to shake his. He looked at me with a half-cocked smile and returned the gesture.

"Hi. Joshua, Joshua North. You're not quite what we expected," he said with that same annoying grin as he eyed my attire and footwear.

"Well, what did *we* expect, exactly?"

Not realizing he would be forced to begin his day describing his prejudices, he looked a smidgen embarrassed. "Oh, it's nothing. It's all in good fun. We're just glad you're here. I sit across from you. Let me know if you need anything. I know this is probably a different world from the one you're used to. You know, where people do everything for you. You'll have to get your own coffee, I'm afraid," he said, turning around and heading to his desk.

I could have let it go, probably even should have. I could have let him sit his little wrinkled khakis down and sip his little brown-wrapped coffee and prop his feet up with that smirk across his face. I should have. But I didn't. I did, however, let him get good and situated, let him think for one brief moment he had left me speechless.

Then I rounded the corner of his cubicle.

"I did think about bringing my mother to work with me today. You know, to keep the *mean* people away," I said in mock fear. He spun in his chair to face me. "But then I remembered that I've never asked my mother for anything. In fact, I started my first job when I was fifteen and was elected president of my high-school student body—without using any of my mother's food or money to bribe the fellow students. I was the president of my college student body as well, and I didn't even need her to campaign for me. Then, lo and behold, I went off and won a publishing contract," I finished, leaving out the fact that she was totally responsible for that.

He leaned back in his chair as if to enjoy the show, which irritated me all the more. "Then I made a decision all by myself. Can you imagine that?" I said, slapping him on the shoulder and nearly knocking him out of his chair. "I made a decision and I decided to forgo book advances and fame and fortune to come here, to work beside you, to write stories that would influence the hearts of this city. I did it all without my mother's influence, letter of recommendation, or coercion. Instead, I decided those values she instilled in me would work fine on their own. And you know what? They did. Because here I am. Right beside you! Aren't you excited?"

"Extremely," he replied.

"And no pomp or circumstance, just me, all alone. Why? Because I'm totally capable on my own. Now for you, my new friend, the name is Savannah, not 'Victoria's daughter.' I get my own Cokes because, for your information, I don't even like coffee, and if I did, it would be from my father's coffee shop. If you have any more questions, remarks, or unsolicited comments, restrain yourself. I'll contact you when I have the time to discuss them." With that, I turned on my Kate Spade heels and headed back to my Styrofoam world.

CHAPTER TWENTY-FIVE

stared at the ringing apparatus on my desk. Was I supposed to just say, "Hello"? Was I to introduce myself? Was I even supposed to answer it at all? After the fourth ring, the voice that belonged to the flip-flops came from the other cubicle. "You might want to answer that."

I picked the phone up as if it might be an explosive and said, "Savannah Phillips."

"Hey, Savannah. This is Marla at the front desk. I know we haven't met yet, but we'll get to know each other soon. But right now, I need to tell you that there's a man on the phone for you. I'll transfer him."

"A man, well, OK . . . how do you transfer him exactly?"

"Well, you just hang up the phone. Your phone will ring again, and when it does, you answer it just the way you did a minute ago and he'll be on the other end. OK?"

"OK," I said, hanging up the phone. I waited for about three seconds, and the phone rang again. I answered the same way, adding a hello.

"Yes, Savannah. This is Richard Cummings."

I froze. I had hoped he might call. But I had never considered what I'd say or how I'd say it, let alone what he might say in return. I didn't even know where to begin, so I just started with the first thing that came to mind. "Yes, Mr. Cummings. I didn't know if I would hear from you or not."

"Well, I am still appalled at your allegations and your intrusion. I wanted to catch you first thing this morning to let you know how out of line you were. You are extremely nosy, but you seem like you try real hard," he said with mock appreciation. "Now, past things are past things, none of which needs stirring up around here. You need to let things that have been laid to rest, simply rest. Nothing but trouble will come from your accusations." His anger had been giving way to weariness. "I'm asking you to simply let this be."

"I don't think it needs to just be, Mr. Cummings."

"Well, this thing was settled years ago. And if you try to stir up things now, we will have some trouble to deal with."

"Are you threatening me?"

He chuckled at that. "My dear girl, I'm too old to threaten people. I'm a successful, established businessman in a reputable community. My family and I are part of the fabric of this city, and to have a child from Savannah make such allegations against us is merely more than an annoyance. As for you, however, well, it would probably not be the wisest move."

"Well, I've learned that when people are duped by a person they put great faith in, they usually appreciate the knowledge of such things in the long run."

"I don't believe anything my family has done has 'duped' any-one. But I do believe your meddling will ultimately contribute to the well-being of no one," he said, his even voice full of hidden meaning.

"Are you saying that the things you have done have not had long-term ramifications on others' lives?"

"I didn't say I had done anything. But I do believe that any

215

decision made by beauty pageant judges affects a young lady's life for one year. That's all. It's just one year out of her life. So don't waste your time on temporal things, my dear. Go write stories on things that really matter to people. That's all I have to say to you."

I jumped in before he could hang up. "Let me remind you of someone this story really matters to, Mr. Cummings. Her name is Emma. And your son's decision, your son's greedy choice, precipitated by years of your own greedy choices, have caused her to spend the last six years regarding herself as worthless. Did her own choices have something to do with that? Yes. Were your son's decisions the catalyst? I believe they were. Are you innocent? I don't think so. He followed in your footsteps, made the same choices you made for others countless times before. Besides the fact that you dictate destinies, you are a greedy man."

"Don't talk about what you don't know."

"Oh, I know. You chose a dollar over a life. You, Mr. Cummings, are the one who has let the temporal affect your future. You let one moment of decision, one pivotal moment of choice, determine that your life would be not one of character, but of compromise."

"You're treading on dangerous ground, little girl."

"Maybe so, Mr. Cummings. But you should be old and wise by now. Instead, you've missed what really matters. You've missed the opportunity to be a man of character producing children of character."

And with that, I heard a click from the other end of the line.

The bed-head from next door peeked around the corner and said with a quirky smile, "Do you talk to everyone in condescending composition form?"

I sat my elbows on the corner of my desk and laid my head in my hands. "No. No, I'm in rare form today. I'm sorry about earlier. Not a good way to get started," I said, looking up into his face.

His smirk softened. "Well, it was deserved, considering my smart-aleck comment. How 'bout we try again?" He stretched out his hand. "Hello, my name is Joshua, Joshua North."

I shook his hand as confidently as I could, trying not to act as defeated as I felt. "Hello, Joshua, I'm Savannah Phillips. Nice to meet you."

"Nice to meet you as well, Ms. Phillips. Do you need any help?" he asked, kneeling down beside my chair.

"Yes, I need a story. Because my first one just went bye-bye," I said, putting my head back into my hands.

"It can't be that bad. Maybe you just need to pursue it from another angle."

"The only angle I have not pursued would involve breaking into a bank or using my influence with Judge Hoddicks to retrieve information that really wouldn't produce a public-interest story. Except for maybe the *Star.*" I tried to laugh but proved totally unable.

"Well, if it's any consolation, my first story was a total disaster. I was writing about a meeting of the Savannah Chamber of Commerce and called your mother for some background. Then I referred to her in the article as "Vicky Phillips." It passed the editor, but I got a phone call at home at around six a.m. from one irate Vicky Phillips. It was pretty horrendous, and now I think your mother refers to me as 'the young man with deplorable research skills.'" He grinned.

"You know how to make a first impression," I said, looking at him and laughing as well. "If you only knew how much my mother detests being called Vicky. That's like calling Queen Elizabeth 'Beth.' Some things are just forbidden."

"Well, your father must not have minded, because he called me and told me he thought I did a good job for my first story."

"So you've already met my parents."

"Well, I wish I would have just been introduced to them as a normal person, but most around here would say I got what I deserved, and that I was anything but normal," he said, standing back up, as if he had revealed enough of himself.

I stood up too, feeling as if I needed a good stretch, and it wasn't much past nine o'clock. "Well, don't worry, by the time everyone here gets to know me, you and I will be in good company. Shoot, by the time my first article comes out, Vicky will probably be calling *me* a young lady with deplorable research skills. Trust me, she is no respecter of persons." Even as I said it, I wondered if that was true, considering her surprising response to news of my story the previous evening.

"Well, hang in there. It really will get better. You'll figure out your story. You'll write it, and everyone will love it. By what I hear, this town is crazy about you anyway. So, just do whatever it is that you've done for the last fifteen or twenty years, and I'm sure you'll be just fine. I have to get back to work, or whatever it is they have me doing around here. I think I'm covering the school board meeting this morning at ten."

"No more Chamber of Commerce meetings?"

"Oh, no! I got taken off of that beat immediately. Hey, maybe you can cover them," he said with that same sarcastic smirk.

"Or not!" I said with my right eyebrow raised.

"How did you do that?" he asked, trying to raise his own eyebrow and putting his face through hilarious contortions instead.

"Just one of those God-given talents. I have a few, you know. Despite my inability to communicate, there are a few things I can do."

"Well, that is too weird. I'm going to have to see that again sometime."

"I'm sure you will!"

"Well, I'll see you later. Don't work too hard."

"How can I? I still haven't figured out what I'm working on. Maybe I'll just sit here and decide which of my family members has secrets interesting enough to reveal to the world."

"That shouldn't be a hard decision," he said picking up his notepad, pen, and tape recorder. As he walked toward the door, he said, "See you later," and gave me a backward wave as the beautiful sound of flip-flops carried him away.

The latter part of the morning brought a sweet, timid girl named Margaret to my desk to give me an overview of my computer. She showed me all of its ins and outs and rehearsed me on the interoffice linkup and my deadlines for copy. We finished up around noon, and her parting words sent shivers up my spine. "You need to have your first article to Mr. Hicks for editing by two tomorrow. All stories will go to press by five. You're lucky, Savannah; two is his latest editing slot. He always gave it to Gloria. I didn't figure he would give it to you, but he hasn't said to change it." She smiled a sweet and gentle smile. "You'll do great here. Don't let them bother you about your mother, either. She's one of the nicest ladies I've ever met."

"When did you meet my mother?" I asked, afraid to know the answer.

Margaret's shyness evaporated. "Oh, one afternoon, right after I moved here, I decided to ride one of the trolleys and take a tour to learn the history of Savannah."

"A trolley tour, huh?"

"Yeah, little did I know, but I was sitting right by your mother. She was dressed in a pink linen dress, with a big straw hat and matching lipstick, fingernail polish, and pale pink shoes. She was the prettiest thing I ever did see, and I just couldn't quit staring at her. I didn't even hear the tour guide for staring at your mother. Finally, she told me who she was and what she was doing, but she made me promise to keep it a secret."

"I'm sure that wasn't hard."

"Actually, you're the first person I've told. Anyway, I shared a little bit about myself, and she took me to lunch and got me this job. So, any time anyone says anything about her, I just tell them to hush up. I say, 'You don't know anything about Miss Victoria, and you surely shouldn't be talking about things you don't know.' That hushes them for a while, and then, well, you know how people can be. But I just love your mother, and I'm sure I'll love you too."

"Well, thank you, Margaret. You've been a wonderful help, and I'm sure we'll get along great. Is there a set time that I can go to lunch?"

"Oh, people go whenever. Mr. Hicks just wants the work done right and on time. The rest is up to you. Well, have a great day. I hope I haven't talked your ear off," she said, lowering her head as if she was all of a sudden embarrassed at her candor.

"No, it was wonderful. Thank you for sharing the story about my mother."

"She really is a wonderful lady. Now, take care, you hear. And call me for anything," she said as she turned to leave.

"I'm sure I will." And I knew I would.

CHAPTER TWENTY-SIX

My breakfast Coke had settled itself in the most uncomfortable of ways. I headed down the hall to the restrooms and turned right at the first corridor, certain that this was where they were. Yet no friendly stick figures with skirts or slacks beckoned me. By the time I had rounded the fifth corridor, I was welcomed to the world of mayhem. It was the sports department. People were just loud in there. They talked loud and called each other by sport names: "Champ," "Sport," "Superstar." Televisions blared all around with golf, tennis, baseball, even reruns of last year's football games.

Now, far be it from me to be critical, but who in the world wants to watch a sporting event when you already know the outcome? Like me, these sportswriters had their own cubicle world, but theirs was red and black, the color of the Georgia Bulldogs. Seemed only fitting. There were a few black ones thrown in to add a flair of the Falcons. Yet, for all their excitement, they were none too observant of the fact that I was about to have to cross my legs and plop down on the floor right in the midst of them unless someone delivered me. Finally, a friendly soul took note. "You look lost."

"Desperately."

"Where were you headed?"

"The r-e-s-t-r-o-o-m."

"Ooh, that bad huh?"

"Uh-huh."

"Right down the hall, then take the first left."

I nodded in appreciation. As I made my way down the hall, it opened back to the place where I had begun, and there before me was a lovely left turn I should have taken instead of the right one I chose. I kept walking, hoping no one would notice that I had made a complete circle of the first floor.

My cell phone rang as soon as I put the key in the ignition. Mother's work number came up on the caller ID.

"Hello."

"Hello, darling. I hope you're not too busy."

"No. I'm actually just leaving to meet Paige at Clary's for lunch. What are you doing?"

"Oh, I'm just heading out to a meeting and wanted to see how your first day is going."

"Well, wonderful except for the fact that I'm not sure what to write," I said flatly.

"Why not? Have you not heard from Mr. Cummings?"

"Actually, I have. He called me this morning as soon as I sat down at my desk. He let me know in no uncertain terms that I really didn't want to pursue this story any further." I sighed. "I could call Gregory and we could dig a little more, but this whole thing is just out of my league. Part of me thinks I've missed the whole thing, wasted people's time, pursued the wrong story. I don't know. I should probably be writing books. I could ruin Gloria's legacy if I don't do a good job on this first piece. I just wanted it to be so perfect."

"Savannah Phillips, I have to say, I am ashamed of you at this very moment. You have said nothing but negative things since you started this job. You can do this. You will do it, and you will do it well. You will not let some old coot threaten you, and you surely won't embarrass me or Gloria by the article you write. But you will quit this pity party and write your story. Now, don't you say another negative thing, or your very words are going to trap you. Go, kick butt, and take some names."

"I know you did not just say, 'kick butt and take names,'" I said, laughing hysterically.

"Isn't that what they say?"

"I don't know who 'they' are, but you should not be saying 'butt.'"

"Well, whatever you need to be doing, start doing it. You are Savannah Phillips, and you are not a negative child. Now quit with all that doom and gloom and get in there with some heart and some life. Do you hear me?"

"Yes, ma'am, I hear you perfectly."

"Good. Now your mother's glad she called you. You must have needed to hear what I had to say. I love you. Will you be home for dinner?"

"I'm glad you called. I love you too. And yes, I plan to be home for dinner, but I might be late, working on this story."

"Well, I'll wait and have dinner around seven, so you can take your time. Now, chin up, young lady."

"Yes, ma'am, chin up," I repeated, laughing. "I'll see you tonight." And with good-byes, she hung up. Margaret was right. She really was a great lady.

By the time I reached Clary's, I had convinced myself I could write a story. Somehow, the pieces would come together, and my story would be what it needed to be and say what needed to be said. Paige was already inside at our usual spot, had ordered our food, and had a Coke waiting on me.

"Thank you, thank you, thank you," I said once I could breathe. My eyes watered from the powerful intake. "How is it possible you arrived before me?"

"I was bored. How are you, stranger? And where are your real clothes?" she asked.

"I found out that I can bring a Coke to my job, wear flip-flops, and work in the park if I want to, as long as my work gets done. You couldn't ask for anything better than that," I said, taking another drink.

"So how totally awesome is your office?"

"Well, it's not exactly an office."

"But you said it had big windows and overlooked Bay Street."

"Actually it has no windows and overlooks the path to the bathroom."

"You've got to be kidding me. You're taking Gloria's place. Do they think you can just work anywhere? Well, you can't, and you should tell them. So what's it like exactly?"

"It's exactly like a cubicle made of gray Styrofoam."

"Oh my stars. You poor pitiful creature. Are you totally depressed? If I had to look at gray all day, I would be totally depressed."

"I'm more worried about what I'm going to write inside those four pitiful, dreary walls."

She rested her elbows on the table and leaned in not to miss a word. "Right. Your first article. Tell me everything."

I tried to sound totally confident. "Well, I don't know exactly. But it's going to deal with beauty queens, a rigged pageant, and all of that."

"Savannah, I knew that a week ago. What is the story going to say?" she asked, looking disappointed.

"Well, I haven't worked it all out yet. But I will have it completed by tomorrow at two, and you can read it Wednesday morning with the rest of the city," I said with a smile.

"You have nothing, do you?"

"No! That is not true! I have a lot of somethings I've yet to combine into a perfect something. Just trust me. It will all come together. I promise."

"I hope you're right!"

"We must be positive, now. I'm sure I'm right."

Helen brought our BLTs and chocolate shakes, Paige caught me up on her weekend, and I told her all about mine. She had already heard about Emma from her mother, who had spent the majority of the weekend with my mother, shopping and working in their gardens. Paige said that Vicky had told Sheila that I was up to something that she had no idea about, but that she was going to find out as soon as I got home. I told Paige how Mother and I had talked, and then an hour was gone. I was not used to lunch on a time frame. But I felt like I needed to toe the line for at least the first month, then I could make everything more flexible.

Heading back to the paper, it dawned on me that Mr. Hicks had yet to visit my flavorless world. He had probably forgotten that I even started today. But I would let him seek me out. There was no need for me to go looking for trouble today.

I returned to my desk and decided to contact each involved party one more time. My first call was to Mrs. Harvard from Atlanta, hoping some twinge of compassion for me might cause her to reassess her reluctance to tell me everything she knew. I left her a brief but pathetic-sounding message on her answering machine, along with every number I knew, including my mother's cell phone. Who knew when she might break. The next call rang only twice before it was picked up by a determined two-year-old.

"Hewo . . ."

"Hello, is Emma there?"

"Hewo."

"Yes, this is Savannah. Is your mother home?"

"Mama go potty."

"Oh, that's nice. So is your mother in the restroom?"

"Potty, potty."

"OK, I got that part. Is your brother or sister there?"

"Hewo."

Finally, the line went dead. I decided I would try one last time to get Katherine to talk.

"Hello," said the voice on the other end of the phone.

"Hello, Katherine, it's Savannah."

"Well, hello, sweet girl. I haven't seen you in way too long. You must be working up a storm. You started your job today, didn't you?"

"Yes, I sure did."

"So, how are things going?"

"Well, to keep it positive, I believe I'll have something to talk about by tomorrow. No one has been willing to reveal anything much so far, and I'm trying to avoid becoming a sleazy undercover journalist."

"I'm glad you have chosen the path of least resistance."

"*Chose* is a harsh word." I paused, hoping she would ask about the pageant the other night.

"So, how was the pageant the other night?" Perhaps my tide was turning.

"Interesting, to say the least. But my mother is a former Miss Georgia United States of America, so I've had to endure them quite often in the past."

"Yes, I knew she was."

"You did?" I asked, feeling as if a door had been opened.

"Yes, that is pretty common knowledge here. Well, I'm sure you'd better get back to work. Was there anything else?"

"No, I was just calling to say hello," I lied. "I'll see you soon." As soon as I laid the receiver down, the phone rang, almost projecting me out of my seat. I looked at the clock in front of me. Three o'clock. I picked up the phone and this time actually said, "Hello."

"Savannah, hey, it's Marla again. Mr. Hicks just called down and would like to see you in his office."

Oh yeah, just the breather I needed. Carbon-monoxide poisoning. "OK, I'll be right there." I hung up the receiver and headed for the back staircase by the elevator. I needed stairs for this. I needed blood-circulating movement, brain-cell-birthing activity to deal with whatever was about to ensue.

After catching my breath, I passed the empty secretary desk and knocked on the half-open door.

"Come in," came the same gruff voice.

I opened the door, trying not to swing too hard. "Hello, Mr. Hicks," I said, reaching out my hand.

"Well, hello, Savannah," he said, shaking my hand in a professional manner. "Savannah, sit down. Uh, please, have a seat," he said, motioning awkwardly to the seat behind me.

"Oh, thank you," I said, taking a seat and trying to act in total control.

He took his own seat and began slowly. "Savannah, how's your first day?"

"Oh, it's been fine, sir. Everyone has been helpful and friendly. I'm really excited to be here," I said, thankful he'd asked a question I could answer.

His hands began shuffling papers around his desk.

"And how's your first story coming?"

"Wonderfully. My article will be on your desk by two tomorrow." Maybe this would be easy after all.

"So what's your piece about?" he asked as he created stacks of what I assumed were other writers' stories.

I hoped my face didn't reflect panic. "Well, I'm still working out the details. I feel that to discuss it now, knowing that things could change, might just confuse things." I examined my need for a manicure.

Mr. Hicks aligned a stack of papers with a brisk tap against the desktop and cleared his throat. "Savannah."

I looked up at him once more. "Yes, sir?"

"I took a great chance in putting you in this position." He looked me square in the eye and delivered this last statement with perfect clarity. "Now, I need you to deliver."

"I know you did, Mr. Hicks, and I promise you that I will." I stood, breathed deeply, and headed for the door. Feeling his eyes still staring at the back of my head, I turned to add, "And I appreciate the opportunity you have given me."

I got back downstairs and had no more than sat down when Curly Locks spoke. "Well, well, she has returned from the third floor alive."

"Did you doubt that I would?"

"I doubted a lot of things, Ms. Phillips. I doubted a lot of things."

"Then I'm glad I'm here to put your troubled mind at ease. I've got to get to work, if you'll excuse me." And I returned to my inanimate, passionless cubicle. Thankfully, he retreated as well.

Three thirty. I decided I should at least start working on something, anything that could be described as a story. I ignored the IBM and fished my Mac out of my backpack. Mr. Hicks would want a hard copy anyway, so it didn't matter what computer it came from. For the next hour and a half I stared at a blank screen. I tried to write something, but there was nothing to write. About five o'clock, Curly Locks made his way to my desk.

"Are you going to just stare at it or actually write something on it?" he asked, leaning against the partition.

"I'm actually going to cut it off and pray that between tonight and tomorrow a miracle occurs," I said, closing it up to pack and take home. I stood up, grabbed my satchel and purse, and waited to walk out the door with Joshua.

"You really can do it, Ms. Phillips. I'm sure that if you can talk like you do you can surely write well enough for somebody to want to read it. You just got to pull it out from your gut."

"You mean more like pull it out of my . . ."

"Savannah! don't you even," he interrupted.

"*But,* I just got to find something worth pulling out."

"It's in there. You've just got to find it."

"Is your name Victoria?" I asked, stopping to stare at him.

"Excuse me?"

"Never mind. Thanks for everything today. I'll see you tomorrow." He started to round the corner. "Joshua?"

"Yes?"

"Why do you call me Ms. Phillips? It is totally annoying."

"I just think it sounds like you. And as long as it's not Victoria's daughter, I think you should be happy."

I threw my hand up at him in a passing motion and headed to my car. I knew Vicky was holding dinner for me, but all I wanted to do was go home, close myself up in my room, and sit on the floor counting my new shoes.

I pulled up to the side of the house and turned off the car. Through my rearview mirror I saw her—Miss Amber Ruby Sapphire headed out of Clary's, flanked by two rather attractive gentlemen, headed toward my house. They were walking down the sidewalk that would cause them to pass right by my car. Doing the only thing I could think of to avoid detection, I hid. I tried my best to cram my five-foot-six frame all the way under my steering column. The last thing in the world I felt like facing was Miss Tape and Spray. I just didn't think I would survive that, not tonight.

Just when I was about to get my head fully under the dash, there was a knocking on the passenger-side door. Knowing who was there, I didn't rush to get up, but I still couldn't avoid banging my head on my steering column. My disheveled head turned to face the opposite window and there she stood, grinning from ear to ear in a key-lime-pie linen pantsuit that would have made Paige hungry. As soon as her eyes met mine, she waved as if she were ten blocks away trying to get my attention. I just rested my head on my steering column, thinking surely she couldn't be for real.

She opened the passenger door and positioned herself firmly in the seat next to me, having lost her suitors somewhere along the way. I didn't have the strength to raise my head, so I just kept it there, firmly planted on the steering wheel. I knew I looked fright- ful. I didn't care.

"Savannah, you look ghastly. Did you have a bad first day at work?"

I nodded.

"Did you finish your story?"

I shook my head.

"Are you going to be finished in time to do lunch tomorrow?" she asked with a pathetic mousy-sounding voice. I didn't hesitate.

I shook my head again.

"Well, don't you worry. We'll just shoot for Wednesday."

I nodded only to avoid actual conversation.

"You just get your story done and then we'll catch up on everything we need to. I've had such a busy day. I had to handle some things down at the tourism office. Your mother wasn't happy with some of the guides' descriptions of our fair city, so we had to do some rearranging today. Your mother, she runs a tight ship," she said as serious as she could be. "And tonight I have to go help this little girl down on Tybee Island with her talent for the Miss Georgia United States of America Pageant. I'm sure you're wondering why I'm helping another contestant."

I shook my head, but she didn't care.

"She's just pitiful; someone has got to help her. She used to sing. Poor child was tone-deaf. One time she even tried to do sign language with her song. People said she would have scored higher if she would have just signed and nixed the singing altogether. So, I told her she was going to have to change her talent. I tried her on the trumpet, but the sad soul about blew her brains out. I didn't think I would ever find anything she'd actually be good at, but finally I found something."

I allowed my right eyebrow to feign interest.

"I taught her how to play the cymbals. I just put one big cym- bal in one hand and one big cymbal in the other. I gave her a tape of the "Star-Spangled Banner," and on about every fifth beat she clangs those cymbals with more enthusiasm than me getting a new dress. I still haven't told her it really isn't a talent, but poor child couldn't do anything else. I know she won't win, but I had to help her find something. But I've seen worse talent win."

I gave her another brief eyebrow raise.

"Yes, I have, I tell ya. It was my second time in Miss Georgia United States of America. The girl that won played the drums. Now, no lady should play the drums. You have to sit there with your legs spread-eagle and bang around and shake your head until your bun falls down. I don't even know the song she was playing. She clanged so loud on those cymbals and beat that big ol' front drum so hard you couldn't even hear her music. She was horrible. And she won. I sang an aria, fluttered around that stage like a gazelle, and didn't miss a note, including the climax of a C above high C. I have a tape of my song in my bag. Would you like to hear it?" she asked, eyes brighter than an exploding Fourth of July.

I should have stopped her there. But no, ridiculous me gave a nod. I just thought a head shake would be entirely too rude. I have no idea why I even cared. But I did. This was an unfortunate creature in front of me. She had no life. Well, no real life. She lived in a world of sequins, teased hair, and fake everything. And me, stupid me, gave her pity at the wrong time, because my nod took me to a place few should ever have to travel.

Now when someone tells me she has a tape of her song, my first thought is that she is actually singing on tape. Simply having to listen to a taped copy of her talent presentation would be persecution enough, but what actually happened teetered on the horrendous. This was no tape of her singing; this was her *accompaniment*. The actual singing was going to be done live and in person by Miss Savannah United States of America herself.

She hit an opening note that was so loud, my head flew back and embedded itself in the headrest of the driver's seat, where it stayed for the rest of the performance. For the next three and a half minutes, she performed an operatic aria, right there in the front seat of my car. She had motions; she had expressions; she had earth-shattering, only-dogs-could-hear piercing notes. Passersby stared at us. What was I to do? I did the only thing I knew: I waved.

At one point Amber became so animated that I actually believe she forgot she was sitting in an automobile, on the side of the road, *in front of someone's home.* I thought those few minutes would last an eternity. I thought I would never hear the final note. And when it finally came, I thought for sure every window in my car was going to shatter. I had just been presented an entire talent presentation. When she finished, I simply remained in my impacted, strained-neck, totally frazzled position and prayed for rescue.

"Now, can you imagine that being beaten by a drummer? She won and I left with some money and soon-to-be-dead flowers. The whole thing's rigged, I tell you. Because honey, the day I lose to a bong-bong player, you can bet your sweet rose-smelling britches that pageant is rigged."

With those words I should have jumped. I should have tackled that moment like Ellis Johnson tackles Steve McNair, but suddenly it just didn't seem to matter. The entire thing rested on the ridicu-lous. Grown women prancing around a stage, vying for the atten-tion of five people, each trying to get the judges to view her as better than the one before. Grown women singing their talent numbers in the cars of virtual strangers. What did it matter? Why had I bothered with something so preposterous? Even I, for one fleeting moment, wondered if Mr. Cummings's words weren't true. Maybe it really didn't matter. Miss Amber Topaz didn't get it. So, maybe none of it really mattered. Maybe this whole thing had been a waste of time.

"Well, toodleoo, Miss Savannah. I'll see you tomorrow, and we'll figure out what we're going to do for lunch on Wednesday. You take care. You might need to get some major rest. You look a little stressed." And with that she closed the door and skipped her happy little self on down the street and out of sight.

I waited until she was completely gone to extricate my head from the headrest. It was now close to six, and I went promptly into the house and up to my bedroom. I laid myself across the bed.

When I woke up, the clock beside me read one a.m.

I decided to go downstairs and get a bowl of cereal. There was a note on the kitchen counter from my mother.

Savannah, I was going to wake you for dinner, but you looked exhausted. I hope your day went OK, and just remember that you were created for this job. I love you, Mother.

I still wasn't sure why she was so happy for me and this job, but at this moment I was too hungry to care. I poured a bowl of Cocoa Pebbles, walked over to the sofa, and turned on the TV. Tan Beautiful was being advertised. It is amazing how quickly those infomercials can snare you in their tangled web. Before I knew it, I had ordered two bottles with rush delivery.

When I finally returned to bed, I lay there staring at the ceiling and began to think of the stars of my beauty pageant story, and of how different each woman was: Victoria, so together; Emma, so traumatized; Katherine, so over that stage of her life. Very different women all uniquely touched by the same bizarre experience.

I bolted up in bed. That was it. My story wasn't so much about the pageants as much as it was about the people *in* the pageants. The thoughts began to come so fast and furious that by the time I fell asleep, the whole story was neatly written in my head.

CHAPTER TWENTY-SEVEN

I headed downstairs around seven forty-five. Mother had prepared my favorite breakfast: chocolate gravy and biscuits. Trust me on this one. It is absolutely the best stuff I have ever put in my mouth. She makes homemade biscuits, then prepares a chocolate gravy, similar to what you would use as icing for a cake, but not quite as thick.

It is because of Vicky's culinary skill that we even supported her decision to write a cookbook. She wanted to compete with her good friend Paula Deen, who owns The Lady & Sons, one of the best restaurants in town. Paula has her own cookbooks and her own show on the Food Network, which is perfectly charming and perfectly Savannah. One night after dinner, we were going on about what a fabulous cook my mother is, and she decided that since we loved her cooking so much, maybe she should write a cookbook. We all agreed, thinking it would keep her out of our business for a while. Well, it did, and the result is *Dining with Victoria*. We tried to get her to call it *Victoria's Vittles,* but she didn't think that sounded Martha Stewart enough. I know in the back of her mind she is trying to build her own

Martha Stewart conglomerate of the South. Well, maybe not so much anymore.

The cover picture has her standing in our kitchen holding up one of her silver platters with pork tenderloin, southern mashed potatoes, and green beans. It was pre-hair-fallout, when the color was still red. She was wearing a beautiful yellow suit, accessorized to perfection. She did look stunning. But now that she's chestnut, she wants to take a new cover picture. For that reason alone, it will probably never be published. If she took a new picture she'd have another hairstyle by the time the book came out anyway. It would be a cruel and vicious cycle for some local photographer, pity the soul.

And trust me, we will never mention the word *television*.

"Thank you for not waking me up last night; I was exhausted," I said, taking a plate from the counter.

Mother turned around at the sound of my voice. "Oh, I could tell that you were exhausted. I'm sorry things haven't turned out like you planned," she said, opening the refrigerator and pouring me a glass of milk. She walked over and pulled out the chair beside me. "When is your story due?"

I took a drink of milk before responding. "I must deliver my copy into Mr. Hicks's hands by two. So I have from now until then to create a story."

"Well, you need to remember that these are people, Savannah, not characters. You're writing truth, not fiction."

Now, where did that come from? I didn't have time to investigate. "Speaking of characters, I saw the lovely character creation of your own yesterday."

"Savannah Phillips, bite your tongue. I did not create that child. She is a creation of . . . I'm not sure what yet. She cracks me up, though, and I think she stands a great shot at becoming Miss Georgia United States of America this year."

"Don't you think she would have won by now if she could have?"

"I think there's a timing for everything in life, Savannah. Sometimes we think things should happen at a certain time, in a certain way, but there is a master plan. So we brush ourselves off and learn from our mistakes, and try not to make the same ones again, all the while doing what we feel it is we've been called to do."

"So at what point is it fair to ask yourself if maybe, just maybe, you aren't following the master plan? I mean, if I had tried to write three different books and none of them ever got published, I would start to wonder if that was what I was supposed to do."

Victoria smiled at me in the way she does when she is about to say something truly profound. "Yes, and you should. But only you can figure that out for yourself. What if all of those books that failed gave you the idea for a fourth book, the one that gets published? Then you could reasonably say each rejection paved the way to success. See, Savannah, you have to be careful not to put destiny into a mold. Each life has its own."

Then back to the world of Mary Kay we went. "Anyway, Amber really does do a wonderful job. She has the perfect personality for tourism director and she's delicate with the adjustments that have to be made over there quite often."

"Yeah, she told me about your adjustments. You need to leave those poor people alone, Mother. You have them so nervous! One day you're going to be on the back of a trolley and they're going to spot you and send that trolley right into the statue of General Oglethorpe. It's not right what you put those people through."

"Well, you don't need to worry about what I do in this city. I have it perfectly under control," Vicky said, standing up and pretending to put away dishes.

"Under control? Wait a minute. Aren't you the one who climbed into the horse-drawn carriage and screamed so loud when a wasp flew up her dress that the poor horse had to be sedated before they could hook him up to a carriage again? That's just wrong, Mother."

"Is that all you remember about me? Can you not recall sometimes the multitude of good I do around here?" She pretended to act all pouty, but I could tell she got a kick out of the memory too.

I wiped my mouth and took my plate over to the sink where she was. "Trust me, I know all of the wonderful things you do, and taking care of us is the most wonderful of all. Especially this," I said pointing to the empty plate in front of me. "I've got to go. I'll remember what you said." I kissed her on the cheek and headed out the door. "I love you," I called out on the way.

"I love you too, darling," I heard from a distance.

"Well, I guess you're ready to write that story?"

"Ready as I'll ever be."

Dad paused for a moment, then closed the top of the Coke machine and stepped aside to let me have my fill. He leaned against the counter, and by the look in his eyes, I knew he had something to say.

"You can say whatever it is you're wanting to say, Dad. Mother had her turn; feel free to take yours."

"You know you can tell me anything, Savannah. In fact, until now, you have always told me everything. When you were little, you actually told me more than I really wanted to know, from every stubbed toe to broken heart to bad prom dress. So why have you had trouble letting me in on this one?"

"What do you mean?"

"Telling me what this story is about. Your mother won't even tell me anything, and that woman is incapable of keeping a secret. But apparently she feels strongly that it should come from you," he said with an expression I'm not quite sure I had ever seen on his face before.

It wasn't a look of hurt so much as it was of perplexity. I could see in his eyes; he was wondering if the time to let me go had come yet again. I had slipped from his arms to the hairy halls of preschool; I had kissed him good-bye and climbed into the car with Grant for my first real date; I had closed my college dorm-room door behind him when he left me there to enter the world of adulthood. But I had never closed the door to our conversations.

I had always told him everything. But today, Vicky knew something he didn't. The poor man had to be suffering.

I hadn't realized until that moment that I was changing. Not everything would be known to my parents anymore. Not every detail of my life would be disclosed, because there's no need, really, to expose parents to unnecessary knowledge. Who wants her parents to carry her hurt when she knows she will recover, while they might not? Today was our shifting. It had happened without fanfare or even true awareness. I had become the protective parent; he had become the curious child.

I smiled at the concern in his eyes. "You know, when I was little you wouldn't let me watch something on TV because you didn't want it to scare me."

"That's because you were scared of your shadow."

"Still am. Then there were also the times when someone would be in here early in the morning talking about something, and you would quiet them because you didn't want me to hear."

"You were very nosy."

"Still am. But even though I didn't understand, I knew it was for my own good. I guess this is one of those times. But this time I've been protecting you. Not from anything horrible or sordid," I said quickly when his look of concern grew exponentially.

"See, I've been trying to protect you from the need to protect her. So, before you ask, just know, I will do nothing to hurt her, harm her, or cause her pain. As for us, maybe the tide has turned. But nothing will ever change the way I feel about you," I said, encasing him in a bear hug. Then I whispered in his ear, "I'm growing up, Dad. I won't be able to tell you everything anymore. But I'm sure I'll still tell you far more than you'll ever want to know." He held on a little tighter than he had in years. When he let go, his face registered that he understood.

"Are you ready for another day at work?"

"No."

"Are you ready for your story?"

"No."

He paused for a moment, not sure if he should ask any more questions, so he settled for the one he already knew the answer to. "Would you like another Coke?"

"Yes!" I said. He took the glass from my hand and filled it up. He looked at the clock, which read 8:15.

"Take this Coke. Grab a banana off of the counter if you're hungry. Get in your car, gather your thoughts, and go to work. And when you are there, take yourself, your very talented self, go to your office, and write an article like this city has never read," he said, his eyes just hinting at tears. "Do that, Savannah, and this transition will have been worth it."

I had spent my life knowing that my father was the finest of men. But there are encounters in life that take things we've known forever in our heads and channel them into the chambers of our hearts. I call it the "second look" moment. Most people stop at first looks, never taking a second glance to really see what has transpired in an experience.

Today, my father became a person, a person to discover, a person to cherish. In that moment my father became Jake, not just Dad. In my car, I gathered myself and wiped away the tears that had begun to flow down my face. I didn't know what awaited me today, but the unfolding of a story could never match what had just developed in the last few moments of my life.

"Hey, you must be Marla. I'm Savannah Phillips," I said, holding out my hand to the sweet face smiling behind the receptionist's desk.

"Well, Savannah Phillips," she said, refusing my hand and proceeding to get up and walk around her desk to face me. "I feel like I know you," she said, grabbing me in a bear hug. "You are just the cutest thing I've ever seen. We're so glad you're here. Mr. Hicks is a tad concerned, but we're thrilled to have Victoria Phillips's very own daughter working right here among us," she said. "Now, I'll just be right here, behind my little desk. I'm only a phone call away. So you just ring-a-ding me if you need anything," she said, returning to her place.

"Thank you. I think I'm good for now. But if I need you, I'll be sure to call. Oh, but would you mind holding my calls today, Marla? This is my first story, and I want to make sure I make it good."

"Not at all, dear. You just go write this paper one amazing story."

"Thank you. I'll do my best." When I arrived at my new home away from home, I pulled a stack of books from my bedroom library out of my backpack. A girl needed to have something inside this monotone mausoleum to add a little color, and nothing added color like books. I stood them up neatly and made a mental note to acquire some bookends. Curly Locks flip-flopped in during my designing moment. I could tell he wanted to have a conversation, but I stopped him before he started. "Don't. I've got too much work to do. I've got a story due by two, and it's got to be perfect," I said, holding out my hand and never looking in his direction.

"Your computer isn't even on."

I reached down and pushed a button. "It is now." He disappeared for the rest of the morning.

And for the rest of the morning, I shut myself off from the world. I typed, retyped, wiped out, started over, and all but turned the thing inside out and upside down until my first story was fully complete.

When two o'clock came, it was finished—a human-interest story that would set Savannah on its ears. When the last page had printed, I grabbed my "copy," as they call it in the newspaper world, put it in a folder marked "Savannah Phillips," and headed to the third floor.

After only one wrong turn, which put me in a broom closet, I arrived in the proper place, but Mr. Hicks was nowhere to be found. His secretary wasn't there either. For a fleeting moment I wondered if Mr. Hicks actually had a secretary. After much reflection, I set my folder on his desk and walked out. I had done my job. Mr. Hicks would now have to do his.

"Where have you been? Taking attendance in traffic court?" I asked, refusing to look up as Curly Locks appeared.

He pulled his uninvited chair up to my desk. "You are a regular comedian. No, Ms. Phillips, I am capable of more than paint by numbers. So. How do you feel now that your first work of art is in Mr. Hicks's hands?"

"I feel good, I think." I was surprised that I felt nervous. "We'll know tomorrow, won't we?"

"Yes, my dear, we sure will. Your critics will be silenced, I'm sure."

"Critics, I have critics?" I asked, thinking he was just trying to get me to react and hating myself that I was.

"Well, maybe skeptics is a better word."

"Well, they've been mighty silent."

"To you, yes."

"But not to you?"

He got up from his chair to return to his desk. "Let's just say, tomorrow they'll be silenced."

Poor Marla had been holding my calls since morning, so I went to her desk to thank her and see if I had any messages. She greeted me with a handful of pink While You Were Out notices. There were seven in all, each one from Miss Amber Topaz Cubic Zirconia Rhinestone Childers. She just wanted to make sure that we connected today to make plans for lunch tomorrow.

"She's a persistent little thing, Savannah," Marla said with a furrowed brow. "Just a persistent little thing."

"Yes, she is, dear Marla. I sure appreciate your intervention."

"Savannah, this switchboard is my domain. What I say gets through, gets through. And what I desire to hold, I will hold. What I say gets lost, well, it gets lost. And may I say, it has been my

241

pleasure to get Miss Amber lost. Actually, I've lost her on a couple of occasions in the *last fifteen minutes!*" she said, trying to control herself.

"I'm really sorry."

"Don't you be sorry, Savannah. I'll protect you." With those words the phone rang and she returned to her seat. As I walked away, I heard, "Listen here, young lady. Miss Savannah is taking a lunch break. She needs her nutrition and cannot be bothered. And you have tied up my switchboard long enough. Now, I don't want to hear from you one more time today. Do you understand me?" I couldn't help but laugh all the way back to my Styrofoam paradise.

Mr. Hicks had not called me to his office by the time five o'clock arrived. That meant that either he was using my story or he was in desperate search of a replacement. I could only hope for the former.

The pink card underneath my windshield wiper was embossed with the words *Amber Topaz Childers, Miss Savannah United States of America.* I was being stalked by a crazed former beauty queen. Surely there were laws against women with big hair stalking women who were just trying to do an honest day's work. The note read, "Sorry I haven't been able to reach you today, but the lady at the switchboard is an absolute irritant. I'll just swing by tonight and we can make our lunch plans. Love ya, Amber." I made mental note to search out a good therapist. I might need one sooner than later. Just two weeks ago I was a healthy young woman. Now it seemed as though my mind was slowly becoming debilitated by mind-warping tales of marimba players and magicians—or was it ventriloquists? See, it was already happening.

I drove home, desperate to find something to do other than go home. I called Paige and asked if she wanted to go to a movie and grab some dinner. She was a go, so I risked a quick stop at home.

When I walked through the door, I could smell dinner. I knew Vicky would be disappointed that I wasn't staying, but she would eventually get used to this new rhythm of my life. When I walked into the kitchen, she was standing in front of the sink rinsing a dish, and Dad was behind her with his arms wrapped around her waist, saying something in her ear that had her giggling.

Dad noticed me first. "Hey, sweet girl," he said, coming over to give me a hug. My mother turned around too.

"Well, hey, darling," she said, walking to the stove to remove what smelled like green beans.

"Hey!" I said and hugged Dad back.

Dad went over to the table, pulled out a chair, then sat down in the one across from it. "Savannah, sit down and tell us what happened today. We want to know all about your story."

I sat down and went over the same thing that I had determined to tell everyone. "Well, you'll be glad to know I actually wrote one."

"Well, we thank the Lord for that," Dad said, laughing and taking a drink of his iced tea.

I stood up and walked over to survey what good food I might be missing. "But I really want you to wait and read it in the morning. That way everyone can have an objective reaction."

"Well, Savannah," Dad said, "we look forward to reading it in the morning then."

"And, Mother, I hope it's no big deal, but I really need a mental breather tonight, so Paige and I are going to go see a movie and grab a bite to eat."

She hid her disappointment, gave me a kiss on the cheek, and told me to have a good time.

Then I remembered I had one item of undone business. "Mother, by the way, your happy little director of tourism will be stopping by. Please let her know that I have been busy and will meet her for lunch tomorrow at The Lady & Sons at noon."

That night as I was leaving Paige's apartment, I noticed a small painting lying next to the door.

"When did you do that?"

"The other day. I was just trying something different."

"I love it. The color is so vibrant and bold."

"What would you expect?"

"Nothing less from you."

"Do you want it?"

"I can't take it."

"Yes, you can. Consider it a congratulations gift for your new job."

I scooped it up in my arms before she had any second thoughts. "OK. That sounds good. You hadn't gotten me anything yet anyway."

Home was wonderfully quiet. In less than ten minutes my head was on my pillow. My mind tried to run wild with all of the what-ifs that the morning could bring. But I put a halt to that and simply said a prayer of thankfulness that I had been able to write anything at all. Sleep came quickly, and it was the sweetest sleep I had known in quite a while.

CHAPTER TWENTY-EIGHT

For an instant, I forgot that today was the day that my first article would appear in the paper. But then I was fully awake. Today was the day that Savannah would realize that I was or wasn't a human-interest writer, was or wasn't a suitable replacement for Gloria, was or wasn't any kind of writer at all.

I jumped up, put on some jogging clothes, brushed my teeth, and ran downstairs. I grabbed the leash and attached Duke to it, grabbed the newspaper from the iron console, and didn't stop running until I reached a bench on the perimeter of the park's east side. I sat down and slipped Duke's leash over the arm of the bench so he wouldn't drag both of us after some fair lab. Opening the paper directly to the local section, there on the front page was my picture with my name under it: Savannah Phillips.

I was shaking so badly, I almost didn't think I was going to be able to read it. I tried to breathe in about six or seven times and refocus my eyes, but they were getting blurred from sudden light-headedness. I leaned back against the bench and enjoyed the fact that at least Mr. Hicks liked some of it. I mean after all, my picture was there, so he had to have kept at least part of it. Sure, maybe he had edited it to smithereens, but if he used my picture, he at least had to have used my premise.

"Just read the story already, Savannah!" I said out loud. I looked down and began to read the product of my so-called investigation.

I have lived most of my life never quite understanding beauty pageants. Not that there is anything wrong with them; there just doesn't seem to be anything necessary in them. They don't solve world hunger; they don't change the political climate; they don't even do much to affect a city. But I have recently come to realize that no institution truly changes any of these things either. Hunger organizations don't feed world hunger; people giving of their time, money, and energy do. The government doesn't change the landscape of this nation; people who care about issues, who serve in blood banks and listen to the needs of the elderly in small corner cafés and play with children and repair dilapidated playgrounds, they do. And cities don't change themselves, but people who love them, who give of their time and care about every detail from the trolley tour to the airport lobby, who build corner bookstores and open up coffee shops, and who raise the next generation to love their neighbor, they do.

So, as unnecessary as beauty pageants may seem, by this standard everything is unnecessary. What makes anything of value are the people who are a part of it. And yes, believe it or not, countless women who enter beauty pageants every year are some of the most productive, viable, and life-giving forces behind the very causes that matter most to each of us.

The time I have spent considering the relative value of beauty pageants has proven enlightening. I will spare you the many horror stories I have been forced to endure over recent days: tales of manufactured cleavage, dresses worn backward, and cymbal concertos. No, today I want to suggest that even though beauty pageants hardly fortify the fiber of a nation, they can shatter the life of an individual. And when a life is so shattered because of pride or greed, when it is thrown off its destined course, the fiber of a nation will ultimately be weakened.

Consider the story of one of the most beautiful women Savannah has ever seen. Today, her beauty is gone. Her glory is such a distant memory that I have wondered if even she recalls it.

Savannah's jewel once won every pageant, every homecoming, and every heart. Her inner spirit was as beautiful as her physical self. I know, because on one of my more desperate days at the tender age of thirteen, I was the unexpected recipient of her compassion and kindness. But as I stood at her door just days ago and stared at her dirty T-shirt and uncombed hair, as I witnessed her grim outlook on life, I didn't see how this could be the same person I once knew.

She had a dream too. A dream to be Miss Georgia United States of America. But when that dream was taken from her, the loss was too much to bear.

She came home, married a man who abused her, had four children, and has spent her life since forging a dreamless existence. I went to her home the other day, and as I wiped old Cheerios from the sofa, I tried to force her to see herself as she was, remind her of who she had once been. I wasn't eloquent. Frankly, I wasn't really even nice. But I was honest.

After I left her home, my anger at the people who had done this to her began to grow, so I went searching.

And what I uncovered was an age-old story of greed, deceit, and lies, all in the name of money.

Some of you may blame her for allowing such a "petty" loss to destroy her own life. But I would challenge all of us to consider our power to affect others' destinies. When we are entrusted with the life of another—to direct or guide or lead or aid—and we deem anything greater than that life, then we have devalued the greatest treasure any of us could ever have the privilege to bear.

If I could give Savannah's one-time reigning beauty anything, I would restore her ability to dream. I would wrap up a crown, place it on her head, and assure her she is a princess. I would wash her face and comb her hair and try to help her remember her true beauty. But what's done is done. We can't go back. The choices we make to affect people's lives are done. We can alter the future, but the path is forever littered with reminders of past losses.

I have much more to say, but today, I will urge you to nurture the personal destinies that fall within your realm of influence. Speak life into them, and help them find their wings. Because the life of a city is determined by the destiny and character of its individuals.

Until Friday,
Savannah Phillips

I sat back and realized I'd been holding my breath. I couldn't believe it. Mr. Hicks had edited me more lightly than I could have hoped. Not only was my story intact, but most of the words were mine too. I grabbed Duke, kissed him square on his nose, grabbed his leash, and took off toward home.

I took the first eight steps of the staircase by twos. "Vanni, if that's you, Mom wanted me to tell you that Amber is going to meet you at The Lady & Sons at noon," Thomas said sleepily. I stopped dead in my tracks, took a breath, and continued my climb by twos. Not even Amber would be able to ruin this day.

I showered and dressed in a giddy mood. And I don't do giddy. I sang every Barry Manilow song I knew. I danced around my bedroom like a woman unleashed. I swung on bedposts, tap-danced on the tile floor in my bathroom, even struck up a chorus of "I Write the Songs." I've never written a song in my life, but by George, I wrote an article. And it was a good article.

I flitted to the closet and picked out something extremely "out of control." I picked out a dress. Then I actually put it on. A black linen dress, but it was a dress nonetheless. I don't know what came over me, but something did. And then I picked out a pair of Kate Spade shoes in black, which I had come to adore, that still flipped when I walked, but weren't technically flip-flops.

"Somebody stop me!" I screamed at the mirrors that covered my sliding closet doors. Then I swirled around and about whipped myself too hard again, but this time I recovered with nothing more than disheveled hair freed from a ponytail holder. Hold on, Hannah. Savannah has let loose and traded her pulled-back do for a straightened mane of dark hair. I had forgotten how long my hair had become. I ran my hands through it, wondering if I could handle an entire day with this flopping around my head.

Well, today anything was possible. With one last gander at myself in the mirror, I took off down the stairs.

The seventh step from the top, my flip-flop-clad feet slid out from under me. The rest of the trip down was endured by my backside, though I tried to stop myself with one hand on the railing and the other descending the stairs beside me. I made such a commotion coming down that I thought surely the neighborhood would come in to check on me. Sitting on the floor in sheer agony, hoping for someone to kiss my boo-boo, it occurred to me that no

one in the world would be hailing my latest achievement if they
had witnessed my ungraceful fall.

The silence of an absent audience encouraged me to gather my
dignity and my bruised behind. I headed out the door and shouted
for all the world to hear, "Miss Grace has left the building."

CHAPTER TWENTY-NINE

In the mouth of the foolish lies one's arrogance, but the lips of the sensible will preserve them." No sooner had I read the words on Dad's board than Judge Hoddicks walked over, grabbed me by both arms, and pulled me to him in a bear hug. I couldn't breathe well, but at moments like this, you simply endure.

"Betty, I can't tell you how wonderful I thought your article was. I laughed. I . . . well, I didn't cry, but I thought about it. I just thought it was wonderful. I'll be honest: I loved Gloria. I wasn't sure you could pull it off, but you did. In fact, you more than pulled it off; you nailed it, baby. Caused me to think about how I treat those ol' ornery criminals. I can't wait until Friday. I cannot wait until Friday."

I waited for more congratulations, but none came. Everyone seemed rather preoccupied with customers and all. Even Duke didn't offer a lick, a wag of the tail, or a would-you-take-me-to-do-my-business look. I headed into the back to get a Coke and pulled Dad by the arm along with me. "OK. So tell me, what did you think?"

"I got up early to read the paper without interruption, but it was gone and so were you and Duke." I slapped my forehead and groaned. "I heard your mother get up earlier, around five, and I wanted her to have time to digest whatever you had written by herself."

"She read it already?" I asked wide-eyed, anticipating some dramatic retelling of every word and sigh and tear.

"Yes, she read it."

"Well, what did she say?"

"Nothing."

I considered this. "Well, did you know I was doing something about the pageant?" I finally asked, nudging his arm.

"That didn't take an Einstein, Savannah. An investigative journalist you may be; a subtle one you are not." That made us both laugh. "So, I got ready, told Thomas to bring Duke on his way to the courthouse, and sat here with a cup of coffee and the morning paper. I wasn't sure what you would say, Savannah," he said, his eyes more intense than I had seen them in years. "I knew you wouldn't hurt your mother, but I also knew that you wanted a story that would declare your legitimacy. I wasn't quite sure how you could protect one and accomplish the other." He paused for a moment. "And to be honest, I'm not so sure you did."

Every ounce of my energy left. I put my drink down and tried to speak. "What . . . what do you mean? I didn't say anything bad about Mother. I didn't even talk about her."

"This isn't about your mother, Savannah. This is about Emma."

"I didn't say anything untrue about her. I didn't even use her name."

"No, maybe not technically, but you described her according to your opinion. Do you think anyone doesn't know who you were talking about? And did she ever tell you she wanted to be talked about? Or that she wanted her life told in the paper? Or that she even cared if she had lost the pageant at all?"

I stood there trying to get my taxed brain to register his barrage of questions. I had been through so much. It had been a long week. I had just fallen down the stairs, for goodness' sake.

"I thought I would be helping her. Trying to find out who did this to her and why. Putting a face to her pain."

"Savannah, you needed to know that she wanted a face to her pain. Now the only face she might see when remembering her pain is you."

That was so far from my intent that I hardly knew what to say. "Do you really think this will hurt her? I tried not to even make it about her."

"But it was, Savannah. The message behind the whole thing was Emma, or a bunch of Emmas. Or not becoming an Emma. Can you imagine someone writing about you, about how horrible your life would be if you became a Savannah?" He stopped, realizing that his words were cutting me to the core.

"But I didn't mean to hurt anyone. I would never have intentionally hurt her," I said, feeling the sting of tears forming in my eyes. "I wouldn't knowingly hurt anyone," I said, letting the tears fall freely now.

"I know you wouldn't," he said, wrapping me in his arms. "But I believe you probably did today. And you're going to have to make it right."

Dad released me and headed toward the front of the store, but stopped to add, "I love you, Savannah. I wouldn't hurt you for the world either. But you still have things to learn. You still have wisdom left to gain. And the best place to begin is in learning to guard your words. They are now more powerful than I believe you know."

I made my way to my desk undetected. Who knew how many other people would feel like my father? About the time I got to my seat, two girls I had seen before but never met walked by my desk giggling and whispering until they spotted me. I smiled, but they didn't. In fact, their faces went pretty much stone cold, expressionless. Not angry or malicious, just indifferent. Those two would probably take effort. I had no energy for effort today.

I wanted to hang my new picture. I had picked the perfect place, just to the left of my books on the top shelf. That way, anytime I needed a pick-me-up, I could just look up and catch a glimpse of its vibrant tones. But why hang it up when I would surely be fired before the day's end? I left Paige's artwork leaning against the bookcase and spent the morning trying to look busy, while Friday loomed like a stalker with pink stationery. If anyone felt half as much concern as my father, the only thing left to write was a formal apology to the city, Emma, Ichabod over the door, and resign myself to becoming a tour guide.

To my great relief, Joshua never appeared. Marla called me around nine thirty to tell me she had just "loved every little word" I had written on those pages. "It was like a painter had created a masterpiece." Then, she added, "But the lady who's headed back to you now, well, she might not feel quite the same way."

Emma, in fine form for a Spray and Wash commercial, rounded the corner while I still held the receiver in my hand.

"I can't believe you," she hissed, waving her newspaper in my face. I stood up to at least be able to block any blows she might be contemplating. "How could you?"

"Emma, I know. It was kind of insensitive . . ."

"*Kind of* insensitive? Who do you think you are?"

"Ooh, whoa doggies. Let's go outside and talk. We don't need to bring the whole office into this."

"Are you kidding me? You brought the *entire city* into this! I just want to know, Miss Priss, who died and made you judge and jury? When did you decide that I needed you to take me up as your cause?"

"Well, I was trying to—"

"*I'm not a cause,* Savannah; I'm a person. A person you single-handedly turned into a complete and utter laughingstock," she said. Every blood vessel in her face pulsed beneath her pale skin.

I caught her eyes. At once I saw both anger and hurt. Dad's revelation became my own. "Emma, you're right. I'm so sorry. I'll retract everything on Friday."

"Your retraction won't help, Savannah. It's done. It's all done. You can't undo it. You said it yourself, with your own words, in your own little paper. 'The choices you make to affect people's lives are done,'" she mimicked. "'You can alter the future, but the path is forever marked with reminders of past losses,'" she said, throwing the newspaper at my feet.

The sound startled me. "I said all that?"

"Yes, you said all that. Well, take a close look at what you've accomplished. Not only have you embarrassed me, but my children, Savannah. My children now get to go to school and listen to what other children say about their mother. You think about that, Savannah. Even if you had no thought about how this might affect me, I would have hoped you cared more about my children." And with those words, she turned her greased locks around and left me to wallow in my own misery.

"Long day?" Curly Locks appeared from nowhere, picking up the scattered paper and throwing it away.

"You don't know. And I don't want to hear your comments about my article," I said, flopping to my chair and laying my head on my desk.

I could feel him kneel down beside me. "Well, it wasn't all bad. I mean it was bad, but not all bad."

"Any bad negates any good," I said, starting to cry.

"Not all the good."

"Yes, any good."

"At least she didn't hit you."

I tried to stifle my laugh, but I couldn't. I sat up.

"Ooh, Ms. Phillips needs a tissue."

"Sorry," I said, reaching across my desk for a tissue. I blew hard and wiped off my face. "I didn't realize I would hurt her. What was I thinking? I am a complete idiot."

"A complete idiot. That's harsh. Partial idiot, certainly. But I'm not sure what you were thinking either. I mean, what were you thinking?"

"I don't want to have this conversation with you. I've had a long morning, and I'm tired, and I really can't stay here anymore," I said matter-of-factly.

"What? Are you going to quit after your first article?"

"I have no choice. You heard what I did to her. Have mercy! I have affected her children! I should have stuck to fiction." I stood up, feeling the anger rise. "I was supposed to write books, to make people laugh and smile. To tell stories of crazy people that weren't real. That way, at the end of the day, no one would be hurt or angry or remove their children from my path when I walk by. This is all my mother's fault."

"Obviously, you have deeply rooted, unresolved issues with your mother."

"Oh, that's good, Sherlock. Do you charge for your therapeutic services?"

"You couldn't afford me."

"Well then it's a good thing I don't need you." I turned on my heels and headed to the elevator. "I don't need counseling. I know what I have to do."

"You may know what you have to do, but you definitely need counseling. And if you want my opinion, you're making a mistake. And this isn't about your mother." I threw my hands over my ears and continued in forward motion, singing "la, la, la."

Of course, there was no secretary at Mr. Hicks's office. I knocked on his half-open door and waited for him to allow me to enter.

"Come in, Ms. Phillips."

"Mr. Hicks, I just wanted to let you know that I'll be taking my things and leaving today. I know I've done nothing but desecrate Gloria's good name, and I won't put you through any further embarrassment or shame by having my name associated with your paper. I'll write a brief apology for Friday and you don't have to worry about paying me."

"Oh, really."

"Yes, really, and truth be known, I should probably give you money for rent space. So, anyway, thank you for the opportunity. I'm sorry I wasn't capable of more, but I appreciate your taking a risk on me at all. Good luck, Mr. Hicks. I hope you find someone worthy to take Gloria's place." I began my exit.

"I did find someone worthy to take Gloria's place," he said, stopping me in my tracks. "And if she would learn to give other people a chance to speak before she makes such hasty exits, she might learn a thing or two along the way." He stood and pointed to a chair. "Sit."

He sat on the edge of his desk, arms folded neatly across his belly. I took the seat across from him. "You're a good writer, Savannah. You tell a story. You teach us lessons. You even taught me a lesson. You challenged me to see the potential in the people who work for me. It is precisely because of what you wrote in that article, Savannah, that I'm not letting you walk out that door and go home."

"Because of what I wrote?"

"Yes, when I first read your piece, I was furious at your carelessness. The things you said about Emma were downright indefensible."

"Yes, they were."

"They may have been true, but not your truth to put into print. But the other things you said made me realize you are one of those people within my realm of influence. You are one that needs to be guided and grown and matured. I'm here to help you do that. And today, you've learned the lesson you needed to learn."

"Remind me again of what that is."

"You've learned you have much to learn. That will make you from this day forward a better writer than you ever dreamed of being. You won't leave. Instead, you'll go down there and write an article for Friday—better, wiser, and more powerful than the one you wrote today. Now go. And I don't want to see you again until you deliver me your article tomorrow afternoon."

"Thank you," I said, swallowing my tears. "Thank you. You're a good man, Mr. Hicks. I'll see you tomorrow."

The clock on my desk said noon. The Lady & Sons was waiting. I would go. But only after I hung up my picture.

CHAPTER THIRTY

It wasn't hard to locate my lunch companion. She was the one in the back, standing on her tiptoes, wearing a bright purple pantsuit with lipstick that matched her suit perfectly. "Yoo-hoo! Savannah! I'm over here." I sighed and made a point of avoiding eye contact with anyone. Today of all days, I didn't want the Purple People Eater yelling my name across a crowded restaurant.

I tried to sit Amber down with the wave of my hand, but she continued making a spectacle until I took my seat across from her.

"Savannah Phillips," she started, "I had no idea in this world that you were going to write an article on beauty pageants. I mean, you should have interviewed me. I could have told you a thousand stories," she began in her animated way, not stopping to breathe. "I mean, Savannah, I have competed in more pageants than most women this side of Decatur." And then she laughed a ludicrous laugh; a laugh that totally appreciated the fact that she probably *had* competed in more pageants than the sum total of all the women I know.

To my inexpressible relief, the waitress came quickly. I ordered Coke and asked her to keep them coming. I also ordered the baked spaghetti, voted the best in the South by *Fodor* magazine, even though I hardly had the appetite for it. Amber ordered a salad with no dressing but, true to her word, caved in and had sweet tea. "This is the only place I break down to have sweet tea. But I just can't help it," she said, as if this life necessity needed justification.

I stared at her in pity. This poor child was probably going to live her entire life eating less than a toy poodle. Chatty Cathy started up again, reminding me that the only pleasure in lunch with her was knowing I could eat without ever having to say a word.

"Savannah, I didn't realize everything Emma has been through. That child just sounds plumb pitiful."

I wanted to tell her she looked plumb pitiful, but it didn't seem appropriate.

"I think one afternoon I'm going to stop at her house and offer to take her out or something. I might even go to that Katherine's Corner Bookstore and buy her a book."

"You read?" I asked. I felt bad as soon as it came out; she was unfazed.

"Well, sure. I mean, just yesterday I was reading *People* magazine. Do you ever read that, Savannah? I just love hearing about the lives of the stars. I mean, did you know that Jennifer Aniston—"

I held up one hand. "Amber, there's one thing you need to know about me. I don't live in the land of need-to-know, unless someone deems I need to know. So let's not spend lunch talking about people. Why don't you tell me about you? Tell me about your job."

"Whatever you say, but you told the whole city about Emma."

I tried to catch my breath. Amber had just shown me myself. But she didn't stop to ponder the revelation with me. "Oh, I just love my job. You know, your mother helped me get it. Miss Victoria is just the sweetest thing I've ever met. She saw me at the pageant my last year and we got to talking. I had already been out of school for a year and was working at the bank. I knew I could do so much more, but nothing had opened up yet. When your mother mentioned the job as director of tourism, I saw doors swinging wide open. So I jumped at the chance, and between the two of us we have made this place come alive." I barely heard her, still mulling over my need-to-know revelation.

"But you know my greatest goal, that is if I don't ever win Miss United States of America, is to win *Mrs.* United States of America," she said, actually stopping long enough to take a sip of her tea.

"Do what?!" I asked, fully present again.

"Oh, yeah. When I get married—and I've got my eye on a fellow now—but when I get married, I want to be Mrs. United States of America. I mean, surely I can win that. I've already got the wardrobe. That's why I try to keep my figure, you know." She pointed to the uneaten salad before her. "Yeah, the pageant's in California, so once I get married, all I have to do is just keep rehearsing my talent and staying up on current events. You never know when you might snatch Mr. Right, and you need to be ready.

"I practice all the time anyway," she continued. "I practice walking in my evening gown and answering questions on stage. I just stand in front of the mirror in my bathroom and use my brush for a microphone, then I ask myself questions, like I'm the emcee. Then I step to the other side of the bathroom and answer the question I just asked. I did really good last night. I got all the answers right." Spaghetti about flew out of my mouth on that one, but I recovered. "So when I get married, it will just be a natural recession." I do believe a noodle lodged in my throat at that exact moment.

"You know, Savannah, you could have interviewed me," she said, getting all pitiful.

"Amber, my story wasn't about the quest to win a pageant," I said, trying to sound as diplomatic as possible.

"Oh, I know. It was about losing pageants."

"No, it wasn't just about losing pageants. Did you read it?"

"Yes, I read it. I do read, Savannah," she said, acting slightly irritated. "But I've lost pageants. I know what that's like. I could have shared my story."

"I told you, Amber, the article wasn't just about losing. The article was about different things. It was about the treasure of a destiny, the loss of a destiny, and the lessons we learn along the way. And a multitude have been learned by me today, trust me."

"What are you talking about? What have you learned?"

"Multitudes. But back to you. After your losses, did you make any life-changing decisions, other than just to compete again? I mean, if you don't win Miss United States of America, or Mrs. United States of America, are you going to start a Mrs. Senior United States of America?"

"You should bite your tongue. But actually there already is a—"

"Oh, please, tell me it's not true," I said, throwing my head back in utter disbelief.

"Well, I can't help it, but there is," she said, patting me on the arm and forcing me to look up at her purple mouth. "But I made a decision too, Savannah," she said, laying her fork down. "I made a decision after each loss, the decision to keep going, to keep trying. I'm not sure why. To someone like you, it probably sounds silly.

"But I determined a long time ago that of all the things I really wanted, I really want this. I really enjoy it all. Every aspect. Every moment of success erases every time I didn't hear my name called. So I keep trying. I keep waiting for the moment that some magical host will sing a song just for me. And everyone will stand around the stage and for that one moment, I will be the most special person in the room. Fortunately, I'll have the opportunity until I'm dead." She laughed in amusement at her ceaseless opportunity.

It struck me that inside Amber lay a desperate need to be approved. "But you've heard your name called, Amber. Every local pageant you've won has given you that moment, several actually. When will it be enough? When is it enough applause or enough adulation or enough praise? At some point, the need to be approved by others has to bow to the need to simply appreciate yourself, don't you think? You're beautiful. You're a tad extreme, but you're a nice young woman. You're talented. You have a great job. You get to take people into an unfamiliar place and make them feel at home."

"You think I do all of that?"

"Yes, you do. But I get the sense that's not enough for you."

"Not enough?"

"Well, is it? Let me tell you: I believe that inside each of us is a hole only one thing will ever fill. You can try to measure out its space and search the world over, but you won't find it there. It's an eternal purpose, and only eternity can fill what it created. No tiara or applause or walk down the runway with Lawrence Welk's bubbles will fill what heaven created in you. Every pageant judge this side of Dallas might declare you a perfect ten, but until you realize that's not true victory, you will never be happy. It's time to look up, Amber. It's the only place eternal things are found."

The tears that sat on the brim of her counterfeit eyelashes were proof that she had, for the first time, really heard me. And for the first time since I had met Miss Amber Topaz Childers, she was speechless. I was pretty wasted myself. Because as much as I was speaking to her, I was certain I was also speaking to myself.

Her brief inability to communicate gave me the opportunity to look at my watch, which read 1:10.

"I'm so sorry to have to leave, Amber, but I've got to get back to work." She still never spoke. And I wasn't quite sure what to do with her there. So I stood up, grabbed my purse, and put my hand on hers. I knew I might hate myself in the morning, but at that moment, there was only one appropriate response. "I'll be your friend, Amber. A real friend. I won't always tell you what you want to hear, but I will always tell you the truth. I'll get lunch. And we'll talk soon."

She looked up at me with dark brown eyes covered by green contact lenses, making them a lovely shade of ocean. She smiled slightly. A genuine Amber smile, not a smile of competition, not an interview moment. I returned it, understanding in that moment we really weren't so different after all.

CHAPTER THIRTY-ONE

W e need to talk. I have the information you want. I believe it is time you knew the truth. I'll meet you at the fountain at Forsythe Park at 2 p.m."

I would have completely missed the typewritten note had it not fallen to the floor when I laid my purse on my desk. I didn't know what to do. Should I run around screaming, "I've got the story. I've got the story!"? Should I call the police and request an escort? Should I even go at all? And was this even the story that should be told? After the fiasco of that morning, who knew what really needed to be told? But I knew I had to go.

My mind began to race. Maybe Mrs. Harvard had a change of heart. Maybe it was Mr. Cummings . . . or Katherine, finally ready to talk after what she had read in the paper today. Maybe she hated me now and wanted to slap me around. It was only 1:20. I would go stir-crazy before two. There was no way I could stay here. I had to get a Coke, get something.

I grabbed my purse and headed out the door, calling to Marla as I passed, "If anyone needs me, they can call me on my cell. I'm closing in on my story, and I'll be back later."

"You got it, girlfriend."

Curly Locks emerged from his car with a cup of coffee that looked mighty familiar. It was from Jake's. I knew he would want to talk, but there was no time. So I just answered his questions before he asked them. "I'm going to get a Coke. I have a lead on my story. I'll be back before quitting time, and I'm glad to see you finally got you some real coffee." With that, I got in my car and sped in the direction of Jake's. I grabbed my cell phone out of my purse as I navigated myself through Reynolds Square.

"Jackson County Courthouse," someone crooned.

"Gregory Taylor, please."

"One moment."

"Gregory Taylor."

"Grisham, it's Savannah," I said. "I believe something is about to break. My first story was a bomb, according to some, but maybe not everyone, but definitely my father and definitely Emma, and I'm not sure what my break is, I'm not even sure it is a break. I'm not sure even if it's anything at all; it could be nothing; it's probably nothing. No, it can't be nothing; I have to have something by tomorrow!"

"Would you stop and breathe? You're wearing me out, and I don't get paid enough for such nonsense. Now, take a breath and start at the beginning," he said.

I pulled the car in front of Dad's store and cut the engine. "I'm not even sure what the beginning is."

"Well, just start somewhere—you're driving me crazy," he said.

I started with the phone call from number III and went all the way up to the note on my desk a moment ago. "So anyway, now I'm going to get a Coke, because I couldn't sit in my office until two doing nothing except draft my 'Apology of a Loser.' So who do you think the note's from?"

"I have no idea."

"What do you mean you have no idea? I called you because I figured you'd know. Lawyers always know. And even if they don't, they act like they do. So start acting like you do!"

"Well then, I have a couple of ideas. Did Cummings act like he was in town?"

"No. Well, he never mentioned that he was. Not that he would have. You don't think it is him, do you? I mean if it is, I might need to take someone with me, just in case."

"Savannah, that man is not going to hurt you. He is old, well-known, and not in the business of killing local reporters who have never actually reported a thing a day in their lives."

"Oh, thanks! I'm just a fanny load of encouragement now!"

"You are so dramatic. Has anyone ever told you that you should really have been an actress?"

"Has anyone told you you should really not try to be a psychiatrist and dissect people's personalities?"

"Honestly, Savannah, I really don't know who it is. It could be anyone or no one. Do many people who aren't actually related to this story know what you are up to?" he asked.

"No, no one actually. I mean, I just told my dad the whole story. My mother knew, but she must be solving world hunger because I haven't even heard from her today." I gasped. "Oh my Lord, have mercy!"

"What? What?"

"I haven't heard from my mother today! Do you have any idea what that means?"

"I have absolutely no idea what that means."

"That means at this moment, my mother is somewhere in this city planning a party bigger than Texas. And she will have circus men and airplanes flying banners, and she's liable to have a billboard bigger than life with my face and name splattered across it. As soon as this is over, I have got to find her and stop her. She's the reason I'm in this mess in the first place."

"Savannah, it's time to let your mother go. You just go to the park, face whatever it is head-on, and see what it holds. You can handle it. Of that I'm sure."

"Do you really think I can?"

"You've proven it already. Look back, Savannah. Look back at all you've done this last week, and you'll know that nothing you can meet today will be more than what you've already had to face. Chin up, young girl. Counsel says, pursue," he said with a laugh. "But call me immediately."

"If you don't hear from me . . ."

"Trust me, I'll hear from you."

"Did this cost me? Because you were really weak today."

"Yes! For unappreciation I charge triple."

"OK, the check's in the mail."

Duke came over and put his head under my hand as soon as I sat down at a front table by the window. That was his way of letting anyone know he needed petting. Obliging, I took his head between my two hands and got up close, where his big black nose was almost touching mine. He thought that meant I needed to be kissed. Only my quick reflexes saved my face from being lovingly slathered with dog drool.

"Duke, do you have any idea how lucky you are?" I asked. His expression assured me he knew I was trying to give him a valuable life lesson. "People feed you, bathe you, kiss you, walk you, and pet you. You have no job, no bills, no responsibilities. Granted, you have issues with Vicky and that darling lab up the street, but don't we all? On the whole, you really have it made.

"And you are loved. Deeply loved. Maybe not by the people who have to buy a new pair of tennis shoes every other month, but by most. The women adore you." I could have sworn he smiled at that one. "And Dad, well, Dad would be hard pressed if ever forced to choose between you and Vicky. Don't take this for granted. Savor it, relish it, chase cats up trees, roll around in the mud, retrieve whatever your little heart desires, take baths in Vicky's pool. My stars, lick yourself if you want to. After all, that's what dogs do. You have only one life, Duke; live it well."

"You might want to see a counselor for that," Dad said as he sat down in the chair across from me.

"I've been hearing way too much about counselors lately."

"They make movies about people who talk to animals."

"You're thinking of movies about people who can hear animals talk. I only wish I knew what this old fella was thinking."

"No, it's probably best we don't," he said, laughing. "Especially for your mother's sake." I couldn't help but laugh at that. "What in the world are you doing back here in the middle of the afternoon? Please don't tell me you've lost your job already."

"No. I tried, but he refused. I'm here for the caffeine," I said, rising to go into the back. Duke followed me, hoping I might need more time to talk through things while rubbing his head. Dad followed too.

"I hear they have a Coke machine down at the *Chronicle*."

I reached the back room, pulled a glass out of the cabinet, and proceeded to the ice dispenser. "Actually, I have a two o'clock appointment at the park and had a few minutes to kill."

Dad came around to the side of the Coke machine where he knew he would be in my view. "What's going on?"

"I don't know," I told him, grabbing a straw from the straw box. I unwrapped it, placed it in my glass, and took a long drink. Then I backed up so I could lean against the counter. "I thought I had written a good story. But obviously it lacked wisdom. I got scolded by you and reamed out by Emma. My resignation was refused, I do believe my mother's planning a party bigger than one she would throw for 'Bushie,' and I'm headed to the park to meet a stranger who might want to kill me. And the day isn't even half over."

"So you have no idea who you're meeting at the park?"

"Absolutely no idea," I said, taking another long swig of my Coke. By then he was reaching for a Coke himself.

"Emma wasn't very happy, huh?"

"Madder than the wasp that flew up Victoria's dress."

"Let you have it, huh?"

"Both barrels."

"Still going to write a story about a rigged beauty pageant?"

"That or Dead Woman Walking."

CHAPTER THIRTY-TWO

The fountain stared at me from the south side of Forsythe Park. One fifty. It was time to do the work of a journalist. It was time to discover my story.

Unfortunately, it couldn't be done here in the car, even though my sore behind had finally found a comfortable position on Old Betsy's pillow. I wasn't sure I wanted this story anymore, or this job or this chaos or this changing relationship with my father. I wasn't sure I wanted anything to change. *Maybe I should go back and get my doctorate in how to become a professional student. Maybe I shouldn't move out. Maybe I'm pressuring myself to grow up before I'm ready. My word, I'm only twenty-four. I'm just a babe. Babes shouldn't be putting their lives in danger for a dumb beauty pageant. Babes should be curled up on chairs with their mothers. Sharing stories with their fathers. But I am not a babe. I, Savannah Phillips, am a grown woman.* Extricating myself from the car, I began a slow but determined walk to the fountain.

At five 'til two, I saw her at the top of the main path leading to the fountain. She was wearing a beautiful peach linen pantsuit. I stopped before she saw me. This was no time for a Vicky encounter. I was too frustrated to see her anyway, and whoever was meeting me didn't want to have to deal with two Phillips women at once. So I withdrew to the other side of the sidewalk. I watched her for a minute from behind some shrubbery. At least she wasn't tucked away in her office coordinating hula dancers and knife throwers. *You need to go to a meeting or a walking tour or a trolley ride or something.* But she wasn't with anyone. She was standing in front of the fountain as if she were waiting.

As if struck by a flying tiara, the realization hit me: She was waiting for me. Vicky was my appointment.

My thoughts ran out of control. *What did she know? Had she been a part of something? Did I know my mother at all?*

Must a woman have all her life-changing moments in the course of one day?

I looked at her again. Even from here I could see the concern on her face, the intensity of her brow. Now granted, Vicky was always intense, but this was a different expression. I saw a mother about to play a different role in her daughter's life than either had ever known.

I could run, but no number of miles would ever create enough distance to leave behind what I had seen at the fountain. I knew that going forward was the only option. Vicky knew too. I reset my step.

She turned around and saw me coming, then smiled at me in a bashful way never before directed toward me. Dad had received this smile a thousand times. It was half "I'm sorry," half "You'll appreciate me after you hear what I actually have to say" kind of smile.

"Hello, darling, I can only imagine what you're thinking," she said, trying to offer a faint laugh.

"I'm not sure that you can. I don't even know what I'm thinking." I stared at her blankly.

"Would you like to walk?" she asked, motioning to the side of the fountain.

"Sure." I followed her lead.

"I haven't really been able to sleep since our conversation the other night. And after your conversation with Mr. Cummings and after reading your article in the paper, I knew you needed to know the whole story. I wish I had told you earlier. It could have spared all of us pain, especially Emma."

"You know something that could have stopped me from writing that article?"

"I just need you to listen to me."

My agitation grew. "I'm not sure that I want to listen to you."

"Savannah, watch your tone. I'm sure you've had an eventful day, but I'm still your mother."

"Eventful? Eventful? I would say so. I've been reprimanded by my father, screamed at by Emma, and embarrassed in front of my entire office. And now you're here with information that could have stopped it all. Why now?"

"Why now am I telling you, or just why now?"

"Why, after all these years of sticking your nose into *everything* from the very beginning, would you wait until now, after a tombstone's being carved with my initials?"

"Savannah, what in the world are you talking about?"

"Don't act like you don't know what I'm talking about. You know good and well what I'm talking about!"

"I know good and well that my hand is about to meet your face if you speak to me that way again."

I tried to pull back my tone, but I was so angry that trying to contain twenty-four years of whys was virtually impossible. "You're why I'm here. I wouldn't be going through any of this if you would have just stayed out of my fiction contest at school. But no, you had to get involved. You couldn't just let me win on my own."

"You think I helped you win that contest?"

"Mother, please, let's lose the drama. I know you had everything to do with me winning that contest."

Vicky hooked her arm in mine and tugged my rigid frame along beside her. "You think you're all grown up, don't you, Savannah? You think you know everything, I can tell. Well, you walk and listen; I'll talk. Understand?"

I harrumphed. "Talk away." Her heels made an irritating clicking sound on the sidewalk.

"During my reign as Miss Georgia United States of America, I found out that the pageant was rigged. One night during my preparation for the Miss United States of America Pageant I was over at Mr. and Mrs. Todd's house going over my schedule of appearances. Mr. and Mrs. Cummings were there as well. I had found out the families were good friends, but I had never thought much about it. That night, I left them at the table after dinner and went to the bathroom. As I was returning, I heard Mr. Cummings mention to Mr. Todd that the sale of the program pages had been extremely high. Something inside me told me to just stop and listen. So I stayed tucked away in the hallway where they couldn't see me.

"Mr. Cummings asked Mr. Todd what he had done to encourage such high sales. Mr. Todd started laughing and said that *somehow* the girls had gotten the idea that the more pages they sold the more likely they were to win. He said the girls had set themselves into competition with each other before the pageant had ever started. 'It's so funny, isn't it?' he said. 'Watching those girls try so hard, knowing I decide the winner on the final night myself. The god of the pageant, that's me. I know who I want, and I have to live with her for a year, so you bet I'm going to choose her.'"

"He said that?"

"Hard to believe, isn't it?" After all this time, judging the pageant had been about nothing but power. The craziness of it all was just settling in when she continued. "Well, then Mrs. Todd asked Mrs. Cummings if she had received her thank-you note and gift. Mr. Cummings answered for her, saying she had and that was what made him realize they had sold a substantial amount of pages."

"So it was true."

"Yes, it was. Mr. Todd thanked Mrs. Cummings for her company's fine printing job and laughed again and called it the most expensive comped service anyone had ever been given. At that point, I didn't know how I was ever going to return to that room without my face giving away what I knew."

"How did you do it?"

"I just summoned all my acting experience and gave the best performance I'd ever given," she said, putting her hand on her chest.

I almost said, "Up to that moment," but I didn't want to stop her momentum.

She continued. "When they saw me come around the corner, they immediately changed the subject to the Georgia weather. Everyone finished dinner, and Mr. and Mrs. Cummings left. I told them I needed to leave as well. I climbed in my car and cried the whole way home. At that moment, I knew I hadn't won legitimately. I had been picked by two sickening individuals, not by five legitimate judges, and certainly not because of my all-around talent and personality."

"And you do have that."

"Well, I think so. Anyway, I didn't know what I was going to do. I didn't want to tell anyone, because I was so mortified. How could I tell people that I wasn't really Miss Georgia United States of America, but I was Miss Money Market Miss?"

"I know you did not just call yourself Miss Money Market Miss.'"

"Yes, I did. I felt cheapened, violated. I felt like someone had stolen my greatest dream from me."

I couldn't let her go with that. I slipped out of her arm and made her look at me square in the eye. "I can't believe that was your greatest dream. And I don't mean any offense, but I don't know how you can compare losing a beauty pageant to what I've lost. I mean, it is nothing more than a group of women strutting around in bathing suits, vying for five people's approval, and sauntering across a stage in expensive and hideous gowns."

"Not all of them are hideous."

"Mother, honestly, how can that be your greatest dream? Those women are a bunch of overcooked, overemotional, over-the-top phonies."

"That's enough, Savannah Phillips!" Mother said with a tone I had heard only in moments about to involve extreme contact. "Sit down and let me explain before you make me out to be some mindless twit."

She sat down and turned to stare me straight in the eye. Now she was scaring me.

"I've always known you have never understood pageants. I've always known that you thought I was whacked, or whatever word you girls use these days, simply because I enjoyed competing in beauty pageants. But let me explain it to you as clearly as possible, Savannah." I sat quietly. "It was never about fame or fortune to me. It was never about people's applause or even their approval. It was about being part of an organization that offered me opportunities to take the things that I believed in, that I enjoyed, and bring them to a more visible stage. I knew if I ever became Miss United States of America, that it would open doors for me like nothing else could ever do. And it was fun, Savannah. Believe it or not, it was just a lot of fun."

"Fun?"

"Yes, Miss Priss, fun. I got to meet wonderful women. They're not all as you say, Savannah. And after all of that—after the sequined dresses, big hair, and tacky talent costumes—I was able to travel the state and meet people and talk to them about my dreams and my ideals. And do you know what, Savannah? People listened."

"I have no doubt you captured their full attention."

"Well, they didn't listen to me because my name was Victoria Musick. They listened to me because I was Miss Georgia United States of America. Granted, times have changed. Granted, the women's movement has tried to make us look like a bunch of hollow, high-heeled, out-of-touch simpletons. But some of those women today are just like I was over twenty-five years ago. They have goals and dreams. They have things to say that people need to hear. And they see beauty pageants as the avenue to open those doors."

"I'm sure not all of them feel that way."

"Sure, some of them have other goals. Some of them just want to say they're the best at something, at anything. But there really are some who, just like you, want to author books or write articles to reveal to the world that they have something of value to say. Is it old-fashioned? Maybe to some. Is it still enjoyable to others? Absolutely. Does it hurt anyone? Obviously it does. Do we all have to know how to win gracefully as well as lose gracefully? Eventually. Because each of us will do both at one point or another. And I think you've learned that yourself today."

"Yes, ma'am. I think I have."

We are good women, with good hearts, though some push the limits with their obsession. But some . . . no, *many*, Savannah, are women just like you, except their book is a pageant. Their story is a song or a ballet or a moment in front of a willing audience. They may never get a record deal, or tour with the New York Metropolitan Ballet, but to their parents, every moment was exceptional."

"As it should be to any parent."

"And it is with yours, rest assured. So for that one magical moment they are living a dream. Now, you can dilute that to mind-lessness if you'd like, but you'd have to include me in your sweeping generalizations. And I may enjoy things that are different from you, Savannah, but that doesn't make me any less capable than you. It just makes me different. I have always encouraged your dreams. It is time that you at least try to understand mine." She paused. She breathed. But she did not cry. "For many girls, Savannah, losing can cause them to feel their lives are over."

"Mother, how can losing a pageant cause someone to think that life is over?"

"It's the death of a dream, Savannah. It's me watching them crown someone else Miss United States of America, when all my life that is what I thought I would be. It's you watching Grant marry someone else, or writing your first article for the paper and it not being received the way you had hoped. It's not that you don't think better things will come your way. It's that this one thing is lost forever. And like anything, it is a loss that you grieve. And for one moment, I thought I had lost my dream."

My anger flared up again, "I hope you can remember that feeling, because that's how you made me feel. You stole my greatest dream."

She looked at me exasperated, wondering, I'm sure, if I had heard one word she just said. "I didn't rig your contest, Savannah. A friend of mine from college noticed your name and where you were from and called to see if you were my daughter. He just happened to be the head of the publishing company. We hadn't spoken in years. I told him you were and that you were an excellent writer. I let him know, however, very clearly, that I didn't want you to know we had even spoken. If you didn't deserve to win that contest, then you shouldn't be the winner, regardless of our friendship."

"But your name was on my notification. I called them. They thought I was you . . ." Even as I said it and replayed the conversation, I realized that Mr. Peterson had said nothing to indicate that Mother had asked for their special favor in any way. It was only my assumption. My assumptions made me give away my publishing deal. My stupid assumptions made me write an article that should never have been written. My assumptions had me sitting on a park bench with my mother, realizing I had just totally and successfully screwed up my life. "I threw it all away!" I buried my head in my hands. "I threw it all away to prove a point to you!"

She sat down and wrapped her arms around me. "Well now, you're experiencing the loss of a dream. It hurts. And it blinds. But there was a greater plan for you, darling. And you found it, wrapped in a newspaper. You're a great writer. Today's experience will make you a more compassionate writer. Don't lose what you feel today, because it will forever change who you are and what you write."

I looked up at her and saw my mother in a different light. She was not trying to manipulate this moment. She was trying to help me encounter her feelings. She had stated her case, and I could accept or ignore it. But it wouldn't change it. This was who she was. She was a woman who'd experienced dreams and losses. A woman like me.

We would never dress alike, walk alike, talk alike, or ever think alike, rest assured. But we were still the same in this regard. Her dreams led her down runways; mine led me down hallways. Hers required lipstick and hairspray; mine required laptops and Post-it notes.

"Forgive me, Mom," I said, looking at her very similarly to the way I had looked at my father earlier that morning, knowing our relationship would never be the same.

She stared back at me. "'Mom.' I like that."

"All these years I couldn't understand what this fascination was, this craving for this type of life. Then I met Emma and Katherine. Each of you walked the same road and yet are so different. You are not mindless, and please don't ever think I have thought that about you. But today I've seen something in you I've never seen before. I see me."

"Well, now, that took a while, didn't it?" she said with a smile.

I laughed. "I always thought I got my drive from Dad, and this idea that I have a destiny, a place, an actual calling. But I got it from you."

"That knowledge is in the core of each of us, Savannah. And at the end of the day, there really is only one dream: to touch some part of the world with something of eternal value. The only thing that differentiates the call is the method."

"I love you. If I become half the woman you are, I will have achieved great things. Will you tell me the rest of your story?"

"Sure." We stood and continued our walk. "I called your father after I gathered myself. We hadn't been dating long, but I knew I was going to marry Jake the first time I saw him." She still spoke his name with tenderness, even after twenty-five years. "I've never met a stronger, yet gentler, man. He holds us together. He's that quiet strength. I'm that flamboyant moment!" Her face revealed a delicate smile. "He just did it for me. You know what I mean?"

"Would you stop trying to talk like a teenager? I do not want to know all of your intimate feelings. I know you love him. Now, focus. On with the story."

"OK, OK. But you're a lucky girl to have two parents who love each other like we do."

"Yes, I am," not adding how lucky we all were to have Jake to balance the chaos.

"Anyway, he told me that I needed to get to the bottom of it. Even if it meant finding out I was an illegitimate winner. He let me know that I couldn't be a part of something that was a lie. And if it meant giving up my dream, then I would have to give up a dream and wait for another to replace it. So the next day I went straight back to the Todds' house and told Mr. Todd what I had overheard the night before. He assured me I had misunderstood, that none of it was anything more than two old friends cracking jokes and acting crazy, that I had been the unanimous choice. I didn't know what else to do but believe what he told me. Your father and I agreed that I would continue with my preparation, and we would just try to find out anything to the contrary that we could."

"So Dad's known about this all along as well?"

"Yes, he has."

"You two are good."

"We know," she said matter-of-factly. "Anyway, for the next six months I prepared for the Miss United States of America Pageant and your father tried to find out anything he could to disprove what Mr. Todd had said. But we were young. We didn't have any connections with anyone and very little spare time. He was in graduate school full-time, and I was an eighteen-year-old dreamer. We were more concerned really with seeing each other when we could. And honestly, Savannah, once I met your father, all I was really excited about was getting married. Then, when I didn't win the Miss United States of America Pageant, I just wished the next six months away."

"When it was time to give up my crown, there was a beautiful young lady competing that year. She was so petite and talented, and people had been talking about her all over the state. She had emceed numerous local pageants and the word was that she was magical. She could captivate an audience. Well, everyone compared her to me," she said with a big smile, apparently proud that she was captivating and magical.

"But for some reason, every time her name was mentioned by anyone, Mr. Todd got irate. He accused her of taking another girl's song for her talent competition. I know it's totally ludicrous, but no one even gave her the opportunity to defend herself. Looking back, I believe it was her character in general he had a problem with. Word got back to me about another girl who was competing for her third time in the pageant. Mr. Todd had nothing but wonderful things to say about her. So I decided I would just watch. Not being in the middle of it gave me the ability to be far more objective.

"During the competition, the petite one just captured everyone's heart. She was a lady. She was extremely talented and even won the swimsuit competition. The other girl was beautiful, don't get me wrong. But the petite one stole the audience. But when the evening ended, the one Mr. Todd loved walked away with the crown. The whole audience gasped at the announcement. And I left knowing I was going to get to the bottom of that mess," Her southern indignation rose even now.

"Two days after giving up my title I went back to their house. I told him I didn't believe what he had said, and that I was going to be keeping my eye on them. If they were up to anything, I was going to make sure that they didn't ruin another girl's life in any way, shape, or form.

"I guess my naiveté thought mere talk would work. But it wasn't until Emma lost that I realized what they were actually doing. That year, I went into undercover mode. I used all the influences of Judge Hoddicks, got all of the bank records with the listing of every deposit made into Patricia Cummings's account from Mrs. Todd's account, knew every deposit and every note and everything imaginable. It was documented and categorized. I mean, they were so silly. They didn't even try to really hide anything. I finally got all of the past score sheets, and they revealed that in each illegitimate win, Mr. Cummings III or IV had scored a woman fairly in the preliminaries so he wouldn't rouse suspicion among the other judges, then gave her ones in every phase of competition on the final night."

"And you had actual proof of this?"

"I had every piece of evidence needed not only to prove but to prosecute."

"What did you do with it?"

"I gave it all to Judge Hoddicks. I asked him not to prosecute unless forced, because I really didn't feel Emma needed her name slathered in scandal with everything else that she was going through."

"Unfortunately, I took care of that for you."

"Yes, you did. But years ago I even went to her house and tried to help her, but she refused. She broke my heart, Savannah. Judge Hoddicks went down to Jackson. He met privately with Judge Tucker, and then they met privately with Mr. Todd and Mr. Cummings III and IV. Judge Hoddicks said it wasn't pretty, but it was gratifying. They reached a private settlement and all of them were forced to leave their positions. None of them have any part in the pageant anymore, and only by Judge Hoddicks's mercy are they not serving jail time.

"So that's what happened. That is all of it," she said, sitting down on another park bench and dabbing her forehead with a tissue.

I sat down beside her and turned to ask, "How did you feel when you saw your scores and realized that you had only won because they made you win, over someone else?"

"Well, that didn't happen in every situation. In the year I won and about nine other pageants through the years, the person that actually won had indeed been chosen to be the best by all of the judges. I had actually been the winner. Now, could I have handled it if I wasn't? I don't know. It's a question I never had to ask."

"You could have. I'm certain of it."

"I hope I could have. I hope that by now it would be enough for me to be the wife of an incredible man, the mother of fascinatingly passionate children, and a woman who is making a difference in the city she loves. But I'll never really know the answer to that question, Savannah. I'll never really know." We had come full circle, and she stared at the fountain in front of our bench.

"Why did you wait to tell me all of this?" I asked. I wasn't angry anymore, just puzzled.

"Because I was hoping you would see the bigger picture here, Savannah. There really is one."

"You're not the first to say such a thing."

"Then you might want to listen. The intrigue is great. The stories of mayhem would be entertaining. But are those the things you want people to leave with? Did you leave fiction writing to just uncover real fiction, or did you leave fiction writing to make a difference, to change a city?" She stood up. "What did you give up your dream for, Savannah? Beyond proving something to me?" She bent down, kissed me on my forehead, and simply walked away.

I called after her. "So all those contests I thought you influenced, I really won on my own merit?"

She just raised her hand and shrugged her shoulders. I knew her well enough to know. And I watched as her Coach embroidered sling-back pumps clicked all the way home.

I laughed out loud. I got myself so tickled I couldn't get up off of the bench. I laughed until my side hurt. I laughed at taping and dresses worn backward, at strange women singing in my car, and at the last week of pent-up anxiety. I laughed at the people who looked at me as if I were crazy. I laughed at the insanity of my life. I laughed at the thought of having to write another story by tomorrow afternoon.

Finally, I headed back to my office to pick up my computer. I had a story to write. Could I do it? Well, I am Savannah from Savannah. Victoria is my mother and Jake is my father. Oh yeah, I could do it. Wasn't sure I really wanted to, but at least I knew I could.

CHAPTER THIRTY-THREE

Girl, well, what can I say? You just did an amazing job. I'm not even sure that *I* would have been more interesting. There is a possibility, but I'm truly not certain," Paige said on the other end of the line.

"Well, not everyone appreciated it."

"Oh, the Emma thing. That was a little risky, but it was true. And you have always been a declarer of truth."

"Yes, well, I about declared my truth all the way to the unemployment line."

"You almost got fired?"

"Not exactly, but really I don't want to talk about me today. What have you been doing all day?"

"Well, I've eaten breakfast, eaten lunch, and jabbered with every plaid Bermuda shorts, kneesock-wearing gentleman that has a hotel reservation in this city tonight. But I sold three pieces of art, and that, my friend, is enough to take the rest of the week off."

"Ooh, I think that's a great idea. You should treat yourself."

"We should both treat ourselves. How about we go grab some dessert after Bible study tonight? You want me to just pick you up?"

"That sounds great. Come about six-thirty."

"OK. I'll just honk."

"I'm sure you will."

"Bye."

"Bye."

I entered the side door on the first floor and came up the back stairs that lead into the kitchen. There was no reason to return to work because the day was already over. Mother was busy preparing dinner and talking on the phone at the same time.

Dad and Duke apparently weren't home yet, and Thomas, well, who knows where he was. As I went upstairs to wash my hands and freshen up, I heard Vicky say, "I know. She's just fabulous. I think I might take out another one of those ads to surprise her. You know, in all these years she's never guessed that it was me," she said, laughing. The poor woman had no clue. I wasn't going to give her one either, but I would have a long talk with my dad about making sure she never placed another ad again.

The Wednesday-night message was timely. With excerpts from Jim Collins's book *From Good to Great,* the sermon revealed, "The only ones who accomplish great things that last are those who live a life not swayed by trends, but who hold fast to what they know to be true."

In the car, Paige put her key into the ignition but didn't turn it. "Savannah?"

"Yeah?"

"Do you think what I do has any real eternal value?" she asked in a rare moment of introspection.

"I think you have done exactly what you were destined to do. You've been given an amazing gift, and you've put it to good use. And each time someone steps into your gallery and purchases one of your amazing gifts, you give them joy and pleasure every time they pass by it hanging in their foyer or hallway. There is eternity in that."

"You think so?"

"I should know. I have an original hanging in my office."

"Did you get permission for that?" I asked, laughing at the two entertaining creatures sprawled across the sofa. Their heads perked up simultaneously at the sound of my voice.

"We don't have to get permission for anything, do we, Duke?" Duke simply laid his head back down on his side of the sofa, knowing he didn't need permission from anything or anyone other than the man by his side. "I think you forget who's in charge here," Dad said, patting Duke on his hind end.

I walked over and took a seat in the chair next to the sofa. "I'm not sure if it's you or the hairy creature lying next to you."

"It's both of us. When I'm too tired to be in charge, Duke steps into his rightful place."

"What about Thomas?"

"Duke has more authority because of his actual time spent on the premises. Pretty good sermon, wasn't it?"

"Yeah, it was great. It seems like that place has grown so much since I've been gone."

"Yeah, it has. They really have the pulse of this city. They're reaching people who haven't had a place to belong. They've given them a type of family. Those of us who have good ones forget some people have never known what that's like." He continued petting Duke without looking at me.

I scooted to the front of my chair, getting as close to Dad's head as possible. "Speaking of our family, I overheard a conversation with Vicky, I mean Mother, and one of her friends. Seems she's planning to put another ad in the paper."

Jake snickered.

"Dad, please. She doesn't even think I know it's her, and I wish I could put a stop to this. But you and I both know you're the only one that can pull the plug on her madness. People who aren't too excited that I have this job will be even more unhappy when they realize it's still mine on Friday. And the last thing I need is Mother making a declaration that she thinks my employment at the paper needs to be celebrated in print."

Dad cocked his head. "Trust me, you will see no more ads in the paper."

"Thanks." I stood up, leaned over and kissed him on the head, and turned to leave the kitchen. "You do know you are not only helping me, but you are sparing innocent generations to come. My children will thank you." He raised his hand that was petting Duke, then put it right back where it had been.

It was around nine-thirty when I made it to bed, and I was exhausted. For some weird reason I was thankful for all that had transpired this day. Thankful that even though it had been difficult, it had still been good. I finally fell asleep.

Somewhere in the wee hours of the morning I dreamed that when I showed up at work, everyone was standing in front of the door holding up the front page, which boasted a full-page ad of congratulations and a half-page picture of me and Vicky when I was eight and she had us dressed alike for Easter. We wore matching floral dresses with dangerously large bows planted on the side of our waists, I in black patent-leather shoes and she in her black patent-leather pumps. I woke up about three in the morning in a cold sweat. I ran downstairs and scoured our picture albums for any photo that could be totally humiliating if it were to appear in a newspaper. I put them all in a folder, took the folder to my bedroom, and hid it in the bookcase behind a stack of books.

I enjoyed dreamless sleep the rest of the night.

CHAPTER THIRTY-FOUR

We have a mini YMCA on our first floor, which Vicky designed years ago. When the world decided it was fashionable to do aerobics, so did Vicky. She bought Savannah out of every leotard it had, and when she couldn't find any more in town, she had someone design them for her. No one understood as well as Vicky did the importance of looking good when working out in your own basement by yourself.

A trainer from one of the finest state-of-the-art gyms in Atlanta designed her a fabulous workout facility. He did one whole wall of mirrors and about every weight you could imagine, along with a treadmill and a rowing machine. But the only thing Vicky ever did was aerobics. That lasted, in total, forty-eight days.

Every morning at six a.m., she came out of her room in full makeup, totally coiffed hair, and manicured nails. In exactly sixty minutes, she returned upstairs. The amazing thing was, she never came out perspiring. I assumed she never actually moved enough to produce perspiration. But regardless of what she actually did while she was down there, after forty-eight days exactly, she never returned to do it again. Not to say that she doesn't go down there.

Oh, she goes down there, all right, and we hear her singing at the top of her lungs. Usually it's when she's had a really bad day, on which she usually sings show tunes. On the days that have been significantly challenging, however, we are treated to Vicky's version of "Nobody Knows the Trouble I've Seen." Reality is, the only ones with troubles are the afflicted creatures upstairs forced to endure such recreation. Duke retreats to the top floor and hides under Dad's bed.

This morning, it poured outside. I silently prayed the rain would wash away the horror of yesterday. I spent time lifting a few free weights, for which I was sure I would pay the next day, then spent thirty good minutes on the treadmill, perspiring profusely. When I returned upstairs, I found Duke sitting dejectedly at the door. The one thing that rain brought him was the inability to be walked at all. He knew today was going to be one of those days.

"I'll see you tonight," I called into the kitchen to Mother as I raced for the door.

"You'll have to start dinner without me. I've got a five o'clock meeting tonight. I had to call an emergency meeting because some developer wants to tear down one of our houses and put in a singles' bar. Can you imagine me letting that happen? These people and their crazy ideas. I don't know what city they think they've come to, but this isn't sin city. This is Savannah. And it doesn't happen here unless it comes through me."

"I'm sure they'll figure that out soon enough."

"Yes, they will. And no singles' bar will be replacing a historical home in the heart of our city. I guess the next thing they'll want is adult entertainment and bathhouses. These people need to go to church. If they want to meet someone worth meeting, that might be a fine place for them to start. Singles' bars! When I was young, people didn't need help meeting people." She turned back to the sink, and I was certain the conversation could go on without me. I sneaked out.

My phone was ringing as I made my way to my barely pigmented world. "Savannah," I heard Marla say from the other end, "I just sent a lady back to your desk."

I pulled out some framed pictures of Paige, college buddies, and my family and placed them on the far corner of my desk. "Is she as uptight as the one yesterday?"

"No, she seems a lot calmer than yesterday's adventure. A little cleaner too."

"Well, thanks for telling me. I hear her coming." I braced myself, not certain who would appear around the corner. Much to my surprise and anxiousness, it was Katherine, looking perfectly stunning.

"Good morning, Savannah. I'm sorry to bother you at work."

"Oh, it's not a bother at all. Please have a seat," I said, motioning to the chair just inside my modular wall.

"Actually, the rain has stopped. Would you have a moment to take a walk?" *Wish Emma would have wanted to take a walk,* I thought.

"Sure. That would be nice. Here, we can just go out the back door," I said, motioning to the door that wasn't far from my desk.

"Cute cubicle."

I opened the door, and a blast of Savannah heat caught us off guard. "Well, it's not much, but it's mine. I guess you're here to talk about my article."

"I've known about your article since the day you invited me to the pageant. You're not the most subtle person I've ever met," she said gently.

"Pretty pathetic, aren't I."

"No, pretty fearless, I would say. I'm wondering how long you've known about me?"

"I found Gloria's tape of your interview the day that I went through some of her files. So when I came into your store the second time, I realized the voice on the tape was yours."

Her flesh-toned mules clicked in rhythm as we walked. "Why didn't you just ask me about it?"

"I honestly just wanted to get to know you. But now that we're talking about it, may I ask why you didn't tell Gloria your story?"

"Because for me, the real story wasn't about a rigged beauty pageant. It was about the decisions I made for my life after the pageant. I read your article, Savannah. You had some good points in there, but you had the wrong premise."

"What do you mean?"

"My heart breaks for Emma, it really does. And I do think your point about people in positions of authority using them wisely is a story in and of itself. But Emma's decision really had nothing to do with the decisions the judges made. The ultimate decision was Emma's and Emma's alone. Let me tell you the difference between disappointment and defeat."

"I'm listening."

"We all have moments of disappointment, Savannah. But we don't experience defeat until we invite disappointment to stay with us. Emma allowed disappointment to define her life. She made a home there; she got married there and had children there. She held hands with disappointment and it led her to abuse, lies, torment, and more unhappiness than she ever intended. Disappointment gave way to her defeat."

"I think I understand."

"It only takes one moment of real confrontation with the truth to force defeat out."

"I guess that's what you did?"

Katherine nodded slowly. "Yes, I met up with disappointment. But when I realized it was a thief, I made it leave." She paused to see if I was listening.

"So how did your moment of disappointment come?"

"Well, about thirty years ago, I competed in the Miss Georgia US of A Pageant."

"Did you just call it US of A?"

"Yes."

"That's not sacrilegious to you?"

"No," she looked at me as if I needed to be examined.

"Just checking. Go ahead."

"Anyway, I was twenty years old and had two more years of school left. A couple of friends who had competed in the pageant before talked me into being in it myself. Well, I had never been in a pageant in my life," she said, raising her hand in amusement. "But they told me they were going to do it again and we could all do it together. That made it exciting enough for me."

"You and I have different interpretations of exciting."

"Well, when I came away with the title of Miss Savannah US of A I was astonished. Are you sure you want to hear this?"

"Absolutely. Go ahead." I had been around beauty queens all my life, and I mean all my life, and Katherine was like none of these. I may have been mistaken about her story being the one I needed to tell, but it was still a story I personally wanted to hear.

"Well, the director of the Miss Savannah US of A Pageant took the Miss Georgia US of A Pageant extremely seriously. The day after they had topped my head with a tiara and announced me the winner, the director and I met to begin my preparation for the next competition. As far as she was concerned, I needed a total overhaul, and she had less than nine months to get me to competition level."

"Competition level?"

"My question exactly. All I knew was that I had sung in a borrowed dress, walked around in a two-year-old swimsuit, and interviewed in one of my mother's suits. I figured if that worked for Miss Savannah US of A, it should work for Miss Georgia US of A. But she was sure it wouldn't.

"So for the next nine months, every weekend I met with the former Miss Savannah US of A to go over every aspect of competition. She assured me that I had what it took to win. And by the end of nine months, with a new hairdo, fabulous clothes, a knowledge of every current event and any other event of most of history, I was ready to sing my heart out with my version of 'Where the Boys Are,' designed to make grown men cry. It even had choreography."

"Go, Katherine."

"I did. I won both the interview and evening gown competitions. But then I didn't even place in the top five. I was shocked. I had grown from a young lady who had won Miss Savannah US of A on a dare into a woman who was taking this event seriously. After they announced the winner, the night shifted into slow motion."

"How so?"

"I don't remember them crowning her, her walk down the runway, or the emcee saying good night. I just stood there in shock, wondering how in the world I had not only lost, but hadn't even placed. Somehow I got back to my hotel room, and I found a copy of the auditor's sheet underneath my door. Those sheets revealed something that to this day I've never told anyone."

"What?"

"I had the high scores in every category of the pageant. Beyond the interview and evening gown, I had also won talent and tied for first in swimsuit. Can you believe that?" she asked more of herself than of me. "But on the final night, for some reason, one of the judges gave me a one in every single category. Somewhere between Friday night and Saturday night, this judge was convinced by something or someone that I wasn't the one who needed to leave that evening as Miss Georgia US of A."

"But how do you know it was an actual copy of the auditor's sheet?"

"Well, each judge has to sign the bottom of their scorecard for authenticity and sign the final auditor's ballot as well. Earlier that week I had participated in my personal interview with the judges' panel. As a contestant, one of the greatest things you can do is to leave your personal interview with a memorable thought. So at the end of my session, I told the judges I was starting a time capsule that I would open in thirty years on my fiftieth birthday, and I wanted this experience to be a part of that. I had brought my pageant program book and placed it underneath my chair. I pulled it out and told them that each contestant had already signed it for me, and that it would be an even greater memory if they would be willing to sign it for me as well. You could tell they were all flattered, and I had obviously come up with a rather ingenious idea."

"All these years, I thought my mother had come up with that concept herself. I should have known better." We both laughed.

"So when I got a copy of the auditor's sheet, I was able to compare it to the signatures in my book. Each one was exactly the same."

A drop of rain hit my cheek, and I suggested we turn back. "Who would want you to have that information?"

"I've asked myself that same question a million times. It had to be either a judge or an auditor. Someone who realized what had happened in retrospect, or someone who had a conscience check a little too late."

"I know who gave it to you."

"You do? Who?"

"Mr. Harvard. He and Mr. Wilcox never audited for that pageant again," I said. Every piece of the puzzle was beginning to form a perfectly fitted whole.

"Why do you think it was Mr. Harvard?"

"Well, I actually met with Mr. Harvard's wife, and I'm sure that is why my questions upset her so. I do wonder, though, why he would give it to you. What could you do with it?"

"Well, I've had thirty years to ask myself those questions. I honestly believe that they hoped I would make this public so they wouldn't have to. They believed what had happened was wrong but didn't want to be the ones to reveal it. They probably thought I would be mad enough to go tell anyone who would listen."

"Why didn't you? Why didn't you go to a paper then or question the pageant directors or contact the judges or auditors?"

"I thought I would give it a couple of months to settle in, get over the shock, and then evaluate what I wanted to do. By then, I had started my last year of school and that is when I met Jim."

At the very mention of his name, it seemed Katherine left for a place reserved for only the greatest of lovers. As I watched the shift in her gaze, I knew that until my heart held that respect, that divine regard, for another man, I would remain alone. Having witnessed that kind of love truly exists, I would be foolish to settle for less.

She caught me taking in her transformed countenance, and she blushed. "Honestly, once I met him I didn't think about much else until years later. Meeting him was the best thing that ever happened to me. He transferred in from Mississippi State for his senior year, then he graduated. He went to the University of Alabama for only that one year. If I had been Miss Georgia US of A, I wouldn't have returned to school. The one year I would have missed would have prevented me from meeting the man I fell in love with."

"And you wouldn't be here today. Walking with me in Savannah."

"No, I wouldn't be a lot of things. But when I finally opened the time capsule, it seemed maybe it was time to tell my story. And Gloria seemed perfect. But sitting there, it was clear the better life had been lived."

"So would you say your loss was part of a better destiny?"

"Oh yes. Even though I could have spent the last thirty years being called a former Miss Georgia United States of America, I much prefer being called Mrs. Owens. And you can say that in your article if you want to. That love was my greatest achievement, gained only because of what seemed at the time to be my greatest defeat. I truly believe, Savannah, that a divine presence guided my life for an eternal purpose." Katherine finished her story just as we arrived at the back door to the paper.

"I've taken enough of your time; I'm sure you need to get back to work and I need to get back to the bookstore."

"You're an amazing lady, Katherine Owens," I said. "And I'm sorry for your loss—not the pageant, but Mr. Owens."

"To have a love like we had, Savannah, I don't deserve anyone's sorrow. I just hope you find someone to love that way in your lifetime."

"After today, there isn't any other option." I reached out and wrapped her in a hug.

"Don't settle for the Ishmael," she said in my ear, "when you can have the Isaac. In anything, Savannah."

I held on for a moment longer. She let me go. I tried to blink away my tears. "I'll come see you soon."

"I'd be disappointed if you didn't." I watched her go. The real story had found me.

CHAPTER THIRTY-FIVE

Before I walked into the paper, I took a moment to take in my city. It was different to me somehow. It took a moment, but I began to appreciate the fact that it wasn't really the city that had changed; it was me. I wasn't Betty anymore; I was Savannah. Savannah from Savannah.

I had somehow grown into myself, grown into the things about me that I liked and the things I had refused to see. The things that I had respected about myself and those denied would both have to be accepted. They were all me—the good, the bad, and the Vicky. They all made up Savannah.

As I made my way back to my prosaic world, even it didn't seem quite as flat as it had when I left. I tried to envision amazing things happening within my makeshift cosmos. But first, a stop by the ladies' room.

The voices coming into the bathroom after me were obnoxious and giddy. "She about got her prissy little behind fired, is what I heard," one of the voices said. "Every time I see her headed to Mr. Hicks's office, I just leave. I can't believe he hired her in the first place." This must be the always-invisible secretary of Mr. Hicks.

And the prissy little behind was undoubtedly the one now trapped in this stall.

"Well, don't be too hard on her," said the other, a very sweet, lovely young maiden.

"Oh, she needs somebody to set her in her place. Her mother thinks she rules everything around here. She's even trying to make my parents get rid of their satellite."

OK, girls, hurry it up. I looked through the small crack and noticed they were painting their faces.

Miss Two-Faced Tilda packed up her beauty makeover kit as my legs began to shake from the extended squatting period, then added, "Well, she's met her match with me."

Finally, they left, only to be replaced by a new visitor who headed to my stall. The hand pushed hard on my unlockable stall door, forcing me to fall firmly onto the very toilet seat that up until then had successfully been avoided.

"Oh, I'm so sorry," I heard a somewhat familiar voice say.

By then, my tumble signaled the automatic flusher, which plunged with such force I was sure I would end up somewhere the far side of New Jersey or it had just sucked a hickey on my hiney the size of Texas. Reaching for nonexistent toilet paper to wipe off every rudiment of germs, I moaned in agony.

"No paper?" came the voice next door.

"No."

"I'll send you some."

"That would be nice, because if you don't, I'll be forced to use this toilet tissue attached to my shoe."

I saw her hand come from underneath, bearing enough toilet paper for a small country. "It ain't quite that big," I said, and we both just died laughing.

I had less than two hours to complete my story. People came and went by my prefab world, but everyone could tell I was too busy to talk. Even Curly Locks left me alone. I saw him peek his head around the corner once around lunchtime, but I didn't look up. After the last couple of days, I needed a day off from conversation in general.

At one forty-five, the final page printed off. What needed to be redeemed was hopefully complete. I headed up to Mr. Hicks's office to turn in my story. His secretary was missing in action again. Mr. Hicks, however, was working diligently at his desk, so I knocked on the open door. He looked up and invited me inside but never looked up.

"Got another story ready, Savannah?"

"Yes, sir. I hope it will repair what I screwed up."

"I'm sure it will," he said still engrossed in what he was working on. "So what's your next article going to be about?"

I'm almost certain that my heart stopped beating and my blood stopped flowing through my veins. It was really true: I was going to have to work this hard to come up with a story every week. What in the world had I been thinking? This workaholic, crazed individual would never allow a moment's peace. I gathered myself enough to say, "You'll have to wait and see."

"Meet me in front of your dad's store as soon as you can," Claire said from the other end of the line.

"Why?"

"Because the apartment above his store has just been purchased and the new owner wants to rent it out."

"The Culpeppers' place? Dad never even said they were thinking about moving."

"Well, they moved out about two weeks ago. Mrs. Culpepper needed a little extra care and couldn't handle the stairs any longer. They sold it for not much more than they paid for it. I heard they really like the buyer and didn't want a long drawn-out process. But the new owner asked to remain anonymous, because they feared people might think they had taken advantage of the Culpeppers, when really the Culpeppers felt like they were keeping it in the family."

"Well, it doesn't matter. You know I can't afford something on a square. Those are the most expensive properties in the city. Your front yard's a square, for crying out loud. Look some more; this won't work ..."

"Savannah Phillips, don't you hang up on me. Get down here now and at least look at this place."

"Well, meet me around back then. I don't want Dad to know anything yet."

I met Claire around the corner in front of the Lucas Theater. The Lucas Theater is Savannah's gift to the fine arts. Mr. Lucas built a number of theaters through the years in the South. But the one in Savannah is the only one that bears his name. After a ten-year restoration project, it reopened in 1998. I would tell you that Mother had something to do with it, but unfortunately, someone else thought of it first. However, the rumor floating around town says they stole the idea from her. One can only imagine how such rumors get started. As for me, my imagination is vivid and often accurate.

Across the street from the Lucas Theater is the Olde Pink House. The eighteenth-century mansion-turned-restaurant is a designated National Landmark and is, of course, pink. Its claim to fame is that the Declaration of Independence was read there for the very first time, and it's pink because the scored stucco was never removed and the color of the red brick is bleeding through.

Grant and I used to eat regularly at the Olde Pink House. He always ordered for me. He would hold my hand across the table and share his thoughts about life, his childhood memories, his dreams for the future. We had a regular table, from which I could see the Lucas Theater marquee, clearly in the winter and more partially in the summer, when all the leaves have taken their places on the trees. The last time we ate there it read, "Savannah Chamber Orchestra, June 28."

Claire touched my arm, returning my thoughts to the present, and we headed to the back of Dad's store, where stairs went up to the apartment. "So how can I make my rent payments if the owner is anonymous?" I asked her, not caring who owned it as much as whether I could afford it.

"They have an escrow account set up down the street at the SunTrust Bank. You'll just go there and pay to an account number each month."

We climbed the stairs. Despite thirteen years of memorizing every line of this entrance, I had never climbed the stairs to the Culpeppers' home. Claire opened the door. It was perfectly laid out and pristinely kept. It had old refurbished hardwood floors, high doors, and beautiful moldings. There was a living room and dining area, and in the back was the kitchen with what seemed to be brand-new appliances and a built-in breakfast area. One more flight of stairs took us to the two bedrooms, separated by a small hallway. The master was a little larger than the second bedroom, with an incredible master bath and a claw-foot tub haloed by a curtain rod that allowed one to draw the shower curtain all the way around. The other bath was ideal as a guest bath. The place was perfect, and perfectly out of my price range, I was sure.

"Claire, how in the world do you think I'll be able to afford this on my salary?" I asked, still perturbed that she would even show me this place.

"Well, that's what you're not going to believe. The owner got such a good deal, he's only asking $850 a month. Do you think you can swing that? This is the deal of a lifetime. If you don't take it, I'm going to!"

"There's no way this place is $850. You just didn't hear him right. This place has to be at least $1,850. You'd better go back and tell him he gave you the wrong price."

"I checked and double-checked, and he assured me that the rent was only $850. All he wanted me to do was find someone who would take care of it and not ransack the place with wild parties, like those that go on everywhere else around here."

"Well, I won't even get a paycheck for another two weeks." I ran my hand up the trim of a doorframe.

"Well, it gets better. And stop looking at me as if I'm some lying girl from lower Savannah. He said that he was so concerned about the kind of person that lived here, he would rather hold it for the right one than rent it for the sake of renting."

"Is there a candid camera about to pop out on my head?"

"No, silly. I told him I had a wonderful friend who had moved back to town and is one of the best southern girls I know," she said, smiling a ridiculous smile, "and she is looking for a place, and this would be perfect for her. He told me to just let him know what you thought. So, what do you think?" she asked me, grinning that "I already know what you're thinking but I'm going to ask you anyway just to be totally obnoxious" kind of grin. "You love it. I know you love it."

"Yes, I love it," I said, laughing. If there had been furniture, I would have flung my body on it in total disbelief. But since there wasn't, I just twirled around in absolute amazement at my good fortune. As I did, my eyes landed on something familiar. A tennis ball. A drool-encased tennis ball. The common bond between man and dog. A man and dog I knew very well.

The box on the top step declared my Tan Beautiful had arrived. I planned to try it that night, but when evening fell and I remembered the fright of tomorrow, a small spot of mildew in the far corner of my shower ruined me for two good hours.

When I finally got ready for bed, I remembered my Tan Beautiful. It recommended using gloves for application, but I didn't have any. So I just slathered myself from head to toe and went to bed expecting to wake up looking like I had spent the last week on the beach.

Sleep came easily after my two-hour workout. But somewhere in the wee hours of the morning, I began to smell smoke. It seemed faint at first, then it got stronger and stronger. I jumped out of bed and ran though the hall toward the door, screaming, "Fire! Everyone get up! Get up, THE HOUSE IS ON FIRE!"

Dad was in the hall in no time. Mother came out trying to tie a robe around herself all while carrying her mother's pearls and her own wedding album. She started screaming for Dad to wake up Thomas. We all started running down the stairs trying to find out where the smell was coming from, but none of us could see any smoke. We searched and searched, but the smell just wouldn't leave me. Mother scurried around the house trying to retrieve all of her priceless possessions. She threw things out windows and the front door and ran around snatching up baby booties and crowns boxed in acrylic.

Dad and Thomas were walking around with a fire extinguisher when, somewhere in the hubbub, I caught a sniff of myself.

I was the fire.

Tan Beautiful was the fire. I was the one that smelled like fire.

I put out a call far and wide for everyone to come into the foyer. Each one ran in frantically from different directions, Mother in her high heels with an eye mask perched atop her head, Dad and Thomas skidding to a halt in the foyer, Duke on their heels, convinced this whole escapade was a party. I simply stated, "There's no fire." With that I turned around and headed up the stairs.

Dad panted as he leaned over double, "Savannah, how do you know there is no fire?"

"Just trust me on this one, Dad, there is no fire." With that the stairs carried me back to my asylum. I'm sure it took my mother three hours to retrieve everything she had thrown onto the sidewalk, and I'm certain Dad kept looking for the fire anyway. I myself went to bed with the declaration that no other living, breathing soul would ever know the truth about that moment.

CHAPTER THIRTY-SIX

I woke up early and headed downstairs to begin what I was sure would be my Wednesday and Friday routine—at least until I moved and could read the paper alone at my own breakfast table. Duke was waiting at the door. Since I had returned home, Dad had an excuse not to walk him. "Why should Duke be walked twice?" he asked. Duke merrily led the way out the front door, and I saw the paper resting safely between the iron railing and the boxwoods, perfectly placed by a hurried paperboy.

About the time we hit the sidewalk, I spied Grant's image two blocks down, coming my way. I did a one-eighty, ducked, and tugged at Duke's leash to follow. I climbed the stairs in a crouched position and headed safely back inside. As I closed the door quietly, I tried to catch my breath.

"Good boy, Duke," I said, reaching down to pat his head and feeling nothing. "Duke!" I screamed at the end of a leash that disappeared to the other side of the door. I opened the door just a crack. Duke was staring at me in disgust. I opened the door and snatched him in as quickly as possible. Then I waited. Duke sat by me, stoic and calm, while his master was fidgety and anxious.

"It's really nothing," I assured him. "We'll leave in just a moment. It simply didn't feel like the right time."

After a good ten minutes, Duke and I headed to the park where we nestled ourselves on the closest park bench. It still gave me chills to see my picture on the front page of section B with my name underneath, knowing my mother had nothing to do with it. Duke was thankful for the breather, and I strapped his leash around my ankle and began to read the second and final part to my first human-interest story.

I tried to savor it, knowing I'd experience this first only once. For all the pain of the week, I had come to realize how little I had appreciated first things. My first kiss, my first love ... even my first public failure. These moments pass too quickly, moving from magic to familiarity. So I read slowly and appreciated every dotted *i,* comma, and period.

I owe this city an apology. But first, I must apologize to the woman who was the subject of my Wednesday column. To act as if it was my right to tell someone else's story was presumptuous and arrogant. It is a privilege to know a person; it is an honor to know her story. And it is a treasure to be given a person's time, which is what you offer me on Wednesdays and Fridays. Wasting it with thoughtlessness was inexcusable. I assure you, if you would entrust your time to me once more, I will handle it with grace and caution.

I have learned a great deal over the past twenty-four hours. I have learned the real human-interest story I sought had nothing to do with the story that I spent days investigating. There is much even for me to learn about my treatment of those entrusted to me. In a way, Savannah's beauty queen was entrusted to me, and I failed her. In desiring to help her fly again, I clipped her wings instead. I hope she will forgive me.

I've also spent the last twenty-four hours asking

myself many questions about loss and disappointment and defeat. No one wants anyone to see his or her failures. And by exposing another's, I lived my own. The lesson was hard. But the outcome will hopefully make me more aware—aware that failure and loss, when accompanied by a true desire to learn, is often the necessary road to achieving a dream.

We experience loss every day. I lost a book deal because of a misguided attitude. I lost a good human-interest story because of arrogance, and I almost lost this opportunity to commune with you, right here on these pages, because my failure tempted me to throw it all away.

My greatest failure, however, was the misconception that another's loss paled in comparison to my own. A fine lady taught me that one. She caused me to realize that even if the dream isn't yours, the death of it is no less significant.

This beautiful city boasts at least two women who know the secret of weathering loss. One stands on the corner of one of our squares, selling books and dispensing smiles. Katherine Owens has faced the loss of a dream and the loss of her love. The loss of a dream introduced her to the man of her dreams. And the loss of that man propelled her into yet another new dream. She could have wallowed in her world of disrepair. But she knew, even on dark nights, that opportunity awaited her. And morning always showed up. Mrs. Owens will tell you that to lose is only to begin something new, to discover something you would have missed had success taken you down a different path.

The other woman has taken on challenges I would never have the courage to face myself. My mother has loved her husband and children, breathed life into this city, and found jobs for people in whom she's seen hidden potential, and all this after losing her own greatest dream. Yet Victoria Phillips refused to allow that loss to define her future, and as a result, her life has touched the lives of all of us who live here, and none more than mine.

We experience loss in families, in football games, in the stock market. But what if in the midst of those losses we could remember the successes? What if in the moment the marriage seemed to be crumbling we grabbed hold of each other and remembered the wedding day, the birth of our children, the sharing of dreams, the telling of secrets, the love that we've made, and the heartbreaks we've shared? Could focusing on the fulfillment of the past allow us to realize that today's conflict will pass as well?

Today I challenge you to reject loss and disappointment as your companions. Let's resolve to face our crippling moments with the courage of Katherine Owens and Victoria Phillips. We will face lies and deceit, unfairness and cruelty, bad economies and sickness. What we do in the face of such circumstances is what will set our course. It is what will lead us to a corner bookstore or to the Chamber of Commerce. What will you do in the face of your life losses? Whatever you do, rest assured you will never be the same for having met them and faced them well. Nor will the life of our city.

Until Wednesday,
Savannah from Savannah

Someone sat down beside me and started petting Duke. When Grant's face registered, paper, park bench, and me all about went flying. So much for avoidance.

"Have mercy! you about scared me to death," I said, crumpling the paper to my chest so I could grab my heart.

"Well, you were so focused I didn't want to bother you. So what did you think?"

"What did I think about what?"

"About your article."

"Oh," I said, embarrassed that I had been caught reading my own work. "Well, I just wanted to see if it had to be edited much."

"Savannah Phillips, I know you. You would read me everything you wrote. You would call me at three in the morning just to read me something, whether I was cognizant or not," he said, laughing.

I couldn't believe he would bring all of that up. They weren't things I wanted to remember just then. "Well, that was a long time ago," I said. I stood as if to go.

"I'm sorry. Just wanted you to know you made the right decision. Well, I'm sure I'll see you soon. And I would really love for you to meet Elisabeth."

"Well, I'm sure we'll meet eventually. I really need to hurry. I hope you have a good day. It was nice to see you," I said as I walked past him.

"It was nice to see you too. Nice tan," he said as he headed in the opposite direction. I turned to watch him jog away and knew I must choose how this loss would define me. There was the convent option, which might afford me a teaching position at Saint Vincent's Academy. That wasn't appealing. There was the "I'll never love again" recluse option. Paige would never allow it. Or there was the option to live my life, write well, and perhaps one day meet a man who would rock my world like Jake did Victoria's, or Jim did Katherine's, and experience that cataclysmic risk of marriage. Or maybe not.

I stared into my closet. Each color represented some-thing to me. Khakis reflected my nature of somewhat predictability. All the black represented my desire to fit in while standing out.

And my flip-flops represented my need to feel free. Today, I wanted to reflect something different. Something less safe. Something, dare I say, more Savannah. Today required a dress, a blue denim sleeveless wrap dress. So I put it on and slid my feet into my cute leather-between-the-toes Kate Spade sandals with matching bag.

Vicky was pulling out of the garage as I came out the side door. She backed up to position herself beside my car, stopped, and rolled down her window. "Savannah Phillips, you look absolutely breathtaking. Have you met a man?" she asked, staring at me.

"No, it's Friday and I feel like wearing a dress. I do that sometimes, you know," I said, opening my own car door and sitting down where I could see her eye to eye. "I was hoping I'd see you before I left. Would you have time to go to lunch today? I have somebody I'd like you to meet."

"You must be ill! Do you have a fever? We need to get you checked. Maybe you have Lyme disease. You know, Duke is probably loaded with ticks and you might have gotten one on you. Get out of the car, go upstairs, and let me take your temperature. That thing could be sucking the blood out of your brain as we speak," she said, turning off her car.

"Mother, please. I am fine," I said, starting my own. "And Duke doesn't get out enough for a tick to even find him. Seriously, I want you to have lunch with me. Today is a special day."

Well, that stopped her ranting. "Then yes, Savannah, I would love to have lunch with you, and it is a special day. Your article was one of the nicest things I've ever read. I am supremely proud of you, supremely proud. But promise me, if you ask to go shopping with me too, we will head straight to the emergency room."

"Would that really be so shocking?"

"As shocking as if you said you had always had a secret desire to enter a beauty pageant yourself."

"If I ever say that, I'll need more than an emergency room, I'll need to be admitted for psychiatric evaluation. I'll see you at noon. Let's meet at The Lady & Sons."

"I'll see you at noon. Get checked, honey. Really, get checked," and she drove off in her Mercedes coupe convertible that she bought purposefully so Duke could never ride in it. Dad bought the SUV so Duke could ride in it whenever he wants.

I placed another call on the way to Dad's shop. Another invitation to lunch. It was accepted. Then I called Claire. I told her that I should have enough money to move into the new place in about a week or so. I asked her to see if that would be OK with the landlord. She assured me it would. But I told her to check anyway.

CHAPTER THIRTY-SEVEN

As I pulled into a parking place a couple of stores up from Jake's, I saw the back of a man leaning over and petting Duke. Duke's tail was wagging feverishly. As I approached the gentleman from behind, he stood up. It was Joshua.

"Oh, hey, Ms. Phillips," he said, startled.

I tried not to act as surprised as he. "I see you've met the master around here." Duke got up to greet me and I patted him on the head.

"Yeah. Thanks to you I've become more addicted to your father's java than I was St—at that other place. I think that's what you call it." He started swirling his cup around as if he didn't know what to say next. "Do you smell something burning?"

Apparently Tan Beautiful's promise of a lasting tan wasn't the only thing that lasted.

"That would be Duke. He lost his ball in the fireplace and was bound and determined not to let it escape."

I turned to look inside the store, and when I did, every head whipped around. Surely they had far more interesting things to do today at work than glue themselves to the window.

"You must have been pretty busy yesterday. I didn't see hide nor hair of you," I said, walking to the door as two of the ladies who work at the courthouse came out with their coffee in hand. They said hi to us both, and after they passed Joshua, they turned around to check him out.

"Yeah. I had to contend with two board meetings and a local petition about satellites brought up by the Chamber of Commerce."

"I heard about the petition. That must have made for an interesting afternoon."

"Actually it made for an interesting evening as well." He reached down to pet Duke again, who was persistently nuzzling Joshua's hand.

I decided to take the opportunity to ask what I felt was a rather pressing question, since he had brought up the satellite issue. "Joshua, do you know Mr. Hicks's secretary very well?"

"Why, have you met her?" he asked with a slight smirk.

"I wouldn't say we have actually met," I said, thankful that she hadn't witnessed my encounter with ceramic in the ladies' room, "I hear she doesn't care for me much."

"Ms. Phillips, I told you earlier, not everyone is thrilled that you're here. I know it's hard for you to believe, but not all the world is going to celebrate you."

"I don't need celebrating. It was just a question."

"Well, you worry too much. She's just a silly girl with a stressful job. She probably wanted yours. But don't worry. You'll win her over in time. Might be a long time, if I know her, but eventually you'll become friends, I'm sure. And if you don't, you'll still have the likes of me to run around with." He gave me an obnoxious wink. "Well, the tourism department calls." He said as he gave Duke one last pat on the head and began to walk past me.

"You cover the tourism department?" I gave him a slight smirk of my own.

"Yes, I have had it for the last year. Can't say I enjoy it though. The new director has a crush on me." He wrapped his satchel crossways around his rather defined chest.

"Well, that's flattering," I said, trying to stifle my growing smile.

Joshua and Miss Amber Topaz? The mere thought of the two of them together made me laugh out loud.

"Laugh if you want, Ms. Phillips. But I have job to do, a professional job. And I can't have a giddy director of tourism winking at me when she needs to be directing meetings. Not to mention it makes all the other journalists there slightly jealous." He turned back around to continue his walk to his bike that was parked up the street.

"Well, flatter her. I bet she's a fine young lady."

"Aren't they all, Ms. Phillips, aren't they all?" His voice trailed off down the street. I didn't know what it was about these newspaper people always repeating themselves. "Good article, by the way," he called out, turning around with an incredible smile. I refused to act like I even heard him.

I wanted to stop there for a moment and take in what had happened to me with his smile. But had I stopped for any length of time I would have invited a set of twins, an aged African American, and an anonymous landlord to hit me with a thousand questions, none of which I had either time or desire to answer. So instead of stopping to think about anything, I walked straight in and straight to the back and only acknowledged the stares with a casual hello.

I poured myself a Coke and was putting the lid on it when the only one brave enough to come back and ask questions entered the room. "He seems like a nice guy. Do you see much of each other at work?" Dad asked.

"Inquisitive, aren't we? But that's not why I'm here. I found an apartment."

"Yeah? Well, tell me you can afford it!" he said, coming around the counter to sit down.

"Don't you want to know where it is?" I asked.

"Of course."

I grabbed his hand and said, "Well, come out here and I'll show you." I dragged him out the front door, and even Duke jumped from his slumber when he saw us headed to his location on the sidewalk. I turned Dad around to face the front of his store and said, "Look up!"

He turned his gaze upward and said, "What am I looking at?"

"The Culpeppers' place. It's going to be mine," I told him, punching his arm and jumping up and down like a teenager.

"Savannah, are you sure you can afford that?" he asked, still looking up.

"I know! I didn't think I could either. But apparently the man who bought it just wanted to have a responsible kind of person living there. That would be me." I pointed to myself as if I were a two-year-old. "Do you know who bought it?"

"No, uh . . . I heard he likes to keep to himself though." He returned to the shop.

"Well, don't you love it?" I asked, following him back inside.

"Yes, I think it's perfect. If you can afford it, I think it's perfect. But I really think you just wanted to be a hop, skip, and a jump from your father."

"Don't kid yourself; I wanted to be a hop, skip, and a jump from free Coca-Colas and Duke."

"So how soon are you moving?"

"Well, my, my, don't we seem quite anxious?"

"Well, it's not like I'm getting rid of you," he said, looking up.

"I should have my money together after I get my first paycheck. Hopefully I'll get paid by next week, so I should be moving out in a couple of weeks, maybe sooner. Won't you be a happy man?"

"Oh yes, now I will have one Phillips woman to dictate my days and another my nights. Won't I be the lucky one?"

"Yes, because now you really can sleep at the store if you need to. I'll have an extra bedroom anytime you need a break."

"So back to this Joshua kid."

"There's nothing to him. He's annoying and arrogant and we have to sit right next to each other." I would not allow this conversation to become interesting.

"Well, anyway, I didn't get to see you before I left the house. Your article was wonderful, Savannah. I can't tell you how proud I am of you. You did exactly what you needed to do," he said, leaning back against the counter on the other side of the Coke machine.

"All I did was write down my own questions," I said, turning to look at him. "I figure if I'm asking them, surely someone else is asking them or has asked them. I just hope that with all the questions there are some answers in there as well. Life hasn't given me many experiences. I mean you and . . . Mother have sheltered Thomas and me from a lot of things."

"I think it came across loud and clear. I've got to get back up front. I'll see you for dinner. You're welcome to invite your friend sometime," he said with a wink as he headed out the door.

"Paige would love to come by. She was just talking about you the other day," I yelled loud enough that he could hear me even though he tried to act as if he couldn't.

As I passed Dad's "Thought for the Journey" on my way to the car, the words resounded with my new discoveries: "In his heart a man plans his course, but God determines his steps." Nothing clearer needed to be said. Nothing truer either.

Marla was already busy answering phones. She gave me a thumbs-up sign as I walked through the door. I headed back to my desk and sat down to open up my laptop and rack my brain for a new story. I might as well resign myself to a life of sleepless nights.

Paige's, Jake's, college-student-turns-human-interest-writer were the best story possibilities that occurred to me in the hours I sat typing out asinine concepts. I looked at my watch to discover it was almost lunch time, but I wanted to speak to Mr. Hicks before going. As my feet exited the elevator, I saw his secretary's petite frame actually sitting where I imagined it was supposed to. I stopped at her desk and introduced myself, extending my hand.

"Hello, I'm Savannah Phillips. I don't believe we've met."

She looked up at me said, "I know who you are," and turned around to put a file in the cabinet behind her. This one would definitely take some effort. I proceeded to ask if I could see Mr. Hicks. "Mr. Hicks is busy at the moment. You should have called before you climbed all those stairs with your delicate legs."

I was looking forward to a good day, and getting into it with this little girl wasn't on my agenda. So I simply said, "Actually, I took the elevator."

The back of her head replied, "Whatever."

"I'll just come back later."

All would have gone off without a hitch if she just hadn't added under her breath, "Oh yea! She's coming back later."

I was halfway down the hall when I heard it. I promptly stalked back to the desk of that bleached-blond, overdone Prissalina. "Do you have a problem with me?"

She turned around, and gave me a rather menacing glare for such a little one. "Yes, I do have a problem with you," she said. "You prance yourself in here, demanding a job you don't deserve. You walk around here like you are the queen of the world and think everyone is supposed to jump when you say jump. Well, I won't be jumping. You'll respect the rules around here like everyone else. There are no exceptions, and no one gets to that man in there unless they come through me. I only wish I would have been here on your first visit, because I would have made sure that meeting never happened. So you can act like you're some cherished prize around here, like your mama does, but you ain't all that, sister, and neither is she."

Why can't some people just leave well enough alone? Attack me, talk about my clothes, make cracks about my flip-flops, I don't care; but for heaven's sake, when they talk about my mother, they leave me no options.

"Number one, I don't prance. Number two, the only thing I've ever been queen of was the okra seed–spitting contest. Number three, my dog doesn't even jump when I tell him to, let alone any human I know. Number four, I've always respected every rule, every law—well, except an occasional breaking and entering—but that's none of your business. And lastly, sister, my mother *is* all that."

She shook her head and tsked at me! "Don't suck your teeth at me. Victoria Phillips is everything she thinks she is and more. And I want you to know something. I got this job because Mr. Hicks gave me an opportunity, just as I'm sure you have yours for the same reason. I don't want your job. I don't want your attention. But I do expect your respect."

"Dream on . . . dream on."

"If I need to speak with Mr. Hicks, you'd better make sure he gets the message. And if I turn in an article to you, you'd better make sure he gets it exactly the way I left it. And if you ever, and I do mean ever, talk about my mother to me or anyone else, well, let's just say there is not a set of stairs high enough that I won't find you and deal with you. So let's make a truce here. You don't have to like me. You don't even have to talk to me if you don't want to. But you will respect me. And I will respect you. I'll call for appointments, and I'll turn my stories in on time. We can get along. But that choice is yours."

She looked puzzled, but I knew she was just trying to sidetrack me. "You are a weird child."

"Well, you're whacked."

"What did you say?"

"I said, you are in lack. In people skills, that is. So, if you can, would you tell Mr. Hicks I need to see him. I'll be downstairs." While I was still standing over her desk, I heard the click of Mr. Hicks's door.

"What's going on out here?"

Miss Thing put on the most phony smile I had seen since the Hinesville Pageant. "Oh, nothing, sir. Ms. Phillips just came up without an appointment, and I was trying to explain to her," she said, rolling her eyes at me, "that she needs to have an appointment."

Mr. Hicks chuckled and said, "Thank you for guarding me, but I don't mind if someone needs to talk to me." He reached over and patted her hand, which had a death grip on the edge of her desk. Then he turned to me. "Savannah, I have a few minutes now, would you like to come in?"

"Yes, sir, it won't take a second."

He motioned for me to go in front of him. I offered one last smile to the warden, hoping it might soften her. It didn't.

"Savannah, have a seat." He shut the door behind us. "Jessica is a little rigid about how she wants things to run around here. I imagine she'll lighten up in time." I sat down in one of the two worn blue leather chairs in front of his desk. "Did you need to talk about your next story?" he asked with a delighted smile on his face. I wasn't sure why he was so anxious to hear about my next story. He acted more anxious than me, if that was possible.

"No, sir. I'm here to make sure today's article was OK."

"Actually, I thought it was an improvement," he said, leaning his larger frame down into his own blue leather desk chair, as every spring let out a sound of extreme tension. "You still have a lot to learn, but at least you won't bring on needless litigation."

"Well, I'm learning."

"Well, we'll learn together," he said with a smile I'm sure he had given to a multitude of young dreamers who had stood in this same office many times before. "Time will teach you the difference one person can make."

"One person can't make that big a difference."

"Oh yes, they can. Look what Gloria did for years. One person can light a fire under a multitude of people. You need to remember that every time you write an article."

Well, that was just a glorious ounce of pressure added to an already draining morning. "Thank you for that pep talk. Well, I've got to head to lunch. I'll see you later."

"Have a good one. By the way, I noticed the book on your desk when I walked by the other day. You'll enjoy it."

He was referring to the new book I picked up after Wednesday's debacle, Peggy Noonan's *When Character Was King: A Story of Ronald Reagan*. "Didn't think it could hurt, with my track record and all."

"Never hurts any of us. Have a good lunch. Oh, when you pick up your next Coke, tell Duke I said hello," he said with a sly grin.

"Point taken, sir."

Jessica was standing by her desk sifting through some papers as I walked by. And suddenly I was overcome by exactly what I needed to do. So I walked right over to her, grabbed her by her shoulders, planted a big ol' kiss on her cheek, looked her straight in her eye, and said, "I'm going to make you like me." And I walked back to the stairwell and down the stairs, laughing all the way.

Victoria eats at The Lady & Sons about once a week, just to trade recipes with the owner, her good friend Paula Deen. She says Lady & Sons knows how food should be cooked; no boxed stuff found here. When I pulled in, she pulled in beside me. I got out of my car first and walked over to open her door.

"Hello, darling," she said, removing her blue floral Kate Spade mules from the car first, then lifting the matching bag from the other side, and finally bringing her blue-suited self out of the car.

I closed her door and wrapped my arm around her to walk into the restaurant. "This suit looks almost identical to the white one you had on yesterday."

"That's because it is. I loved the style so much, I bought three; a white one, a blue one, and a pink one. So how was your morning?"

"It was more interesting than you can imagine." I opened the door so we could go inside.

"Well, what in the world happened?" she asked. She was quickly sidetracked, however, when Miss Paula greeted her at the door. They caught up for a few moments, talking about Paula's boys, Miss Paula's new television show, and Thomas and me as if I wasn't there. When they were through catching up, I asked if we could have a table in the back. When we sat down, and I positioned myself where I could see the front door. Mother ordered a sweet tea and I ordered a Coke. "Now tell me, young lady, what in the world happened today?"

Her ringing cell phone spared me from answering. The only

thing that was mentioned was TV crews and that she would be there when she was finished.

Katherine walked to our table as my mother ended the call, looking as good as I hoped to in another twenty-five years. She was wearing pressed khakis with a black sleeveless sweater, a black belt with a simple silver buckle, and another sweater draped over her shoulders. Her silver hair fell fresh and naturally around her face, framing her beautiful smile. I wrapped my arms around her and gave her a warm hug, which she returned as warmly, and then I was able to introduce two of the finest women I knew to each other. "Katherine Owens, this is my mother, Victoria Phillips."

"What an absolute pleasure to meet you," Katherine said as she took my mother's extended hand and placed it inside both of hers. "Can I give you a hug? I feel like I know you."

Victoria smiled as the two women shared a greeting. "Absolutely. I feel like I know you as well."

"I thought you two needed to meet," I explained. "After all, I wouldn't be here without either one of you." The emotion of the moment as I looked into the faces of these women I had grown to love and admire was almost overwhelming.

"Now, that's not true," Katherine said. "You know, Savannah, your determination to make your own way is what brought you here."

"Isn't that the truth?" Mother replied.

"But that's not why I've stayed," I assured them. "I stayed because somewhere between proving points and losing dreams— not to mention torturous pageant stories—I realized this is where I was really meant to be."

We all got a chuckle at our pageant horrors.

"Amazing, isn't it?" Mother added. "Look at us. Three very different women, all having lost something. And yet we've each discovered, because of our willingness to believe in an eternal purpose, that every loss eventually reveals something better that we've gained."

This table and my life revealed plenty.

CHAPTER THIRTY-EIGHT

The blaring date on my cell phone seemed to be important, but I couldn't quite remember why. Then the memory lured me back to a party in New York I would have attended this evening. Today, however, I was confident I had made no mistake. I was home.

To many, my home exists in a time gone by. But Savannah has its own rhythm. Life still happens here. People still die. Babies are still born. Dreams are still shattered. Successes achieved. You can find it all here. And I'm not sure that changing the world was ever really my goal anyway. I just wanted to touch a soul, so that he or she could touch another, and the ongoing cycle—the cycle of life, the reason for living—would produce change. And I was glad at this moment, with the almost-summer sun beating through my window, that Savannah had welcomed me home.

At the office, I saw the pantyhose-covered legs and cranberry sling-back pumps before I turned the corner of my tiny cubicle. When the full body came into view, I found myself face-to-face with Amber, decked out in a cranberry suit with tiny fabric-covered buttons running up the front of her jacket. Her hair had not moved since I saw her the other day at lunch, and her jewelry reflected her, shall we say, illuminating personality. As soon as she saw me, she stood to her feet. "I'm sorry to bother you, Savannah. I know I shouldn't just stop here without even calling first. I just wanted to see you for one minute since we haven't talked since lunch the other day."

"It's OK," I said, setting my satchel on the far side of my desk. I motioned for her to sit back down and pulled my chair up to sit across from her. "What's up? You look beautiful."

She looked down at herself with a surprisingly shy smile. "Oh, this is an old suit. I've had it since I competed in Miss Georgia United States of America the third time," she said, lowering her head. "Pretty sad, isn't it? That's how I remember the time frame of major events in my life, what pageant I was in."

"We all need points of references. Mine are ads in the paper. So how have you been?"

"I've been good. Really good," she said and I believed her. "I've done a lot of thinking since we talked. You said some hurtful things, Savannah," she said with a pouty look. "But they were true. Every one of them. I've spent my entire life allowing other people's opinions to define me. And I made a decision that I'm not going to do that anymore. I mean, the last time I lost Miss Georgia United States of America, I went home and sat in front of the TV eating an entire chocolate cake and replaying the pageant video in my VCR over and over. In the middle of the forty-ninth viewing, I called my mother and said, 'I've watched this thing forty-nine times and I still haven't won.'" She broke into a light laugh. "It was really pitiful. I realize now that only one thing will give me that kind of self-worth. You called it an 'eternal perspective,' I think. And thanks to you, I believe I've been able to find that."

"So are you hanging up your pageant dresses?"

"Well, no. I'm just getting a new perspective. I'm going to do pageants for the enjoyment alone. Because I do enjoy them. Just like you enjoy writing. But I'm just not going to do it for approval. I'm going to tell myself, 'Self, you are beautiful. You don't need these people's approval. You don't even need to win. Now, it's OK if you do, but you don't have to win. So, self, you just go out there and sing your little heart out, answer your questions, and let the whole world see those great legs. And if you win, you need to tell those other girls how wonderful they were and not to let the judges' decision make them feel worthless.' What do you think about that?"

I just smiled at her sincerity, patted her skinny knee, and said, "That's a wonderful place to begin."

"I thought you would agree," she said. "So I've got to get back to work. And I've got a busy weekend because I think I might get asked out soon, and I also need to practice changing from my swimsuit to my talent competition outfit. I've got my time down to a minute and thirty seconds, but I really think I can cut ten seconds off of that. If it wasn't so hard getting my swimsuit unstuck, I could probably do it in a minute flat. 'Always be prepared.' I learned that motto in Girl Scouts. And I hear the Mrs. United States of America Pageant has a lot less time to get ready than you do in the Miss Pageants. Who knows, I could be there by this time next year."

I knew the next thing we might need to work on was her motivation for marriage. I also wasn't about to be the one to inform her of Joshua's feelings for her. So I simply raised an eyebrow and stood up. She continued to talk incessantly until I had to use more abrupt measures by saying, "Amber, it was great to see you, but I've got to get back to work."

"Oh, I'm sorry," she said, standing up with a slight, very slight, hint of embarrassment. She straightened her cranberry attire and headed around to the other side of the cubicle. As she turned the corner, Joshua's nameplate that hung on the side of his cubicle caught her eye. "Savannah! that's him. That's the man I think I'm going to marry. Oh, my side. If I knew that was his cubicle right next to yours, I'd have gone weak in the knees. And if he would've heard us! Oh, heaven help me, I would've had to have a face transplant and move to Katmandu." Her face morphed into that of a lovesick pup. "He's the most beautiful thing my eyes have ever beheld. The way his hair kind of flops on his head. And those curls. Oh, they are just like a bowl of noodles. And his hands, have you ever looked at his hands, Savannah? They are the strongest, most breathtaking hands I've ever seen. I bet they could hold your hand in theirs, and you wouldn't even be able to see your fingers. I need to go. I'm getting annihilated."

"I'll see you later," I said, laughing, knowing even I had never seen "exhilarated" in quite that way. I watched as she half swayed, half strutted back up the aisle. I hoped she wouldn't introduce herself to Marla, because she'd probably never make it through the door again. *Well, Rome wasn't built in a day,* I thought as she disappeared into a sea of gray.

I peered around the corner of Joshua's cubicle. It was totally sparse except for a University of Florida banner hanging on one of the Styrofoam beams and a picture of him and a group of guys about his age. There was little to reveal the full character of the man that rested in this chair. I figured what I didn't know, Miss Amber Topaz would reveal. The ringing of my phone called me back to my desk.

"Hello, Savannah Phillips."

"Vanni, you were worried about your next story?" came a unique tone of excitement, so rare, in fact, the last twenty-one years had never revealed such enthusiasm. "Well, I've found it. Get up here to the courthouse as soon as you can."

"What is it, Thomas?"

"Just get up here, now."

"OK, I'll be right there," I said, reaching for my satchel.

"And Vanni."

"Yeah?"

"Don't be shocked when you get here, but Mom has chained herself to it."

"I'll be there in three minutes," I assured Thomas and hung up.

I grabbed all coordinating paraphernalia and my cell phone. "I've got to get my attorney on speed dial," I muttered. I left, not sure if this was the story I would want or not. But a reporter must go. A reporter must go.

ACKNOWLEDGMENTS

Most of you can skip these pages. After all, the only people who will read it are those who are dying to see if I mention their names. So, for those who read it and you weren't mentioned, I can only blame such reprehensible actions on my weary being. For the rest of you that I did mention, my words are sincere and words that I hope I have said to you personally at one time or another and not just on the written page. If I haven't, I'm glad the opportunity arose that I could.

Many authors would tell you that they had some profound idea when they began writing a book. I did once. However, that book received a substantial amount of rejection letters, thirteen to be exact. (But who keeps a count of such things?) So, I simply wrote this one instead. It didn't start with a prolific idea. I simply knew beauty pageants and thought a story of one being rigged would be an enjoyable adventure. Since I began this idea almost three years ago, many other books with tiaras gracing the cover have been published. But like any good writer will assure you, I had mine first!

This book was written because of a dream I thought I had lost. My multiple rejected manuscript was how I wanted to be introduced to the publishing world. It seemed that it would offer true hope on this chaotic adventure. But no one wanted to publish it. A wiser person might have given up on writing books altogether after the thirteenth rejection letter declaring her book "Not what we are looking for." A statement which cuts as deeply as "She's got a great personality." But call me crazy, or stubborn, neither would be foreign to me, but I believe it was those closed doors that allowed me to get quiet enough to hear the direction the Lord had for this time in my life. That direction is Savannah.

I can honestly say I've fallen in love with these characters. Partly because they were created and developed in one of the darkest times in my life. They gave me laughter and an outlet to be creative and produce a work that I can honestly say I am proud of. I feel like I know them. Even gotten sick of them a time or two. But I must clarify here and now that they are not me, nor my mother, or any beauty queen I have even known, and any resemblance thereof is totally due to way too much Coke consumed during the writing of these pages.

Speaking of my mother, few things of life are possible without one. Life itself being the main thing. But for me she has been a wonderful example of grace and beauty in a world where those words are used to describe very few things. And my father, whose love made it easy to believe Jesus loves me too. For the cars you bought me, for the college you sent me to, for the trust you had in me (because if you had known better, you would have locked me in my room until I was forty, as you threatened), and for letting me climb in an old dilapidated Saab of my own and spread my wings to the hills of Tennessee. I love you and I thank you. But for allowing me a safe place in a dark time and being true believers in miracles, and for giving me a heritage in Jesus, I love you and thank you even more.

To the two grown men who are my brothers, one of which I will forever boss around and the other who, even though he is almost a foot taller than me, will forever be know as "the baby," know this book is not about you and you, and no, you cannot receive any royalties. But you can forever know that it is a privilege to call you on the phone, laugh at your stupid jokes, and pray with you for our needs and dreams.

To my priceless friend Deneen—I know you hate to read, but at this point, until there is a book on tape, you have no choice. You helped finishing this become possible. Through your prayers, through your love, and through your belief that God could somehow use the likes of me. Few people will live this side of heaven and know such a treasure as our friendship has given me. I'm glad I didn't have to wait until there to find it.

To the two women who have been friends and sisters—Beth and Joan. Distance has prevented our getting together as often as we would like. But it will never prevent us from our wonderful memories and invaluable friendships. You two are a part of my best moments.

To Esther Fedorkevich—this would still be lying on a shelf in my office if it hadn't been for your belief, dedication, and hard work. And often persistent attitude. (Aren't we a pair!) This was part of God's plan for both of us. I will always believe that. And I will be forever thankful that He let us have this new path in our lives together.

To Ami McConnell, my editor—I knew you were my kind of girl when you asked if it was "McDonald's calibration system." That was just plain freaky. You have made me mad. You have made me laugh. You have made me better. And you have believed in Savannah like I did. I didn't think people did that unless they were married to you, gave birth to you, or owed you money. But you just got it. From the first day you got it. Here's to believing you'll get the next one as well. Shoot! Here's to believing I'll get the next one as well.

To Bridgett O'Lannerty—thank you for your energy and effort. You were a joy to work with.

To Erin Healy—thank you for making Savannah dance. You

were gentle and "surgical." You took the heart of something and made it beat more powerfully. You are a master at what you do. And such a kind lady. Even though you edited out my husband, you redeemed yourself in fabulous ways. I look forward to seeing what you do with the next one.

To Allen Arnold at Thomas Nelson—what a risk taker you are. How grateful I am. I'm proud to be part of your team.

To the rest of the Thomas Nelson team—Jenny, Amanda, Andrea, and Rebeca—you are here because of your talent. Thank you for sharing those talents with me.

And to my sister-in-laws Janey and Deborah, my cousins Patty and Carol, and my wonderful friends, Heather, Jackie, Valencia, and Cyndi—first thank you for being women of prayer. Your prayers held me up and kept me alive. But also thank you for selflessly reading my book and critiquing my book. Even though I told you a thousand times this is not autobiographical, I know you still don't believe me. I thank you and love you.

To my precious mother-in-law—your strength astounded me. Your faith challenged me. And your life taught me invaluable lessons. I love you for who you are and the treasure you gave me in your son.

To Hannah, Lauren, Abigail, Daxtyn, and the newest addition Jake, Aunt Niecy or Aunt Nina—whichever it is you call me—wants you to know that your destiny is going to be powerful and you are going to be a part of changing this world. I can't wait to see what you will become.

And to the rest of my family, extended and immediate—our treasure is our heritage. Our joy is having the privilege of shared experience and love. All that I know is a part of who I have walked this journey with. I'm thankful God allowed me to be a part of you. And I'm thankful I come from such fine people.

And to my Pastors Rice and Jody Broocks—you loved me, prayed with me, and believed with me. I count it a privilege to walk with you in ministry and to call you pastors. To Pastors Tim and Lechelle Johnson—you challenged me and loved me at the same time. Then, assured me, "No one's getting out of the boat." I know that is true. You have proved it. To Pastor Jim and Kathy Laffoon—your prayers have been felt, and the word of the Lord you have spoken over my life has been foundational in allowing me to continue to believe. To David and Sandy Houston—thank you for giving us such a beautiful love to emulate and the defining words of "original intent." To John and Maretta Rohrer—you have loved me with an undeserving love. You gave when I had nothing to give in return but my gratitude. You grieved and rejoiced with me. I smile when I think of you, and am glad this journey will be traveled with you. To my Bethel family—I am never more proud than when I'm riding down the road and catch a glimpse of those two distinctive hands touching each other, declaring that we are "Reaching a City to Touch the World." I am honored to be a part of such a beautiful body of believers.

And to those who dwell under my roof. My Maggie and Chloe, who have let me cry in their fur and laugh at their inability to ever tire of chasing a ball from one end of the room to the other. Thank you for being just as excited to see me if I've been gone for two weeks overseas or ten minutes to the grocery store.

And to the man I fell in love with in what seems a lifetime ago. Marriage is a journey. It will make us smile, bump and bruise us, challenge us, grow us, and hopefully, at the end of the day, lead us somewhere. My prayer is that it leads us to our original intent. Thank you for your sacrifice to let me pursue the gifts I felt God had given me, even when they seemed to cost more than they brought in. And thank you for being a man with as much character as talent. Your abilities amaze me. But your heart amazes me more. And at the end of the day, when our children sit on the steps as we swing on the front porch, we're going to tell them the stories about how Mommy and Daddy kept loving when everything in the world screamed at them to stop. And then we're going to tell them how they fell off their bikes and we patched them up, how they had dreams and we nurtured them, and how their hearts got broken and we helped mend them. And then "when there are lines upon our face, from a lifetime of smiles, and when it comes time to embrace, for one long last while, we will laugh about it, how time really flies. We won't say good-bye 'cause true love never dies. You'll always be beautiful in my eyes."

And to the Man who lives in my heart: Jesus Christ. You've taught me much these past years. You've broken me to pieces, then graciously rebuilt me. You've disciplined me, then held me. You've listened to my secret dreams, then given me new ones yet to share. And You've loved me. When I wasn't sure anyone could see my failures and really love me, You showed me that not only could You, but You did. At the end of the day, the only thing that matters is that You are pleased with me: with my life, with the way I love, and with the way I use my gifts. My greatest desire has always been for You to use me, someway, anyway. Thank You for allowing me to be used in a way that I sincerely love. You are the Christ of my soul, the Healer of my heart, and the Deliverer of my dreams, and the One I can't wait to see.

SAVANNAH
COMES UNDONE

CHAPTER ONE

My mother is in chains. Chained to what or for what I have no idea. Thomas only said, "Mother is chained to it."

I didn't ask.

I looked down at the denim bow that tied up my wrap dress. It was slightly tilted, so I straightened it. Now, the bow is an amazing accessory, the way it holds things together. Tying a bow is one of the first achievements of childhood. How unfair: a child, learning how to hold things together. I traced the perfectly symmetrical loops with my index fingers. I thought of childhood and sanity.

The phone rang. Again. I jumped. I snatched up my ringing satchel off the hood of Old Betsy and found my phone conveniently resting on the bottom.

"What?"

"Where are you?" my younger brother, Thomas, asked.

"I'm on my way."

"You said that five minutes ago."

I plopped into the driver's seat. "Are you the clock police?"

"Get down here now. Are you a human-interest writer or not?"

"I am and I'm coming. Just take a breather. I'll be there in a minute."

Welcome to my world. The world of Savannah, where a mother in chains for any reason is no great cause for my alarm.

I pointed my declining Saab away from the newspaper office and toward the courthouse. Something off-kilter hovered in the muggy Savannah humidity. Today I suspected something other than the steamy afternoon sun lured people outside their stores, cooling themselves with makeshift fans. I was certain it had to do with "the woman in chains."

A plump, elderly, floral blur almost attached herself to my front bumper. "Watch where you're going!" I hollered at the closed window. She scampered on up the street, oblivious to the fact that she had narrowly escaped a lovebug's fate.

As I tried to pull up to Wright Square—where both Dad's coffee shop and the U.S. Courthouse stand—I encountered an impassable bottleneck of cars, SUVs, trolleys, and a few unhappy horses toting gawking spectators. This jam was a phenomenon not even experienced on parade day, because cars aren't allowed into the historical district on parade day. But today Savannah had apparently plunged into the depths of downright delirium.

I pulled into the covered parking place at the back of Jake's. My little brother (or rather, *younger* brother; the child stands six feet tall and towers over my five-foot-four-inch frame like a bamboo stalk over a tulip) snatched open the car door.

"Vanni, get out of the car! You've got to get to the courthouse."

"How did you even see me?"

"I've been looking for you for fifteen minutes."

"You only called five minutes ago."

"I called you twice." He grabbed my arm and slammed the door behind me. Thomas, the only one in the world allowed to call me Vanni, dragged me out of the alley and onto the sidewalk in the direction of the courthouse. "What were you doing anyway?"

"I have a job, Thomas. An important job. I have things to finish up before I can just run from my office and jump to the streets."

"Give me a break. You were probably checking your hair."

I would die a thousand deaths before admitting how close he was to the truth.

"Just come on, because you are not going to believe what Mom has done!"

I tried to keep pace with him and actually talk at the same time. "Trust me, I'll believe it. And slow down, I don't run well in heels."

"You shouldn't be wearing heels. The combination is dangerous to society. And trust me, sweet child, you would never have guessed what you're about to see."

We turned the corner and met a scene not witnessed since Tom Hanks sat on a bench and ate a box of chocolates. I could hardly even catch a glimpse of the marble courthouse for the mass of people gathered around something—or dare I say someone—in front of it. ABC and NBC news trucks had arrived. People milled and jabbered like schoolchildren at recess.

We took refuge from the blazing sun with fifteen other shameless gawkers under a live oak near the edge of the square.

"She's in the middle of that, isn't she?"

"You bet your sweet britches she's in the middle of that."

"Does Dad know?"

"Oh yeah, he knows."

"Where is he?"

"He's out there with her."

"Is he angry?"

"Doesn't seem to be."

"Am I going to have to move out of town?"

"Move? Are you kidding? We haven't had this much excitement, since . . . well, since Mom tried to pass that law to neuter all golden retrievers."

"I believe the opposition defined her actions as 'discriminatory.'"

"You should know"—he gave me a beautiful white smile and winked a green eye at me—"Ms. Opposition."

"Just because Duke isn't a lapdog doesn't mean she can ruin his existence." I said, looking around for the golden retriever that had been my mother's nemesis since the day Dad brought him home. "Where is Duke anyway?"

"Tucked away inside Dad's shop."

"Lucky boy. What did he do? Go potty on her Persian again?"

"No, he just can't endure both this squelching heat *and* Mom. A dog can only take so much in one afternoon." Odd but true: Duke had no idea he was actually a dog.

We moved along the sidewalk that passes in front of the courthouse, and a few people parted enough for me to make out the lovely vision I left less than an hour ago after a perfectly normal lunch at The Lady & Sons. Her blue capri slacks and floral Kate Spade mules came into view before her face did.

"Does she have a chain wrapped around her?"

Thomas laughed and folded his arms across his chest. "Yes, that would be a chain."

"What's that big stone thing that she's attached to?" I asked, not certain I wanted to know.

"That, my friend, is a six-thousand-pound stone monument of the Ten Commandments."

"You are not serious."

"Dead serious. Judge Hoddicks brought it in yesterday afternoon. Had it delivered right here."

"Who's he trying to be, Roy Moore?"

"Judge Moore called him earlier actually. Right before I left Judge Hoddicks's office." Thomas wiped the beading sweat off of his forehead and pushed it up through his short, sun-kissed brown hair. "Judge Hoddicks says the case belongs to the people, not the courts. So he wants to keep it in the limelight."

"Is there a reason he's not chained to it instead of Mother?" I watched Mother's beaming smile shine over all. She flitted her head from side to side as if she were ringmaster of this circus.

"Well, a suit was filed against the monument and Judge Hoddicks first thing this morning by some attorneys from Athens and by the ACLU. Judge countersued. Mother suggested the judge take care of the legal matters, and she would take care of the monument."

"You mean public relations."

"No, I mean the monument."

I looked down at my own pretty shoes, trying to avoid the eyes of the very woman who had purchased them. "And Jake said?"

"Haven't heard yet. You can ask him yourself." He pointed to Dad, who was standing on the right set of stairs that entered the courthouse. He was talking to Judge Hoddicks and smiling.

Dad caught Thomas's delighted smile and my mortified stare and winked. My gaze followed his secure gait as he walked over to my mother, whispered in her ear, gave her a kiss on the cheek, and brought his striking six-foot-one frame our way.

Dad patted me on my shoulder and was about to walk past me. "Where are you going?"

He stopped to smile at me. "Back to work."

"Back to work! You've got to be kidding me!" I chuckled. He matched my chuckle with his own.

"No. I'm not kidding."

"You mean you're going to leave her here, strapped to a piece of stone, to be aired on the nightly news? Our reputation will be left here on the sidewalk to be feasted on by water bugs!" I added extra effect to my statement by crushing the water bug that had bravely, yet stupidly, made its way to my area of the sidewalk.

He kissed me on my cheek then brushed his hands through his slightly graying brown hair. "Yes, that's exactly what I'm going to do."

I stared at the disappearing image of my father as he casually sauntered back to his world of coffee and calm, khakis and polo shirts.

My father, at the age of fifty-four, had indisputably gone insane. "But
... how ... why?" I turned my face upward. "Why me, Lord?"

"Take it easy, Vanni. You've got a story and we've got drama,"
Thomas said, patting me on the back and heading over to our
mother like an overgrown adolescent enjoying the spotlight.

"But I don't need drama." I called out, gesturing to no one in
particular. "Really, I can create my own. Who needs extra?"

But then extra arrived. Amber Topaz Childers, the reigning
Miss Savannah United States of America, came up from behind
and goosed me. I screeched. She giggled. And her aqua-colored
eyes, a combination of natural brown irises and artificially colored
contact lenses, made taking her serious very difficult.

"Is this not the most exciting thing ever?" she squealed.

"Right up there with an enema," I muttered.

"Right up there with a what?" She crinkled her perfect nose.

"Right up there with an evening at the cinema."

"Oh my word. Are you telling me you, Savannah Phillips"—
as if my name were lost on me—"have had more exciting times
than this?"

"In abundance."

"All with your mother?"

"Right at the center of it."

"Are you the luckiest girl alive or what?"

"Or what." I looked at this beauty in her little pink pantsuit
with matching lipstick and earrings. She could have been mistaken
for a flamingo had her hair not been quite so ... shall we say, lively.
But even it was held back with a matching pink grosgrain ribbon.

And with nothing more to say, she flounced along to meet the
other present reigning royalty. The former Miss Georgia United
States of America. Mrs. Victoria Phillips. Vicky. My mother.

Every other eye was glued to the vision in blue gracefully
chained to a monument in the middle of my city. And in one
moment of horror, the vision saw me and waved. A few people
turned to see who had her attention. I turned with them, hoping

it was clear that I didn't know the fettered beauty in front of me. But then she called my name.

"Savannah, darling. Savannah! Yoo-hoo!" She waved like a maniacal Barbie. Amber tried to help her get my attention. It was painful for all involved.

I hoped these people would think the woman just wanted to say hello to her city, Savannah, while the cameras were rolling. I didn't lift my eyes to check on their potential gullibility. But I did notice my bow had come undone. And my dress flap had flown open and exposed my slip. I jerked it closed and held it together in my fist.

"This day had better be no reflection of my week to come," I warned the heat. It laughed. Yes, I'm certain it laughed.

CHAPTER TWO

It's no great feat for a television crew to distract my
mother. But when distraction is accompanied by airtime, well,
it technically isn't a distraction anymore, now, is it? At least not in
her world. Call it what you will. In my book, it was my chance to
escape.

As I returned to Jake's, I turned around for one more glimpse
of the square. Wright Square was the second square laid in
Savannah. It was originally named for Lord Viscount Percival. But
in 1763, it was renamed for Savannah's royal governor, James
Wright. Of course, now he's buried in Westminster Abbey, and
Tomochichi, the Yamacraw chief who helped Oglethorpe establish
Savannah, is buried here in Wright Square. And the large rock from
Stone Mountain that sits atop his grave—something I avoid at all
costs—was given by the Colonial Dames on the sixtieth anniversary of his death. Of course General Oglethorpe, a poor man who
came here to deliver us from craziness, has his statue in one square
and his name on another. Go figure.

So, maybe today isn't the first day Savannah has done something ridiculous.

"Mr. Phillips, you can trust me. I'll have you a new dishwasher in here first thing tomorrow morning." The young man in a blue uniform picked up his tools on the other side of the kitchen door.

"That will be great, Ron. I'll be here around seven thirty, so if we could get it earlier that would really help us out. Tomorrow's liable to be a crazy day." Dad peered out the window toward the spectacular spectacle across the square.

"I know. I'm going to spend the night out there with everyone else tonight. Need to make sure these people trying to steal our rights know what we stand for, you know, Mr. Phillips."

"Yeah, well, thanks, Ron. Do I need to pay you anything today?"

"Oh, if you could pay for half today, you can give me the rest when I get it installed in the morning." He bent over to pick up the pen he had just dropped. Poor child showed more of his exposed behind to Dad's staff than anyone should be forced to endure. Louise let out a groan. Her twin sister, Mervine, a snicker. Richard cleared his throat and slid his ebony hand over his eyes. Duke whined as if in pain.

Ron stood and hiked up his britches. I couldn't have been more thankful than a seventy-five-year-old Southern woman on beauty-shop day. Because after all, this city has enough attractions.

Dad wrote a check for Mr. Ron, who left a receipt on the counter. Dad proceeded to help himself to the coffeepot, which brewed underneath the blackboard that featured "Jake's Thought for the Day."

"Watch your words and hold your tongue; you'll save yourself a lot of grief."

I didn't really care what it said today. This man calmly pouring himself some java, as if the entire world hadn't turned upside down on his front lawn, wasn't going to quiet me with his renowned blackboard wit. "Surely you are not going to stand here pouring coffee while *your wife* is chained to a monument large enough to crush a small village?"

He kept pouring. I picked up Ron's receipt on the counter. An emblem of a fish was embossed across the entire piece of paper.

I set it down and then followed my question in case it was lost on him in some form or fashion. "Have you noticed that no one is even here?" I said, motioning to the empty tables and coffee bar. "Every other creature within a thirty-mile radius and probably other states is over there, watching her. Why aren't you?"

"Savannah, your mother doesn't need watching."

"Obviously you are mistaken. The woman is chained to a monument, for crying out loud. I think she has needed watching for years!"

He walked to a window table and sat so he could view the spectacle from his chair. Duke followed close behind. Duke has been a virtual "store prisoner" since the incident last summer when mother caught him coming home carrying a bag of empty beer bottles and pork & beans. She wasn't the only one that saw him, however, and the whole episode had the city abuzz with rumors of Victoria Phillips's dog, "the tootin' alcoholic." That, accompanied by last week's dip in her pool, has pretty much kept him staring out the window too. He looked up at my father as if ready for an explanation of this crazy afternoon as well.

"Your mother is using her free will to express herself, well . . . freely." He laughed at his own amused self.

Duke came over and nuzzled his head up under my hand. I obliged and rubbed his ears. "You laugh. Well, I hate to be the one to break it to you, but I don't need this right now. I just started my job at the paper. Shoot, half of them don't even think I should be writing human-interest stories, and the other half look at me as Victoria Phillips's daughter, *the* human-interest story. So, however you want to break this debacle down, she should be restrained."

I stared into those green smirking eyes that had produced both Thomas's and my own.

"She is, actually."

"Ever the comedian, aren't we?" I looked out the window myself only to see two other television trucks make their way to our newly adorned square. "Great, now every network's covered. CBS and FOX have arrived."

"Savannah, the world doesn't revolve around you, in case you haven't noticed." I heard the twins and Richard make their way to the back room. "And this has nothing to do with you, personally." He turned his attention back to the window.

I walked to the front door and opened it, trying to hide what was boiling inside me. "Well, that is where you're wrong, brother. It has everything to do with me. And you. And my mother. And the fact that we are already talked about in the paper more than your average criminal, and in this city, more than the mayor himself."

"That's not true." He took a casual sip of his coffee.

"It is true. And it is about me. And whether you like it or not, it's about you too. Because half of you is across the street in mules and pastels and will have your name and my name on every nightly news network before our heads hit our pillows."

"Don't you need to get back to work, Savannah?"

"Actually what I need is a Valium."

His head jerked around to scold me. "What did you say?"

"If you would have let me finish, I was trying to say, 'Actually, what we need is to go tell 'em to stop this madness.' But I guess no help is going to come from this side of the square." With that inane salvage I walked out the door.

The Ten Commandments of our Lord were being defended by the same woman who came with me to basketball tryouts and spent the entire time yelling, "Good shot, darling!" while I was dribbling. She sat in the stands on a towel, holding her hands out to her side, not touching anything. I don't know who they found more amusing: me, or Vicky and her antibacterial gel. By the time she started hollering "You go, girl!" and all I was doing was sitting on the bench, I decided to cut myself from the team.

I decided to take up a quieter sport. A sport where the people in the stands weren't allowed to say anything. I became a tennis player. I told her it was uncouth to talk at all while people were playing tennis. I didn't even let her think she could cheer between points. So, for four solid years, at every match, Victoria sat on the stands, on a cushion, and never said a word. It was heaven.

And now here she is, fighting for a piece of it.

I looked across the street, and mother was nowhere to be found in the madness. Camera lights were beaming everywhere and microphones were waving in the air, and my life offered more excitement than a recovering beauty queen. Or maybe not. Because the former Miss Georgia United States of America, nestled across the street in chains, was evidently having a pretty exciting afternoon herself.

I walked to the back of Dad's coffee shop and climbed into Old Betsy. The parking space belonged to the apartment above Jake's, an apartment only a paycheck away from being mine. I, Ms. Savannah Phillips, or "Savannah from Savannah" as my mother calls me, was getting her own apartment. Granted, it was above my father's business, but it was out of my mother's house. Liberation, no matter how you defined it. Even though I had only been out of graduate school and back home for just a little more than two weeks, the walls had closed in and were strangling the life from my vibrant, young soul.

My next-door cubicle buddy and self-appointed affliction greeted me in the narrow passageway before I had a chance to enter my redecorated haven of cardboard. I had attempted to make it more homey with the addition of a few books and one Paige Long "original" oil painting. A gift from the painter herself, who happens to be my best friend.

"Have you heard what's going on at the courthouse?" Joshua's annoyingly overconfident, perfectly white smile gleamed down at me, and a loose black curl hung in front of his left eye. I didn't much like men anymore. Since Paige informed me last week that the only man I had ever really dated—or even loved for that matter—is marrying some chick from an all-girls' school, I have sworn off men in general. So, men in general have moved to my *tolerable* category of relationships.

"Could I at least get through the door and sit down?" I pushed him aside.

"You don't have a door. You have a cubicle." He let me pass.

"Is this comedy hour?" I tossed my satchel on the floor next to my chair. I dropped into it and it squealed.

"My, my, my. To have had such a good morning, you sure deteriorate fast."

I stared at my blank computer screen. Now was not the time to discuss the last hour with The Man among men who irritated me so. Turning to look over at his tanned face, piercing dark eyes, and frantic curls, I said, "You know, I really don't need your analysis of my moods, or my days. We both have jobs to do, and that should keep us busy enough to stay out of each other's way. Don't you have a deadline or something?"

"Or something. Okay, well, if you don't want to tell me, I'm sure I'll find out in the morning with the rest of the city."

"I'm sure you will."

"But I could tell you my news if you told me your news." He invited himself in and pulled up the lone chair that rested underneath Paige's painting.

I didn't even look at him.

"So you don't want to know who's coming on Friday?"

I picked up the phone to dial anyone who would rescue me, even though there was no one I knew well enough that would. My only friends here so far were the receptionist, Marla, the sweet little pixie who got her job because she befriended my mother on a trolley car, and this man next to me. Other than these two, few people around here desired my presence at all.

"I guess that means you don't want to know. Okay. Well"—he

stood, performing a pitiful attempt at dejection—"I guess you don't care that the president is headed this way Friday for a visit before he heads off to Sea Island for a meeting with world leaders. Word has it the mayor was going to invite your mother to attend the president's luncheon."

My head swiveled in time to see his right hand grab the corner of my cubicle, showing off the well-defined muscle that ran from his hand to his elbow and disappeared underneath his shirtsleeve.

He knew exactly what was going on in this city. He knew that my mother was at the center of it all. And he wanted me to be the one to tell him all about it. Well. He could read it in the paper. But no matter how perfectly toned his bicep was, he wasn't getting it from me.

CHAPTER THREE

On the drive home, I avoided Wright Square and the dead man's tomb. But I could not avoid the fact that Savannah had officially turned upside down. And this time it had nothing to do with a best-selling book about a murder, or a University of Georgia win.

The behavior that rippled through Savannah today was so unorthodox. I mean, there is only one time a year that the people of Savannah attach a scurry to their step, and that is in preparation for the annual St. Patrick's Day parade. Other than that, this town's pace is set apart by its ability to accomplish even the most pressing tasks in slow motion. Stores actually close for months at a time with nothing more than a note in their window: "Got an itch and will return when the fall clothes arrive or the beach gets too cold."

Truly, there is nothing electric about this place, except what you might see during a thunderstorm. Or during any activity related to my mother. And occasionally during a well-publicized murder. But today, I could practically see the electricity buzzing along the very sidewalks and alleyways.

Pulling on to Abercorn Street, I glanced at Clary's restaurant across the street from my parents' home. The absence of a dinner-time rush offered more proof that something was amiss in the South.

I walked through the second-floor doors of our rather substantial home. Some would consider it a mansion. Vicky considered it a compromise. She had wanted to live in (I kid you not) the Victorian district. But my dad, wanting as uneventful a life as possible with a woman who calls her daughter "Savannah from Savannah" refused to spend the next twenty-some-odd years listening to his wife introduce herself as "Victoria from the Victorian district." So, she settled on this lovely house, a house on the Historical Register large enough to accommodate a small village. Don't tell her I said that. She would think I was making some snide reference to Hillary Clinton's first book.

Home has a smell. Well, it used to. It used to smell like beef roast with potatoes and carrots and gravy with a side of butter beans and macaroni and cheese. But not today. No pungent aromas accosted my senses when I opened the front door. No flurry of activity in the kitchen, no loud conversations. It was then, for the first time, my mental faculties registered the fact that no Victoria meant . . . no dinner. No one else in this entire family knew how to do much more than pour a bowl of cereal.

We discovered this absence of talent the night my father had the brilliant idea of informing my mother that "the only thing someone inherits who stirs up undue trouble in their own house is the wind." In essence, he informed my mother she was a bag of hot air. All because he wouldn't eat the crumbs at the bottom of the potato-chip bag before he opened a new one.

And I do believe he capped it all off by calling her Vicky. My mother hates nothing more than being called Vicky. But when it came from my father's mouth, well, let's just say, "Hold on, Hannah!"

My mother had paused briefly at this comment. She attempted to regather and reload. But nothing came out. She tried. She tried hard. Even stamped her foot a couple times like a horse about to charge. But the poor woman didn't have a comeback. A verbal comeback, that is. She came back all right. She didn't cook for a week. And after he tried to make us a dinner of canned tomato soup by mixing it with water, well, let's just say I didn't even like him much myself at that point. So we ate cereal. Three times a day. I suggested that next time he should make only those observations that would result in his sole punishment.

I walked up the stairs to the sound of my own feet. No patter of paws followed. No, "Dinner's ready!" No smart comment about the fact that my body was actually encased in a dress. I would have welcomed the persecution. But none came.

As I entered my bedroom and proceeded to my bathroom to wash my face, the stress of my mother's antics finally captured me. Toothpaste from the morning brushing had not completely made its way down the sink, and a blob of blue Crest lay on the oil-rubbed bronze drain.

I couldn't help it. I grabbed the Comet, a toothbrush, and a few extra-strength Tylenol and busted up in that bathroom like it hadn't seen in a good two days. I scrubbed faucets. I scrubbed shower tiles. I scrubbed floor tiles. I scrubbed things you wouldn't even know existed unless you got down on all fours and examined the plumbing. By the time I was through, that placed shined as if Mr. Clean on steroids had come through.

The chime from the door alarm declared someone's entrance. I figured I should greet the intruder. My twenty-four-year-old frame felt the two hours of squatting and cleaning, and I required extra care in removing the kneepads and rubber gloves. But you can rest assured, there was not a microscopic remnant of any germs, fungus, or hardened toothpaste to be found.

Thomas, Duke, and Dad came up through the downstairs door from Thomas's floor of the house, otherwise known as a basement.

The child inherited it after I refused it. He'll be there 'til Vicky buys him a house or Dad kicks him out. The former will only happen because of the latter.

I met them in the kitchen. No Vicky. No hope for normalcy inside these four walls this evening.

"Where have you three been?"

Thomas went straight to the refrigerator and pulled out a Dr Pepper. "We've been talking to Mom. She is so into this thing!" He was acting as if this was the greatest thing he had been a part of since he shaved his head for his "knob" year at The Citadel military college. I couldn't hide my disgust.

"When is she coming home?"

Dad looked at me with undisguised disbelief. "Savannah, your mother is staying there until they remove her or the monument."

"You've got to be kidding me."

"I think it's great," Thomas quipped.

"Ever the juvenile, aren't we, Thomas?"

"Ever the girl with the stick up her—"

"Thomas," Dad interrupted. "That's enough."

I nodded. "I think you need to get out more." I turned my attention back to the once-sane leader of this questionable family. "Seriously, Dad, she can't stay there. What's she going to do, sleep outside all night?"

"It looks that way."

His calm demeanor dismayed me. "You mean, you are going to let her sleep out there all night?"

"Savannah, I'll take care of your mother. You don't worry about her. Now, I'm going to get her and me something to eat." He began to make his way to the stairs to perform his usual after-work ritual of a shower and change of clothes. "You want to come have dinner with us?"

"What? And risk a picnic caught on tape? I don't think so."

He continued upstairs. "Have it your way."

"What are Thomas and I going to eat?"

My brother headed downstairs only to call back, "I'm going with Dad."

I looked down at the golden four-legged creature next to me. "I guess we're on our own." Duke remained for one brief second, and then became a golden blur as his flapping furry tail followed Thomas downstairs. Even Duke knew who would really eat dinner tonight.

The kitchen was empty. "Like I said, I guess I'm on my own."

I sat down at the edge of the bar and rested my elbows on the black soapstone countertop. Putting my face in my hands, I let out an extended sigh. But I wasn't totally alone. I was joined by the presence of official Phillips-family collapse. I stared at the empty dinner table where someone always sat. I stared at the empty oven that always had something baking in it by this time of the evening. I stared at the empty pathway between island and counter that always had a woman flittering up and down it. Tonight, my mother was outside on a Friday evening, and not for a dinner engagement.

Well, come to think of it, it was going to end up a dinner engagement.

I stood. Wiped away my cares and declared to the empty room, "Well, this will just get me in practice for living on my own. No one will be there to cook me dinner. So I'm just going to seize the moment."

I called Paige to see what she was eating.

"Do you have any food?" I asked, flopping myself onto one of her two new chocolate-brown leather sofas with stainless-steel legs that flanked her fireplace.

"Child, when have you known me not to have food?"

I let the soft leather cradle my head. "I mean real food. Not Doritos, dip, and Diet Coke."

"Savannah has had a bad day?" She came over and sat on the edge of the sofa beside me and patted my head. "Poor baby needs real food. Real food it is."

With that she called out for pizza delivery and bounced back down on her brown and Tiffany blue velvet-covered ottoman that served as her coffee table. Her perfectly messy short blond hair bounced with her. Not that it's her natural color. But it does look natural on her.

She has had the same great short cut since I met her in sixth grade. Except for our eighth-grade year, when we both had failed attempts at perms. I tried short once. But only once. I looked like a boy and spent the next year suffering through insufferable grow out. No more haircuts above the shoulders since.

"Okay, tell me all your troubles."

I looked up at her in total shock. "You mean you don't know?!" I asked as I reached down to scratch my itching foot.

"What are you doing?"

"I'm scratching my foot. Do you know what that means?"

"It itches?"

"No, it means you're going to walk on new ground."

"You got all of that out of an itching foot?"

"It's just something my mother has always said. She got it from her mother, I think."

"Okay, well, whatever. Just take me with you. Now, back to what I know. Of course I know. My mother's been out there with your mother all day. But you just need to get it off your chest. That's the only way you will heal."

"The only way I will heal is to leave town and change my name to Villamina Venzinhoffer."

"Oh, that wouldn't attract any attention, now, would it? So, your mother's getting a little attention . . ."

"A little? Have you been down there?"

"Actually, I couldn't get through the crowd, but she'll be home by evening. I mean, do you honestly think Miss One-Thousand-Dollar-Suit, Never-Let-Them-See-You-Without-Your-Makeup Woman is going to spend the night outside?"

"Well, Dad said he was taking her dinner. What do you think she's going to do?"

"I think he'll take her dinner and she'll give the evening shift to some poor soul from the Savannah College of Art and Design, along with a crisp hundred-dollar bill and the promise of a great job upon graduation."

"You're absolutely right." I sat up straight on the sofa. This revelation gave me the desire to pace and talk. "Victoria Phillips would never spend the night outside. That lady's idea of camping is a two-star hotel. Shoot, I remember—well, you know, how she takes her own sheets to hotels, Miss Has-Sheets-Will-Travel."

Paige rolled her eyes. "Yes, because of the *20/20* episode on hotels and gyms. I totally know."

"Well, a couple of weeks ago, she went out of state to judge a pageant, and apparently the hotel was more like, well, like a *motel*."

She crinkled her nose. "Oh, don't tell me. The doors were on the outside."

"Yes, sweet sister. The only door on the inside led to the toilet."

"You mean she didn't pack her bags and pay for her own hotel somewhere else?"

"The only other place in town was where the contestants were. So she had no option but to leave. And we are talking beauty pageant here."

"Oh, how silly of me. Please continue. But sit down. I can't stand it when you pace or clean."

I sat back down on the sofa and used my hands to continue my story. "Well, apparently she put her sheets on the bed."

"The five-hundred-dollar set?"

"Are there others? And she slept with a light on all night. In case of bugs."

"Bugs?"

"Yeah, didn't you hear about her friend Cyndi?"

"Cyndi who?"

"You know, Cyndi who found that tick in her ear."

"No way! That is sick!" She shivered as if she had the chills. "Do not tell me any more about that. Just get back to your mother."

"Well, Vicky is petrified something's going to crawl in her ear at night."

"Stop!" She made a gagging sound.

"Yeah, isn't it? Anyway, she puts her sheets on the bed, only to hardly sleep because of the tick thing." I snicker now. "Then, for three straight days she doesn't even let the cleaning ladies in. But, on the fourth day—"

"Oh, Lord, what happened on the fourth day?"

"She forgot to put the 'Do Not Disturb' hanger on the door."

"I'm taking it she got disturbed."

"Honey, when she got back they had made her bed and thrown her sheets in a wadded up pile on the sofa."

"Ew, the sofa."

"Yep, where behinds have sat for centuries."

"Did she wash them?"

"Honey, she threw them away and made them take her to a store so she could buy new ones. She said they were totally unsalvageable."

"And you think this woman would spend the night, outside, on hard concrete, where any kind of bug imaginable could crawl in her ear? Well, you aren't thinking clearly."

The doorbell rang and Paige retrieved our pizza. I followed her to her galley kitchen to prepare our feast. "You're right. What was I thinking?"

"Obviously not much. Here, eat." With that, we devoured our pizza and chattered about endless nothings. She told me all about her new coffee table, who made it, how it was made, and we created a fabulous layout for my nonexistent furniture, for my yet-to-be-mine apartment.

Then she talked about the cute boy who moved in down the hall. She didn't know his name but she had deciphered his cologne. Even though we were supposed to have sworn off men, she had never been very good at resisting tan legs and white smiles.

I walked home enjoying the still warmth of a spring evening. After pizza and Coke, life seemed . . . well, just plain okay.

CHAPTER FOUR

Pulling the covers from my head and hugging my pillow, I looked out the window to see what action Abercorn held this morning. Not much. A few joggers passed, tugging at me to join them. As I washed my face, the silence caught my attention. Eight a.m. on a Saturday in the Phillips's house usually boasted far more activity than seemed to be developing this morning.

My sneakered feet walked out of my bedroom and stopped on the landing. The bed was made in Mom and Dad's bedroom. Nothing new. Vicky never left her bed unmade. She blames the habit on one unforgettable experience before she married when she left her apartment messy and the maintenance guy saw her underwear on the floor.

"So, Savannah, whatever you do, always pick up your panties, always make your bed, and don't call strangers to come fix your toilet."

I can honestly say, in all my life adventures, those three occurrences have never run in tandem.

No lingering smell of chocolate gravy and homemade biscuits lured me to the kitchen. For a moment that fear of ages past gripped me. It first captured me around eight years of age, the fear that the Rapture has taken place and I alone inhabit the world. I had searched the house and yard desperately but found no one. My recent dip into the *Left Behind* series only increased that fear. This morning, I stifled the desire to scream loudly or run up and down the street, knocking on the doors of the most holy people I knew.

Somehow my heart steadied itself and made its way out the front door for a jog and some tilling time. My iPod played my CeCe Winans library. About halfway up Bull Street toward Forsythe Park, Granny Daniels, one of the godliest ladies I know, came walking out of her house right into my path. I stopped right in front of her. Grabbed her with both arms and gave her a big ol' bear hug.

"So good to see you this morning, Granny Daniels."

Trying to catch her breath from my assault, she grabbed her chest. "Well, Savannah, my Lord, child, you look like the Rapture's come and you're the only one left."

"Oh, that's funny!" I said through my nervous laughter of relief. "Wouldn't that be awful?"

She extricated herself from my hold and started walking up the street. "Tell your parents hello for me."

"I will. See ya tomorrow." The heaviness of my trepidation lifted, and I increased my pace. The smell of mothballs stayed with me long after Granny Daniels left. I've never been certain why she smells like them so, though rumor has it she heard they kept snakes away. As far as I know, not many snakes make their way up to the homes of Savannah. Mothballs would be my weapon of choice, however, if I knew they would keep water bugs away. I stared at the ones on the sidewalk, struck down by morning joggers.

The smell of mothballs makes its way into just about everything that comes out of Granny Daniels's house. She once fixed us a big ol' pot of fresh garden-picked butter beans, and Vicky threw them out, because they, too, smelled like mothballs.

And like her odor, her authenticity is just as impossible to miss. You can hear it in the prayers she prays when you sit in front of her at church. Or see it in the weathered Bible that rests on the table by her weathered recliner. But it shows most vibrantly in her letters, which go out at graduations and weddings.

Mine arrived on a Sunday. She slipped it into my palm with a "piece of money," as she liked to call it. She let me know her prayers had followed my mother and father "everywhere they have ever been" and that me and Thomas were in her prayers too. Then she reminded me that there was a "work" for me to do, and that I needed to "live humble and never let pride have no place in your heart."

Then she apologized for her handwriting and asked me to pray for her. So today, I remembered and did some tilling time for Granny Daniels too.

Tilling time is my time to pray, reflect, and listen. I set aside the first moments of the day to get my mind (or soil, as Pastor Brice defined it) focused on an eternal perspective in a temporary world. Duke and I usually till together. Well, to be honest, God alone knows what Duke thinks about while we jog, except I can say he's a hard one to hold when any four-legged female passes by. But Dad must have taken him this morning.

So, between my conversation with Paige and my run-in with Granny Daniels, my steps seemed lighter. Today was bound to be a lovely May day.

I paused a moment on a park bench to enjoy the stillness of the dissipating spring. A ball flew through the air and caught my attention. Joshua. But he wasn't alone. He was accompanied by a beautiful golden retriever.

He never told me he had a dog.

Come to think of it, he's never told me much of anything.

I watched as the boy and his dog played catch. Joshua hardly stopped laughing as he called out to "Shelby," who was clearly a girl. It's not hard to tell these things. They played. They tumbled. I spied. It was weird. I felt like an intruder. But I couldn't turn my gaze. Then I watched in amazement as he held up his finger at that dog and yelled "Bang!" and she fell right to the ground like she was dead. Then she high-fived him. But the be-all and end-all was when he turned his back and that dog grabbed his leg with her paw and tripped that grown man.

Unbelievable.

Well, Duke ain't worth much compared to that. All he does is chase a ball and lie around waiting for food to fall from the counter or ice to fall from the ice maker.

I didn't know he had a dog. He knew my dog. Then, he and Shelby packed up and headed home. I watched. Shameless, I know, but I did it anyway.

I love to walk the streets of Savannah, and the day was too flawless to drive for my morning fix. After a shower I grabbed a book and headed for Dad's shop, which harbored my McDonald's Coke machine. Dad had it installed for me shortly after the cheerless discovery that no McDonald's existed in the Historical District.

The enjoyable route to Jake's runs up Abercorn Street past Lafayette Square (which holds the Hamilton Turner Inn), then past the Colonial Park Cemetery (which holds a few Hamiltons and Turners itself, I'm sure). I don't hang out there much; sister don't do dead people. So usually I hang a left at West Harris and then a right on Bull, which deposits me at Wright Square with York Street and State Street completing the four corners.

It's amazing how a place you know so well feels so excitingly new some mornings. Even though I've passed the same antique stores, women's clothing stores, restaurants, and corner cafés probably a million times through the years, some days the city just feels different. New, fresh . . . dare I say inspiring? Today felt that way. At least it did until I passed Bull and realized things were, new, fresh, and definitely inspiring to someone. Wright Square was as active this morning as it was yesterday.

Crossing York Street, I couldn't see Mother, even though I was certain she was there. She probably started her day off with coffee at Dad's and then wandered back to relieve the pitiable creature who endured the elements of the evening. I crossed to the opposite side of the square in front of the Chatham County Legislative Offices because it kept me away from the fray.

I gazed up at the two iron banisters flanking the French doors to my apartment above Dad's store and assured her it wouldn't be long 'til Mama was home. One more paycheck, one simple conversation with Vicky, and it would be mine. I entered Jake's through the back door so I could get straight to the Coke machine.

Louise and Mervine, the two twins who had worked with Dad since the day he opened eleven years ago, had their backs to me as I entered. They came out of retirement "because your dad was so sweet and cute," they confessed. In fact, all of Dad's employees have worked with him since he opened. Never lost a one.

Oh, well, there was *that* one.

When Dad first opened Jake's, Mother decided she would be the hostess. Dad assured her a coffee shop didn't need a hostess. She assured him it did. She lasted four and a half days. She was fired with these words: "Lady Wisdom builds a lovely home; Lady Fool comes along and tears it down brick by brick."

I think it was the fool part that got her. She grabbed her Louis Vuitton satchel, because we all know you need one to be the hostess at a coffee shop, and the entire place held their breath until the clicking of her Stuart Weitzman heels could no longer be heard from the other side of the square. Remarkably, the place didn't fall apart.

"What are you two doing?"

"That crazy man hasn't gotten here with the dishwasher yet," Louise said, swinging her head around and wiping her face with a suds-covered hand.

I fixed a cup of ice and poured a Coke. Duke ran to my side, chomping at the pieces of ice that fell. "I'll deal with you later." I wagged a finger at him then turned my attention to the Madge wannabes up to their elbows in Palmolive. "I thought Mr. Ron was bringing the dishwasher this morning."

"So did we. But all we've got is a hole." She pointed to the space where the machine used to be. "So, you're looking at the dishwashers." Mervine just looked up and smiled.

"Well, maybe he'll be here shortly."

"I'm sure he will, or I'll hunt him down and strap *his* behind to this sink."

I gave them each a kiss and headed to the front. Richard greeted me with a wink as his black eyes did their customary dance. His dark hand extended a refill to the customer who sat at the window.

Duke returned to me affectionately with his wet mouth. "Give me a high-five, Duke." I grabbed his paw and lifted it to touch my palm. He jerked his leg from my grip.

Dad laughed. "You can't teach an old dog new tricks. Don't you know that?"

"Well, I'm going to. Duke can't do jack." I patted his cute but uneducated head. "You should have taught him how to do more than just retrieve people's trash and chase a ball."

"What else does he need to know?"

"Something more than he does, that's all I know. And you could have left him with me this morning. I would have brought him in."

"Oh, well, we've been here all night." Dad poured some coffee for a kid on the other side of the counter who looked too young to be drinking coffee.

I walked over and set my latest reading material down on top of the granite. It would take a good afternoon to be finished with Peggy Noonan's book on Ronald Reagan, *When Character Was King*. Duke followed me to the counter, walking more slowly than usual, as if his night might have been better spent with me.

"What do you mean *we've* been here all night?"

Dad returned the coffeepot to its warmer. "I mean, I wasn't going to let your mother sleep outside by herself."

I started laughing and slapped the counter. "Oh, you're good. You had me going there for a minute. But you weren't thinking when you added the mother-slept-outside part."

"Think what you will Savannah, but she did. And so did I. And so did Duke. Didn't you, Duke?"

Duke looked up at him, tucking his tail between his legs and scrunching closer to my chair. Maybe he wasn't completely stupid after all. I mean, the poor creature was forced to spend the night outside with a woman who loathes him because he's not a lapdog named Magnolia.

"Wished you'd stayed with me, huh?" His tail wagged as he looked up in acknowledgment of his great error. I turned my attention back to my Dad. "And what did you sleep on, may I ask?"

He headed back into the back room. "You may, and I brought sleeping bags."

"You are too much. So, Victoria Phillips, the Victoria Phillips, former Miss Georgia United States of America, head of the Chamber of Commerce turned City of Savannah Diva, spent the night, outside, in a sleeping bag, with no way to take a bath, redo her makeup, or change her clothes. And you think I'm going to believe that?"

"Go see for yourself."

"I will. I'll just go see for myself. Come on, Duke." We headed outside to peer across the square. He was reluctant but came when he realized my arms were free of sleeping paraphernalia. It was necessary to move in closer because my petite mother was easily swallowed whole by the crowd, which was definitely larger than yesterday's. People sat around talking; reporters stood in front of cameras. We stopped to watch a kid too young to drink coffee take his place in front of a news camera to deliver the latest information.

"Standing here in front of the United States Courthouse on Wright Square, in the heart of Savannah, we are waiting on the latest order to be issued from the federal courts on whether this monument, like many before, and I'm certain many after, will get to stay or have to go. At the center of this case is a federal judge by the name of Judge Hoddicks. He brought in the structure late Thursday afternoon, after most courts were closed and people were headed home from work. He is fighting this on the legal end, and Victoria Phillips, the head of the Savannah Chamber of Commerce, is fighting this on the human-rights end along with hundreds of other crusaders. She has been here all night. Many others have gone home to shower and return to work, but she remains, looking exceptionally fresh, I might add. And totally capable of staying until this battle goes one way or the other. Now back to you, Sarah, in the studio."

The camera quit rolling and he plopped down in the grass and took a long swig of his coffee. "Why do I always get the gigs where you have to stay outside?" he asked his cameraman.

About that time the people parted enough for me to catch a glimpse of my mother. She sat on a rolled-up sleeping bag in the same blue suit she had had on yesterday.

At no time in my twenty-four years had I ever, until that exact moment, seen Vicky in the same outfit two days in a row.

Trying to stand back among the others, not wanting her to see me, I observed that she did look exceptionally well for having spent the evening outside. I managed to spot a small stain on the bottom left-hand side of her jacket, and her makeup looked a little tired, but her hair was perfectly fixed. But if she stayed here much longer her hair would probably start to look more like her outfit. I wouldn't put it past her to change her hair to match her outfit, even though she'd become a tad more cautious since the hair-breakage-on-the-pillow incident.

She was talking to Sergeant Millings. And he didn't look really happy. Nothing new. He always looked rather constipated. Of course, he was afraid of my mother. Weird, as she was always exceptionally nice to him, in spite of his customary ability to annoy. Maybe the oddity of niceness was enough to freak out the former Sears security guard.

He stood there, legs spread, one hand on gun, free hand on hip. That stance shouldn't be allowed in public. He was letting her know something clearly and adamantly, until a rather looming federal agent who stepped out of the courthouse tapped him on the shoulder.

"You have no jurisdiction here." The federal agent's booming voice carried all the way to my ears.

"This sidewalk is my responsibility, young fella." I was glad Sergeant Millings hadn't called the six-foot-six man "little fella."

"No sir. We're in front of a federal building, which makes this my jurisdiction."

Mr. Looloo would not give up. "I'll have you know that this sidewalk has been a part of my jurisdiction since before you could spell 'bubba.' So, either you go back inside that courthouse or I'll be seeing you in court."

"I think you should remember that the courthouse is my jurisdiction too."

"Are you threatening me?" Sergeant Millings asked, hand shifting on his gun. A few gawkers stepped back.

"You need to take your hand off your gun, sir. Now."

He shifted his hand casually to his belt buckle, as if it were all his idea. "I'll have you know I've already issued Mrs. Phillips here an Order to Disperse."

"You have not!" Mother protested.

Millings pulled out a notepad. Scribbled on it. Ripped it out and handed it to my mother. "I have now." She refused to take it. "Not taking it, Mrs. Phillips, doesn't change the fact that it's an order."

"Wanna bet?"

The federal agent reentered the conversation. "Sergeant Millings, why don't you and I go have a talk with Judge Hoddicks and see what we can come up with."

"We'll go talk to whoever we need to, sonny, to get you off my sidewalk." He turned his attention back to my mother. "You have until Friday, Mrs. Phillips. If you're not out of here by Friday at five p.m., I will cart you off to jail."

Mother stared a hole into him, causing him to back into the federal agent, who pushed him back toward my mother. I just prayed she wasn't within reach of his gun.

CHAPTER FIVE

C ome on, Duke. Let's get out of here." Duke turned
himself around, appreciating that he wasn't going to have
to spend the afternoon sleeping on sun-soaked concrete too. As
I turned around in a bit of a hurry, an exotic-looking beauty
careened into my shoulder, spinning me around.

"Oh, excuse me," she said, turning around to make sure I was
okay.

"Sorry, I didn't see you." She wasn't from around here. Her
accent was Southern, but her look was metropolitan, classy, almost
L.A.-like. I tried not to stare, but her long black hair, pulled back
into a sleek ponytail, made her striking features and light brown
eyes stand out even more. Her flawless olive skin had probably
never needed a bottle of "Tan Perfect," the new tanning regimen
for the scaredy-cats of Savannah.

She just nodded and continued up the steps of the courthouse,
perfection slipping through the glass-and-gold antiqued doors. Her
all-black attire was exceptionally odd for a Southern spring. But
there wasn't much room in my closet for criticism. Until two weeks

ago, about the only color I possessed came from the lone red blouse my mother bought me six years earlier for one of her memorable Christmas parties. I might have done red, but this lovely blouse was adorned by enough layers of ruffles around the neck to cover my face to my hairline. Red has never since adorned my body.

The heat of the afternoon encroached on the countless souls forced to take cover under umbrellas or live oak trees with their Spanish moss. Mother, however, was exposed to the elements. The grand hall of justice would not shield her from the sun until late afternoon. She raised her umbrella, which matched her Kate Spade handbag and shoes.

"Duke, we need another Coke. And I'm going to teach you how to get your own ice." He agreed and led the way to safety.

Richard was cleaning off the two front tables when I entered. "Those people are crazy out there. That's a three-ring circus," I declared.

"Now, Savannah, those are people doing somethin' they believe in. You ought not be callin' them crazy." His gray hairs glistened in the sun that streamed through the front window.

I continued my walk to the back and the fountain of sanity. "Whatever you say. But it looks like craziness to me."

Duke and I took a moment to gather ourselves. I grabbed his paw and used it to slap the ice dispenser attached to my Coke machine. Ice cubes fell to the ground and he ran off with them. I sighed. So easily sidetracked. We would work on his focus later.

A rather loud, Southern female voice distracted me from Duke. I peered through the slats in the swinging door to see who had entered Jake's. Duke, who put away the ice in one swallow, resumed residence beside me.

"I'll have a double espresso, please." She offered my father a smile. The corners of her mouth barely moved. And her eyebrows may as well have been paralyzed. She was a BOTOX butcher block.

"Sorry, young lady, but we just serve regular old coffee."

"Just coffee?" She snickered. Her snicker seemed rather contrived, not to mention unnecessary. "Are you serious?"

"Yes, ma'am, I am. We just keep it simple around here. But I promise you whether you like decaf or the real stuff, you won't get any better anywhere else."

"Well, I don't have time to go anywhere else. So just give me a large of the regular."

Jake turned around to pour the stranger a cup of his magic. "It will be my pleasure."

About that time Duke let out a growl. I had not heard Duke growl since Vicky made him get out of one of the chairs at the dining-room table. "Duke, chill. We'll go out there in a minute."

BOTOX lady carried on for ten more minutes, sipping and drinking and talking and putting her hand up against her bosom like some dainty Southerner. And touching my father no fewer than *ten* annoying times. He tried to be polite. He always was.

She revealed she worked for one of the national affiliates and was there to report the events at the courthouse. On her way to the door she turned around to flash Dad a *vavoom* smile half a dozen times—and with all that collagen, those lips took up half her face. But Duke and I had a moment of satisfaction when she ran smack-dab into the half-open door as my raven-haired stranger entered.

"May I have a decaf, please? Black, no sugar." A lady who appreciated the simple things in life. I liked that. She stood there so elegant and ladylike. It's not that we don't have ladies or elegance in Savannah. It's just most of the time they're adorned with linen and heavy perfume. But she was different, understated, Southern, and by all appearances important. I looked at the bracelet on her right wrist and noticed it was just like the David Yurman bracelet I had been given for graduation. She also had a matching ring on her right ring finger. Nothing on her left hand.

The board above Dad's head caught her attention as she sat her monogrammed leather satchel on the counter to retrieve her money. "What is that?"

He placed her coffee on the counter. "Oh, that's just a little board where I post a thought for the day. Gives everybody a little something to reflect on before they get started."

"Sounds like a religious saying. 'Keep mercy and truth with you always. Wear them as a necklace, write them on your heart. They will keep you respected by both God and man.' Lot of *that* going on around here, huh?"

"Where are you from?"

"Atlanta."

"Oh, I used to live in Atlanta."

I looked down at Duke, whose expression was still sour, for a golden retriever. "What is your problem, Duke?" He answered with another rather nasty growl.

"You lived in Atlanta?"

"Yeah, owned a company there but got tired of the pace. Moved here to slow down and learn how to enjoy living." He leaned on the counter. "What brings you here to Savannah?"

"Oh, I'm here to represent the voice of the people over this monument issue. I represented the last controversy in Jackson, Mississippi, and was asked to handle this one."

"I knew she was important," I said, slapping Duke on the head. I think he might have snarled at me. "Lighten up, old boy. How old do you think she is? Early thirties? Wonder what the *A* stands for on her bag?" Duke crouched as if ready to pounce.

"What voice do you represent exactly?" Dad asked.

"I work for the ACLU. But I won't be here long. The courts will have that thing out of here by the first of the week." She took a drink of her coffee. I caught a glimpse of her expression as the first swallow went down. Sheer satisfaction.

"Well, I hope you find what you're looking for." Dad pushed off the counter and gave her change.

She put it in her pocket and headed for the door. "Just look-ing for justice."

"Just find you a little truth in your justice," he said about the time her hand caught the handle of the door. I could see her turn around and stare at this new stranger. Then she walked out.

Duke and I came around the corner after the sounds of the bell announcing entrances and exits ceased. I took a stool at the counter, and Duke managed to pull himself up and balance pre-cariously on the one next to me. "Neat lady, huh?"

"Yeah, I'm sure she is. Probably a lot like you. A young woman trying to do her job and figure out what she believes."

"Seems like she knows what she believes. Looks like she has a pretty good job too. Those bags aren't cheap."

"Well, after you work at your job for a while, you can afford nice bags too." He wiped off the counter.

"She liked your coffee."

He laughed. "You noticed that, huh?"

"It was written all over her face. That was the best-tasting stuff she's ever had."

"I know. I could tell."

"Now for the other character. You should lock your doors next time."

"She won't be back. She likes espressos."

"No way, champ. She'll be back. She likes Jake. Plus, she's so processed, the shock of something unprocessed will send her into a tailspin."

"You need to quit the name-calling. And your mother wants to know why you haven't been out there to see her." He prepared more coffee, for tired, hot people who were too addicted to realize that they should be drinking cold drinks in the eclipsing spring.

I turned my stool around to gaze out the front window and watch the action across the street. "Dad, I don't want to go out there. No one needs me in the middle of that."

"No one has asked you to get in the middle of anything. But you could at least go tell your mother hello."

"You and I both know if I go over there to tell her hello, I'm going to end up on the front page somehow as the cause of this entire episode."

"No, she already made the front page of today's paper."

I raised my right eyebrow and turned to stare at him. "Why would I have doubted?"

"Anyway, this is about more than a person, Savannah. One day you'll realize that. So get over yourself and learn from the book you're reading and go tell your mother hello. And that is coming from your father. Now, go."

"Wouldn't you like us to go look at my apartment first? You know, just kind of get an idea about what kind of furniture I might need."

"You don't have any money to get any furniture."

"Yes I do. I got paid yesterday."

"Well, I see your new apartment every day when I come to work, and I doubt one paycheck is going to get you moved in. But you haven't talked to your mother since yesterday. Now, get, and don't come back until you've seen her."

"I'm way too old to be scolded."

His right eyebrow mirrored mine. "You're way too old to need to be scolded."

"Well, huh! Let's go, Duke." Picking my book up off the counter, I pointed my dejected soul for the door, and the second soul wagged his tail the entire way.

"Duke, you're staying here," Dad called out to his loyal companion. So my dejected soul headed to the door alone, and the second dejected soul flung himself to the cold, hard concrete of his coffee-covered world.

CHAPTER SIX

Sheila Long, Paige's mother, stopped by Vicky's latest residence. Dropped in to say hello, I suppose. I stared across the square and watched as my mother pulled a tissue out of her purse and wiped off an area of the sidewalk for Sheila to sit down.

I knew perfectly well that this tissue had been wadded in her purse, probably since last Sunday at church. It's what she always does. And she always says, "It's clean."

How a wadded-up tissue in the bottom of a woman's purse can be considered clean is beyond me. But apparently Sheila fell for it, because she sat down beside Vicky.

Since Mother had a visitor and it was way too early in this beautiful day to throw myself into her world of chaos, I decided to eat. Dad wouldn't be home until evening, if then, so it seemed the perfect opportunity to delay obedience. I would obey eventually. Now just didn't feel like the right time. It felt more like teatime.

Saturdays are perfect days for tea. Even though afternoon tea in Savannah is left mostly to tourists and dainty Southern women,

I continue to enjoy it. A yearning for hot tea accompanied by crab cakes led me to the Gryphon Tea Room by way of Paige's. And no, hot tea and coffee are not the same.

I walked into Paige's small studio behind her parents' antique store across from St. John's Cathedral on Abercorn Street. She was wrapping up a painting for a miserably attired elderly couple. One vintage tourist had bejeweled herself with enough baubles for a family of four, and her companion had inadvertently, or maybe not, forgotten the no-white-knee-socks-with-walking-shorts-and-Florsheim-shoes rule. He smelled of an Old Spice train wreck and she looked as if she'd allowed a three-year-old to apply her blue eye shadow.

Paige slipped the sweet-looking gentleman his receipt, and he tried to insert it into his stitched-shut back pocket. He gave up after several attempts and stuffed it into his front pocket. His wife had similar struggles with her white vinyl bag, whose screw-in clasp didn't want to screw. By the time they were both through, I do believe they were winded.

Yet the wind continued to blow. They talked loud and long, and Paige loved every minute of it. Truth be known, she just liked old people. If all else failed for her, she would start a chain of nursing homes. She would teach the art classes. But she was totally perfect for this setting. She was lively enough to attract all kinds, down-to-earth enough to make them comfortable, and talkative enough to keep them entertained. The colorful duo left totally thrilled with their new purchase.

"Do you smell that?"

She sniffed the air. "Smell what?"

"That. Old-people perfume."

"You are weird. There is no such thing as old-people perfume."

"Oh yes there is. Every old lady that sits down in front of me on Sundays at church wears the same old-lady perfume. Just like old men do."

She moved over to her stool that sat in the corner and picked up a paintbrush to start back on a modern abstract landscape she was working on. "Why are you here? To dissect my clientele?"

"Okay, you made a sale; let's go eat!"

She ran her left hand through the front of her hair the way she always does, as if straightening it. Yet the very essence of her hairstyle is to look as if it's always messed up. "I can't."

"Why? You're the owner. You can do whatever you want to."

"Yes, you're right. Well, no, technically you're wrong. My mother is the owner and continues to inform me of such, and my father informed me, just a few moments ago actually, that if I am going to run a business, they would require some things of me."

"Things?"

"Yes, Savannah, things. Business-owner things. Like punctuality, reliability, those kind of things."

"Ooh, there's a cute guy about to come in here, huh?"

She turned her back to me and walked over to a half-finished canvas and picked up a paintbrush. "I don't know what you're talking about."

"Liar!" I laughed.

She turned back with a grin. "Yes I am. Their son is on his way."

"Excuse me, did you see her and smell him?"

"Yes I did, smarty-pants. But I saw him too." she said with a giggle. "He passed by with them a little while ago, and I saw him through the window." She paused for extra effect. "And he is, shall we say, extremely eligible and extremely fine."

"So you're choosing 'fine' over me and crab cakes?"

She laid down her brush, walked over to me, placed her hand on my back, and pushed me toward the door. "I know it's hard to believe, but it's true. I am about to forgo food to meet this handsome stranger."

"So fickle we are. Well, I hope the boy isn't crazy about the color blue."

"I saw flip-flops."

"Okay. He'll do. So, is that your final answer?"

"Yes. Now, take that little book you have tucked up under your arm and go have you a lovely lunch. By the way, what did your mother say last night about her little adventure?"

"Well, so much for you and your predictions, but my mother slept outside all night."

"I know. Mine slept out there with her. Came home walking like she was ninety. Holding her back and fighting tears."

"Are you serious?"

"Yes, our prissy-wissy mothers—and I say that totally respect-fully—slept outside, all alone . . ."

"Oh, no, they weren't alone."

Paige's face contorted. "What?"

"I mean, my father slept outside too."

"Oh? Oh . . . oh . . . isn't that the sweetest thing you have ever heard?"

"Sweet? Ridiculous maybe, but sweet, give me a break. Grown adults, one strapped to a slab of stone, sleeping in sleeping bags on a sidewalk. Not to mention I hear it made the front page. There is nothing sweet about that."

"Ooh. Like you aren't in the paper enough," she said, making shameless reference to the number of times my mother chooses to publicize my performances in print. My cell phone rang. It was my mother. I sent her to voice mail.

"Your mother?"

"Yes."

"She'll call again."

"She always does. But back to you . . . this isn't about me, this, oh yes, this is totally about my parents." I waved my cell phone at her chest. "And yours too, apparently. Because your mother is with her again today." I made for the door and turned back around. "Anyway, I'm changing my last name first thing Monday morning."

"There's not a soul that would blame you, honey."

"I know."

"Eat a crab cake for me."

"I'm eating two."

"He should keep his religious convictions to himself," one storeowner quipped to another. The streets of Savannah were still busy with murmurs.

"Why? So you can be comfortable? That's part of the problem, isn't it, that everyone's so comfortable the truth that used to make us uncomfortable doesn't anymore?"

"Who are you? God?"

I walked past, losing them somewhere between yelling and cursing. It was evident not much work besides eating, exercising, and engaging were getting done today.

At the Gryphon Tea Room I took a seat in the raised area that looks out the grand picture window at the front of the store. It's an old apothecary, which still reflects the practice of an era gone by with its deep, rich, wood-encased window seats and chairs. Small drawers line the back wall. Today it is known more for its crab cakes and desserts than its medicine. Of course, their cheesecake can cure anything that ails as far as I'm concerned.

After placing my order, I took up my book and ignored the blinking message light on my phone. But a rapid movement drew my eye off the page and out the large window. Had I realized before I turned who it was, I simply would not have looked. My book would have become as interesting as a McDonald's Coke after a twelve-week fast. But no, inquisitive me, Miss Can't-Let-a-Maniac-Pass-by-a-Window-Without-Looking, looked.

There she stood, dressed like she was going to a parade. The reigning Miss Savannah United States of America, my newfound friend, beamed at me. I call her "friend" because I told her only a couple days ago at lunch that is what I'd be, her friend. She looked pitiful that day. She suckered me in. And now, seeing her out there waving like a hummingbird on speed, I knew with certainty that friends were an evaporating commodity in her world.

I smiled as best I could, hoping she would be appeased and prance on by. No such luck. She pranced herself right up to my table and plopped her prance right down beside me.

"I can't believe you're here! Sitting right where we did only a couple weeks ago, when our paths crossed for the first time. I just can't believe it. This is like fate or something. It's like our two-week anniversary!"

Eyes darted in our direction, causing my own to grow large. In this day and age, that wasn't a remark I wanted misconstrued. "Please don't say that so loud." I smiled at the gawking patrons. "Anyway, you look mighty nice for a Saturday."

"Oh well honey, with all the television cameras happening around here, it's best to look your best." She giggled, beside herself with the possibility of celebrity. Sun-streaked tresses teased her bare arm, and her flirty brown fifties-style sundress with a pink ribbon waistband spread pretty as a picture on the padded pew. "You know I heard Julia Roberts was discovered on the streets of Smyrna, Georgia, just for her smile."

"You don't say? Well, I didn't know that." I noticed a tourist across the room taking in the beauty next to me.

"No, I'm joking. But she should have been. She really moved to New York after she graduated from Campbell High School in 1985 and got her first role in the Western *Blood Red* in 1986. Anyway, people say I have that same fabulous smile." She grinned from ear to ear, just in case such information was lost on me. "Okay! Enough about me. Can you believe what your mother is doing? I just think it's awesome. Miss Victoria is such the heroine. Such a woman of power and confidence. I just think she's amazing. You should be so proud of her, out there strapped to that monument like a beauty queen strapped to a rhinestone." She slapped me rather forcefully on the arm.

I rubbed the spot. Didn't we have this conversation yesterday? This caused me to wrinkle my forehead and tilt my head. A move

I learned from Duke. Maybe he did know tricks. My food came at that moment, so I didn't have to worry about pretending to respond to her tribute to my mother, even though none of it warranted a response.

She wrinkled her nose at my beautiful crab cakes, but looked a tad more receptive to the salad. She picked up my unfortunately closed book and studied the cover. "Well, what are you reading? Ooh, Ronald Reagan. I just loved him."

I stared at her, knowing that the only thing she read was *People* magazine. "Oh, you did, did you?"

"Oh, yeah. His life was so interesting."

"And what exactly do you know about his life?" I took a big ol' bite of my delicious lunch, all covered in a mayonnaise-based dressing.

"Ooh, that's disgusting," she said, staring at my mouth as I chewed, but losing interest quickly. "Okay, what do I know about Reagan?" She clasped her hands together and sat more erectly. "Well, he was born on February 6, 1911, as Ronald Wilson Reagan. His mother was Nelle and his father was John, and they had him in Tampico, Illinois."

I stopped chewing and looked behind me to make sure no one was feeding her this information. I comforted myself with the fact that anyone who knew much about history could know this information. Not that I had remembered it, and I was actually reading a book about him, but that didn't matter. However, I felt confident that there was no way Miss Amber Topaz herself could know all of this. She was a beauty queen, for crying out loud.

"Well, that's nice." At least I could act appreciative of her knowledge.

"Yes, I know that's nice, but I know tons more from his days at Eureka College, where he played football and starred in their theater program. After he graduated, he married Jane Wyman and had two beautiful children, Maureen and Michael." I stopped eating and sat back in my chair, crossed my arms, and stared in amazement at this MAC-covered walking encyclopedia.

"So in '52 he married Nancy, and the rest of their life was lived in front of us."

She paused to breathe and I was about to congratulate her, when she started again. Now, I thought her pageant stories were bad. I mean, try to sit with this woman through her tales of beauty queens who tape their boobies, wear dresses backward, and spray "sticky tack" on their behinds to keep their bathing suits from riding up, and you just want to cross on over. But I didn't like history in school, and I really didn't care to hear the book I was reading recited to me by a beauty-queen bombshell. No matter how long I lived, I would always believe she was fed this information through some earpiece connected to a lunatic outside in a black van.

"He turned to politics eventually and became governor of California in 1966, and then he became the fortieth president in 1980. He had 489 electoral votes to Jimmy Carter's 49. How is that for kicking some bu——. Ooh, I almost said the *b* word. How unseemly for a lady."

Other than that she didn't miss a beat. "But nothing can compare to that moment when Reagan stood behind that podium"—and with those words the queen herself rose, put her hand over her heart, and hollered loud enough for the people outside to hear—"MR. GORBACHEV, TEAR DOWN THIS WALL." However, when Reagan said the word *wall,* I'm sure it didn't have two syllables.

The entire restaurant seemed to contemplate whether they needed to rise as well. I'm certain a myriad of thoughts such as saluting, standing, or slapping ran through more minds than my own, because by the time she said *Gorbachawf,* everyone had whiplash. She sniffled and wiped her eyes of either real or artificial tears. Who could be sure?

She leaned into me. I withdrew. "That very speech, Savannah Phillips, set those people free. Set me free too." She giggled. "It helped me win the title of Miss Catfish Stomp Festival Queen when I ended my interview competition with it. Those poor judges were ready to enlist by the time I got through."

If I doubted it before, I now knew for sure that another Victoria actually existed in this world. Amber reached down to pick up my book and studied the cover again.

"Ooh, Peggy Noonan wrote this. I love her too. This is her fifth book, you know?" I can honestly say, I had no idea. "Yes, it is. Her first book was *What I Saw at the Revolution* followed by *Life, Liberty, and the Pursuit of Happiness*, then *Simply Speaking*." She set the book down. "Oh! And my favorite, *The Case Against Hillary Clinton*, and now the one you're reading."

Finally it seemed that she was finished. My mouth hung somewhere around my chest.

She reached down to pick my book up one more time. I swept in and snatched that puppy away and pulled it to my chest.

"How?" was all I could come up with.

"I know you don't think I read, Savannah. But to graduate with a 4.0 you have to read sometimes."

Had I been eating, I would have choked.

She noticed my expression. She had a response. She always has a response. "And if you ever compete in a pageant interview"—she couldn't be that bright to even conjure up such a scenario—"you'll know, that one shall not tread those waters ill-prepared. Well, gotta run. So great to talk with you on our two-week anniversary. Your stories always intrigue me." She leaned over me in a whisper. "Kisses, kisses." And with that, the personification of Trivial Pursuit for Beauty Pageants made her exit before an audience no less flabbergasted than yours truly.

I hadn't even graduated with a 4.0.

Truth be told, my writing scores were high, but most other grades proved how inept I was at anything other than telling a tale.

I eyed my cold crab cakes, which didn't look as appetizing as before. Then the same voice that had filled the restaurant with a Southern-belle rendition of Reagan let loose with a shriek.

"Stop him! Stop him! He stole my purse!"

CHAPTER SEVEN

'm going to stomp you into the pavement, you little
sucker!" screamed the woman who was too ladylike to say *butt*
only moments before.

I took off after Amber in a full-speed run, which wasn't so easy
in flip-flops. But the long-legged maniac in heels was so close to
the little fella, I was certain he could smell her Altoid. Obviously,
she could run as furiously as she could wave. Her sundress flowed
behind her as if created for such activity. And her head was back,
Forrest Gump–style. I declare I heard the *Chariots of Fire* sound
track playing in my head.

The thief rounded a corner, and a couple men from the store
across the street got into the chase. But no one could keep up with
Wonder Woman. As if in slow motion, I saw her hand reach out
and grab his ponytail, a rebellion he would live to regret for the
rest of his adult life. That and the fact that the crotch of his jeans
flopped around his knees, preventing a long stride. He clung to his
waistband and her purse with equal measures of desperation.

She yanked him to the ground in one tug, hiked up her skirt,
and sat on top of his chest like she was The Rock in a cage match.

The three of us in pursuit reached them and doubled over trying to catch our breath, while Amber barely panted. The top of the rather unintelligent youth's wide-eyed head stuck out from one side of her flowing sundress, and his tennis shoes pointed out the other. He wriggled in vain. Her knees pinned his arms, and she perched her hands atop her rather wee waist.

"Who's your mama, young man?" None of us were quite sure what information she sought from this kid who would just as soon whip out a gun as look at you.

He screamed a response anyway. "You are!"

"I'm not your mama!" She slapped him upside the head with her hand.

"Ow!" I said, before he could let out a holler. But his holler followed shortly thereafter. He squirmed some more.

"You may as well forget about getting away from me!" She snatched her pretty little brown and pink bag from his hands. "I could give you a karate chop right in your throat and maim you for the rest of your existence, you little creep. Think you're going to steal my purse?" She finally tried to rise. The two out-of-breath gentlemen quickly found their composure and swooped over to help the damsel, who obviously didn't need it but accepted theirs with her Julia Roberts smile and rapidly returning manners. "Oh, thank you. How sweet."

The bewildered youth tried to stand, but before the two men could grab him, the crazed queen grabbed him by his ponytail and pulled him to her side. "No sirree, little fella." Her six-foot frame towered over his prepubescent self. "You are going with me, and we are going to find your mama!"

So she really *did* mean, "Who's your mama?" She brushed off her skirt, flung her bag back over her shoulder, and thanked us for our assistance, albeit nothing more than emotional.

"How . . . did you . . . run like that?" I asked, still leaning and panting, as she dragged this weary roamer back up the side street.

"Oh, number-one sprinter in track and field. If he'd have gone for distance I'd have never made it." She flashed that smile and winked.

Really. She was probably number-one in the Boston Marathon as well.

She tugged at the boy's ponytail, and I knew no one would ever be so glad to see his mama compared to the Mary Poppins that had a hold of him right now. Amber Topaz, Director of Tourism, was about to give him a tour of Savannah, in a way he had never experienced.

"I know you think I'm impotent," she said underneath her breath to the poor thief. The gentlemen fidgeted and darted their eyes downward at the sound of those words. "But you're about to see how potent I am, little boy."

"She meant *incompetent*," I assured the gentlemen.

They still looked scared.

"And she got a 4.0," I told them. "Go figure." I followed the perfectly coiffed and statuesque beauty who had a death grip on a ponytail and tried not to laugh. No doubt these two wouldn't be running to another woman's rescue anytime soon.

And every person on this street now staring out of windows and gawking from street corners knew for certain they would never try to steal the handbag of one Miss Amber Topaz Childers, the reigning Miss Savannah United States of America.

I myself kept my eyes out for a black van.

The crab cakes had lost their cakiness, the salad its crispness, and the hot tea . . . well, it wasn't so hot anymore. The message light on my cell phone still blinked. In the commotion I had left all of my possessions at the table.

"Darling," came the voice on the message, "I'm so sorry we didn't talk yesterday. The events here just went so quickly I didn't even have time to grab my floss. But you're never going to guess who's having me on their show tonight. I'm going to be on Rita Cosby from FOX News. I would love for you to come watch. She's just the cutest little thing. Anyway, I missed you last night for dinner. And I want to see you today. I love you. Make sure you eat, darling. Call me if you get time. Or just stop on by. I'm not going anywhere." She concluded with an annoying giggle.

Lord have mercy. If she starts getting interviewed, she might just run the rest of our lives from the sidewalk.

I picked up my book. Maybe if I could actually finish reading it, I could find some solace from a quiet, confident man. He didn't say much. But he meant what he said. Maybe I would try that. Not speak often, just speak wisely.

I took back to the streets of Savannah. The United States Courthouse and its activities drew onlookers to the square as magnetically as Frodo's ring drew others to darkness. As I approached the square, I noticed that a small lectern with microphones perched all over it stood nearby.

What a grand scene. The backdrop is truly one of the most majestic settings in Savannah. The stately building is made of Georgia marble and is only three stories, but it takes up an entire city block. The front reads "United States Post Office and Courthouse" and was built in 1898, but the post office was closed years ago. Remnants of it exist in the prestigious foyer, however, where empty, aged boxes line the front wall, their secrets locked up forever.

The sidewalk that spreads out in front of the courthouse is lined at the street with fresh flowers and tall evergreen trees. Black iron poles are evenly distributed from one end of the block to the other, as if they were hitching posts for horses in an era that whispers down back alleys and lives on in women's conversations.

The building can be entered from huge arched doorways at the far left and right of the building. Under each arch, two large swinging glass doors with aged brass trim and handles usher people into the world of security guards and metal detectors, as it has been since the building was turned over to the Federal Courthouse.

Six large windows line up between the two brilliant arches.

Above each arch, on both the second and third floors, architecturally timeless balconies indicate the judges' chambers. In front of the building, part of the sidewalk expands into a half moon, where the monument of the moment and my mother made their stand.

Judge Hoddicks came out of the imposing right front doors and descended the marble stairs.

Every journalist, even those who had been catnapping only moments before, rushed the podium, yelling questions and waving microphones in total pandemonium as the judge prepared to speak.

He raised his sixty-eight-year-old hand to quiet the crowd. It worked. I searched for a glimpse of my mother, but the crowd from this morning had probably grown by fifty or so. Judge Hoddicks tapped the microphone. I could hear just fine even at this part of the square. He spoke.

"Ladies and gentlemen. Thank you for being here. We just received word from a federal judge who says this monument, like the ones before it, violates the Constitution's ban on government promotion of religion."

The crowd went crazy. Some were cheering, others were booing, and the reporters started screaming questions as if Judge Hoddicks might actually start answering them. He raised his hands again. His piercing blue eyes scanned the swarm of reporters and flock of pilgrims.

"Please, ladies and gentlemen, I am not through. The order informed us that we have exactly six days to remove this monument, or it will be removed for us."

The onslaught started all over. Standing back in amazement, I found myself interested to watch this moment in history unfold around me. Even little children too young to have convictions of their own beyond food and TV preferences were out here yelling the convictions of their parents.

"I know, I know." Judge Hoddicks started again. "This is a very emotional topic for us all. But please know that I will be petitioning the Supreme Court to stop this order from being enforced. As details become available, I will keep you informed. All I ask is that each party in this extremely passionate issue respect each other. Thank you."

Judge Hoddicks walked over to the vicinity of the monument and my mother. The reporters followed him until he returned to the steps of the courthouse and vanished inside.

The journalists turned their attention to my mother. Sergeant Millings stood in the background, slapping his nightstick against his leg.

"Mrs. Phillips, Mrs. Phillips! How long will you be out here?'

"As long as it takes." She grinned from ear to ear.

I can't wait to see that.

"Why are you doing this?" another hollered above the rest.

"Because this is our heritage. And I want it for my children, for my daughter—"

Please don't . . .

"—Savannah, or Savannah from Savannah as she is known here, and for my son, Thomas, who works with our wonderful Judge Hoddicks."

I am certifiably ruined.

I prayed for a quick end. Lightening. Earthquake. Sergeant Millings's bullet. I would have even settled for a dart through the chest. But the woman had found a television camera willing to record and a crowd willing to listen. It was a full fifteen minutes before the reporters returned to their trucks or their naps.

And me? Well, my next human-interest story had found me. Right on Wright Square.

CHAPTER EIGHT

The reporter couldn't hide his admiration for the raven-haired, expensive-handbag stranger. I, too, watched her closely. Her gestures were few but graceful. Her laugh was feminine and seemingly genuine. And her rapport with the journalist made them seem lifelong friends. Before he could ask his final question, she patted his arm and departed into the courthouse.

I turned to leave when the sight of two young lovers heading my way distracted me once again. Since I found out my longtime-love, Grant, was getting married, and not to me, something inside me had begun to notice the expressions of love. And these two were virtual CliffsNotes. Looking closer, one face seemed awfully familiar. Grant. I ducked behind one of the trees but kept an eye wrapped around the trunk of the live oak. I knew our paths would cross now and then. In 2.2 square miles of history, it's inevitable. But why did it have to be today?

Seeing him walking up the street in khaki shorts and a T-shirt, brown leather flip-flops generating Savannah's only breeze, the overwhelming feeling of loss rushed through me again. To lose one of your best friends, who also happens to have the name you hope to share for the rest of your life, is hard for any young woman.

Of course our relationship dissolved over years of drifting apart. But I had been so self-absorbed that the drifting was lost on me until I found myself clinging to a piece of driftwood and watching the *Titanic* go down. But here was proof. We had drifted so far apart that this flaming redhead had easily docked her little long-legged self right between us. This was the first time my eyes had seen her. The child had hair as auburn as a Southern sunset. It was strikingly beautiful, in a ratty sort of way. A tad poofy. I pulled the ends of my stick-straight mane around to inspect it. I noticed a split end and stuck it in my mouth to try to chew it off. It was that or the fingernails.

She was so tall, and leggy and anorexic. Poor child probably didn't even eat. Couldn't hardly keep her pants up. She had an ample bosom. I was certain they were fake, and instinctively crossed my arms in front of my chest. Paige and I had already determined before we even saw her that she had to be fake. Any girl who goes to an all-girl college could have nothing better to do than sit around and inject things into herself.

I called her a prepackaged Barbie who would probably be a "four-foot-eleven, forty-five-year-old mother of two," if relieved of all her processed beauty.

Paige declared I was talking about my own mother.

I told her not to compare my mother to this woman. That the only thing not real on Vicky was her hair color. Of course we knew that was a lie.

I tried to reach Paige on her cell. She didn't answer. As they came down the street, I gradually scooted around the tree to keep myself hidden.

"Who you hiding from, Savannah?" The voice ran down my spine like ice. Turning around wasn't necessary to know Mr. Curly Locks himself had entered the square.

"Shh. I don't want Grant to see me."

"Who's Grant?"

"None of your business. Now would you please go away and leave me alone?"

"Oh, an old boyfriend." His eyes scanned the square, stopped. "Well, old boyfriend looks like he has a new girlfriend."

"Fiancée, actually. Now get!" I said holding on to the trunk.

He kicked out the kickstand on his blue bike and made it evident he wasn't going anywhere. "Do you know what you look like?"

"A woman annoyed? Because that's what I am."

"No, a girl who's seen one too many bad *Charlie's Angels* flicks."

"What do you know about love?"

"I know it doesn't usually involve hiding behind a tree, chewing on your hair."

I spit my hair out of my mouth. Then I noticed Grant and little Merry Sunshine were walking into the vicinity of my mother. "It was!" I turned to glare at him. "Yes it was love! But not anymore."

"Looks like the new lady's getting to meet your mother," he said, nodding in their direction.

I turned and watched in horror as the love of my life introduced his flaming redheaded future squaw to the woman who, by all intents, purposes, and DNA, was my mother. Vicky leaned over and hugged Grant and then—ugh!—hugged the woman next to him.

"Ooh, looks like they might get invited to dinner."

I turned back to my thorn. "Do you take pleasure in my pain?"

"Pain?! You've got to be kidding."

"No. I'm not kidding. Now would you *please* take your little bike and your little mind and your little self and go away?"

"You are going to have to see them eventually."

"I'm going to have to do a lot of things eventually, but I would prefer not to have to do all of them in one afternoon. Now *get!*"

He placed his perfectly tanned hands on his handlebars, using the most beautiful part of any man—his arms—to lift his body onto his bicycle. His khaki shorts revealed nice legs, but I refused to look.

"Well, I'll see you Monday."

"Yeah, yeah, Monday! And if you want to know, Mr. Smarty Pants, my dog can get ice out of the ice maker all by himself."

He crinkled his brow, contemplating the sheer looniness of my statement. "What are you talking about?"

"Are you still here?" I asked, lifting my hands and bobbing my head.

"You are so odd." I could hear him riding away and turned to notice that he was looking back at me as well. Before I knew it I had stuck my tongue out at him. I was walking in the land of the mature today, for sure. So much for becoming a woman of few words and great wisdom. He threw his head back in laughter, almost running right into a ninety-year-old woman walking her dog. I threw my head back in mimicked disgust.

My mother was now alone. She had even ditched the umbrella, as the towering building now shielded the great summertime aggressor. But there were two who weren't alone. I watched the hand-in-hand lovebirds as they walked up Bull Street. How fitting. He slipped his arm around her waist to pull her toward him, the same arm that had pulled me to him a thousand times. Sickening. My eyes wanted to turn away, to escape from the memories. But they couldn't. They were held captive by recollection, the recollection of a love let go. That flew away, and unlike that stupid saying, never flew back home. Of course my bird feeder was empty and rather nasty, so who would blame the poor bird for finding someone more willing to feed it.

Action near the lovely slab of marble resumed, seizing my attention and relieving it of pathetic metaphors and poor misguided notions.

"You are wasting the taxpayers' money and the people's time, and on top of that you are alienating people who don't share your beliefs, virtually attacking them in their own city."

The voice that responded belonged to the woman of high-heeled mules and now-rumpled blue suit. "Honey, if anyone knows the people of this city, I do."

"Do you really?" I watched as the alluring raven-haired woman walked over to my mother in some rather sharp-looking black open-toed sling-backs.

"Yes, I do really." Mother tugged a tad at her chains.

Her adversary inched closer. "If there ever was a time that cities across this nation needed to operate in unity, it is now."

"Are you calling me divisive?" Mother asked, getting as close as her leash would allow.

"Misguided maybe." The beauty stopped within striking distance of my mother. And by the look on my mother's face, that might not have been such a wise move.

Red flashing lights atop television cameras helped Mother regain her composure. "Well, honey, I'm sorry you feel that way, but your litigation could be considered just as misguided and divisive, depending on whom you ask."

I wondered if intervention might be necessary. I searched the crowd for a suitable arbiter. Sergeant Millings leaned against the side of the courthouse, picking his nose. No option existed but one. Me. So I marched my flip-flop-clad feet into the combat zone.

Now, the last thing I wanted was to be on the evening news for a situation that I honestly cared nothing about. So, I tried to stay calm. I laughed a half laugh as I approached, trying to make mother cool down and back off. But then, she had to speak.

"Oh, Savannah darling. I was wondering when you were going to come see your mother." She squealed, reaching out to me. I stayed beyond her reach, preventing her from stroking my head.

Why do mothers stroke their children's heads? Is it a reflex? Is it a vitamin deficiency? Is it a superiority complex? It's the same way a man greets his golden retriever: "Look at my baby; isn't he a good boy?" So I just left her there. Arms extended and hands moving in a pitiful stroking motion through the air.

The stranger tried to place my face. The craziness of her line of work probably had her encountering a thousand unknown faces.

"Hey, Mother. Why don't you calm down?" I said this under my breath while trying to grin at both the cameras and the striking stranger. "She's just trying to do her job, like you're trying to do, well, whatever it is you're trying to do."

"I'm making a statement, Savannah." Mother dropped her hands, most definitely using her outside voice.

I continued to whisper, hoping it would be infectious. "Yes, ma'am, I see that you are."

The whispering didn't catch on. And Mother turned her attention toward the stranger instead of me. "A statement that apparently this young lady needs to hear!"

The other young lady spoke just as loud. "It's one I've heard, ma'am, a thousand times by a thousand different people and in a thousand different ways."

"Well, you obviously didn't get it!"

I looked at the dark-haired lady. "Sorry, she takes everything that happens in this city very personally."

"Savannah, don't you dare apologize for me to this woman. She has an agenda just like I do, just wrapped in a different package." Mom's voice turned snide for a lady in expensive shoes and a designer suit. "She chooses subtlety. She sneaks up on you. I choose a forward march." Well, it would have to be a forward march in place, apparently. The chain only extended so far. I expected Amber to appear any moment and inform our new tourist of her need to "Tear down this wall!"

"Yes, Mother, you do." I agreed. "Anyway, this will be fought in the courts. We don't have to fight on the sidewalk." I gestured to the sidewalk I desperately desired to melt into.

"Savannah, think what you will, but this is where battles are won—not in courtrooms, but in the daily lives of sacrificial, everyday, ordinary people."

In twenty-four years I had never heard my mother describe

herself as ordinary. Replaying the speech in my mind, I wasn't certain if she intended the adjective for herself or the situation in general. But it was a milestone nonetheless.

Raven spoke again. "You're right, ma'am. This is an issue people are willing to fight for. And it is an issue people have died for. And I am here to fight for the people who need a representative. We are going to fight civil-liberties violations any time and any place we see them occurring. The Bill of Rights will be protected as long as we have a voice. We are here doing the noble thing. You are here trying to take people captive once again to the prison of narrow-mindedness."

"Young lady," Vicky said, tugging at her chains like Duke on a leash, spotting FooFoo the cat, "we are not violating anyone's civil liberties. We are simply trying to make it clear that we have a voice. That there is a right and wrong. That this nation was built upon laws that were intentional and clear, and we are going to stand up for them, whether that interferes with the *agendas* of others or not."

I wasn't sure why I was still there. If I had it my way, I would be sitting in a park, reading a book, looking forward to going home and eating roast and potatoes or pork tenderloin and wild rice. Instead I was standing in the Savannah heat, surrounded by reporters (my least favorite of all people, though I was one myself), a mediator between my temporarily insane mother and this interesting visitor. Trust me, this was not my idea of how to spend a Saturday.

About the time Vicky was to go at it again, raven-lady's cell phone rang. "Ms. Austin," she answered with undue calm. "Yes. Okay. Hold on one moment." She turned her attention back to us. "If you ladies will excuse me, I've got to take this call. I'm sure we'll see each other again soon." And with that she left us alone. Well, as alone as one can be with television cameras, photographers, sojourners, a crazy white woman, and a gigantic slab of marble.

CHAPTER NINE

My reunion with my mother could have been spent debating why it had taken twenty-four hours for me to actually come see her. But that didn't appeal to me, so I chose another option.

"Well, Mother, if this doesn't work, you can take your case to the president."

Her eyes glazed over and the biggest smile swept across her face. To see a grown, married woman with a crush, well, it border-lined on just plain sad. "Oh, I just love him, don't you?"

"Well, I have some amazing news for you," I said shamelessly.

Her brown eyes danced, as she clasped her bound hands together. "Bigger than Rita Cosby?"

I let my eyes get as big as her own and spoke as if to a five-year-old. "Yes, ma'am, bigger than Rita Cosby. You, my sweet lady, are going to get to see the president on Friday. He's coming here."

My mother screamed in sheer delight. "Bushie is going to be here on Friday?" She started to run her hands through her hair and over her wrinkled pants. It was a woeful attempt to fix herself up.

"No," I responded. "The president of the United States of

America is going to be here on Friday. *Bushie* is the pet name of a wife for her husband."

Then she grabbed her chest. "Savannah, don't play with me. If you're playing a joke, I'll whip you from here to South Carolina."

"I'm not." I laughed, though the thought of her whipping me was not attractive. This woman used a flyswatter, the most disgusting thing imaginable to discipline a child with. You wouldn't think this antibacterial champion would want children with fly innards attached to their tails going around town. Thomas was still scarred from his last encounter with it. He was thirteen and in the shower and showing a bad attitude, banging his fists on the wall, and the petite little fireball snatched open the shower door and unloaded on his pubescent body with reckless abandon.

But that was a distant memory. The woman was downright full of glee, clapping her hands together like a three-year-old being exonerated of bath time. "Bushie is coming? You have got to be kidding me." She slapped me on the arm. I had moved too close. "I can't believe this! This is unbelievable!" She reached up, threw her arms around my neck, and cameras could be heard clicking all around.

I whispered into her well-adorned ear. "If this is on the front page of any paper, I will not be happy."

"Oh, get a grip, Savannah." She pushed me away. The woman might be bipolar. "The president's coming. Oh Lord, what will I wear?"

I looked at her in astonishment. "It won't matter what you wear if you're still in the middle of this square, chained to a monument, now, will it? You won't even get to see him."

"Oh, yes I will. I'll see him. We'll just make sure he has to come by here if this matter isn't resolved before then." Of course "we" would. The woman ran this city. Who was I to think she wouldn't dictate the president of the United States' very itinerary?

But I needed to bring her back to more critical matters. "I know you are not staying out here an entire week."

She retained a significantly steady resolve in her eyes. "I'll stay out here as long as it is necessary, Savannah. You do those kind of things when you believe in something."

She couldn't be well. We needed a doctor that made house—I mean, sidewalk—calls. She needed to be medicated. Or maybe she was medicated. Maybe this was like the time we flew to L.A. and hit severe turbulence, and she took enough Xanax for a three-hundred-pound man. They were drugs her friend Theresa gave her when Mother mentioned she had panic attacks when she flew. Not that drug-swapping is a crime or anything.

By the time we landed, she was so out of it she needed Dad to carry her to the car. But he refused. Well, it wasn't his fault. He had warned her clearly as she popped three of the things into her perfectly painted mouth. "If you take those things and don't wake up, I will leave you right here on this plane."

And he did. But when faced with the choice of leaving her on the plane and letting her fly to Kalamazoo, or planting her behind on top of a luggage cart, Thomas and I saw a delightful opportunity. We just smiled at the flight attendant as we carried her off the plane. Thomas had her upper body and I toted her feet. Had she not just recently cut her hair all flippy, then it could have covered her face and salvaged a minute amount of her reputation. But those red lips were in clear view.

We threw her dead weight over the basket of a luggage cart and pushed her right through the terminal, arms and feet dangling like a Charlie McCarthy doll. I made Thomas take pictures so we could blackmail her later. We took pictures of her in the men's bathroom. We took pictures of her picking her nose. We took pictures of her sitting in the race-car machine in the arcade. We took pictures of her sprawled out on a terminal bench with a *GQ* magazine spread across her chest. We didn't stop until Dad called us from his cell phone in the car, where he was waiting at the curb.

By the time she woke up, about three days later, the pictures had been printed in duplicate, one set strewn across her bed. She never told us where she put them. We never asked. We both just always knew that there were duplicates at our immediate disposal.

"Are you doing drugs?" I asked.

"Savannah Grace Phillips, I should just as soon slap you as look at you for that comment."

"You didn't answer my question."

"I'm fixing to answer your question with my hand upside your head."

"Why is it you can ask me if I do drugs, but I can't ask you?"

"Because I'm your mother. I can ask you anything I pretty well please."

"Well, whatever you're on, I hope you come off of it soon and come home, where you should be."

"Where are you going?"

"I said I would come by and say hey. So hey. Love ya. Talk to you soon. I've got to figure out what we're going to have for dinner for the *next week*." And with that I left Vicky to figure out what to do with her "matter." But she wouldn't miss me now. Bushie was coming. Who was I compared to him?

"I need a lawyer."

My new friend Gregory's voice came on over the other end, calm as always. Gregory is a law clerk from Jackson, Mississippi, who helped me out on my last article about rigged beauty pageants. "You have one. Bought and paid for with a buck, remember?"

"Do you have craziness in Jackson?"

"Not until you came here and brought your craziness with you over a rigged beauty pageant."

"I think you just called me crazy."

"Maybe. Judge Tucker has talked to Judge Hoddicks. I hear what's going on over there," he said, sounding as if he was chewing something.

"What are you eating?"

"Lunch."

"Oh, that was clever. Anyway, why don't you come down here and do some lawyering stuff, get my mother unchained from this granite, and make my life less eventful before Monday."

I was certain his chocolate legs were propped up on a desk or sofa or ottoman somewhere as he snacked on whatever it was he was snacking and a beautiful white grin emerged across his face.

"Girl, you couldn't find less eventful if you were a contestant on *The Amazing Race* and searched the world over. You don't know anything but eventful."

I continued walking up Bull toward Forsythe Park with my book tucked safely under my arm. "I do. And I love that show, by the way. Actually tried to be a contestant. Me and Thomas sent in a video. Didn't even get a call back."

"Did you speak on the video?"

"Of course."

"Then that might be why you didn't get a callback."

"Do you hate me?"

He laughed. "No, silly, I don't hate you. But say what you will, you're weird. And you talk too much. But I will tell you that, knowing the law and the previous cases and their decisions, this monument case will probably be remedied sooner than later."

"By Monday?"

He laughed.

"Don't laugh. I'm serious."

"No, Sherlock, this won't be finished by Monday."

"Why? Why do you judicial types take so long to do anything? Just so you can bill people?"

"Honey, if I billed you for all the needless energy you drain from me, you wouldn't see your own apartment until you had private quarters six feet under."

"Aren't you full of yourself today. But I need you. My mother is chained to a monument, harassing a sophisticated lady from Atlanta. Really, this needs to come to a close quickly."

"Well, I might see you this week. Judge Tucker is thinking about coming down to help Judge Hoddicks."

"Oh good. So, be thinking then."

"About what?"

"About how to speed this thing up."

"Okay, Savannah, I'll be doing just that."

"Call me if you think of something good."

"You just wait by your little phone."

"I will, smarty butt. I will." With that I hung up, thankful that I had been able to say *butt* without it being recorded for the evening news.

"Oh, I'm so sorry," I said to the blur that careened into my shoulder as I turned the corner onto Drayton Street.

The blur didn't respond. But it looked vaguely familiar. *It can't be. She doesn't have food hanging from her shirt. There's no way. You think? Maybe it is.* It was. Emma Riley. She and I had experienced another run-in of sorts last week. Actually, I had taken it upon myself to tell her wretched story to the entire city without bothering to care whether she wanted it told. She cared. Oh, did she ever care. The extent of her care reminded me now that it would not be in my best interests to reintroduce myself. No need to make an otherwise miserable day more miserable. She continued up the street, and I headed in the direction of the park, thinking maybe a pinch would prove whether I was just having a nightmare of a day.

"Ow!" I hollered. Yep. Sure enough. I was *wide* awake.

CHAPTER TEN

Saturday and parks go hand in hand for most of us in Savannah. Not so much today. Maybe it was the growing stickiness and encroaching summer temperatures. Walks would be done in the relative cool of the morning or the doable steaminess of the evening. But the action up the street played a greater role in keeping people away today, I was certain.

An empty bench on the front pathway of the park gave me a perfect view of the fountain in the middle, as well as the Oglethorpe Club on Bull Street and the Armstrong Building, which houses the law offices of Bouham, Williams, & Levy, directly across the street from it.

The Oglethorpe Club is the oldest gentleman's club in Georgia. They have two prohibitions. One: No female members. Two: A woman can come with her husband, but she has to wear a dress. And an unwritten law: Your money must be old. Old money looks down on new money. For some reason, if you weren't born with it, it's not legitimate. Never quite made sense to me, because somewhere down the line it was new to somebody. Famed Savannian Jim Williams couldn't get into the club, so he just bought the monstrous Armstrong Building right across the street.

This city and its money have always intrigued me. Most complain about what they don't have while the minority can't seem to get enough. Either way, everybody's trying to get more, causing one to wonder if there ever really is such thing as *enough*.

The lady who sat down on the park bench beside me forced me back into the present. "Beautiful day, isn't it?" she said, wiping her black brow with a yellowed hanky. She hummed softly. A familiar melody, but one I couldn't place.

"Yes, yes it is."

She reached into her well-worn straw bag and pulled out an apple. "Would you like a bite?" she asked, extending her snack.

I giggled, wondering if she would want it back after I had taken a bite. "No, thank you. I just ate actually." Well, had attempted to anyway.

"Okay."

I watched as she stared off into the blue sky that could be seen through the row of houses that lined Drayton Street. She looked intently at the large house on the corner of Drayton and East Gaston, which Charlize Theron used as her residence in *The Legend of Bagger Vance*. The newcomer took up a large portion of the bench. Her worn dress, with a large floral print pattern and faded yellow background, had seen happier days. While perusing her petals, I realized that this was the lady that I had almost hit yesterday in the street. Her straw bag looked as if it had carried apples to park benches for years, but I had never seen her before yesterday.

She took her plump hand with its dirty fingernails and tried to smooth the wiry gray hair poking out from her strained attempt at a ponytail. Her haunting dark eyes seemed older, mysterious, and strange. But friendly. And peaceful.

"Ever wonder what goes on inside these houses?" She gave a

nod to the million-dollar homes. Her enunciation was precise and her dialect truly Southern.

I studied her dark face and watched the movement of her lips as she took a huge chunk out of the front side of her apple. I turned back to my book, hoping to make it clear I really didn't want conversation.

"No, ma'am. I really haven't."

"It's a shame. I would bet you, if I were a betting lady, that is, and not a churchgoing woman"—she gave a determined nod—"that most of the people inside of these homes are in need of something."

I wasn't sure what she meant by that. Her eyes stared so intently down the street that I might have believed she could see straight through the walls.

"Yes ma'am, people in need of something, I'm certain."

She didn't care that I was reading. She hadn't even noticed I was reading. And I was so overcome by curiosity, I had about forgotten I was reading too. I closed the book on my lap.

"Why do you think that?"

"Oh, sweet child, you can see it on their faces." Her ebony hand brought the apple to her lips again. A small dirt smudge on the top of her right cheek marred her otherwise flawless complexion. "They're tired. Just look around their eyes. You can see it. Exhaustion is everywhere. They even walk around like they're tired. And they drive like maniacs trying to get nowhere fast." I felt the sudden urge to cough.

"You all right, child?"

I nodded.

She continued. "This generation is either in a whirlwind rush or a state of utter fatigue. Most of them with sad stories to tell."

I couldn't recall seeing too many whirlwinds in Savannah since moving here years ago. "Hmm . . . hadn't really seen all that." My slight laugh caused her to look at me.

"Even you, little one. You're so young and cute, yet you're tired too. You try too hard. You think too much. You need to enjoy an apple, smell a flower, read a book." She pointed down to the book I would have been reading had we not been having this conversation. "I loved that Mr. Reagan. See what you can learn from him." She stood up to leave. "I'll see you again. Hope you're wearing a bigger smile next time."

Her plump cheeks rose with a smile, causing them to look like the apple she had just finished off. Yet her dark eyes pierced me one more time, causing me to stop and pause. But her smile was infectious. I returned it. Then I watched as she walked up the street and took another apple out of her bag, humming once again.

A tiny little man came rushing past her with his briefcase in his hand and cell phone plastered to his ear. I watched him as he approached my bench, jabbering as if the world was surely collapsing today, right here, in the middle of Forsythe Park around us both.

"What do you mean, you might lose this deal?!" he screamed into the phone. "You lose a sixty-million-dollar deal and you may as well close down the office!"

He sat down on my park bench, totally ignoring me and my book. He flung open his briefcase to find some piece of paper that was either clinging for dear life to another or was wadded up somewhere in the bottomless pit.

"You don't lose deals. You only make deals, Ken. You aren't playing with the little boys anymore; you're playing with the big dogs."

The voice on the other end made futile attempts to secure vindication. "I don't want to hear it. Do you want to keep your nice car and your private jet? Do you want to keep your fancy suits and your big house? Huh? Well, then don't screw up. Jesus, man, don't think for a minute there aren't a thousand men and women ready to take you down and get their name on your office. You better get it together and fast."

His hand finally pulled out a paper, and just about everything in his briefcase came with it. In frustration he threw the mess across the park bench, causing some of it to hit my leg. I pushed it back, which was the first time he even noticed me. He gave me an angry look as if somehow I had invaded his space. My raised right eyebrow made it clear who arrived first.

He grabbed all of the scattered papers and crammed them back into the abyss. It could be years before he ever found what he was actually looking for. He marched onward, still yelling at some lamentable creature all the way. He ascended the stairs of the Oglethorpe Club and disappeared.

I spent the walk home peeking in windows and looking down alleys expecting some precious Allen Funt wannabe to scream at me, "Smile! You're on *Candid Camera!*"

I smiled bigger than I had in years. Looked over every corner of that park, even stood up and held out my arms in case they didn't know I was ready to hear the truth. But no one came. No Allen Funt appeared. No nothing. Reaching the top step of home, I looked back one more time just in case. The only thing that appeared was my shadow.

Either I'm losing my mind, or either . . . well, I'm losing my mind. There really was no other option.

CHAPTER ELEVEN

A mirror can be a cruel thing. It can mock you. Even laugh at you. Today the thing was plumb near hysterical. I scowled at it in return. Looking back was a stranger. My tired, worn, twenty-four-year-old face mocked me. The lines on my forehead must have crept into place in an afternoon. Because they certainly weren't there this morning.

Who did this to me? Who stole my youth? I crinkled my brow up and down. Pulled the side of my eyes back only to discover I would make a woeful-looking Asian. And the process did nothing to remove the deeply embedded crow's-feet. My green eyes drooped and the corners of my lips turned downward. *I need BOTOX. I might need a facelift before I'm thirty. I need to find out who Mother's miracle worker is and stop this madness.*

As I let the corners of my eyes fall back to their basset-hound positions, the apple lady's words echoed in my mind. I was old and tired, ragged and worn, and it took a stranger to let me know. Even my golden brown hair didn't seem to shine. It, too, scoffed at me. My eye caught a sight in the far corner of my shower. It looked like mildew. My right eyebrow raised and the perils of "cleanliness is next to godliness" set in. Retrieving my rubber galoshes, knee pads, and rubber gloves from under the sink, I tore into that bathroom and scrubbed as if I were an exfoliant attacking a buildup of over-obsessing mothers and apathetic fathers.

Hours later I heard a sniffing noise near my behind, which was protruding from the commode, where my efforts were finishing off the pipes that connect the water to the toilet.

"Duke, if you're remotely dirty, you better get off my tile!" He laid himself down and rested his head flat against the tile, eyes looking up at me. "How was your day?"

He raised his right eyebrow.

"Long one, huh?"

He looked down.

I turned around to face him and removed my weapons of war. "Me too! Come on, let's go eat."

We trotted down the stairs, where Dad was putting some dishes in the dishwasher. "What are we going to do for dinner tonight?" I asked.

"I'm doing the same thing I did last night, Savannah." He turned around and leaned against the counter.

I sat down at a stool on the other side of the island. "How long is this charade going to continue? Pretty soon we're going to need clean underwear. What are we going to do then? I say we hire someone to clean the house, fix us dinner, and wash our clothes."

He laughed and crossed his arms. "Savannah, your mother has never let anyone clean her house in her life, and you know it."

"Oh yes, she did. Once."

"Key word in that phrase is *once.*"

No one likes to reminiscence about the day we had a housekeeper. It was the longest day of all of our lives. Victoria is a neat freak. I mean you can move a chair and before you've gotten up from it, she'll put it back to where it "should" be. Everything has its place. Everything has its order. And everything must match, coordinate, or complement. And everything must be clean. We were stupid to even think for a moment that she would appreciate someone's aid.

Shortly after mother went to work at the chamber of commerce, Dad lovingly convinced her that she needed a housekeeper. "I wouldn't dream of having her cook," he assured Vicky, "but at least let someone take some of the load. You can't do it all." He really had her best interests at heart.

Well, she assured him she could do it all and all of us would have been better off for believing her. Because for eleven years, mother has never ceased to resurrect the memory of Mrs. Gonzalez on cleaning days. As for Mrs. Gonzalez, every time she sees mother coming, she hightails it quicker than a cat caught in a tree facing a fire hose. Mrs. Gonzalez is the best in the business. Mother heard about her from Sheila, Paige's mother. In fact, Sheila still uses her to this day.

Mrs. Gonzalez hadn't been in Savannah long and at that time her English was still, shall we say, expanding. She arrived promptly at eight thirty. Mother felt it necessary to take the day off to show her how *she* cleaned the house. By noon Mrs. Gonzalez had done nothing but observe mother clean the house herself. They were doing sign language to communicate. Somewhere around three, Mother made it clear to Mrs. Gonzalez that she didn't think she was going to work out.

"You're . . . just . . . too . . . slow . . ." mother said loudly and slowly, as if volume would remedy Mrs. Gonzalez's inability to understand. Mother added to the insult by showing her the book *The Tortoise and the Hare.* When Mother pointed to the turtle and then to Mrs. Gonzalez, well, let's just say I wish I knew Spanish. But her sign language was interpretation enough.

For kicks, Paige and I will sometimes hug Mrs. Gonzalez and then just whisper Vicky's name in her ear so we can hear the beauty of the range of the Spanish language. Our combined ten years of Spanish study does us no good, but our imaginations fill in.

My dad's continued evaluation brought me back to the kitchen. "Besides, you, Thomas, and I are more than capable of cleaning this house and washing our own clothes."

"You left out meals."

"That is why God made take-out."

"Well, you are missing a wonderful opportunity here. And because mother is totally obsessive-compulsive and thinks no one can clean as well as she can, we could use this opportunity to relieve her of the stress. And on the days that she doesn't feel like cooking, like today, we would have someone here to help us."

"Savannah, I thought you were about to move out."

"I am, but not this week, and tonight I need food."

"I would say for someone so close to moving out, it's high time you wash your own clothes and fix your own meals. What did you do in college?"

"I took everything to the cleaners and ordered takeout or ate in the cafeteria."

"No kidding?"

"Does this look like a face of jest?"

"Girl, it is time you grew up." He walked past me and picked his car keys up off the table.

I turned my legs around in my stool to face him. "Well, I'm sure I can fix something."

"I'm sure you will. Your mother said she saw you briefly today. I expect that to be an everyday occurrence."

He walked over and kissed me and left me there sitting on the stool. Duke followed him, because it was evident who would be eating well tonight, and dogs have their priorities. He would endure stone for steak. He apparently would even endure Vicky. See, he wasn't real bright.

In the refrigerator, the only things that looked familiar were the condiments and the drinks. There was some dip in there that goes great with Doritos, and some sour cream that would be good on a baked potato. *You can do this, Savannah. You're about to be out on your own. Just give it a shot.*

Lady & Son's Cookbook rested on the bar by the telephone. Page 30 offered a lovely looking dish. Some kind of pasta bake. Remembering that most things start with boiling water, I pulled that off without much fanfare or pain. Mother had frozen some homemade ziti noodles and had homemade spaghetti sauce canned and in the pantry. An hour and a half later I pulled a pan full of pasta bake out of the oven.

Except there wasn't much more than a bowlful in the center of the baking dish. It looked nothing like the picture. Something was missing. Scanning the kitchen, trying desperately to figure out why my creation didn't resemble the picture, the tubular noodles resting in the colander in the sink caught my attention. I had a pan of simply "bake."

"Hello, is this Mr. Wong's Chinese Palace?" I asked as soon as I heard the connection. "Do you deliver?"

CHAPTER TWELVE

The biggest problem with Chinese food is that you're hungry two hours after eating it. So by eleven o'clock, I was back to square one. The other problem was that the news wasn't about to help me fall asleep. By the time a person made it to the weather, they were usually too afraid to fall asleep. That's why Leno and Letterman had such high ratings; they catered to all the paranoids too scared to sleep.

Tonight, however, hunger and not fear would keep me awake. That and the picture of my mug that had shown up on the local reports. It appeared shortly after the glib little overprocessed Katie Couric wannabe introduced me as an "episode."

Now, Vicky's name has been attached to the word "episode" on numerous occasions. And her face can find a way to plaster itself across the television screen at any opportunity. Shoot, she could create an occasion. Which is basically what she did here. In fact, she created enough "episodes" in the past two days to sustain her own network. Sit inside any room within the Savannah cable district and turn on your television to public access and you will find Victoria giving a tour of this city through her heavily shaded brown eyes.

She came up with that idea when she decided tourists needed an easy way to get quick information about the sights to see and things to do while in the city. And since it was her idea, well, could there be anyone else to host? You have to ask such a silly question. I mean, she is the head of the Savannah Chamber of Commerce.

So she stands in front of the Andrew Low House in a peach ensemble, and next she's in front of a square in something from the cranberry family, and then she's in front of Lady & Sons wearing floral, and before you know it she's giving a tour of her own office in the Savannah Chamber of Commerce, having donned her favorite color, cream. If cream is even a color. Each ensemble is accessorized and immaculately kept. And for a tour of the city squares themselves, the lady dons a hat bigger than the state of Texas.

So to have to sit here in my own room, in my own home, and view the two of us on camera together, me looking lost and her looking smudged, and labeled together as an "episode," well, it made me downright angry. And the fact that I was sleeping in an empty house on a Saturday night, starving, and that my future husband had walked away with a redhead whom my mother actually embraced, and that I was forced in front of a camera only because my mother had no common sense . . . it was all more than I could bear.

Then came the coup de grâce. An interview with my mother in which she referred to—who? Could a turnip truck carrying turnips be more certain? She referenced me, her Savannah from Savannah. In fact she mentioned just about every accolade I had achieved since potty training. I think she even mentioned that one. *Well, I guess advertisements in the newspaper will never again compare to what she has just accomplished here this evening. Thank God this was only local news.*

I pulled out a pair of jogging shorts and a white T-shirt, and then slipped on my tennis shoes. I would deal with this insanity once and for all. The Phillipses were not going to be the headline news and bathroom folly any longer. Not on my watch.

Grabbing a peanut-butter-and-jelly sandwich, I headed out to stop the madness. The jaunt took a little longer because there was no way sister was walking past the cemetery at the hour of the dead. Yet, even at eleven, the streets of Savannah were still alive. People enjoyed the nightlife here, the restaurants and lounges and music. There was that other coffee shop, which stayed open until past the "godly hour," and parties going on in houses with open doors. You could almost just walk on in. Most people didn't know each other anyway, so what was one more stranger?

Savannah has its own clock. Its own reality. Its own rules. Some hate them, some love them, and others just tolerate them. The people now spread across the square and the small grassy-knoll area in front of the courthouse apparently comprised a few of all three types.

The camera trucks hadn't moved and a few bright lights still glared. But most media members had gone to bed with the eleven o'clock news. A few lonely feeds for the West Coast remained. And Rita Cosby from FOX News. She was chatting with my father. Then I remembered. My demise was confirmed. I, Savannah, had certainly transcended the realm of "local" personality this evening and been thrust into the world of "national." All by the descriptive powers of my mother.

Ms. Austin was standing at the corner with one of our local merchants having a cup of that other shop's coffee. They behaved as if they had known each other for years, until she was interrupted by her cell phone. I continued scanning and noticed Dad was wrapping it up with Rita. He gave her a pat on the shoulder. The man never met a stranger. Then he made his steady but slow stride over to my mother.

Vicky was unpacking her evening gear, silken-clad neck pillow, eye mask, ear plugs, and cream taffeta sleeping bag. I wanted to walk up and shake her out of her obvious delirium. But truth be known, I was too tired to fight.

The rest of the square looked surprisingly clean, considering all the activity. I expected it to be blanketed with paper cups, dinner trash, and empty bottles. But it was just blanketed with people and, well, their blankets. The moon made its way over the square, and its full brilliance spotlighted the stone monument, as if making a statement. Some of the sojourners were ready to rest. Others prayed quietly in groups. And others were talking quietly, holding candles.

Crossing to the sidewalk in front of the courthouse, I stopped when I saw Mother rest her head against the back of the monument. She adjusted her silk eye mask atop her rather smashed tresses. Only a moment later, Dad's head rested next to hers. There, encased in moonlight and looking up with a teenage smile, Dad nestled his arm behind mother's head. They both continued to look into the face of the moon.

The dog and young man lying next to them were in peaceful dreamland and obvious rapture. Duke had even scored his own pillow. Thomas had scored two sleeping bags.

"This is what it was like when we were teenagers." Mother's voice broke the silence.

"Yes, it was. Except I wasn't actually a teenager."

They both laughed. He was eight years older and a "cradle robber" as my grandmother called him.

Vicky nodded at the moon. "It's a shame it takes an event like this to get us to stop long enough to appreciate something so beautiful."

He pulled her toward him. "Yeah, we've been too busy, haven't we?"

"I know I have. You're better. You stop when you need to. I keep going like the Energizer Bunny." She giggled.

"Maybe it's time to make first things first."

"We do, on the whole. We always have dinner together. We take Sundays off, and our children have grown up to be givers instead of takers."

"Yes, but you've still got to let go of some of your responsibilities. You can't do it all."

"I don't try to do it all."

"Oh yes, you do. And I think you do it because you're afraid."

411

"I'm not afraid." She straightened to make her point. "What would I have to be afraid of?"

"Afraid life might not work if you're not in charge of it. Afraid this city will crumble if you're not there to hold it up. But you don't hold Savannah up now, Victoria. You just think you do."

"I do not." She crossed her arms.

"You most certainly do." Dad nudged her stiffening arms. "You can't hold on so tight. Because at the end of the day, all you can control is you. And Savannah isn't yours. You live here. But it's not yours. And you need to quit making it the most important thing in your life."

"Jake Phillips, how dare you say this is the most important thing in my life. You know you and my children are the most important thing to me."

"Victoria, I know we're important, but you won't even take a vacation because you're afraid this place will fall apart when you leave."

Score one for Jake. I used to will myself to believe that Vicky wanted to direct the chamber of commerce so she could create an atmosphere of true Southern hospitality for visitors to our fair city. Part of me still believes that's true. However, the other part of me thinks that she thinks the city can't make it without her. And I do believe she has convinced most of the city of the same.

Maybe her powers of persuasion are in the perfectly coiffed hair or pristinely applied Mary Kay. They might even be in the way she puts her hand on your arm and laughs that small feminine laugh and stretches one-syllable words into two, like *light* into *lie-it*. Who knows what it is that makes people crumble so, but she is the queen of her domain. And she works in the grandest structure on Bay Street as well.

"I am not afraid of any such thing. This city would be just fine without me. I just . . . I just . . . well, I just don't like turbulent situations. I want the city to know I'm here for them." She pouted and apparently forgot about the moon.

"Turbulent situations? Give me a break. You believe Savannah will slip into the ocean if you leave it for a moment. I mean, think about it: Who is chained to this monument and plans to run her office from here the entire week if necessary? Who makes sure everything runs right around here? Who thinks she has to be at every meeting, make every decision, and be the head of every event?"

"Is this a trick question?"

Dad laughed at her naiveté. "No, this is an adequate assessment. I'm just saying you need to ask yourself some questions, Victoria. And I can't think of any better place to do it than here, outside, looking at that amazing moon." He lifted her chin to the brilliant light that was making its way to the other side of the square.

"I think you're off-base and out of line, Jake Phillips." *Ooh, both names. That's never good.* "Why are you here?"

"To protect you. To keep you warm. To cover you," he said, pulling her close.

"I'm not a child."

"No, you're not."

"Then don't treat me like one."

He pulled her in closer, placing his mouth at her ear. It was a whisper, but I could still hear him. "I love you more than you could ever know."

"I know," she responded, trying to resist his effect on her. It didn't work.

He kissed her softly on the lips and nestled her back under his arm, and fingered her unusually carefree hair. "You could never truly know," he whispered.

Those words hovered in the air like familiar love lingers over the words of a song. They rested there like the knowledge of their love rested in each other. For a child watching such interaction between her parents, it was, well, disgusting. But for a woman to watch such a loving exchange between two people, it was defining.

Their gazes lifted to the moon, and mine fell to the sidewalk. I journeyed to my bed with a new definition of love, commitment, and character. These were the people I had come from. Their love had made me. Their character had defined me. And their choices would affect me.

But my choices would determine where this new revelation would take me.

CHAPTER THIRTEEN

"Vanni, if you're riding with me you better hurry up."

I wet my hand to press back the golden brown lock that was protruding from an otherwise pristine ponytail. It was Sunday and I could drive myself, but it was about the only time Thomas and I even got to talk anymore. I peered in the mirror one more time and made sure my white suit jacket laid neatly across the matching white skirt, and appreciated the way the delicate black pinstripes elongated my five-foot-six frame.

This suit accomplished in an instant what Pilates could only do in four years. My rather pitiful legs stuck out, but the strappy white sandals (with a heel rather high for my taste) made them look a little better. Usually by this time in May I had a golden tan. But after my smoky run-in with Tan Beautiful last week, and now the revelation that I looked old and tired, well, I would have to rethink the whole tanning ritual. I could only wish for the olive complexion of Ms. Austin.

Thomas was waiting at the bottom of the stairs, and Duke waited by his side. We walked out the front door to his Jeep. "What do you think Duke does on Sundays when we are all gone?" I asked.

Thomas opened my door and shut it behind me. He crawled in the other side. "Oh, after his last two nights, he'll probably sleep."

"I've always pictured him sitting at the table, drinking coffee, reading the paper, then going for a dip in the pool and blow-drying himself off in Mom's bathroom."

"You are weird."

"Weird, but it's still possible. He's that smart, don't you think?"

"No dog is that smart."

"But Duke isn't stupid, is he?"

"No, he's one of the smartest dogs I know. Why? Are you trying to get him on a stupid-pet-tricks show?"

"No, I just think he does amazing things when we're not looking."

"Make sure you get prayer for that this morning."

Thomas's Jeep jerked as he took off from the stop sign and headed toward Tybee Island and our interdenominational church.

Thomas got his Jeep—which he has named Leroy, no one knows why—for high-school graduation. Mother had visions of a four-door LTD, but Dad would have nothing to do with it. She was stirring up enough trouble over Thomas's choosing of The Citadel. Believing Charleston to be the illegitimate child of the South, she warned him she wouldn't even visit.

Don't let her fool you. He's going into his senior year and she's already made over the bookstore, brought in a new line of Citadel dishware, and was even asked to represent The Citadel in trying to dissuade the first female applicant from attending.

Vicky herself went to the girl's hometown, took her to lunch, bought her a dress, and did her best to get the young woman to go to a school that would make her appreciate "being a lady."

"They are forming men there, honey. Surely you don't want to spend your life with people thinking you're a she-boy." To this day I am not quite certain what a she-boy is, was, or will be. But Vicky was sure that would work.

Two weeks later Shannon became the first woman in the corps. Vicky was mortified and still to this day calls it an "all-male" academy.

In her quarterly column in The Citadel's *Pass In Review*, entitled "The Making of an All-American Man," Vicky wrote, "If those girls want to be treated like men then I'll just call them men." And so she does.

Anytime she passes a girl on campus, she simply smiles and says, "Well, hello, young man." Hasn't phased them a bit. Downright near sent Mother to the halls of Washington. Fortunately for Washington, she's afraid to fly.

The church was already bustling. It had grown so much over the past year that Pastor Brice decided we needed to go to three services. As I watched the people enter, I was amazed by how many young people there were. Dad greeted us at the door and handed us a bulletin. The usual big hat and red lipstick and happy greeting from the other side of the door was conspicuously absent.

"Savannah, you look beautiful," Dad said, kissing me on the cheek. "Your mother wouldn't have wanted to miss this." That creeped me out. It was as if we were talking about someone who had passed through the eternal gates of glory.

I gave him a raised right eyebrow, and Thomas and I entered the sanctuary. "Where did all these college students come from?" I asked.

"A lot are from the Savannah College of Art and Design. Pastor Brice said the other day that he gave his heart to Jesus over twenty years ago, and he wasn't going anywhere. So, if the music was too loud or the service needed to be a little different to reach his kids and their friends, he was okay with that."

"That's a rather different perspective," I mused. "What's Granny Daniels think?"

"I heard she attends their Sunday-night youth services and keeps up with the best of them."

I laughed, certain he had accurate information. "I wouldn't doubt it. Seems weird today, huh?"

Thomas sat down beside me on a pew in the middle of the left-hand side. "What, with Mom not at the door?"

"No, with her not telling us to take our seats and sit quietly or spitting in her hand to wet your cowlicks down." We both laughed.

The music began, and the very essence of it seemed to lift me. It started with an up-tempo song about faith. The multiracial choir swayed from one side to the other. By the time they were through, the volume had been brought down to a powerful yet reverent conclusion. Our associate pastor, Tom Jackson, was speaking this morning. The former Washington Redskin, with whom my father liked to chat football, rose to take the platform. His forty-year-old physique oozed professional athlete. And his African American heritage gave him beautiful skin and a magnetic smile.

He towered behind the Plexiglas podium, where he sat his Bible down and took in the thousand pairs of eyes staring back. He moved to the right of the podium and leaned against it. And I looked forward to some inspiring moments away from Vicky and the events of the last two days.

I was not to have them. For the next forty-five minutes, Pastor Jackson delivered a message entitled "Declaration of Dependence," offering insight and reflection on the events transpiring in our city. No one could get away from it. Yet no one else's mother was keeping quite the vigil mine was. I wouldn't be getting away from Vicky until this madness was over.

Thomas started the Jeep. "What are you doing for lunch?"

The question brought revelation. There would be no Sunday roast today. No country-style steak. No rice. No gravy. No homemade biscuits. No nothing. Just take-out.

"I'm going to go find a housekeeper that cooks."

"Dad got a big dinner from Lady & Sons last night and put it in the refrigerator so we could have it today. We're taking it to the square and having lunch with Mom." He noticed my disgust. "Just think of it as a Sunday dinner on the grounds."

"When have you ever been to a Sunday dinner on the grounds?"

"We used to when we would go to Granny's country church."

"They had ants."

"Are you ever positive?"

"Yes, smarty butt, I'm positive you will have a wonderful time. Don't worry about me. I'll get something."

As he pulled up in front of the house, he turned to look back at me. "You really need to get over this pride issue you have. If you are proud of anything, it should be over our mother standing up for something she believes in, no matter how she may look to others." He didn't wait for a reply. He just left me there sitting in the Jeep staring at his backside.

Thomas had been mean in the past. We didn't even like each other much until I left for college. I think we even had a few knock-down, drag-outs that ended with the words "moron!" and "Well, what do you know? You were an accident anyway." Both of which hurt my feelings and left me screaming for my father.

But Thomas had never said anything that stung like those words just did. "Pride? I'm not the one with the pride issue. The one with the pride issue is the silly woman sitting in the middle of a square, holding the city hostage. That's who has a pride issue. You're telling me what to do? I'll do what I want to do. I'm a grown woman who's about to have her own apartment. You're a little bald Citadel boy. Haven't even finished school yet. Need to teach you some manners."

Two fanny-pack-toting tourists on the street watched me quizzically as I ascended the stairs to the front door.

The Sunday newspaper was lying atop the breakfast-room table, where Dad had obviously read it with a morning cup of coffee. Or possibly where Duke had left it. I needed to see if Joshua's dog could do that. By it rested a note and a take-out dinner. *Enjoy your lunch. We'd like to see you today.*

The cover of the paper only caused the anger of last night to return. There I was, betrayed by my own employer. My backside was on the front of the paper, with the beaming face of my mother peering over my shoulder. It would resonate with the world that I agreed with her. I would never wear that outfit again and would do whatever I could to prevent the world from knowing it was me.

Then I noticed the caption underneath. "*Victoria Phillips, head of the chamber of commerce, embraces daughter, Savannah Phillips, in front of Ten Commandments Monument.*"

My cell phone rang. I sent her to voice mail once again. *Does US Air fly to Tanzania?*

CHAPTER FOURTEEN

I wasn't hungry for anything but vengeance. I had two plans of attack. And they were vicious, but well deserved. One: Get a housekeeper. Two: Get a housekeeper that cooks. To sort through strategies, I had always walked. So I walked straight up West Jones Street instead of going near the courthouse. That was nowhere on my agenda today. Con me with food or not, I wasn't biting.

Mr. Fisher was outside his house, trimming the ivy that had overtaken the iron-gate entrance to his spectacular garden. Mr. Fisher's house, a beautiful aged, burnt brick with rich tones and streaks of black, had a side-porch entrance more common to Charleston, South Carolina, architecture. The black shutters and ebony-stained wood door that led to the porch, complemented by a brass lion's-head door-knocker, had all been maintained with extreme care.

Charleston homes were originally taxed based on how many windows they had in the front of their house. So the Southerners got frugal as well as savvy and built all of their homes with side-porches, which served as the main entrance. By building the houses sideways, the "fronts" had as few windows as any other part of the house.

But Vicky's issues are deeply rooted in her competitive spirit with the other "Sister of the South." Stepsister, if you ask her. The fact that any house in Savannah resembled a Charleston residence is a fact Vicky fought tooth and nail, and well, I do mean literally tooth and nail.

It happened one beautiful fall day a couple of years after our arrival here from Atlanta, and only months after I decided to picket in front of our house because there was no McDonald's near our home. About the time Mr. Fisher and his wife were having their furniture unloaded, Mother pranced herself up the street and threw herself on top of their baby grand piano as the movers were trying to carry it into the house.

"What in the tar hill are you doing, young lady?" Mr. Fisher screamed. The young lady part almost caused mother to completely forget why she was there. But the jolt of the piano brought her back to reality.

"I'm saving you!" she replied with great animation.

"You're violating my piano! Now get yourself down!"

The mover provided extra incentive. "You might want to do what he says, lady, because we're about to have to turn this baby on her side, and then you won't be on the top any longer."

"Well, wait just a minute!" she said, still atop her perch. "You don't want to buy this house."

"I already bought it, lady!"

"Well, you don't want to move in."

"And why wouldn't I want to do that? Are you going to tell me it's haunted or something?"

"Lord have mercy, no. I don't like ghosts, and I pray them out of town any chance I get. Even walked a street or two getting them out of here."

"Lady, you're crazy. Now get off of my piano!"

About that time, the dainty Mrs. Fisher walked out with her pretty bobbed gray hair, and pants that looked like jeans but weren't. "Oh my Lord, what is she doing on our piano?"

"She's preparing to get off!" her husband assured her.

"Lady, I'm warning you," the mover said, straining beneath the added one hundred and ten pounds of peculiar. "We are tipping this puppy on three. One, two, three." And with that, three grown men turned the top of the antique baby grand piano on its side, and one Victoria Phillips on her bum. They didn't stop to check on her or survey the damage; they just continued straight in the house.

Mr. Fisher just stared at my mother, but Mrs. Fisher ran over to help her up. "Young lady, what is all this about?"

Mother tried to salvage as much grace as she possibly could after being dumped off a piano. "You live in Savannah. Why in the world would you want to buy a home that looks like Charleston?"

Mrs. Fisher let out a chuckle. "Is that what this nonsense is about? What is your name anyway?"

For one minute, or so the story goes, Mother hesitated. After all, to say that she was the head of the chamber of commerce might make for rather embarrassing dinner conversation. But then again, that revelation wasn't enough to forgo her great pride in her position. "I am Mrs. Victoria Phillips, head of the Savannah Chamber of Commerce."

Mr. Fisher let out a humph. "You have got to be kidding me. Is this how you welcome everyone to the city? If it is, tourism will be destroyed in six months." With that he and Mrs. Fisher left her there with a bruised ego and a bruised bum.

Vicky walked back to our house. Rumor has it there were a couple more similar episodes involving dressers and a dining room table, but the episodes ceased after the washing-machine incident made it on the front page.

Mr. Fisher's voice threw my recollection. "Savannah Phillips, how do you like my garden? Not bad for a Charleston house, huh?" A pretty good memory for his seventy-five years.

I peeked inside the gate and admired how beautifully landscaped and sculpted it was. "Oh, it's beautiful. You've been working hard, haven't you?"

"Oh yeah. Takes up most of my time. But with me still working, it gets away from me and I have to attack it whenever I have free time. Where you off to? Trying to get away from the picture in the paper?" He smiled knowingly.

I picked invisible lint off my khaki capris and made my way up to my white T-shirt. "Just taking a walk before I eat lunch."

"Lunch?" he asked, putting down his trimmers. "Why on earth are you not eating at—oh, that's right, your mother's down at the courthouse. Is she lying on the monument or just sitting beside it?"

That made us both roar with laughter. "She's actually gone to sitting these days," I finally managed.

He took out his hanky and wiped the sweat from his gray bushy eyebrows. His blue eyes were crystal clear and shimmered of a stolen youth, but also of a life still flourishing inside. "Why don't you come eat with me and the Mrs.? She has enough food for us to eat off all week. We're having fish."

"No, that's okay really. I appreciate it. But I've got to do some work this afternoon for my next column, so I'm just going to grab a quick bite at home."

"You sure?" He picked up his clippers.

I patted him on his damp white T-shirt. "Yes, sir, I'm sure. Thanks anyway."

"Will do."

"Uh, Mr. Fisher?"

"Yes?"

"Does Mrs. Fisher ever rent out her cooking services?"

He laughed. "You're asking for trouble, Miss Savannah."

"You think?"

"I've gone a round with your mama. I know."

"Well, tell Mrs. Fisher I said hello."

"You tell your family the same." Fortunately for Victoria, Mr. Fisher was able to let go. Too bad the letter to the editor he wrote about her welcoming party took them four years for the letting go to begin.

I would eat on the stoop. If I sat in the garden, sequestered by ivy, I couldn't really see what was happening on the streets. So, I went out to the stoop and sat on the steps. This is virtually the only way I am like my mother. I do like to see what is going on around me.

Come to think of it, Dad does too. He likes to plant himself at the table by the window in the hopes that some weary straggler will need to bare his soul. He'll act all casual, sitting there petting Duke. Someone will walk in for a quick hello or cup of coffee, but before you know it Jake's helping with marital problems (which he denies having), adolescent terrors (of which he declares he's had many), or financial difficulties (which he overcame). By the time they leave smiling, Dad's sitting back at the window, smiling too.

About two bites into my first piece of catfish, my park-bench friend arrived. I heard her before I saw her. She was humming that same melody she had departed with yesterday. She wore the same dress as yesterday too, carried the same bag, and didn't look much different than she had twenty-four (or forty-eight!) hours earlier. This week anyway, she and Vicky had a thing or two in common.

"Well, well, young lady. Where's your book?"

I laughed, finding it hard to believe she remembered me. "Inside." I motioned to my house. "I didn't bring it for this journey."

But she didn't really care about my book. She didn't care about the house either. Didn't care about Victoria's lovely iron balconies, or stately wooden, black-painted doors. Couldn't have given a rat's rear end for the pristine ivy growing over our own brick wall that surrounded our fortress. No, her eyes were on my plate. She was like Duke eying a tenderloin. I wanted her to pull out her apple and get to eating her food. She walked up a few steps and planted herself next to me, still fixated on my food. "Ooh, you got a nice Sunday dinner there, don't ya?"

"Yeah, you can get some at Lady & Son's. It's just up the street." I was even gracious enough to point her in the direction.

She wasn't paying a lick of attention to my lead. "Yeah, well maybe I'll try to get over there." But she didn't move. How could she when she never even looked away from my plate?

Well, it was Sunday. "Would you like some?"

She turned away, embarrassed. "Oh no, baby. I don't want to eat your food. You need your food. You can tell I get all the food I need." She patted her stomach. I wasn't going to argue with her. Then she turned quickly back around. "Well, if you really want me to have some, I don't want to hurt your feelings."

I laughed at her sweet expression. "Here. Take two. Who wants to eat Sunday dinner alone anyway?" I laid a napkin out for her. Gave her some catfish and a homemade biscuit. By the time she was through, Garfield couldn't have accomplished cleaner bones. "What's your name?"

"Oh, my name is . . ." She looked off into the distance as if trying to find something to jog her memory or offer her a name. "My name is Joy. Yes, it's Joy." She finally answered as more of a declaration.

"Oh, that's a beautiful name. Here, take a drink." I handed her the tea I had yet to enjoy and offered her the opportunity to wash down what she had virtually inhaled.

"What's your name, precious girl?"

"Savannah," I said, scratching my nose.

"Nose itch?"

"Like crazy. My mother says that means somebody's coming to see you." I raised a right eyebrow at my dinner guest. "Guess she got that one right, huh?"

She looked at me inquisitively. "Well, I think Savannah is a beautiful name for a beautiful girl."

"You don't want to crack a joke about it? Everyone else does."

"Now, who would crack a joke about a beautiful name?"

I wiped my mouth and gave her the rest of my plate. It seemed she needed it more than me. "You'd be surprised."

"I'm surprised by a lot of things, Savannah. I'm surprised by how people rush to and fro. Hardly stop to breathe. Or give thanks for the ability to breathe. So busy working and doing and never simply resting or enjoying. I see the lights on in their windows until late in the night. They type on computers and rummage through papers. All the time doing and never living. And then the one moment, the one day the world is told to rest, it just keeps on moving. We all need rest, Savannah."

"You're telling me."

She looked back at me, not seeming to remember. "You look kind of that way. Like you need some rest."

"You said the same thing yesterday. I didn't realize how bad I was looking until you informed me."

She chuckled, causing her belly to move with her. "Ooh, I'm sorry, baby. I didn't mean that you look bad like you were ugly or something. It's a furrowed brow. It's a heaviness of the eyes. It's seeing the weight someone carries by the mere look in their eyes. But it doesn't have to be that way."

"You aren't going to try to sell me some Anthony Robbins tape series are you?"

"Who's Anthony Robbins?"

"Good."

"No, I don't have anything to sell. Life isn't about selling and buying. It's about knowing and doing. And I'm not talking about the twenty-four-hour-a-day, seven-day-a-week doing. I'm talking about the heart knowing and the life doing."

I leaned my elbows on the step behind me. My mind was so tired. And all of this was just making me more tired. "I'm tired of doing."

"I see you've had all you can take, my sweet Savannah." She rose from her side of the stoop and laid my empty plate neatly beside me. Then she rose and picked up the half glass of tea to take it with her. I couldn't help but smile at her mature innocence.

She seemed so wise, yet her eyes looked so young and vulnerable. "I'm sure I'll see you soon," I assured us both.

She turned and headed to the corner of the house. She stopped and turned back around. "Being, Savannah! That's the word. Not doing, but just being, baby."

I watched her as her skirt shifted tightly across her backside with the movement of her round legs. And I wondered who this stranger was and where she had come from. The thought of a strange elderly woman walking up some street, drinking my tea and singing, caused me to laugh at the absurdity of the last couple days. I would have asked her if she would like a job, but the way she was always hungry, it was evident cooking wasn't her forte. And the blur that passed by me forced my attention elsewhere.

You don't see a lot of lawn mowers in downtown Savannah. Few people actually have yards to be mowed. Most people's yards aren't lawns; they're gardens. And gardens need maintaining, mulching, even manicuring, but nowhere do they need mowing. And if they do, the areas are so small that they pretty much only require a weed eater.

But the city does mow the town. Savannah takes great pride in the preservation of the squares for the enjoyment of the tourists, and the homeowners that claim them as front yards.

The young man driving the mower that zoomed by my house didn't look too happy about his afternoon assignment. I followed him in sheer wonder of this most ordinary activity. He was probably a young college kid desperate for summer money. On a beautiful day like today, a kid his age had a thousand other things he should have been enjoying.

But this one kid now arriving at Lafayette Square, he was commissioned to mow. I sat down on a bench to observe. I don't know why. Wasn't much else to observe, well, nothing that I wanted to get in the middle of now. The grass flew up on the pavement in front of me, making a scattered green hedge along the edge of the sidewalk. The new design would have to be removed by the young worker after completing the first stage of his duty.

I bore easily. As I got up to work my way down the street, the edge of my flip-flop scraped some of the freshly laid hedge back onto the lawn. At least, on the edge of one square of one of the four sidewalks, this small section would not require his attention. It might not save much time, but it may save him a moment.

The two women in front of me didn't quit talking, nor move from my path the entire way to the courthouse. Their hands were loaded down with shopping bags, and they rambled on incessantly for three blocks.

"What are you doing the rest of the day?" the stately, elderly woman said to the medium-built, stout younger one.

"Working. I've got final exams to finish grading before tomorrow. What about you?"

"The same. And next year will only be worse. We are going to have to submit weekly lesson plans."

"Every week? I'm doing good to get mine submitted once a month."

"It's just gotten absurd."

And on and on they went for three straight blocks. They waxed eloquent on everything from how the last week of school would run to who had lunch duty. By the time they were through, I needed a nap. Their incessant rambling made me decide not to think about work until tomorrow. After all, my story wasn't going anywhere. It rested right down the street on that square alive with activity. And all I had to do was sit and observe. By Tuesday, Mr. Hicks would have an article on his desk.

I had no idea yet what I was going to tell people about the upheaval of our city, but I knew that story would consist of a thousand strangers, a large piece of granite, and a woman who claimed to be responsible for my physical birth. She would probably be the one responsible for my occupational death.

CHAPTER FIFTEEN

When the courthouse came into view, I was shocked at what I saw. In a part of the nation known as the Bible Belt, Savannah's church- or cathedral- or synagogue-going population is probably right up there with the likes of Nashville. The name of God is mentioned in most conversations and everyone knows of Him, believes in Him, or knew of Him at one time or another, or at the very least attaches His name to their profanities.

But today, in Savannah, Georgia, church had come to the square. As I scanned the mass of people, most were stretched out, lying with their faces touching cement or the very dust of the earth. And a sound was rising from every corner. Wright Square was enveloped in prayer. The sound of it was overwhelming and amazing. And as if on cue, every prostrate pilgrim rose and began to sing the anthem of ages past, of saints and sinners alike, "Amazing Grace."

I caught sight of Thomas and Dad, apparently headed to the same place I was.

"Brought church to the square today, huh?"

Dad smiled and responded. "Sounds like it, doesn't it?"

We met up on the corner. As the final chorus ended I caught Dad's eye. We each paused. Moments like this weren't textbook, even for the South. None of us rushed it. Who would want to? For or against, some moments in life required everyone's respect. This was one.

"Are y'all going inside the store?"

Dad wrapped his arm around me. "Yeah, I wanted a cup of coffee and it's free at my place. But let's go in the back. I don't want anyone to think I'm open."

Dad opened the back door. The aroma of coffee was so ingrained into the very wood that even on days when it wasn't being brewed, Jake's smelled like coffee. Even the hole where the dishwasher was supposed to be smelled of coffee.

"Did your dishwasher man take off with your cash?" I asked.

Dad shook his head, unable to hide his slight frustration. "Who knows? I've tried to call him three or four times, but he still hasn't responded."

"Didn't you see him on your outing last night?"

"No. He didn't show up there either."

"Mervine and Louise will want a raise."

"And you can bet they'll let me know about it too." He laughed. He put on a pot of coffee and Thomas sat on top of the stainless steel worktable that rested in the center of the room. Duke tried to join him, but lost his footing, only to end up in a pitiful clump on the stamped concrete floor.

"Duke, you're pitiful, ol' boy." I patted his head but refused to pat his boo-boo. "So what did y'all do all afternoon?"

Thomas curled his feet up under him as if he were ten and turned his ball cap around backward. His green eyes became expressive with his recounting of their "picnic on the grounds."

"We ate and told old stories. Mother told me things about her life when she was growing up, stories I don't think I've ever heard."

I tried not to act all that interested and turned around to fix myself a Coke. "Like what?"

"Like about how she would go out behind her house and smoke when she was little."

I turned back around in amazement. "No way! Victoria Phillips never smoked."

"Oh, yes she did! But if you told anyone, she would deny it."

I sat down beside him on the table. The coffeepot began spattering and sputtering, and the fresh aroma of coffee began to take over the aroma of yesterdays.

"There is no way our mother, Miss No-Cigarettes-No-Alcohol-No-Nothing-but-Coffee, would ever have smoked."

Dad poured his cup of coffee while looking amused at our exchange.

Thomas added. "She did, I swear! She said she could have even been addicted."

Dad laughed out loud.

"She could not!" I slapped Thomas on the arm and went back to my Coke. Duke looked up once again just to make sure we hadn't changed our minds about inviting him to join us on the table. Dad poured his coffee and leaned against the side of the counter by my Coke machine.

Thomas took my Coke from my hands and took a sip big enough to force me to have to get more. "Yes, she could have. She said it herself. You'll have to get her to tell you all about it. It is hysterical." He jumped down off of the table.

"What else did she tell you?"

"Oh, lots of stuff. About her parents. About how her mother started going to church when they moved next door to one. How their lives changed. How she felt when they died. All those kinds of things."

"Well, sounds like a nostalgic afternoon. Mine was pretty interesting too."

"That's nice, Savannah. Okay, Dad, let's go back. Mother's going to be singing a special."

"Heaven help us all."

"Plus the judge is working around the clock to make sure this monument stays. And I wouldn't mind catching another glimpse of that Ms. Austin lady. That woman is—" Dad gave him a playful slap on the back of the head.

I tried to hide my hurt at their lack of interest by pouring myself some more Coke.

Thomas turned around to look at me. Hiding my feelings from him seemed a wasted effort. He took no notice of them anyway. "Are you coming with us, Vanni, or heading back to your hole?"

I raised my right eyebrow at him in total disgust at his disregard for my choice to have a life. "No thanks. I really need to get home and start putting together my story."

"Whatever you say."

Dad locked the door behind us and put his arm around me to walk down the alley and back to the square. "Did you have a good afternoon?"

I stopped to ponder my tea-stealing stranger. The thought of her made me smile. "I had an interesting one, to say the least."

"Good, I'm glad. We missed you though. Your mother was disappointed."

I knew what her disappointment was: extreme sighing, dramatic chest clasping, pouty red lips.

I gave in. After all, this square was my story. "Well, let's go see what the crowd out there is up to, shall we?"

"Yeah, let's do."

The size of the crowd seemed double that of yesterday. Apparently most people had Sunday off. Except for the lawn boy, the schoolteachers who weren't even going to let their minds rest today, and Mr. Fisher. But a large portion of Savannah's workforce seemed to be standing shoulder to shoulder, making clear their passion toward a monument of ancient truths.

Judge Hoddicks came out of the courthouse about the time

we made it to the end of the square. Even the newsmen who sat through the hymn rose to take note of Judge Hoddicks's arrival.

The judge cleared his throat as he stood behind the makeshift podium. Beside him stood a distinguished-looking gentleman with smooth, dark skin and hair sprinkled with gray, suggesting wisdom. His tiny gold-framed glasses and steady eyes solidified his importance. I paused and tried to determine who he was and why he was here. Then I saw the familiar figure beside him. He saw me at the same time and tried to hide his white smile beneath his chocolate skin while acting dignified and important.

So it was clear now: Judge Tucker from Mississippi had indeed come to support his old friend. I was certain Gregory had come along for the sheer entertainment value of it all.

Judge Hoddicks introduced Judge Tucker to the captive audience. Well, at least one was truly captive. After giving an uninformative "update," he motioned to someone in the crowd. For a brief moment I expected my mother to heave that monument atop her back and follow. But instead I watched as Ms. Austin headed his direction. She had traded her cascading ponytail for cascading curls that reached midway down the back of her brown sleeveless top. Her lean legs covered in matching slacks followed the judges and my partner in legal battles, Gregory, up the stairs.

"That's her," I mouthed. "ACLU lady."

His face made it clear he didn't mind following her at all. And I suspected that every man within a two-block radius—maybe except for Jake—wished at that moment they were an old judge or a young law clerk from Mississippi.

My mother looked as if her mind was processing a thousand things. Which wasn't any great phenomenon because she did usually have trouble focusing on one thing at a time. Her appearance, in contrast to the raven-haired beauty, had never before looked quite so unkempt. Granted, her level of unkemptness would pale in comparison to most people's, because on a good day she was

Queen-of-England caliber. In other words, she looked like a normal woman on a Saturday. The rushed makeup job. The not-going-to-iron-because-it's-Saturday wrinkled clothes that had been lying in the floor, but looked remotely clean. The hair-will-do syndrome.

But on Vicky, well, let's just say it wasn't pretty.

Her blue suit was extremely wrinkled. And the two stains from yesterday had apparently been poorly attacked with some Shout wipes, only to leave water marks and were now joined by three new stains. Her makeup looked reapplied and was nearing the "hard" arena. Her hair had lost its "edge" and was now teetering on the squashed, might-need-a-wash brink. And this was my mother. Sitting in front of that monument, with as much pride as a mother watching her child graduate from college after three previously failed attempts, was my mother.

It was obvious she hadn't seen herself in a mirror in two days. Because if she had, she would be like any common criminal who holds up their handcuffed arms to shield their face from the cameras. The wide-brimmed hat, in a complementary shade of blue, had replaced the umbrella and averted a few prying eyes.

"Does she know how horrible she looks?"

"Savannah, your mother doesn't look horrible. She looks, well, she looks alive."

"Oh, that's a new line. Try that one on her and then hand her a mirror and see whose going to need the new apartment. And another delicate matter I've been pondering . . ."

"And what would that be?"

"How does the woman go to the bathroom?"

"Very well actually."

I punched his arm. "You know what I mean."

"Ever heard of a Porta Potti?"

"There is no way."

"Trust me, there is a way."

"Victoria Phillips would not use a Porta Potti in the middle of a Savannah square."

"You don't know your mother like you think."

"Please tell me I was adopted."

"It's never too late." Dad began to head in her direction. "Now come tell your mother hello."

"I will later. I'm not into crowds."

"You mean you're not into uncomfortable," he said, leaving me to myself. My rather uncomfortable self.

CHAPTER SIXTEEN

Elderly tourists are easy to spot. They have a walk. A slow, stop-and-look-at-things-that-don't-even-matter walk. The elderly tourists that had been at Paige's yesterday were coming down the street away from the square I had yet to vacate. No sign of their son, Prince Charming. Paige hadn't mentioned him at church earlier today, though she did enter smiling and depart quickly. Nor did she answer her cell phone when I called to invite her over for my "picnic on the stoop." Who knew? But this twosome could be perfectly captured in a comic strip with their attire teetering on ghastly and plunging over the wall of tacky.

Then I watched as he patted her tushie. It was a soft pat, a love pat. A pat that happens between two people who have loved each other way past the point of teenage desire. Or at least one should hope. But it was the familiarity that caught me. She slapped him teasingly, and by the up-and-down movement of her shoulders it was evident she still got a kick out of him.

He wrapped his arm around her and tugged her toward him. It wasn't a smooth movement, the way Dad took Vicky in his arms the other night. No, this was an eighty-year-old's tug. A shaky tug, because of the old-people tremors. A cushioned tug, padded by years of good eating. But it was real. It was engaging. It was as it should be.

An ache formed in my gut. The ache of longing for that kind of familiarity. For someone who knows how you like your steak cooked and what makes you scared. For someone who knows even the things about you that you are too proud to admit.

It was a Grant ache. I flipped open my cell phone and speed-dialed Paige.

"Where have you been?"

"At the mall."

"I've tried you for *two days*."

Paige sounded perturbed. "My phone hasn't worked."

"Why?"

"Why? Well, that would be because I flushed it down the toilet."

"Ooh, nice."

"Yep, real nice. Happened on my date."

"Ooh, tell me all about it."

"He went to one bathroom. I went to another. Leaned over to flush with my bag strapped over my arm, and out went the phone. It's somewhere in the Atlantic now, or lower Savannah. Who can be certain?"

I was laughing hysterically. "Why didn't you reach in and get it?"

"So funny, aren't we? All I could do was let out a scream. My date was waiting at the door with a rather perplexed look on his face."

"He heard you, huh?"

"The whole thing, I'm certain. Got home from Tybee Island quicker than if I'd have driven myself."

"Scared him, huh?"

"I think it was when I yelled, 'Don't make me come in there after you!'"

"Well, no need in both of us losing our men. We've got to develop a plan."

"Hello to you too."

"I can't just let him get away, walk into the arms of a stranger without a fight. What am I thinking, sitting around here like a doormat? I'm smart and talented and sometimes funny. Don't you think?"

"I think you are all of those things, dear one, but don't leave out 'borderline insane.' He is only weeks away from getting married."

"So? I know people who stole fiancés only a week before the wedding. Even left notes on church doors saying, 'Due to circumstances beyond our control there will be no wedding here tonight,' when they couldn't contact all the guests. Why should this be any different?"

"That's a good point."

"I thought so too. I mean, he is my soul mate. We have loved each other our entire pubescent lives and then some. So, what's your idea?"

"What's my idea?"

"Yes. *What. Is. Your. Idea?* You always have great ideas. You know men. You love men. Not so good with phones, but I don't need an idea for a phone. I need an idea for a man. I've got to win back his heart and get rid of that redheaded annoyance."

"Ooh, catty. I like it. Okay, let me think. I'll get back to you."

"Don't take long. Time's a-wastin'."

"Time's a-wastin'?"

"Just get to work or I'm liable to have to go home and clean something. By the way, have any suggestions on a cleaning lady who cooks and isn't named Mrs. Gonzalez?"

"You sure are needy today."

"Not as needy as you'll be if that pastel-plaid-arrayed duo become your in-laws."

"You don't have to worry about that. I wasn't crazy about him anyway. Poor fella was cute, but still lived at home with Mommy and Daddy. At thirty-five-years old—"

"*Thirty-five?!* My word, that man is old."

"Ancient, I know. But anyway, forget about me and let's stay focused. We've got to get your man back. Stay close to your phone and I'm going to the drawing board."

"You're going to go paint?"

"I always think better when I paint."

"Well, whatever works. Call me soon."

"Bye." And she hung up to rescue me one more time.

Needing a bite of something sweet, I walked down York Street to get a key lime square from Wright Square Café. Opening the door, I was shocked to see Ms. Austin standing at the counter. She turned around holding a key lime square and bottled water.

She looked at me and smiled a beautiful smile. Her lips were covered in a rich red that accentuated her perfect smile and rich complexion. "Savannah, right?" Her soft Southern accent kept the words lingering for a moment.

"Yes, Savannah," I said, pointing to myself as if discovering who I was for the first time. "And you're Ms. Austin."

"Oh, please call me Faith."

"Okay. Well, I see you've found one of the best things in town." I winked at Eric, the college student who worked here during the summer. He stood behind the counter, unable to take his eyes off of our new guest.

"What is that?"

"That square of sheer delight you hold in your hands."

She studied the key lime square between her fingers. "Oh, is it good?"

"It's beyond good; it's divine. I came in for one myself." I thought that might be Eric's cue to get me one too, but I had to actually ask before he turned his attention back to me.

"I'm sorry about my mother," I said, paying for my dessert.

"I deal with people that fana—that dedicated all the time." She took a seat by the window. "Would you like to sit down?"

"Sure. So, how long have you been a crusader?"

She laughed and opened her bottled water with her perfectly

manicured left hand. "Well, I've never thought of it that way." Faith twirled her single strand of pearls as she looked out of the large, paned window. "A crusader, huh? Well, ever since I graduated college almost, oh Lord, well, almost ten years ago now."

"You've been out of school for ten years? You look great."

She raised both eyebrows. "Well, I'm not that old."

I felt my face flush. "Oh, I'm sorry, I didn't mean it that way."

"It's okay. Thirty-two sounded ancient to me when I was your age. How old are you? About twenty-two?"

"Twenty-four actually."

I watched her take a bite of her square. "Oh my goodness. This thing is delicious." Eric leaned over the counter as if he would have wiped her mouth himself. I squelched my intense desire to roll my eyes.

"So, will you be here long?" I asked.

"Until this is over. Probably only about a week. I figure the courts will remove the monument soon and life will be back to normal."

"Normal. Now, that's a concept."

"You have a rather adventurous mother, I take it."

"Oh, let's just say she is involved."

"Well, it seems like you have a great head on your shoulders." She finished up her square and wiped her mouth. "You were right, Miss Savannah. That was one of the best key lime squares I've ever eaten. I think I'm going to take another for the road."

"You're going to eat two?" I asked, amazed that she could maintain such a figure while eating sugar slathered across some graham cracker crumbs. Might as well just slather it on my thighs.

"I do most anything I want, Savannah." She gave Eric a wink as he failed miserably in catching his drool. "I have to get back to work now. I hope I'll see you soon." I scratched my left hand. "You okay?" she asked.

"Yeah. My hand's just itching. But it's a good thing. It means you're going to get some money."

"Ooh, well, call me when you do." She eyed me suspiciously.

"Yeah, I'll do that." I laughed a dorky laugh. Fortunately she was already answering her ringing cell phone and was oblivious to my world of dork.

"Take care."

She offered me a wink and a mouthed, "You too."

I walked back to the cooler, debating another Coke. I consumed excessive portions of the sugar-laden caffeine drink each day. Here at the café, it looked beautiful sitting in that cooler all chilled and inviting. I had never debated such a concept before. And Ms. Austin had just given me permission. So, I didn't tarry long. As I handed it to Eric, he looked rather perturbed.

Once he slammed the cash register shut, he and three vibrant young men came running out from the back and watched Ms. Austin all the way up the street. I looked at them with nausea, threw my napkin away, and had to part them to make my way to the door.

"You do that every time I leave too, don't you?" I quipped. They never responded. The dark-headed siren, sauntering up the street, rendered them deaf. And the tired, old, worn-out-looking twenty-four-year-old slipped out utterly undetected.

CHAPTER SEVENTEEN

The familiar face came around the corner with a smile. He nodded at Ms. Austin as he passed her while he headed in my direction. I gave Gregory a hug. "Okay. Now tell me what happened in that meeting and how quick this is going to be over."

He turned around to walk with me up the street. "I'm not supposed to talk about what goes on inside a meeting like that."

"Why? We're friends."

That caused Gregory to chuckle. "We're friends? Wouldn't that be a good ploy to suck information from lawyers. 'Oh, but sir'"— he made a pathetic attempt to mimic my voice—"'we're friends.'"

"Okay, smart aleck. I don't want to know anyway."

"Well, just be careful."

"Be careful with what."

"That woman there." He pointed to Ms. Austin's disappearing back. "She's got no shortage of venom underneath that sweetness."

"Oh please. She's obviously very talented. She wouldn't be here representing an entire organization and body of people without being good at what she does."

"She's good all right. Which is why I'm just warning you."

"Whatever. How long are you here?"

"We're heading back now."

"Now? I thought we could grab dinner and talk."

"Sorry, no time. The judge needs to make it back for a Sunday-afternoon nap."

"You won't get back before evening."

"So he'll have to forgo the nap and just go to bed early. I'll talk to you this week."

"Okay. But if I need you, I'm going to be calling you."

"I don't doubt it." He started to walk off and I grabbed his arm.

"Ooh, don't turn around. I don't want him to see us."

He turned around of course. "You don't want who to see us?"

I jerked him back. "That curly-headed guy, Joshua."

He turned around again.

I slapped him. "Would you stop that?"

"The guy with the golden retriever?"

"Yes," I said, pulling him back up the street toward where we had just been. "He works with me, and he is rude and annoying."

"Oh, he is?"

"Yes. He's condescending and has a dog who can do tricks."

"Oh my word," he said, stopping dead in his tracks. "Savannah Phillips. You're crazy about him."

I stared at him in wide-eyed wonder. "I'm what?!"

His white smile beneath his chocolate skin was just too pleased, as if his ridiculous revelation was some kind of epiphany for the world. "You're crazy about him."

"I am in love"—I straightened my chest—"with a man I have loved since I was a child. And I will get him back. Don't you have to leave?"

He laughed a caustic laugh. "Yeah, I've got to go. And you, my friend, need to come to grips with reality. Fantasy only exists in beauty pageants." He winked and sauntered away. "Just remember to send me an invitation."

"I'll send you an invitation all right, mister!" I yelled at the back of his head. "An invitation to . . . to a therapist who helps the delusional!!"

He raised his hand but never turned around.

I gave him a good hand raise myself.

As I sat in the house alone, again, going another night without food, again, I knew I had to move. I mean, it was coming eventually, so why not this week? I had to take charge of my world. Construct my chaos. Tailor my tune. Okay, that was stretching it, but one would rather starve and be alone in her own place than die a slow, drawn-out death in a home where a family *should* be. And because I had a pretty good week in which Victoria would be preoccupied with other matters, it might be wise to make the most of it. I was fortunate enough that my soon-to-be-home was already vacated and waiting. And my anonymous landlord had made it so affordable that as few as three paychecks would at least get me moved in.

One week. One good week to move out while my mother was, shall we say, tied up and unlikely to come up with any campaigns to keep me at her home.

Only one problem: I had only one paycheck. So two more long pay periods stood between me and my first month of freedom. But I knew someone who had money. And she must have known I was thinking about her. Because after waiting on her all day, she finally called.

"Okay, I've got it. It's perfect." Paige's excited voice came on the other end.

"Tell me; I need to know."

"I can't. I'm still working out details. I'll tell you at lunch tomorrow."

Monday was our standing lunch-date day. "Oh, my Lord! Tomorrow is Monday!"

"Yes, Savannah. It's Sunday . . . then Monday . . . then Tuesday."

"Paige, please. I have a story due by Tuesday and I don't have a clue what I'm going to say."

"Nothing odd about that. But I would think you'll be writing on what is happening down there at the square. My word, you can't get any more human interest than that."

"Well, yes, but I haven't even formulated my thoughts, interviewed anyone. Well, basically I haven't done a thing."

"Just voice both opinions. Make clear the controversy. Let the people decide. Just make the humans interested, and the rest will take care of itself."

"Hmm . . . I'll think on that. Anyway, are you crazy? I can't wait until tomorrow."

"Well, you'll have to. Just trust me, it will be perfect. Now sleep tight, precious."

"I'll have to take something."

"No, you just rest knowing that your man's coming home to mama."

"You think?"

"I know. Now, good night."

"Good night. Oh, wait, one more thing. How is your bank account looking these days?"

"Why, Savannah? Has my mother been asking you questions?"

"No, I just want to try to get out of here before Mother gets unshackled. It will make for a much more peaceful transition. Except I don't have a pot to pee in."

"Ooh, I don't need to be informed of all your issues. Plus, I hear you could borrow your mother's."

"Nor do I need to be informed of all *her* issues."

"How much?"

"A month's rent and enough to turn on my utilities and the chance to pay you back in installments, no interest. About twelve hundred dollars."

"Sounds good."

"You'll do it?"

"Of course. I'll even help you move."

"I love you."

"I know."

"I owe you."

"That you do. Tomorrow."

"Tomorrow."

As soon as I hung up, the phone rang again. Thank the Lord for caller ID. Mother obviously needed to say good night before she spent another evening under Moon River. Her message thanked me for coming by yesterday and delivering such wonderful news. She added how she loved her picture in the paper, except for her eye makeup. She left me suggestions on my article for Wednesday's edition and offered to do an exclusive interview with me if necessary. After all, she had just spent another evening with Rita Cosby and was all warmed up. She felt most people would be interested in her as a human, and as I was a human-interest writer, well, it might look good on my résumé.

I deleted her ideas from my voice mail and ordered my dreams to be sweet. They were. Grant was in them, walking with me through Forsythe Park. Then we were holding hands and kissing on a bench. It was like old times. Except that when he left, he rode his bicycle home.

CHAPTER EIGHTEEN

Y ou need to go to the dentist," I informed the stank-breath mutt who was perched atop my bed, staring at me. "I hate Mondays." He sat up, making it clear he agreed. He hobbled off the bed.

"Moving a little slow, are we?"

He cocked his head. The poor soul looked weary. He was used to sleeping on a down pillow in the air-conditioning. The concrete didn't agree with him. Okay, I wouldn't make him learn a new trick today. The poor soul just looked too beat-up.

Making my way to the bottom of the stairs to head out for some tilling time, I picked his leash up off the Asian altar table that takes up a large portion of the main foyer wall. Duke sat at the top of the stairs, simply staring at me.

"Don't you want to go walk?"

He didn't budge.

"Just a short jog?"

Was he glaring at me? This animal had never refused a stroll. For him to refuse the opportunity to sniff schnauzers and fire hydrants could only mean he had suffered severe psychological damage in just a few short days. I climbed the stairs to try to coax him. I attached the leash to his collar.

"Come on, we haven't been together in days." I headed down the stairs. That dog would have none of it. He planted his feet, and by the time I got to stair number twelve, his leash fully extended, his stationary weight forced me back to stair eight via my haunches. I looked back at him from my now-seated position. All four of his paws had scooted up to the front of his body. I was surprised he hadn't wrapped himself around the iron railing to hold on for dear life.

I crawled up the stairs so I could stare at him directly in his deep dark eyes. "You really don't want to go outside?"

I heard a brief whimper and then he dropped to the floor with a sigh as only his eyes looked up at me.

I rubbed his head. "She's not out there."

He raised his head slightly.

"I promise. I will not take you to the courthouse, or even make you walk on the sidewalk. We can trot in the grass if you want to."

He sat up on that one.

"I will protect you from the crazy lady."

It took some more coaxing, but he did walk slowly to the door. But as I opened it, the poor soul just couldn't bring himself to walk through it. And I would not be remembered in his beautiful strawberry blond head as the woman who led him to undue anguish. No, Vicky would keep that title.

I walked out the door not knowing if Duke would ever till with me again. It was a sad day. Until I remembered my conversation with Paige. Then, the hope of redemption swept over me in my prison of unrequited love with the calming effect of a southern siesta. Well, if you're from southern Mexico.

The sounds of Josh Groban filled my iPod. In the middle of his and Charlotte Church's rendition of "The Prayer," I began to say some of my own. But tilling today felt exceptionally challenging. Somewhere between naming and claiming my destiny with Grant, and binding my mother's reckless foolishness, the receiving end of my tilling felt rather . . . empty. I pressed on anyway. Today was Monday. Not that I thought heaven had Mondays. But just in case it did, I would give it the benefit of the doubt.

Classy and elegant hangs in the closet across the hall.

Classy and elegant has not been seen in my closet since I purged it of such nonsense after a quarrel over my refusal to wear a suit to a two-year-old's birthday party.

As I scanned my closet for something to wear I longed for classy and elegant. Who knows why. I just felt the need to get away from anything in the dark and dreary family. I had been shopping last week at Banana Republic on Broughton, so I sifted through the new assortment, longing for something a little un-Savannah.

Tucked in the back behind my new acquisitions was a straight-lined khaki skirt of brushed cotton. It had been a gift from Paige, who once ate one too many bags of Doritos and couldn't get into it the next morning. In her fit of frustration, I gained some rather cute separates. It was a fitting compliment to my calves, falling just below the knees. I matched it with a baby blue cotton button-down with three-quarter sleeves.

As I slipped on my flip-flops and studied myself in the mirror, the word *dowdy* came to mind. The look was sleek, but the shoes didn't fit. But the khaki opened-toed Coach-emblemed slip-ons with a small heel, purchased by my mother, were a perfect complement. As I tucked my standard flip-flops back into the closet, I resolved not to tell anyone what I discovered today.

Feeling a little flirty, I pulled out a strand of pearls worn only on Sundays or to the occasional Saturday wedding. Today they seemed fitting. Finishing it off with dainty pearl-stud earrings, I studied myself one more time. Sleek ponytail: classic. Pearls: elegant. The entire look was, dare I say, perfection. I could compete with the best of them. This look could turn heads in windows. And I'm not talking pet-store windows either.

"Well, Savannah Phillips, you look like you stepped out of some kind of fashion magazine," Louise said, stopping her dishwashing midstroke as I entered the back door of Jake's.

I looked down, running my hands over my skirt, trying unsuccessfully to smooth out the two wrinkles that the trip over here had created. "It's not all that."

Then Dad walked through the doors and stopped midstride as well. "Well, what do we have here? I thought you already got a job."

"So are you saying I only dress up for job interviews?" I refused to look at him and focused on my morning breakfast out of a fountain.

"I'm just saying it's either an interview or church, and it's not Sunday. Or it could be a funeral, but unless it's slipped by the prying eyes and listening ears around here, no one's died lately."

"Somebody's about to die." I thought I heard Louise mumble as she returned to her dish washing.

I took a long sip of my Coke. "You're crazy. I'm a working woman. There is nothing unusual about me looking nice to go to work."

"Whatever you say. Well, have a good day." He kissed me on the head and started back to the front.

"Still washing dishes?" I asked.

Louise mumbled again. This time I was pretty certain a death threat was involved. Even Mervine wasn't smiling today. And that is enough to cause anyone to ruminate over the current state of affairs. I scurried to the front, before Louise was finished mumbling and Mervine took to imitating a scene from *Psycho* with that knife she was washing.

"Anyone willing to listen to correction that can lead them to life can consider themselves in company with the wise." Jake's thought for the day. Dad watched me as I read. "How do you know everything?"

"Savannah, you're the crazy one. I don't know half of anything."

"Yes, you do. You know all of most, and the rest of all."

"I just want to be prepared."

"Prepared for what?"

"Prepared for living."

"You're prepared, for everything from skinned knees to natural disasters."

He laughed. "I've had a lot of practice."

"Am I prepared?"

"Only you can answer that. Are you? Are you prepared for your article tomorrow?"

I rested my chin in my hands and looked up at him. "I know the topic. But not the details. How is that for prepared?"

"Shaky, but at least you have a topic. Anyway, if you can't think of anything, at least you'll look like a professional."

"Well, I'm so glad I've given all of you something to talk about today." I said with a smirk.

The chime on the door announced the entrance of the cappuccino-loving television personality. Every head turned in tandem.

"Told you she'd be back," I stated with shameless pleasure. Dad's face filled with regret. "Ooh, look. Maybe I'm smarter than I thought." Our raised right eyebrows mirrored each other's, and I headed to a place that would respect my newfound discernment and my professional attire.

Old Betsy hiccupped when I turned her off. The Saab still looked good (on the outside at least) for its eight years of age and close to 150,000 miles. Reaching across the seat, I grabbed my taupe Coach handbag that matched my shoes. I laughed at my mother's diligence in making sure I possessed some sense of style. With her out of sight for a while, I could enjoy carrying it without her taking credit for instilling me with good, albeit expensive, taste. I opened the car door and practically collided with the last face I needed or wanted to see, standing there grinning at me.

"Why are you in the parking lot when you ride a bike?"

"I don't want it to get scratched." His grin absolutely grated. "And how was your evening?"

"It was fine." I would try to ignore him. Taking a step forward, my perfect grace and elegance was held back by the fact that I had shut my skirt in the car door. My attempt to walk jerked the ensnared skirt so hard that the force pulled my feet out from under me and flung them underneath the car. My purse flew out of my arms, and all of its contents ended up at Joshua's feet. And there I was, held in place by the fabric of my skirt, elbows digging into pavement and sleek ponytail covering my face.

"Oh, Savannah!" He tried to catch me, yet unsuccessfully thwarted my fall. "Here, let me help you." He opened the door and my knees came down to the concrete with undue pain and suffering.

"Ow!" I declared of both my pride and my body. He helped me squirm out from underneath the car and lifted me to my feet. He was about to brush the gravel from my now miserably stained skirt and shirt. I slapped his hand. "Well, pardon me, but I am more than capable of wiping myself off."

He tried to hide his intense delight but proved totally incapable. I brushed the residue of embedded gravel from my unfortunate apparel and looked in horror at the contents of my purse, displayed across two parking places. We both saw them at the same time. The feminine items. Everyone knows a woman has feminine issues that require feminine products, but no one wants them exhibited across a parking lot and stared at by their latest affliction.

But he never made a remark as he picked up every item, including those "products," and placed them back inside my purse. I snatched it from him and straightened, refusing to give him any glory in my plight. Then I tucked the dangling hair back behind my ears and made a mental note to fix that as soon as I could get to a bathroom.

He opened the back door for me without saying a word and let me go to my desk without further comment or insult. As soon as his back was turned, I made my way to the ladies' room. Long gone was the classic and elegant look of the morning. Here in the mirror stood a pavement-stained skirt, gravel-pitted blouse, scuffed-up sandals, ratted hair, and bleeding knee. The trashed pride wasn't even worth mentioning.

Halfway into trying to salvage any semblance of being well-groomed, Jessica—my boss's abrasive secretary—walked in. *Just what I need to top off my morning.*

"I'll come back when you're through," said the snippy petite blonde.

"I'm through. Trust me." I made my way to the door.

"You might want to rethink that." She said in a perfectly pain-in-the-behind tone while backing away from me.

"What? Are you afraid I'm going to kiss you?" I referred to my kissing her on the cheek last week, assuring her I would make her like me. Looking back now, I wasn't sure of that small fact at all.

"No!" But she backed up even farther. "You better not anyway."

"Well, as I said, I'm through." And with that I walked around her to head out the bathroom door that she was holding open. I lunged for her as I walked through. Poor child about crashed into the paper-towel dispenser. I didn't even feel like laughing. So I just walked slowly to my cardboard world that needed walls and a door and an intercom system so I didn't have to come out until all the world had fallen into the ocean.

CHAPTER NINETEEN

My Styrofoam world had only been mine for one week today. I had tried to make it home the best I could. It wasn't great. How could any office without a door be considered great? But at least there wasn't quite so much gray.

I was going to be a writer. A writer of books. Actually, I did write a book. *The Road to Anywhere* it was called, about four girls on a road trip. Won a huge competition. A competition that would have made me a published author. A competition I was certain my mother had rigged. She hadn't. Didn't find that out quick enough. So, here I sit. A journalist for the *Savannah Chronicle*. A new destiny. But today it felt rather daunting. I was filling the shoes of an icon. A lady named Gloria Anderson, who had written stories that were life changing and thought provoking.

My most recent article took two long weeks to produce, and I do mean long, so long an entire book could be written about them. Come to think of it, I might just do that someday. But first I have to figure out what to say in the article for this week.

What part of the story shaping up on Wright Square would challenge a person, truly change a person? The events represented so many opinions and passions that it wasn't clear to me how to effectively portray their real breadth to my readers. And, after only one week on the job, I still worked in prove-yourself territory.

Even though this city has known about me and my achievements for years because of Vicky's incessant need to recognize me publicly—mostly in this very newspaper through, shall we say, rather large announcements—this effort of mine was different. And the world seemed to be watching. Every network-news team and several cable stations had collided in the heart of Savannah, giving me unprecedented opportunity to prove to the world my rational side, to be an effective and unbiased journalist. To portray the facts. Let the readers form their opinion. Let all humans reading this newspaper garner their own perspective by the views that had made us a city in the spotlight.

"That's it," I said to the ashen wall staring back. "I'll just state the views, the perspectives. Let the readers form their own opinions."

I got to work, trying to succinctly base the foundation of my story on the manifold conversations I heard around that square over the last three very long days. It was a human-interest story based on multiple humans.

By noon my computer screen was full but my stomach was empty. The cold Pop-Tart that I found stuck inside one of Dad's desk drawers in his study hadn't proven to be a substantial breakfast. The Coke had helped. But to be honest, I considered it an extraordinary achievement that I had been able to concentrate on anything other than how to bring my love home.

Paige and her plan awaited.

As I packed up my bag, the chatter of two girls a couple of shelters up strayed over the top of my own.

"You are so paranoid," one announced. "Who in the world will care if you take an hour or an hour and a half lunch break? No one will even notice you're still gone."

"I'm not sure I should appreciate that observation."

"Oh, you know what I mean. We work hard; we deserve to

take however long we want to for lunch. Now go and have fun. You can show an hour on your time card and no one will know the difference."

"Well, I'll think about it."

I headed out the door, certain that after only a week, I wasn't going to be pressing any luck with that one. At least not yet.

Clary's was our constant. Our North Star. Well, it wasn't all that, but their BLTs were the bomb. Helen had our drinks waiting. A Coke for me and a fake Coke for Paige, who pranced in late as always.

"Don't drink. Just talk," I told her.

She took the straw that was touching her lips and sucked on it long and hard and bugged her eyes out at me. "You're just nasty lately. Are you PMSing it?"

"Permanently! But enough about me. Let's talk about your plan for me."

"Well, at least you give me credit for the plan."

"I'm feeling generous." I smiled.

Helen sat our plates down in front of us. Her eyes darted between Paige and me. "Savannah, child, you look too thin. I'm getting you a milkshake." With that she darted back behind the bar to prepare me extra caffeine.

"Am I Two-Ton Tilda or what?" Paige asked loud enough for Helen to hear. Helen chose not to.

"Don't worry about her, I'll share. Now go on."

As she began her strategy for our conquest, the young man at the table next to us began to raise his voice at the other two elderly men sitting with him. "Do you have a medical degree?" he challenged. He expressed little regard for the fact that either of the two were old enough to have been his father. "No, you don't. You don't take people's hearts out of their chests and hold them in your hand and then put new ones back inside and save their lives. Do you do that?"

"You can lower your voice, Peter," one of the gentlemen encouraged.

"I'm not going to lower my voice," he assured us all. Apparently he was clueless that I had a plan to hear and he was getting in the way of it. "You two come in here trying to tell me what procedures I can and can't do in my operating room, while you push bureaucratic papers through, trying to keep Joe Public happy."

"Paige, just talk a little louder."

"Huh?"

"TALK A LITTLE LOUDER!"

"I CAN'T TALK OVER THAT!"

The snot-nosed surgeon continued to attract the attention of the entire restaurant and even got a few *shh*'s from different directions. Had Helen not been in the back kicking up a milkshake for me, she would have come out here and thrown him out on his keister.

Looking down at my watch, I realized my lunch hour was evaporating. And unlike some people, I didn't have the luxury of being tardy. Finally, with no relief in sight, I took relief into my own hands.

"Excuse me, Paige."

"HUH?"

"EXCUSE ME!" I got up. Placed my napkin back on the table, pried the backs of my legs off of the plastic-encased seat cushion and entered the firing zone.

"Sir?"

He didn't look up.

"Um, sir." I cleared my throat. He wouldn't even look in my direction.

"SIR!" That one got him and just about everybody else. About near startled myself.

"What do you want?" he snapped.

"I, no, we"—I motioned to the now totally engrossed audience—"we want you to either pipe down or leave."

"I beg your pardon?" He rose from his seat. He was a pretty big fella.

"Please don't get up unless you're going to leave."

"I don't know who you think you are—"

"I'll tell you who I am. I am a patron of this restaurant, and I have thirty minutes to eat, hear a story that I have been waiting all day to hear, and get back to work before my lunch time expires. You have just wasted ten minutes of my time. And unless you hold the ability to heal *broken* hearts, then your discourse on all your other skills won't do me a lick of good. So, if you will please keep it down, the rest of us could get back to our nice lunch and not have to endure your insufferable self-righteousness and obnoxious behavior."

I got quite a few "amens" on that one from the other parties in the dining facility.

"George, let's go," the elderly gentleman said to his quiet friend.

They both rose, and the gentleman who had yet to add anything to this basically one-sided conversation stood. He looked at the yapper and said, "Peter, you may be a wonderful doctor. You may even be a gifted surgeon. You may have the knowledge of the latest innovations in the medical field. But you have not been nor will you ever be a 'savior' to anyone. That is one thing you should never forget."

The two left, and the irate man in front of me could have procured the role of Michael Douglas's character in *Falling Down II*. But I didn't wait to watch. I went back to my table and made Paige pick up where she left off, at the beginning.

"That was good," she said, finishing off the last of my milkshake. Even Helen hadn't noticed that Paige had consumed my shake, until she turned around, because she, too, had been frozen beside our table during the exchange. When she did realize Paige's ungrateful behavior, she slapped her on the back of the head with her dirty towel.

"Gross."

"You deserved that." And away Helen went to prepare another.

"Okay. I'm a desperate woman; now talk."

For the next twenty minutes we ate, and Paige laid out one of the best plans I had heard in a while. Well, actually the only plan. It was subtle but effective, and it would take place tomorrow night. As we walked up the street to our cars, we finalized the details. "So can you get all of that done before seven o'clock tomorrow night?"

"I think. Dad closes the store down at five and he'll be with Mom by six, so that should give me plenty of time. But let's do seven thirty to play it safe."

She scanned my attire and her eyes rested on my skirt. "Okay, seven thirty it is. But you need to come without grease stains."

"You're funny. Seven thirty, and I'll look fabulous."

She headed back to her studio, and I longed for five minutes to run into my house and change, but I was still behaving like a good little new employee. Set a good example. Get there on time. Don't overdo lunch. And avoid the boss at all cost.

"Mr. Hicks wants to see you in his office." The grating voice of his assistant came over my phone no sooner than my purse hit my desk.

"Okay. I'll be right there." My first attempts to learn my way around the building were met with a few detours through broom closets and men's lavatories, but my confidence was building. This trip was successful. Unfortunately, the welcoming committee wasn't all too welcoming. In fact, all Jessica did was snarl and remind me of a four-legged hairy creature that had taken to sleeping on sidewalks.

She hated me all because I was the daughter of Victoria Phillips, who also happened to be the woman trying to force Jessica's family into getting rid of the enormous satellite that resides in their backyard and can be seen from three different streets. Or so Vicky says.

"Savannah, come in and have a seat," Mr. Hicks's gruff voice summoned me from the other side of his glass window. "Close the door."

He seemed exceedingly irritated. The fact that I was on a four-week probation period meant it wasn't in my best interest to attract attention. But as he held up a stack of papers and flopped them back down on his desk, I was overcome by the sense that his irritation was all about me. "Savannah . . ." He paused, eying my tainted appearance. He simply shook his head and made his way to the edge of his desk. As he sat, the desk moaned and his tummy came to rest, albeit after a few bounces, over his belt. His suspenders did the rest of the work. "Savannah, papers on the whole try to remain fair and impartial."

I eyed him carefully, thinking few newspapers I had ever read in this world were capable of such a feat. "We do have columns, however, that reflect definite opinion. But for a human-interest writer, it's best to capture the sides of human interest without defining your own personal parameters quite so clearly."

"I'm not sure what you're talking about sir."

He held up the cover of yesterday's paper. "This is what I'm talking about."

"But you wouldn't have known it was me, if someone hadn't put my name in there."

"Well, Miss Victoria Phillips's daughter"—he waved the stack of papers in front of my face—"these are e-mails incensed about your presence there."

"Well, who approved my name in the caption?" I asked. "Apparently someone wants me to fail, wouldn't you think? Or at least portray this as something it's not. You are the editor, are you not?" I tried to remain as respectful as possible even though my face was flushed with anger.

"Yes, I did approve it. Because it happens to be one of the biggest news stories we've had in a while." He also tried to stay calm. "So you don't adamantly support your mother's position?"

"My mother's position is that of a woman standing on a side-walk chained to a slab of concrete. Would you support that position? No, I support the position of feather beds and duvets."

He crossed his arms and stared at me. "Savannah, you know what I'm talking about."

"Yes, sir, I do. But my mother was hugging me because I told her President Bush was coming to town. The people who wrote those e-mails have done nothing more than derive opinions from false assumptions. But frankly, I've had to deal with that since I got here."

"Well, I just felt you needed to know what was going on." He moved back to his squeaky leather chair, which immediately propelled him backward.

"I'm doing the best I can. I don't know why people care what I do anyway."

"Savannah, people need a winner and loser; they don't like draws. And if they don't agree with the outcome, they need someone to blame. If you don't want to be blamed, don't put yourself in a place of opinion."

"That's kind of hard with what I do."

"But not impossible. You tell the story. Let others form the opinion. And believe it or not, it is possible to do that while having a clearly defined opinion yourself." He winked. "You're a writer, Savannah. Tell the people a story. Make the moment real. Make the people real. And then make the revelation real. You'll have an opinion. And it will be clear. But what matters is the journey people take in order to get to theirs."

I'm not sure I had one clue this side of Saluda what he was talking about. But at the rapid rate things were declining around me, it came as no real surprise. I stood up to leave. "Am I getting fired?"

His belly bounced with his chuckle. "No, Miss Savannah, you are getting educated."

His secretary had disappeared. I wasn't surprised. Truth be known, she had taken my picture and turned it in herself. Truth be known. I didn't care. Truth be known. That was a lie.

CHAPTER TWENTY

If that had been the e-mail, Lord be with the mailman. I tried to keep my mind busy. I ordered my notes and decided to focus on the great debate and clearly portray both sides. Fairness and balance would hopefully silence my critics.

Curly Locks left me alone. Either he was too busy to bother me, or he didn't want to associate with Savannah's newest source of disheveled contention.

I picked up on one of Vicky's calls by mistake. She had resorted to calling from someone else's phone. She was good.

"Honey, do you want to have dinner with us tonight? It's like having a dinner party with strangers. You'll love it. This has been the most fun I've had in years. And if it weren't for the noise of the protesters it'd actually be peaceful."

"Well, I'm glad you're enjoying yourself. But actually, well, I, I really have to work on my story. It's due tomorrow at two and I'm still putting it together."

"Are you sure you don't need to interview me?"

I had to be quick with this one. "Well, no, not for Wednesday. Maybe I'll need some comments for Friday's story."

"Well, you know your mother always wants to see you. And I think there are a couple new people coming to spend the night tonight. So, it could be fun. At least come by and see me if you don't stay."

"Well, I'll have to see. I've got a lot of work to do."

"You can't work all the time, Savannah," she said in a Southern drawl that was drawn-out even for her. Miss Working Twenty-Four/Seven.

"Who is taking care of your job?" I asked, trying not to sound catty.

"Honey, I'm in control of my job. Ran me an extension cord into the courthouse and plugged in my cell-phone charger. Your father brought my laptop, and I'm a working machine. If that little diva from Atlanta would leave me alone, I might get more work done."

"You've talked with her today?"

"Oh, she has something to say to me every day. Most of the time she does it all nice and syrupy." The mere mention of syrup caused me to lick my lips. "She tries to act like Ms. Perfect. But she's perfectly evil I tell ya."

I couldn't picture such a refined woman speaking evil things to a woman attached to a monument in the middle of a city. The heat was getting to her. "Well, I've got to run. I'm getting buzzed by Marla."

She ended her performance in a perfect pout. "I love you, darling. Come see Mother soon, okay?"

"Bye, mother." I clicked over right before Marla gave up. Her own Southern drawl came over the phone. "Savannah, I have some messages up here for you."

I wasn't sure why we didn't have voice mail around here, but with Styrofoam walls, who was surprised? "Be there in a minute."

Upon arrival she handed me a stack of pink slips.

"All of these in a half an hour? Please tell me they're from the beauty queen."

"Wish I could, but most are from not-too-happy Savannians. But don't worry, honey. They'll get over it. They always do."

As I started to the back, I noticed a little odd-looking doll-like creature Marla had sitting on her desk. "What's that?"

"Oh, this?" She picked up the odd-looking creature. "This is my good-luck charm. I got it on my thirteenth birthday and have had good luck ever since. It helped me win ten thousand dollars on *The Pyramid*; then I won the showcase showdown on *The Price Is Right*, and the biggest thing it has done is got me in the audience at Oprah's 'Favorite Things' Christmas show."

"No way! That show is like the bomb! People try anything to get in the audience of that show. How in the world did you accomplish that?"

"Saved up for a whole year to go see Tom Cruise on her show, and then she surprised us when we got there. And I wasn't even disappointed."

"I'd say not. Sounds like you need to hang on to that little thing."

"If it weren't for this thing, I wouldn't have had any of that happen."

"Well, I don't know about that, but you at least have some great stories to tell. Did you meet Donny Osmond?" I asked, trying to hide my secret attraction.

"Yes, honey, I did, and that man is"—she leaned across her desk and whispered—"well, he's just plumb perfect."

"He is kind of cute, huh?"

"Ooh, honey, and when he hugged me after I won that ten thousand dollars, I just held on as long as I could without looking suspicious."

I couldn't help but giggle. Her innocence and Southern charm were so refreshing. "Have a great night. Thanks for the notes."

"It'll die down. There'll be something more interesting tomorrow."

"Hope so."

I stopped off at Jake's on the way home. Louise and Mervine were already gone for the day. At seventy-five they deserved to leave whenever they wanted to. Richard was heading out to his car when I pulled up behind the store.

"Your dad's already gone, Savannah."

"I figured. Just wanted to grab a Coke before I went home."

"You don't have any Cokes at your house?"

"We don't have much of anything left at the house. The milk's sour, I ate all the leftovers, and we've been out of Cokes since Saturday."

He paused as his dark brown hand grabbed the doorhandle of his new Ford Taurus. He said the dealership gave him an incredible deal, but he really thinks Dad had something to do with it all. "You don't know how to go to the grocery store, Savannah Phillips?"

"Okay, Richard, that's enough. Don't you start in on me too. Yes, I know how to go to the grocery store. It's the cooking part that has me stumped. Know of any good cleaning ladies that can cook? I'm desperate."

"Savannah Phillips, your mother would have your hide if you brought someone into her house, let them into her kitchen, and had them changin' her sheets. Now, you know that would be the undoin' of all undoin'."

"They would just be, shall we say, filling in."

"Child, you ain't like no other child I've ever seen. But there ain't no way I'm recommendin' anyone to step into your mama's kitchen. She ain't gonna be handcuffed to that thing forever. She will come home one day."

I laughed. "You're a chicken."

He chuckled. "Call me what you will. But stupid I ain't." He gave me a wink and climbed in his car.

I walked over to a park bench across from the courthouse to eye the day's activities from a distance and took a long, burning swig of my Coke. The sound of it fizzing inside the cup was like a childhood comfort. And the burning was like a purging of the yuck of the day. I watched as two women came out of the legislative building with their sleeping bags rolled up under their arms. They sat down quietly about a yard in front of my bench and proceeded to establish their accommodations for the evening.

Listening to the low sounds of continuing conversation, it wasn't hard to gather this city's opinions, because few people talked about anything else. For all intents and purposes, the world of Savannah had stopped except for right here, on this square. And on the front pages of the *Savannah Chronicle*, of course.

I peered into the store next to Dad's shop. Through the window I noticed two kids fighting over what seemed to be a sucker. Their mother leaned down to take it from them. Her again. Emma. Savannah's rumor mill said that Emma hadn't been seen on the streets in years without a cigarette hanging out of her mouth or hair that needed scrubbing. But I could see that sister had obviously found the ashtray and the shampoo. Her blond tresses were pulled back into a neat ponytail, and her lips were painted the same soft pink shade as her floral Lilly Pulitzer sundress. I needed to talk with her. I couldn't avoid her forever. I decided to wait until they came out of the store.

A hand on my shoulder about caused me to jump out of my skin. It was none other than my new park-bench partner in her customary floral attire. "Well, hello, baby. That's a lot of commotion going on over there, isn't it?"

"Sure is, Joy." I so longed to blurt out, *Why in the world are you still wearing that same dress?* But fear that it may be the only one she owned caused me to refrain. "What have you been doing all day?"

She paused and turned to look at the ceaseless activity by the courthouse sidewalk. "Observing. What about yourself?" She eyed my stained outfit.

I tried to ignore her stares. "Pretty much the same thing. Except I was writing down my observations."

"You're a writer, Savannah?"

The mere word *writer* pricked me. After leaving college and letting go of my dream to become a novelist, the thought of what I had let go of was a tad overwhelming some days. "Well, I guess so. I write for the paper."

"What kind of writing?"

"Human-interest stories."

She chuckled, and the flowers across her belly shook. She nodded to the events across the street. "Well, you've got your work cut out for you, don't you, sweet girl?"

"You would think so, wouldn't you?"

Joy's attention was diverted for a brief moment to Miss Sally. Miss Sally is a peculiar creature. She pushes her Yorkie in a baby carriage and walks her canary. I lie not. Would I lie with a monument sitting across the street declaring, "Thou shall not lie"? She actually carries the canary in its cage in one hand and walks it around as if it needs fresh air. I can't help but be thankful she doesn't have a cat. Poor thing would have declawed *itself* by now.

"What is that?" Joy asked, wide-eyed.

"Crazy in the flesh. Ever seen it?"

"Just did." Then she was back to the things that really mattered. "So, what are you having for dinner tonight?" I wasn't sure if she thought we would be having dinner together every night, or if this was just the next step in our conversation.

I looked toward the monument, growing increasingly irritated. "I have no idea. I've had to eat out a lot lately."

"Ooh, food issue has Savannah a little testy."

"Yeah, sorry. It's just a sore spot with me."

"Why so, baby?"

"Well, you see that big mass of people over there?" I nodded to the clump surrounding the monument. She turned to look. "Well, hidden behind all those people is a petite fireball who happens to be my mother. And as long as she is strapped to that monument, I'm eating out."

Joy squinted, trying to find my mother among the masses. "Your mother is strapped to that monument?"

"Chained, is more like it."

Her expression changed to grave concern. "Oh my. What did she do? Commit a crime?"

I patted her hand and giggled, trying to relieve her of her worry. "No. Sister Vicky committed no crime except that of abandoning her family."

"She abandoned your entire family?"

"Well, actually, the rest of my family is probably out there right now gathering dinner to take to *her*. I think they're just creating a bigger monster."

"Don't you call your mother a monster, Savannah. I don't care what she's done."

"I'm just frustrated."

She turned to look at me with her deep brown eyes. I had no question a theological revelation was on the horizon. But she paused extra long. Her eyes looked past me, through me, as if she was remembering something. Her own experience. Her own moment.

"Miss Joy, you okay?"

Her eyes registered with mine once again. "Oh yeah, baby, just thinking."

"Thinking what?"

She stood up and tugged at her skirt to try to get it to come down from where it had bunched around her waist. Then she tugged at her stockings uselessly. "Thinking I probably need to go."

"Oh, well, okay. I guess I'll just see you later."

She stopped. Her gaze went up the street and stuck on something that was probably invisible to those of us in this world. "Parents, Savannah, don't always make the right decisions. But they make the best decisions they know. And at the end of the day, the choice is yours to honor them or not. But don't forget that every choice has a consequence, be it good or bad."

As if her other realm dissipated, she turned her gaze back to me. "A lot of people waste time being angry when anger affords no results. Your mother's not trying to hurt you, Savannah. She's trying to rescue you. That's what good parents do; they rescue. They rescue their children's futures. They rescue their children's heritage. They rescue their children's hopes. They don't always do it in the way you think is best. But they do it the best they know."

She left me there on that park bench as confused as I was when I left Mr. Hicks's office. She waddled through the square, humming that familiar tune, the one that was now officially driving me crazy because I couldn't place it. She patted people's heads as she went, each person lighting up when they saw her. By the time she disappeared up the street, she had been given a 16-ounce Coca-Cola, what appeared to be a sandwich, and an entire bag of Doritos. If Paige spotted her, Joy would be the one having to share *her* dinner this evening.

Sometime during my conversation with Joy, Emma had slipped away. Not that it mattered; I had already forgotten her.

CHAPTER TWENTY-ONE

The sea parted long enough for me to catch a glimpse of my mother. Poor thing was looking downright pitiful. Surely if she had any real idea of her present state of disgrace, she would be hiding *behind* the boulder instead of displaying herself in front of it. She stood there with her hair having been haphazardly brushed out and standing on end. Even from this far away I could see her mascara.

Her blue suit would probably have to be burned after this incident. Miss Savannah United States of America, one Amber Topaz, was at her side, posing for the cameras. She was looking exceptionally fabulous in a black strapless sundress with a white ribbon around the waist. Her golden tresses cascaded down her shoulders from a matching ribbon headband. As I stared at the two of them, it was hard not to wonder if maybe they should have been mother and daughter. After all, they both loved pageants, accessories, and high heels.

Clearly, that didn't work for me. In fact, pageants had never worked for me. Amazing enough since they had once been the core of my mother's world. I boycotted pageants effectively for over ten years until last week, when Amber invited me to one. I was working on a story that made the pageant a mandatory affliction. Had it not been for that, I would still be on a pageant "fast" as I called it.

The fast began at the age of fourteen, after my mother's attempt to get me to be a part of the "pageant system" as it is identified by anyone who knows a thing about them at all. The mere shock of it forged in me a fear of anything that sparkles, a fear that still pretty much exists to this day.

It was a Victoria and Savannah "date week." I should have boycotted. I should have feigned a seizure right there in the middle of the marble-covered foyer. But Vicky would have called a paramedic and delivered me to the pageant à la ambulance, via stretcher. She'd have propped me up with a drip if necessary. But either I was going to a weeklong pageant, or I was going to be grounded from Coca-Cola for the week. I figured, how long could a week be? Had I known, I would have sacrificed Cokes for a month.

She sat me on the front row and she wore her tiara. I won't even tell you the battle that precipitated that final outcome. But the curtain opened that first night with the "Salute to Broadway" serenade, and the reigning queen belted out the song "One" from *A Chorus Line* while somebody's fishnet-stocking-covered leg kept kicking out from the side curtain. Well, a person would rather have her toenails pulled out with pliers.

"How long does this last?"

She elbowed me. "Sit back and enjoy, Savannah." Then she sang along and beamed from ear to ear.

"What is that?" I asked in horror as the two grown men came out from each side of the stage and sang Don Quixote's "Man from La Mancha." Just imagine Rick and Bubba doing such, and you pretty well get the picture. Except one poor soul had a hairpiece that he should have sued over. They were joined by two old women. Well, at fourteen, forty is old. And they all sang in unison until the final note. When they gave a downright unfortunate attempt at four-part harmony, I decided they should have just kept that puppy uni-son the whole way through.

"You should ask for your money back," I told my mother.

"You should act like a duchess and keep your mouth closed if you can't be nice."

I thought that was nice. Far nicer than what I had been think-ing anyway.

Each contestant began to introduce herself. One child seemed to crack herself up just by saying her own name.

"Do they think we're deaf?" I asked as each passing participant screamed into the microphone above their head. "Look like a bunch of strained-neck whooping cranes, if you ask me."

"I didn't."

For an entire week I endured swimsuit competition, talent presentation, and evening gown. Some women with thighs the size of Georgia pranced around as if they were Tinkerbell. I was certain the stage was shaking.

Talent presentation took the cake.

"Does she know she's tone-deaf?" I asked the pageant profes-sional seated next to me.

"It's the monitors," she assured me.

"Ooh, whoa, girl," I almost hollered as a tap dancer turned one time too many and about ended up tapping via her backside.

The operatic aria, in Italian I presumed, offered more fodder. "You do realize she could be singing pig latin for all we know."

Mother looked at me incredulously. "No, she couldn't, Savannah. Because *I know* pig latin."

When the violinist took the stage and played a number that I'm sure the original composer never intended to be interpreted in such a way, I couldn't help but ask, "Can you hear her?"

"Oh, yes. Isn't it amazing? She just started two weeks ago."

"Ya think?"

The poor emcee, a local news personality, introduced each contestant like a Southern gospel preacher. "And-a ladies and gentlemen-a, please welcome-a, The Very Golden-a, Miss Golden Highway-a!"

But when Miss Upper Georgia took the microphone and tried to sing like Whitney Houston, I had to squint from the pain. About downright scraped the leather off the armrests of my chair. "Please tell me it will be over soon."

"Not soon enough." Even Vicky had had enough by evening three, for a totally different reason, I assure you.

I watched, drugged, the final night. And I do mean drugged. I laid in bed all day, moaning in agony, sheer agony. Agony from the knowledge that I had to endure yet another evening. Mother gave me half a Valium. That and the revelation that this would be *it* gave me the fortitude to endure.

After the top ten were announced, I was certain that beauty contestants and flight attendants went to the same school.

"Where do you learn that?" I quizzed.

She wouldn't even respond to me. But when it came to the final onstage question, Sister Savannah came to her apex. Even though I was half-comatose, I was aware that Miss Merry Christmas had taken the stage in a rather bright red and green ensemble.

"Miss Merry Christmas-a," the evangelist asked, "do you-a think-a women who have been abused-a are better suited to speak out about domestic-a violence-a than women who haven't-a?"

Well, nothing could hold me back. From my front-row seat, I jumped to my feet, and you would have thought I was in the parade of contestants myself as loud as I got.

"You have got to be kidding me!" I screamed, throwing my hands up to slap my own head.

Vicky reacted immediately. She threw her hand across my mouth, but I was ready for a fight, and this one she would not win. "Yes, genius! I want a woman to be beaten, just so she can be better qualified to speak out against domestic violence! And that's what it's called—'domestic violence,' not 'domestic-a, violenc-a!'"

I left freely and waited in the foyer. I do believe Mother

crawled out underneath the chairs during the final song, when the Rick (or was it Bubba?) impersonator came out donned in a multilayered crinoline evening gown and blond curly wig as Glenda the Good Witch from *The Wizard of Oz*. It was the beard that gave him away. We didn't speak for a week. But I was eternally relieved of all pageant-going responsibilities.

The chamber of commerce is the sponsor of the Miss Savannah United States of America Pageant. This could be the very reason Vicky wanted to be the head of the chamber. Even now she attends every summer with the reigning queen for two solid weeks.

She always invites us to join her. But who would forfeit two weeks of sheer pleasure? Junk food! Unmade beds! Late-night movies! Duke sleeps on Victoria's side of the bed. I even try to get Dad to put Duke in Vicky's Jacuzzi tub. Give the dog some real enjoyment. But Dad didn't want dog hair to come flying out of the jets during Mother's next soak, so he refused. Duke abhors Vicky's return. She even has to fight him a couple good evenings to rescue her pillow from him. Usually, after she threatens to buy a cat, the poor thing takes a dump in her slippers and gives her her bed back.

Secretly though, I know she pines for someone who would enjoy her world of whipping with her. *Whipping* is the coined phrase for what those girls do when they turn themselves around so the judges can catch them from all sides. Now, staring at her and Amber Topaz Childers, the reigning Miss Savannah United States of America, I was certain that Amber would have made a much more suitable daughter.

"Vanni, looks like you're thinking too hard," Thomas said as he kissed me on the cheek.

He was the lucky one. The one who escaped being named George. Mother wanted to introduce him as "My son George from Georgia," but Dad saved him from such a fate by naming him after himself, Thomas Jake Phillips II. So, he failed to deliver me from my curse, but going through life as a girl named Tommy probably wouldn't have made my life much better anyway.

"No, just remembering." I said wiping off the perspiration the mere memory had caused. "I didn't even see you."

"I could tell. Ooh, you look like you've been trampled." He ran his hand through his lengthening hair. Every summer away from the hallowed halls of the Citadel, Thomas would grow out his hair and refuse to cut it all summer. Then football camp came, and bye-bye went the mop.

"Thank you. You look nice yourself." I stared at his frayed khaki cut-offs and his wrinkled T-shirt bearing the face of one Mr. Rogers asking, 'Won't you be my neighbor?'

He motioned to the rowdy protestors and asked, "Did they do this to you?"

"No. They are not to blame for these smudges. So where are you sleeping tonight? On the left or the right?"

He sat down on the stool beside me. "Oh, I'm sleeping at home tonight. That concrete is killing me." He rubbed his pained areas. "And I hear Amber's sleeping out there, and the last thing I want is a slumber party with that girl."

I laughed. "Well, you haven't totally gone mad then, have you?"

"So how about I have dinner with my sister tonight?"

I stood up to head back to my car. "I would like that."

He got up to follow me. "Would you mind changing first? You might embarrass me."

"Oh, I'm sure that would happen." I laughed. He wrapped his arm around me and walked with me to my car. "Oh, did I mention I'm moving this week?"

He laughed. "You are either extremely brave or extremely crazy."

"Do I get to choose which?"

"What bank did you rob?"

"I didn't rob a bank, just borrowed from one."

"Dad?"

"Now who's crazy?"

"Paige?"

"It's none of your business. But I figure if I'm going to starve, I may as well starve in my own house."

He opened my door for me and headed around to the other side of the car. "You could learn how to cook yourself."

"Yes, I could." And that was the end of that conversation.

CHAPTER TWENTY-TWO

Bistro Savannah would feed me tonight. I was thankful. We walked into the quaint atmosphere of the bistro on West Congress Street. Thomas wanted to come here because he had just gotten paid. And every good-ol' American boy wants a steak on payday. So where else would we go but the restaurant that was voted "Georgia's #1 seafood restaurant" by the Zagat Survey. Rest assured, they do steaks as well as they do seafood.

Thomas gave me a chance to change. And dinner gave us a chance to talk. We walked into the bistro, located in the historic market area, and ordered dinner. Now, staring across the table at him over a fabulous plate of potato-crusted salmon with chive butter sauce, it was hard not to notice how he had grown. Not necessarily matured, but definitely grown. Our years together had afforded us each other's confidence. Even though we easily irritated each other, we trusted each other. When we first moved to Savannah, we were pretty much each other's only friend. He found new ones quickly. I found Paige. Thomas loved her. First, because she got me away from hanging out with him and his friends. Second, because she got me away from hanging out with him and his friends.

He is the lover of the family. He's always kissing and hugging on people. He is also the schmoozer of the group. He can schmooze you out of something—usually money—before you know you've even been schmoozed. Dad is onto him. Vicky's a sucker. Me? Well, he learned most of his tricks from me, so I'm totally not snared in his tangled web.

He looks a great deal like our dad. And it seems that people have the same attraction to him as they do toward our father. Thomas has won the hearts of most of the older assistants at the courthouse—all women. Broken the hearts of quite a few of the interns—all women. And most of the judges assure him he needs to be a lawyer and needs to attend their alma mater—all ego. I've always thought he would be a great lawyer, because he will argue his point until you give in, give up, or slap him. The trait of debate he got from the one who birthed him. That even he cannot deny.

"I got some great songs off of the Internet today free. It's like Napster used to be."

"Are you hanging out with a rapper?"

"Do you live in this century?"

"Last I checked."

"Honestly, sometimes it's like a ninety-year-old woman crawls out of your body and lands into my conversations."

I placed the fork back on my salad plate. "Is there something in the water about relating me to old people?"

"Napster was a Web site where you could download free music until some law got rid of that as an option. But people still find a way to do it."

"Sounds illegal."

"No more illegal than what record companies are charging for CDs."

"So, what songs can you get?" I asked, taking a bite of the salmon that sat before me and letting it melt in my mouth.

He didn't bother to stop chewing the steak that he had just put in his mouth. "Any song. Just click and it's yours."

"Can you get Donny Osmond songs on there?"

"See, I knew it! You really are ninety. There is no way you, a twenty-four-year-old woman, should even know Donny Osmond songs. You should be singing Bon Jovi songs, or I'll even give you Boyz II Men or that Jonathan Pierce guy, who's not half-bad. But my Lord, woman, not Donny Osmond. Next thing you know you'll be talking about Barry Manilow tunes."

"I actually love—"

"Don't say it, Savannah. I swear, I'll dig you a hole in the ground when we leave here."

"*I'll dig you a hole in the ground when we leave here.*" I mimicked. "I am not old. And you shouldn't swear."

"See, you sound just like our mother. And to top it off you're wearing pearls on a Monday." He swung his fork at me, causing a piece of his potato to swat me in the face.

"Would you put that down before you gesture, please?" I wiped my face with my napkin. I had forgotten to take my pearls off when I changed clothes. They didn't really match my jeans and T-shirt. "I'm trying to look more professional."

"You're trying to look like that Ms. Austin lady. And you will never look that good," he said, not looking up from his plate.

"I am not. And I will too."

He looked up at me with a totally annoying-brother kind of look. "You want to refuse who you are, to become something you're not. And you don't even know if what's on the cover is an accurate representation of what's on the pages. Are you getting me here? Because I'm trying to relate to your world."

"Whatever."

"You like what you see, but you don't know that what you see is all you will get. And once you get all that you see, you might not like it."

"You have just crossed over to loo-loo land."

This dinner wasn't enjoyable anymore. I got up to go to the restroom. My cell phone rang on the way.

"Hello?"

"Where are you? You sound like you're in a well," Paige's voice declared.

"I'm in the restroom."

"Gross! You're not using the restroom and talking to me at the same time, are you?"

"Like you haven't done that to me a thousand times. And no, I'm standing here at the sink. And you better not be calling to tell me our plans have fallen through."

"Actually, my darling, I'm calling to tell you that I have successfully contacted Grant. And I will have him at the door of Jake's promptly at seven thirty."

"You are fabulous."

"Yes, sweet girl, I am. You owe me big."

"He'll owe you bigger," I assured her.

"Now go get on with your business."

"I'm going back to get dessert."

"Ooh, have some for me."

"Sure. My pleasure. Thank you, my friend. Love ya."

"You too. Tomorrow."

"Tomorrow!" I declared in sheer delight as an elderly lady walked through the bathroom door, only to back herself right back through it upon my outburst.

Back at the table, Thomas appeared in no way disturbed at our conversation. He was just stating the facts as he saw them. He was like Vicky in that way. Neither realized or even concerned themselves with the immediate effects of their words. They just simply stated how they felt, what they observed, and that was that.

"I'm not in denial, and I know who I am. And I'm not old. So I would advise a man who desires to live eternally with his mother to quit dissecting my personality and talk about other things. Like this free-music stuff."

"Oh, it really is amazing. Just pick a song. Download it. And bam! You've got new music."

"Could I just download them to my iPod?"

"Anything you want."

"Anything?"

"Even Donny Osmond." We shared our desserts and speculated how Amber and Mother would spend their evening under the stars. We came up with many options and expressed thanks that we would be present for none of them.

CHAPTER TWENTY-THREE

Television at ten, featuring Mother and Greta Van Susteren, was a bad idea. I tried to turn it. But like a train wreck, it held my attention. Old Vicky did pretty good until the end, when she didn't know the microphone was on and she asked Greta who had done her fabulous eye job. Then she offered poor Greta the number of her hairstylist so she could get some help on that end while she was in town. But since I didn't hear my name surface one time during the interview, I didn't even care that Ms. Susteren had been insulted.

As I sat on the sofa, curiosity got the best of me. I'd witnessed Mother sleeping outside, but Miss Amber Topaz sleeping on a sidewalk was something that needed to be seen. Thomas refused to accompany me. He said it would take weeks before his body recovered as it was. Mother had called us during dinner, but I made Thomas talk to her while I ran to the bathroom again. That way he could honestly say I wasn't available.

The commotion around the square had died down. Propped up against the monument this evening were Victoria and Miss Gemstone. Dad was across the square, talking to a couple men who looked like journalists packing up for the night. Mother and Miss Gemstone had their silk eye masks propped on the tops of their heads, obviously confident their assignments for the evening had concluded. Mother was looking ever the worse for wear, and they were gabbing it up at ninety miles an hour. It wasn't clear to me how at the end of the day there was still so much left to be discussed. My vocabulary ceased after dinner and abandoned me until after my first morning Coke. But these two, these two incessant chatty Cathys, seemed to find conversation in mere conversation.

"Does this concrete not leave marks?" Amber asked, rubbing her backside.

Mother giggled. "Honey, my poor body will never be the same after this. I'm glad I'm so physically fit."

I tried to stifle my laughter. That woman had only used her in-home gym once. Once. Hadn't even gone down there since to see if anything was even still there. And here she was declaring that her physically fit body was helping her. The only thing that kept her fit were the countless miles she logged from walking all around these squares, making sure things ran the way she deemed they should run.

Amber looked up at her. "Well, I'm thankful I started those Pilates videos last week. Ooh, that's what I should do. I should show you some of those moves that I've learned."

I thought for sure mother would protest. It would have seemed appropriate. But she didn't. And the next thing I knew, two grown women perched themselves atop their sleeping bags and began doing Pilates. It was ugly. If that was Pilates, someone should be charged. Amber had my chained mother doing things in public that should be downright illegal. Cirque du Soleil wouldn't be auditioning them anytime soon. Eventually, Dad finally noticed them and made them stop. They were flabbergasted at his request, but he didn't leave it up for discussion. He simply told them to get back in their sleeping bags and get to sleeping. At least all of his good sense didn't leave with this new way of life that had overtaken our world, our Savannah. Duke growled at Amber when she tried to get him to lie on the end of her sleeping bag. Instead, he walked all the way over to the other side of Dad and plopped himself down with an extended sigh. If he knew Thomas was at home in a warm cozy bed, Thomas would suffer the ill effects of chewed-up underwear for no less than a year.

"I wish Savannah were here," I heard my mother whisper.

"I do too." Amber pouted.

Those women were certifiable. I sat down to make sure I wasn't spotted and leaned back against one of the stately live oaks. It was kind of nice out here. Neither the death-grip of summer nor the "love bug" infestation had yet to truly seize us. And the evenings of quickly dissipating spring still held gentle breezes and sometimes a need for a lightweight jacket.

"May I join you?" came the voice of Faith Austin.

"Sure, it's a big tree." I scooted over. "So, where do you rest your head at night?"

"Well, not out here, that's for sure." Her dark tresses seemed to reflect the light of the moon. "I'm staying over at the Westin Resort. It has computer access, which helps. Why aren't you up there with your mother, supporting her cause?"

I chuckled at the thought. "Well, my mother and I aren't much alike. She likes the spotlight; I prefer lowlight. My mother has a way of continually moving toward the press, wherever it might be at the moment."

"So you think that's the only reason she's up there?"

"No, couldn't be."

"Why?"

"'Cause she wouldn't sleep outside four nights in a row if it was just about media exposure. No, she adamantly believes in what she is doing."

"So you don't support your mother's views?" she asked, digging a Snickers out of her purse.

"There are a lot of views my mother has that I don't support. Then, there are some I simply don't understand. In this case, I simply fail to see the necessity of chaining oneself to a statement."

"Want a bite?" she asked. It was nice for someone to offer *me* food for a change.

"Sure." I took a bite out of my portion of the Snickers. "How do you eat all of this stuff and look like you do?"

"Who knows. Good metabolism. Always working. Never enough sleep. All of those good things." She took another large bite.

"Do you work like this all the time?"

"You have to in this world, Savannah. But I love work. Even thrive on it. It defines me. Plus, you have to work hard if you want to stand out among the rest."

"You don't have much trouble standing out among anyone."

She laughed softly. "You're kind."

"Why are you really here, though?"

"I told you. Because this is my job." She gazed at the silk-masked ladies who were still chatting.

"I don't mean here in Savannah; I mean here, in the middle of this controversy at all."

"Savannah, one day you'll realize that life isn't black and white. Absolutes are relative. Most only restrain you. Kind of like your mother is over there."

"She would be restrained all right." I watched as Vicky tried to find a comfortable position beneath her down sleeping bag and her chains.

"Well, I was restrained long enough. Don't have any desire to do that again." Her gaze wandered off for a moment. But she was back as quickly as she had gone. "And the church doesn't belong in the states' business. They're clearly separated by the Constitution. I mean, nowhere is God mentioned in the Constitution. Church people need to keep their stuff inside their churches and out of schools and city squares."

"So that's why you're here, to make sure church and state don't mingle?"

"Pretty much, Savannah. Just trying to keep those lines clear, you know."

"But if there are no real absolutes, then how can the separation of church and state be so cut-and-dry?"

"Touché, Savannah. It basically comes down to this: The courts need to effectively be able to do their job without a conservative few dictating a nation's way of life."

"Sounds diplomatic enough." I finished off my half of the Snickers. "I had to learn diplomacy in college. I was the president of the student body my senior year in undergrad. So I can relate to the need of taking an important issue with two clearly defined opinions and trying to make the best of it."

"So you understand what I'm saying."

"Yes, in part." I let my mind wander off to those beautiful days of college. I returned. "But I never negated what was true to appease either side. That's because I believe in absolute truth."

"I guess that's where we're different." She picked up her thousand-dollar handbag that sat next to her.

"Yeah, I guess that's where we're different. But so long as everyone can respect each other in spite of their differences, I guess we're really not that different at all."

We were interrupted by Mr. Shelton from the market up the street. "Oh, Ms. Austin, I didn't think you would be out here so late."

"Yes, Mr. Shelton, just enjoying that Snickers I got at your store, with my new friend." She gave me a wink. It was clear Mr. Shelton was entirely smitten.

"I've got more if you'd like me to go open up the store for you." He grabbed a key ring the size of a horseshoe from his belt loop.

She held her hand up in protest. "Oh, no sir. That's all right. I think we've had enough for the evening. I have to go get some sleep anyway, before another busy day tomorrow." She turned her attention to me, apparently having forgotten what I just said to her. "Well, if you ever want to come see what we're all about, you can always come to Atlanta."

"I used to live there actually."

"I know. Your father told me. A nice man. A little over-the-top with the board and all, but a really nice man. Cute too."

"Whatever." I laughed.

"Well, when you come, you'll have a new friend to visit." She wiped off her brown-and-khaki-striped linen pants.

"We'll see you tomorrow?"

"I'm sure." And with that her perfectly manicured hand slid into Mr. Shelton's arm as they strode up the street together. She was stopped no fewer than six times by people who obviously wanted to talk to her. Eventually, Mr. Shelton bid her good night. I watched as she disappeared toward the Riverfront and one of the last evening ferries that would carry her across the river to the Westin. Mr. Shelton watched too.

The beaming floodlights of the eleven o'clock news finally all shut off, and the steady music of the crickets lured me to sleep.

I woke up in the dead of the night, covered in dew and hurting from the top of my head to well below the caboose area. I leaned against the rock to help me stand and tried to wipe off the dampness and bark. Then I caught sight of it: I had been leaning against Tomochichi's rock. I tried to stifle my screams. But the jig I did around that rock, beating my backside from any remnant of dead people, didn't go unnoticed. I shivered no less than twenty times and looked like a bad Jim Carrey impersonator. Those around me stared in their own postures of terror.

I tried to compose myself to make it home. I looked back once more at the concrete monument that had stolen my family. There lay two women with an umbrella perched over their heads to capture the dew (a concept lost on me), silk eye masks over their faces, (another concept that would forever be lost on me), and my dad curled up by my mother with his arms wrapped around her.

Looking at this scene, hearing the sounds of people snoring

and seeing sleeping bags strewn from one entrance of the courthouse all the way to the other, and hearing the low murmuring of those who were praying through the midnight watch, I was struck by the lengths people would go to express their beliefs.

Ms. Austin had made it clear why she was here. At least I think she had. These people were making their reasoning clear as well. They were standing for principles others had given their lives for. They were fighting for what judges only a couple years before had been fired for. They were doing that which America so beautifully allowed people to do. They were standing up for what they believed in.

I had yet to understand the breadth of it all. The extremity of it was beyond me to begin with. But I knew that in the end, all would reveal itself. Life always does that. In my case, many of those revelations came through my mother. No matter how crazy she drove me, or how different she was from me, she deserved admiration. And the man lying beside her admired her the most. He didn't always agree with her, but he completely admired her.

As for me, well, I went home dancing a few more involuntary jigs along the way.

CHAPTER TWENTY-FOUR

Forsythe Park is the essence of our city to me. It seems to embody the heart of Savannah. Every element of our character seems to merge here and is represented somewhere in this two-block area. Tilling here with Duke—this morning he was desperate enough for sanity that he agreed to accompany me—was such a perfect way to start a day. The manicured shrubs lined the perimeter, the branches of towering trees cascaded over the sidewalk, the soothing sound of the fountain bubbled out of the center. The kaleidoscope required one to focus on something central.

Every morning it brought me to focus on communing with my Creator. Not some life force that gave us morning beauty and evening splendor. Not someone who only mattered when recognized, but who recognized us even when we treated Him as if He didn't matter. It was our time. His time to remind me of eternal things. My time to remind Him of my much-needed graces.

Somewhere between my attempts to make more headway than I had the day before, a redheaded flame passed me. She was wearing short shorts and had legs up to heaven. Her curly mane was pulled back in a ponytail. She had her earphones on but was singing. It was clear she wasn't tilling, because she obviously didn't realize how loud she was.

She didn't recognize me, or at least didn't let on if she did. I'm sure Grant had a picture of me somewhere. As many memories as we had made on film, it wasn't possible he had removed every trace of me from his existence. After she passed me I slowed up, forcing Duke to retreat with a gagging sound, as I hadn't forewarned him.

You have no idea your world's about to be rocked, do you, sister? Well, I don't want to have to hurt you, but love is difficult.

"Isn't it, Duke?" He looked at me, seeming a tad irritated and confused. "Love is difficult. Don't you know?"

Of course he knew. His gaze wandered to a poodle coming up the sidewalk. But he couldn't fool me. I knew every dog made him dream of Lucy. He had pined for that dog since she got antique-store broken. But Mr. Newman knew Duke's reputation. Duke has a wandering eye, that must be admitted, which is why Dad has to keep such a close eye on him. And why Miss Alberta carries her Chihuahua in her purse. Rumors of his philandering float the streets of Savannah. As do a few suspicious-looking mixed-breeds.

This distraction from my tilling was rather frustrating. But it did affirm that my evening plans would be worth all the heartache I'd endured.

We entered Jake's through the back door. Duke began growling at the swinging doors immediately. I peeked out to see none other than Miss Television Time perched at the counter, talking to my father.

"She must really like it here." I patted Duke on the head. He growled again. "What's into you, anyway?"

"He doesn't like that little lady," Richard said as he came out of the stockroom with more napkins.

"Growls at her every time she comes in," Louise said, looking up from the dishes she was washing.

"How often does she come in?" I asked.

"Oh, three, maybe four times a day. Only wants your father helping her. She likes him."

Their drama cracked me up. "She's a silly lady. She knows my father is married."

"Savannah, child. Some women don't care 'bout that kind of stuff," Richard said, putting away some cups that Mervine had just dried.

"Please, what would that woman want with my dad? He's old enough to be her father." I took a quick peek out through the slats of the door. I patted Duke on the head. "Come on, boy, let's try to get ice out of the ice dispenser again." He wasn't interested. I sighed and turned my attention back to the manual dishwashers. "Anyway, when is that dishwasher getting here, ladies?"

"I called that little twit again this morning. He said he would have it here this afternoon," Louise said, becoming slightly more aggressive with the cup she was washing. "I told him if he didn't he would have me to contend with when I showed up on his front porch."

"Ooh, call me before you go. I'm needing a good human-interest story." I headed to the door.

"Better not have to go. And you could do an interest story on all these demanding people that keep coming in here, wanting stuff we don't have. If one more young'un asks me for a Frappuccino, I'm going to beat his big old—" Mervine slapped her wet hand over Louise's mouth, leaving Louise to spit out soap suds.

"Well, you two just keep that woman away from my dad," I shouted as I went to close the door.

"Hard to keep women away from a good-looking man, Savannah." Mervine spoke with a sly smile.

"Oh, that's disgusting."

I heard Mervine laugh. That was about all she offered. Probably wouldn't hear from her for another week.

As I walked out to my car, I could hear my mother's voice talking lively and loudly. Turning slowly so as not to attract attention, I saw the top of her red mane shooting out above possibly ten microphones. It was when I heard my name mentioned that red blood cells in me began to swim upstream and land inside my face. I was tired of being her topic of discussion. She wanted me to interview her for my article. There was no need to. She had given me everything I needed to know in her sound bites.

"Gave up on the heels today, huh?" my office partner asked as he stared at my brown leather flip-flops. "And the pearls? Where are the pearls?"

"Do you monitor everyone's clothes, or do you just need someone to irritate at the crack of dawn?"

He couldn't hide his perfectly white smile, even though he tried to feign disinterest. "Well, only the attire of those who like to dangle beneath cars, and it is nowhere near the crack of dawn."

I sat my Coke down on my strip of desk that ran from one end of my Styrofoam heaven to the other. The metamorphosis of my cardboard world to some semblance of an office was slow, menial, and probably impossible.

"You are such the comedian. Do you work or just walk around?" I turned my back on him and sat down to cut on my computer.

He produced a pathetic mimic. "*Do you work or just walk around?* Actually, I work while I walk around, and bike and sit and all kinds of things. So what are you going to write about?" He pulled up a chair.

I turned to look at his black curls, which were drooping into his eyes. His tanned and masculine hand pushed them away, leaving his black eyes to stare at me. The richness of them caught me off guard and I looked away. "Did I invite you here this morning? Because trust me, I've met my irritation quota for the day."

"No, but I'm not invited to most of the places I end up. Anyway, you're too young to be irritated so early in the morning. So quit avoiding the subject. What are you going to write about?"

I began to check my e-mail so I wouldn't have to look at him. "I'm going to write about what everyone is talking about. It would be rather odd for me to act as if nothing is happening around here, wouldn't it? Especially after I was highlighted in the *paper!*"

"Well, I'm sure there is plenty to say. So are you going to talk about your mother?"

I finally turned to him. He sat there with his elbow leaning on my desk and his face resting in his hand, like a two-year-old just needing to talk. "You can read it with the rest of the city. Now, would you please go away?"

"You don't look like you want me to go."

His words startled me. I stopped, not knowing where he was getting his imaginary information. "You . . . you are beside yourself this morning, mister. Trust me, I want you to *go!*" I said, adding a little push to his arrogant arm that rested underneath his chin.

His face fell but he lifted it with an evil smile and got up, returning his chair beside the door. "I gotta get to a meeting anyway. I'm going to cover the chamber of commerce."

"I thought you couldn't cover them anymore since you referred to my mother as Vicky in your first coverage."

He peeked back around my opening. "She won't be there now, will she?"

"Touché."

"Adios, Ms. Phillips. Adios."

Adios, Ms. Phillips. Adios. I don't want you to go? You must be out of your mind. I am a woman in love with a wonderful man who is going to be thrilled that I have finally come to my senses. You need to get over yourself and join up with the woman who loves you. Miss Amber Topaz. You wll be perfect for each other. Then she can finally be Mrs. United States of America.

494

The pace of a newspaper seems consistently frantic. There is always the sound of a printer echoing in the hall. There is the sound of the pecking of computer keys. The smell of coffee. The fizzing of Coke. And the chatter of televisions. I wasn't used to this pace. I was a person who stole away and wrote in parks. Who sat in cafés and sipped Coca-Cola and snacked on chips. Most deadlines I created for myself. But now things were different. Life was different.

I stared at the computer screen in front of me and could make out my own image in its black reflection. Even though I had just written a story one week before, the simple task of turning yesterday's stream-of-consciousness efforts into an article suffocated me. I turned my hands over and watched as the dampness seeped its way into the lines on the palm of my hands. I had expected different things in my life.

I had expected Grant to marry me. I had expected to be a novelist. I had expected the circle of life to end up, well, in a circle. But somewhere Savannah's train had missed the junction, and I was heading into a land of uncharted territory and frightening change.

My fingers crawled gingerly up to the keyboard. And with the steady well of irritation that had been pent up for the last five days, the dam burst. What I had feared, flowed. I typed like a crazy woman. I typed and laughed and grimaced and typed. It was downright cathartic. I didn't need to make a revelation of ideals. I just needed to talk about the human factor. After all, I was a writer of human interest. And nothing was more of human interest than interesting humans. And my word, there was a human factor on that square bigger than all get-out.

By my two p.m. deadline, my third human-interest article was printed and tucked neatly away in a folder and placed on Mr. Hicks's desk. The truth about this city would be revealed by one of its very own, Ms. "Savannah from Savannah."

CHAPTER TWENTY-FIVE

My stomach was calling for lunch. A Greek salad sounded good today, so I walked across to River Street and headed to Olympia Café. The lunch rush was gone. But tourists lined River Street at any time of the day in the summer. Passing by Savannah's Candy Kitchen, one of my childhood staples, I saw the floral-clad Ms. Joy staring into the window.

"What do you see?" I asked.

She turned to look at me and her face lit up. "Oh, I was just admiring those caramel-covered apples." She turned back to stare into the window. "I used to eat those all the time when I was a little girl."

"Well, go get you one," I encouraged her, not wanting to tell her I was headed to get lunch, lest she want to make it a family affair.

"Yeah . . . yeah, I'll do that." But she didn't move.

I felt such sympathy for this woman. I wasn't sure why. Maybe it was the same dress, or the old straw bag. Maybe it was the direct words encompassed by the compassionate tone. But I was certain why she wasn't moving. It was the same reason she wanted to know what I was having to eat every evening for dinner. "You know,

Ms. Joy. I was thinking how good a caramel apple would be too. Why don't you come in and let me get us both one."

She let her head dip low and said, "Oh, baby, no, that's okay. I can get one later."

"No, you won't," I said, putting my arm through hers. "This is my treat to you today."

"Well, if you really want to." She giggled and we walked inside.

Savannah's Candy Kitchen is two storesful of any kind of candy you could want or remember. We filled up two large bags for her of all different kinds of gumdrops and jawbreakers and caramels from the huge barrels that sit on one side of the store. As we walked to the middle of the store, we got her a small, ice-cold, glass-bottled Coke from the large barrel that held the pieces of heaven amid the cold ice cubes. Then we got her some homemade fudge and topped it off with a caramel-covered apple.

She stared in amazement at the taffy conveyer belt, which made taffy on one side of the room and wrapped it and sent it across a conveyer belt that runs across the ceiling and deposited it in another barrel.

Then she and I strolled to the other side of the store and took in the wonderful ice creams and watched for a few moments through the paned glass that allows curious eyes to survey the culinary masters at work on indescribable fudge. She missed nothing. She was like a child having her senses filled with every pleasant part of childhood. When I left her at the small iron table that sits outside in front of the window, she had her two bags of candy, a small Coke, and was chowing down on a caramel apple, with her fudge tucked safely in her straw bag. She would save that for later. She never even noticed me leave.

The smell of Greece was so inviting that the Greek salad I chose required accompaniment. I added some gyro meat, pita bread, onions, and sauce to my salad. I didn't care who I had to talk to the rest of the day. This child was hungry.

Mr. Euzinidas came over to say hello.

"This protest thing driving you crazy?" I asked.

"Honey, I've made more money these past few days than we make most of the summer. Your mother can keep this up until January for all I care."

He could tell by my dejected expression that didn't interest me in the least. He left me to look out the window at the waterfront and enjoy my lunch. Until I saw the curly head flash by the window. He saw me too.

"Savannah!" he panted, doubling over at the entrance of the door. "Come on! I've got to take your car."

I sat my fork down and looked at him. "I just stopped to eat. Can't people leave me alone for two seconds and just let me have lunch?"

He came over to my table and grabbed my plates with one hand and my arm with the other. "You can eat in the car." He informed me. He asked Mr. Euzinidas to wrap up my lunch quickly so I could take it with me.

I jerked my arm from his grasp. "Joshua North. I'm not going anywhere. I'm going to sit down here and finish my lunch." I tried to get my plates back from Mr. Euzinidas.

"No!" Joshua took them away from me and gave them back to the poor man behind the counter who was ready to go sit down and eat my lunch himself. "I have to borrow your car."

"Why in the world do you need to borrow my car?" I asked, reaching one last time for my plates.

"Savannah, please." He calmed down yet kept pulling my hand away. "Trust me, please. I need you to just take me up the street. It will only take a minute. I just need your help, Savannah!" he finally said, exasperated.

I could tell he was serious. We grabbed my lunch and headed to the car. I handed him the keys, then snatched them back. "Do you even have a license?"

He reached for them. "Yes, Savannah. I ride a bike because I want to."

I offered them back hesitantly. "Where are we going?" He came around to open my car door.

"There's apparently been a shooting," he said as he climbed into the driver's seat.

"Joshua." I unbuckled my seat belt. "I am not going to any shooting."

He pulled the seat belt from my hand and buckled it back in, but I held on. "I've got to go. If I ever want to cover anything other than meetings with people who are half-dead or half-crazy, I've got to prove I can do something more."

I noticed something in his face that I had yet to see. A vulnerability. Mr. Curly Locks had passion. "Okay," I said, taking my hand off of the seat belt. "Go wherever it is you feel you need to go."

"Thank you." He started the car.

We drove about five minutes outside of the Historical District. And I turned to look at his face. His complexion was olive and baby smooth. His dark eyebrows framed his black eyes as if they were made for his face. Well, you know what I mean. And his eyes were focused today, not dancing like they normally do. He was thinking about something other than his bicycle or my issues.

I broke the odd silence. "Do you have any idea who got shot?"

"Not sure of his name, but apparently it is the boyfriend of whoever is Miss Chatham County United States of America."

"You're kidding. Wonder if she knows?"

"I'm almost certain. If my sources are right, she's the one who pulled the trigger."

"Oh my Lord, have mercy." I stared straight ahead. We drove for what felt like another long, awkward silence. "So what are you trying to accomplish with this?"

"I'm trying to get this story first." He glanced over at me to see if I had a response. I didn't. "I want to get it written and on

Mr. Hicks's desk before anyone else, so he'll take me as a serious journalist." He stared straight ahead now.

I turned in my seat to see him more clearly. "You don't think he takes you seriously?"

He paused for a long moment. "Honestly, no, I don't. I don't think many people around there take me seriously. They see me as a guy who can't afford a car and who wears flip-flops. Mr. Hicks has even said as much, so I've heard." I could see a glint of something in his eyes. Some remnant of frustration.

"Don't believe everything you hear. Lord knows I don't."

He laughed. "I bet you hear all kinds of things. Like how you only got your job because your mother agreed to buy lifetime advertising."

I raised my right eyebrow. "Actually, no, I haven't heard that one."

He looked at me and winked. "Well, don't believe everything you hear, right?"

I changed the subject. "How long have you been at the paper?"

"Almost two years. I started after I graduated from the University of Florida."

"Oh, is Florida where you're from?"

"Yeah, my family's from Jacksonville. Lived there my entire life."

"How in the world did you get to Savannah?"

"Insanity, I have come to believe."

"Me too," I said under my breath.

"Needed to get away from home. Find my own space. I'd driven through here quite a few times and just thought I'd try it. Got a job pretty quick. Liked the people and haven't left. But Mr. Hicks told me he would let me start doing hard news stories last year, and I'm still covering school-board meetings."

"Shoot, I hear those can be hard news themselves anymore," I offered.

"Mr. Hicks doesn't give me the time of day. So I figure the only way to make him notice my work is to give him some work to notice."

He pulled the car over to the curb on a narrow side street and cut the engine. "Okay, let's go see what we can find out."

Before I knew it he had grabbed his satchel and was around to my side of the car with the door open. I got out and looked at him. "Thank you," I said, trying to avoid the awkward moment.

"Let's go." He turned to walk up the alley, making it clear it wasn't any big deal.

We came out directly opposite a house that had more activity going on around it than any square in downtown Savannah. Except the one my mother occupied, of course.

Two police cars sat in front of the house. And people strained to catch a glimpse at the activity. About the time we emerged, a van passed us with "City Morgue" written across the side.

I felt every part of my body go weak. "Uh-uh, no, brother, this sister don't do dead people." I turned on my heels and headed in the direction of the car. I wasn't even sure if my legs would get me there.

He grabbed me and swung me around. "It's okay. We won't be here long." I wasn't reassured.

"Serious." I tried not to sound as afraid as I really was. "Dead people scare me. Like that movie when the little boy said, 'I see dead people.' Just the preview made me drive home with my interior car lights on. I had to call my dad to meet me at the curb and walk me to the house." I bounced up and down trying to stay as calm as possible. Failing miserably.

"Are you seriously that afraid?" Glints of compassion and laughter passed through his eyes at the same time.

"Yes, I'm serious." I tried not to look at the morgue van and tried to hide the burning tears that were rising to the surface of my eyes.

"Okay." He placed his hands on my shoulders. "It's okay. I'm sorry I brought you out here. I had no idea. Really. Just go sit in the car. You won't be able to see anything, and I'll be back in just a few minutes to take you back to the office."

"Promise?" I said, looking at him for a moment as if he would really protect me.

"I promise." And I believed him. "I'll be back in one minute."

I tried to gather my composure and turned around to head back to the car. But as much horror faced me in that direction. Because I spied, with my little eye, something coming up the street fast and fabulous. Miss Amber Ruby Diamonique, driving up the street in her Mercedes coupe, and I was with her man. "This can't be happening!" I said loud enough for Joshua to hear.

"What? What's wrong now?" he asked, coming back to me. I think the poor man was afraid I was about to hurl.

"It's Amber. She's coming up the street!" I said, doing one of those yelling whispers as if she could hear me inside of her car.

"So? Don't worry about her. Just go on to the car."

"Don't *worry* about her?" I yellspered. "She is in love with you and she thinks I'm her new best friend. If she sees me with you, she will think we . . . we . . ." I said, moving my index finger back and forth between us frantically.

"Think what? That we like each other?" he asked incredulously.

"Yes, Mr. Ambulance Chaser! That we like each other!"

"You worry way too much." He turned his attention back to the scene in front of him. "Now, either go back to the car or stand here while I go get the information that I need for this story."

I jerked his tablet from his hand and threw it up in front of my face. Amber had just gotten out of her car and was headed in our direction. I could only pray her two-and-a-half-inch heels would get stuck in a crack in the concrete and contain her until I could get to the car. No such luck. She spotted Joshua. Then she spotted me. Only after Joshua jerked his notebook from my hand and proceeded to leave me. She gasped. I did too. Both for entirely different reasons.

CHAPTER TWENTY-SIX

O ne man exited each side of the city morgue van. They opened the back and pulled out a gurney with a wadded black mass laying on top. I looked over at Amber, who was looking in horror at the scene. Maybe she would forget all about the fact that Joshua and I had been standing there together.

I watched her eyes get wider and reluctantly turned my attention back to the door of the house. I resisted the urge to watch the events play out through cracks in my fingers. A petite, disheveled blonde young woman in jeans and a T-shirt was being led from the house by two police officers. Her hands were behind her back as they walked to the back of a patrol car.

"That's her, Savannah. That's Courtney White," Amber said in total disbelief. I had never seen her so subdued.

"Miss Chatham County United States of America?"

"Yes, Miss Chatham County United States of America," she murmured.

As soon as the police car pulled away with Courtney in the back, the two men from the van exited the house with their gurney and what was undeniably a body underneath the black bag.

"Oh my Lord, Savannah! He's dead!"

I couldn't move. The insides of my stomach begin to churn. I instinctively turned my head away. "Are you sure it's her boyfriend under there?" I asked over my shoulder.

She didn't move either. We carried on our conversation staring straight ahead. "I'm absolutely certain. You know my friends Tina, Miss Swainsboro United States of America, and Trina, Miss Sandersville United States of America. The twins." I knew them. Sad but true. "Tina said he was cheating on Courtney; that's why she shot him."

The twilight zone that surrounded me had begun to play music in my head. Things were coming in and out of focus. Before my rationale returned to extricate me from this entire experience, Amber interrupted the Muzak.

"Oh, Savannah," she said, a moment of genuineness transforming her. "She was such a nice girl."

"Amber, do you even know for sure if it's her boyfriend?"

She looked at me as if I were absurd. "Savannah, Tina and Trina live with police scanners attached to the sides of their heads. Trust me, if they say it is Miss Chatham County United States of America's boyfriend, it's Miss Chatham County United States of America's boyfriend.

"Let's get closer." She jerked at my sleeve. I jerked it back.

"No way, sister. I was just about to leave."

"Well, I can't go over there by myself; it would look too inconspicuous."

I patted down my sleeve and kept my face turned from the scene playing out in front of me. "I think you mean *suspicious*. And why do you want to get closer anyway?"

She came around to look at my face. "Just because," she said, trying to tell me something with her tilted head, pursed lips, and wide eyes framed with fake eyelashes.

"Because *why?*" I pressed. But I knew. Her eyes darted over my shoulder. I turned slightly to see the man eagerly scribbling down information on his stolen legal pad.

But there was no need for us to go to him; he was now coming to us.

"Hello, Amber." He nodded politely.

"Joshua." She was unable—or maybe simply unwilling—to hide her attraction.

"Savannah, you ready? I think I have everything I need."

"Oh?" Her eyes became wider. "You two came together?"

"Well . . . we . . . actually . . ." I started.

Joshua finished. "Yes. I needed to get here to cover this story, and Savannah was the first person I spotted with a car."

Truthfully, coming from his lips, it was clear how totally uninteresting her discovery actually was. And it seemed to be enough for her.

"Well, I'm glad you are getting to know my new best friend. Isn't she the greatest?" She grinned from ear to ear so we could both enjoy the glow of her Crest Whitestrip–bleached ensemble.

"The greatest. Okay, Miss Wonderful, I really need to get this story back before I'm too late."

Before I could help myself, I blurted out, "Oh, just go ahead and take my car. I'll catch a ride with Amber."

He looked at me as if my personality number two had just effectively risen to the surface. But this would rest better with Amber. And it would prove to anyone in doubt that I had no interest in Joshua North whatsoever.

"That would be just fabulous," Amber offered.

"Whatever." And with that he was gone with no hesitation.

As the people began to clear, I saw Miss Tina and Miss Trina themselves walk down the street and hop into matching yellow VW bugs. Amber and I proceeded to her luxury vehicle, a perfect replica of my mother's except for the color.

Amber turned the car in the direction of the paper. We were

both peculiarly quiet. As we pulled up to the sidewalk, I opened the door and turned back to notice a tear had formed in the corner of her eye.

"What's wrong, Amber?"

"A man just died. And a girl I know killed him."

"I'm really sorry."

She never looked at me, just stared straight ahead. "I know we seem catty and petty. But we're like family, really. Even though you want to win and think you hate the person who does, you still want the best for them."

I couldn't help but smile at her simple view of life. "But you never wish this on anyone," she continued. "I mean, you wish ripped seams, or broken straps, or even dresses put on backward, but nothing like this. I'll have to go see her. Yeah, that's what I'll do; I'll go see her."

"I think that would be nice." I said as I held the car door in my hand.

Crocodile tears began to fall down her face. She looked at me. "You think so?"

"Yeah, I do."

"And I'll encourage her, Savannah. I'll encourage her like you encourage me."

"Well . . . I . . . I don't quite know what to say, Amber. Thanks."

"Do you want to come with me?" she said, begging with her deeply set aqua-colored eyes. "You could encourage her so much better than me."

"No, Amber, I think this might be something you need to do yourself."

"Should I take Tina and Trina?"

"Probably not."

"Okay. I'll just go by myself. I'm glad you were there, Savannah. It just made the whole thing easier."

"I'm glad I could be there too," I blatantly lied. Well, it was almost a lie. "I'll talk to you soon."

She pulled a tissue out of her purse, dabbed her eyes, and then blew her nose like a foghorn. "Thanks for being my friend."

"Thanks for letting me. Call me if you need me." I knew she would.

Making my way up the stairs to get a Coke, I knew what the headlines would read in the morning: "Beauty Queen Kills Boyfriend." And yet the world wouldn't stop. Even now, as a family was about to hear tragic news, the world would keep moving. People would keep laughing. Men would keep telling coarse jokes. Children would keep learning lessons in schoolhouses. Businessmen and women all around this city would keep on working. Vicky would stay chained to a monument.

And me, well I'd keep on climbing stairs, going to vending machines, and drinking Cokes.

But one family's world would be changed forever. Dinners would never be the same. Holidays would miss a person to open presents. Grandchildren would never have their son's eyes. As brutal as the reality was, it was still reality. The world stops for no one. Even on days like September 11, when the majority of people were paralyzed in front of their television sets, mothers were still in hospitals, giving birth, and doctors were still on call to make sure that life entered the world.

It felt downright wrong to continue living. I'd never seen a body bag. I'd never been that close to death. Burying a pet gerbil named Dufus just doesn't count. The guy in that bag was somebody like me. The girl who shot him was somebody like me. As real as the death was, so for a brief moment was the murderer. A girl for a moment gone crazy. Her life would never be the same either.

My phone rang.

"Are you getting excited?"

"Excited? About what?"

Paige reacted in complete horror. "Savannah? You have got to be kidding me."

"Oh my gosh, yes, I almost completely forgot. This has been a . . . well, shall we say, rather eventful day."

"Well, I don't know how something could be more eventful than what you are about to embark on tonight. Do you have everything ready?"

"Yes, everything is ordered, outfit is pressed and lying on my bed, and every womanly weapon I own, checked."

"You have womanly weapons?"

"I thought I did. Do I not?"

"I haven't seen or heard from them in a while."

"Me either. But they're ready. Maybe a little rusty, but they're ready."

"Well, I'll be there on time, so you just make sure you're ready."

"I'll be more than ready, honey."

"Okay, call me if you have any questions."

"I will. Bye."

Five o'clock found me walking to my car in attack mode. But the smell of my forgotten lunch had turned into a disastrous stench. Driving down Bull Street, however, my mind was so focused on my evening of resurrected love that I forgot the smell and nearly hit the flowery mass that walked right out into the street. Slamming on the brakes, I was propelled with such force that my lip hit the steering column and started bleeding. I looked up to see my bumper only inches away from Joy. Déjà vu.

I jumped out of the car and ran to her, instinctively throwing my arms around her. "Joy, are you okay?! I could have killed you!" Stepping back to survey her, she seemed fine as a Georgia peach. "What in the world were you doing just walking out in the street?! Did you not see me coming?!" I reprimanded her like a child.

She smiled her silly grin. "Oh, Savannah, I'm sorry, baby. I didn't mean to frighten you. I just wasn't paying attention, I guess. But I'm okay." She giggled at my arms, which were still holding on to her.

"Well, I'm glad. But you have got to be more careful." I released her from my grip. "Now, why don't you just get in the car and let me take you home?"

"No, baby. I'm fine. I've got a few places left to go today, and a few people I need to see. You just get back in your car and head on home. I promise I'll be more careful."

"You'd better. You scared the heebie-jeebies out of me."

She reached her hand up to my face. "Your lip's bleeding, baby. Are you okay?"

I touched my lip, which felt like it had swelled to half the size of my head. "Yes. It won't make for an attractive evening, but I'm okay."

About that time a car honked having obviously discovered we were both okay. I looked back and gave them a raised right eyebrow and walked Joy over to the sidewalk.

"Now, Savannah, you need to be careful too. You seemed rather preoccupied. And preoccupation is often a sign of misplaced priorities."

"Okay, Joy, thank you. But I've got to go now. You be more careful." I walked back to my car and opened the door, then glared at the obnoxious car behind me.

"I will, Miss Savannah. But remember, nothing's worth consuming yourself over. Everything has its place. And when everything is in the right place, nothing is out of place."

"That's real good. Now, stay on the sidewalk."

I watched her climb onto the sidewalk and begin to sing quietly. I drove home trying to figure out how much makeup it would take to disguise my ever-growing lower lip.

Life was going on.

CHAPTER TWENTY-SEVEN

The lip protruded like a bad collagen job. But by six o'clock I was cascading down the front staircase and back to my car looking, shall we say, like "a Southern lady fit for dining." Which was pretty much exactly what I was about to be.

"Well, what do we have here?"

I stared straight into the face of my father and tried to regain any amount of composure I might have possessed. I had taken great lengths to avoid anyone who knew me, because such attire at six o'clock on a Tuesday evening would pose questions for which there were no appropriate answers.

"Oh, I juth haf a meething thif evenith."

That wouldn't do. He took a stance like he had nowhere to go fast. "What kind of meeting?" He scanned my pale blue stretch-cotton skirt with white embroidery and white capped-sleeve v-neck sweater.

"Oh, jthuth a thinner meefing. Buf ith's nofing importhanth." I gave him a quick kiss on the cheek, causing a searing pain to shoot through my lip. "Ow."

"What did you do?"

"Jthusth a booboo." I answered, dodging eye contact and starting in the direction of my car, trying to walk gracefully in white two-inch heels with only two thin straps holding them into place. "I'll thee you lafer. Mayfee I'll come fee you and Muffer," I added shamelessly.

"Savannah Phillips."

I hated it when he did that. I turned around, reminding myself to look nonchalant. The shoes prevented it. "Yef?"

"I hope you aren't up to something you shouldn't be. And I *will* expect to see you this evening." With that, his suspicious stare disappeared with him into the house.

How in the world do they always know? It's downright sick, I tell ya. And why in the world would he think the worst of me? I'm a grown woman just going to a meeting. What would he want me to wear, blue jeans and flip-flops? Heaven forbid I would actually take pride in my appearance. The monologue continued down six alleys, past three squares, and into a safe parking place an entire street removed from Jake's coffee shop.

I made sure the coast was clear and entered the coffee shop with a wonderful story about why I was there, should anyone need to hear it. I was thankful that all parties had departed. All the front blinds were closed, which was a blessed sight. It would prevent Jake from passing by and seeing anything out of the ordinary going on inside his little retirement office.

I opened my bag of goodies and sat them on the counter, releasing a sigh of relief at the fact that I had carried these to the car earlier. The questioning with my dad would have resulted in downright accusation had he seen me bearing picnic gear. The back table that sat against the far wall would be the safest. It would prevent anyone on the street from seeing the flickering of the candlelight through the closed blinds.

I shook out the white linen tablecloth and smoothed it with my hands. I retrieved two beautiful yellow bamboo candles, borrowed from Mother's stash, and placed them in two silver candlesticks. I placed Mom and Dad's white china trimmed with silver neatly at each place and finished it off with Baccarat stemware.

"Wellf fath looths faubulus." But my lip did not. A quick glance in the mirror made it clear the swelling wasn't going down. Cramming a piece of ice into a paper towel, I placed it gingerly on my lip and headed to Bistro Savannah to pick up the dinner order I had inconspicuously placed last night on a trip to the bathroom. While picking up two seared beef tenderloins with shiitakes, scallions, and crisp corn pancakes topped off with horseradish sauce, I tried to avoid as much conversation as possible. By my return it was already seven fifteen.

"Are you ready?" Paige's voice came over my phone.

"Yesf."

"Why are you talking like that?"

"Don'th askf."

"You've hurt yourself, haven't you? Miss Grace, you might need to get checked. Do you at least look okay?"

"I lookth butiful."

"Well, do you have it on ice?"

"Yesf."

"Good. Well, don't worry; it will be okay. We'll be there at exactly seven thirty. Have the door unlocked. Your life's about to change, sweetheart."

Bathroom to window, window to bathroom, I paced, trying about fifteen different locations in the store for ideal placement upon Grant's entrance: leaning against the counter looked too desperate; sitting daintily at the table looked too not-me. I even tried a striking pose across the bar. That just plain hurt too bad. Anyway, all would have proven fruitless anyway, because I had to go to the bathroom. Thus, I was officially indisposed when I heard the bells on the door.

As I came from the back room, I could hear Grant's shock. "Why did you bring me *here,* Paige?"

Then his eyes caught a glimpse of me. From the neck down I

looked pretty good. From the neck up, well, let's just say I could have done a commercial for an ambulance-chasing attorney suing over a plastic surgery catastrophe.

Paige's eyes caught a glimpse of the same and rolled.

His poor green eyes protruded frighteningly and made their way from me to Paige, eventually returning back to me. "Savannah, what are you doing here?" Then his eyes caught a glimpse of the table and the candlelight and the dinner. The expression that began in the eyes and worked its way down to his beautiful mouth made it altogether clear: Grant knew he had been set up.

"Well, my job is done. You two have a wonderful evening," Paige said, patting Grant on the back. She left with a wink and a thumbs-up. He protested. She wouldn't hear of it. And she left us there all alone.

There we stood. Two familiar strangers. I decided to break the awkward silence. "Wouf you wife thoo thith thown?" I asked, motioning to the two chairs that flanked the cozy table, arranged in such a way that two old loves could rediscover one another.

Grant stared at me and walked slowly to the table and sat down. "What did you do to your lip?"

Well, at least we could get that out of the way early. "I hadth a liffle affithenth. Wuff you life sofing thoo thrink?"

"That would be nice." Then, as if he had come to his senses, he stood. "No, Savannah, I don't want something to drink. I don't want anything but to know what this is all about."

I looked at him in disbelief. This wasn't part of the script for the evening. I had gone over it a thousand times, and this wasn't in it. "I thjuth wanfed thoo thalk wif you."

"Savannah, this isn't about talking." He motioned to the room, then picked up one of the silver forks at the table. "This, Savannah, is about far more than talking. And this isn't part of what we do anymore. Now, either you can tell me what this is about, or I'm going to have to leave."

For a moment I felt a sting rise up in my throat. But I pushed

it back down. "Thith ith abouth uth." I tried to keep my composure. "Thith ith abouth you mafing a therrible misthake. Thith ith
abouth uth noth ruining our wifes."

"What? Our wives?"

"No, I said, our wifesth!"

"Savannah, I haven't ruined my life. I haven't made a mistake
either. I just went *on* with my life. And I only made that decision
the day you sat at that table right there"—he pointed to the table
for two at the front window—"and let me know that school was
your priority. Do you think I would marry someone while I had
unresolved feelings for another woman? If you think that, then you
never really knew me at all, Savannah." The expression in his eyes
was one of hurt, which I had only seen from him on a couple of
occasions. But there was something even different in them tonight.
A resolve. He had thought this one through, and long before he
walked in a few minutes ago, hoodooed by Paige.

"Buff thif wafn't how if waf thuppothe thoo be. We were thuppose thoo be thogether forefer."

"What?"

He was making this painful. "You're killingth me here. *I saith
. . . we were thuppose thoo be thogether forefer!*"

"Supposed to be together forever? So, I was just supposed to
wait until you got through doing everything else you wanted to do
and then, when you were ready for me, I was supposed to be right
there waiting for you?"

I looked at him with a look Duke has used on me many times.
A look that said, "Well, when you put it that way, it has a slightly
different ring to it."

"Don't cock your head at me. That is exactly what you thought.
And I knew you thought that. And the mere fact that you thought
that proved you didn't love me the way I loved you."

As he said that, his expression softened. And he walked over to
me and put his hands on my bare arms. But he hadn't even noticed
my lovely spring attire. No, he was looking straight into my eyes.

"I loved you from the time we got caught in Wesley Monumental Church at midnight with Pastor Mason. I loved your quirkiness and your clumsiness." He pointed to my lip. "I loved everything about you. But that day, sitting in this very place, I realized you didn't love me that way."

"Buff I—"

He placed his finger in front of my face. "Don't talk anymore. It is painful for you, obviously, and painful for me to decipher." That made us both smile. "It's okay, Savannah. It's okay that you had dreams and visions and plans. And it's okay that you weren't ready. But I've changed. I'm not the kid you caught fireflies with or skipped school with or got your first kiss from. I'm a man. A man in love with a wonderful woman. A man fortunate enough to have loved two amazing women in his lifetime. But our chapter is over."

I studied his gaze to see if there was any hint of doubt in his own words. One glimmer of apprehension was all I would have needed to grab him and hold him and share the gentleness of a kiss we had once known. But there was none. No doubt. No hesitation. No second thoughts. I suppose I had known that already. "Now you go out there. Change the world. Love will find you. When you're ready, it will find you." He laughed. "I'm not sure it can handle you, but it will find you."

He kissed me gently on the cheek. And a small tear fell from the corner of my eye that surprised even me. He took his thumb and gently wiped it away. As he held my hand and led me to the front door, my mind raced with what this man had been to me. He would never know he held my greatest secrets and my *only* kisses. He would never know that years down the road, stories would be written about him. He would just never know.

He opened the front door, let go of my hand, and turned back to me. "This is over, Savannah. It's time for you to start writing the next chapter of your life." With that I watched him slowly disappear up the street and take his place in a world of past conversations and onetime loves.

"I wuff you," I said quietly.

Unfortunately it was loud enough for the harassing curly-headed pedaler to have heard. He had apparently witnessed the entire parting episode. He and his dog. He pulled his ringlets right up next to me and stopped. Peeking his head inside the coffee shop, he leaned back and shook his head.

"Shuffup!!!" I declared straight into his smirking face. I might have even sprayed him with a little spit, but who cared? My soul was broken, floating on the barren sea of heartbreak. I slammed the door closed and locked it before he could dare to enter.

Jake's had lost its sparkle. Jake's felt cold and lonely. Jake's had apparently held Grant's heartbreak years before, and mine today. What a wretched place. Once my place of joy and laughter, now my home of bitterness and woe. Packing up two cold steaks, I put them in the refrigerator so Duke could at least experience some pleasure in what had come to be his concrete world. Duke and I were more alike than woman and beast ought to be. Our worlds were colorless and our meals takeout. After folding the white linen tablecloth and placing it neatly atop the other items of lost hope, my picnic basket felt like a heavy pack of burden. This wasn't the way moments like these were supposed to end. It wasn't the way my practiced ending had transpired. I had us slow dancing to the music we would hum together. Our new song, "Ready to Take a Chance Again" by Barry Manilow. What I like is none of Thomas's business.

I pushed the table back to its place and walked through the swinging doors that led to the back room. I turned off the lights, and with them the light of my heart. As I closed the door behind me, I knew it would be years before I could ever enter Jake's again. Well, okay. I'd show up tomorrow morning for a Coke. But only because it was utterly necessary.

CHAPTER TWENTY-EIGHT

Talking was too painful. Both physically and emotionally. Paige let me sleep on her sofa. She consoled me and helped me wipe away my tears. Well, there weren't any more tears, but there was a lot of slurred whining. However, our top ten list of "Why Savannah was a better catch than Miss Redhead"—made in conjunction with the viewing of David Letterman—was rather cathartic.

Morning came crashing in hard and furious. My head was killing me from a caffeine overdose. The only highlight was that my lip had retreated to a somewhat normal level. And the lowlight was my mother's message regarding my depiction of her in today's column.

I stared at Paige's check in my hand. Two thousand dollars. Liberation.

Ms. Austin was on the morning news. The local newscaster found it hard to believe that she was born and raised in the South.

"Why? Southerners aren't all big hats and afternoon tea. Some of us like our coffee as espressos and some of us favor black to pastels. There is a progressive voice of the South that is unmistakably being voiced and heard."

The recent journalism-school grad responded, "I can see where that would be true."

"I'm just trying to help people from my part of the world realize that the conservative mind-set of the old South isn't what this new generation needs or truly desires."

"What *do* you feel this generation desires?"

"Someone who listens. And actually hears. Then fights to help implement their concerns and ideals. And who helps their voice to be heard."

"Well, we're glad you had a few moments to spend with us this morning. Ladies and gentlemen, Ms. Faith Austin."

Faith smiled that perfect smile. She had it. Whatever *it* was. She had it.

I tilled alone. It was best. God and I had a lot of talking to do. He seemed quiet. Again. So I just kept the conversation going. Reminding Him how miserably last night had transpired. Nothing to my liking. And nothing to His, I was certain. Reminding Him that if He was passing out more *it,* I would like some of my own. By the time I was through, the only consolation I could imagine was Coke. Coke and flip-flops. No pearls today. *It* hadn't rained down. No use in trying to pretend. At least for now.

The question slammed into me as soon as I entered the back door. "I expected you last night. You said you would be there."

"No sir, I said I would try."

He leaned against the steel counter that held my liquid delight and extended a cup.

I took the cup from his hand, filled it full of ice, and watched the dark, powerful fluid flow. "My meeting took a detour and I had to regroup." I leaned against the counter while the events of last night came back like a stampede. I took a long swig of my Coke, which burned all the way down. Nothing was so good. "Whoo! That's good stuff."

"So, your dinner with Grant didn't go as you expected?" he asked with a perfectly stoic expression.

Had I possessed any remaining liquid in my mouth, it would have surely escaped through every cavity in my head. "I'm not sure I know what you're talking about."

"Savannah, did you know that not telling the entire truth is really not truth at all?"

I pursed my lips and wrinkled my brow and turned to stare at him. "How do you know everything?" He started to give a quick response. "No, seriously, Dad. How do parents know everything? Is there not one thing I can do that you wouldn't know of?"

"You know how we know, Savannah? Because there is part of us inside of you. And we know ourselves very well." He tapped me on my nose, then proceeded to head back into the front of the shop. "By the way, your article was . . . interesting."

I headed straight to the paper and snatched a copy of the morning news from Marla's desk. I greeted her quickly but friendly and headed to my hallowed haven. But I wasn't to sit. No, Jessica buzzed me as soon as I entered my hole; Mr. Hicks wanted to see me.

I would be fired. I was certain. Who wouldn't be certain? I couldn't do anything right. Except create a blaring headline. Oh, yes, I had mastered that one. I walked slowly. Even wanted to scream, "Dead woman walking!" But who would care? Most would be glad. I would give Paige her money back. I would live with my mother and die old and wretched.

Jessica had disappeared into obnoxious oblivion. I was grateful. She made me weary. Mr. Hicks was snacking on a country ham biscuit and had more crumbs on his tie than around his mouth.

"Oh, Savannah. Come in, come in." He tried to brush away the remnants of breakfast from his face unsuccessfully. "I wanted you to know you did a great job with your story. You gave me a kick," he said, chuckling. "I wish I could have seen your mother in a silk eye mask. I didn't even know all the activity that was happening around there."

I sat down across from him more confident. "Well, thank you, sir. I'm glad you liked it."

"Yeah." He placed the other half of his biscuit aside and brushed the crumbs from his desk. "I thought you would give us some 'sidewalk sermons' like your mother has been giving on the evening news. But you branched out, young lady. Gave us a laugh and kept self-righteous opinions to yourself. Couldn't have written it better myself. Now, go get ready for tomorrow's deadline."

"Well, thank you, sir. Really, thank you so much." As I started out the door, I noticed a yellow file on his desk bearing Joshua's name and a "Dated Material" stamp. Joshua's story. Unopened. I couldn't help it. "Did you not read Joshua's story?"

"What?" He looked down, confused. "Oh, this?" He picked up the file. "No, I haven't gotten to it yet."

"But it's dated. It was for today's paper!"

"Oh, I didn't notice."

"How could you not notice?" I asked, incredulous.

"Because I *didn't*, Savannah," he snapped.

"Well, you should have. You really should have."

I left, my cadence not as enthusiastic as Mr. Hicks's compliments of my work warranted. And the nuisance coming up the aisle conjured the usual dread. Jessica turned the corner and headed in my direction, with none other than Faith Austin at her side. The city's new darling looked exceptionally fabulous today. Her long dark hair spread symmetrically across her shoulders, and her camel-color pants and matching lace top looked almost tie-dyed.

I hesitated for a moment. I felt too casual next to this woman in my flip-flops and white capris. Jessica didn't even notice me until we were practically flip-flop to Ferragamo.

"Hello, Ms. Austin," I said with a nod. "Jessica."

"Savannah," Jessica snipped.

"Hello, Savannah. How are you this morning?"

"Doing great, thank you very much. Just heading back to work. What are you ladies up to this morning?"

"We were trying to have a conversation," Jessica snapped. "And I believe this conversation was between *A* and *B*"—she pointed to her and Ms. Austin—"so why don't you *C* your way out of it?"

I raised my right eyebrow and fought desperately not to laugh in her face.

Ms. Austin had trouble hiding her smirk as well and spoke to me anyway. "I liked your article today. I expected a downright assault. But you were rather refreshing. The Pilates episode got me good."

"Well, I'm glad you enjoyed it. I'm still trying to wrap my mind around the whole thing though."

"That shouldn't take too long." Peanut gallery.

The two mature ones tried to ignore the child.

"Ms. Austin!" came Mr. Hicks's voice. He was smiling like a child with a crush on the teacher. "Come on in here and let's get this interview going." He ignored both Jessica and me as he took Ms. Austin by the hand and began to lead her to his office.

She looked back with a smile. "Maybe we can have dinner soon." Her cell phone rang as she turned around. She answered it with a rather perturbed, "Hello?"

Mr. Hicks closed the door behind them and left Jessica staring at the veneer.

"I guess you'll have to *C* your way out," I said with a shameless giggle. I deserved to laugh.

"Be careful with those two," came the voice over my shoulder as I descended the stairs. The same voice that had snickered over my shoulder yesterday as Grant walked out of my life and into the land of regrettable remembrances.

"Well, I would think you would find both of them stunningly

beautiful," I said, ignoring the bounce of his curls that I was certain were following me.

"You clearly have no idea what I find beautiful. I can see right through women like them." He kept his steps on my heels.

"Oh you can, can you?"

"Yes, and I can see through women like you too."

I opened the door to the first floor and turned to stare him down. I expected a smirk. Even a wide-eyed smile. But he just stared back. It was a look I'd never seen on his face in the less than two weeks we'd known each other. It forced a nervous laugh. Odd for me, with this annoyance. "See through me? What are you talking about? Everyone else seems to like my article, Mr. North."

"I'm not talking about your article. That is an issue in and of itself. I'm talking about yesterday at the coffee shop. You acted pathetic, Ms. Phillips."

"How dare you talk to me like that? I don't have to listen to this, coming from a man who doesn't even have a car." I turned on my heels, or not, to my pitiful world. My word. I had just defended this man to my boss. I knew he would follow. I knew he would reply. But he didn't. He left me there. With *pathetic* and *Ms. Phillips* dangling like piercing participles in the air.

CHAPTER TWENTY-NINE

A person should be allowed to enjoy lunch. It should be an unstated law: Lunch hour is to be enjoyed. Add that as commandment eleven, and Vicky would willingly stay chained the rest of the year. Despite Joshua, this was a good day. And I was going to enjoy the rest.

Coke from Jake's for lunch was the only thought on my brain. Until I got the Coke. Then the thought of food began to cross my mind. I opened up the refrigerator to see if Richard or the twins had brought anything desirable from home. Only the aluminum wrapper of two cold-hearted steaks caught my eye.

I closed the refrigerator and stared at my hand that held the handle. Then I opened it again. Snatched the steaks out of the refrigerator, laid one in Duke's bowl, and took the other one along with the morning paper and my Coke to the park bench directly across from the coffee shop. A raised hand was all I offered those who greeted me as I passed.

As I sat down, a tune caught my ear, and my new bench buddy caught the corner of my eye. I hid my steak beneath my paper.

"Savannah, I had no idea I had met a star."

"Good morning, Joy. You haven't been walking into any more streets, have you?"

Her floral belly shook. But her hair looked neatly combed. She sat down on the bench, oblivious to the fact that I was about to have a moment to myself.

"You wrote a nice piece, Savannah."

"Actually I was just about—"

"But it wasn't clear what you really think about what is happening." She pulled an orange out of her purse and began to peel it.

"It's not really about what I feel. It's more about what I observe through the lives of others."

"Is it?"

"Yes, stories are about what interests people. I try to tell others' stories."

She continued to peel and never looked up. "Well, you told other people's stories all right. Your poor mother hasn't smiled all morning. And that tall, beautiful, but extremely loquacious girl that follows her around carrying a tiara didn't fare too well either. And pity the people who were in their company this morning."

I stopped and looked at her. She apparently needed me to help educate her on what newspaper reporters actually do. "I just tell it like life lives it."

"But isn't life really about how events affect us and change us?"

"Yes, life is, but not necessarily human-interest stories."

"So, you don't want your stories to change people?"

"Well, yes, that is the intent of all my stories. That was why I wanted this job. Because the lady who did this before me . . ." I paused for a moment and thought of Gloria Richardson, who had held this position prior to my arrival. The brief time that had transpired since Gloria's death and my first day on the job blew by me and came to rest inside my thoughts. I looked down at the paper lying on my lap and my picture staring back at me in the same place Gloria's had through my six years of college and graduate school. "Yeah, my stories should change people," I muttered.

Joy put a piece of orange in her mouth and chewed slowly. She wouldn't speak until every morsel was dissolved. She was a lady that way. Forcing me to wait.

"Well, if you want your stories to change people, then they first have to change you. Your story was witty and charming. But it didn't say anything. You just told me what I can come down here and see for myself. See, I need you to tell me the things I don't notice. I need you to reveal to me what I've missed myself." She stopped for a moment and that distant look took over her face again as she stared at the large group of people that still surrounded the monument and my mother.

"All this, Savannah"—she motioned across the street—"This hasn't changed you, Savannah; it's just annoyed you." Well, I would beg to differ; she was the one to annoy me. She must have read it in my face. "Now, don't get mad at me, baby. I've grown fond of you. But take it from an old lady: Living should change you. It shouldn't leave you apathetic or annoyed, or dare I say, cynical." Apparently she dared. "It should leave you changed. I'm not even sure this event has changed this city yet either. So far it's just transpired in the middle of it. But everyone will be changed before it's over. I guarantee you that."

"Changed, huh?"

She wrapped up her peeling inside a napkin and stuffed it in her purse. Then her black eyes looked up at me to make sure I was listening. "Yes, but you can't be changed until you know what you believe, Savannah." She knew I was listening.

She bent over and tugged at her drooping stockings before she stood. She pulled her dress down as she rose and took her tired straw bag in her hand. Those eyes looked straight into my soul and refused to look away without one final parting Joy thought. "Yeah, you need to figure out what you believe, Savannah. But it's even more important to know why you believe it." With that she left to greet a news reporter camped out underneath a nearby tree. Wonder what he needed to change.

I stood up and threw the steak away, because I had lost my appetite. I tucked the paper underneath my arm. I had no need to read it. Joy had just made it clear what it said. A bunch of nothing.

I would have returned to Jake's, but the memories were simply too painful at this time. I had no desire to enter the newspaper either. Entering meant interacting, and I was downright tired of interacting. Didn't care if I saw another woman carrying snacks in her purse or another curly-headed coworker.

I flung the newspaper onto the passenger's seat. The front page unfolded, and staring back at me was a beautiful young woman with long flaxen hair and breathtaking green eyes. Next to her, the picture of a nice-looking boy with hair close to the same color. Both looked to be in their late teens, early twenties. The headline declared, "Local Beauty Queen Arrested for Alleged Murder of Boyfriend."

I had forgotten. Over a nonexistent dinner with a hopelessly former love, and then a morning of enjoying my own weak press, I had forgotten. Life was supposed to have been altered forever by yesterday's events. I had declared it myself. But life happened, just like always. I had dressed myself up, bought dinner, gotten dumped and then humiliated, and spent the evening mentally trashing a woman I didn't even know. And this morning I had debated over heels or flip-flops, bought a Coke, got puffed up, and then had my balloon popped by a practical stranger, all while worlds just around the corner had stopped.

My selfishness and shallowness slammed into me and stuck like a stretched flower around Ms. Joy's upper thigh. It was what it was. Not one for avoiding confrontation, confronting myself seemed far less desirable.

So much for avoiding interaction. Because interaction didn't care a thing about avoiding me. It greeted me at the front desk. It greeted me rounding the first corner. It greeted me even in my little Styrofoam world.

"Oh, Savannah. I'm so glad you finally got here. I just need you. I'm having nightmares. I can't eat. I can't sleep." Miss Amber Topaz was pacing. And if she wasn't careful, she would run right into my Styrofoam wall.

I knew why she was really here. I was certain that this whole thing was nothing more than a brouhaha to see Joshua. She was in love with him. I still wasn't quite sure if that was because she really liked him or because she saw him as the shortest distance between her and the title of *Mrs.* United States of America. And since her discovery that his desk was perched directly across from my own, I could never assume her visits were simply to see me. No, her dropping by would be for one reason alone: to run into Mr. Bike Boy. I was no fool. Maybe a witless wonder, but not a fool.

Then she started to cry. *Well, maybe she is here to see me.*

"Oh my, I think I'm going to hyperventilate." She collapsed into the chair by my small orifice that would have been a door had a person been privileged enough to have an office *with* a door. "I might need mouth to mouth." I was certain she peeked across the corridor.

I grabbed my chair, pulled it up next to her, and sat down. "Amber, get a grip or I'm going to have to slap you."

That got her attention. "Why would you slap me?" She sniffled.

"Because that's what people do to people who act hysterical. Now, what in the world is going on?"

"It's just yesterday, Savannah. The whole thing. The body, the police, Miss Chatham County United States of America in handcuffs. I even went to see her!" she wailed.

That one got me. "You did? What did she say?"

"Oh," she said, blowing her nose and trying to gain her composure. "I couldn't go in. A guard wanted to search me. Well, my Lord have mercy, Savannah." She sat upright in her chair and straightened the skirt of her teal sundress. "I've never had a man touch me in such places in my life, and I wasn't about to have the first time happen by a complete stranger in a jail, now, was I? No, I'm waiting for Mr. North when he makes me Mrs. North and, well, let the party be—"

"Please!" This child was crazier than I. "You and Joshua getting married isn't even a present reality. Stick to the facts. So, you didn't go see her?"

"No, I just couldn't." She started tearing up again. "But I'm going to. I just want you to go with me. I *neeeeeeeed yooooooou,* Savannah." She wrapped her arms around my neck and threw her head down in sobs.

Her head was bobbing from her heaves. I removed her arms from my neck. "How is it you are so hysterical today, when I heard you were back outside with my mother last night trying to do Pilates again?"

She cocked her head at me as if that was the dumbest question she had heard since the mayor emceed the Miss Georgia United States of America and asked her to tell why she should be the next Miss Georgia United States of America. Shouldn't the answer be piercingly obvious? "Savannah, I called your mother last night because I was in such a mess. She asked me to come spend the night with her, and she spent our entire dinner encouraging me and giving me advice, and then she held me while I *criiiiiiied.*" She started blubbering again.

"My mother did all that?"

"Yes. Then she had me laughing, telling me crazy stories about when she was young, and before I knew it I was showing her more Pilates moves. It's not like I just walked up and said, 'Okay sunshine, let me teach you some Pilates.' I mean, please, Savannah, I'm not totally callous."

Ooh, right word. Right way. "Well, I'm sorry. I shouldn't have just assumed."

"It's okay." She grabbed a tissue and snorted loud enough to alert the Atlantic's ships of fog. "Your mother's really special, Savannah. I'm not even her daughter and she makes me feel like I am. You should be nicer to her."

But before I could respond, the sound of a familiar voice came up the hall. I stood up and peeked around the corner. Ms. Faith Austin was walking down the hall, accompanied by Mr. Hicks's "charming" secretary once again. Looking down at Amber's lovely dress in teal, it became clear to me that she was too . . . well, too teal. But I didn't want to miss the opportunity to speak.

"Hello Faith. What has you at the paper so long today?" I asked as they walked past my door, clearly on their way to the elevator.

Jessica would not let the poor woman speak. "Savannah, Ms. Austin and I are in an extended meeting with Mr. Hicks, and we don't have time for chatting."

Faith stopped anyway. "Oh, Mr. Hicks and I are just going to wrap up our interview from this morning."

"Well, I hope it has gone well."

Amber blew once more. "Oh, excuse me. This is Amber. Uh, my friend." I tried not to wince from the pain of the proclamation.

"Nice to meet you, uh, Amber," Ms. Austin offered.

"We really need to be going," Jessica snipped.

Amber ignored her. "Well, hello. I'm Amber Topaz Childers. I've seen you, haven't I? Down there at the monument."

"Yes, I have work I'm doing down there."

"Well, I hope it goes well. You just let Ms. Victoria know if you need a thing. That lady would do anything for anyone. Well, ladies, I need to skedaddle. Have to sort out some things down at the visitors center. We have some issues with this group out of Atlanta, AFUCLA or something. Probably a bunch of sorority girls trying to stir up the dickens. Well, gotta run. Nice to meet you. And you too, little one. Whatever your name is." I thought for a moment the six-foot Amazon Amber might actually pat Jessica on the head.

"Bye, Amber. I'll talk to you soon. We'll figure something out."

"I know. You always do." And with that her teal skirt reflected fluorescently off of the drab gray carpet and white walls until she safely turned the corner.

Jessica chimed in first. "What an idiot." She flung her hair around.

"She's not an idiot, Jessica."

"Sounded like you thought she was even in your own column today," she sneered.

"You missed the point."

"No you missed *a* point." She took Ms. Austin's arm and they continued to the elevator. Ms. Austin turned back with a wink. I had nothing to offer in return. Therein lay the whole problem.

CHAPTER THIRTY

T hese are for you." I turned to see Mr. Hicks standing in the doorway of my cubby. He laid a thick legal-size envelope on my desk and then looked casually around my partition-style walls. "Well, you've made this rather homey, Savannah."

"Remember that probation period we talked about when I first started last week?"

"Yes, I do." He placed his arms atop the set of twins he was packing above his belt.

"Are these"—I pointed toward the folder he had laid down in front of me—"Are these going to cause me to hasten my departure from these homey quarters, or could I dare bring in a few more items of hominess?"

"Well, ignoring the fact that *hominess* isn't a word, you should know not all the correspondence in that folder there is negative. And today's story partially redeemed you. And controversy sells newspapers, Savannah." He headed back up the hall toward the elevator that would lead him to his real door and his beautiful view of Bay Street.

He didn't answer my question. But I had a lot of questions that needed answers. And obviously to him and the little bundle of sheer delight that answered his phones, being hated one day and liked the next was no big deal as long as people bought newspapers.

Perusing the stack of letters, I was shocked by how much people actually cared about what happened on the cover of a newspaper. The opinions were straightforward and strong. People cared one way or the other about what was happening on Wright Square. People had opinions that I had ignored for one reason alone: evasion. I was a chicken.

Gloria Richardson had never been a chicken. She talked about things that were uncomfortable. Told stories that ignited passion and compassion. And I wanted to be well liked at other people's expense.

You have to know why you believe what you believe. Joy's words wouldn't leave me. So I would confront them. I would make a business trip this afternoon. I might come out with stink all over me, but it was a trip that must be traveled.

"Savannah Phillips, you haven't been to my house since the day you picked up that last pot of butter beans I made you."

Granny Daniels never changed. She had always looked old. But not old in a bad way. Just old in an old way. Some people just always look old. You didn't age with them. You didn't enjoy their early years. You just know them old. Well, that is how Granny Daniels has always been to me.

I also never quite remembered what she wore, except that there was always a hat, a black hat. But I couldn't recall the style of hat, or what was under the black. At that age, most of the people she knew were dying left and right. I imagine she decided to simply stay dressed for the occasion.

But today I noticed. Today I wanted to notice. I wanted to notice detail. Not my own, but someone else's. She didn't have a hat on today, and her gray curls were neatly pressed, tight up around her head like a knit cap. She wore a simple coat-style dress in a pretty bright shade of pink. No belt, no buttons, just a zipper up the front, and short sleeves cuffed at the bottom.

The shoes were similar to Joy's. In the sandal family, black, and with pantyhose sticking out from the toes. She was thicker than I had ever realized. But she was wearing fewer clothes than I had ever seen her wear before, either. Her toy poodle yapped at me as soon as I entered and sniffed my legs for the first thirty minutes of our conversation.

"Do you mind if I come in for a few minutes?" I asked, standing at the red front door of her modest white-siding home.

"No, honey. You come in here and sit your little self down and let Granny Daniels fix you some good eatin'."

I couldn't do it. I could sit here and smell mothballs, but I couldn't put them in my mouth. "Oh, that's okay. I'm not hungry."

I sat down at her small kitchen table while she fixed her a plate and I tried to disguise the noises coming from my stomach area.

"Well, what brings you here, sweet girl?" she asked, sitting down next to me at the table. Her plate looked so good. Fresh biscuits, fried pork chops, cabbage, and some kind of potato casserole. This meal and her age were proof: Lard doesn't necessarily kill you young. It could have been one fine meal. But I was certain it looked far better than it would taste. Of course, with the smell so thick inside the house, I might not even be able to smell it in the food. But it just wasn't worth the risk.

"I don't know. Just had some questions."

"What kind of questions, honey?" Butter dripped down her fingers as she lifted that steaming biscuit toward her mouth.

I tried not to lick my lips. My eyes glazed over, and for a moment I lost my train of thought. "Uh, well . . . I was . . . I was just curious what you thought about everything that's been happening around here?"

"Well, it has been rather eventful lately, hasn't it?"

"Yes, ma'am, it sure has."

She leaned back in her chair and took a long sip of her sweet tea. "I've got a lot of thoughts, Savannah. You don't live this long and not have a lot of thoughts on a lot of things. I mean, let's face it: I'm old. Pretty much have always felt old." She chuckled, and I kept my thoughts to myself. "But we're facing times, Savannah, that will probably determine the future for you and your children."

"What do you mean?"

"I mean your mother and hundreds others like her are out there trying to preserve a defining line for you and your children."

"Chaining herself to a monument is defining me all right."

"Is that all you see, Savannah?"

"Is what all I see?"

"Is all you see that your mother is chained to something? Do you not see the bigger picture?"

"There's always a bigger picture for my mother. But the manner in which she chooses to state her cases is usually all I can focus on."

"Then you've probably been robbed of a lot of powerful revelations."

She noticed my pause and she continued. "You are so focused on your fear that your mother will damage your life or reputation that you forget she's her own person. Do you know what's really happening around that square?"

I was certain this was a trick question. "Let's hear your thoughts."

"Life, Savannah. People are declaring life as they have chosen to live it. Some are saying they have chosen to follow the principles carved in that piece of stone. Others are saying anything of a 'Christian viewpoint' has no place on public property. But do you know where the Ten Commandments reside as we speak?"

"No, ma'am, I can't say that I do."

"They rest on the floor of the National Archives Building. And a picture of Moses holding the Ten Commandments—or 'the tablets of the law,' some say—is on the outside of the building that houses the U.S. Supreme Court. Do you think when 'In the Year of Our Lord' was written into the Constitution that some hidden meaning, some hidden god, was being referred to?"

I wasn't sure if this needed an answer.

"No, it was the one true God." See, it didn't. "People can argue all they want that God isn't mentioned in the Constitution. But He is the basis for the Constitution, Savannah. It was written because of who He is."

"But what about the separation of church and state? Isn't that also part of the core of who we are?"

"Well, that's nowhere in the Constitution."

"Yes it is!"

"Where?"

She had me there. "I have no idea."

"Because it's not. That phrase was originally taken from a statement in a letter by Thomas Jefferson that said there should be a 'wall of separation between church and state.' So in a move totally separate of Congress, the courts took what had originally been a prohibition against the Congress establishing a national church and changed it into a prohibition against any acts of religion by the state government—or anyone affiliated with it."

This woman was good. "But in spite of all of that, how is anyone really listening, when everyone is screaming their positions?"

"Some people will never listen, Savannah. Some people will set their course and die for what they believe in."

"My mother would."

"Yes, she would. But she listens too. She may not always act like she's listening," she said with a slight laugh. "The question is, what are you listening to? Truth, or your own set of ideals?"

"It depends who you ask."

"But the answer doesn't change what is true. A person's opinion, even perception, doesn't change truth."

"I know, you're right. Truth is the one constant, isn't it?"

"It is."

"And you might just find it on a slab of concrete strapped to my mama."

That made her chuckle, causing her thickness to shake. "Yes, Savannah, you just might."

On my walk back to the office, I noticed Vicky's countless touches in the streets of Savannah. The landscaping in the squares reflected her taste. The tongues of the passersby often held her name. The Pumpkin House that faced me as I turned the corner held her animosity.

Four years ago, a man from Atlanta purchased the stately home, which required substantial renovation. He began by painting it a lovely shade of Halloween pumpkin orange. Once the update began, Mr. Atlanta ran into some financial troubles. Thus the renovations were completely halted for two years and have run at a virtual snail's pace since then.

Had he known my mother, he would have known that getting approval for the color on the streets of her city would prove rather difficult. About as difficult as his money woes. As a member of the Historic Review Board, Vicky was certain pumpkin orange was not a period color. So, in a rather precise letter, the board informed him that he must repaint his house in a color that was truly representative of the historic period.

They didn't know who they were dealing with either. Mr. Atlanta had done research of his own and proved that his "Pumpkin House" was indeed a period color. Well, Vicky is still confident he fabricated the whole thing, even forged history books, but don't be fooled by her frustration. His house is still orange.

So, seeing her touch everywhere reiterated to me her passion. The same passion that was denying her of down feathers and hot showers was the same passion that propelled her to aid underprivileged families to tidy up their neighborhoods and preserve their dignity. The same woman that was out there praying, singing, and having evening dinner parties was the same woman who had taken this city to new heights in, dare I say, the eyes of the world.

Though *ordinary* on any scale cannot be found within sight of her, extraordinary shows up quite often. The world may laugh. People may ridicule. But in the end, for those who know her, all eventually conclude she's an all right kind of lady.

"Okay, Mr. Attorney, I have a few questions."

I could hear Gregory's heavy sigh on the other end. "What now, Queen of Denial?"

"I've never been the queen of anything, except the okra-seed-spitting contest, and Vicky refuses to allow me to mention it."

We both laughed.

"Seriously, I have a few questions. Sergeant Millings has issued my mother something called an Order to Disperse. He said if she doesn't hightail it home by Friday afternoon at five, he will put her in jail. Can he really do that?"

"Is he a federal officer?"

"No, he's a Savannah officer who should have retired years ago. But after all this attention, he will probably stay around for the next ten years."

"I would think this would be a federal issue, with her being in front of a Federal Courthouse."

"They're still wrangling over that one. Sergeant Millings is fighting them tooth and nail to be the one who gets to handcuff Victoria Phillips right back up. Of course, if she got too close to him, poor soul would have a coronary. But could my mother really go to jail? I mean, the woman's good, but Martha Stewart she ain't. My mother would crumble at a strip search."

"Well, if he gave her an Order to Disperse, our Criminal Code Section 39-17-305 says she could get arrested for disorderly conduct if she doesn't comply. I'm not sure if it's the same for Georgia."

"So you're saying she very well could."

"Yes, my friend, she very well could. I'm surprised they haven't gotten her for Section 39-17-307, obstructing a highway or other passageway."

"She's on a sidewalk, Gregory."

"Yes, a passageway to the courthouse."

"I couldn't stand to see her get thrown in jail. That just wouldn't be right. Plus, the local police shouldn't be forced to endure her for thirty days. Maybe we should break into Sergeant Millings's office and find that order and throw it away."

"That—"

"That would *not* be stealing; that would be misplacing."

"You need help."

"I know. I need yours. Will you come defend my mother?"

"She'll have to pay me more than you."

"She has more money than me, genius."

"Sure. If it gets that far, call me. Now, have you dealt with your other issue?"

"I don't have any other issues. Ooh, I think my phone's beeping. Check your calendar. We'll need you by Friday."

"Savann—"

"Ooh, gotta run! Beep, beep, beep! Bye."

"Yeah, Mr. Hicks received almost a hundred letters about her picture in the paper." That little snide secretary made sure I could hear her.

"Hello, Savannah." Ms. Austin was apparently leaving and looked rather startled as I rounded the corner.

"Hello," I responded to her and the tormented one. The little tick turned up her already upturned nose and asked. "Ooh, what's that smell?"

"It smells like mothballs," Ms. Austin said.

"Yeah, I smell that in the foyer every now and then too," I assured them.

"Well, I've never smelled it before," Jessica said.

Joshua came around the corner right behind me and about knocked us all down. I was actually glad to see him. He bumped into Faith and gave a quick "Excuse me" but offered nothing else to any of us.

Ms. Austin scanned him up and down, and her eyes followed him down the hall. I found it rather uncomfortable. "Who is that good-looking man?"

"Oh, that's Joshua North," Jessica responded. "He is one of the cutest things around here. Doesn't pay much attention to anyone though. Trust me, I've tried for years . . ." she recalled the two of us were present. "Oh," she said, semiembarrassed.

Ms. Austin's cell phone rang. "Ms. Austin . . . Yes . . . I know. Would you lay off? I told you I'd call you when I got through." She slammed the phone shut.

Jessica jumped. "Well then, if you'll excuse me, I need to get back to Mr. Hicks. The paper never slows down for anyone."

"Sure. Thank you, Jessica, for your hospitality today." As soon as Jessica was out of earshot, Ms. Austin unleashed. "My God, that woman is simply insufferable. She's been breathing down my neck all day long. Well, Savannah. Always good to see you. Let me know if we can get together soon."

Her outburst startled me. I watched her as she walked away. Granted, Jessica was condescending, downright annoying and, well, a pain to be certain, but hearing someone else say it felt a little awkward. The woman in the thousand-dollar outfit and bust-the-bank cosmetic line left. I watched her leave. After all, that's what people did.

CHAPTER THIRTY-ONE

D o you want me to come help you pack?" Paige asked over the phone.

I looked out my car window and stared up at my house. I'd spent a long afternoon staring at a blank computer screen. Tomorrow, my friend and real-estate agent, Claire, would bring me keys for my new place. Yet the whole moment felt slightly overwhelming. "No, I think this is something I need to do myself."

"You sure?"

"Yeah, I'm sure."

"Are we still moving you out tomorrow night, though?"

"Yeah, Thomas has agreed to help. Not much to move though."

"We'll have to move your whole bedroom suite."

"Yeah, but that's about it. I don't have anything else. And with what I have to pay you back, I'll be eating sitting on my bed for the next year."

"You'll be surprised how quickly things will change."

Thinking back to all the happenings of this week, I knew things had already changed. "I'm already surprised."

"Well, have fun. It's a new day."

"Yes, it's a new day. I'll call you later."

"What are you going to do? Plop you a monument in your front yard?" The younger man asked the elderly gentleman as they walked past my house.

"If I need to, I will. Wouldn't hurt you anyway, young man."

"You are so totally out of touch with this generation, Grandpa."

Their conversation rounded the corner as they did. But the pitch of the grandfather's voice made it clear who was in touch with whom.

I stood at the bottom of the steps to my house for what seemed like forever. I looked around at the ivy. It was so perfect. It ran neatly up the brick wall that surrounded the Abercorn side of our house. Each shrub had been maintained by Jake and his good friend Wayne, who had helped him for years. Every detail was attended to. Everything had its order. Its place. Just like my father. A man of order and detail. He commanded the whole while paying attention to the one. Looking at his handiwork, I was confronted with how much I'd yet to learn about life, about love, about work, about this family. Lord have mercy—about pretty much everything. I couldn't handle one thing, let alone one thousand things. My stars, I couldn't handle myself half the time. I heard a hum.

"You going in, or just going to watch the ivy grow?"

Poor sister always gave herself away before she even said a word. "I'm going in eventually."

"Things have changed, little one." I could feel Joy staring at me.

"How can you tell?"

"See it in your face."

"Look older, huh?"

"You're an old soul, Savannah; a person can't help that."

"Could we talk about something else?"

"Want to talk about dinner?"

I turned and looked at her wide black eyes. Then I cracked up. I laughed until I was doubled over. I even had to hold on to Joy so I wouldn't fall down on the pavement. People were watching, but I didn't care. I deserved to laugh. Somebody needed to laugh. Things had gotten way too serious around here. Before I knew it, Joy was laughing too. We were both trying to hold each other up, but we couldn't, so we finally surrendered and plopped ourselves down on the bottom step. And by the time we were through, neither of us could even remember what had been so funny.

I leaned back on the stoop. "Joy, ahh, you make me laugh. How do you do it?"

"Do what?" She used one of her plump arms to try to lower herself down onto the step beside me. I reached out and helped steady her down.

"Stay so happy. I mean, you're always singing or smiling. Every now and then you get a faraway look, but you're just full of . . ."

"Full of what, baby? Joy?"

I laughed. "Yeah, crazy, isn't it? You are your name. You're just a joy."

She looked at me as if this was no revelation to her at all. "Well, what else would I be, Savannah?"

"Well, I know, but what if your name was Suzy? You'd still be full of joy."

"Ever the clever one, aren't you? Destiny's in a name, Savannah."

Here we went again. "You think?"

"I know. Ever met a child whose parents called him *stupid* all of his life? Stupid is what he turns out to be. Ever met a kid whose parents told him he wouldn't amount to anything? I bet if you looked him up now, you'll find he hasn't amounted to anything. But tell a child he can do anything, and he won't know any better but to believe you. Call a child a champion, or a hero, or a young girl a lady, or a woman of grace, and see what she grows up to be."

She turned and looked at me with that look. That Joy look. That "I'm about to say something you should write down" look.

"Or name a girl Savannah, and she will forever have a destiny for that city. You were meant to be here, baby. You were meant to affect this city. Just like your name says, that is what you were created to do."

"You think?" I asked again, except this time with a totally different attitude.

"I know," she answered, still as confident as she was the last time. "Just like Victoria is meant to bring people to victory. Your mother knew what she was doing when she named you, Miss Savannah from Savannah."

I stared across the street into the window of Clary's. To think my name had a purpose. To think what I called people had an effect on them. Well, that just created a whole other set of issues for me and my life.

"What about Jake?" I asked looking at her.

"Now, that's a man's kind of name."

"That pretty much defines my father, a real man. What about the name Mr. Hicks?"

She snickered. "I'll have to look that one up, Savannah. But today, why don't you just think about who *you* are. What you're here for. And why you were given such a substantial name. Maybe because you have a substantial purpose."

With that she got up and hummed her way down the street. I went inside to close a chapter of my life. And contemplate this new challenge.

As a writer, it is interesting to write the end of a chapter. You want things to be neat and tidy. You want dilemmas to be solved and your characters to be okay. You want your reader to end satisfied. As if the last drink offers the most satisfaction. But unfortunately, that kind of ending creates little anticipation. So you create drama, conflict, questions.

That was what this was for me. As much as I wanted to leave home, create my own life, have my own space, I was scared. I was torn. I was homesick. I was hungry. And I knew a few of those things would only get worse. But it was a necessary closing. It was a necessary journey. I couldn't stay here forever. Victoria and Jake were where Savannah had come from. But it was time for Savannah to clearly define where she was going. I had to fly, grow, change, somehow. And this was the next step in all of those things.

As I walked up each step leading to the front door I decided to make this moment different. I would memorize and remember. And that is what I did. I knew I would be alone to accomplish it. The rest of my family was having supper on a sidewalk. So I took my time. For an hour I did nothing but walk around my house and remember.

Our parlor (or living room, if you're normal) beckoned me. In truth, the monstrosity of a picture over the fireplace—my mother in her tiara, draped in her Miss Georgia United States of America sash, and rather expansive hair—forces one to look. It caused me to smile. It used to cause me to pity her. But tonight was different. Tonight was not about just her. It was about us.

I remembered birthdays and arguments. I remembered sneaking out of windows with Paige and sneaking Grant in for midnight conversations. I remembered countless dinners around the table that had seen far less action than this week and remembered Jake and Victoria and Thomas and Duke and how life had been made better because they were in it. Not perfect. Nothing can reach such standards. But Savannah perfect. Perfectly fit for me. Perfectly created for me.

I walked to Dad's study at the back of the house, across from the kitchen, tucked beside the powder room on the other side of the stairs. I sat down on his leather sofa and looked at the perfect door that only years before had to be entirely replaced. It was the day of Victoria's garden tea. Who knows what for. And who knows who was there. But one person, or canine rather, had been banned and sequestered in Dad's office. Vicky thought that would work. Mistaken child. Duke could see them from Dad's window. First he barked at them. Vicky shut the blinds. Then he howled at them. Vicky turned on Harry Connick Jr. Then he flat decided to come through the door. She hadn't prepared for that one.

And a grand entrance he made with half of Dad's study door wrapped around his neck like a rather large flea collar. She tried to pull him inside. He pulled the other way. It was a tug-of-wills. Duke lost, but only after he had successfully knocked over two tables, feasted on overpriced caviar, and peed on an elderly lady's leg that looked amazingly like a tree stump. I can't help it; the woman had substantial calves. Then he was taken away by Thomas to Dad's store, where he spent the next week in "time-out." Truth be known, Duke probably didn't lose after all.

I walked up the stairs and noticed the gash in step number six. That took place during a rather lively discussion I was having with Thomas that prompted the throwing of a stapler. It had been unsuccessfully patched. I had been successfully disciplined.

I climbed into the attic and retrieved the necessary boxes to pack up my room. Scanning my wall of bookshelves behind my bed, I took each book down carefully and laid it in a box, remembering something about each one. The sight that followed was really not surprising. Hillary Clinton's book *Living History* lay hidden behind all of my other books. No need to ask who put it there. No need to ask why. Because standing upright next to it was Dick Morris's book, *Rewriting History*.

"Sad lady. Sad lady." I laughed.

My eyes were drawn to one of the eye-level shelves and the works of C. S. Lewis. Of all the authors I have read, few have captured the essence of the soul like Lewis. I looked at each of his books stacked neatly in a row in alphabetical order by title.

I picked up *Mere Christianity* and leafed through its pages, chuckling at the oxymoron of the title, pondering the thoughts of Lewis as he decided to place that label on the weight and depth of those pages, making it clear in such relevant terms that Christianity is anything but *mere*. I recalled his statement in *The Weight of Glory*, where he said, "If you have not chosen the Kingdom of God, it will make in the end no difference what you have chosen instead."

I read over and over the underlined text and my own thoughts, written in the margins. Each of them trying to understand what I was reading, even while experiencing revelation. I thumbed through *The Screwtape Letters, The Problem with Pain,* and *The Great Divorce.* And by the time I was through, it was evident why my tilling time had been so nonproductive over the last week. Because tilling had been all about Savannah.

Not about a bigger plan, not about a greater purpose, not about a discovered destiny, but about me, my wants, whims, and selfishness. Joshua was right; that's why he drove me mad. He saw through me. I knew it, and he surely knew it. And the whole thing drove me crazy.

I wasn't an evening tiller. But tonight I didn't have a choice. I had some core issues to settle. I had some demons of my own to purge. I had some monuments of my own that I needed to chain myself to for a while.

As I ran through Forsythe Park, the tears flowed freely. The comprehension of my own lies and idols and pride were almost more than I could handle. But I didn't care. He who handles tilling time could handle this. And He did. He stopped the world for me. He spoke and I listened. He challenged, and I was willing. He rebuked, and I knew it was all true. He reminded me of my limits, and I agreed. He offered His strength, and I gladly accepted.

And then I noticed, for the first time since I had returned to Savannah almost three weeks ago, the most beautiful rose garden I had ever seen, right in the middle of the park I ran through every morning.

I approached the white-columned enclosure with reverence. The iron gate that surrounded it was willing to let me enter. The two iron benches that sat on either side of the garden were available. But the stone bench that sat in underneath the concrete arbor was invit-ing. Next to the bench was a small plaque declaring, "Everyone needs to stop and smell the roses."

I remembered Joy's words of wisdom. "You need to stop, smell a flower . . ." I hadn't smelled a flower in years. I hadn't stopped in years. I probably hadn't listened much in years either.

I leaned over one of the most beautiful yellow roses I had ever seen, suddenly understanding why an entire song was written about them. It was stunning. Perfectly opened. Smelled like, well, like a rose, and before I knew it I was dancing around that garden like Julie Andrews in *The Sound of Music.* I smelled the white ones, the red ones, the pink ones, the pink with white ones. And then I sat down on the bench and just smelled them all. For the first time in years, Savannah smelled a rose. And for the first time in weeks, Savannah was listening. Really listening. And amazingly enough, when I fell quiet, a wealth of wisdom waited.

CHAPTER THIRTY-TWO

"Hey, child, smelling flowers?"

She always found me. Every time I stepped outside, she found me. "Yeah, I am, Joy. I'm smelling flowers." I turned to look at her. Yet her expression seemed lost. She looked at me like a stranger. "Joy, you okay? It's me, Savannah."

"Yeah, yeah, Savannah. Hey, baby." Her eyes sparkled with the recollection of me. "I see you found my secret place." She sat down on the bench. Her side squeaked under her weight.

"It's beautiful. Can you believe I never noticed it?"

"You wouldn't be the first. Most people around here haven't noticed it. No one has time. Too much craziness going on." She patted her fading floral. I watched her drift off in thought. "Emily Dickinson, though, once wrote a friend that 'consider the lilies of the field' is the only commandment she never broke."

I chuckled. "I'd just have to add it to my list."

"Mine too, baby." She laughed. "Mine too."

Finally, it was too much. It had to be asked. "Joy, why do you wear that dress every day?"

She looked at me, puzzled. "This?" she paused. "Oh, well, I don't really know. I guess I just have a couple of the same kind. Just comfortable, you know. So, what's your favorite one?"

She was back to flowers by choice. I would respect that. "Couldn't pick if I tried."

She stood up to leave. "Well, enjoy my secret garden."

"Where are you going?"

"Oh, got a lot of work to do. A lot of people left to see this evening. You take care of my special place, now."

"I will." I assured her. She wandered away. Looking lost. And without commenting on food or facial defects. And no humming. Something was amiss. But she wasn't ready. I would know when she was.

Paige was sitting on the steps of my house as I cleared the side of Clary's. "Why in the world are you running in the evening? Are you still dealing with deeply rooted issues?"

I proceeded up the stairs past her, into the foyer. "I am a deeply rooted issue."

"Well, how much have you packed?" She followed me up the stairs and into my room. "Oh, you've packed five entire books. Don't really want to go, do you?"

I turned to look at her; then I looked into my bathroom and spotted some toothpaste splatters on my mirror. "My bathroom looks filthy."

She grabbed my arm and jerked me back. "Oh, no you don't, Miss Hygiene Freak. You will not avoid the question."

"What question?"

"You know what question."

I sat down on the bed and looked out of my window and stared up Abercorn Street. "It's not about wanting to go; it's about having to go."

"Is this going to get real deep, because I might need some Doritos and a Diet Coke."

She made me laugh. I couldn't help it. Looking at her cute

549

little button nose and perfectly messy bleached-blonde short tresses, she cracked me up. "No, not deep tonight. Come on, help me pack. Grab a book." I tossed her one from the bookcase. "So, what are your parents doing tonight?"

"Oh, I think my dad went to hang out with your dad at the coffee shop and play some cards, while Mom is at a Mary Kay party with your mother."

"Oh, that's right. I forgot about that," I said laughing. "I should have known Mother would have it no matter what. I bet that's a sight—a group of women painting themselves up while one poor soul is in shackles."

As soon as it came out of my mouth, we both stared at each other. And without a word we threw the books in the boxes and took off down the stairs and across the black marble floor of the foyer and slammed the door behind us. We didn't stop running until we hit "Monument" Square.

"Do not let them see us," I said, panting and squatting behind a tree. It was close to seven o'clock and the sun had a good thirty more minutes, but they didn't care; there were enough television crew lights for the seven o'clock news that a 747 could have landed on the sidewalk.

"Lord, if they see us, we'll be their guinea pigs."

"They'd take us on as their goodwill project."

We leaned against the tree, Paige on one side, me on the other, but each of us with a good enough view to enjoy the production. And a production it was.

Each woman had donned a lovely white terry-cloth headband. Except Miss Amber Topaz; she had chosen a pale pink one. The Mary Kay representative had them eating out of the palm of her hand.

"Now, ladies. This is the latest in skin care. This mask will continue to purge your skin of its deepest blackheads long after you've gone to sleep."

"Now, that's a visual," Paige added.

And before we knew it, each of the nine women was covered in white cream, looking like a white version of the Blue Man Group. And there they sat, for the next ten minutes, while tiny blackheads screamed for refuge across all nine of their little faces.

"I want them to get to the makeup," Paige said.

"Be patient. Good skin care is essential to your daily skin regimen."

She looked at me as if a poltergeist was about to come out of my body. "What do you know? You use Noxema."

"Do you forget that is *my* mother up there?"

"Oh, right."

The Mary Kay consultant continued. "Now, ladies, apply your foundation smoothly, and make sure it matches your skin tone."

"I don't wear foundation," I offered.

"What's to cover up?" Paige asked.

"My ever-increasing age, I hear."

"Let me look." Paige came rather close to my face. "Nah, you look great. Need some waxing done, there on your lip"—she rubbed the top of my lip, and I slapped her hand—"but besides that you don't look a day over twenty."

"You think?" I asked, patting my face.

"Absolutely. Oh, *don't do it!*" she yellspered in terror toward the entertainment. But Amber wasn't listening and with the speed of an expert had applied bright blue eye shadow to her lids.

"Looks like my grandmother," I said.

"Not as bad as I thought. Kind of a retro-nouveau look. Everything comes back, you know." She squinted to get a better look.

"Some things shouldn't," I assured her. But it did look good on Amber. Of course, that girl would look good in a floral print muumuu.

"Ooh, look at that lipstick," Paige said, eying the pale pink color that Amber was applying to her lips.

"Ooh, that's nice. I could wear that."

"Oh, yeah, that would look great on you, with that pink toe nail polish you always wear."

"Oh, and look at that blush."

"Maybe *we* should have gone to this thing," Paige said, then looked at me. We both busted out laughing.

As the women finished, applause rose from those pilgrims who had gathered around to watch. Amber struck a pose or two, and mother tugged on a chain. But she did look the best she had looked in weeks. If the poor soul could get her hair washed and that outfit changed, she'd look downright clean.

"Let's go finish packing."

Paige stood up to follow me as we headed back to the house. "I could sneak my mother's Mary Kay book out of the house or get one from that Mary Kay lady and we could order some of that stuff."

"I don't think they have books. That's Avon."

"Oh, well, I like Avon too."

"And they're called consultants, not 'Mary Kay ladies.'"

"Well, I still want some of her stuff, whatever I need to call her."

"You just like to spend money."

"Other people's, preferably."

"Me too!"

"Yeah, I know."

CHAPTER THIRTY-THREE

The mind is a frustrating instrument. If not for the necessity of it, I'd have banished it long ago. But then I would have become the witless wonder Thomas has declared me to be for two decades. See, the mind never stops. It harasses you. Take the simple task of getting up and trying to brush your teeth: it forces you to stare at the toothpaste splatters on the mirror and quizzes you over when you're going to clean them.

Or the simple task of driving to work: Which of the three routes there will you choose? And once you choose, it questions whether you've chosen well. It teases you with the possibility that another option would have had less traffic or fewer red lights. And when you pass the window of Katherine's Corner Bookstore, the mind sends you down a memory lane of your own vanished opportunities for literary fame and store-window showcases.

The mind never leaves you alone. When you're trying to read, it barges in with to-do lists. When you're trying to listen, it barges in with your next question. And when you're trying to let go of love, it barges in with every reason to keep fighting.

But when I need a Coke—well, in large part my mind and I

are usually in agreement. Until lately. Lately it has been making an issue of Coke. Coke! As if it were an addiction. As if it mattered. As if I would care. As if everybody didn't deserve one. I mean, compared to the addictions I could have chosen, my mind shouldn't be harassing me. Trust me. I would be a witless wonder before I would be a former Coke consumer.

"Where is our dishwasher?!" I heard Louise asking rather clearly and with an extra dose of volume. The man staring back at her just tried to smile, looking as if he couldn't determine exactly what the problem was. When she flung her hand out of the soapy dishwater and splattered suds across the front of his shirt, she didn't apologize, and I think he determined the problem.

Jake rounded the corner from his office. "Louise, I'll handle it from here." And Louise let out a rather loud *humph* and returned to her dishes. I thought about staying hidden, but I didn't want to miss anything. So I proceeded to stand by the Coke machine.

"Mr. Phillips, the dishwasher will be here this afternoon, I assure you." He gave my dad a slap on the arm. "Doesn't hurt a woman to wash a few dishes."

I leaned back against the counter and took a long swig of my Coke and flung my eyes toward Louise. She and Mervine both turned around on that one, and the little man seemed to shift closer to my father.

"Ron, you have told me that every day for a week." Dad calmly wiped his hands on the towel draped over the tie of his apron. He was smooth.

"I know, sir. But I promise it will be today!"

"Well, you know what? That's not good enough."

"What do you mean?"

"I mean exactly what I said, Ron. That's not good enough."

"Well, I don't know what else to do."

"I'll tell you what you can do: you can write me a check for the deposit I paid you and consider our business finished."

"Well, that isn't possible. I've already paid for the deposit on your dishwasher."

"Then you should get your money back from them, after they've given you the runaround." Jake paused. "Unless, of course, they never told you they could have it here the next day. If that's the case, then this is apparently your problem and your problem alone."

"Well, I think you're being hasty." The little man began to twitch nervously.

"I don't think I'm being hasty, Ron." Dad sure liked to say his name. "I'm just making you keep your word."

"I'm getting you your dishwasher, Mr. Phillips! That *was* my word!" the man said rather rudely.

"No, your word was you would get me my dishwasher by last Saturday. Today is Thursday. On Saturday you said it would be here Monday. On Monday and Tuesday and Wednesday you simply decided not to return our calls. And you are only in here today because I dragged you in here after I saw you in the market. In fact, I haven't seen hide nor hair of you since I wrote you a check. A substantial check." By this time Jake was leaning against the counter himself.

Mervine and Louise and I were just enjoying the whole scene. The little fella was becoming progressively smaller and increasingly more fidgety. "Well, I think you just have unrealistic expectations."

"Well, if expecting someone to do what they *say* they're going to do is unrealistic, then yes sir, Ron, I guess I do." Poor soul would know his name by the time Jake was through with him. "But if you had told me it would have taken a week, then we wouldn't even be having this discussion today. You should have just been honest with me from the beginning."

I was about to feel sorry for the meager man when his lower lip began to twitch. "I just haven't been able to help it, Mr. Phillips. See, my wife and my kids—"

"Stop it right there. Don't you try to exploit your family. Your wife and kids are fine. I have seen them out at the square almost every day. But haven't caught a glimpse of you, come to think of it. So this is where this conversation needs to end. I want my check, and I want it now."

Dad never raised his voice. Never really even changed his tone. But you would have thought he had stood over that man and berated him like a schoolboy, the way ol' Ron shook when he reached for his checkbook. As he ripped out the check and laid it on the counter, he turned to leave. But before he did he tapped my Coke machine and said, "If you ever need a new one of these, I know where to get you a good one at cost."

"Ahh!" I said, pulling my Coke from my mouth and slapping his hand. He jerked away quickly. Wise move. "Don't you even think about it." I glared at him.

He walked to the door. But Dad wasn't quite through.

"One more thought, Ron. You might want to remove the fish emblem from your invoices. There's something downright distasteful about using a symbol of integrity to manipulate people into thinking it represents your character as well. I would think about that, sir. Because I've learned something in the business world." Well, I guess Dad had two more thoughts. "All your giftings might get you to the front of the line, but if your character's not in order when you get there, it can destroy you."

The little man morphed into a wee little man as he left with his tail between his legs.

"Louise, Mervine, I'm sorry. I'll have a dishwasher in here by tomorrow morning," my dad said. Then he kissed me and headed back to the front of the store.

His heart was heavy, I could tell. Jake didn't like hurting anyone. He was a tender spirit. But he was the real thing too, a man. So to receive any less from someone else wasn't acceptable to him.

"Are your hands shriveled prunes?" I asked as I gave them both a sideways hug.

"No, we've just been mumbling. Truth be told, your father and

Richard have washed as many of these dishes as we have. We're just spoiled," Louise said with a chuckle.

"Me too," I mused. "Me too. But had that man touched my machine again, I would have kicked his heinie."

"Savannah Phillips! Watch your mouth," Louise snapped.

"What? I said I would have had Duke lick him shiny!"

Mervine tried to stifle her grin. I didn't. "Child, don't you have a job?" Louise laughed.

I headed to the door to go check on my dad. "So they tell me. So they tell me."

As I opened the door, I noticed Dad and Duke sitting together at the front table. Dad was in a chair; Duke was at his feet. Although no one would have been surprised had Duke been sitting in the chair opposite him. He really was an immensely talented dog. These two had an unusual bond. You could tell just by observing them. Dad sat there rubbing Duke's head while they both stared out the window. Who knows what they were thinking. But by their identical expressions, it was probably about the same thing: spending another night on concrete.

I'm sure their perspectives of it were very different. But Duke would do anything for my father. And my father would do anything for Duke. He had been purchased for Thomas, but he had been treasured by my father. They go everywhere together. And when Duke must make way for Vicky, he ain't at all happy about it. And when Vicky has to deal with red dog hair, she ain't too happy about that one either.

But there Jake is. Loving the dog. Loving the woman. And adored by both while the two drive each other ferociously insane.

As I rounded the corner to head to the office, I noticed a slight commotion in front of Walgreen's. A short, fair-haired maiden was letting loose on one Sergeant Millings. Poor thing shouldn't have stood a chance with that man. But from the looks of it, the poor man didn't stand a chance with Paige. I drove by with a beep and a smile.

"I heard they stole her purse. Poor kid probably needed it. That girl has enough of her own. She should have just given it to him," Jessica said into her cell phone as she made her way in front of me through the front door.

"Don't feel bad, Savannah," Marla said as she saw me come through the door behind Jessica. "She never speaks to me either."

I made my way to my cubicle to work on my story. All newspaper systems were go. Feet were scurrying. Fingers were pecking on keyboards. The sounds of a soda can being opened and a tug-of-war with a bag of chips was coming from the cubicle in front of me. I sat down at my computer to lend my talents to this pressured world. After my talk with Granny Daniels, the issues were coming into focus. I would dive in and see what I came up with.

By the time I came up for air, she was my human-interest story, and her knowledge of history, happenings, and life would surely be as interesting to the readers as they had been to me. I printed it out around eleven and set it on my desk. But I wasn't going to deliver it until I got back from lunch. I had only been here for two hours, but it felt like a full day. I made a motion for an early lunch. There were no objections.

"My, my, child. I thought you just left here," Richard said as I entered the back door of Jake's.

"It's been a long morning already, and I needed a Coke. Thought I'd take an early lunch." I was distracted by a growling noise staring at the doorway into the shop. "Is she back, Duke?" I asked, walking to pat his ornery head.

Much to my surprise, Jake's was empty, except for Dad's persistent admirer. I guess everyone had paused to check out whatever was going on across the street, and few people partook of lunch at eleven. So, that left Jake and his new friend alone. She looked rather striking today, her brown hair coiffed in an updo, her microphone still attached to her flowing blouse, waiting for the noon report, I figured. She was sitting at the bar and was rubbing the side of her cup, in what was a rather flirtatious, dare I say provocative, move. Dad stood behind the counter refilling the coffeepots for the lunchtime crowd. His business had grown along with the group outside.

"So, how long have you been married, Jake?"

"Twenty-five years, Susan. Can you believe that?"

"Oh, they've gone to first names," I told Duke, patting his head. He was stiff as a board.

"Are you happy?" She rubbed the side of her coffee cup again and tilted her head.

"She's downright shameless!" I said. Duke looked up at me with a "Where in the world have you been?" kind of look. By this time an old African American and two ancient twins were peering over our shoulders.

"As happy as one can be in this life. I have more than I could ask for."

"Haven't you been lonely this past week, with your wife out there strapped to a pillar of concrete?" She batted her false eyelashes, over what I was now certain were eyes of equally false green.

"Actually, I've been out there with Victoria every night. Almost feels like camping."

She gave a vain attempt at laughter. "You are a remarkable man, Jake Phillips, a remarkable man." She stood up and patted his hand softly where he had laid it on the counter. I'm almost certain *I* was growling at that point.

"Well, have a great afternoon," Dad offered as he removed his hand and headed around the counter to wipe off a table by the far wall. The next action happened so quickly that about all five of us fell out of the doorway. As Dad made his way to the table, she cut him off at the edge of the counter, grabbed him by the edge of his apron, and laid one on him as if she were Angelina Jolie. Well, poor

Duke had absorbed all a canine could take. That gentle golden retriever took off before any of us could stop him. In the meantime Dad had grabbed a hold of Susan's arms and pushed her away. Duke finished her off. He pounced between them and had that Mary Kay reject flat on her back in two seconds flat. He hovered over her like a scene from *Scooby Doo*.

"Way to go, boy!" I screamed, dancing a jig to meet them. "Tripping?! What is *that?!* *My* boy can lay a woman flat on her back!" Then I stopped, the shock of it all setting in. My father had just kissed another woman. Well, maybe not technically. After all, she did grab him, by the apron no less. We were throwing that thing in the trash before day's end.

"Duke, get off of her!" Dad shouted.

Duke didn't pay him a lick of attention. He stood atop her, growling from ear to ear. Every time she tried to squirm, he would flinch in that direction. That poor woman whimpered like a trapped puppy.

"Duke! I said get down, now!" Dad demanded. This time Duke obeyed, but he still hovered right beside my father, snarling and growling all the way. Richard, Louise, and Mervine had indeed fallen through the swinging doors at my departure and were standing exposed by the counter, staring at the raucous affair. I'm sure we all looked like a *Girls Behaving Badly* episode. We stood, mouths agape, and eyes wider than a hoot owl's.

Dad graciously lifted up the wanton woman. "I'm sorry, Susan," Dad said, trying to stifle a laugh. She wasn't laughing.

"You need to get that dog under control." She wiped off her skirt as best her trembling hands could manage.

"I think *you* need to get *yourself* under control," Dad said to her.

"Well, it's about time!" I offered rather loudly. Dad looked at me as well.

"Savannah, stay out of this."

She gave us both a glare that would have made mouths drop open and eyes bug out, had that not been a preexisting condition.

She snatched up her purse and headed for the door. Dad gently took hold of her arm and made her turn around. "Susan, you are a beautiful woman. But when someone has given not just a pledge but a commitment to someone else, you need to respect that."

"You need to come into the real world, Jake Phillips. My Lord, man, you don't even sell iced coffee, Frappuccino, or cappuccino. Do you know it is the twenty-first century?"

"Yes, I do. I also know that just because years pass and trends come and go, some things aren't up for modification. There are some absolutes. Coffee being one of them." My word, don't insult the man's coffee! "Whether you like it or not, they still exist. And the covenant I made to that 'concrete hugger' across the street is one of them."

"Well, then you deserve her."

"No, I don't deserve her, Susan. But I am thankful she's mine."

She didn't stick around for any more of his discourse. Duke followed her to the door.

"Okay, show's over," Dad said as he passed the four of us and went into his office. The man had had a rough day. Duke stared at Susan from the window. She looked back only once. Duke snarled. She winced. Dog, one. Naughty newscaster, zero.

CHAPTER THIRTY-FOUR

The park bench gave a little as I sat down. The scene had expanded immensely over these full six days. Each side had grown larger and louder. Each sign had grown bigger and bolder. Each prayer was offered with greater passion and fervor. And each opposition to each prayer was offered with greater passion and fervor.

I heard the slow shuffle of black sandals and the swooshing sound larger thighs make when the nylons they are wearing brush together as one is walking. And I knew my lunch partner had arrived.

"You need to go talk to her, Savannah. At the end of the day, she's your mother."

I knew Joy was right. I needed to deal with my mother. She was out there fighting as hard as she could for what she believed in, while her daughter ignored her and other women kissed her husband. She deserved my respect. She had gone to great lengths this week, in large part for me alone. Well, for me and Thomas.

I didn't respond to Joy verbally, but actively. Walking toward my mother, I noticed the raven-haired beauty was rather close to her. I might have recommended she rethink this, as Mother had spent a week's worth of evenings in the humid outdoors, in the same attire. Granted, her makeup was fresh from the Mary Kay adventure, but the rest of her was disintegrating rapidly.

I approached unnoticed. That wasn't hard anymore. Things around here had grown to such a chaotic level that no one noticed much except what was blasted from a bullhorn. I slipped in under the volume of the other conversations, the protests, and the prayers. But in spite of the noise, I did hear Faith. I heard words that I'm sure were meant for my mother alone. But I heard each one of them. And let's just say, what followed wasn't pretty.

"You're nothing but a self-righteous, self-promoting little woman who has made herself a laughingstock in front of the entire nation. You should be more like your daughter and try to see at least some of the humor in this situation." As she backed her charcoal tresses up, her thousand-dollar designer pantsuit didn't look so attractive anymore. But the expression on my mother's face locked itself in my memory for what I knew would be forever. After all, who could ever forget the look of a shocked pig as it discovers that it is, well, a pig.

That raven lady could talk about this city. She could talk about my writing. She could talk about me, for crying out loud (which she had, and rather nicely). But now she had talked about my mama. If Faith were a Savannian, she'd know better than to talk about my mama, or to label my mother's actions as self-serving. Only I can do that. Plus, "self-serving" may have gotten Vicky here, but if I knew anything, I knew "self-serving" wouldn't have kept her here.

I stepped forward and startled the two beauties. "You need to step back, Ms. Austin."

"Savannah, this doesn't concern you. You've proven you're nothing like your mother," she quipped, no longer trying to hide her blatant disdain for Vicky. And she turned to go.

"So, is that what you do?" I asked. "Explode all over people and then walk away without giving them the opportunity to respond?"

She turned back around. The friendly look that she once

bestowed upon me had gone bye-bye. "You had an entire news-paper article to respond, Savannah, and you couldn't even come up with any passion of your own. Granted, it had humor, but there wasn't any substance in it."

"Don't bring me into this," I said getting rather uncomfortable with where this was going.

"Yeah, this is between me and you, sunshine!" my mother yelled, tugging at her chains.

"Mother, please." I motioned for her to move back.

"Well, isn't that what you and your mother do? Seek attention from the city? Use it to promote yourself?" She crossed her arms. I liked her better from the back.

"We don't use this city, *Ms.* Austin." I made sure the *Ms.* came out with a hissing noise. "We love this city. And no one loves it more than my mother. And she's not self-righteous. She lives what she believes."

"Give me a break. You're both hypocrites. You want to point out everyone else's sin and not admit to your own."

Well, if I had thought about confessing any sin, I wouldn't begin here on a sidewalk in the middle of a Savannah square. Because if I wasn't mistaken, every journalist in the place had just moved in about ten feet closer.

"That's what you people do, isn't it, Savannah?" she said, hissing to herself. "You sit your self-righteous bodies in position of power and try to determine the standards by which the world should live, while hiding the ghosts in your own closets." She began moving in closer. I wasn't sure whose closets she had been snooping in, but me and sister Vicky don't do ghosts. Or dead people. I began looking for Duke. He had already about eaten one woman for lunch today; he could go two for two. He wasn't anywhere to be found. Why would he be? I was standing next to my mother.

She moved in even closer. We were about to touch noses. And hers was a perfectly proportioned nose, I might add. But her eyes weren't quite as inviting as they had been in the past. "So why don't you quit hiding behind your little monument"—she turned to look at my mother—"and quit trying to make me look like the bad guy, and let the world know what you're really like, Savannah Phillips"— she turned back to me—"because this Miss Perfect performance has gone on long enough."

It was more than I could bear. It was as if a dam burst, and before I knew it, I threw both hands in the air, lifted my face to the sky, and screamed, "Okay, I STOLE A CAR DADDY!" Some gasped. Others cheered. Some laughed. My mother grabbed her chest, did a Fred Sanford move backward, and Ms. Austin didn't try to disguise her smirk. Every camera within the square started rolling, and pictures were snapped like I was Anna Kournikova.

"Yes, I stole a Sugar Daddy!" I confirmed to the listening world. "I saw a little girl licking it. It looked good. I begged for a lick, and when she finally held it out in her little hand, I snatched it and took off like a streak. Are you happy now?"

"Grow up, Savannah." She started walking off again. The crowd roared. But I wouldn't let her off so easy. Cheers or no cheers. I would follow.

"I have grown up, Ms. Austin. And I grew up in a whole new way this week alone."

She turned around one more time, not happy that we were having this song and dance. "Savannah, let's drop it. This will be over by the weekend anyway. The courts will get this monstrosity out of here, and you children can all go home to your million-dollar mansions and million-mile denials."

"You're the one in denial. And I'm not dropping it, because you started it." Another group cheered on that one. "I may have stolen a Sugar Daddy when I was seven, but you try to steal a person's good name and reputation, something it takes a lifetime to create. You destroy it with a sentence. I may have my own demons to deal with, but I would say you do too."

"I do not. And I don't steal Sugar Daddys *or* reputations."

"You just tried to no more than five minutes ago! You just

stood in front of a thousand television cameras and declared to the viewing public that my mother was here for no other reason than to get exposure. Well, that right there was breaking Number Nine, sister. And I've seen every other commandment broken this week too, in this very town."

"You need a life, Savannah."

"No, I've just learned to observe, Ms. Austin. In less than a week this city has lied about one another and stolen dreams, purses, and employers' time. I've listened to people who think they're God and then heard God's name used in more horrible ways than should be legal. I've watched women worship "lucky" dolls and Coca-Cola. I've even watched children shamelessly disobey their parents." Mother glared. I traveled to more comfortable ground. "I've even seen a woman try to commit adultery with—" I stopped. Well, maybe that ground wasn't too comfortable either.

"What?! What did you see?!" Vicky asked with eyes still in animated horror over the Sugar Daddy revelation.

"Well, that one doesn't need to be delved into right now. But my Lord, have mercy, someone was even killed this week. All of that, right here in the heart of this city. In the heart of *my* city," I declared, with a finger that tapped my own chest. Then I opened my arms to encompass the entire span of nuts. "This entire city has fallen apart in less than a week."

"Then you've said it yourself, Savannah. You can't, and these people can't." She motioned to those who had closed in around us. "None of you can even live by the very principles you're fighting over. Stealing a Sugar Daddy." Her laugh was only half-mocking. "I still say you're nothing but a bunch of hypocrites."

At those words, my mother tugged at her chains just far enough to grab the back of my shirt. She snatched me away and looked me square in the face and said, "Sit down, and sit down now. I will handle this from here. And when I'm through, I'll handle you and whoever this Sugar Daddy fella is that you've stolen."

I was about certain at that moment that the entire square gasped. The woman in chains had taken a deep breath and morphed into a woman that few had caught a glimpse of this week. Everyone stepped back and the path between her and Ms. Austin cleared.

"Ms. Austin, come here," Vicky summoned.

For a brief moment, Ms. Austin looked downright terrified. "I'm really through here."

"No, you're not through. Now, please, please come here, Faith." With those words mother's voice softened to that of just a mom. Not a monument percher, not a chamber of commerce president, not a city of Savannah commander and chief, just Victoria Phillips, a mother.

Ms. Austin inched closer, still uncertain whether the woman would leap. "You know what, Faith, you'd be right." That one made her stop. It made about everyone else stop too.

Ms. Austin coughed out her question. "About what?"

"You're right about the hypocrite part." Most everyone on the square gasped again, then leaned in closer. This was going to be good. "We do have things to learn. I learn ways I've screwed up every day. Well, almost every day." She was at least trying to be diplomatic. "But we all have things to learn. And right now *you* need to learn that I'm not self-righteous or self-serving. I'm out here for this little girl behind me." She pointed in my direction.

At times a mother's reference to you as her "little girl" fills you with warm, childlike euphoria. Standing in front of Ms. Austin, camera bulbs flashing and television cameras rolling, was not one of them.

"She's old enough to take care of herself." I wanted to agree with Ms. Austin there, but now didn't quite feel like the right time.

"Yes, she is," Mother said, looking back at me with a goofy smile. "But life is different now, Faith. You and my daughter belong to a generation that believes truth is a relative mind-set. It isn't."

"You and I have different opinions on that."

"Then we have fundamental differences, Faith."

"And, I've never stolen a Sugar Daddy," she spat like a two-year-old.

"Neither have I." Mother glared at me. "But trust me, that will be dealt with. And trust me on this, Faith: just because life changes, truth doesn't. Paint it black and call it brown and it's still black. Paint it mauve and call it aubergine and it's still mauve." I rolled my eyes. "That's what this means to me." She walked over to the monument and placed her hand atop it, never minding her chipped manicure. "But even if this monument crumbled into the sidewalk, the truth it holds at this moment would still be the truth."

Ms. Austin's phone broke the silence. "Ms. Austin." I was grateful for the reprieve. "What?!" she screamed into the phone. "I don't care! I don't give a flying flip what you want or what you think! I told you I would let you know. That means when I know something, you will know something! And right now I know I'm sick of answering this stupid phone!" And with that Ms. Austin's phone took a flying flip of its own, right across about six heads, skimmed a rather large swooped updo, and crashed into the wall of the Federal Building.

Ooh, sister's got a few issues with her cellular. Sergeant Millings woke up from his horse nap and grabbed his gun. That could have proven dreadful, had I not screamed out at him, "Whoa, doggies. Whoa. It was just a cell phone."

He looked around as if he was going to rid this city of all cellular activity, but he calmed down after a moment.

Ms. Austin's face began to grow redder than it had when she was screaming in the phone. Even strands of her hair had shaken loose from her ponytail during her breakdown. When she regained her composure, her mortification was apparent to all. I didn't mind. I needed the company.

She didn't ask again if Mother was through. She just turned quickly and walked away quickly. I watched her go. I liked her. I could have been her friend. Shoot, I could have been her. I didn't know what circumstances had brought her to the choices that framed her perspective. But I knew her decisions had determined her future.

Mother was still leaning against the monument. I realized now that she had been here for me, and for Thomas. All her efforts this week had been about preserving something of value for us to be able to preserve for our children. How strange. That was the same thing this monument was offering.

The treasures of what we have and have become can be found in the faces of those who raised us. Yet some never find a treasure there. So they fight forever to escape the faces of abuse. Others fight forever to run from faces of addiction. Some of us will even fight against faces that are just plain extraordinary. But looking at my mother, I realized ordinary would be boring. Who would want that?

I sneaked off before she remembered me. It would take her two hours to realize that Sugar Daddy was a candy and not a strange man I had stashed under my bed since I was a child. And I didn't need any other misunderstandings in the paper. So, I left her to return to work. But I would be back. I would be back to check on her soon.

"You left out something," Joshua's voice came as I rounded the corner to the back alley to head to my car. He was leaning up against it.

I was too tired to brush him off. "Did you hear all of that?" I asked, half-embarrassed, half too stressed to care.

"Every word. But you missed one."

I leaned up against the car and stared back. "And what *one* would that be?"

"The last one. The one about wanting what isn't yours."

"Joshua, just drop it." I opened my car door.

He shut it promptly. "No, Savannah. If you're going to deal with your 'demons,' as you call them, deal with all of them. And a perfect place to begin would be with this incessant desire of wanting something that isn't yours. You don't want Grant for any reason other than the fact that he belongs to someone else."

"You don't know what you're talking about!" I snapped.

"Yes, I do. You don't even look at him the way a woman looks at a man she loves."

"You don't know how I look at him."

"Yes, I do." He was as perfectly sickening as a half-rotten cucumber. "I saw you. You looked at him like a woman who was sad she had lost."

I abandoned all calm. "I love him, Joshua North! And how dare you try to make six years of commitment so . . . so meaningless and petty!"

"I didn't. You did."

"Leave me alone!" I said, trying to pull the handle to my car door, but he wouldn't move his arm to allow me to retreat. I wanted to cry. I wanted to scream. I wanted to slap him. I wanted to kiss him. I wanted to wrap my arms around his neck and lay one on him. And he knew I did. And that made it all the worse.

"You don't love him, Savannah," he said as he inched closer to my face. I could feel his arm behind my back as it held the door firmly closed. I refused to let any part of him affect me. I returned his cool demeanor with a cold stare. "He doesn't make your eyes dance. I've seen them dance. And it wasn't when you were looking at him." I felt his breath across my face. He let those words settle in the air between the two of us. We both knew what he meant. "Let him go. Let your pride go. Let this so-called hurt go. Let the desire to have what isn't yours go, just because it isn't yours. You're passionate Savannah. You deserve passion in return." He removed his arm from my car door. The very presence of it as it brushed my shirt created a feeling I refused to allow to surface.

"Are you finished?"

He got on his bike and headed down the alley. "I'm finished," he called back.

He and I both knew things had only begun.

CHAPTER THIRTY-FIVE

I collected myself in Katherine's Corner Bookstore before heading back to the office. Few places brought such comfort. Few things as well. But books, well, books were living entities to me. They triggered as many memories as poorly chosen love songs or badly splintered park benches. They brought to mind vacations and good years, and I enjoyed just looking at them. And if I could get a few undistracted minutes, maybe I could actually finish the one I've been reading.

"Savannah, I haven't seen you since lunch Friday."

"A lot has changed since Friday, Katherine." I smiled at the striking, petite, middle-aged storeowner approaching me with her undeniable freshness.

"I hear your mother has been at the monument since then."

I tried to focus on the new-books section. "What you hear is true."

She walked over and replaced a misplaced book on the shelf in front of me. I watched her graceful olive hand with short red-painted fingernails. Katherine was a former beauty queen herself. But she defied every stereotype known to the common population of man. Victoria was the personification of rhinestone tiaras, mascara cries, ridiculous talent costumes, and post-traumatic stress disorder. She is what every good novel or bad press coverage would define as the typical beauty pageant contestant. But Katherine, she was different. She was elegant and calm. Self-assured yet humble. Stunningly beautiful yet perfectly unassuming. We had met two weeks ago, when I discovered this world of hers for the first time. She had given me some of her secrets. But best of all, she had given me her friendship.

"How are you doing with that?" she asked me. "With everything that is going on at the courthouse?"

"I don't know."

"You mean you don't have an opinion?"

"Oh, no, I have a multitude of opinions. I'm just not sure what I know about all the opinions that I have. Couldn't you tell by my article?"

She laughed. "Savannah, you are too young to be so complex."

"And I hear I look the worse for wear because of it."

"Who told you that?"

"A stranger in a floral dress. She said I looked old, or maybe she called me tired. No, actually I think *worn out* were her exact words."

She giggled at my pouty lips and droopy demeanor. "Savannah, you look beautiful. Are you talking about the elderly African American lady with the straw bag?"

"That's her! Has she been in here too?"

"No, but I've seen her on the street a couple times. The dress caught my attention."

I sat down on the steps that led to the fiction section of the bookstore. "What do you think is up with her?"

"Probably lonely. Maybe retired, or her spouse has died."

"But don't you think her children would tell her, 'Mother, let's please don some different attire'?"

She laughed. "You crack me up, Savannah." She sat down beside me, and her pressed khaki pants slid up at the ankles, fully exposing her cute little black slip-on sandals.

"And she follows me."

"She follows you?"

"Yeah, and she wants my food."

"What?"

"Serious. I had to share my lunch with her on Sunday. I mean, I didn't mind, but with Mother up there strapped to cement, I've been a little sensitive about the whole food issue."

"Well, who knows? Maybe she's sent to teach you something. Get yourself a good book and put your mind at ease."

"I've got one I can't find time to finish. Besides, everything in life shouldn't be a lesson." I stood and scanned the books. The title *Ten Minutes from Normal* jumped out at me. "I'm glad Karen Hughes knows where Normal is. I couldn't find it with a wall map and a day to waste."

"Well, you could ask her where it is. I hear she'll be with the president tomorrow."

"Oh, my word, I forgot the president was coming tomorrow. He's one president I won't have to read about. I already know his life story."

"You do, huh?"

"Oh, yeah, Vicky has the hots for him."

"Savannah," she said, giggling, "you shouldn't talk that way about your mother. She is in love with your father."

"She may be in love with my father, but I shall not tell a lie after the kind of day I've witnessed: the woman would love to be Laura Bush for a day."

"She would whip your heinie for that."

"I wish she was home to whip my heinie; that would mean she was cooking too."

"You could cook for yourself."

"Tried it. Didn't work."

"Some things have to be tried more than once."

"And some things are better left to the experts." I gave her a good-natured wave, and the bell gave its *ding-a-ling-a-ling* at my departure.

"You sure can find a way to get into the middle of things," said a strange voice as I closed the door.

"Emma!" I was unable to hide my shock. "What happened to you? I mean, you're clean . . . I mean . . . you're . . . well, you're just clean."

"You made your point." She tried to stifle a laugh. "Are you always so honest?"

I felt my face flush. "I'm sorry. It's a curse. Man . . . you just look . . . you look fabulous. I thought I'd seen you around town a couple times. I just wasn't quite sure it was you."

"Well, it's me." She ran her hands along the seams of her tailored khaki sundress. The black piping lay strikingly upon her golden skin. The sallow tone present just last week was gone.

"What happened?"

"Uh, humiliation maybe?" She looked straight at me.

I tried not to flinch. "Are you going to yell at me again?"

She smiled. "No. I was harsh. But you deserved it."

"I deserved worse, actually."

"I probably did too." She lowered her head and fingered the bow at her delicate waist. I tried to change the subject.

"You been eating?"

"What?"

"You just look a little healthier."

"Yes, I've been eating."

"Do you want to go eat with me sometime? Maybe talk, like normal people?"

"No," she said flatly.

"No?"

"No. I'm not really ready to be your friend."

"Eating lunch together would make us friends?"

"Yes." She turned to go. "Well, try not to add to anyone else's troubles."

"I'm really sorry for hurting you, Emma." I hoped she knew I meant it.

She turned around to look at me with the beauty I remembered from her high-school days. "It didn't turn out all bad, Savannah. Look at me." She held her arms out at her sides.

I nodded. "Yeah. Look at you."

She left, but I would see her again. And one day I'd buy her lunch.

Peggy Noonan's book was lying on the corner of my desk. I lifted it up in my hands, and it opened to page 65. The red underlines from my own pen caught my eye. They marked her reflection on Reagan's character as it related to his stance on communism.

"It was in this drama that Reagan's character was fully revealed," she wrote. "In a time of malice he was not malicious; in a time of lies he did not falsify; in a time of great pressure he didn't bend or break; in a time of disingenuousness he was clear and candid about where he stood and why. And in a time when people just gave up after a while and changed the subject, he remained on the field through all the long haul."

I laid the book down and saw my article still resting on the corner of my desk. After the events of my lunch hour, it didn't feel like the right story to tell. No, as backward as it sounded, the human-interest story I really needed to explore was mine: the story of the bystander, the uninvolved, the ill-equipped, the student, the one who hadn't broken under the pressure but avoided it altogether. Maybe exploring this story would help to establish the depths of a relationship, the trust that comes with a writer and her audience. Maybe it would help them to understand me. Maybe it would help me to understand me. The city and I had both suffered our share of upheavals this week. Maybe in a few paragraphs I could help us both discover what we'd learned.

I worked hard until two o'clock. And at the last moment, with no time to spare, the pages slipped out of the printer, and I headed to Mr. Hicks to meet my deadline.

Jessica all but ducked under her desk when she saw me come around the corner.

"Hello, Jessica." I peered over the corner of the low-walled cubicle that surrounded her desk.

She didn't respond.

"You can't stay under there forever."

She didn't respond again.

"I'll catch you when I come back." I proceeded to Mr. Hicks's open door and knocked lightly.

A loud thump came from behind me. "Ow!" And the blonde carpet inspector came up rubbing her head.

"Come in," Mr. Hicks offered. "What's so funny, Savannah?"

"Oh, nothing much," I said, trying to control myself.

"Is this your article?"

"Yes, sir. All finished."

"Are you pleased?"

"Pleased? Let's just say I've come to terms with myself."

"Well, let's hope that's a good thing."

"It is." I turned back to the door and paused to ask a final question. "Am I going to be on the cover of the paper tomorrow?"

He looked up from his desk with a slight smirk. "From the reports from the field I have received, yes ma'am, I believe you are."

"Arms spread-eagle."

"That's the one."

"Declaring I'm a thief?"

"Very probable."

"I figured."

"You did?"

"Yes, sir, I'm pretty good at figuring nowadays."

I sneaked into the ladies' room before I went back to my cubicle. Three Cokes and no lunch made for an uncomfortable situation. I peered underneath the stalls just to make sure I didn't walk in on any unsuspecting soul. There were feet in two but none in one, three, four or five. I settled for three. As I locked the door, another pair of feet came to occupy four.

I like to look at feet underneath stalls. Even wrote an entire short story on them for my junior year creative writing course. "The Stories of Shoes in a Stall," I called it. Today's feet both wore flip-flops. Stall number two's flip-flops were black, and the toes were short and plump. They housed their small, unpainted toenails with great padding and protection. As if they just plumped right up around them. Stall number four housed white flip-flops.

I love this place. The owner of the white flip-flops had long toe-nails painted a deep metallic rust. The nails hung slightly over the toes and were long and narrow. Downright weird. Toenails tend to be a reflection of the individual. Vicky wears red. Always red. Paige wears clear. Always clear. I wear pink. Always pink. In-your-face Victoria. Always-brutally-honest Paige. Always trying to be not quite in your face and hopefully honest, at least when possible, me.

As we each arrived to wash our hands at the same time, I had known before I saw them what they would look like. Their feet had given them away.

"Knock, knock," came the voice on the other side of my nonexistent door.

"Hey, Claire. Welcome to my office. Come in and have a seat." This friend of mine was solely responsible for acquiring my apart-ment with her fabulous real-estate skills.

"I don't have much time. I've got to go show a house in a few minutes. I just wanted to drop off your new keys so you could get your stuff moved in." She held out the two keys that hung from a long metal loop with a Cora Betts Realty marketing tool at the end.

"This is it, huh?" I asked, holding out my hand cautiously.

She dropped them into my hand. "Yes, my sweet friend. These are the keys to a new way of living." I looked at them as if they were some medieval torture device. "I'm not sensing an overwhelming rush of excitement."

I looked up at her pretty yet uniquely proportioned face. "It's just all happened a little quick."

"This has been years in the making, Savannah."

"Yeah, I guess." I glanced down at my toes, then returned to her pleasant smile. "Where do I drop off my rent again?"

"Here," she said, handing me a sheet of paper with a ten-digit number on it. "Go to Bank of America and make a deposit into this account. That's all you have to do."

"You still won't tell me who it is?"

"He doesn't feel it's necessary. Makes his life less complicated if everything goes through me. Now, enough worrying. I'll stop by later, when I get off work. I'll help you move if you need me."

"Oh, no. I think I'll be fine. I don't have a lot of stuff. Thomas and Paige are helping me."

"Well, call me if you need me." She lifted my chin and put her other hand on my shoulder. "This will be one of the most exciting things you have ever done."

"Do I have the look of someone who needs added excitement?"

"This move is about you, Savannah. Not your father, not your mother, just you. This is a grown-up thing."

"I need to be grown up?"

"Yes, you do. Now I've got to go." And she gave me a hug and walked off.

"I'll miss my mommy," I whispered. But she was safely out of earshot. I was glad. I was wishing I hadn't heard it either.

CHAPTER THIRTY-SIX

Police dogs were sniffing a Shih Tzu. And she wasn't any too happy about it. The entire strip of Bull Street was blocked off by the secret service and local police squads conducting a sweep of the Historical District in preparation for the president's appearance here tomorrow. Their presence forced me to go on down a block farther to Lincoln Street and cross back down East State Street to get to Jake's. In the hubbub of the last week, I had failed to ask why in the world the president was actually coming here. Victoria probably knew every last detail of his schedule. She did have Internet access, remember.

I pulled into my covered parking place. The Culpepper's Buick no longer resided here. That had left almost a month ago now. And it was no longer the *future* home of Old Betsy, but the present home of one Savannah Phillips and Old Betsy. Old Betsy had never seen shelter a day in her life. If no one else appreciated this new stage of our journey, she would.

I didn't even go into Jake's. Everyone had left already anyway. I slowly climbed the stairs up to the back entrance of my new residence. There is a front entrance as well, a door to the side of

Jake's. But this one closest to the carport would be the one I'd use most.

I put the key into the door and for a brief moment hoped it wouldn't fit. Then I could regretfully delay this transition of life. But it turned with ease. And as the door opened, so the next page of my life's book turned. I had no clue what it would tell.

I walked slowly through the halls and through each room. I opened cabinets and turned on lights. I tried to imagine how life would play out here. But some moments in life aren't even imaginable. Some you can only experience. This would be one.

I sat down in the middle of the bedroom floor, and the enormity of this moment slammed into me like a lovebug on the windshield of a semi. I cried. I'm not sure why. It just felt like what I needed to do. So it is what I did. And I continued until I lifted my head and caught sight of the green tennis ball lying in the far back corner of the closet, whose door was opened. Then I began to laugh. That ball reminded me that I wasn't really leaving home. That ball confirmed that my "anonymous" landlord and his "golden" companion would always be just one floor below. And inside my heart after hours.

"When did you get here?" I asked Paige as I got out of the car. She was sitting on the bottom step of my parents' house.

"Oh, about thirty minutes ago."

"Do you keep office hours?"

She scrunched her lips and crinkled her nose as if this question required deep thought. "No."

She followed me into the house, and we heard Thomas pull up as we headed inside. You couldn't help but hear him. His Jeep was rather loud. Vicky lost her battle for an LTD the same way she lost the one to get me in a Lincoln Town Car: vanquished by Jake. Her argument for me was safety. Her argument for Thomas was if he was going to a military school, he should have an American-made car. She made this point one afternoon as she climbed into her powder-blue Mercedes two-seater convertible. And Jake went and bought Thomas a Jeep and let her know that it *was* made in America.

Thomas bounded up the stairs and came into the room. "You two ready to get moving?"

"Why are you in such a hurry for me to leave?"

"Because he wants your bathroom," Paige said.

"You better stay out of my bathroom with your filth," I warned him clearly.

"I have my own bathroom, in case you two forgot. And truth be told, yours isn't my shade of yellow. Now, grab a box and let's get this party moving."

"What's this?" Paige asked as she picked up the tiny tan box with orange stripes and white lettering.

"Give that to me!" I snatched it from her hand.

"It's empty, Savannah."

"No! It's not empty." I looked at it, trying to stifle the lump in my throat. "It's full! It's full of memories. Memories I'm not ready to get rid of!"

Thomas walked over and stared at it, squinting. "It looks like the box to a tiny halogen light bulb."

"That's exactly what it is." I jerked it out of his sight and turned my back.

Paige jerked me back around. "Who gave you that?"

I refused to answer.

"Savannah Phillips, who gave you that little box?"

"Grant! Okay, Grant gave me this box."

"Well, no wonder you dumped him, if that's his idea of romance." Thomas sat down on the floor, realizing we weren't going anywhere fast.

I sat beside him. "It was romantic, Thomas. It went to a lamp we had found in an alley on our first date."

Paige surrendered to the moment and collapsed on the floor as well. "Wait. You were walking in an alley on your first date?"

I looked at her with disdain. "Yes! He was walking me to my

car that I had left behind Dad's store. And the Culpeppers had left this great lamp by their trash. He picked it up and said we should restore it. That we'd have a memento from our first date."

"A lamp from a trash can was your memento?"

"We were sixteen, Paige. For crying out loud, we didn't have a pot to pee in."

Thomas quipped, "You would have if you'd gotten a job."

"My occupational past has nothing to do with this conversation."

"So why in the world do we have to keep this box?" Paige mused.

"Because for four years we never could find a lightbulb. We had repaired the lamp, made it absolutely beautiful, but it never worked, because it needed this specific kind of bulb that we couldn't find."

Thomas fell back on the floor and closed his eyes. "My Lord, this is a long story."

"It's a story of love, Thomas. They don't occur in ten-second sound bites."

"They should."

"Well, one day, during my sophomore year, I'm in my bedroom studying, and I hear this knock on my door. When I opened it, Grant was standing there. He holds up this little box and says, 'I found it!' 'Found what?' I asked him. 'I found the bulb. I finally found us a bulb.'"

Thomas let out a moan. I kicked him.

I held the box up and felt the tears return to the brim of my rather long eyelashes. "Grant drove all the way from Clemson just to tell me he had found us a bulb. So, now you know why there is no way in the world that I can ever throw this box away."

"Oh, baby!" Paige said, wrapping her arm around me. "You keep that as long as you want to. That's a precious story."

"It's a stupid story! And you're both pathetic," Thomas said as rose to his feet and slapped us both on the tops of our heads. "The boy is getting married, Savannah. Give it up!" He was starting to sound annoyingly like Joshua.

"It ain't over till he's walked down the aisle," I informed him.

"Whatever you say, little dreamer. Now, grab a box." He tossed one to each of us. I tucked my little memory inside my purse and shoved Joshua's ridiculous accusations to the back of my mind. I would find a safe place in my new home for one. And a trash can for the other.

For the next two hours we loaded up every last piece of my furniture and made trips to my new apartment. The one that required us holding the mattresses on top of Thomas's Jeep was a rather interesting haul. Paige refused to sit on top after Thomas declared her behind too big. That caused a few moments of tension. But we just hung out of the windows and rested our elbows on top, while Thomas meandered through a maze of roadblocks and men in black.

By eight o'clock we all collapsed on the floor of the living room. And when I entered the kitchen to drink out of the faucet—since I had no cups or anything else to put in a kitchen for that matter—I was welcomed by a sight of a stack of plastic cups, plastic flatware, paper plates, a bag of ice, Cokes, and a large cheese pizza. Oh, and there was a note. A note from my new landlord, welcoming me to my new home. Signed, well, "Landlord." A trip he must have made in between our final loads. And a pizza just like I would like it. A pizza that only a father would know.

"Dinner is served." I distributed pizza to my hungry helpers.

"Ooh, let's sit on the balcony and eat. That way we can see what's going on across the street," Paige said as she flung open the French doors to the balcony. We had a perfect view of the square. And a perfect view of my mother.

"This is like dinner and a movie," Paige said, ripping into her pizza. "It would be perfect with Doritos."

The child was ill. "Mom looks kind of nice," Thomas said, guzzling down some Coke.

I patted him on the back as our feet dangled over the balcony.

"You are a sweet son, you know. To find 'nice' in that is optimism in it's finest form."

"Well, she did freshen up her makeup," Paige added. "Maybe that's what he's noticing."

I looked hard. I wanted to see it. But the harsh floodlights on the sidewalk that saturated her with unflattering shades of white made her look, dare I say, plumb nasty. "She needs a bath. I mean, this woman might see the president tomorrow, and she looks like Homeless Hannah."

Paige nodded. "But in very expensive shoes."

"Yes, and matching handbag. Don't forget the handbag," I said.

"Oh, yes. Of course."

"She needs a mint, too." Thomas responded. "She's battling Duke for just plain stank! Shoot, I bet that's what the people on *Survivor* smell like."

"*Survivor*! Oh my gosh, she missed *Survivor* tonight!" I said in total shock.

"No, she didn't. She's got a TV out there. Look, she's watching it right now." And she was. Battery-operated TV. Headset. And she was talking to the TV. She was watching *Survivor* all right. "And it will be over in perfect time for her interview on *Hannity & Colmes*."

No one was surprised.

"Oh, I think that Sean Hannity is a fine specimen of a man," Paige offered, drifting away.

"He is cute," I offered. "I think he should have won sexiest newscaster."

"He would have if that MSNBC man hadn't shamelessly promoted himself," Paige retorted.

Thomas threw his two cents in. And trust me, that was a high estimate. "You think anything that walks and breathes is fine."

Paige retorted. "I do not. You aren't all that."

"*You aren't all that,*" he mimicked.

"Just tell me she's not going to have another *Survivor* party this year," Paige said.

"Not if I can help it," I assured her.

"Well, it's your fault, Savannah," Thomas added. "If you hadn't told her to watch that very first season finale, none of us would have to endure it at all."

"It's not my fault," I protested. "I was just trying to help her branch out."

"Well, you better hope this season isn't in Africa, because I'm not giving Jeep rides to a soul," Thomas assured us both. Like we were the ones who would ask him.

"Well, I'm not wearing a colorful sarong that calls my tribe *Victoriajumanji* either."

"I guess we should just be grateful that she's never tried to enter herself. Watching her audition tape would make safari tours in my Jeep feel like a bearable punishment."

I comforted him. "She couldn't audition. Contestants are allowed only one luxury item. That woman would vote herself off by day two if she couldn't wax, pluck, and inject."

He nodded across the square. "I would have agreed with you there last week. But not anymore. She has effectively brought to ruin any notion of what I thought she would and would not do in this life."

The mere observation caused each of us to groan.

Paige interjected. "Neither of you should complain. At least you get pizza every Thursday night."

"On china plates," I informed her. "And I did not say *Chinette*."

"And I didn't say your mother wasn't half-crazy. I just said you got one night to eat something that came out of a box."

"But it is made from scratch," I assured her.

"Whatever."

"I think I'm going to buy me a sundress."

Paige's face contorted. "To wear to your mother's *Survivor* party?"

"I'm not talking about *Survivor* anymore, Paige."

"There are drugs for that."

"So, should I?"

"Should you what?"

Thomas broke in. "Should she buy a dress, Paige. My word, even I know what she's talking about."

"That's because your illness runs in the family."

He flicked her. She flicked back.

"Why do you want a sundress?" she asked me. "You hate dresses."

"I don't know. I just think they're . . . well . . . kind of pretty. Maybe it's stupid."

"Yes, it's stupid," Thomas said.

Paige glared at him. "It's not stupid. It would be lovely on you. Okay, enough fun," she said as she began to rise. "Ow, ooh, oh, that hurts." She moved slow for a vibrant woman of twenty-four.

Thomas showed no mercy as he stood up. "You're pathetic."

"She's an old soul, Thomas."

"With old parts, obviously."

Paige reprimanded us both. "Would you two quit talking about me like I'm not here?"

"You need to work out," I told her, setting our plates on the counter. I'd need to get a trash can.

"I don't work out. I'll mess up my sleek lines." She ran her hands across her stomach and the little pouch that had formed after her four pieces of pizza. "And I wouldn't have this pouch had your landlord brought Diet Coke."

"You're sad," I said, giving her a hug.

"Well, you're a homeowner." She hugged me back.

"Renter," I corrected.

"Whatever. You don't live with your mama anymore. What are you doing? Is your foot itching again?"

"Yes. It means—"

Thomas answered for me. "It mean's she's going to walk on new ground. And if her hand itches, one means she's going to get pleased; the other means she's going to get money. And if her nose itches, someone's coming to see her. And if her head itches, it means . . . that she's realized it's empty."

I slapped him.

"I know what it means," Paige said. "She was doing it the other night at my house. Sister might need a new pair of sneakers with all the walking she's going to be doing."

"Well, you two girls have fun. I'm going to check on Duke."

"Yeah, I've got to go back to the house for a few last items."

"Toilet paper?" Paige asked.

Toilet paper hadn't crossed my mind. They could tell. "Are you sure you'll survive?" Thomas asked.

"She has to. She owes me money," Paige said. And we laughed our way to the sidewalk.

"Oh," I said, bounding back up the stairs. "I forgot to lock the door."

I heard Thomas in the distance. "I'll give her a week."

Paige's faith in two weeks wasn't any more affirming. I shut the door and searched for the keys. They were sitting by the still-open balcony doors.

"I've got to do better than this," I muttered. I looked out over the packed square, and the sight of my mother reached my eyes like a lighthouse beam through a settled fog. The very woman I was trying to escape was as close to me now as she had been on most evenings. Yet seeing her here felt reassuring, dare I say comforting. No, I wasn't moving from her—I was moving toward me. But truth be told, I would sleep better tonight knowing she was right outside.

CHAPTER THIRTY-SEVEN

My bedroom looked different. The shelves were empty, save the dust that had collected from the lack of attention since Sister Victoria had become Savannah's patron saint. I walked around the hardwood floors that echoed with the flipping of my flops. I peered out my window at the familiar scene of Clary's and the cracks in the sidewalk and the street I had awakened to every morning.

I left the drapes up. I didn't know how to hang them anyway. And I had to leave Vicky something to do for me when she was released. I wandered over to my bathroom and stared into the completely clean space. There wasn't even dirt to imagine. It was spotless. And my galoshes and knee pads were packed up.

I sat down in the middle of my floor. I peered at the perfectly round smudges on my yellow walls from countless games of fetch-the-slobber-ball. There was the small dent in the door frame that I made with Thomas's head after a mean battle of wills over who was going to get to the first pool party of the summer. I lost by default. There were the notches I had made in the windowsill, recording the times I had sneaked out through the years. Vicky thought I was keeping track of most-outstanding-student accolades. Jake knew and eventually put an alarm chime on my window. I disconnected it right after installation.

The thought of that made me laugh. The memories were really priceless to me. And no matter how many times one dreams of spreading her wings and flying away, or up the street, the actual event means one has officially grown up. College isn't growing up. College is a supervised transition. You still live off of Mom and Dad's money. Well, some of us do; there are always exceptions. And you live with a bunch of other mindless, overexalted youth like yourself.

But moving out. Paying rent. Sleeping alone. Those are grownup things. Waking yourself up for work. That is downright elderly. But necessary. And my growing up was happening today.

The distant sound of thunder caused the hardwood to vibrate underneath me. It brought me out of my soap-opera moment. I stood up and walked over to the windowsill and flaked off a small wood splinter sticking out from one of my last notches, brought on by a need to have ice cream with Paige and Grant at a godforsaken hour of the morning.

The sky over Savannah had turned pitch black. It was already almost ten, but there had been stars out on my last trip home. Looking up, I was met with another clap of thunder that felt as if it had just landed on top of my house. My entire body shook. And before I knew it, rain was pouring from the sky like Savannah hadn't seen in over a week.

The rain felt poignant for the moment, a washing of the old to begin the new. Then the reality of what was happening struck me about the same time the lightning hit the tree across the street.

"Oh my stars, my mother!" I screamed as I looked out of the window.

The next few minutes were a flurry of activity. I ran around that house like Robin Williams with his fake boobs on fire in *Mrs. Doubtfire*. In less than five minutes I was flying up the street only to be blocked by yellow barricades. I swallowed the desire to curse and instead drove around the block and parked on the curb behind the courthouse. If they wanted to come out in this mess and tow my car, have at it.

People were scampering under makeshift shelters, running for cover under local shop awnings, and scurrying up the street, racing the cockroaches. I reached Mother only to find her resembling a wet rat. It wasn't pretty. It was downright grisly. Her umbrella offered no escape from the blowing rain. And the tent the local funeral home had loaned was being chased across the square by a couple men. Vicky's Mary Kay had slid to her chin. Her hair was plastered to her scalp, goo stung her eyes from the way she was batting them, and her clothes were waterlogged. And the poor thing had taken to crying. Well, more like blubbering, but I wasn't about to throw stones. I hadn't been outside for almost an entire week and had still done substantial blubbering today myself.

"Hurry, help me set this up," I commanded my father, who was running up the sidewalk. In a few minutes we were all soaked but sheltered by Thomas's camping tent, with only the end of a chain sticking out on the other side.

"Thank you," my mother cried and gasped at the same time. "Thank you, darling, for saving your *mooootheeeer* . . ." She wailed and threw her head in my lap.

"It's okay, Mother," I said, patting her head. I picked up my hand and tried to sling off the product that she had apparently thought should be added each day. "This is disgusting," I mouthed to my father, who rested on the other side of her in our tent.

"Be nice," he mouthed back with a smile.

"Don't leave me, Savannah. Please don't leave me," she cried, never looking up. It was a most heart-wrenching moment.

"I won't, Mother. I won't." I rubbed her rain-drenched arm and watched as the water dripped from her elbow onto her pants.

"I'll leave you two girls for a while."

"You sure you want to do that?" I asked, my eyes making clear what I desired him to do. Stay.

"Yes, I'm sure. I better check on Duke anyway. He's probably floating up Abercorn somewhere. I'll be back later." And my only remnant of sanity walked out into the deep, dark, night.

"Okay, you need to get up now," I said, trying to pull her by the elbow.

"I don't wanna," she moaned.

"Mother, seriously, who's the parent here?"

"It should probably be you at this point." Her sounds were muffled as they tunneled from the side of my leg.

"Really, get control. We need to make you beautiful." I tried to tug her again.

"That's impossible. Have you seen me?"

So she had seen herself. This was worse than I thought. The woman had seen herself and still stayed out in public. "Yes, I've seen you. And you look . . . well, you look worn."

She wailed louder. "I've paid a heavy price for freedom."

"People have paid heavier, I assure you."

"I *know!*" and she wailed one more time. This made me laugh. "Don't laugh at me. I'm bruised."

"I'm not laughing at you, I'm laughing . . . well, with you."

"That's impossible! Because I'm not laughing."

She had a point. Who was to know what was water running down my leg and what was snot at this point. "Please, Mother, seriously. Get up." I tugged with great effort, and the battered and tattered former Miss Georgia United States of America rose with her own hair looking as if it had formed itself into a matted tiara of its own.

"Ooh, nice."

"Savannah Phillips. Do not laugh at me. I'm not in the mood. I'm sore and I'm wet. And I haven't had my own cooking in a week."

"Well, let's not even go there. This could ruin a perfectly good evening."

"Do you know what I would fix for dinner if I were home?" she asked, eyes glazing over, tongue fluttering across her lips. "I'd fix a chuck roast, slice some potatoes and carrots in there. Cover it with a little flour, salt and pepper, add some onion gravy and mushroom gravy. Bake it at 350 for three hours." She was hallucinating. "Fix some butter beans, corn, macaroni and cheese, get out some hot peppers and make homemade biscuits."

I was hallucinating. "Stop it! Stop it!" I snapped my fingers in front of her face. She came back to our world. "I will not talk with you about food one more moment. If you do, I will leave."

She grabbed hold of me in a death grip and started to wail again. "Please don't leave me, darling! Please! Please!"

I jerked her up again. "Now, get a grip! I am here for one reason and one reason alone. I am here to make you beautiful."

"Look at me, Savannah. Are you blind, child? I am permanently maimed. My beauty is a forgotten treasure. My song a forgotten cadence in the Savannah atmosphere."

"Okay, drama queen, enough." I squared her at the shoulders and faced her head-on. "I have starved this week. I have had to turn my underwear on inside out. And I have had to sleep in a house by myself. So, we have no place for drama this evening."

"Why are you here?" she asked, brown eyes looking like the local lush's after a ten-day drinking binge.

"I'm here because my mother is not going to meet the president of the United States looking, well, looking like . . ."

"Go ahead, you can say it. Like a former beauty queen."

"Actually no, I was going to say, like a streetwalk—"

"Savannah!"

"But, if former beauty queen makes you feel better, then that's what you can have."

"You better have magic in that bag with that kind of talk."

"Sister, I've got anything your heart desires. But we are starting from the top down. We begin with the hair," I said, pulling some shampoo and conditioner out of my huge duffel bag. "The rest of you is wet, so let's get this hair cleaned up."

"How will I rinse it?"

"You will stick your head outside this tent in that downpour and let nature have its way."

"Ooh, good idea."

She about drowned on the final rinse. But I told her if she put herself facedown instead of nose up, she might be able to breathe without water going up her nose. I scrubbed that head like one would scrub Duke after a mud bath. We wrapped a clean towel around her saturated head, and then we got to work on that face. We cleaned it from top to bottom, and then we dealt with the breath issue. I treaded sensitively and did not subject her to any comparisons to Duke before he got his two rotted teeth pulled.

"Now, how are we going to change your clothes?" I asked, studying the once pale baby blue pantsuit that had turned a lovely shade of burnt teal.

"Oh, that's an easy one," she responded nonchalantly.

"Oh it is?"

"Oh sure. I've got the keys to the handcuffs right here in my purse. I can just take them off and change real quick and then put them back on."

"You mean for six days you have worn the same outfit every day when you could have changed clothes?"

"Duh, Savannah. Do you think I would let someone else keep the key to these chains?"

"Please don't say *duh.*"

"Okay. Uh, Savannah"—she could be a total smart aleck—"I couldn't very well change clothes every day. Wouldn't that have made a real statement. This process has meant something to me, and I wanted to make sure people realized that."

"Well, nothing could have said that more than Victoria Phillips in the same outfit for one week straight."

"My sentiments exactly," she said, nodding and thankful I had finally discovered her obvious intentions.

"Well, you can't wear that tomorrow to see the president."

"You don't think?" she asked, looking down. It was kind of like the look a person gives you when you question whether they have gained weight. Because it came upon them gradually, they don't quite see the degree to which they really need intervention. And the hand passes over the body as if feeling for themselves to make sure the other's assessment is accurate.

"No, that outfit, my sweet child, will have to be burned."

"Burned?!"

"Yes, burned."

"Do you know how much this cost?"

"I have a good idea, but this outfit is ruined. And this is not Burger King, so, you can forget about having it your way today."

"Blah, blah, blah." She could be so childish for a forty-five-year-old. "Well, I don't have to decide that today." And she didn't. I would decide it for her. Because it was going in the bag I had, and she would never see it again.

"I brought you some pajamas." I pulled some beautiful pale pink cotton pajamas out of my "magic" bag.

"Ooh, I didn't know I had those." She eyed them like a bowl of Ben and Jerry's chocolate-brownie-chunk ice cream after a four-month chocolate fast. Then her delight turned to puzzlement. "Why didn't you bring me a nightgown?"

"Because you are sleeping on the s-t-r-e-e-t."

"Oh."

She had her a nice sponge bath and put on her warm pajamas, and because of the safety of her makeshift home, no one was the wiser that for the first time in a week, Victoria Phillips was free from chains. I looked down at her once beautifully jewelry-adorned right wrist, which had been handcuffed to her chain, and noticed it was now adorned with a huge red strip of swollen skin where the handcuff had rubbed her for the last six days. But as soon as she slipped into her pink pajamas, she handcuffed herself once again.

"Mother, no one will know you don't have those on. You could sleep without them for one night."

"I would know. That would be enough." She pulled her arms

up around her, enjoying the feeling of being clean. "My pillows are soaked." She pointed to the pillows that sat next to her rolled-up sleeping bag that we had pulled from the rain.

I gave her a wink. "I've got extra." I pulled two perfectly fabulous down-feather pillows from my bag.

"You got drugs in there too. 'Cause I think you're high as a kite." Her brow crinkled.

"Would you hush and let me dry your hair?" I jerked the towel on her head. We decided instead to let her hair dry naturally to avoid electrocution from the downpour. Then we would use the battery-operated curling iron that I had brought before she went to sleep. We could fluff it up again in the morning. But at least she was clean.

We dried off her sleeping bag, tossed her foul clothes in the bag, and sealed them up. When those were safely tucked away, I laid out a beautiful pink suit that I had brought, with cream pumps, for her viewing of the president of the United States tomorrow.

I pulled us out two bottled waters, but she declined hers. "I try not to drink much. You know. The bathroom thing and all," she whispered. She hurt my heart. Until tonight I hadn't thought about all she had been going through.

We fluffed out our fresh pillows and laid down on the sleeping bag. "This was fun, Savannah. Thank you. Ooh, my right hand's itching. That means I'm going to get pleased. But I couldn't be any more pleased than I am right now." She looked up at me, smiling.

"You know, I think we're going to have to deal with that."

She gave me a look of an exasperated child. "Now what?"

"That old wives' tale stuff. It's either number one or two on here," I said, tapping the concrete monument behind us. "I'm not sure which. But we shouldn't be believing in it."

"You don't think?"

"No, I really don't."

"Well, my Lord have mercy, I'm sitting here chained to this monument, and I'm breaking these commandments even as I breathe."

"It's okay. We're going to do better." We nestled down into our sleeping bags, and I stared up at the ceiling of the red nylon tent. "Tell me a story, Mother."

"What kind of story?"

"You know, like the stories you told Thomas on Sunday."

She giggled. "Oh, about my antics as a little girl?"

"Yeah, those kind of stories."

"Well, after that we need to talk about your little-girl antics."

"Oh, the whole city will be talking about that tomorrow; let's save something to talk about for then."

"But, Savannah, who is this 'Sugar Daddy?' Did you have a crush on Virginia Cooper's daddy, Sug?"

I belly laughed. "Are you for real?"

"Are you depraved? My stars, child, you were just a baby."

"For your information, crazy woman, a Sugar Daddy is a piece of candy, and Sug was Virginia's mother's pet name for her husband, Larry. I stole candy, Mother. Now, get over it. No more talk about it. Please."

"Well, thank the Lord and call off the cavalry, because I was about to search your room from stem to stern, and see where Sug was hiding." She giggled after that. She may play stupid, but we both knew she was smart as a tack.

For the next two hours my mother shared some of the funniest, silliest, and greatest stories I have ever heard. And for the first time in a week, I slept like a baby. Who cared that the newspaper would declare I was a thief tomorrow. Who cared that I was sleeping on the sidewalk, in a tent, in front of the courthouse, with a crazy mama. She was *my* crazy mama. And I was immensely proud of her.

CHAPTER THIRTY-EIGHT

O w, pain." I tried to stretch my body out.

Mother pulled her earplugs from her ears. "What?"

"I'm battered and bruised," I said, rubbing my backside.

"I know. I'm permanently debilitated," Mother said, rubbing her eyes. "But you get used to it." This from a woman who takes her own sheets to hotels.

"There ain't no way."

"Don't say ain't."

"Don't boss me around at the crack of dawn."

She laughed. "I am bossy, aren't I?"

"Totally," I said, leaning up on my elbow to look at her.

She rolled over on her side so we could talk face to tired face. "Your dad thinks I'm a control freak."

"You are."

Her eyes widened in complete shock.

"I'm certain of it."

"What makes you think that?"

"You are chained to a monument. What makes you ask?"

"But this isn't about being in control. This is about fighting for what I believe in."

"I'm sure it is. I'm sure it is. Now let's make you beautiful again." I sat up to help pick out her mushed do.

"It really is, Savannah. I know you don't believe me."

I started fluffing her hair. "No, actually, I don't."

"Why?"

"Because you are always in the middle of everything. And you couldn't be more in the middle of this unless you had been chiseled into that monument yourself."

"But this isn't about me," she said, trying to pout.

"I didn't say it was about you. I said it was a control issue. You don't think anyone could do it like you, so you think you have to do it yourself." I took her by the arm and unzipped the front of the tent. "Look out there, Mother."

"Ooh, pretty day."

"Not at the sky, at the people. These people slept out here last night too. Any one of them would have been just as capable as you of chaining themselves to this monument."

"But they wouldn't have—"

"There. See, you don't know what they would or wouldn't have accomplished. Because you didn't let them."

"You think they wanted to?"

"I'm not sure. But I know at least some of them would have."

"Well. Even so, I do believe in this." She ducked back inside the tent.

"I know you do. I do know it's not *just* about control. About controlling the city anyway. Part of it is about controlling me. My destiny. My decisions."

"You think I did all of this for you?"

"For me, for Thomas, for other people's children. You said exactly that to Ms. Austin."

"But I did it for me, too, Savannah. I did this because I believe in those words up there. I try to live them the best I know. I fail miserably and often. I do try to control too much. They should have made that commandment number eleven: Thou shalt not control. Then I would have successfully kept from breaking four."

Ooh, she had me wondering now. "Which three of the real ones have you not broken?"

"The ones about killing and the stealing. And the one about adultery. Who would want something else, when you already have the best?"

"You've used the Lord's name in vain?" I asked in complete shock.

"It slipped." She clearly felt shame over this.

A smile crept across my face as I looked at this naïve, bright, frighteningly pure woman. "I love you."

"You what?"

"I love you. You're completely strange, and completely abnormal, and completely perfect," I told her.

She started sniffling.

"Do not cry. We have to make you beautiful. You are going to see the president today."

Poor thing sucked up her tears and beamed in a most lamentable way for such a grown woman. But by the time we unzipped that tent and removed it from around her, she was beautiful. I mean, she was "local dignitary" quality. And she knew it. Those around her gasped. She beamed.

"Now, go get 'em."

"And where will I take 'em when I get 'em?"

"To the heart of who you are."

"You think they'll see it?"

"As long as you let them share it with you. They won't miss it."

I gave her a kiss. Packed up my tent. And left her there to think. And she was thinking. You could always tell. Thinking for Vicky required extreme quiet. A rarity. And extreme furrowed brow. A BOTOX miracle. Who knew what she would uncover in the process, but at least she would look good doing it.

I slipped away to till, making a stop at my old house for Duke and some clothes. Duke looked refreshed from his and Dad's evening indoors. About halfway around the corner I saw the long raven ponytail of one Ms. Austin flopping in front of me. I slowed my pace as she continued around the park. After yesterday's adventure I wasn't too sure that she would want to see me. Or I her, for that matter.

I eyed her as she headed around the corner of the back end of the park. When Duke and I turned the corner shortly thereafter, she had made her way to a park bench, facing the artsy-district side of the park. I would have to take either the mature route of pass and acknowledge, or the favored route of hightail it and run. With my very maturity questioned yesterday, I tiptoed onward.

"Hello, Ms. Austin," I said as I neared her bench.

"Savannah," she stated as if noting a minor detail in a mundane event. Just, "Savannah." Flat, dry, colorless. Not, "Hey Savannah!" with a singsong effect. Not, "Hey, Savannah!" with surprise. She wiped her face with a towel.

"May I sit down?"

"It's a public park. Public bench."

"Is that a yes?"

"That's an I-really-don't-give-a-flip." Well, at least she was offering some expression. "I'm leaving anyway." She stood.

"Please wait," I said, reaching out for her arm. I let go of her and sat down on the bench. She hesitantly followed. "This is Duke." Maybe his charm could ease the tension.

"I don't like dogs." So much for that. Duke heard her and turned his back on the both of us.

"I just wanted to talk about yesterday."

"Everyone will be talking about yesterday. Your picture is on the front page declaring you a thief, and your article pretty much identified everything you've discovered in this situation. And you made it clear what you thought of me too."

"I didn't even mention your name."

"No, you referred to me as a 'type.' Yes, I believe that was your word."

"No, I referred to your position as a 'belief,' Ms. Austin."

"My name is Faith," she said as if my calling her Ms. Austin was patronizing. She was right.

"I'm sorry. We all believe in something, Faith. And I said that in the course of this debate over whether this monument should stand or not, the core of people's beliefs are the issue."

"You know what I don't get, Savannah? This nice act of yours. You know, the one you like to play on people. As if you are so naïve and innocent."

"I think I made it clear in that article that I can manipulate with the best of them. Trust me, I learned a thing or two about myself this week." Then I noticed the look on her face. I could tell she thought I had tried to manipulate her. "I genuinely liked you. And you have the same 'nice act,' as you call it, need I remind you."

She glared back. "What are you talking about?"

"A few people warned me you could be vicious, but I didn't believe them. Then I caught a glimpse of it in your opinion of Jessica, and then with the cruel things you said to my mother."

"You never liked me, Savannah. You were looking for a story the entire time. I figured you out the first day I met you."

"Then you need to gear up on the discernment, sister. Because I not only liked you, I admired you. Your style. Your beauty. Your professionalism. My word, I even tried to dress like you."

"You did not." Surprise replaced her offense.

"Did too."

"You did?"

"Didn't work."

"Didn't?"

"Ended up under a car."

"What?"

"Long story," I assured her. "But you know what? I like you

now. I don't agree with you. I don't believe in your cause. And I sure don't like your technique. But I have to appreciate your passion. "

"You have a great deal of passion yourself, Miss Sugar Daddy Stealer." She laughed.

"I can't believe you got that out of me."

"I can't believe you shouted it in front of rolling television cameras."

"And snapping flashbulbs. Please don't forget the flashbulbs." We both laughed. "You know, it's funny. You resent in me the very things I resent in myself."

"What are you talking about?"

"Oh, the hypocrisy," I said, leaning back on the park bench. "The expectation that someone should be something that I have trouble being myself. Like the anger I felt when you talked about Jessica—I've called her worse in my head. The things you said to my mother's face that I've probably thought a thousand times. But I do try. I try hard to live the things I believe."

"I used to believe like you, Savannah. I used to have Sunday dinners with my family too, like you said in your article you have with your family. Back before Sunday ran like any other day of the week. We didn't work. We didn't fuss. We just were." She leaned back against the park bench herself, and you could see her mind drift back to those memories.

"Where were you raised?"

"The suburbs of Chicago."

"Cold?"

"Bitter. But home."

"You miss it?"

"I miss living. I'm tired of schmoozing and acting like I like people. And always being on call. And my cell phone always ringing."

"I think you already took care of that small matter."

She chuckled. "Yeah, I guess I did."

"I would think your life would be total excitement."

"Parts are. The travel. Many of the people. But some days I just want to live. Live for me."

"I read something one time."

"You do a lot of that, I notice."

"Can't help it. I'm addicted."

"Could have a worse one."

"I do. Coke."

"Savannah?! You?"

"Coca-cola."

"Oh, girl, you better be careful how you say that."

"I'd say you're right. But anyway, one of my favorite writers is a man named Frederick Buechner. Brutally honest novelist. Has scared his share of people in the evangelical world. But he's just real."

"I like real."

"Me too. He said in *Now and Then* in the last analysis all moments are key moments, and life itself is grace."

"You remembered that?"

"Couldn't help it. Changed me too much to forget it."

"You really believe it?"

"Have to. It's always been true."

"You mean every moment in your life has been a key moment?"

"Every one has led me to where I am now. Every moment of joy—like getting my job at the paper. Every moment of shame—like being exploited by that same paper," I said, trying to wipe the frustration from my face. "Every moment of pain—"

"You don't know pain, Savannah. Your life is too perfect."

"No life is perfect."

"My life was." She paused, eyes staring across the street at nothing. "Everything was perfect, until one day my perfect husband came home to tell me our perfect life was perfectly over."

"I'm so sorry, Faith."

"Oh, I don't care. He was a jerk who sat on the second pew of our local church and was remarried to the blonde choir member on the third row, fifth seat, in no less than three weeks, when she was three months pregnant. All that in a church."

"Could happen anywhere you find a human. Do you have any children?"

"Thank God, no." She turned her attention back to me.

"Be careful what you say. That stone monument might have influenced you more than you know." I smiled at her.

She chuckled. "Need to guard my figures of speech I guess."

"Not having a child sounds like a gift in a situation like that." She stared deep into me. "A key moment of grace." I studied her. "You know, we're not that different."

She turned and looked at me. "Yes, we are, Savannah. We're very different. You want a fairy-tale world to be a reality. I want a world that is progressive and moving forward, not trying to revert to stereotypes, slavery, and a takeover by a small fraction of society's extremists."

"Is that what you see?"

"From this side of the bench, that's what I see."

"That's funny. Because that's not what I see from *this* side of the bench. You know what I see?"

"I doubt that is a rhetorical question."

"I don't see fairy tales; I see a heritage. Ronald Reagan said Winston Churchill had the gift of vision, the willingness to see the future based on the experience of the past. I think if you throw away the past, Faith, you throw away the ability to rightly determine the future."

She considered this before standing up to leave. "Well, the court will make the final decision here, and they'll do it today."

"Maybe about the placement of a one-ton piece of stone, but not about the indelible imprint its engravings will leave on a heart."

She turned around. She had heard me. And I believe she knew they could strip every monument from here to Hawaii and not be able to erase the commandments from our hearts. "You're odd to me. You make me crazy, in fact. But you do have a sense of grace about you, Savannah. You really do."

Her words caused me to stop. More than being named Savannah, my name was Savannah Grace. I thought of Joy and smiled. "It's my name. I don't have a choice."

"What?"

"Savannah Grace Phillips. That's my name. So I don't have a choice."

"You need rest."

"My names declare me a woman with a calling for this city and hopefully the grace needed for the people here. Do you know what your name is?"

She refused to answer. I did it for her.

"When you were born, you were placed into your mother's arms and she looked at your face, and declared you to be Faith. The very thing you were destined to be is the very thing you have so much trouble with. The faith to believe in something."

"Oh, I believe in something, Savannah."

"Okay, then how about the faith to believe in *someone* again?"

She looked at me. And extended her hand. I responded in kind. This would stop here. I had made my point. She would make hers as well. Only time would tell whether she believed me, a woman who didn't share her views. I may never know for sure. But it didn't change what I saw in her.

"Do you respect me, Savannah?"

Odd coming from a woman whose mere presence seemed to demand it. "Does it matter?"

She paused. "Actually it does."

"I respect passion, Faith. I've just learned that passion and un-bridled anger aren't the same thing. My mother taught me that one. She is passionate. But not angry. That is one reason I can't help but admire her." I paused myself. "And learn from her, I must say. And trust me, I've learned much the hard way this week."

She stared into me. Not with a question. Not with a thought. Just with a stare. "It was a pleasure to meet you, Savannah Phillips."

"And you as well, Faith Austin." I took Duke's leash, but he still wouldn't look at either of us. I hadn't defended him. He was none too happy about it either. I looked up at her as she turned to go. "I hope you find what you're really looking for. And I think when you do, you're going to be shocked that it was really seeking you."

She didn't respond. She just walked down the sidewalk of Forsythe Park and out of sight.

CHAPTER THIRTY-NINE

It was buried in the back. Buried behind the red ruffled blouse and the canary yellow lace pants. I don't know when she bought it for me. Obviously, I had refused to wear it. But today I was surprised that I had hidden it. It was exactly what I would have bought myself. Wearing it could prove dangerous. Mother might think we should start shopping together. Worse yet, she might tell people she was dressing me. But if she could just keep it coming and keep her mouth closed about it, we might form a rather nice relationship.

I slipped it on. The neckline was curved, causing the straps to look as if they laid across my shoulders. The black fabric was complimentary of the rest of my wardrobe. And the dainty white polka dots that covered the entire dress gave it a feminine effect. But it was the pink flower that resided on the left side that down right took it over the edge. This dress was no where near the "tad" category. It took me to the land of down right daring. I looked almost as good as Miss Amber Topaz herself. The flowing skirt fell just below my knees.

"I can't go out in this. It will ruin me. Amber will want to buy a matching outfit." I turned in front of the mirror. I simply looked too good not to risk it. For a moment I wondered if Joshua would laugh. Then I decided I didn't care what he thought. I was free to wear those canary yellow pants *with* the red ruffled blouse if I wanted to, though if I wanted to, I would need to be committed. I was free to do anything, no matter what Joshua North thought. But he would think something. Of that I was sure.

The black, small-heeled flip-flops—or maybe you would call them thongs, who can be sure these days?—with the faux silver buckle at least gave me some semblance of familiarity. I gave myself one last gaze, running my hand over the front of my waist and down the sides of my skirt. Then I remembered. The president was coming. Who in the world would care what I was wearing?

"Nice dress." Mervine spoke.

"Did you know the president's coming today, Mervine?" The humming dishwasher caught my attention. "Duke, I do believe these people have been liberated."

It was the busiest time of the day at Dad's shop, people clamoring for their morning coffee. I filled up Duke's water bowl and checked to see if he had eaten the steak. He had. Only the bone remained. And that was being generous. Apparently he felt life had returned to normal. If normal is eating steak out of a dog trough at eight in the morning.

I reached for a Coke. A ritual of mine for the last 365 days of each of the past nineteen years of my life, and a few more if you count leap years. But today as I looked at the fountain, I wondered who controlled whom. Faith ate and drank anything she wanted simply because she wanted. Until this exact moment I had done the same. But for some reason, today, I felt I needed to make a statement to myself. To my own personal "demons," as Joshua tried to remind me. And as much as I loved that Coke in the morning and, granted, the afternoon, and as an end to a perfectly good day, well . . . if it controlled me, then I had to change.

No one wants such change. To stare a new revelation in the face and deny it is for some an everyday occurrence. But with what I now knew, especially what I had realized over this past week, that would not be possible for me. I took my shaking hand and got some ice. A magnetic force tried to pull me to the Coke. It was a war like few others my mind had ever waged. But it was one I would win. I wasn't giving up Coke. I was just letting it know who was boss. I drank water.

For the first morning in nineteen years, I drank water. Had anyone seen me, they would have had me committed. Had I not just lived through this entire week, I would have committed myself. The only thing I knew was that Savannah Phillips had learned something: any priority above the ultimate priority is out of priority. Well, Joy had said something to that effect. Maybe I would have her just write it all down.

Dad's eyes scanned me. "Nice dress, Savannah."

"Did you know the president's coming today?"

He laughed. "Yes I did, actually. So, did you have a nice evening?"

I tried to sit down at the counter. "A painful one."

"Painful how?"

"There are two kinds? Oh, yes, we are speaking of Vicky now, aren't we?"

"Savannah, it is *Mother* to you, not Vicky."

"Oh yes, I believe you're right. Actually, Mom was tolerable. It was the sidewalk that was painful." I took a long swallow of my water. It didn't burn, but it was appropriately pleasurable. "Ahhh. I see your dishwashers have retired."

"Thank the Lord. We got it in yesterday."

"You gave that poor man Ron a fright."

He motioned in the direction of the twins. "Honey, I paled in comparison to what he endured from those two creatures."

"I can only imagine."

"Hey, you! You're that girl from the park. The one that listened to my conversation and sat on my bench." A finger-pointing little twit headed toward the counter. I recognized him as the one who made the berating phone call in Forsythe Park.

"Excuse me?"

"Yeah, it is you. And then you wrote about me today in your little article."

He had me on that one. I just couldn't believe he remembered me. Or that he knew I was talking about him. Well, what do they say, admission is the first step to change. Or change is the first step to admission. Or something like that.

"Yeah, what was it you said about me exactly?" He questioned snidely. "Oh, well, why don't we read it word for word." He snatched up Section B from the table where he had been sitting before he rose to annoy me. "Let's see here: 'I listened to a man as he berated an apparent employee on the phone in the middle of Forsythe Park. For him, life was about money and making it. It was about winning or losing. It was about being the "top dog." But my friend Joy reminded me it isn't about either; it's about just being. Just being kind. Just being faithful. Just being a friend. Just being available. Available for Sunday dinner and baseball games. Available for graduations and recitals. How can any man be those things when the very premise, the very foundation of his living, has been focused on the wrong hero?' "

"I think that's pretty good, don't you, Dad?" Surely Jake could shore me up in these here murky waters.

"If it's what you heard, it sounds good to me."

"Good?! You call that good! It wasn't even accurate."

"I just call it how I see it."

"I was talking to my father, you idiot. He's the owner of the company, not my employee."

"Then I would say your tone isn't the only issue you need to be dealing with, mister."

"I could sue you."

"Wouldn't do any good," Dad assured him. "Last I heard, she's in the hole as it is."

"He's right. I don't have a penny to my name. And no one will know it's you," I said, attempting to console him. "Unless *man* is your middle name." I turned around on my stool and left him to snarl at the back of my head.

"Jake, you better get control of this . . . this . . . this little Sugar Daddy Stealer," the man spat at the back of my head.

"Now you're getting personal," I said to the man behind me while looking at my father in front of me. "And those who live in glass houses shouldn't throw stones."

"Savannah, that's enough." I could tell my dad was trying not to smile. "Todd, I'll handle Savannah; you just try to have a good day at work."

He left. But he made a whole lot of ruckus in the process.

"You are an incorrigible child."

"You liked my article, and you know it. Or you would have told me first thing."

"You did a good job, baby girl," Dad said, sitting down beside me and picking up the paper. He began to read aloud.

I'm not here to write about choosing a religion. I'm here to share my experience that one can begin a journey unsure of the destination. But when the fork in the road comes and one path or another must be taken, a choice will have to be made. I had to choose. Not to choose would prove apathetic, a trait no one today can afford to have. And I could not choose a path that abandoned the beliefs I hold dear.

But the path I did choose led me to a very valuable revelation: Should every monument be hauled away, what I believe is etched in me. And I learned it this week by walking with three different women. One made me smile, taught me with her ever-present wisdom, and ate my food. The other caused me to think, challenged me with her divergent belief, and shared her Snickers. The third has offered me her food and her wisdom for the last twenty-four years. And each week I learn to respect her more as the woman she is, and not just because she's my mother. Each woman came to her own fork in the road. Each woman chose the path that reflected the core belief of who she is.

In the end, only one path will prove right. I chose the voice of experience on this one. And I followed the one of my heritage. The heritage of my family, and at the end of the day, the very heritage of my nation.

Until next week.

Savannah from Savannah

Dad put the paper down and stood up from his stool. He walked over and gave me a peck on the top of my forehead. "Good job, baby girl."

"Thanks. I'm listening."

"Would help if you showed it more often," he said, right eyebrow raised.

I met his challenge and then posed the ever-looming question. "Have you seen me on the front page of the newspaper?"

"Yep."

"Well, two stories about me in one day. I just might become my mother after all. Lord help us all." And with that I left him. Him and his little thought for the day in chalk above his head. *He who guards his way, guards his life.*

CHAPTER FORTY

I felt every stair. Yet I continued to climb to my new home. Opening the door, reality swept over me once again: life as I knew it was gone. Well, that had actually begun last Friday, so technically I was being prepared in advance.

Everything was as we left it. Sparse. I walked into my new bedroom, which felt nothing like home except for the fact that everything I owned in this world was in it. But then, 90 percent of what I owned, I had not actually purchased. Sad.

The small tan box with the orange stripe and white lettering rested safely on my nightstand. I picked it up and let it turn gently in my fingers. I knew I would come across pictures. I would find letters. I would battle memories. But I had to start somewhere. And as much as I detested the remote possibility that Joshua *might* be a smidgen accurate, I knew he was.

I had loved Grant. As much as I was capable of loving anyone up to this point in my life, I had loved him. But it wasn't the kind of love that included a lifetime of commitment. Grant had known it years ago. I wouldn't admit it until I knew he was gone. I could fight on. But what for? Pride? Jealousy? Resentment? The mere fact I didn't want to lose to a long-legged maiden? And I did love Grant enough not to cause him any more pain, or at least any more wasted evenings.

I walked over to the small stainless-steel trash can that I had brought up, with permission I might add, from Dad's shop. I stepped on the small black lever that opened the lid. To my chagrin the dumb thing worked. The lid opened. I dropped my small lightbulb box, and with it any chance of marrying the man who I had just assumed would wait for me forever.

He was just what I knew. Now I wasn't sure I knew anything. Well, I did know one thing: Joshua North would never be allowed the satisfaction he hoped to find in this moment. He may make me tingle. But I would die a thousand Vicky-induced deaths before he would ever have the satisfaction of knowing it.

Today's agenda: Avoid Joshua. Don't read the newspaper. Pretend that front page didn't even exist.

I set my goals too high. Joshua was on the receiving end of the door as it slammed into him when I opened it. And the newspaper was spread across my desk.

"Wouldn't have hit you if you had gotten out of the doorway." I passed by him and his conversation partner from the sports room and went straight to my four portable walls.

Then I picked up the paper. At least I looked good. Arms stretched out, head tipped back, not quite as tired as the day before. Outfit was a bit wrinkled, but besides that my hair was lying nicely around my face. It was the caption, however, that allowed me a moment of satisfaction: "Columnist Savannah Phillips, Researching the Very Heart of the Matter." He did like me. I knew it.

I was about to sit down when I caught a familiar face in the bottom right-hand corner of the paper. Right under the copy that read, "confessed to stealing a Sugar Daddy as a youth." I would come back to that later. The picture was Joy. Joy was in the paper. I sat down to scan the article, but the headline gave me a wealth of information: "Atlanta Family Widens Search for Missing Mother and Grandmother." My little Joy was a runaway.

"Wonder why?" I asked myself. Wouldn't have even had to ask myself had I read the article first. Seems that Joy was suffering from long-term memory loss, the result of a head injury she had sustained during a car accident a couple months ago. Her family feared that she had wandered off and forgotten her way home.

I ran to Mr. Hicks's office without stopping to get permission from Jessica. She didn't like it. I didn't care.

"Mr. Hicks," I panted. I hadn't waited for the elevator, painful thighs or not. "I know this woman," I said, laying the paper down in front of him.

"What?" His head was spinning from the flurry of activity that had just entered his office. Because Jessica was on my heels in adamant protest of my arrival.

"I know her. This lady. Joy. She ate my catfish!"

"Would you calm down?"

"I can't! I have to find her. And call her family! That's why she wears the same dress every day." I was talking to myself, but he didn't catch on.

"Savannah, if you will calm down one moment and speak sanely, we might get somewhere."

"Okay. Okay. I *knoooow* this lady. She's been wandering the streets around here for a week."

"This missing grandmother?"

I started pacing, and Jessica left. It was best for us both. "Yes. We talk every day. She's like, well, like my friend."

"Is she the lady you talked about eating your food?"

"Yes!" I collapsed into his leather chair, because that was all the energy I had left. "Yes, she's the one."

"Well, why are you sitting down?"

"What? Just because I'm a confessed candy stealer, now I can't even sit down? And I do owe you one for that headline." I smiled.

He winked but continued with his protest of my sitting position. "No, Miss Paranoia, you need to get up and go find this lady."

I jumped up, wondering why the thought hadn't crossed my mind. "Oh, right! Good idea."

"Now, listen. I'll call the number here in the paper. You bring this lady back here to my office, and I'll try to get her family to come here and pick her up."

"Her name is Joy. She has a name."

"*Okay,* Savannah, you . . . go . . . *find . . . Joy.*"

I put my hand on my hip and raised my right eyebrow at his drawn-out mockery. "I'm not a third grader."

"Would you listen? For one minute, just listen. Go find Joy. Bring her back here and quit making everything a discussion."

"Right. I'll get her. I'll bring her back. She'll have her family, and you can put a new picture of me on the front of your paper. 'Candy Stealer Redeems Self. Finds Missing Grandmother.'"

"Would you please go?"

I drove around like a crazy person. And when that was no longer possible because of the ridiculous number of roadblocks and police pandemonium due to the presidential visit, I simply got out and ran. Not easy in a sundress and wedged Stuart Weitzmans. I couldn't find her anywhere. She wasn't in the square across from the courthouse. She wasn't near Katherine's Corner Bookstore. She hadn't taken up outside of Savannah's Candy Kitchen. So, I headed back to our first encounter, Forsythe Park. There, lying on the bench amid "her" flowers, was one Joy Odom.

I knelt down by her bench. She was killing it. I hadn't heard snoring like that except from Duke. I wanted to see her as a helpless child, lost and alone. But with sounds coming out of a person that could raise the dead, well, let's just say I had to wake her up before she scared *me.*

"Hey, sunshine. Wake up." I tapped her arm. She startled with a snort and a jerk. "Whoa, missy. It's just me, Savannah."

"Savannah, my Lord, baby, you about scared the daylights out of an old woman."

She made me smile. Even when she lusted after my food, she made me smile. I just liked her. Everything about her. Even her old ugly floral dress.

"Ow," she said, rubbing her back. "That's a small bench for a big woman like me."

She moved over to the right side, and I was able to sit down. "Have you been sleeping out here every night?"

"No, a lot of nights I sleep out by the monument. But I was out here last night praying in this beautiful garden, and just got too tired to walk back." I realized at that point there was no telling how far Joy had walked this past week. Savannah may be built on twenty-two squares, but it is 2.2 square miles of squares, and nothing is as close as it seems. The poor thing should be skin and bones by now. Although, with all the dinners she'd been having, she was liable to have gained weight.

"Who do you sleep with out at the monument?"

"Some nice man with a golden retriever always has an extra sleeping bag. He lets me use it when I'm there. Gives me free coffee too. I really like him. He's pretty nice-looking too."

Ooh, this was odd. And after the kissing episode the other day, I was already dealing with undue trauma. I changed the subject. "How would you like to come hang out where I work today?"

Her face lit up. "At the paper?"

"Yeah. See what we do. How the paper is printed. Meet my boss. All those kind of neat things. Maybe even have lunch together, and maybe even buy a new dress. What do you think?"

"I think that is a glorious idea, baby." I helped her up off of the bench and took her arm to walk her to the car. "What are we having for lunch today, Savannah? Got some catfish?" Her eyes were like a two-year-old's.

I giggled at her innocence. "How 'bout we go get you a cup of coffee and a muffin at Jake's, and then I'll take you to Lady & Sons for some catfish or fried chicken for lunch."

"It's going to be a glorious day, Savannah. I feel it in my very bones. Just a glorious day." She had no idea.

Richard opened the door for us. "Ms. Joy, what are you up to today?"

"Oh, nothing, Richard. Just spending some time with this sweet girl."

"Who? Savannah?" he chided with a wink.

"Yes, this baby is taking me on a tour today," she said with genuine appreciation.

Dad walked from behind the counter and gave us both a peck on the cheek. "Just like you like it, Joy," he said, handing her a cup of coffee.

"This is a fine man," she said, poking me with her elbow. That was a rather disturbing glint in her eye.

"Joy, please, this is my father. I don't want to talk about him being fine, handsome, or kissable. I just want to think about him being a father."

"This is your father?"

Dad smirked.

"Yes, and he's not fine. No offense, Dad."

"None taken."

"He's just a dad. My dad. Who doesn't need women swooning over him all day."

"Well, my Lord have mercy. I should have known you come from such quality."

"Thank you, Joy." He gave her another peck. "And thank you for appreciating me too," he said, giving her a wink. He was becoming downright shameless.

The door opened, and Granny Daniels entered. "Savannah, what are you doing here this morning?"

"Just brought my friend in here for some of Jake's coffee."

The two women looked at each other. Granny Daniels's face lit up. "Joy! I missed you last night." And with that the two friends linked arms and walked to a corner table. Mervine and Louise took them a breakfast of muffins and coffee. Dad sat down beside me at the bar.

"They've both been sleeping out on the square?" I asked.

"Every night."

"That's amazing."

"Yes ma'am, it is."

"Did you get in touch with her family?" Dad asked quietly.

"How did you—" I whispered, getting successfully cut off by the rattling of the paper on the counter.

"I read the paper too, Savannah."

"Oh yeah, right. Yeah, Mr. Hicks is calling them. They should be here quickly. But she has no idea."

"Well, go show her a wonderful morning."

"I will."

"You like your new place?"

I couldn't help but smile. "Yeah, needs furniture. But it's going to be great. You can come see it after work."

"I'd like that."

"Me too." Even though we'd never let the other know, we already knew he had.

CHAPTER FORTY-ONE

I treated Joy like a princess. She toured every spot of that facility. Met Joshua. Liked him immensely. (She had been hit on the head, remember.) Didn't think Jessica had very good manners for a Southern young woman. (So maybe she wasn't hit real hard.) Loved to watch the printing press. Got her a snack in the break room. The woman couldn't pass up food if she was muzzled. She and Paige would have been soulmates.

We stole away to Jezebel's and got her a great yellow linen ensemble. Then I stole her away to my parents' house for thirty minutes to let her shower and to make her beautiful. If the newspaper thing failed, I definitely had a fallback career: personal stylist to street people. She was still beautiful but greasy by the time we finished lunch at Lady & Sons. But Miss Paula Dean made over her like she was royalty. Joy told her she had some recipes she would send, but she couldn't quite remember where they were right now. Miss Paula told her to mail them when she got the time.

By our return to the paper at noon, a page came over the

loudspeaker, asking me to come to Mr. Hicks's office. I knew what this meant. Joy was going home, I left her at my desk for a minute so I could make sure everything was okay upstairs. It was. And when I returned to fetch her, she had neatly folded up Section B with my article on top and laid it on my desk.

I touched her arm, and she looked up at me with a smile. "I'm proud of you, baby girl. Real proud."

I tried to fight the burning in my nose and the swell of tears in my eyes. "Come on, Joy. Let me take you to see my boss's office. He has the best view in the place."

"Oh, I'd like that, Savannah." She hooked her black arm around mine, giving them an Oreo effect. "I sure have enjoyed this day."

I smiled at her sincere black eyes. "Me too, me too." I put her black hand in mine and appreciated the nice way we had cleaned up her short nails. Her hair looked good too, for the rush job we did.

"Think we can do this again?"

I knew that after today I might never see my new friend again. "Sure, I would love that." And I meant every word.

I could hear voices coming from Mr. Hicks's office. And as soon as we rounded the corner, a fortyish man ran out of the room and down the hall. "Mama! Oh, Mama! We've looked and looked for you. Thank God you're safe."

When he reached her, he wrapped her in a death grip. And his arms made it all the way around her. I could see her eyes as her head rested on his broad shoulder. They were searching and almost frightened. For a moment I wanted to reach out and protect her; she thought he was a stranger. But this was his mama. He had lost her, and now he had found her. And he wasn't letting her go.

Finally she pushed him away and stared blankly into his matching dark eyes. He looked at her with such an ache. I couldn't imagine the pain of not being recognized by the one who took you to preschool and taught you to tie your shoes (or in my case, buckle your pumps). But then there was a flicker beneath the bewilderment. And her sweet and smooth hand went up to his face and touched it. "Baby boy," she said. "My baby boy."

And with that he fell back into her arms and began to cry. And she patted his head, just like a mama would. And he wept.

"Hush, baby. Mama's okay. Mama's just fine," she assured him as she stroked his head. By then her other children had surrounded us, and I stepped back to let them have this moment to themselves. I did notice there was no Mr. Joy. Just children. But no matter why Mr. Joy didn't exist, she still lived her name. Even *that* untold story refused to deter her from being Joy. Her children gushed over her and patted her and loved her and scolded her, and she just loved the whole thing. She laughed and talked and patted and told them stories. Oh, the stories she had to tell.

As they made their way to the elevator, I wiped my tears on the back of my hand. They thanked me and Mr. Hicks, even Jessica, because she had witnessed the whole thing. I didn't even care. Who would care about that at this point? I might care about it later, but right now it was all okay.

I listened to Joy's familiar swooshing sound and wished I had one more plate of catfish that we could share. I watched as the yellow ensemble made its way up the hall and planned to burn her old one with Mother's blue number upon my arrival home. I saw Joy reach her hand over to her oldest son and stop him. She turned around and looked at me.

She held out her arms. And I gladly accepted. I walked over to her and buried my head in her ample bosom, one I was certain had held many the head of a child through the years. My head fit perfectly. I tried to stifle my tears but couldn't. Again, I didn't care. I leaned up and whispered in her ear. "I'm going to miss you, Ms. Joy."

She whispered back. "I'm going to miss you too, Miss Savannah." She pulled me back and looked me square in the eye. Her eyes pierced me one last time. At least I hoped for a while. The woman had about worn me out.

"You see that man over there?" she asked me, pointing at Mr. Hicks.

"Yes, ma'am."

"His name's Samuel. I saw his placard on his door. Do you know what that means?"

"I have no idea."

"It means 'man who heard from God.' And men who hear, Savannah, teach. If they are any men at all," she said, peering up to give him a clear message.

He winked at her in response. She replied in kind. She looked back at me. "You're going to see a lot and do a lot, baby girl. You're going to touch people and tell people's stories and share more dinners with strangers." She was tickled with herself, and her belly bounced. "But you learned something this week. You're learning how to *be*. 'Cause you've *been* something to me."

I wanted to be stoic. I bit my lip in a vain attempt. But the tears fell freely. "And you've *been* to me, Ms. Joy. I've seen and heard every word. I'll never forget you."

"I wouldn't want you to. 'Cause we're going to do this again, remember?"

That made me laugh. She was telling me to remember. "I remember."

"And you chose the right road, baby," she said with a knowing smile. "You're right, every treasure you need for *being* is etched right here." She tapped her finger on my heart. "And no one can ever steal what is in your heart." She kissed me on my cheek and gave me one final penetrating look.

I stared into her beautiful dark eyes, which revealed her very soul. "You're an angel, aren't you?"

"No, baby girl. I'm a mother." She took the hand of her oldest son and turned to leave. She left humming.

That familiar tune rolled around in my head. Finally it hit me. "I know it!" I hollered loud enough to frighten us all. "I know what you're humming!"

"Took you long enough." She turned around with a sly smile.

"'Rock of Ages.' That's it, isn't it? It's 'Rock of Ages.'"

"You got it, baby girl. 'Rock of Ages.' And that won't change, no matter what happens up the street."

CHAPTER FORTY-TWO

Jessica was trying to hide a tear. Imagine that. My word, the child was actually human. I was beginning to think she was a short-circuited Stepford wife. "Gotcha, didn't it?" I said to her.

She flitted herself around to stare at her filing cabinet. "I don't know what you're talking about."

"Yes, you do, Jessica. See, you're not so mean after all."

She spun around. "I've never been mean."

"You don't call putting pictures of me in the paper in embarrassing and misunderstood situations mean?"

"I don't make the decision of what gets in the paper around here, Savannah. He does." She pointed to Mr. Hicks, who was still trying to recover from Joy's departure. She was right, of course. At the end of the day, Mr. Hicks made the decisions. I looked at him. He looked back. Joy had gotten him. I could tell. The grown man's eyes were sweating.

"Savannah, she's right. The buck stops with me. And about your picture. Well, I'll try to make sure that in the future your picture appears only above your article."

He nodded at me with a smile. Jessica wore no expression at all.

"One more thing, Savannah. Tell Joshua North I'll be talking with him shortly."

Joshua was at my desk when I went to grab my purse. He had, once again, invaded my personal space and was looking at the picture of me and Paige from a trip we took a year ago to Greece for part of the Olympic games.

"Did you knock?" I picked up my bag.

He set the picture back down and turned to face me. "Very funny."

He stopped and stared at me. The look in his eyes made me uncomfortable. "What?"

"You look . . . well, you look rather nice today." I knew he'd notice. He thought he had me pegged. I could tell.

"I've got to go," I said, heading back out.

He grabbed my elbow. "You can't ignore me forever," he said, trying to hide his smile.

"No, but I can ignore you for today. And I can deal with you tomorrow." I removed my elbow from his grip before offering him my hand upside his head as well.

He brushed past me on his way back to his own cubbyhole to answer his ringing phone. Mr. Hicks. "I'm not going anywhere."

"Well, I am."

"You're a mess." He laughed.

"I am not. I look much better today than the other day," I said, passing my hands over my skirt.

"I didn't mean the way you look; I mean you. But you're figuring it out. I can tell." Well, wasn't he just some master of life.

"Oh, well, I'm so glad you approve. Because at the end of the day, my greatest desire is for your approval." I tried to be as snide as possible. I exited with no further parting words. I didn't care to ever see him again. Not again today anyway.

"Ooh!" I let out my frustration as I straightened my cushion to sit down in Old Betsy. She let out a similar sound, and we were on our way.

Most every street from the newspaper to the courthouse was blocked. It didn't matter. I would walk. It was hard to park nearby on a typical day anyway. The sidewalks were packed because the streets had been cordoned off with rope and police officers, so the presidential motorcade could drive directly up to the courthouse.

"Betty?!"

I turned to see Judge Hoddicks walking up the sidewalk with some men who were sweating underneath their black suits and death-grip neckties. He had called me Betty since I petitioned to change my name to Betty in the eighth grade. From that day forward, the name Savannah had never even crossed his lips.

"Judge! I haven't gotten to see you all week. Tied up, huh?"

He chuckled, wiping his sixty-five-year-old white eyebrows with his handkerchief and wrapping the other free hand around me as we walked. "I would say your mother has paid the tied-up price for me."

"You got me there."

"Are you heading over there to see her?"

"Yes, sir. Want to make sure she looks okay. You know, with the president coming and everything."

"She's proud of you, Betty."

"I know. And I'm proud of her."

"You should be. She's shown us what she's made of this week."

I looked at his tired eyes. Wonder what Joy would have said about him. "Looks like you have too."

"It's been worth it. We might not win here, but the message sent by the people who have flocked to this square is proof of what they're willing to fight for."

"You did good." I put my arm through his and rested my head on it as we walked.

"It's not hard when you love what you do."

The path cleared before us as Judge Hoddicks made his way to the courthouse. There were some pats, some cheers, and a few rather snippy remarks. Sergeant Millings raised his nightstick at the protestors, as if he would know what to do with it. I paused across the street from my mother while the judge went on inside the courthouse. Vicky was standing, talking animatedly with some women who were gathered around her. She looked beautiful, stunningly beautiful, considering the sweltering humidity of this first day of June. Of course, she was underneath her umbrella and holding a tiny motorized fan to her face, but in spite of that, she looked fabulous.

I didn't want to bother her. I just wanted to enjoy her. She loved these people. She loved this city. Her love showed in every gesture and every hug and every question about someone else's children. True, she wanted to control it, but at the core, she just wanted to see it succeed.

A lady on the roped-off sidewalk caught everyone's attention. "Watch it. Watch it. The president. That's his car. Look, look, the president's motorcade!"

All the action on the sidewalks and around the courthouse ceased. And in that moment in time, it seemed as if the entire light of the sun shone on one Victoria Phillips and the monument she protected. Everybody backed away from her, and she stood in front of the monument, waiting to meet the president. She looked regal. Almost queenlike. Handcuffed, perhaps, but queens had passed that way before as well.

I heard the sound before I realized what was happening. The roar of an engine. The squealing of brakes. I turned quickly from my position across the street from my mother. In one lightening-flash moment, the third car in the motorcade broke loose and headed directly for my mother and the monument.

The air was sucked out of the square. All I saw were the whites of Vicky's eyes, larger than life. They were like a Shih Tzu's with its ponytail too tight. In an instant, the car broke through the iron hitching posts and crashed into the monument. The sound of crunching metal, crumbling concrete, and piercing screams could be heard on Bay Street. Then silence. For an eternity no one moved. All that was heard was the hissing of the radiator of the engine and the clanging metal as the rest of the bumper detached itself and landed on the sidewalk.

"Mother!" I screamed as I ran across the square. Bile rose in my throat at the thought of what I would see. Before I knew it, two men who looked for all the world like morticians, grabbed me and pulled me away. The back door of the limousine flew open, and out climbed two secret-service men, followed by the president of the United States.

The president's car had killed my mother! The president scrambled out and ran toward the monument. The secret service men were in front of him and behind him. I broke free from the two men holding me and ran in terror to find my mother. As I rounded the side of the car, I noticed movement underneath some of the granite. My father rose from the mess, and underneath him lay my mother, virtually lifeless until she heard the president's voice. Then those Mary Kay mascara eyelashes batted open. The secret service men pulled my father up. He had a noticeable cut across his elbow and a small cut on his cheek. Other than that, he was mostly dusty.

The president then reached down to help up my mother. She wasn't quite the picture of perfection that she had been moments ago. Her hair was sitting predominately on the right side of her head, now a white ashen color. Her face was practically albino, and her pretty pink suit . . . well, let's just say it wasn't so pretty. She had a slight cut above her right eyebrow. She'd milk that one for a month. One heel was broken. She'd milk that for two. And her stockings were ripped to shreds, proving once again the ridiculous notion of wearing clean underwear during a wreck. Who's to say how the mess happens.

She tried to brush herself off. Make herself presentable for the leader of the free world. A vain attempt at uselessness.

And there in rubble, surrounding the woman that had protected it, lay the crumbled monument of the Ten Commandments. For the past week people had prayed by it, sung by it, slept by it, and fought over it. And today it was nothing more than a mass of chunks of marble and piles of dust. No court would decide its fate now. That had been decided by a crazed limousine driver.

Then I remembered Joy's tap on my heart. It was still intact in there, no matter what had happened to it out here. We would fight for the monument again. But no matter the outcome next time, it hadn't been shattered inside me.

CHAPTER FORTY-THREE

Are you all right, ma'am?" the Texas drawl of our forty-third president filled the air.

"Oh, yes, yes, I'm fine." Had she seen herself, she would have known better. Had she seen herself, she would have stayed under the rubble. Feigned death and sent a better picture of herself later. "I'm simply fine, Bushi . . . I mean, Mr. President." Poor soul was still dazed.

I made my way to Dad, who was being attended by a doctor. I would give her and her hero a moment alone. After her week, she deserved this. After her sacrifice, even the Lord had given her a treat.

"Are you okay?" I asked my father, throwing my arms around his neck.

"Yes, honey, I'm okay."

"Oh, thank goodness. How did you get to Mother so fast?"

He removed the ice pack from his lip. "I don't know. I just knew the car was coming and I had to get her out of the way. I grabbed the other side of that chain and just lifted it off of the monument and pulled her away."

"You saved her life, Dad."

"That's okay. She saved mine years ago." He looked at her with a love shared by people who knew what loving meant. We watched her gush over the president while a doctor attended her. The president and she talked and laughed. I couldn't help but notice the extreme sparkle behind the eyes in her dusty face.

"Is that lust?" I asked my father.

He laughed. "No, that's admiration."

"You sure?"

"After what I just did, it better be."

The doctors patched them up. The president gave a warm handshake to my father. "You're a fine man, Mr. Phillips, with a brave and honorable wife."

My father stood and returned his firm grip. "Thank you, Mr. President. I think so as well." Dad smiled at my mother, who seemed to notice him for the first time.

"I really wasn't trying to kill her." He laughed a nervous Texas laugh.

Dad laughed too, easing the tension. "It isn't anything I'm sure many people haven't thought about doing themselves a time or two." That caused both of them to laugh.

Mother didn't laugh a bit. "Jake Phillips!" she scolded.

"I just read a book about Ronald Reagan," I offered. They all stared at me. I was odd. Undeniably odd.

The president extended an invitation to the White House. One I'm sure he would keep after today. One I'm sure none of us would ever live through. With that the Texas gentleman gave a Southern kiss on the chalky cheek of my mother. "Thank you, Mrs. Phillips. What you did here will be remembered by some forever."

"Ooh, well it was the least I could do, Mr. President." She placed her hand against her chest. It was the most Southern of gestures, the lowered batting eyes, the dainty hand-to-chest scenario. Picture perfect. Perfectly Vicky.

Fortunately for the president, he had more than one car. He stopped as he passed me. "Nice dress, young lady." He was a charming man.

"Why, thank you, Mr. President. Thank you very much." With that he left, followed by the rest of his motorcade. Time would reveal the driver of his car had suffered a heart attack, so it really wasn't the "left-wing conspiracy" mother originally declared it to be.

When Thomas met me and Dad, we found Mother, who had slipped away, sitting atop a piece of stone that read, "Shalt Not Steal." She wanted to take it with her as a memento, but she couldn't carry it. She cried quite a few tears of desolation over those ruins.

We waited for her to speak first. "I can't believe it would end this way."

"It's not ever really over," Dad assured her as he gently wiped concrete dust from her face.

"You're right. We'll just go get us another one and start this whole thing over." Her voice grew louder with each word.

Dad took her hand and led her in the direction of home. "How about we just go rest for a little while first?"

Thomas and I sighed.

She let out a relieved sigh herself. "That would be nice."

We gathered Vicky and what was left of her belongings. Most were gathered as evidence. Or offered. She just wanted them to be *sure* it wasn't a left-wing conspiracy, so they took off with her sleeping bags and Thomas's tent. I was certain they would end up in some trash bin between here and the airport.

As we started our walk toward home, or our wobble, depending upon whom you were watching, others began to pack up their memories of the week as well. The cameras were packed away, and the trucks lowered their lights. Sleeping bags were rolled up, and coolers were hauled off. Hugs were given. Tears were shed. High-fives offered. But as we walked in the direction of home, the city of Savannah headed back in the direction of, well, Savannah. Still a little odd, no doubt. But our familiar kind of odd.

The first block, nobody said much. I broke the silence with my good news. "I moved out!" I declared. No better time than the present.

"You what?!" Vicky screeched. "Jake, you let our baby move out?"

"She was going now or in two weeks, Victoria. Why delay the inevitable?"

"It's an amazing place," Thomas offered.

"Really?" She was having trouble believing it. "Do you have furniture?"

"A bedroom suite."

"That's all?"

"Yes ma'am."

"What will you eat on?"

"I'll get a table eventually."

"Where will you sit and watch TV?"

"On my bed for now, I guess."

"Jake, my baby doesn't even have a sofa." She was truly horrified.

"Victoria, that's what happens when you move out on your own. You have to work your way up to those things."

"Darling, don't you worry. Your mama will take you shopping this weekend, and we'll get you set. If you are going to move out, then we're just going to make your new place beautiful." She hobbled along, broken heel in hand and a new mission in mind.

I wasn't sure that was best. It might result in free stuff, but it still required shopping. With my mother. Maybe she could just go by herself and surprise me.

"Maybe you should just get me a key," she said. "Then I could just come and do it whenever I was free." On the other hand, maybe one day of shopping would be better than a lifetime of drop-ins. "And your dress is fabulous, Savannah. Ooh, we could go get you some clothes this weekend." She had said *we*. Someone needed to rescue me.

"Anyone know what time it is?" Thomas asked, giving me a wink.

I looked at my watch. "Five o'clock. Well, Mother, I do believe you have just been saved from serving time."

She looked at us and rubbed her behind. "I did my time, I assure you." That made us all laugh. "But I would have stayed as long as necessary."

As well as I thought I had known my mother last week, I now knew her differently. I now believed that she meant what she had just said. I wrapped my arm around her. She would have reciprocated but her arms were a little tired. She just laid her ratty head on my shoulder. Truth be known, the whole thing had made me tired, as tired as Joy assured me I looked. And this after only three weeks back home. Two weeks at my new job. One day in an apartment I had yet to sleep in. I knew what I needed. I needed a vacation. Surely nothing could happen on vacation.

What could possibly go wrong on vacation?

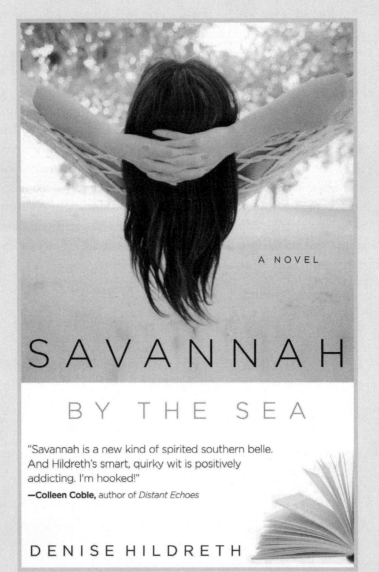

A NOVEL

SAVANNAH

BY THE SEA

"Savannah is a new kind of spirited southern belle.
And Hildreth's smart, quirky wit is positively
addicting. I'm hooked!"

—Colleen Coble, author of *Distant Echoes*

DENISE HILDRETH